ON COMPANY TIME

ON COMPANY TIME

IN THE GARDEN OF IDEN
SKY COYOTE

KAGE BAKER

FANTASY

IN THE GARDEN OF IDEN Copyright © 1988 by Kage Baker
    Printing History: Harcourt Brace hardcover
    February 1998

SKY COYOTE Copyright © 1999 by Kage Baker
    Printing History: Harcourt Brace hardcover
    February 1999

First SFBC Fantasy Printing: February 1999

Published by arrangement with:
Harcourt Brace & Company
15 East 26th Street
New York, NY 10010

Visit The SFBC online at *http://www.sfbc.com*
Visit Harcourt Brace's website at *http://www. harcourtbrace.com/*
Visit Kage Baker's website at *http://members.tripod.com/ MrsCheckerfield/*

ISBN# 0-7394-0152-1

PRINTED IN THE UNITED STATES OF AMERICA

CONTENTS

In the Garden of Iden

For my mother, Katherine Carmichael Baker,

and her mother, Kate Jeffreys Carmichael,

and for Athene Mihalakis,

a Gray-Eyed Goddess if ever there was one

1

I AM A BOTANIST. I will write down the story of my life as an exercise, to provide the illusion of conversation in this place where I am now alone. It will be a long story, because it was a long road that brought me here, and it led through blazing Spain and green, green England and ever so many centuries of Time. But you'll understand it best if I begin by telling you what I learned in school.

Once, there was a cabal of merchants and scientists whose purpose was to make money and improve the lot of humankind. They invented Time Travel and Immortality. Now, I was taught that they invented Time Travel first and developed Immortals so they could send people safely back through the years.

In reality it was the other way around. The process for Immortality was developed first. In order to test it, they had to invent Time Travel.

It worked like this: they would send a team of doctors into the past, into 1486 for example, and select some lucky native of that time and confer immortality on him. Then they'd go back to their own time and see if their test case was still around. Had he survived the intervening nine hundred years? He had? How wonderful. Were there any unpleasant side effects? There were? Oops. They'd go back to the drawing board and then back to 1486 to try the new, improved process on another native. Then they'd go home again, to see how this one turned out. Still not perfect? They'd try again. After all, they were only expending a few days of their own time. The flawed immortals couldn't sue them, and there was a certain satisfaction in finally discovering what made all those Dutchmen fly and Jews wander.

But the experiments didn't precisely pan out. Immortality is not for the general public. Oh, it works. God, how it works. But it *can* have several undesirable side effects, mental instability being one of them, and there are certain restrictions that make it impractical for general sale. For example, it only really works on little children with flexible minds and bodies. It does not work on middle-aged million-aires, which is a pity, because they are the only consumers who can afford the process.

So this cabal (they called themselves Dr. Zeus, Incorporated) came up with a limited version of the procedure and marketed it as truly superior geriatric medicine. As such it was fabulously profitable, and everyone commended Dr. Zeus.

Everyone, of course, except all those flawed immortals.

But about the Time Travel part.

Somehow, Dr. Zeus invented a time transcendence field. It, too, had its limitations. Time travel is only possible backward, for one thing. You can return to your own present once you've finished your business in the past, but you can't jump forward into your future. So much for finding out who's going to win in the fifth race at Santa Anita on April 1, 2375.

Still, Dr. Zeus played around with the field and discovered what could at first be taken as a comforting fact: History cannot be changed. You can't go back and save Lincoln, but neither can you erase your own present by accidentally killing one of your ancestors. To repeat, history cannot be changed.

However—and listen closely, this is the important part—*this law can only be observed to apply to recorded history*. See the implications?

You can't loot the future, but you can loot the past.

I'll spell it out for you. If history states that John Jones won a million dollars in the lottery on a certain day in the past, you can't go back there and win the lottery instead. But you can make sure that John Jones is an agent of yours, who will purchase the winning ticket on that day and dutifully invest the proceeds for you. From your vantage point in the future, you tell him which investments are sound and which financial institutions are stable. Result: the longest of long-term dividends for future you.

And suppose you have John Jones purchase property with his lottery winnings, and transfer title to a mysterious holding firm? Suppose you have an army of John Joneses all doing the same thing? If you started early enough, and kept at it long enough, you could pretty much own the world.

Dr. Zeus did.

Overnight they discovered assets they never knew they had, administered by long-lived law firms with ancient instructions to deliver interest accrued, on a certain day in 2335, to a "descendant" of the original investor. And the money was nothing compared to the real estate. As long as they stayed within the frame of recorded history, they had the ability to prearrange things so that every event that ever happened fell out to the Company's advantage.

At about this point, the scientist members of the cabal protested that Dr. Zeus's focus seemed to have shifted to ruling the world, and hadn't the Mission Statement mentioned something about improving the lot of humanity too? The merchant members of the cabal smiled pleasantly and pointed out that history, after all, cannot be changed, so there was a limit to how much humanity's lot could be improved without running up against that immutable law.

But remember, Gentle Reader, that that law can only be seen to apply to *recorded* history. The test case was the famous Library of Alexandria, burned with all its books by a truculent invader. Technically, the library couldn't be saved, because history emphatically states that it was destroyed. However, Dr. Zeus sent a couple of clerks back to the library with a battery-powered copier disguised as a lap desk. Working nights over many years, they transferred every book in the place to film before the arsonist got to it, and took it all back to 2335.

Even though the books turned out to be mostly liberal arts stuff like poetry and philosophy that nobody could understand anymore, the point was made, the paradox solved: What had been dead could be made to live again. What had been lost could be found.

Over the next few months in 2335, previously unknown works of art by the great masters began turning up in strange places. Buried in lead caskets in cellars in Switzerland, hidden in vaults in the Vatican Library, concealed under hunting scenes by successful third-rate Victorian commercial painters: Da Vincis and Rodins and Van Goghs all over the place, undocumented, uncatalogued, but genuine articles nonetheless.

Take the case of *The Kale Eaters*, the unknown first version of Van Gogh's early *Potato Eaters*. It wasn't possible for the Company to go drug Van Gogh in his studio, take the newly finished painting, and leap home with it: nothing can be transported forward out of its own time. What they did was drug poor Vincent, take *The Kale Eaters* and seal it in a protective coat of great chemical complexity, paint it over in black, and present it to a furniture maker in Wyoming (old USA), who used it to back a chair that later found its way into a folk arts-and-crafts museum, and later still into other museums, until some

zealous restorer X-rayed the chair and got the shock of his life. Need-
less to say, the chair was at that time in a collection owned by Dr.
Zeus.

As it happens, there are all sorts of chests and cupboards in lonely
houses that don't get explored for years on end. There are buildings
that survive bombings, fire, and flood, so that no one ever sees what's
hidden in their walls or under their floorboards. The unlikely things
that get buried in graves alone would astonish you. Get yourself a
database to keep track of all such safe hiding places, and you too can
go into the Miraculous Recovery business.

And why stop there? Art is all very well and can fetch a good
price, but what the paying public really wants is dinosaurs.

Not dinosaurs literally, of course. Everyone knew what happened
when you tried to revive dinosaurs. But the Romance of Extinction
was big business in the twenty-fourth century. To sell merchandise,
you had merely to slap a picture of something extinct on it. A tiger,
for example. Or a gorilla. Or a whale. Crying over spilt milk was de
rigueur by that time. What better way to cash in on ecological nos-
talgia than to revive supposedly extinct species?

In May of 2336, people turned on their newspapers and learned
that a small colony of passenger pigeons had been discovered in Ice-
land, of all places. In Christmas of that same year, four blue whales
were sighted off the coast of Chile. In March of 2337, a stand of
Santa Lucia fir trees, a primitive conifer thought extinct for two centuries, was found growing in a corner of the Republic of California.
Everyone applauded politely (people never get as excited over plants
as they do over animals), but what didn't make the news was that this
species of fir was the only known host of a species of lichen that had
certain invaluable medical properties . . .

Miracles? Not at all. Dr. Zeus had collected breeding pairs of the
pigeons in upstate New York in the year 1500. They were protected
and bred in a Dr. Zeus station in Canada for over half a millennium
and then released to the outside world again. Similar arrangements
were made for the whales and the fir trees.

Anyway, when the public imagination was all aglow with these
marvelous discoveries, Dr. Zeus let the truth be known. Not *all* the
truth, naturally, and not *widely* known; business didn't work that way
in the twenty-fourth century. But rumor and wild surmise worked as
well as the plushiest advertising campaign, and the Company didn't
have to pay a cent for it. It got to be known that if you knew the right
people and could meet the price, you could have any treasure from
the past; you could raise the lamented dead.

The orders began to come in.

Obsessive collectors of art and literature. Philanthropists sentimental about lost species. Pharmaceutical companies desperate for new biological sources. Stranger people, with stranger needs and plenty of ready cash. There were only two or three questions.

Who was running Dr. Zeus now? Even its founders weren't sure. Its most secretive inner circle couldn't have said positively. Suddenly they were surrounded by the prearranged fruits of somebody's labor on their behalf—but whose labor? Just how many people worked for the Company?

Also, were they now faced with the responsibility of making sure history happened at all? Quite a few species had been declared extinct, only to turn up alive and well in unexpected places. Were these Dr. Zeus projects they hadn't been aware of? Someone went digging in the Company archives and discovered that the coelacanth was a Dr. Zeus special. So was the tule elk. So was the dodo, the cheetah, Père David's deer. And the Company archives had an unsettling way of expanding when no one was looking.

Finally, where do you get the support personnel for an operation the size that this one had to be? Besides the cost of sending modern agents to and from the past, the agents themselves hated it. They said it was dangerous back there. It was dirty. People talked funny and the clothes were uncomfortable and the food was disgusting. Couldn't somebody be found who was better suited to deal with the past?

Well. Remember all those test-case immortals?

A team from the future was sent back to history's predawn, to build training centers in unpopulated places. They went out and got children from the local Neanderthals and Cro-Magnons, and shaved their diverse little skulls and worked the Immortality Process on their little brains and bodies. They brought them up with careful indoctrination and superior education. Then they went back to their own time, leaving the new agents there to expand the operation.

And what did Dr. Zeus have then? A permanent workforce that didn't have to be shipped back and forth through time, that didn't suffer culture shock, and that never, never needed medical benefits. Or, to put it in the corporate prose of the Official Company History: slowly these agents would labor through the centuries for Dr. Zeus, unshakable in their loyalty. They had been gifted with Immortality, after all. They knew they had a share in the glorious world of the future. They were provided with all the great literature and cinema of ages unborn. Their life work (their unending life work) was the no-

blest imaginable: the rescue of living things from extinction, the preservation of irreplaceable works of art.

Who could ask for anything more, you say?

Ah, but remember that Immortality has certain undesirable side
effects. Consider, also, the mental discomfort of being part of a plan
so vast that no single person knows the whole truth about it. Consider,
finally, the problem in logistics: there are thousands of us already,
and as the operation expands, more of us are made. None of us can
die. So where are they going to put us all, when we finally make it
to that glorious future world our creators inhabit?

Will they allow us in their houses? Will they finally pay us sal-
aries? Will they really welcome us, will they really share with us the
rewards we've worked millennia to provide them with?

If you're any student of history, you know the answer to *that*
question.

So why don't we rise in rebellion, as in a nice testosterone-loaded
science fiction novel, laser pistols blazing away in both fists? Because
in the long run (and we have no other way of looking at anything)
we don't matter. Nothing matters except our work.

Look. Look with eyes that can never close at what men do to
themselves, and to their world, age after age. The monasteries burned.
The forests cut down. Animals hunted to extinction; families of men,
too. Live through even a few centuries of human greed and stupidity
and you will learn that mortals never change, any more than we do.

We must go on with our work, because no one else will do it.
The tide of death has to be held back. Nothing matters except our
work.

Nothing matters.

Except our work.

2

MY NAME, MY age, the village of my birth, I can't tell you with any certainty. I do know it was somewhere near the great city of Santiago de Compostela, where the Holy Apostle's body was supposed to have been found. During the Middle Ages pilgrims flocked there to see the holy relics (if they didn't get wrecked first off Cape Finisterre) and returned with cockle shells pinned to their hats (if they didn't get wrecked going back). There, in that city, the Holy Inquisition set up one of its offices.

Also there, in the enormous cathedral, the Infanta Katherine, daughter of Ferdinand and Isabella, is supposed to have stopped to hear Mass on her way to marry the Prince of England. Now, in this cathedral was a silver censer, big as a cauldron, that swung in stately arcs at the end of a chain; and during the Infanta's Mass the chain broke and this censer hurtled out of the church through a window and exploded like a bomb on the paving stones outside. Some people would have taken this as an omen, but not the Infanta. She went resolutely on to England and wound up marrying King Henry the Eighth. This shows that one ought to pay attention to omens.

Anyway, we lived near there. My parents were thin and desperately poor, but racially pure, as they constantly assured us; and that is about all I remember of them. Racially pure meant a lot in Spain in those days, you see. Presumably to extend the line of Old White Christians, my parents had half a dozen little children, which they soon regretted because our house only had one room.

This is where the story begins.

One day in 1541 (all dates approximate) my mother was sitting by the door, gloomily watching her little White Christians as they

rolled in a screaming knot in the dust of the yard. Along the road
came some people on horseback. They were very well dressed and
looked as white as we did, nothing like Jews or Moriscos, though of
course you could never tell nowadays. They reined in beside the gate
and sat watching us for a moment.

"Good morning, gentle sirs and ladies," said my mother.

"Good morning, goodwife," said a tall lady with red hair. "What
pretty children you have."

"Thank you, gentle lady," said my mother.

"And so many of them," said the lady.

"Yes, gentle lady," said my mother ruefully. (At least, they said
something like this, but in sixteenth-century Galician Spanish, all
right?)

We children had meanwhile stopped fighting and were staring at
the people openmouthed. They really did look wealthy. I recall the
women had those things on their heads like the queens on playing
cards wear. You know.

"Perhaps," said the fine lady, "you have more little ones here
than you can provide for? You would perhaps entertain the idea of,
say, hiring one out?"

Now my mother's eyes went narrow with suspicion. She didn't
know who these people were. They could be Jews, and everybody
knew that Jews bought and ate Christian children. Or they could be
agents of the Church, sent to see if they could confiscate her property
because she was the kind of woman who sold her children to Jews.
They could be anybody.

"Gentle lady, please," she said. "Have consideration for a
mother's feelings. How should I sell my own flesh and blood, which
is very old Christian blood, you should know."

"That is very obvious," said the lady soothingly.

"In fact, we are descended from the Goths," added my mother.

"Of course," said the lady. "Actually, this was an entirely honorable proposition I had in mind. You see, my husband, Don Miguel
de Mendes y Mendoza, was wrecked on the rocks at La Coruña, and
I am traveling around the country until I have performed one hundred
acts of charity for the repose of his soul. I thought I'd take one of
your children into my house as a servant. The child would have food
and clothing, a virtuous Catholic upbringing, and a suitable marriage
portion arranged when she comes of age. What do you think of this
idea?"

Boy, my mamacita was in a quandary. Just what every Poor but
Honest Mother prayed would happen! One less mouth to feed without

the expense of a funeral! Still . . . I can just see her racing mentally down the list of *One Hundred Ways to Recognize a Secret Jew*, posted by the Holy Inquisition in every village square.

"I would have to have some kind of surety," she said slowly.

Beaming, the lady held out a purse, heavy and all clinquant, as the man says, with gold.

My mother swallowed hard and said: "Please excuse me, gentle lady, but you will surely understand my hesitation." She wasn't going to come right out and say, Would you care to stay for dinner, we're having pork?

The lady understood perfectly. Spaniards were as famed for paranoia as for courtesy in those days. She pulled out a little silver case that hung about her neck on a chain.

"I swear by the finger of Holy Saint Catherine of Alexandria that I am neither Judaizer nor Morisco," she declared. She leaned over and put the purse into my mother's hands, and my mother opened it and looked inside. Then my mother looked at all of us, with our gaping little mouths, and she sighed and shrugged.

"Honest employment is a good thing for a child," she said. "So. Which one would you like to hire?"

The lady looked us over carefully, like a litter of small cats, and said: "What about the one with the red hair?"

That was me. That was the first moment I can remember being aware of being *me*, myself alone. My mother came and got me and led me to the gate. The lady smiled down at me from the height of her horse.

"What about it, little girl?" she said. "Would you like to come live in a fine house, and have fine clothes to wear, and plenty of food to eat?"

"Yes," I said like a shot. "And my own bed to sleep in, too?"

Whereupon my mother slapped me, but all the fine folk laughed. "Yes," said the lady, "I'll take that one." So I was taken indoors to have my face washed while the strangers waited, and my mother stripped off my filthy shift and pulled a clean one on over my head. Then she leaned close to give me her last piece of advice before sending me out into the world.

"If those people turn out to have been lying, hija, you go straight to the Holy Inquisition and inform on them."

"Yes, Mama," I said.

Then we went out and I was lifted up in front of one of the men: he smelled of leather and musk perfume. We waved goodbye and rode slowly away into the golden morning. Goodbye Mama, Papa, Babies, Little Stone House!

I didn't cry. I was only four or five, but I knew I was going off on a splendid adventure. Food and clothing and my very own bed! Though before we had ridden many miles, the lady carefully explained to me that what she had told my mother wasn't exactly true: I was not to be a servant.

"In fact, little girl, we are going to do you a very great honor," she said. "We are going to betroth you to be married to a mighty lord. This will be much to your advantage, for then you will no longer be a little pauper: You will be a noblewoman."

It sounded fine to me, except: "I'm only a little girl. Big girls get married, not little ones," I observed.

"Oh, gentlefolk marry off their little children all the time," said the lady serenely. "Little princes, little princesses, two and three years old they hitch them up. So you see there's no problem."

We rode along for a while, past castles and crags, while I mulled this over.

"But I'm not a princess," I said at last.

"You will be," I was assured by the man who held me. He wore riding gauntlets with the cuffs embroidered in gold wire. I can see the pattern to this day. "As soon as he marries you, you see."

"Oh," I said, seeing nothing at all. But they all smiled at one another. What a slender, elegant lot they were, with their smiles and secrets. I considered my cotton shift and my grubby sandals, and felt as strange as red wheat in a vase of lilies.

"Why is this lord going to marry me?" I wanted to know.

"I told you, I'm arranging it as an act of charity," said the lady.

"But—"

"He loves little girls," laughed one of them, a very young man, his face still downy over the lip. The others all glared at him, and the lady rode between us and said:

"He too is a very charitable man. And life will be splendid for you from now on! You'll wear gowns of fine velvet and shoes lined with lamb's fleece. You'll have a bed all to yourself with sheets of the whitest lawn, the counterpane embroidered with ruby pomegranates and golden lilies. You'll have a servant to lift you into it each night. The pillow will be filled with whitest down from the wild geese that fly to England in the spring."

I stared at her. "What land is he lord of, this lord?" I asked finally.

"The summer land," said the lady. "Beyond Zaragoza." I didn't know where that was. "Shall I tell you about the palace where you'll live? The most beautiful palace of Argentoro, which is not least among the palaces of the world, being made of blocks of pure white marble veined with gold. The park around it is seven by seventy leagues to a side and filled with pleasant streams and walks; there are orange groves and pools where swim gold and silver fish. There are Indians and monkeys from the New World; there are rose gardens. Everything a little girl could want."

"Oh," I said again.

And again they all smiled at one another over my head.

Well, that had me floating on air. Except, in all the stories I'd ever heard, little princesses had big troubles. It was true that handsome princes usually came and rescued them, but the troubles came first and sometimes they lasted a hundred years.

Anyway, we rode on through green mountains, I asking questions and they laughing at me. By nightfall we reached a big old house set far back from the road, darkly shadowed by oak trees, and there wasn't a castle or an orange grove in sight.

They took me inside this dark house, and I must admit I had the biggest meal of bacon and onions I'd ever seen, all to myself. But when I asked them where the great lord was, they told me he'd be there soon; he was riding from a far country and it would take him days yet to arrive. Then they put me to bed alone in a room, all to myself—another promise kept—and for all my doubt I slept soundly.

I lived with those people in that house for maybe a week. I knew there was something odd about the household but, being a peasant child, didn't know that it was unusual for gentlefolk to live in a remote house with nearly no furniture, no servants, and no visible means of support—in that century, anyway. They had plenty of food of the finest quality (in my opinion), and their clothes were not threadbare. These weren't impoverished nobility; their purses were heavy with gold that never diminished.

They made no attempt to train me in any kind of work. In fact, I was left to myself to wander through the empty rooms of the house all day, while they came and went on mysterious errands. They were more and more evasive in answering my questions. Sometimes they gave conflicting answers, or fanciful ones a baby wouldn't have believed.

By sitting quietly where they didn't think I could hear, I gathered that the house was only a temporary place and we wouldn't be staying there long. The red-haired lady seemed to be their mistress; they all deferred to her. There was to be some kind of party soon, at a place called The Rocks, where other persons would be waiting for us.

The ring was turning my finger green, as the saying goes.

Then, one day, I was alone with the youngest man of the party. He was the only one who would play with me; he talked so much, the others were always cautioning him to silence. Watching from my cupboard window, I had seen the lady and her friends ride away that morning. I climbed out of bed and padded down the creaking stairs.

The young man was sitting on the empty kitchen floor. He had just opened a bottle of wine and raised it in a toast when he saw me peering around the doorway.

"Greetings, little one," he said, and drank deep. I stared at him. His doublet had small white birds and red hearts embroidered all over it. The hearts were silk and looked shiny-wet, like candies.

"I'm hungry," I told him.

"So eat." He pushed a tray across the flagstones with his boot. It had bread and cheese and radishes on it. I picked up a loaf of bread.

"It's too big." I pulled vainly at the crust.

He sent his dagger clattering across the floor toward me. I took it in surprise. Didn't he know that little children weren't supposed to play with knives? Suppose I planned to rob him? But I managed to slice some bread without taking off a finger as well and sat there chewing, staring at him thoughtfully. He kept on drinking the wine. By the time I had eaten most of the bread and cheese, his eyelids were drooping and his mouth was silly. I decided to try asking about my future one more time.

"What about this husband I'm supposed to have, señor?" I prodded.

He looked blank. Then he giggled and laid a finger beside his nose, which was the sixteenth-century body language equivalent of a broad wink.

"Well," he said. "Little lady, I'll tell you a great secret. He arrived here in the night."

"He did?" Oh, how my heart leaped up. "Where is he?"

"Ssh. Ssh. He's asleep. If you wake him, he'll be angry! He'll come down and strike you with a thunderbolt! Eh? So don't bother him. Anyway, you'll see him soon enough."

"When?" I wanted to know.

"Tonight." His smile got sillier. "At moonrise." And he took another long pull at his bottle. I sat there and fumed. Thunderbolts! Who did he think he was fooling?

He chuckled to himself for a while and finally took a long slow slide down the wall. When he arrived on the floor, he arranged his hat for a pillow and went unconcernedly to sleep. I headed for the staircase at once. I had to have a look at this great lord. Up the high bare creaking flight narrow as a ladder, I went; round and round to the top of the house.

At the end of the passageway was a shut door. I ran and pulled it open.

No lord there, with riding boots and sword propped beside his bed; no fine aristocrat pale against the bed linen. No. Only, leaning in the corner, the figure of a man all braided together out of sheaves of wheat. He was large as life and decked with colored ribbons, bright and frivolous as festival time.

Writing this down, I can still feel the howl of disappointment rising in me. I tiptoed into the room—God knows why I tiptoed, I could never wake him—and looked very closely to be sure.

A big straw dolly was all he was, like the play figures folk put up to decorate their houses at harvest time and burned later. I remembered seeing them. I remembered the priest scowling and telling us these were things of the Devil.

I had been crying quietly but clapped my hands over my mouth as Light Dawned on me.

Crash of cymbals for dramatic emphasis here. Actually, there had to have been quite a lot of crashing and other commotion going on downstairs at this point, but all I heard was my own heart pounding. These people were witches. The Devil gave them powers and that was where all the gold came from and of course all witches dressed in splendid clothes. No, wait, wasn't that secret Jews? Was it Jews who sacrificed little children to idols and witches who ate them, or the other way around? Whichever, I had to find the Holy Inquisition as fast as I could.

I turned and scurried down the stairs, arriving at the bottom landing to behold the hallway full of big men, booted and spurred. Two of them were dragging the young man out of the kitchen. He had puked all over his doublet in terror, and hung limp between them. A grim-looking fellow leaned down and said:

"Señor, the Holy Inquisition is waiting for you. It seems they wish to discuss a matter of faith."

"Are you Inquisidors?" I inquired, peering through the stair railings. All their heads swung up in astonishment.

"Yes," said the grim man.

With a cry of relief I ran down and hugged him around the legs.

He stared at me in shock. I can't imagine he got that kind of reaction from people very often.

"Thank you, Holy Inquisidor!" I babbled. "These people are witches and they were going to kill me and there's a big scary devil-thing upstairs, I saw it, and I didn't know how to find you but here you are! Please save me, señor!"

There was a moment's silence before he turned to his men and said:

"Seize this child also. And search the house."

Well, I didn't think anything was wrong, even when they hauled me out and set me on a horse and bound my hands to the pommel. After all, everyone knew the Holy Office played a little rough. I was so grateful to be saved, I didn't mind in the least. All I had to do (I thought) was explain everything to the Inquisidors and they would understand the danger I had been in. All would be well. Of course.

They brought out the young man—he was crying now—and tied him to a horse too. They brought out a big bundle containing everything they had found in the house; I could see the trailing ribbons of the wheat man.

"See, señor?" I pointed as well as I could with my hands bound. "There's the bad devil-thing. Are you going to burn this bad man, señor? Are you going to tell my mama and papa?"

But they wouldn't answer me. They all mounted; a man vaulted up behind me, and away we rode at a gallop. Just as before, my heart was bright and light. I was rescued! I was safe! Goodbye, dark house under the oak trees!

Well.

We came to the great city of Santiago in broad morning, by country lanes and by narrow city streets where not a soul moved, even in the light of day. I remember a city white with dust and blazing in all its stone ways: no people, I suppose because of the heat, but also because the Holy Office was secretive and came and went on near-deserted streets. The streets glared all the brighter for their emptiness. It hurt my eyes to look.

But soon enough we went under a big archway, the horses' hooves echoing back, and down steep stairs into darkness. And that was the last I had to worry about the sun hurting my eyes for a long time.

I was locked in a tiny dark room. There was a sort of wooden tray on the floor, filled with straw, to lie down in; there was a crockery pot to do something else in. No other thing in that room at all; no windows. The only light came from the grated window in the door.

So there I was, in the dungeons of the Inquisition.

3

IT REALLY WASN'T so bad at first. I was full of optimism; I sat there in the straw rehearsing all the things I would say to the Inquisidors when they sent for me—any minute now, I was sure—with a particularly dramatic rendering of how I found the wheat man at the top of the stairs. And at least I still had a bed to myself, though this one had a moldy smell.

And it really didn't bother me (at first anyway) when hours and more hours went by and nobody brought me anything to eat. I was used to that, I could manage. Sometimes at my mama's and papa's we went a day or two without eating. But after I had slept and woken three or four times, I was very thirsty, so I went to the door and yelled up at the little window.

Eventually there came a clumping of boots, and a big nose poked through the grate. I could just see a scowl behind it.

"I'm hungry and I want some water," I told the nose.

"You shut up," it said, "or I'll bring the gag in here."

"But I want something to eat." I backed away from the door a little.

"Got any money?"

"No." I blinked. Was he serious? I'd never held so much as a maravedi in my hand in my whole life.

"Then you may ask San Fructuoso to bring you some," he said, and clumped away. I sat down and cried. After a while I went back to sleep in the straw and was awakened by the sound of the cell door opening. A hand thrust through the blinding crack of light and set a pitcher of water on the floor; then it withdrew, and the door bumped shut. I scrambled to the water and drank greedily, until I got sick and spilled half of it on the floor.

After that I wasn't doing so well. I slept and woke and still got no food; I was beginning to feel very strange, very bad. The next time I woke to see the hand putting water in, I cried at it:

"Please, I need to have some bread!"

It hesitated, and a voice replied: "Your mother is supposed to pay for your food."

"My mama!" I was so excited. "Is she here?"

"Well, yes," said the voice.

"Tell her to come get me! Right away!"

The voice laughed and the door shut.

I got through the next few sleeps in happy anticipation of my mama coming for me, until once again the truth began to insinuate itself, whispering nastily behind its hand like the Devil in the paintings. I don't know how long I was a prisoner there. I couldn't see the sun; time had altered its pace with me. The Holy Office, I was to discover, had a whole different perception of time from the rest of the world.

Time had a few more tricks to play on me, as will be seen. That old devil Chronos.

At some point my door crashed open and brilliant light streamed in. I rubbed my eyes and tried to sit up. The figure of a man appeared in the light and looked at me.

"Little girl? Get up and come with me."

"You get me some food first," I croaked, glaring at him. He took a step or two into the room and crouched down to look at me. And though I know he had to be speaking Galician, because of course I couldn't speak Cinema Standard yet, I swear to God I remember him saying:

"Wow. You're in bad shape, aren't you?"

"Nobody has given me anything to eat since I've been in here!" I tried to yell.

He looked at another man, who was standing just outside the door. "Why is this?" he asked.

"Her mother, the woman Mendoza, has not made any provision for her keeping."

"She's not my mama!" I exclaimed. "She *bought* me from my mama! I don't have anything to do with her and she's a witch."

"Well, she says she's your mother," said the first man.

"She isn't either! She is Bad. I am Good. She's a witch and I told you all and you mean I've been stuck in here because nobody listened?'' In my rage and frustration I beat my fist against the floor.

The man regarded me with interest. He was short, stocky, and dark, like a Biscayan, with a close neat beard. His clothes were good but rather sober and nondescript.

"Days and days down here without any food and you're pretty mad about that, huh?'' he observed. I was so angry, I just stared at him in disbelief.

He gave a wry sort of smile and glanced over his shoulder at the other man. He gestured. The other man ostentatiously turned his back and stared at the opposite wall. From inside his doublet the Biscayan took a thing like a little book, and from its leaves he extracted something small. With great deftness he slapped it behind my ear before I could see what it was. I reached up to feel it, but he struck my hand away and said:

"Don't touch it. Maybe later you'll get some food, but right now the Holy Inquisition wants to talk to you.''

"Good,'' I said sullenly as he picked me up.

"You think that's good?'' He raised an eyebrow at me.

"Yes. I have a lot to tell them.''

He nodded thoughtfully and said nothing for a while as he carried me through endless stone passageways. Finally we came into a high room, very fine, with paneled walls and a distant ceiling. I felt swell and feared nothing.

There were three other men in this room, older than the Biscayan. One was a priest. One was dressed all in red. The other was mousy plain and I couldn't see much of him behind the lectern where his pen scratched. I was put down in a chair, and the others sat at a table to face me.

"So,'' said the priest. "You are the child Mendoza.''

"No, I'm not,'' I said.

Raised eyebrows. "May we ask who you are, then?'' asked the man in red.

"I got kidnapped by that bad lady, and *her* name is Mendoza,'' I said. "She's a wicked, terrible, evil lady. And a witch.'' The man in red looked interested. The other two exchanged glances. The priest leaned forward and said:

"Little girl, tell us the truth.'' And, that first time, there was nothing terrible in the phrase, no ominous reverberation.

Well, I told them the truth, the whole story, just as I'd rehearsed it so often in the dark. I enjoyed the attention. They only interrupted me once or twice, to ask questions. I finished quite cheerfully and concluded:

"Can I go home now, señors?"

There was no reply. The man in red was flipping through some papers on the table in front of him. "This seems very clear to me," he said. "Look here, at the inventory of goods taken from the house. A straw image of Satan. Various tools of witchcraft. Stars chalked on the floor."

"But how many points on the stars?" asked the priest.

"Some had five and some had six," conceded the man in red. The priest smiled tightly. The man in red went on, "Therefore, in my opinion, this is genuine witchcraft. The woman and her confederates were courting the powers of the Prince of Darkness and intended to sacrifice this child at a Sabbat."

"Yes," I confirmed.

"I think otherwise," said the priest, ignoring me. "With respect to his Grace, the Holy Office does not concern itself with superstitions. These are modern times, señor. Peasants believe in witchcraft; the odd corrupt nobleman plays at it; but it is not a thing to be feared."

"Surely you don't deny the evidence of the *Malleus Malificorum*?" demanded the man in red. His face was red too, and his eyes were bugging out a little.

"We disregard it entirely, señor," said the priest. "I mean, really. Women flying through the air on brooms. Toads that speak. What intelligent person credits such nonsense?"

"The Bishop, for one," said the man in red hotly. The Biscayan's smile twisted deeper into his beard, and the priest sighed and rested his chin in his palm. The man in red went on: "Do you deny that demons can be raised to give powers to those who worship Satan? The German, Paracelsus, was carried off by just such, as all men know. These things have been witnessed and proved, worthy Inquisidor."

"You are treading on very shaky theological ground, señor." The priest placed his hands flat on the table. "I would not, if I were you, assert that the Devil has powers equal to God's."

"I never said that." Now the man in red went white.

"Good." The priest nodded. "So, to the matter in hand."

"Nevertheless, we should remember that certain deluded souls do form cults to *attempt* to practice witchcraft," said the Biscayan diplomatically. I lifted my head to stare at him. This time he had spoken in flawless, erudite Castilian, with just a little Biscayan accent. "And the evidence found in the house resembles such things as these cults use.''

''That is possible, that they were cult objects,'' admitted the priest. ''But there are other dark rites that involve, for example, stars.'' He rounded on me. ''I believe this child is a secret Jew.''

Well, my hair stood on end. I couldn't get a word out, I was so terrified.

''Now, how have you arrived at such a conclusion, worthy señor?'' the Biscayan was asking in an intrigued voice.

''I think that house was a nest of secret Jews,'' said the priest. ''Look, in all this inventory you will find not one Christian object of worship. Those that dabble in sorcery keep inverted crucifixes, defiled hosts, and such trash. All their cult is based on Christian belief. But the secret enclaves of Judaism find such things abhorrent. Then, too, the woman Mendoza has consistently testified that this child *is* her child. I point out to you that they both have hair as red as Judas's beard. I think the child is lying, to disassociate herself from the others in hopes of escape. And you may depend upon it, she is our best hope of getting at the truth.''

I shook my head numbly. I didn't understand, they didn't understand, and what did all those big words mean? The man in red was looking considerably deflated, but he rallied enough to say (yes, I swear he did):

''She doesn't look Jewish.''

''None of them do anymore.'' The priest pointed at me with a sneer. ''Insidiously they have married into our noblest families and polluted the most ancient racial stock of Spain. Even here in the north, where the Moors never conquered! She may well have fair skin; it's only the more likely there's polluted blood there. The Jews have no interest in honest Spanish yeomen. They want noble wives, with rich dowers.''

''No!'' I yelled. ''I'm very poor! But pure, señor, my mama says so, we're descended from the Goths!'' Whatever they were, I certainly didn't know, but surely it was important.

''Tell us the truth,'' said the priest.

''I am telling the truth!''

''Who is your mother, if not the woman Mendoza?'' asked the Biscayan.

My downfall was coming, the consequence of spending my brief life as one of a swarming knot of children. ''She lives with my papa and the others. Our house is made of stones. It has tiles on the roof,'' I stammered.

"But what are your parents' names?" pressed the Biscayan.

"Mama and Papa," I said.

"What is your family name?"

I stared in confusion. The truth was, our house had been remote from the village and I had never heard anyone address my parents as Señor or Señora Anything. And my parents had been in the habit of addressing each other as Papacito or Mamacita or Mi Esposa. Very affectionate, I'm sure, but it sank me in deep waters. I sat there racking my brains.

The priest smote the table with his palm. "What is your name?" he said slowly.

"Hija?" I said at last. I had a long sonorous baptismal name, I knew I had, but I couldn't remember what it was.

"What is the name of your village?" tried the man in red.

A memory floated by and desperately I grabbed at it. "It's not Orense because Mama comes from there and she says it's better and she wishes she could go back."

"But where do you live?"

"I told you, in a little house. With a fence. And we have a goat."

Well, it went on like that for what seemed hours, with the dry quiet scratching of the pen taking it all down, establishing only that I was a little girl of unknown origin and apparently no Christian name. The priest seemed very excited, very happy. The man in red fumed. The Biscayan just looked fascinated by it all and kept pressing me for details, which of course I didn't have.

Then abruptly, in the middle of a question, he stopped and peered at me.

"Are you going to faint?"

"What?" I stared at him. But lights were dancing in front of my eyes.

"The child has had no food since the time of her arrest," he explained to the others. "It was assumed that she was the child of the woman Mendoza and her food would be paid for accordingly. However, no arrangements were made." He looked encouragingly at the man in red. "Which could be an argument for your point of view, señor. Surely, if the child was really her daughter, she'd have paid to send the child some food?"

"An oversight," the priest objected. "The woman has been in continuous interrogation since she was arrested. It could easily have slipped her mind."

"On the other hand, if the child's story is true, then the Holy Tribunal has the responsibility of providing her meals, assuming that she is, as she says, a pauper.'' The man in red tapped his finger on the documents in front of them.

The priest glared at him. "We have not yet established that her story is true in any respect."

"Worthy señors," the Biscayan started to say, at which point I swayed forward and threw up bile all over the floor. So the man in red, acting as the Bishop's representative, was able to authorize a loan with the Tribunal that I might buy a supper of milk and broth. The Biscayan took me off to a little side room and watched me as I dined.

Before I drank, he took a flask of something from within his doublet and poured it into my milk. I grabbed it and gulped at it.

"That tastes funny," I said suspiciously.

"What do you want, Rhenish wine?" he replied. "Drink. It'll make you strong. And believe me, you're going to need to be strong."

I shrugged. He leaned there, watching me. The intensity of his watching made me angry. There was no malice there, nor any sympathy, nor any human reaction at all that I could identify.

"You know, they put the woman Mendoza on the rack today," he remarked. "They're torturing her. To make her confess she's a secret Jew."

Was he trying to make me cry? I'd show him. I shrugged.

He studied me. "Doesn't upset you, eh?"

"She's a bad lady. She was going to kill me. I told you that."

He just nodded. "They're going to try to make you confess to being a Jew yourself, you know."

"But I'm not a Jew. I told them that," I said wearily. "If they would only take me back to my mama, she'd tell them."

"But they don't know where your mama is. You can't remember."

He had me there. I blinked back tears.

"Come with me now," he said, and held out his hand.

We went back into the other room, he sat me in my chair, and I glared at them all.

"Little girl, tell us the truth," said the priest.

"I told you the truth already," I said.

"If you do not tell us the truth," he said, just as if I hadn't spoken, "you will be severely punished."

"I did tell you the truth," I squeaked.

"Are you a Jew, little girl?"

"No!"

"When were you first taught Jewish rites?"

"What?"

"Have you ever been inside a Christian church?"

"Yes."

"That proves nothing." The priest made a gesture of dismissal. "The Jews go to Mass to mock the Sacrament. Many have confessed to it. What creed have you been taught, little girl?"

What was a creed? I sat mute.

"How often does your mother change her linen?"

"Oh, lots," I said. "She has to wash and wash, all the time." I meant rows and rows of little diapers drying on the bushes, but that hadn't been what *he'd* meant.

"She washes, eh? And does she wash your food, also, before she prepares it?"

"Sometimes."

The priest shot a triumphant look at the man in red. "You see? Even considering the child's age and mendacity, certain things may be discovered." Apparently he had scored a point of some kind. I looked from one to another of their faces, trying to guess what I'd done. The secretary got up to light a taper, because the room was filling with night. In this pause, the door opened and in came another Inquisidor.

"Excellence." He bowed. "The woman Mendoza has testified."

"And?"

He looked cautiously at me, but the priest waved him on. "She has confessed that she is a practitioner of sorcery and stole the child from her parents."

"See!" I yelled, and the man in red positively grinned.

"She has also confessed, however," the Inquisidor continued, "to being a secret Jew, to being a Morisca, to being the concubine of Almanzor, and to being the Empress of Muscovy." There fell a disgruntled silence.

"Continue the inquiry," ordered the priest. "Persuade her."

The Inquisidor bowed and left. "This always happens," remarked the man in red.

The priest swung back to me. "Do you see what happens to liars, little girl?"

"Yes," I said.

"I don't think you do." He stood up. "We must show you."

They got up, and the Biscayan took me firmly by the wrist, and we left that room with the secretary scurrying after us, fumbling his paper and pen. We went along some halls to a dark place that smelled bad. I could hear crying, loud crying. I remember a little window high in a wall. They opened it and lifted me up to look through. It was dark in there, but as my eyes got used to the darkness, I could see glowing coals . . . and other things I would prefer not to describe.

My eyes hurt. And I couldn't breathe. The priest put his face up very close and said:

"You can save your mother. All you have to do is tell us the truth."

I remember trying to push his face away with my hand because his breath was very hot. I found myself staring at the Biscayan. He was leaning against the wall, watching me, his mouth set, his eyes blank.

I don't remember what I said, but I must have said something to make them take me down from that terrible little window and let me look anywhere else. They didn't take me back to my cell. I was taken to a different room, a tiny place. One chair filled it entirely. Here I was put, and the door was closed. I was left alone in the dark.

But not for long. Briefly the door opened, and the man in red looked in at me. His eyes were full of compassion. "Pray, my child," he told me. "Accept Jesus Christ as your Savior. Take this comfort." He hung something on the inside of the door and closed it again.

A little light slanted down from somewhere, and a figure swam toward me out of the darkness. It was Jesus on the Cross.

A word here about comparative styles in religious art. My little village church had been built in the Gothic style. Stone arches, no plaster, not much decoration. Its furnishings were similarly rude and rustic, for we were, after all, a very poor parish. A few rough saints chopped out of the local stone, smoky candles guttering on rock. The church's great crucifix was old and ax-hewn, stuck up in the shadows behind the altar, and what with the distance and the darkness, Jesus looked as if He were standing in a tree, watching us with alert if yellowed eyes.

But this crucifix, now, was a fine expensive modern thing, from Castile or maybe even Naples. This might have been the Bishop's very own crucifix. It was as real as they could make it. Someone had carved, someone had sanded and polished that poor gaunt body with such care that every bone and sinew shaped out perfect, anatomically precise. Someone had painted it with matte-smooth paint, the color of gray pearls or the skin of a dying man. And not to forget the details: the wounds pink and crusted with black at the edges for dried blood, just like the real thing. The wet yellow stain seeping down from the side wound. The artist who reproduced those thin red lines from the flagellum must have had a tiny brush, fine as an eyelash; yes, and he must have studied real welts, laid on live sweating backs, to show the bruising so well. The matted hair and vicious crown of thorns were reproduced with such veracity that you could see the dust caking the braids, you could see the bright blood drops.

But it was the face, of course, that was the masterwork.

An intelligent face, eyes wide and dark. You could imagine this Christ laughing, or angry, or asleep. Beyond all that, you could see the God shining through the man.

Having given you all this, this living Christ that your heart went out to, the artist put the knife in and twisted it. The mouth was opening in a gasp of pain, the teeth were bared in agony. Those live dark eyes looked out in desperation from that agony to plead, to ask a question I had no answer for. God was being murdered in front of my eyes.

So He hung before me in the gloom, illuminated by one weak beam of light. I was terrified. I couldn't get away, I couldn't.

"I'm sorry, Lord Jesus, I'm sorry, Lord Jesus, I'm sorry, Lord Jesus . . ."

"Why are you causing me such suffering?" cried my hallucination through bleeding lips.

"I don't know, Lord Jesus. I'm sorry, Lord Jesus. Couldn't we get you down from there and get you a barber-surgeon or something?"

"No."

"Couldn't we put bandages on you to make you better?"

"No."

"But why not?"

"Because my suffering is eternal. While men live, they must sin; and while they sin, I must bleed here. I am dying in torment for you. You are the one who pushes these thorns in my flesh by your sin."

"But when did I sin?"

"In the Garden. Because you sinned there, God sent me to be crucified."

"I'm sorry! I don't remember what I did in the garden, but I'm sorry! Can't you come down now?"

"Never." The weary eyes closed for a moment. He was so beautiful, He was in such pain, and I'd have done anything to get those nails out of His hands and feet. But I was so afraid of Him.

"It's not my fault," I wept. "I wasn't even born then."

"That doesn't matter," He explained. "As part of the human race, you are born to Sin. You're one of the daughters of Eve. You can't avoid Sin even if you want to."

"Then no matter what I do, I'll always hurt you?" I was appalled.

"Yes."

"Who made things this way?"

"I did." Sweat glittered on His brow. "I took your state upon myself to redeem you from all Sin."

"I don't think that's such a good idea," I said. "You should go back to heaven and live with the angels. How could I ever be happy again if I hurt you so much? I don't *want* you to suffer for me."

"You will not be saved."

I looked around at the darkened room, remembered my cell and the other room. "But I'm already damned, aren't I? And at least you won't be up on that cross anymore."

"You really mean this?" He looked intently at me.

I meant it with all my heart.

So He shrugged, and the nails came flying out of His hands and feet like bullets. The crown of thorns sprang away from His head like a lute string snapping. His stigmata closed, healed over, were gone. The weals of the scourge receded into His skin.

He stepped down from the Cross, pulled His red robe around Himself, and gave me a courteous nod before striding into the darkness and disappearing. I collapsed back into my chair, overwhelmed with relief. It was short-lived.

The door burst outward and light blinded me. My three Inquisidors stood there, dark against the light like mountains. The priest looked furious. He must have found out that I was talking to Jesus, I thought. "Are you ready to tell us the truth?" he said.

"What?" I blinked at him. He reached in and pulled me out, twisting, by the wrist.

"We have been gentle with you to this hour. We will soon be driven to force if you do not repent."

"I repent!"

"Then tell us the truth."

"I did!"

"We do not believe you. We will go down, now, to show you what will happen to you if you do not repent." And then we went that bad way again, to the bad-smelling place. There the priest set me down and said:

"Now, tell us the truth. Are you a secret Jew?"

And for the first time I wondered: Could I possibly be a Jew and not even know it? Jews were liars, everybody said so. I told lies myself, now and then. Was it possible I'd fooled even myself? Was that why I felt so guilty about poor Jesus? Had I made up a story about Christian parents to conceal my crimes? I swallowed hard and said: "I might be. I think. I don't know."

"I see," said the priest, all smooth now. "And *we* see. *We* know the truth. You're a very wicked child, to have waited so long to tell us." But I hadn't said positively. I stared at him in bewilderment.

"I'm sorry."

"You can save your mother more pain if you tell us everything."

I just stared. I couldn't think up things off the top of my head, I needed time. "But we can continue later," he said, as if reading my mind. "At another time. Until then, you can think about the things you will tell me."

How stupid I'd been, to try to hide anything from such a man.

The Biscayan led me away, back, I thought, to my cell; but halfway there he stopped and put his hand flat on a place in the wall beside us. There was no latch, no subtle engine that I could see, yet a little door clicked and swung inward. "Come with me," he said, and stepped through quickly and pulled me after him. The door closed behind us.

We went into a brilliantly lit room where there was another man. The man wore some manner of thin white surcoat over his clothes. He talked with the Biscayan in a language I did not know. He sounded nervous. When they had spoken together, the Biscayan left. I looked up at the man in the white surcoat.

He took away my rags and shaved my head. He had to put me in restraints to do that, and I thought the end had come. I screamed and screamed. I said I'd tell him everything. He never said a word in reply, but his face went very red. He put needles in my skin. He drew out a tube of my blood. He spent a long time examining my bare skull with calipers.

Writing about this now, I still can't bring myself to laugh at it much.

In time he covered me with a blanket and went away. I was left there trembling under the glaring lights. Much later, the door opened, and the Biscayan came into the room. He pulled up a chair and sat down beside me where I lay. "Well, little Mendoza," he said. "You're not doing so well, are you?"

"Are you going to burn me in the fire?" I asked him.

"No, Mendoza, not I. I am, in fact, your greatest friend in the world right now."

I looked at him in deep distrust. His black eyes were kind, he was turning on the charm, but I had seen him looking on blank while the priest deviled me. "I know who my friend is," I said. "The man in the red clothes. Not you."

"Well, unfortunately he isn't here right now. He's been recalled

to the Bishop for a reprimand. And you certainly know that Fray
Valdeolitas isn't your friend. He thinks you're guilty. I, on the other
hand, know you're innocent.''

"You mean I'm not a secret Jew?" I was dazed.

"No, of course not. You're only a little girl who has been treated
badly for no reason at all. I think that's unfair. I'd like to help you,
Mendoza.''

"Then why didn't you stop the priest?"

"I couldn't, then. His rank in the Holy Office is a lot higher than
mine. But look, I've hidden you away here; and I am prepared to offer
you even more safety.''

"How?" My heart beat fast.

"Let's talk a little first." He pulled his chair closer. "You know
by now what happens to people when the Holy Office finds them
guilty, don't you?''

"Yes," I whispered. "They burn in a big fire."

"And you don't want that to happen to you."

"Oh, no."

"Right. But suppose I let you walk out of here right now. You've
lost your mama and papa. Who will take care of you? Where will you
sleep when night comes?'' My eyes filled with tears, and the Biscayan
patted my hand soothingly. "It's scary, isn't it? But you know what's
even more scary than that? Listen to me, Mendoza.

"You'd go out of here and maybe you'd starve to death in a week
or two, because you haven't got any money, have you? Wouldn't that
be awful? To escape from here and die anyway.''

"Yes." I was glassy-eyed: New Horizons in Fear.

"But, suppose you didn't die so soon? Suppose you lived to be
twenty years old. That's good, yes? Except that it's still very hard to
stay alive. You'll have to do things you don't like, bad things maybe.
And what if you get killed by the plague or soldiers? Terrible, terrible.

"Maybe you'd be lucky. Maybe you'd live to be thirty. Another
ten years. That's not very long, is it? But do you know what happens
when you live to be thirty?'' He took my hand and held it up. "Look
here, look at your nice smooth skin. Some morning you'll wake up,
and it won't be smooth anymore. It'll become cracked, crumpled. It
won't get better. And see, can you see the blue veins here that run
up the back of your hand? One day you'll think, Why are they sticking
out so much? And why are my knuckles poking out so much?

"Only little things, but more of them will come with every year
you cheat death. Your teeth will begin to break and hurt. You'll keep
getting sick. Maybe you'll be beautiful when you grow up, but then

you'll have to watch your looks slip away, year after year. Your flesh will hang and sag. One day you'll see your reflection somewhere and see the flesh has pulled back from your bones and you'll see ghosts: your mother's face, your father's, not *yours* anymore. You'll be very frightened.

"Do you know what happens then, if you live ten more years, or ten more? Such a short time, but do you know what you'll be then?" He leaned close. "Did you ever see the old women with their black shawls who sit in the marketplace? Their mouths are loose and flappy because all their teeth are gone. They're all bent up like little birds, their fingers are twisted like claws. Some of them are blind. All their bones hurt, and they never have any fun. They're afraid to die, but the longer they live, the sicker and lonelier they become. But once, Mendoza, they were children like you. And some day, you'll be just like them."

"No!" I burst into tears. He loosed the restraints and lifted me up against his shoulder consolingly.

"Yes, I'm afraid so," he went on. "If you don't die young, that's all you have to look forward to. But then the day comes when you die because your body is so old. Bad things happen to the dead. Have you seen dead men on the gibbet?" I had. I shuddered against him. "And if you've been good, then you go to Purgatory, and devils torture you with fire until all the Sin is burned out of you. But if you've been bad, you go to Hell. You know what Hell is now, you've seen it. And it's so hard not to be bad.

"Now, there's a reason for my telling you this. I don't like to frighten little girls, I'm not like Fray Valdeolitas. But I had to show you what it is to be a mortal, to be trapped in the round of time. And you don't have to be trapped there, Mendoza. There is a way out, for you."

I lifted my face and stared at him to see if he was lying. But he wasn't smiling at all. "I would like to find the way out," I said, conscious for the first time of what Understatement was.

"Who wouldn't?" He sat me up on the table and arranged the blanket around my shoulders. "But you're one of the lucky ones. I'll tell you a secret, little Mendoza. I'm not really an Inquisidor. I'm a kind of spy. I go into the dungeons of the Inquisition and I rescue little children like you. Not just any little children; if they're stupid, or if their heads are the wrong shape, or if there's anything wrong with their bodies, then I can't save them. But the other ones I save, and I send them to my master, who is a very powerful magician . . ."

"Magician?"

"All right, so he's not a magician, he's a doctor. Such a learned doctor, he can cure you of old age and death. Mind you, you will grow up. You won't stay a little child forever."

I nodded and wiped my nose. This was all right with me; I had no desire to stay small. Children lead a miserable life. "What do I have to do, señor?"

His eyes warmed. "You'll work for the doctor. It's the best work in the world, Mendoza: you'll be saving things and people from time, just like me. What do you say?"

I swung my legs over the edge of the table and attempted to get down. "Get me out of here and I'm all for this doctor, señor."

He laughed and called in a guard. I looked at the guard fearfully, but the Biscayan said:

"This little girl unfortunately died under questioning. It will be some time before her body is discovered." The guard just nodded. The Biscayan sat down and filled out a kind of tag, which he fastened to my blanket, and he stamped my hand with a device in red ink. "It was nice meeting you, Mendoza," he said. "Now, go with this man and he'll take you to my doctor friend. See you in twenty years, eh?"

"Come on." The guard nodded to me. We went into a tiny room that jerked and shuddered and dropped. Then a door opened on a corridor that seemed to stretch away for miles. For all I know, it did. The guard was carrying me by the time we got to the other end; we came out into a great cavern, big as a ballroom, the ceiling vast and distant.

How to turn my eyes back to the eyes of that little primitive and tell the thing I saw? A silver cannon. A gleaming fish. A tin bottle that somehow had rooms and windows in it, studded with rubies that blinked steadily.

Oh, I stared. There were people walking around in silver clothes, too. Over in a corner was some furniture: big, thickly cushioned chairs and a table. Huddled around it were three tiny children like me: blankets, tags, no hair. There were toys scattered on the table, but the little kids weren't playing with them. They clung to each other, silent and owl-eyed. Two of them had been crying. With them sat a lady as beautiful as an Infanta is supposed to be. She was watching them glumly.

My guard led me to them. Turning to us, the lady switched on a bright smile and stood. "Here's the other one," growled my guard.

"Welcome, little—" She tilted her head to read my tag. "Mendoza!" she exclaimed in peculiarly accented Spanish. "Are you ready to come meet some new friends and take a lovely trip?"

"Maybe." I stared up at her. "Where am I going?"

"Terra Australis." Flash, flash went her smile. "You'll like it there. It's lots of fun. Would you like to come sit with the other children now?" So I took her hand (she smelled like flowers) and went to sit down. The children cried and cringed away from me. I eyed them in disgust, looked at the cluttered table, and asked:

"Can anybody play with these toys?"

"Please." She fairly leapt forward and swept them to me. "See, here's a dear little donkey and a horse and here's a sailing ship and these books have pretty pictures on each page. Shall we play together?"

I looked at her, appalled. "No, thank you, señora," I said. "I'll just look at the pictures, all right?"

So I sat and paged through the bright improbable books. There were pictures of children watching other children play games. Children in gardens growing flowers. Children sitting at tables passing each other abundant food. Happy, healthy, laughing children. Not a skeleton or prophet anywhere in sight.

The others sat and stared at me. After a while, one of the boys reached out timidly for the horse. He held it up to his mouth and bit down on its head. I guess he was unnerved.

The people in silver clothes ran around and did things to the ship with silver ropes, feed lines they must have been, and there was shouting and now green lights began to blink with the red. I put down the book and watched, fascinated.

A man came and said something to the señora. She stood up briskly. "Come on, niños y niñas! Time to go off on a wonderful adventure!" The two really little ones let themselves be scooped up like zombie babies, but the boy with the horse clung to the cushions and howled. The señora had her arms full of children and looked on helplessly.

"Shut up, you stupid piece of crap!" I hissed at him. "You want them to give us back to the Inquisidors?"

"He can't understand you," said the señora. "He's a little Mixtec."

A man came and picked up the boy and carried him with us. We all went into the ship, and we children were fastened into our seats with straps. I didn't care; at least, not until the cavern opened above our heads and we rose up through it into the night sky. Then I screamed like the rest of them. Goodbye, Spain. Goodbye, Jesus. Goodbye, human race.

4

THERE WERE TWO ladies on the ship, the beautiful señora and a little woman with red skin, also beautiful. She wore a pendant with a feathered serpent on it. She went and talked soothingly to the little Mixtec in (I assume) Mixtec talk. He calmed down. Afterward she and the señora leaned back on a cabinet and talked wearily, in yet some other language. They sipped something from white cups. Then the señora crunched hers in one hand and flung it into a bin. She came toward me, turning on her smile again.

"How are we doing, uh, Mendoza?"

"Fine." I looked up at her. "Have you got any food?"

"Yes, we'll be serving lovely food in just a few minutes. Are you bored?"

Not me, no, I'd been waiting for the ship to fall out of the sky and kill us all. I shook my head, and she said: "Would you like me to tell you a story?"

"Yes," I said. So she settled into the cushions beside me and began:

"Once, long ago, when the world was very new, there was a queen and a wicked old king. This king's name was Time. Now, he had heard a prophecy that his children would be greater than he was. Do you know what a prophecy is?"

Of course I did. I nodded.

"And he didn't want this prophecy to come true, because he was very wicked and jealous. So, King Time did something very terrible. Do you know what he did?"

I could guess.

"Whenever the queen had a baby, the wicked king would steal it away. And then he'd eat it—whole—just like you'd swallow a grape.''

No way. He'd have to cut them up with a sword first. I folded my hands in my lap and waited to see what she'd say next.

"Yes, it's terrible, I know, but the story has a happy ending. Because, you see, at last the queen thought of a way to fool the wicked king. The next time she had a baby, she hid it, and wrapped a big stone in its swaddling clothes, so the king swallowed the stone instead. The little baby was hidden far away on a magical island and tended by beautiful nurses.

"He grew up into a hero whose name was Blue Sky Boy. He was king of all the thunderstorms. He had a spear made of lightning! But he thought, always, of his poor brothers and sisters who were trapped inside King Time. So, as soon as he could, he went and did battle with the wicked king.

"Oh, it was a dreadful battle! Against his son, King Time sent his years. They were giants, those years, and they fought hard with Blue Sky Boy. His handsome body became thick with muscles, his smooth face became rough with black curly beard. But in the end he defeated the years and hurled a big bolt of lightning right through the heart of Time. Time stopped dead. He fell helpless on the ground.

"And Blue Sky Boy cut open Time and, guess what? Out popped all his brothers and sisters. There they were, alive again. And even though Blue Sky Boy was the youngest of them all, he became the new king over them because he alone had conquered Time. And they were all so grateful to him, they became his faithful subjects.

"Now, this is a very important story for you to remember. Did you like it?''

"Yes," I said. "I know a story also. Want to hear it?''

So I told her the one about a man who kicks a skull out of his way as he goes along the road, and for a joke he invites it to come to his house for supper by way of apology, and that night it comes to his house and tears out his throat at the table. The señora didn't seem to care for it much.

The little red lady was telling the Mixtec boy a story too. Probably something involving a fratricide.

5

I WOULDN'T HAVE said Terra Australis was lots of fun. It was even hotter than Spain. But, oh, was everybody nice to us.

We crossed a lot of water and flew over a dry red land, remote and silent. We touched down within the high walls of Terra Australis Training Compound 32–1800. It had been there about fifteen hundred years when I was enrolled, and had had time to install all the little amenities: air conditioning, laser defense, a piano in the gymnasium. Within its towering walls were gardens and playgrounds and the domes of cool subterranean classrooms. And hospitals. And warehouses. In fact, most of the place was underground.

It wasn't all that different from any particularly demanding boarding school, except that of course nobody ever went home for the holidays and we had a lot of brain surgery.

That was the first thing they did to us, too, the Mixtec and I and a couple of other shaven-headed kids our size. They put us to bed though it was midday, stuck us all over with needles, and the next thing I knew, I was waking up with my head turbaned in bandages. Then everything was different, because they had installed the first of the high-tech stuff, had begun the Process that would transform us from mortal human children into something else entirely. I could now understand the excessively cheery nurses when they spoke to me. They brought me games to play with boxes full of winking lights. I made the right guesses: I touched the right pictures with the light pencil. A doctor pronounced me fit for further processing, and they sent me on down the line.

One day I was given fine clothes to wear, the uniform smock for the neophyte class, with the Company's device emblazoned on the

front pocket, of course. The hat that went with it wouldn't fit over
my bandaged head yet, so I swaggered along after the nurse pretending I was a Morisca. She took me into a big room.

I stopped in my tracks. There were about twenty other little children in the room, each one my size, each one dressed just like me
with a turban of bandage. There all resemblance stopped. I saw blackamoor children and yellow-skinned children and red and brown children. I saw children pale as mushrooms. They were all lined up in
rows of identical desks, and I was ushered to one vacant one. I sat
there staring around. I saw the Mixtec boy not too far away. He met
my eyes and said:

"They cut open my head."

"I know that," I said.

"Did you get cake?"

"Yes."

Then some grown-ups came into the room, and one of them
rapped on the wall and shouted, "Children! Attention please!" We
all fell quiet as mice. Some of us cringed.

They were three big men who smiled at us. They were really
something to see. One was a white man, dressed like all the men I
had ever seen, in an ordinary doublet and hose. One was a yellow
man, in a beautiful silk robe. One was a blackamoor man, who wore
a long caftan. Worked into the snowy cotton of the caftan, and into
the embroidery of the silk robe, and stamped on the doublet buttons
was the same device I had on my uniform pocket.

The men told us their names were Martin, Kwame, and Mareo,
and they were there to welcome us and tell us about Dr. Zeus. In the
splendid polycultural speech that followed, I found out that the most
amazing series of coincidences had occurred! Not only I but *every
single child in that room* had been orphaned, or kidnapped, or abandoned. Every one of us had been facing certain death when we met
a nice man or nice lady who promised us eternal life if we'd let
ourselves be rescued. I wasn't so sure my Biscayan had been a nice
man, but he'd certainly rescued me.

Anyway, here we were, all safe now, guests of a wonderful hero
named Dr. Zeus. This Doctor was very kind-hearted and also very
smart. He wanted to save the whole world. It was a shame he hadn't
been able to save our mommies and daddies, but at least he'd saved
us, and some day we'd all live with him in his magic kingdom, which
was called the future. The future was a long way off, though, so until
we got there, we were going to pass the time being the Doctor's
helpers. We'd save all sorts of things for the Doctor, save them from

the evil destructive mortal people like the ones who'd taken away our families: we'd save beautiful paintings and books, animals, flowers, even little children like ourselves. It would be easy for us to do all this, too, because we'd grow up stronger and smarter than poor defective mortals. And we had all the time in the world to do these things because we would never, ever die, and because Dr. Zeus was the Master of Time.

After they had explained all this to us, smiling with beautiful clean white smiles, other people came in and served us ice cream. If any of us hadn't yet been convinced, the ice cream won us over. We all decided we loved Dr. Zeus.

Later they ushered us out, two long lines of little ones, to the playground. It was in a cavern of white glass, open at the top to show a disk of blue sky, as though we moved under acreage of staring eye. There were trees in this cavern, and vast green playing fields. There were big kids playing ball. Boys and girls, they all wore their hair cropped close to the skull. We cowered together at the sight of them. But then our nurses led us to our own special playground, which made us feel safe because it had a nice high fence all around it. There were playbars and swings painted in brilliant colors, but we were told we couldn't play on them yet because our heads were still healing. So we moped around and stared at one another.

I wanted to look at the blackamoor children up close. I followed one little girl who had retreated behind some bright crawl-barrels to tear at her bandages.

"Did you get left in the bed by Almanzor?" I wanted to know.

She stared at me as though I was crazy. "Who's he?"

"You know, he leaves black babies with people."

She shrugged and went on pulling at the bandages. I studied her. She wasn't black like soot at all but brown, with copper lights under the brown. The palms of her hands were as pink as mine. Abruptly she said, "We look awful in these hats. I hate them. We look like the Smoke Men."

"Who?"

"*They* come in the night. They ride the animals that smell. My daddy went out with his spear and they cut his head off."

"Oh."

"This hat is hurting my hair."

"Your hair is all gone now," I pointed out. "They shaved it off. They shaved everybody's hair off."

She looked sullen. "I know mine is under there. And I won't wear this ugly hat."

"I thought Moriscos wore hats like this."

"What is a Morisco?"

"You know." I was confused. "*You* are."

"No, I'm not," she said firmly. "I'm Spider People. What are you?"

Good question. "I think I'm a Jew," I said at last. "But maybe not."

"What's a Hue?" She put her head on one side to stare at me, tape trailing down.

"It's . . ." I had no idea, after all. She went on:

"You know how I got here? I'll tell you. The Smoke Men rode around and around, like big ghosts flapping, and set fire to all our houses. But I ran and climbed up in a tree. Dogs came and ate the dead people. Then it was night and I woke up in the tree and Spider was up in the tree with me. I could see Him, all black against the stars.

"Well, He said, You know who's down there? Dry Bone Dog. You don't want to go with him, do you? And I said NO.

"So then Spider said, I can steal you away from Dry Bone Dog if you want me to. I can turn you into a cane stick and carry you away.

"But *I* said, I hate You and all Your magic. You were supposed to look after my daddy and everybody. What's wrong with You anyway? Why did You let those Smoke Men come?

"He just went like *this*—" She shrugged again. "And He said, I'll help you now anyway, if you want me to. And I could see Dry Bone Dog down there under the tree. I could see his eyes down there. So I said YES and we climbed up into the Sky Boat, I don't remember how. But He left me, now I'm here and He's gone. And I won't ever be His Spider People again! He's no good." She clenched her tiny fists. "And they put this ugly, *ugly* hat on my head."

"No, no, no, dear!" A nurse found us. "Leave the bandages alone. They're good for you." She produced a roll of tape from nowhere and bound up the trailing ends again, while the little girl glared. "Now, come over here with the other children. Nurse Uni will show you nice pictures and we'll have story time."

So, sulking, we went, to hear all about the wonderful Oz Wizard and the magic body parts he gave people.

In this way our education began.

They didn't waste any time; they made us little geniuses right at the start. Languages, sciences, facts by the zillions, we got them as fast as they could spoon them to us. Speed reading, sleep teaching, hypnosis: when our cranial adjustments were far enough along, they could cram bytes straight into our heads. Encyclopedic knowledge and perfect recall by the age of six. Not bad, eh?

Making us immortal was more time-consuming. Our class had operations the way other students have midterm exams, thirty bandaged neophytes moaning in a ward at once. Always some new symbiote or nanobot or hardware to be put in, or some nasty defective mortal part to be excised. I don't recall anyone mentioning the ugly word *cyborg*, however.

We had years upon years upon interminable years of Phys. Ed.— not to get us into shape, for we were already perfect, but to train the new reflexes that enabled us to dodge bullets at point-blank range. Hypnotherapy to convince us it was impossible we should ever age or die, drugs to heighten our powers of unconscious observation, cellular tinkering I can't even begin to describe.

Do you have some mental image of a gymnasium full of us Überkinder, flawless mechanized specimens training to smash the supervillains of the world with our bare hands? Well, you *would* imagine that, if you were a stupid mortal monkey. We knew better.

Smashing things is the violent way stupid mortal monkeys solve their problems. We were taught so many other ways of resolving difficult situations: negotiation, compromise, bribery, strategic falsehood, or simply running away at amazing speed. You see, being immortal just means you can't die. It doesn't mean you can't be hurt.

Besides, we weren't made to battle villains, because there weren't any. No nation, creed, or race was any better or worse than another; all were flawed, all were equally doomed to suffering, mostly because they couldn't see that they were all alike. Mortals might have been contemptible, true, but not evil entirely. They did enjoy killing one another and frequently came up with ingenious excuses for doing so on a large scale—religions, economic theories, ethnic pride—but we couldn't condemn them for it, as it was in their mortal natures and they were too stupid to know any better.

No, our job was to protect them from their own butchery, and (better still) to protect the other inhabitants of the Earth from the destruction wreaked by human nature.

Pretty lofty, isn't it? Imagine being told that it hadn't mattered whether the Christians or the Moors got Spain! I can still remember my shock. I got over it fairly quickly, though, because by that time I had learned enough history to know that in the long run it never mattered a damn where any particular race of people planted its collective ass. And, really, why should I care? I wasn't one of them anymore.

To be honest, I don't think I would have got on all that well with the human race anyway. The Company did not put that fundamental dislike there. Possibly the Inquisition did. Very likely my Biscayan saw that quality in me and knew it would make the estrangement from mortality easier.

In any case, my aptitude test scores determined that I should not be one of those immortals who works much with human beings. I was trained as a botanist instead. I became one of those cheerful and useful children out of our own books, trudging around my garden project with a watering can, growing big bright flowers.

It was a good decision, because I really loved the things I grew. The leaf that spreads in the sunlight is the only holiness there is. I haven't found holiness in the faiths of mortals, nor in their music, nor in their dreams: it's out in the open field, with the green rows looking at the sky. I don't know what it is, this holiness: but it's there, and it looks at the sky.

Probably though this is some conditioning the Company installed to ensure I'd be a good botanist. Well, I grew up into a good one. Damned good.

6

Mr. Silanus paced across the front of the classroom. On the chalkboard at his back, a few names: MASADA. WARSAW. JONESTOWN. MARS TWO.

"So as we've seen, not one faith has ever lived up to its promises. The world has never become a paradise, quite the opposite, in fact: think of the millions upon millions slaughtered, tortured, imprisoned for this great idea, this good news, this revolution. The visionary who works against human nature to impose his—or her—sweeping vision on the world is inevitably its worst enemy.

"Now, who isn't? Consider the work of certain individual mortals who set themselves simple tasks. They saw no need to raise armies; they saw no need for revolution or bloodshed; they worked instead for realistic goals with the tools they had. And they succeeded, and *their* works have been of lasting benefit to humanity." He erased the board with relish and chalked a new set of names: DICKENS, PASTEUR, LISTER, FLEMING, TERESA, MUIR, KOBIAR, LUONG.

"People like these have done more to relieve human misery than any prophet with a manifesto ever will. They number in the millions, these mortals, but they don't make it into the history books much. They don't do anything sweeping or controversial. They live their lives, contribute their bits of good work, and die quietly in their beds without recognition or reward. Usually. But they make a difference for the good that no true believer ever can.

"Before we meet again on Friday, access the biographies of these mortals and review their lives. Read the complete works of Charles Dickens and be able to explain them in their historical context. Ac-

cessing on your own, see if you can add more names to this list and
be ready to explain your choices. All clear? Class dismissed.''

We drifted out of the classroom, we wonder children.

"Isn't he the most handsome man?" breathed Nancy, twisting at
a lock of her wig. She'd never stopped trying to get her hair to grow.
We'd both vowed to let it grow down to our ankles once the lab techs
stopped tinkering with our brains.

"Double-plus wowie," I agreed.

"I've heard he went to the Crusades to rescue Moslem babies.
I'll bet he looked divine in armor." She pressed the elevator button.
The door opened, and we stepped in, our hoop skirts crowding the
other passengers.

"You couldn't get me to work in the Holy Land for absolutely
anything," I stated.

She clicked her tongue derisively. "As if you had a choice!"

"I do," I said, smug. "I'm fixing it. I'm making my specialty
New World flora, so they'll have to send me there. Hardly any mortals
out there at all. No bloodthirsty zealot fanatic murderers."

"What about the Aztecs?"

"They're just in one part of the New World, aren't they? It's two
big continents and there's miles and miles where mortals have never
even set foot. You can keep your Europe."

She rolled her eyes. "You're fooling yourself. There are mortals
everywhere. You'll have to work with them sometime, you know."

"Not me. Not Mendoza. The only fieldwork I'm doing is in empty
fields. No totally disgusting killer apes for me, thank you very much."

"My, I can see why they didn't make you an anthropologist.
You're headed for trouble with an attitude like that, you know." She
shook her finger at me. She was right, too. And far wiser than I: she
became an art preservation specialist and didn't even have to set foot
in the field until the seventeenth century. And then she got to pose as
a wealthy art patron's Algerian mistress. In Italy. Some people have
all the luck. I wouldn't mind lying around in a gondola in some nice
civilized country but oh, no, I had it all figured out, hadn't I?

The elevator slowed to my floor.

"Oh, um, can I borrow your holo with the footage of Quin Shi?
Something happened to mine in the machine and I've got an assignment on him."

"I'll leave it in your cube." The doors clanked open. "Bye,
Mendy."

"Bye, Nancy."

Ah, the life of a teenage cyborg.

*   *   *

I have an old holostat online somewhere, more crackly and pointy with every passing year, of my graduation class at their Commencement Picnic and Swim Party.

There we are, a double row lined up on a beach in what will one day be Queensland, squinting happily into the imager. Our bathing costumes look particularly ugly and old-fashioned. We don't care, apparently: every one of us is smiling, even Akira who has just had his box lunch dive-bombed by a seagull. Why shouldn't we be happy? Twenty seventeen-year-olds and not one of us has acne.

And there I am, between Nancy and Roxtli. I have won the hair contest: mine waves down my back as far as my hips, while Nancy's only stands out around her head like a dark cloud. But she has grown into a petite beauty and I am plain, plain, plain. And freckled. And unbecomingly tall. Smile on, Mendoza, in the sun and sky and seaweed of that faraway day. If only you had a clue.

As soon as they brought us back and showered the sand off us and handed us our degrees, they gave us our individual appointments with the career guidance counselor.

Bright and early on the appointed day, I rode the elevator down to his office level and put my card in his wall. Moments later, I was bade enter.

The counselor was one of the older ones. He looked no more than twenty-five, like everybody else, but you could tell how long someone had been in the service by a certain facial expression. Moreover, his brow ridges were on the pronounced side. Other than that, his appearance was all up-to-date. His doublet and trunk hose were well cut, and he had on the newer, fuller ruff that was just coming into fashion then. He waved me to a chair and looked at my card.

"Mendoza, Botanist Level One. Well. How are you doing, Mendoza?" We shook hands.

"Great, thanks."

"So." He creaked into his chair. "I've got your specs here, but why don't you tell me a little about yourself?"

"Well, I'm really, really interested in going to the New World," I said at once. "I've made a particular study of the native grain species and I think I could do a lot of good work there. And I wouldn't mind working in the remote areas at all, in fact I'd prefer it. I'd love to get in on the El Dorado operations or maybe even New World One. I've heard some interesting things about Florida, too . . ." He was punch-

ing buttons on his keyboard as I talked, which annoyed me. I shut up
and pointedly waited for him to finish.

He stared at something on the screen for a moment. He reached
for a pen, dipped it in ink, and began to write on a card.

"I wouldn't count on going to the New World just yet," he said.
"Your profile has a recommendation here for Assigned Acclimati-
zation Europe."

"Oh, God." Two years mandatory cover identity working among
mortals?

"That's what it says. Nothing to be upset about, you know." He
kept writing.

"Why would they stick me with a job like that? I'm a botanist.
I've prepared for the New World, not for growing turnips for maniac
religious bigots."

"They're not all like that, you know," he said mildly. "The mortal race has its points."

"Tell me about it. I happen to have been recruited from the dungeons of the Inquisition," I said nastily. My trump card. Top My
Trauma time.

"Is that so?" he remarked. "Ever hear of the Great Goat Cult?"

Of course I had. They were a Paleolithic religious movement
whose principal activities were tattooing themselves and exterminat-
ing their neighbors who didn't. They were so good at genocide that
they nearly wiped out what there was then of the human race, delaying
the birth of civilization by ten thousand years. I looked at his gently
prognathous face and felt hot blood rush into my own.

"Attitude problem. Don't mind me," I muttered.

"It's possible to learn to live with mortals." He took up the pen
again. "Trust me."

I sat there mortified while he jotted a few sentences on the card.

"Besides, if Dr. Z says you have to, you have to," he continued.
"Don't make trouble for yourself. Just be reasonable about it, go
nicely where you're told to go, and in three years the AAE drops off
your file. All you have to do is prove you can handle what's expected
of any operative. Once they know that, they'll be more receptive to
your requests for specific postings."

He tapped up some more stuff on the computer. I watched his
face as he stared at the screen. I could not see the data, of course. No
operative ever sees detailed information on his or her particular future:
even such information as the Company has is sometimes incomplete.
Even kiddies as processed as we are aren't completely documented.
Nevertheless I said resentfully:

"You've probably got it all there in front of you, where they send me and whether I get to go to Florida and what I'll be doing in ninety years."

"That's right." He nodded. "Maybe."

"Why do they bother to call you a counselor?"

"Because I can tell you things you need to know about where they're sending you," he said, keeping his eyes on the screen.

"Well, where are they sending me?"

"England."

"England!" I practically screamed.

England, home of grotesque old King Henry the Six-Wived. As children we'd followed his antics in Current Events with considerable amusement, but when he finally ate himself to death, he left a country as wrecked as his pantry. For years, assorted court cabals had circled each other warily, waiting for frail Prince Edward to reach manhood. We knew, of course, that he'd die in his teens and another era of civil unrest would result.

"What are they sending me to England for?" I cried. "Isn't it, like, very unsafe there? Aren't there going to be all kinds of bloodbaths soon?"

"Not where you're being posted," he assured me. "They want a botanist over there for a very specific project. You're the very one they need. Pretty soon we'll have the opportunity to send European personnel in. You'll be part of a Spanish team. You'll be perfectly safe."

"Spanish?" I narrowed my eyes, doing a fast access. "Now, wait a minute. Edward's sister Mary is going to get the throne when he dies. There's a Spanish connection there. Is that what we're talking about?"

"Yes. The place will be crawling with Spaniards. We can slip you in with no trouble at all."

"It reads like a hazard to me."

"Would we send you somewhere that wasn't safe?" He shuffled papers on his desk. "Anyway. You'll go to Spain first to establish your cover identity, spend a year there, go over to England in"—he leaned over to peer at the screen—"'54. You won't even be alone. You'll be part of a team, and you'll have a facilitator with you."

I relaxed. "That's better. As long as I don't have to interface personally with the killer monkeys."

"Ah, come on." He leaned back. "This is England, after all. The land of, uh, Dickens."

"He's Victorian Era."

"It's green there. Beautiful countryside, I've seen it myself. Best beer in the world. Great cities, like York."

"And London?" I perked up. "Will I get to go to London?"

"Maybe." He smiled. "You might even get to meet Shakespeare."

Dates whirred behind my eyes. "He won't be born for a dozen years."

"Well, you never know; you might get to like England. I've known plenty of operatives who opted to stay on somewhere after their assignment was served, even if they hated it there at first. And England's heading into a Golden Age, uh"—his eyes flicked to my file—"Mendoza. You could be in on it from the beginning."

I thought about it. London was supposed to be the flower of cities all, as Chaucer said, an incredible cosmopolis in an otherwise primitive country. Really fashionable clothing, maybe, for a change. New dances. New music. "It might not be so bad," I conceded.

"You'll see." He smiled. He handed me a stack of printouts. "Now, here's a recommended holo list and an events graph. You can study them privately. The starred entries are mandatory, the highlighted entries are strongly recommended. You'll be issued a field kit sometime in the next two weeks. Your departure is scheduled for July twentieth. Nice to meet you, Mendoza."

I went wandering back to my room. In this present moment I'd fling myself down on my bed to think; in that era of corsets and bumrolls one did no such thing. I perched on a wooden settle instead and looked at the recommended (actually mandatory) holo list.

Might as well start with the history review, I thought. It was starred. I scanned its access pattern, and suddenly I remembered, I had known all along, and I let the information fill up around me like a nice hot bath. Here was the score card, here were the players:

England was a cold, backward, rebellious little kingdom. Its king: Henry the Eighth, remembered principally for his six wives and the chicken legs clutched in his fat fists. Oh yes: and for booting the Roman Catholic Church out of England, though he'd started out as a Catholic, married to our old friend Katherine, Infanta of Aragon. But years of marriage to her produced no son and heir for Henry: only a daughter, Princess Mary. Henry was tired of Katherine anyway, so he divorced her (against the express wishes of the Holy Father) and married Wife Number Two, a court tart with pretensions to trendy radical religious opinions, named Anne Boleyn. Jumping on her Lutheran bandwagon as well as on the rest of her, Henry imported the Protestant Reformation into England.

Next round: Anne Boleyn couldn't produce a male heir either, only a baby girl, Princess Elizabeth, so Henry had Anne beheaded and took Wife Number Three: the devout little Jane Seymour, who, like many of his subjects, was still sympathetic to the Catholics. Before her death there even were rumors that England might go Catholic again. She did die, however, right after giving birth to the long-awaited Prince Edward, and any chance of an early Counter-Reformation died with her.

Endgame: Henry married, in quick succession, three more wives, which sure as hell made rapprochement with the Pope unlikely. By the time Henry died, the Protestant faction was in firm control of the country, especially with the council of regents who ruled for the frail little King Edward.

New game card: the Royal heirs, in order of their respective rights to the throne. Three stiff children with the coldest eyes in Christendom.

Protestant Edward, the boy king, soon to die, his prim face closed and folded shut.

Catholic Mary, sad old maid, with her bulldog face. She'd done a slow burn for years as she watched her father abuse her mother and her Church. She was shortly to get revenge in a big way.

Noncommittal Elizabeth, somber and alert, despised by the Catholics and Protestants alike for her mother's disgrace. Cunning and cautious, she was destined to survive her siblings and inherit the throne. She was famous in our classrooms as one of the Exemplary Mortals, right up there with Charles Dickens. She hated war and wastefulness, and didn't really give a damn what prayers people said as long as the economy thrived and nobody tried to dethrone *her*.

Yay, Elizabeth. I scanned for the current events I'd be concerned with.

1553, June. Edward is dying, lingering on in the last stages of heavy-metal poisoning administered by Mary's adherents. He finally, horribly, dies, and then—

Oh, dear. After a messy interlude involving an abortive Protestant coup, Mary Tudor (a.k.a. Bloody Mary) would be crowned queen. She would make the mistake of assuming that her loyal subjects were all still true Catholics in their hearts, eager to forget the distasteful heretical interlude That Bitch had seduced her father into ordering. But, surprise: a whole generation had grown up sincerely Protestant, and wanted none of the old faith. Riots and rebellion would break out, and here I caught the names Wyatt and Dudley. In desperation, she'd begin burning her disobedient subjects at the stake, earning her nation's everlasting hatred before she died.

But before she died, she'd marry a Catholic monarch in the hope that he'd (1) love her and (2) help her bludgeon the True Faith back into people's hearts. Grimly she yearned for love. She was never to have any love out of him: but in the matter of religion he'd assist her ably.

For she was to marry Philip, most Catholic heir apparent to the throne of Spain, and when he came to England, he'd bring all his pet Inquisidors to share with her. A great respecter of the Holy Office, Philip. Very eager to discuss matters of faith with the English Protestants. They must have run out of secret Jews to burn.

I sat blinking, taking all this in. They were going to send me with Philip's entourage. With all those Inquisidors. The Spanish were going to be as popular as smallpox with their English hosts, and I would be one of their number.

7

IT WAS JULY 21, 1553. Clutching my wicker suitcase to my bosom, I made my way to the transit lounge.

Behind me, the ship blinked and hummed. People in flight-tech coveralls ran around with service hoses. There was no evidence there that time had passed: nothing had changed but me. Now I, too, was beyond change.

I dropped my luggage on a settle and collapsed beside it, pushing my hat to the back of my head so the long comb wouldn't bore into my skull. I leaned back carefully. I was frightened.

This was sunny Spain, land of my birth. A concrete floor, stretching to the other side of the cavern. Three green couches set around a coffee table. A row of beverage-dispensing machines. I thought longingly of coffee and wondered why there were no cups on the stand. Then blared a voice from the steel box directly over my head.

"Botanist Mendoza, please report to the arrivals desk."

I blundered to my feet and looked around. Not ten feet away, the clerk was putting down her microphone, looking straight at me. I glared at her and dragged my suitcase over.

"Reporting."

"Please sign in. Your transport shuttle has arrived."

I signed in. I put down the stylus and looked at her. She was buffing her nails. After a moment she glanced at me, as if surprised to see me there, and said:

"Up those stairs."

I looked around. The stairs were steep, narrow, concrete, and rose into darkness. There was no hand rail. Cursing, I hitched up my skirts and struggled upward. The first few steps were littered with the debris

of any transit area: snack wrappers, crushed paper cups. The treads
had been painted green once. Traffic had worn a path through the
paint, polished the cement to a greasy luster. Cement is one of the
few things that look worse polished.

The light at the top of the stairs was out. I found the VIA panel
by groping and flattened my palm against it for identification, hoping
the panel wasn't broken too. It whirred and clicked, but no door appeared. I turned to shout down that chimney of a stairwell but heard
a gentle whoosh. The door swung open behind me. I stepped through.

I was standing on a rock terrace on a mountainside. Big tumbled
boulders and cliffs of red stone sat there in utter silence. It was seven
o'clock on a warm summer evening, and the sun was low in the sky.
Air warm and heavy as milk, but clear: I could see range upon range
of mountains stretching out before me to the horizon. Where the late
sun slanted on them, they were red and gold. Where it did not, they
were violet. A few stark trees, pines mostly, were aromatic in that
calm air. I was shaking badly. It wasn't supposed to be beautiful.

When I got my nerves together, I picked my way down from
there. On a curve of road below me waited a coach. There were two
horses standing patiently in harness. There was a small man talking
to the horses.

He was the first mortal I'd seen in years. My transport shuttle had
a mortal driver. I would have to put my life in mortal hands. He
looked up and saw me. His eyes widened.

"Señorita!" He swept down low in a bow. "A thousand apologies! You are Doña Rosa Anzolabejar, whom I have been sent to
meet?" That was my cover name. How nice that my one travel outfit
was elegantly cut.

"I am even she," I said in my snootiest Castilian, starting down
the hill. "Pray fetch my luggage, if you will be so kind."

"Immediately, señorita."

While he bustled after my suitcase, I hastily scanned the coach.
Mid-sixteenth-century model, built like a Conestoga wagon without
appreciable springs. No structural defects, though, no weaknesses or
excessive wear in the wheels. I scanned the horses: all eight shoes on
tight, no flaws in the harness, placid healthy animals unlikely to bolt
or fall over dead. Carefully the mortal brought my belongings down.
He opened the wagon door and bowed again, extending a hand to
help me in.

"Allow me, señorita."

I took his hand gingerly. He was young, there were no traces of
alcohol or toxic chemicals in his sweat, his vision was normal, heart-

beat and pulse rate normal, muscular coordination above average. He did have an incipient abscessed tooth, but he wasn't aware of it yet, so it wasn't going to distract him from his task. He helped me in.

"Have we far to go, or shall we arrive before nightfall?" I inquired.

"It is not far to your father's house, gracious Mistress. I will bring you there before moonrise."

"I thank you, señor."

He sprang up into the driver's seat, and we rattled away. Dust billowed. We snaked along the road down out of the mountains. I tracked the landscape fearfully for bandits or other lower life forms but I found none, which was good. Nor had my mortal flown into any chest-pounding homicidal rages yet, nor was he being reckless and driving too fast. So far, okay.

Down, then, to a plain of wheatfields, spreading away empty. A single windmill stood black against the yellow sunset. Where were the dark and crooked streets? The gibbets? The bonfire smoke full of human ashes? This was mortal land, wasn't it?

The sunset deepened to red, and another house appeared on the horizon. As we drew near, I saw people assembled by the front door. Some of them were mortal servants, peering in excitement at the coach. Four of them were my own kind, a man and two women standing together and one man who waited by the gate. He came forward smiling as the coach shook to a stop and I was handed down.

"My most beloved daughter, I am overwhelmed with joy to behold you again!" he cried, opening paternal arms. I made my deepest curtsey and began:

"Dearest and most reverend father, it is with the utmost delight—" Our eyes met, and I froze. It was the Biscayan. He blinked. His smile twisted up into his beard, just as it used to. "—that I return again to your loving care," I concluded, and we embraced with seemly affection. I was as tall as he was. He took my arm, and we turned toward the house.

"And how did you find the Convent of the Sisters of Perpetual Study, my child?"

"Truly, Father, a right holy place, and the good sisters taught me so well that I am *everlastingly* in their debt. And in yours." I shot him an arch glance. He just laughed, patting my arm. The servants were nodding and smiling and trying to make eye contact. I wondered if I was supposed to tip them or something.

The Biscayan waved at them. "Well, here she is, my daughter the most chaste Doña Rosa. You have seen her. Perhaps you will go home now?'' They edged out of the yard, still smiling. ''Anything for some excitement in their lives,'' he told me sotto voce. ''And here, my child, are the others of my household. This is your duenna, Doña Marguerita Figueroa. This is my housekeeper, Señora Isabel Sánchez. This is my secretary, Señor Diego López.''

They had been cast well. The duenna looked swarthily formidable, the housekeeper meek, and the secretary nearsighted. In reality they were a zoologist grade seven, a cultural anthropologist, and a systems technician first class.

''Doña Rosa, we welcome you,'' said the secretary. We all turned to stare at the servants, who got the hint and took off at last down the road into the evening.

''You know, I never connected the name?'' said the Biscayan. ''Little Mendoza, all grown up! So welcome back to Spain. How the hell are you?''

''Immortal,'' I said. ''Glad to see you again. What happened, though, that you had to send a mortal with the transport? That startled me a bit. Regular driver busy?''

''Oh, Juan's all right. He *is* the regular driver, you see. We hire a lot of mortals, it's cheaper. Hey, everybody, I recruited this kid! Must have been, what, fifteen years ago? Small world, isn't it?''

''Right now, anyway,'' said my duenna. ''Come on in, honey, and we'll celebrate. Three whole chickens have been killed in your honor.''

''Plus there's lots to brief you on,'' said the housekeeper as we went in out of the night. ''You'd heard the poor king of England died?''

''Yes, I heard that.''

''So Bloody Mary's got the throne now, and there was the most awful debacle for the Protestants. Half the regents' council is in prison already.'' She led us into a room dark-lit by candles, where a table was nicely laid for five.

''Has she killed Lady Jane Payne yet?''

''Grey. Lady Jane Grey, the little Protestant claimant. No, but that's coming.''

''Golly.'' This was surreal. I was so nervous, I was tracking a radius of two miles, but the house was warm and the chicken tasted wonderful. We did it justice, postponing my briefing until the second bottle of Canary had been opened. My new father lounged back from the table and lifted his glass.

''To your first assignment, Mendoza. All the best.''

Everybody drank. Clearing my throat, I said:

"Thanks. You know, I never learned your real name."

"I guess you didn't, did you?" He looked amused. "My character's name is Don Ruy Anzolabejar, but I've used Joseph as my real name for a long time now. Ms. Figueroa is known among us as Nefer, Ms. Sánchez uses Eva, and Mr. López has been Flavius for almost as long as I've been Joseph." He pointed to each with his wineglass. "Good servants to a good master. You, of course, are my only child from an early marriage, and I am a humble physician who's been knighted for certain discreet services to the Court. I inherited my fortune from an uncle who worked for the Holy Office a few years back."

"Convenient." I held out my glass, and Flavius topped up my wine.

"About the stuff you're supposed to be growing in the back area?" he said. "I have my matrices set up there, but I can move them in a couple of days."

"Am I growing things?" I looked at Joseph.

"You are, as a matter of fact," he said. "This time"—he popped open his chronophase and peered at it—"next year, we'll be in England on our various little missions. We have twelve months to get ready. You're supposed to come up with an exotic plant as a gift for an Englishman."

"What's our objective over there, anyway?" I said, sipping my wine nonchalantly and trying to sound like all the spy novels I'd ever accessed.

"Black-faced sheep!" said Nefer with enthusiasm. She was the zoologist. "We're going after genetic material for the original breeds that won't be around much longer. Well, *I'm* going after them. You're going some place called, what was it, Joseph? Iden City?"

"Iden's Garden," he explained. "Country estate in Kent. Kind of a private botanical garden and zoo. This guy Iden is a retired gentleman who's nuts for collecting rarities. He's got some that are even rarer than he thinks. That's *your* game. We're bribing him to let us come in and take specimens. It would be a nice gesture if you came up with a suitable gift for the man. A showy new plant for his collection, maybe. Something splashy, exotic, impressive."

"Like?" I had another swallow of the wine. It was heady stuff.

"How should I know? You're the botanist."

"Oh." Light dawned. "Right. Improvise. Okay, I'll get going on it tomorrow."

"Good. You've got a year."

"But, really, is this Englishman just going to let a bunch of Spaniards come in and ransack his private garden in exchange for a new plant? Is that enough of a bribe? Won't the English hate us, because of all the burnings?''

"Relax.'' Joseph spread out his fingertips. "We're offering him a lot more than one potted palm, believe me. All will be goodwill and brotherly love where we are, you'll see. The fix is in, Mendoza. That's what a facilitator does. Our traveling arrangements are already made, I'll have you know.''

"That was neat.'' Eva put down her glass in surprise. "The marriage negotiations haven't even started yet.''

"Nah. The Court has seen this coming for years. You want to know something? When the couriers rode in with the news of Edward's death, back on the eighth? Within forty-eight hours, no less than three noblemen I personally know sold their estates: land, dogs, and all. The reason? They figure they'll be able to pick up much better places in England, cheap.''

"No wonder the English will be sore.'' Flavius shook his head. "They don't like invaders, let me tell you.''

"Ah, the lure of barbarian lands for the civilized entrepreneur.'' Joseph reached for a toothpick. "When Philip the passionate pilgrim sails, there'll be one hundred and one Spanish ships crossing the channel, kind of a marital Armada, with (get this) *eight thousand* predatory hidalgos on board, to say nothing of their cooks, confessors, catamites, and''—he placed a theatrical hand on his heart—"personal physicians. Of which I shall be one. Don Alvarado has asked me already if I'll accompany him on the great adventure. He's the one I fixed up with penicillin, remember? I said I'd be happy to go if I could take my household. He said, Why not? He's bringing his confectioner and Señora Moreno. The Emperor is making noises about no women being allowed on the voyage, but nobody's taking him seriously.''

"I hope you're bringing more penicillin,'' snickered Flavius.

"Hey, this isn't the Armada that gets wrecked, is it?'' asked Nefer in sudden alarm.

"They call me El Señorito Milagro,'' mused Joseph.

"No, no,'' Eva assured Nefer. "That's about thirty years down the line. You remember, *Fire over England*, Dame May Robson as Elizabeth?''

"Raymond Massey as Philip. With Laurence Olivier and Vivian Leigh.'' Nefer relaxed. "Okay.''

"Isn't that the holo where they burn Atlanta?'' Flavius grinned at her. He looked over at me. "I'll clean out that back area tomorrow,'' he promised. "Next week at the latest.''

Actually it took him a month, and Joseph was obliged to throw a tantrum about it first. I needed the time to adapt, though, I really did.

It was fortunate I was portraying a shy girl from a convent, because I hid upstairs the first day while our mortal servants came in to work. I could smell them through the floorboards. They were actually in the same building with us, in reach of fire and sharp objects and, and, and . . . Nefer finally hitched up her skirts and stomped upstairs after me, muttering under her breath.

"Will you come down, for hell's sake!" She swung open my door. "It's only the damn laundress and groom, anyway."

"He has an abscessed tooth, and it could start hurting at any time and send him into a killing frenzy," I informed her, looking up from my work. "And the female's in a highly volatile emotional state. Possibly premenstrual. She's also sustained several contusions and is in pain, which could prompt a psychotic episode."

"Her husband beat her up last night, that's all." Nefer came into the room. "Believe me, she's used to pain. Does her work just fine anyway."

"She might suddenly snap."

"And do what? Chase us around with wet laundry? Mendoza, I know this is your first time out, but you can't let the monkeys get to you this way. They're just mortals. In fact, these are our very own hired mortals, security cleared and all. If you can't cope with them, you are surely going to have trouble when we go to Mass this evening."

"When we what?"

"Go to Mass." Nefer grinned. "Every day, rain or shine. Three miles' walk each way. Rainy days we get to use the coach. Don't tell me you weren't briefed on this. We're Spaniards, remember? And you really were one. You of all people ought to know the drill."

"Shit." I put my face in my hands. "They'll be all around us at Mass."

"That's right." She sat down on my bed. "Look, Mendoza. In the entire time I've been in the service, you know how many homicidal maniacs I've encountered? One. And he weighed seventy pounds. Mortals may prey on one another, but they're not all that much of a threat to us. Believe me, sooner than you think, you'll get used to being around them, and you'll find you can actually eat with them, have conversations with them, uh, sleep with them even—"

"You're kidding!" I sat bolt upright. Nefer may have blushed, but with her somewhat Moorish complexion it was hard to tell.

"I didn't mean like that. But . . . well, you know . . . that happens too, actually. Quite a bit, if you want the truth."

"You aren't serious! We were always told, Never Engage in Sexual Recreation Except with Another Operative!"

Nefer looked at the floor, looked at the ceiling, looked out the window. "Sexual recreation with other operatives," she said finally, to the wall, "is . . . sort of dull. And uncomfortable. Say, what are you working on?"

"My assignment. Uncomfortable how?"

"Just, you know, embarrassing. Is that the genetic code for some kind of plant?"

"It's maize. American maize." I displayed the screen proudly. "See? We're playing Spaniards, so we'd have access to strange-looking stuff from the New World, right? And the coloration and viral streaking on this variety are really spectacular. It'll knock that Englishman's eyes out. I can have the seeds ready by January."

"That's great."

"And it can't mess up the biosystem over there at all, because it doesn't grow well in England and it'll never catch on there as a major food source. It's not nourishing enough, for one thing."

"Is that right?"

"Yes. Maize is the biggest of the domesticated grains, but as a food source it's a dud because it's got this incomplete protein, see."

"You don't say."

I was going to tell her about amino acids, but her eyes were glazing over. I looked down at my calculations and sighed.

"I know everything there is to know about New World flora. God, I wish they'd sent me there."

"Oh, well, you'll go one of these days," Nefer reassured me. "I wouldn't mind a good look at a llama myself."

Specialists. One-track minds.

On that long, long daily walk to Mass, Nefer and I had quite a lot of conversations about sheep, as I recall. We became pretty good friends, but her interest in life was hoofed quadrupeds, and to hear her tell it, you could forget about the pyramids: the height of Egyptian achievement had been the domestication of the wild ass. In our endless trudges together I learned things about water buffalo I have since labored in vain to forget. I did my best to introduce her to the exciting world of four-lobed grains, but she kept getting that glassy look in her eyes.

Still, the walks had to be taken, because there was no question of our missing Mass. We made solid identities for ourselves in the neighborhood. We did not become well known, of course; that was not the Company way. Not one of his neighbors could have told you much about Don Ruy Anzolabejar, other than that his uncle had been connected somehow with the Inquisition, and certainly that magic word put a damper on gossip. It was known that Don Ruy traveled frequently to Court. But there were no stories about strange devices or supernatural lights in our windows at night, no indeed. No heretical talk about tolerance or enlightenment or sanitation. We made sure we were an utterly unremarkable Spanish family.

I spent more time on my knees that year than in the rest of my life to date.

I did get used to the presence of mortals. I could sit there at Mass among them, though bombarded by the smells of their humanity: dissatisfactions, diseases, passions, hormonal tides, digestive upsets, religious raptures. I learned to ignore the pathetic beauty of their children and the horror of their old age. And, once, there was a young man, a student by the cut and shabbiness of his clothes, who sat and stared at me with smoldering eyes. I stared back at him, wondering what on earth was the matter, until he mouthed a request at me across the church.

My shock and amusement reverberated loud enough to alert Nefer, who came out of her reverie on bison long enough to look around at the boy and glare at him in a proper duenna way. He averted his eyes at once and slunk out right after Communion. Too silly to be disgusting, but the incident stuck in my mind somehow.

I remember that the weather was hell. The clear and windless night I arrived had been a rare one: most days the wind came roaring across the miles of wheatfields and filled the sky with dust. White haze hid the mountains and hung like a mirror in the air. I developed a permanent squint, which has done nothing for my looks, to keep that furnace glare out of my skull. When summer was over, the wind did not lessen; it only turned cold.

Sometimes, though . . . I remember the sound that that wind made, coming over those fields of wheat. It was like the sea. I used to walk far, far across the open land, till the house was almost out of sight behind me, and stand there in the high wheat only listening. The wind would begin in one place and come across to me, sighing like voices, silvering the tops of the grain.

Then harvest came and men with scythes came and cut it all down. There was sweet-smelling stubble for a while, but the wind did not sing coming across it, and the autumn fogs were thick with dust. The news that winter was that things were already beginning to sour for Mary in England. She had announced her betrothal to Philip, our prince; the English, as everyone had predicted, were furious. Rebellion was working all through the country, and popular sentiment lay not with poor little Lady Jane, the previous Protestant candidate, but with Elizabeth.

Unlikely Elizabeth. For years she'd been a zero politically; no ambitious nobles tried to use her to further their careers, since it was rumored she was a tawdry sexpot like her mother the Great Whore. Suddenly nobody remembered those nasty innuendos: the same people who used to call her the Little Whore now saw her as a virtuous Protestant princess, the Reformation's only hope in England. Elizabeth smiled her cold smile and demurred graciously—she knew what was likely to happen to people who rocked the throne. All the same, Mary didn't trust her not to become the focus of a coup attempt. Just before Christmas she had Elizabeth sent away to a remote country estate where, it was said, the princess was beginning to show signs of heavy metal poisoning . . .

After Christmas came interminable rains that turned the roads to clay. No excuse for us to stay home from Mass; we took the wagon, and still had to slop back and forth from the door, holding our skirts up out of the mud. Only Joseph went out anywhere else, tending his little plots and plans at Court. The rest of us mostly huddled around the fire in the kitchen, accessing novels or holos or staring out the windows at the landscape.

A day came when a man led a horse to the edge of the nearest field. He hitched it to the traces of a plow. Man and horse began to move, and the earth crested and broke dark beneath them like a wave. Away down the plain they went, cutting a long stripe on the land, turned at some point and came back, and at length doubled back again, and so down once more.

All day I watched. By nightfall the field had a weave on it like the fabric of my overskirt. The next day, men came and walked the long lines, casting seed into the furrows. The next day, the field was alive with birds, and the next day, it rained. That was the day I set out my maize seedlings in the earth I'd prepared for them, closed around by the garden wall. There was no more chance of frost now, anyone could have told from the feel and the smell of the air. The earth was black and wet. Bright green as flames were the little blades of corn.

Late in February, Joseph came back from Madrid with the news: open rebellion had finally broken out in England and been promptly squashed. As a further punitive measure, Mary had Lady Jane Grey (still on ice from the previous coup) summarily executed.

"Well, there," I remarked from where I shivered by the fire, trying to make sense of *Tirant lo Blanc*. "I knew she died sometime."

Eva flashed an access code at me. "*Lady Jane*, Helena Bonham-Carter, Cary Elwes, Patrick Stewart."

"Real pointless business, too." Joseph poured himself a sherry. "Mary'd much rather have disposed of her sister, but Elizabeth's too popular with the people. She's got her locked up in London now, letting the poisoners have another shot at her. When that doesn't work, she'll try sending her to the Tower, to see if the English will stand for it."

"Will they?" Nefer moved a pawn, and Flavius leaned forward to study the chessboard.

"No. Mary has no idea how unpopular she really is. She's sure this rebellion problem is confined to Kent."

"Kent?" I registered alarm. "The rebellion's in Kent? Kent where I'm being posted?"

"It *was* in Kent. Was. Past tense," Joseph soothed. "By the time you're there, everything will be dullsville. Would we ever send you anywhere dangerous?"

"You don't think this sounds dangerous?" retorted Flavius. "I'd like to see sometime what you consider dangerous. Every single time I've been shipped over there, they've told me—"

"Take it easy, friends." Joseph held up his hands. "We can but trust Dr. Z, after all. We may catch a rotten egg or two but no sticks or stones, I positively guarantee it. Trust me."

"I don't think I'm happy about going to Kent, Joseph," I said, with considerable restraint I thought.

He surveyed us all with a sympathetic expression.

"What we have here is a morale problem, that's all," he told us. "Poor kids, cooped up with nowhere to go. But I just happened to have stopped in at the transport warehouse on my way back . . ." He hauled his rain-soaked saddlebag up on the table and rummaged through it. ". . . where they just happened to have got in a new shipment." Beaming, he pulled out the silver-wrapped bars and tossed one to each of us.

"Theobromos!" cried Eva. I tore open mine and inhaled the fragrance hungrily. Almost at once the buzz set in. This was powerful stuff, nearly Toblerone quality.

"Highest grade Guatemalan," Joseph informed us. He struck the same pose as the little togaed Greek on the label, waving cheerily.

*   *   *

The fields changed again. There had been a mist, pale and close along the ground; then one day the blades of new wheat stood up green in the sun. Greener. Deeper. A solid carpet of green, going out to the edge of the sky. There was no more rain now, and the green went to silver as the wheat began to come into the ear.

My maize was standing high, setting big ears like clubs, showing bright tassels. I would drag a settle out into the garden and sit for hours, just watching the wind sway the corn. Our mortal servants would come to stare at it in silence; they'd notice me there apparently reading my missal, and edge away with a bow or curtsey.

Another exciting day: I was issued two new gowns for the trip to England. They arrived via courier from the transport station and, once unwrapped, proved to be not exactly the height of current fashion, which was a disappointment. One was a brown broad-cloth thing for working in that looked like a servant's livery. Still, it gave me something to wear besides my peach wool, which looked smashing on me but was fast wearing out.

Was I ever really that bored girl, pining for new gowns? Time, time, time.

Joseph held up his knife, eyed the chunk of potato skewered there.

"I love potatoes," he remarked. "How I used to wait in longing for 1492. Before then you could only get them if you were stationed in the New World. Or occasionally at the transport station commissaries, but then of course they were instant mashed. Little whipped peaks of starch and gray gravy."

We all sat staring at him. The wind howled relentlessly outside. It was June, 1554. He took a little bite of potato and chewed slowly, staring back at us.

"Now, before the Crusades," he continued with his mouth full, "food was even more limited. Bland, bland, bland. Not even cinnamon, except in the bread pudding at the transport station commissaries—"

"When are we leaving?" demanded Flavius.

"Next week. By coach overland to La Coruña, where we have a berth on the *Virgin Mary*. It isn't exactly a stateroom—hell, it isn't exactly a cabin—but I've pulled some rank and greased some palms, so we should be reasonably comfortable."

"England at last!" cried Eva. She was all afire; she'd been to the British Isles before and actually liked the climate. I gathered from

Flavius that that was fairly unusual for our operatives. I went to the window and looked out miserably.

"Next week, eh?" Flavius shook his head. "The diant units won't be ready by then. I have to grow the matrices."

"You what?" Joseph stopped eating. "You've had months!"

"Grow them too long before you're going to use them, and they dry out." Flavius shrugged. "They have to be fresh."

"Dear friend. Old colleague. You get me four working credenzas for England, or I'll personally see to it that you get posted to Greenland for a couple of generations."

"I can try. I can't promise."

"Remember when we used to get stork all the time?" intervened Eva tactfully. "And swan? Nobody ever serves swan anymore."

"You'd *better* promise. You'd better do a green invoice if you have to, understand?" Joseph slammed his fist on the table, but Flavius went right on eating. Joseph growled and clenched both hands in his hair, as if to tear out handfuls. The others ignored him. Eva sighed and reaccessed *Tirant*. She was getting lots more out of it than I had.

"Down on my knees at Court every day kissing the hems of cassocks, and are they grateful? Riding over every rock in the road between here and Madrid, and does anyone care?" ranted Joseph. He didn't give a rat's ass really about the credenza parts, he was just being theatrical. He did that a lot. Isometric exercises to maintain human emotions, I think. I didn't understand then, but I've since learned.

After banging his head against the table a few times, he picked up his knife and continued: "Anyway, I've sent letters to our Paid Friends about housing. Nef, I'm sorry, but there's going to be a delay in your posting. You'll go on standby with us in Kent."

"Hell!"

"They won't be ready for you in Northumberland until next year. I'm sure you'll find something to do in Kent during your layover. That's life in the service, kid."

There were clouds boiling up into the sky beyond the thick little panes of glass. A storm was coming, and I wanted to go see.

"What about me?" Flavius wanted to know. "I suppose I'm getting sent to London. Again."

I put a shawl around my shoulders and went out the kitchen door.

God, the wind, how it scoured and lay flat the little green herbs of the garden: they cowered. The maize tottered and staggered. Beyond the low wall the wheat danced with the wind, all song and combat. It moved and moved like the sea, with the rustle and scream of stiff silk.

I pushed the gate open and walked out into it, finding the rows with my feet, meaning at first just to leave the sounds of the house behind me. Oh, but the clouds that massed in the East were beautiful. They were domed cities and explosions, such meteorological violence touched with the tenderest colors, pink and lavender and fathomless blue. So soft-looking a home for howling angels with flaming swords.

I could never get any nearer that place, though I kept walking, though it moved endlessly toward me out of the sky. In the sough and boom and murmur of the wind it came, and each stalk of wheat circled through its endless arc among the millions of stalks that nodded all around me. The colors in the clouds glowed brighter. Something was about to happen. I wanted to see it happen.

The wind was hot and smelled of orange trees, distant. It smelled of green-cut hay. It smelled of rain and fever. What was going to happen?

Suddenly the wind fell. Click, on cue the summer crickets started up. Then I heard a hoarse cry from far away:

"Mendoza! What in hell are you doing?"

I turned to scowl at them. They were crowded together at the door, staring out at me in consternation. I had left the house farther behind than I'd thought. Joseph opened his mouth to shout again; but the blue flash came and with it the thunder, like barrels rolling downstairs. Rain began to fall, a few big hot drops. There came another blue flash.

I covered that half mile in seconds and stood beside them, trembling, and they pulled me in through the door and slammed it. I stood there in the storm gloom, and they stared at me, their faces shut like books. Joseph was the only one who spoke.

"How about a little talk, Mendoza?" he said. "Upstairs, in the rec room. Now."

God, how embarrassing. I had to follow him up the stairs and sit still while he ran a diagnostic. He said nothing to me while it was running, and I noted the blankness in his eyes. He'd looked just like that when he worked for the Inquisition.

But I tested out normal. He leaned back and looked at me, and let a little human irritation show in his face.

"So, were you trying to get yourself fried? No problem with your evaluation of hazard data, and you knew damn well what those meteorological changes meant. So what's your excuse for generating a Crome field out there, hm?"

"I wasn't!"

"Yes, you were, kiddo, in about a five-meter radius. And if you think this is a way to get yourself sent back to base for repairs so you can get out of going to England, forget it."

"I swear I wasn't!" I was stung. Also intrigued. Was it possible to duck duty that way? Joseph read in my face what I was thinking (one picks up that knack working for the Holy Office) and shook his head grimly.

"Don't even think about it. We're not supposed to malfunction. Dr. Z will excuse you for crying wolf once or twice, but you'll be disciplined. You won't like that. If you're really in need of repairs this early in your career, that's a bigger problem. You won't like the solution to that either."

"Look, I just wanted to look at the storm. It was neat. I didn't do anything wrong. I got out of there the second it got really dangerous, didn't I? So I throw a little Crome when I'm excited. How was I to know that? It's not in my specs. It must have developed since I was posted. I'm only eighteen."

He nodded. "It happens, every now and then. The Company doesn't like it, but it does happen."

"Well, if I'm glitched, it's not my fault, is it? They made me. And what can they do to me if I'm not all up to standard anyway? I'm immortal."

He wasn't smiling. "They'll find a way to use your talents. The Company never wastes anything. But let's just say it's not a career choice you'd ever want to make."

This was distinctly scary. There were stories I'd heard about flawed agents.

"Look, I tested out normal!" I said in a panic. "I'm sure I'm all right."

"Don't let me down, Mendoza," he said. "I recruited you, remember? If it wasn't for me, you'd be out there in the zoo with the rest of them."

"What do you want me to do?" I could feel sweat starting. There was a creepy sense of déjà vu to this conversation.

"Watch yourself. Don't do anything dumb. Be the best little agent you can be, and you'll probably do fine." He decided to lighten up. "To let you in on a secret, nearly every operative I've known has had one or two little kinks. Most can function well enough so there's no trouble. Most."

"What about yourself? Are you flawed?"

"Me?" He smiled. "Hell no. I'm perfection itself."

8

O N THE APPOINTED day we closed up the house, sent away the servants, and rode in the coach, miles and miles and horrific bumping miles through Spain. Days it took us. There were problems with axles and horses. The windows were too small to see much of the passing scenery, which was a comfort to me when we passed into Galicia, because I feared I might feel a pulling, a homesickness or something, and I was now determined to be the most dependable operative the Company ever had. But what little I could see of Galicia looked pretty much like everywhere else. Mostly it just jolted and danced beyond the wooden frame of the window.

And we came to La Coruña on the seacoast, and it stank.

It stank of the lives of mortal men, but also of the deaths of fish, and of rotting, leaking little ships. The crowded stone town was filled, it was true, with sunlight and air, and a brisk breeze snapped the banners in the rigging of the ships, and there were big joyful clouds white as snow in the blue sky. But the town still reeked.

I crawled out of the coach, took one look at the little ships, and yelled in horror.

"We have to go all the way to England in one of *those?*" I gasped. Joseph put his face close to mine.

"Daughter," he said quietly. "Dear. When we board our particular ship, you will notice immediately a number of alarming structural flaws. Do not, I implore you, broadcast this fact to your fellow passengers, the ship's crew, or anyone else you can think of, because if you do, you will be sent directly to the Convent of No Return. Your affectionate father is quite serious. For your spiritual comfort, I can tell you that it is a matter of historical record that the good ship *Virgin*

Mary will not sink until the year of Our Lord fifteen hundred and fifty-nine, when neither you nor any of our party will be aboard. Therefore, my child, a silent and discreet botanist has the best chance of not being throttled on her way to the lamentably heretic island of England."

"Okay, okay," I muttered.

"I came over in a galley my first time," remarked Flavius. "What a panic."

"Cheer up," Eva told me. "Look at all the courtiers! Look at all the clothes!"

Look at all the clothes indeed. The cream of the Prince's court was walking all around us, and it was as if all the cloth merchants of Cathay, Antwerp, and Italy were having a trade war in the streets. All the jewelers, too. Such gold tissue, such brocade and velvet, trimmed silk, figured satin! Such colors! Orange-tawney and sangyn. Primrose. Willow. Peach. Gingerline. Popinjay. Slashes, sashes, and dashes. Peasecods and pansied slops. Picardiles and epaulets. Shoe roses. These were the bright young things, the new generation, not the gloomy old intriguers of the Emperor's court.

There were courtiers walking their little dogs. Courtiers gossiping and sniffing at pomanders. Courtiers in tight silk hose showing off their calves to very attentive sailors. Courtiers directing the loading of their baggage, with screams of alarm for their sweet wines, their sugared comfits, their gold plate. A pair of them, male and female, paraded by in complimenting shades of emerald sewn with pearls.

"I want their clothes," I moaned under my breath.

"I do too," Eva moaned back.

"You don't really. Can you imagine the body lice?" observed Nefer. We glared at her.

Joseph ignored us all and scanned the harbor for our ship. Given the absolute forest of masts and rigging, and the fact that the *Virgin Mary* turned out to be a popular name for ships that year, he was not having an easy time of it. We stood there, clustered protectively around our crates of disguised field gear, and the absurd mortal carnival flowed by on all sides. Just as Joseph thought he had located our particular *Virgin Mary* among the rest, there was a blare of trumpets. All heads turned.

Shouting. People scrambling back.

Make way! Make way for His Royal Highness, the elect of Princes in the whole of Christendom, the most Catholic Philip, Infante of Aragon, Castile, and Brabant, King of Jerusalem, Archduke of Aus-

tria, Duke of Milan and Burgundy, Count of Hapsburg, Flanders, and the Tyrol, Defender of the Faith!

Boom. We all went down on our knees.

And I think a cloud must have crossed the face of the sun, for there was a sudden darkness and coldness. It could hardly have come from the man riding there among his pikemen and priests. He was not even wearing black. Yet we all looked involuntarily to see what was casting the chilly shadow that he was.

But really, now. How could I or anyone else have seen anything that day but a handsome young prince riding to meet his intended bride? Handsome, that is, if you found the barracuda Hapsburg looks appealing. And it is true that the bride he was riding to was nearly forty and no beauty. So maybe he did look a little gloomy. But evil? Did we really see mortal evil somehow incarnate there?

Of our journey, the less said the better. It took us over a week. I will tell you, though, that I would rather spend a month in the dungeons of the Inquisition than a day under hatches. Any time.

Not soon enough, we crossed the channel.

England was gray curtains of rain. When the salvo came booming across the water, all the women belowdecks and some of the men shrieked and wept. Joseph looked up from the detective novel he was reading.

"We must be in Southhampton Water," he remarked. "That's probably the English warning us to lower our flags."

"Good old Britain," grunted Flavius.

"I want to see!" Eva leaped to her feet. "Anybody else want to come?"

I was only too glad to get some air, so we found our way above decks and peered out from under an overhang.

Mist and drizzle. Lots of ships. Some Flemish vessels. Men shouting across the water. It began to rain harder.

"There's England!" Eva was all excited. "The Groves of Amadis!" I peered out but could see nothing distinctly. Rain pocked the surface of the sea, streamed from the ropes and rigging. Sailors shouldered past us, giving us to understand that we had picked the most inconvenient spot on the ship to watch the rain.

"Let's go inside," I shouted in Eva's ear. "It's too wet." She nodded, and we went back below, lifting our skirts well clear of the pools of vomited wines and sugared comfits. So much for England.

* * *

We made landing as darkness fell with more rain, but remained on board that night because the English wouldn't let us come ashore. As we understood it, no Spaniard was allowed to set foot on English soil until Philip himself was officially granted permission; and his serene shadowy Highness was prostrate seasick in his own cabin on the *Holy Ghost*. It was the first inkling a lot of those grandees had that they were in another world entirely. Here was Mary, longing to see her royal intended, and these sons of merchants were telling her whom she could and couldn't have setting foot on the soil of her own country!

The following day, the Prince had recovered himself enough to meet the great golden barge of state when it arrived. We all crowded up on deck to watch the distant scene. Eva quoted ecstatically to herself about burnished poops. Through windy sheets of sunlight and rain we saw the green-and-white figures of the bargemen bring the barge up alongside the *Holy Ghost*. Stiff little gesturing figures in scarlet: those must have been the English lords. Someone descended into the barge from the *Holy Ghost*; shade and dimness, an abrupt fog. Yes, Philip must have boarded. Guns boomed in salute. We all ducked involuntarily.

The golden barge was rowed to shore, and for a while nothing happened, so a lot of people on deck got bored and went below. Eva and I, thus able to see better, were the only witnesses when the wedding party disembarked and took horses on shore. I made out Philip, on a mare with red trappings. Then they all rode off into the countryside, and I swear there was darkness spreading behind them like exhaust smoke.

That was the last I saw of Philip of Spain but not, I regret, of his shadow.

We still weren't allowed to go ashore until the following day, by which time we'd have killed for solid ground under our feet. After hours of jockeying around, we got somebody to row us in with our baggage, under a freezing mist.

"It's July, for crying out loud," I murmured, watching the quay draw nearer. "Doesn't it ever stop raining in this country?"

Flavius just laughed sadly, but Eva said:

"July fifteenth was St. Swithin's Day. The English have a traditional belief that if it rains then, it'll rain for the next forty days."

"I guess it rained then, huh?" said Nefer, wringing out a corner of her shawl.

"What ho!" boomed a voice in English as we bumped up to the

landing. "Two fine magnificoes and their ladies with trains of Spain, all wet. How like you our English weather, Grandees?"

There was a chorus of nasty English laughter, and we looked up defensively, but the speaker was one of our own. A big blond man in a leather hood, he was standing at the front of the crowd with arms akimbo.

Welcome to goddam Sherwood to you too, transmitted Joseph sourly.

Careful. These people are ready to lynch you, they're so frightened. Let's play this scene as a comedy, shall we?

Comedy? All right. One order of broad slapstick served hot. Joseph stood up in the boat and stretched out his arms.

"Por favor, good Señor Englishman, will you not offer us some assistance in conveying our baggage to shore? We have much gold and will pay you well."

"Aye, that thou wilt, I doubt it not." Our representative grinned broadly around at the English, wink wink, who were watching us like vultures. "We'll convey thy Spanish gold any day of the year, will we not, my hearts?" They all laughed appreciatively, and Joseph climbed up the creaking ladder. Our man put out a hand to help him up.

"Ay, Señor, muchas gracias, muchas—" Joseph broke off as they did the stunt: the operative, appearing to assist Joseph, tripped him, and Joseph went rolling neatly into a mud puddle with loud Hispanic cries of distress. Nefer and Eva stood on cue, screaming shrilly, and the assembled mob howled with mirth. Several dropped the stones they'd had ready to pitch at us. We weren't dangerous: we were only comic foreigners, after all.

"Oh, sir, you have rolled in horse dung." The operative went to raise Joseph with a great show of concern. "I am most heartily sorry for it. Let me take you to a fine clean inn I know of where belike you'll have a fine sea-coal fire for drying your fleece, I mean your cloak. Rates very reasonable, sir." The word *fleece* had its subliminal effect on the crowd, and they went off to range along the quay, where other wretched Spaniards were attempting to come ashore.

Nice tumble. You okay? The operative leaned down to Joseph, shaking his hand. *Xenophon, facilitator seventh class. Welcome to England.* Between them, he and Flavius got our baggage loaded into an oxcart, while the rest of us stood shivering and looking around.

I can remember being astonished at how green everything was. Electric green, glowing emerald-green, green growing out of the cracks between the stones, and green crowding in the gardens. Looming tunnels of green trees and green meadows rolling away that pulsed against the eye, they were so green. In Spain and Australia what passed for spring was a sedate olive season compared to this, and it made the green of the tropics look dried out. No wonder the English had a reputation for rowdiness. They must have been drunk on pure oxygen their whole lives.

The other thing that impressed me was the persons of the English themselves. They were the tallest people I'd ever seen and uniformly, man, woman, and child, had skin like rose petals. I saw a grandmother holding up a toddler to curse at us: the old woman's face was no less white under pink than the baby's, and her cheek only a little less smooth. I felt swarthy, with my freckles and Spanish sunburn.

We clambered into the oxcart, and Xenophon drove away with us, chatting subvocally the while. We learned he was taking us to a Company safe house disguised as an English country inn. I could have cried when we pulled up in front of the Jove His Levin Bolt, with the Company insignia carved into its beam ends, and were shown upstairs to private quarters. I saw my first flush toilets in over a year. I leave it to you, whoever you are, to imagine the bliss of a hot shower after so many unspeakable days in the hold of a ship.

When we assembled in the briefing lounge, steamy and as clean as we were going to be for a long while, Xenophon was sitting with a big tray of food and drinks and our assignment dockets. We found seats while he poured out tankards of room-temperature beer and passed them to us.

"Welcome, everyone. Here's a classic English ploughman's lunch for each of you along with our local beer. We brew our own, by the way. We think it's pretty good. Please feel free to eat while we talk; this is all informal. Well, now." He cleared his throat. "I guess you heard some of the things people were shouting at you as we drove along."

"I did get the impression they weren't exactly happy to see us," Nefer said and blew her nose.

"Yes, that's pretty close to it. The thing to remember is, they're just as frightened of you as you are of them. And the law is technically on your side, if one of them attacks you without reason, though of course I imagine you're all too good at keeping low profiles for that kind of situation to develop. If you're from Spain, you may be expecting the same muscle from the local law enforcement you'd have at home. Not the case here. Robin Hood stories notwithstanding, you'll have a fairly hard time getting hold of any sheriff to help you in this shire if you get robbed. So *don't* get robbed. Exercise caution.

Any of you operatives who've been here before—you, I think?'' He
nodded at Flavius, who nodded back. "Yes, well, you're familiar with
the crime in urban London. Don't make the mistake of thinking you'll
be safer in the country. You're much more visible here, particularly
those of you with darker skins. People are frightened, ignorant, and
superstitious, so you might as well have targets painted on your backs.
Travel fast and keep your heads down. London in fact is pretty cos-
mopolitan these days, so you're less likely to have your throat cut for
racial reasons, though of course you still run the risk of having it cut
for your purse.

"So. Enough of the safety lecture. Try some of the cheese, it's
the famous Cheshire cheese. Now if you'll all open your dockets . . .''

Rustle rustle crackle crackle. There was a silence as we all dutifully accessed and integrated. Then one by one we handed the sheets
to Xenophon, who tossed them on the fire. "Nice and tidy. Are there
any questions?''

"Why can't I stay at the HQ in Eastcheape?'' Flavius wanted to
know.

"It was decommissioned fifty years ago. History decrees other
use of the site.''

"Damn.''

"You mean you won't be going where we are?'' I stared at Flavius. It wasn't that I was going to miss him, particularly, but I'd got
used to him.

He shook his head, and Xenophon laughed. "Too much work for
him in London. We need systems techs desperately over here right
now.''

Eva had been sitting with this special little glow on her face ever
since she'd accessed her codes. She was feeling such giddy delight,
it was coming through on the ether. We turned one by one to stare at
her, and Xenophon leaned forward across the table with a grin.

"I see we have a Shakespeare fan here.''

"Stratford!'' she burst out. "Yes! When do I go?''

"You've got a little identity work here, and then we're sending
you off to meet your Arden 'cousins' next month.''

So she was going away too, and to live among mortals. This was
the first time I had any inkling of how alone we really are. I had been
thinking of my team as a family, getting used to everyone's little
quirks. But we weren't a family. Well, I was new then, and hadn't
learned yet that that's life in the service.

"I'll be with you the first year, you and Joseph,'' Nefer told me.
Thank you, Nefer. More livestock discussions.

The briefing went on from there to a discussion of the local currency, to national politics and gossip, to the weather (bad), to the latest field technologies available to us (inadequate, everyone felt), to the merits of British beer over German beer. When the meeting broke up, we stayed by the cozy little coal fire and learned English card games, because the rain resolutely kept raining. As I fell asleep that night, I was thinking that I would have to see if I could spot any cowslips or osiers while I was here. And weirs, I'd read about them in English novels too.

9

JULY 22, 1554. I'd been in the field a year and a day. It was a space of time that figured in old songs and poetry.

We said farewell to Flavius and Eva in the dark of morning before we rode off. I never saw him again, and her I saw only once, a long time after, in a transport lounge in another country. We were going in opposite directions and had no time to talk.

And into darkness we descended, Joseph and Nefer and I, to ride the famous Company underground. It linked all parts of that island in a series of arrow-straight lines, and the operatives on duty in England were terribly proud of it. I thought it was awful, but there was no other way to get from Hampton to Kent on schedule, and it did cut down on our chances of getting lynched.

So we shuttled through shadows on a track in a tiny closet box going twenty-three kilometers an hour. The box thudded to a halt at last in a gloomy alcove, and we groped our way up uneven steps, flight after flight of them, hoisting our baggage well clear of the puddles, until we emerged at the back of a cave.

"This is a cave," I said accusingly. My voice echoed back, and Joseph and Nefer just looked at me. Somewhere ahead a horse whinnied uneasily, and we followed the sound to daylight.

In fact there were three horses in the mouth of the cave, all saddled and bridled, and a little dark man who sat watching the rain. He jumped up when he saw us emerge from the depths and backed off a pace or two.

"*Akai, chavo.*" Joseph tossed him a bag of coins. The man took it and slipped away out into the rain. "Three transport shuttles at the ready, ladies." Joseph smirked.

We rode into Kent therefore on good horses, with our baggage bound around us, in our Company cloaks issued specially against the rain that rained every minute. Most of the journey was a blur of leaves and water for me, so I can't tell you if there were cowslips by the wayside or not.

Still, as the day wore on, we came into an open landscape. Hop fields wide to the horizon, dotted here and there with toy towns, each with its steeple and cluster of trees. Low rolling hills and rivers. At some point we clattered across a little bridge, and Joseph reined in his mount and said, "I guess it's around here somewhere."

Actually he knew exactly where it was, he had directionals fixed and homing, but he never could resist the temptation to pretend he was real.

"Some ride, huh, ladies?" he remarked brightly. "All ready to make a good impression? Are we in character? Mendoza, have you got the whatsit all ready for presentation?"

"The Indian maize," I told him. "It's right here. In a fancy case and everything."

"Great. Nef, your veil is crooked."

"Thanks a lot. Aren't they going to be a little surprised to see us so soon?"

"No. How are they to know just when the ships put in? Xenophon has been sending letters quote from me unquote to our hosts, so they know we're coming, but they don't know when to expect us. Turn right here, I think."

We set off down a green aisle, with green willows looming across our view of the gray sky. Before we had gone a mile, we picked them up, scanning: three mortal males in a highly excitable frame of mind. A quarter mile farther on, they appeared, just sort of stepped out from between the hedges and stood staring at us. They completely blocked the lane. They were bare-legged, blue with cold, and carried great sharp pitchforks caked with manure. They stared hard at us, and Nefer and I shrank back in our hoods.

Get your thinking caps on, girls, transmitted Joseph. Then in flawless South London English he said, "Good day to ye, goodmen."

"Be ye Spaniards?" said one of them. He had very white teeth. So did the other two. I noticed this, because they were baring them threateningly.

"Nay, I thank our Lord Jesus Christ," said Joseph with an easy smile.

"But there be Spaniards come among us now," persisted the man.

"We heard tell from Sir Thomas. And monks come to burn us all."
His friends were staring at our trappings and baggage.

"For very fear of that, good lads, I and mine are removing to
Flanders. *That* for the Pope!" and Joseph spat elegantly, though he
had to wrooch around a little to avoid hitting anyone, because we
were so crowded there in the lane.

"Aye," said the man.

They just stood there.

"Well, we must on. Jesu keep you, good lads, and keep England,
and God save the Princess Elizabeth!" cried Joseph, urging his horse
forward. They let us through.

"You have a ready wit, my father," I said, digging my nails out
of my palms.

"Smooth, that's what I am," he replied. "Good navigator, too.
Here we are."

The way opened out in front of us. I don't know what I had
expected to see, but it certainly wasn't wrought-iron gates four meters
tall, fantastically gilded and ornamented, little pennants fluttering, little weathercocks spinning, and above our heads foot-high letters set
with bright enamel that spelled out

Iden His Garden

And underneath, only slightly smaller, was the legend:

*Here Ye May See Where the Desperate CADE Was Taken,
With Divers Other Curious Marvels Whereat Ye May
Wonder*

"Holy Cow," said Nefer.

Down by the entrance was a small porter's lodge, almost a booth,
you might say, and on its window a placard reading

Penny to See the Great Garden of Wonders

Through the gate we could make out some brick walls, an avenue
of hedges clipped into geometric shapes, and what must have been
the manor house at the far end of it, looking not all that big really.

But here came a man in blue livery, wearing a crucifix the size
of a shovel around his neck, advancing on us with hands outstretched.

"Your worships! Welcome, welcome in the name of the Pope!
Oh, Jesu bless your worships!"

Is this guy one of ours? I inquired of Joseph.

No. *Just a sycophant.* "Buenos días, good fellow! This is then the residence of that worthy friend of Spain, Señor Walter Iden?"

"It is even so. The blessed saints be thanked that you met with no heretics on the way!" He seized our horses' bridles and led us in. "I am Francis Ffrawney and I serve Sir Walter and I pray your worships remember me as a constant friend and a true believer. If you should lack for aught the whiles you stay here—"

"Truly you are a courteous gentleman and doubtless faithful." Joseph grinned at us over his head. "The Pope shall hear good things of you."

The man went pasty white. "H-huzzah!" he got out. "And is it true, then, that you have come to spy out foul heretics in Kent, and intelligence the Pope thereof?"

"Peace, friend. I am but a physician come to gather simples in the garden of good Sir Walter. Though I would be served," and Joseph leaned down and looked very Spanish indeed, you could almost see the auto-da-fé smoke in his beard, "by those with discreet tongues in their heads."

"Oh!" said Master Ffrawney; he went a whiter shade still, an ugly color in all that greenery. By this time we had come up before the house, and there were grooms running to help us. Faces peered from all the leaded windows and over one or two of the clipped hedges, and all those rosy English faces looked terrified. Two men were descending the steps of the manor house. The more elaborately dressed of the two stepped forward to meet us.

"I have the joy of beholding my great friend Doctor Ruy Anzolabejar," he said carefully, putting a not quite audible question in the statement.

"My beloved friend!" cried Joseph. "How many years has it been since we lay at the Seven Ducks?" That was the code response, and Sir Walter relaxed visibly.

He was not a tall man at all, for an Englishman, but his presence expressed itself in at least three contrasting hues in his brilliant doublet. His hose were vivid yellow, the heels of his shoes were built up, and there was a great deal of gold-colored ornamentation sewn all over his clothes. The rather ordinary face that commanded this fashion looked intelligent enough. He must have been about sixty, quite old for a mortal in that era.

We all dismounted, and Joseph went forward and embraced him. "Mi viejo amigo! It has been so long since our youth in the days of the late and sanctified Queen Katherine. Ah, what joyful times they

were, when England and España were one in amity. What high hopes
we have for the present union. It quite brings tears to mine eyes." He
actually dabbed at them with a large lace handkerchief.

"And to mine also," stammered Sir Walter. "You look most, uh,
youthful."

We'd told Joseph he should have grayed his hair more.

"That, my dear friend, you may lay to a certain Greek physick
that you wot well of." Joseph looked at him meaningfully. "Of
which, more anon. But now, let me present to you Doña Marguerita
Figueroa, a woman whose chastity is renowned throughout Valladolid."

Nefer curtseyed, looking regal.

"And allow me further to present to you my daughter, Doña
Rosa." Joseph put out his hand to me, and I curtseyed low. "The
comfort of my middle age and a scholarly child. Are you not, Daughter? She will assist me in my study of your most justly famous garden.
Hija, present to our worthy host the most unworthy trifle we have
brought him for his collection."

Sir Walter looked scared and greedy at once. This was fun. Demure and theatrical as could be, I brought out the fancy case I had
carried so far. With a flourish I opened it and displayed the contents.
Sir Walter caught his breath. Ha, I thought.

It really had turned out especially well, my Indian maize. One
whole ear rested on a bed of harvested kernels. The kernels were big
as marbles and all colors: white like pearls, yellow like gold, red like
garnets, blue like bruises. Sir Walter reached with a trembling hand,
greed winning out completely in his face. He was desperate to grab
it, I could see. This mortal was a serious collector; he would give
anything to have this exotica in his garden, to show it off as it grew
tall and bore strange flowers. The man could not have cared less what
services were said in his chapel. Perfect for use. The Company was
so good at finding these people.

But it wouldn't be mannerly to snatch it out of my hands. He got
control of himself.

"How rare! Here is true magnificence! Pray, what call you this
thing?"

"It is called maize, gentle sir, out of the New World," I said.

"The New World! I have a vine of potato of the Indies, but it
bears no such fruit. Nicholas, you shall tell the guests who pay at the
gate that the savages of Ind do feed on very jewels, and so show forth
this maize! And belike we shall have Master Sampson paint upon a
board a map of the New World, in some several colors, or yet some

figures of men all naked to signify that they be savages—" He controlled himself again.

"Fair Lady Rose, you are most welcome to Iden's Garden. And you, good lady . . . Lady . . ."

"Marguerita," supplied Joseph.

"Even so she is. I bid ye welcome to my poor house, though I may say my garden is a pleasance for kings to command. Nicholas— ah. My friend, this gentleman is my secretary. Master Harpole. Nicholas, hither now."

The other man stepped forward. We craned back our necks to look. He was tall even for an Englishman, and in his black scholar's gown positively towering. He peered down at us sternly.

He was long and lanky but solid through the body, this young man; he had good legs on him. His face was nice too, with high wide cheekbones and a wide mobile mouth, though the mouth was presently pulled down at the corners in an expression of mulish disapproval. He had a long nose with a slight break to the left; his eyes were pale blue and frankly rather small, or at least looked that way glaring at us in icy Protestant dignity.

How interesting, I thought to myself.

"Master Harpole," repeated Sir Walter, with a rising inflection. Master Harpole bowed stiffly.

Oh, how well he moved. And what fresh color in his smooth English skin.

"It is pleasant to meet you, young man," said Joseph brightly. "Sir Walter, shall we see this garden, which is of renown even to the limits of Muscovy?"

I was still holding out the maize in its open box. I shut it and my mouth but did not look away from Master Harpole. I thrust the box at Sir Walter, who grabbed it eagerly and mustered his good breeding to reply:

"Even to Muscovy? Surely not so. Yet, I promise you, you shall marvel at it! Nicholas, pray walk forth and show it them, as you are accustomed."

Nicholas Harpole extended his long black-draped arm and said: "Gentles, will you walk hence?" And though he was being as unpleasant as he knew how, his smooth rich tenor hung on the air like a violin.

So as the grooms hustled our baggage within, I followed Master Harpole into a green confusion of pleaching and pruning and apricocks and yew. The rest of our party came along too, of course, but it should be obvious to you by now that they might have been invisible for all I knew or cared.

The first place we came to was surrounded by a high wall of brick. The area therein enclosed was planted with sorrel, herbs, and a few vegetables. Over in one corner was a dungheap. "The garden, proper, of Alexander Iden, Esquire. A kinsman of our present Sir Walter," intoned Master Harpole. "The very garden where the recreant Jack Cade was taken, in the reign of our late King Henry, sixth of that name. It fell out—"

"But, Nicholas, this is the crown and glory of the walk, the chicfest primature of our attractions! Were it not well considered to hold it forth to the last, being as it were the cake and comfits of our discourse?" cried Sir Walter.

Calmly, Nicholas drew himself upright and folded his arms. "I cry you mercy, Sir Walter. I have but followed the customary walk as presented to our penny-paid guests. What shall it please you I present for the, as it were, bread and broth of our discourse?"

Sir Walter looked at him peevishly. "See you, Doctor Ruy, how it was. This Jack Cade, whom you must know was a most vicious and murdering caitiff, of common low birth, he here being pursued by all loyal Englishmen for his bloodthirsty crimes against our sainted King Henry (who, I would have you know, was a true son of the Church and a faithful friend of the Pope)—the said Jack Cade, hunted all through Kent, in desperate wise scaled this very wall." He ran outside the enclosure, put his leg over the bricks, and slid back in rather awkwardly, as his slops were thickly padded out. "Thus, and went to gather him salad herbs which were here growing, he being in sore need of food. So was the villain engaged when my, uh, kinsman, that famous Alexander Iden, then but an humble esquire of Kent, happed upon him here."

"Verdad?" said Joseph pleasantly. "And what then occurred?"

"Why, they fought, sir. At first the good esquire offered Jack Cade no violence, and would have shown charity to a poor starving fellow, but that the man boasted of his crimes, crimes too hideous to relate here. Wherefore my kinsman took his pruning bill like *this*, and the said Cade drew his sword like *this*—Nicholas, what say you, would it not be better told if we had two mannequins here, in the very posturing of battle, one to figure forth Iden and the other Cade? The better to make it all plain?"

"I will inquire the cost of Master Sampson," said Nicholas gravely.

"Or belike statuary. More expense, but a lasting monument. Well, sir, the fight being over and my kinsman having valiantly slain the accursed Cade, he smote off the head and threw the ignoble body on a dungheap, and bore that same head to blessed Henry where he lay at London. And there, for his great deed of loyalty to his king, Iden was that same day made a knight and given a thousand marks to boot. Such was the king's gratitude! And though the fortunes of the house of Iden have not run constant since that time, mine own success in the wool trade—no valiant work but honest, I assure you—hath furnished me with the means to make suitable commemoration of the Iden valor.''

"I am overwhelmed with astonishment," said Joseph. "And this, then, is the very dungheap where Cade's body lies buried?''

"Why, as to that—'' Sir Walter grew a little red and looked in appeal to Nicholas, "as to that, family fortunes being what they were—''

"The history Sir Walter hath related here is very old, some hundred years or more," explained Nicholas, smooth as music. "In the natural course of time, the original garden vanished, as all things will under Time's crushing heel. Nor could the descendants of Sir Alexander, less favored by fortune than their sire, hold title to the ancient family seat. But when Sir Walter came into this county, having a mind to restore the family greatness, he was assured by sundry persons of good character that this was that same garden, or the place where it had been. All that you see is restored. This dungheap, therefore, hath been placed here solely for your edification.'' He made a slight bow.

"As well as many another marvel unknown in Sir Alexander's day,'' piped up Sir Walter. "Whereas he grew but salad herbs and such things as befit a poor esquire, I with my fortune have made such a collection of wonders, both animal and vegetable, as ye may well exclaim over! Of course, nothing looks its best just now,'' he added parenthetically. "The rain, you know.''

"What would you have them see next, sir?'' inquired Nicholas.

"Oh, my roses. The nonpareils of the world, my roses.''

Nicholas led us deeper into the garden, and we saw a whole arbor where there actually did grow just about every variety of rose that existed at that time, with a couple of variegated petal mutations that were probably unique. I made a mental note to get genetic material from them.

But it was as we were going to see something Sir Walter grew in a hothouse called The Great Engiber Pea Out of Africke that my gaze was distracted from contemplation of Master Harpole's long back. My head snapped around as I turned to stare, and I nearly

collided with Nefer. Ilex tormentosum! I transmitted frantically to
Joseph. *My God, he's got a whole hedge of* Ilex tormentosum *over
here!*

Is that good? Joseph queried. I responded with excited profanity.

What's going on? Nefer wanted to know.

"This hedge here, it is a form of holly, is it not?" Joseph inquired
casually of Sir Walter.

"This? Indeed, sir. Not our English holly, but one I have heard
tell was brought with Julius Caesar from Rome for some properties it
hath, though what they may be I confess I know not. It is not so
common as once it was, I think. In faith, I have not seen it but here
this many a year now."

Oh, what a score. Pharmacologists of the twenty-second century
had three miserable endangered specimens of this plant, source of a
specific for liver cancer, and here was a whole hedge. If Sir Walter
had this kind of botanical loot, what else might he be growing? I
looked more closely and began to spot them everywhere: *Cynoglos-
sum nigra, Oxalis quinquefolia, Calendula albans, Carophyllata
montena, Genista purpurea ascendens . . .* Meanwhile Nicholas was
solemnly holding forth on Sir Walter's prized Portingale orange and
Cathay coriander and even a sad-looking palmetto plant. I had months
of work, fabulous work to do here!

But when the sky suddenly opened and sent black buckets of rain
down on us, we had to turn and run for the house. Only Nicholas
seemed to know his way through the maze, which would have been
difficult to traverse quickly even without the rain, the darkness, the
flight between our legs of a despairing peacock, and the disappointed
wails of Sir Walter.

"So much of my collection yet unseen!" he lamented. "None of
my zoological wonders touched on at all. But 'tis no matter. There'll
be clement weather yet. You must see my unicorn of Hind."

I wondered what that was, but not much. My head was spinning.
Who'd have thought England was such a delightful country?

We made it to the house, and the drafty wooden floors boomed
under our shoes, but there was a roaring fire laid out in what passed
for the great hall. This was indeed a fairly modest little manor, but
the Iden arms were blazoned on every surface.

Everyone crowded to the warmth of the fire, gasping after the run.
I sidled up to Nicholas Harpole. The heat of the room had brought
high color into his face. I must ask you to believe that I had no idea
what had befallen me, there in that garden. My God, that the heart
can be so stupid.

I said to him, in my very best Latin: "What manner of thing is this unicorn, youth?"

He straightened up from the fire and raised an eyebrow at me. Then he replied, in better Latin: "It is no more than a beast, as other beasts are. And how appropriate it is you speak the tongue of Rome."

"Master Harpole," said Sir Walter sharply. "Go thou and see the baggage has been placed in the chamber as I gave orders for."

"I go, sir." He bowed again. "Lady." He inclined perfunctorily to me, then strode from the room. I watched him go. I couldn't fathom it. He smelled good.

10

MASTER HARPOLE DID not dine with us, which was disappointing, but since it was our first meal prepared by a non-Company cook without sanitary preparation training, it was just as well: I needed all my attention for the food. The bread was safe to eat, and the chicken with a sauce of oranges and lemons; but there was a venison pasty that was practically crawling, the meat was so far gone, and a custard dish ridden with bacteria of an extremely undesirable kind. I watched disbelieving as Sir Walter tucked it in happily. His system must have been used to such things.

"My friend, what a bountiful repast!" Joseph pushed his plate away, pushed his chair back from the table, loosened his doublet, and otherwise obscured the fact that he'd eaten nothing more than one chicken leg and a slice of bread. "I am stuffed like a sausage! We have not such fare in Spain."

"It is our custom to dine heartily in England," said Sir Walter smugly. Then he looked uncomfortable. "Though I am sure they do have most excellent feasting in Spain too. And the, um, the vintners of Spain do make a most wondrous Sack, I have heard."

"Ah, yes, the sweet wines of Spain. How I wish I had brought some with me." Joseph looked around to note the absence of servants from the room. He leaned closer to Sir Walter. "And now, old friend, I will be plain with you. Have no fears for your house or your people: I have come into this land, as was told you, only to take simples from your garden and for no other purpose. We will work quietly here and give no offense to any man. Ye may all worship as ye list, or think or speak as ye list; it is all one to me. Only have a care that you be discreet when speaking to other men of who dwelleth here, and we shall all be well pleased alike, you, I, and my masters. Understand my meaning, friend.''

Sir Walter leaned forward until his beard was in the custard.

"Oh, sir, mine are loyal folk—loyal to *me*—and no great talkers but one or two, who love Spain well. For the rest, why, they are young folk and cannot remember Queen Katherine that was, rest her soul, nor the wrongs done her. They fear Spain, aye; but it is a fear that will pass upon greater acquaintance, God willing.''

"Your secretary loves us not, I think," Joseph looked sideways at me.

"A young man, a young man! In truth, he is something stubborn in his . . . um . . . Gospel reading, but he will do as I bid him, I assure you.''

"That is all my masters desire. Come, we shall all be friends. My daughter shall have leave of days to walk your garden and gather what I require. I by night shall distill such liquors as will purge cold heavy melancholy and dry up all unwholesome humors that make a man old.''

"The Greek physick," whispered the old knight.

"Even as my masters promised." Joseph held Sir Walter's gaze with his own.

A silence fell. Master Ffrawney came in, with many a soulful glance at Joseph, and oversaw the removal of the dishes. I scanned Sir Walter, wondering what Joseph was going to do with him. Hypertension, arteriosclerosis, gout, caries, cholelithiasis. Plenty to keep a physician busy.

"I shall require some part of each day cloistered with you privily." Joseph reached for a pear and examined it. Taking out his dagger, he began to peel the fruit in a long spiral. "Perhaps your secretary will assist my daughter in her labors.''

I turned my head to stare at him.

"Doubtless they will find many botanical subjects to discuss." He smiled at me and popped a slice of pear into his mouth.

Pleading exhaustion from the journey, we retired early and were shown to our two rooms on the second floor, nice paneled rooms with a connecting door. Our baggage had been left in the middle of the floor and appeared undisturbed; no danger if it had been, because everything issued to a field agent is disguised to look like something else. Even Joseph's book of holo codes for *Great Cinema of the Twentieth Century* was bound in calfskin with a printer's date of 1547.

"Some bed, huh?" Nefer sank down on the big tapestried four-poster. "I get the window side, Mendoza. Oh, do we have to do that now?" she protested as she saw Joseph pulling out his tool case and setting up the credenzas.

"Yes, we do. Look around for a cabinet or something we can integrate this with. I'd like everything to be installed and invisible before the servants feel confident enough to venture back in here. Especially our friend the very tall Protestant. Speaking of whom . . ." He turned to give me a meaningful look.

"What?" I demanded.

"Oh, nothing. I just thought it might be a nice idea if you took it upon yourself to keep him busy. Change his outlook on evil Spaniards. Show him we're really a bunch of nice guys. And dolls. Get it?"

I didn't know what to say. I stared at the credenza rapidly taking shape in his hands. The drift of our conversation finally sank in for Nefer, who had been hanging upside down trying to read a motto stitched in the canopy.

"Hey!" she cried, sitting up abruptly. "Joseph, really!"

"Really what? He's a hazard to the mission. He obviously disapproves of our being here already. You want the guy walking in on me when I've got his employer opened up like an oyster, installing funny-looking little glowing things? No, no. I want Mister Reformation kept distracted, preferably out in the garden with a little Spanish popsy. And Mendoza did seem rather struck by his personal qualities, if you'll pardon my saying so, kid." He turned to me. "And you're young and healthy and just chock-full of hormones."

Nefer lay back on the counterpane in disgust and resumed her attempts to decipher the motto. I watched as Joseph fitted in the last panel and lifted the unit in his hands, where it glowed a transparent blue. Finding a likely clothes chest, he swung the unit through the side, and it gave a soft beep to let us know integration had occurred. He nodded his satisfaction and went off to his room, whistling the first few notes of "Forty-Second Street."

There was a soft knock on the door.

"Enter, por favor." Nef jumped to her feet. The door opened, and a maidservant edged her way in, carrying a basin and a tall can of steaming water.

"Your washing water, my ladies," she gasped, and set them down on the credenza. From a recess in the expanse of her apron she drew forth a ball of soap—marjoram-scented, what a luxury—and set it beside the water. "There will be a man brings water to his lordship the doctor," she informed us, "but I am to serve you in all things, for clean linen and what else ye require. Have ye aught to be sent to the laundress?''

Boy, had we ever, after that voyage. ''Many thanks, good woman,'' I chirped, as Nef and I pulled open our respective bags and began to fling out a veritable snowstorm of shifts, stockings, and other garments both muddy and malodorous. ''What shall we call thee, pray?''

''Joan, my lady,'' she replied, watching without interest as the stuff piled up. Our clothes looked pretty much like anyone else's, so there was nothing worth her attention, until I, in my enthusiasm, inadvertently snatched up with a bilge-stained underskirt my calfbound copy of the latest issue of *Immortal Lifestyles Monthly* and flung them both on the laundry heap. The magazine bounced once and clattered to the floor, landing open at the new holo releases page.

There in large blackletter was trumpeted the rerelease of *Metropolis* (the silent version, not the 2015 Spielberg remake) with a full-page photo of Maria the Robot in all her brassy glory. I raised horrified eyes to the chambermaid, who was staring fixedly at the picture of the villainous she-mechanism. *Omigod!*

Nef cleared her throat. ''Do not be afraid, good Joan. It is what we call in Spain an iron maiden. You have such things here, have you not, to punish the wicked? In this book it doth depict the torments awaiting sinners,'' she said firmly, scooping up the magazine and snapping it shut. ''For shame, thou, Rosa. Holy monks labored a year to paint this missal for thee, and wilt thou carelessly drop it?''

''I pray you excuse me, Doña Marguerita,'' I stammered. ''For, to be sure, those holy monks paint like the angels.''

Don't overdo it. ''Look you, good Joan, this gown of mine hath been sadly stained by mud.'' Nef thrust it at her. ''I would not for all the world see it ruined. Bid the laundress take some pains with it.'' And she put sixpence in the chambermaid's palm.

Now the chambermaid's gaze did a fast shuttle between the money and the gown, and in the thought balloon over her head Robot Maria was fading, being replaced with an image of all the nice things Joan might buy if she kept the money for herself. Having distracted Joan with this moral dilemma, Nef tucked the magazine out of sight in the depths of her bag.

''That will be all, Joan,'' she prompted. With a half curtsey Joan stooped to gather up our clothes and backed out of the room, muttering her thanks.

''What're we going to *do*?'' I collapsed onto a chest, wringing my hands. "Do you think she'll tell anybody? I can't believe I did that!"

"Oh, it happens." Nef, eyeing the water, stripped down to her shift.

"But they told us in school—"

"It'd be the end of the world if the monkeys saw anything anachronistic, right? Uh-uh." She poured out water, grabbed up the soap, and began to lather vigorously. "I mean—you *know* history can't be changed. So does it matter if an illiterate chambermaid sees something she can't understand? What's she going to do, write to the newspapers? As long as you can explain something away with a good story, you're covered."

"You don't think I'll get in trouble?"

"Nah." Nef groped in her trunk and found a linen hand towel. "Because, you know what? Even when our little mistakes make it into the history books—and it happens, every once in a while—nobody notices. Well, sometimes people do, but if they try to talk about it, everyone thinks they're crazy. In this century, anyway. So don't worry."

I watched doubtfully as she bathed. "But shouldn't we make a report to Joseph about it?"

"I wouldn't." Having finished, she opened the window and tipped the basin out. "Unless you want him to fuss at you unnecessarily."

"Not really," I admitted. I sat there irresolute a moment, grateful for the advice of an older and more experienced operative, until it occurred to me to wonder whether she'd left any hot water for me.

That first night I lay awake in the darkness for hours, listening. There was the beat of rain on thousands of green leaves, outside in the wet night. The breathing of nine mortal souls, slowed and trapped in dreams. A mouse busy in the walls of the kitchen. A clock. The horses in their animal dreams, out in the stable. Distant, chaotic animal thoughts, from farther out.

But *he* did not dream. Four walls away and a floor above me, I could hear the creak of a wooden chair as he shifted his weight from moment to moment. I could hear pages turning, exactly one minute apart, page after page, perfect as a machine. I could hear his breathing and the pulse of his angry heart.

11

NEXT MORNING I packed my field kit, though rain still sheeted down the leaded windows. We had all accepted the fact that it wasn't ever going to stop, but I hadn't let myself think about having to work in it.

Sir Walter was seated at the long table in the great hall when we came down; he was breaking his fast on buttered eggs and fried beefsteak. Nicholas sat opposite him, though he was not eating: they seemed to be having an argument. Nicholas's fists were clenched, making the knuckles white. Sir Walter's face was red, and his eyes protruded slightly. They fell silent as we entered the room.

"Good morrow, good friends!" cried Joseph easily. "And is this the morning meal in England? The famous English beef?" His gaze took in the eggs, fatty beef, and butter, and Nefer and I could hear him ticking as he evaluated what the cholesterol was doing to Sir Walter's arteries.

"It is even so." Sir Walter turned glaring from Nicholas. "Shall I order another mess of eggs fried, Doctor Ruy? Or there is excellent venison pasty, cold—"

"I think not." Joseph smiled. "Our Spanish stomachs are not yet accustomed to English abundance. We eat but sparingly before the midday. Perhaps a little of your English small beer and plain barley bread? What say you, ladies?"

I was dismayed. No coffee? Of course not. Not even any tea, yet. Orange juice?

"There were excellent oranges in your garden," I ventured, curtseying. "I would be most honored, gentle sir, and most grateful, kind sir, to taste of one."

"Fair lady, what you will! You shall have a paste or conserve of orange, or perhaps a dish of cloves and marchpane kneaded up with peel of orange, or a dish made up with oranges boiled with parsnips—"

Joseph was shaking his head at me. "Even a plain orange, simple of itself, please you," I stammered.

"*Raw?*" Sir Walter looked incredulous.

"At some better time, daughter, when good Sir Walter need not send his poor servants out into the rain for such a trifle," reproved Joseph.

"To be sure, my father. Sir Walter, I pray you excuse my inconsideration." Bright pink with mortification, I curtseyed again and sat down. When I raised my eyes, I found myself looking straight into the cold stare of Nicholas Harpole. I lowered my eyes hastily.

"No, no, we will have a new custom now, a dish of fruit to the table," Sir Walter said gallantly. "There are orange groves in Seville, as I hear tell. Are there oranges in the New World?"

"No, my friend, the fruit there is of a different sort from our accustomed fruit," Joseph told him. "There is, for example, the *aboccado*, which doth resemble your English pear, save that . . ." Blah blah blah. I sat there burning with embarrassment. After a while I sneaked a look at Master Harpole. He was still looking at me.

Servants brought in our bread and beer, and I picked at mine, still preoccupied with being a self-conscious teenager. Joseph talked on and on, too boring for words; then, suddenly, there was light in the room, as though God had opened an eye and looked in the window. It took us all a moment to realize that it was the sun.

"Why, look you, the rain hath ended," remarked Sir Walter. "Lady Rose shall have her orange at last, shall she not? And see my garden at its best to boot! Pray you, Nicholas, bear her company and show her what oranges there are."

Nicholas rose to obey, and so did I, groping for my field kit. And so did Nefer, like the good duenna she was supposed to be. "Doña Marguerita!" Joseph spoke up. "By your leave, remain with me. I would discourse with you privily concerning certain things."

She gave him a narrow look and sat down.

"Lady." Nicholas gestured toward the doorway. In silence he led me from the house and out into the garden.

There were still clouds breaking up and rolling back, but most of the sky was blue. The difference was breathtaking. England seemed three times bigger. The garden was, impossibly, more green; the beech trunks shone like bronze. Somewhere near us a river rushed and chattered. Birds cried out. England was aggressively alive, to the point of being intimidating.

By the time we reached the orange tree, the wet grass had soaked our shoes. Nicholas squelched up to the tree and assumed his tour-guide stance.

"The orange, Lady," he told me. I looked for a ripe one.

"Truly I did not think to put you to trouble," I murmured. "I minded not where I was. In Spain it is our custom to have fruit at breakfast."

"Your Spain is not our England," said Nicholas.

"That's true too. I pray you excuse me."

"What needs your excuse? Sir Walter has bid you make free with his oranges. Take his oranges therefore and so make an end of it, Madam."

Green leaves dripped on me. He stood so perfectly still, with such composure, and his voice was so beautiful saying such cold things. I pulled an orange down and showered us both with late rain. He did not even flinch, but watched distantly as I dug my thumbs into the peel and tore the orange into sections. It did not want to be peeled. Juice dripped on my palm, ran stickily down my wrist. "Will you have any?" I held out a piece, vain social gambit.

Without thinking he reached to take the fruit from my hand; then halted and jerked away, with an odd expression in his eyes. He took a full pace backward from me.

I gaped at him. Then I understood. Judeo-Christian mythology, right? Adam and Eve in the Garden, primal woman as tempter to sin. What *subtle* symbolism. Now I hated him.

"Thou ill-mannered and arrogant man!" I exploded. "Thinkest I have read no Scripture and will not see the insult in thy refusal?" I switched to Greek. "And have you read the Gospels in Greek, as I have, uncivil one?" I switched to Aramaic. "Let me tell you, young lord, this is not Eden and you are not Adam but rather Lucifer himself, you are so full of pride, so do not compare *me* to Eve!" And to Hebrew: "Shame on you! I am a stranger come into your country and have done you no wrong." And to Italian: "If you hate the Pope, you may write him an insulting letter for all I care, but I assure you he is not hiding in my skirts!" And to German: "Now I wish earnestly I were again in Spain, for though God knows it is a land of monstrous cruelty, yet folk there have good manners!"

Of course I had to spoil the effect by flinging the orange at him too. He sidestepped it neatly without appearing to notice. The orange sailed out of sight and landed with a soft thump somewhere in the grass.

"I'm sorry," I said at once, in English again. He stared at me a second longer before he recovered himself, setting his scholar's biretta straight on his lank hair.

"Well, I am cast down. The point is taken, Lady. You speak eight languages."

"More," I said resentfully.

"Is it even so? Well, well, there's a marvel. And canst quote Scripture too!" He said it snidely enough, but he came a step closer.

"Folk have tongues to proclaim truth in Spain as well as else-where," I said. "But they dare not. Nor would you, señor, if you were there, lest the Inquisidors come for *you*. And if once you learned a lesson of silence from them, you would not soon forget it."

I was pale and shaking. The adrenaline rush, of course, but it was effective. He came close and peered into my eyes. "Now, I truly crave your pardon," he said abruptly. "But if you do not love your Inqui-sition in Spain, you may imagine how much the less we wish to see it here in England."

"Pray to God, Master Harpole, that you never have such cause to hate it as I do," I said. There. Would the old trump card work?

It did. His hostility was deflected. He took my hand in his own and squeezed it. His hand was warm.

"Well, what a fool I am," he said. "Come you, Lady. Another orange, and shall we walk this garden whiles the sun doth shine? What would you see here?"

I swallowed hard. "I would see Julius Caesar's holly bush again," I told him.

He led me straight to the miracle hedge. I set down my field kit (designed to look like a quaint wicker basket) and drew out my holo camera (designed to look like a pair of horn-rimmed spectacles). I held them up to my eyes and paced slowly along the hedge, shooting the images, grateful for the work to calm my nerves. Nicholas leaned against a tree, watching me.

"Had you your learning from your father?" he inquired at last.

"I had." I broke off a leaf and held it up to the lens, turning it slowly. "He is a doctor, as you know, and a very learned man. I am his only child, wherefore he hath taught me much."

"Ah." Harpole nodded. I groped for my knife (designed to look like a knife) and cut a whole sprig to display for the imager.

"He hath many books, on divers dangerous subjects, which, were they found, he would be burned for a heretic at least," I ventured. Well, it was true. "And, sorrow to tell, he was for some while in the dungeons of the Inquisition." Also true.

"I am sorry to hear it."

"They did not murder him, praise God; but he came from that place a ruined man," I improvised.

"He hath healed himself well, then. He looketh not old," remarked Nicholas.

"That is thanks to a certain Greek physick he hath learned of. I promise you, sir, were it not for that, he'd be in his grave now this many a year." Certainly true again. "There was great learning in Spain once, sir, though none would know now."

He just nodded.

"You have read your Galen and Averroës, then," he said. Was he setting me a trap?

"Yea, and my Avicenna too, howbeit the Moors are not so well regarded as formerly." Under guise of examining the hedge's roots I thrust a soil corer in for a sample. I wrapped it with the holly branch and folded it into the basket. Not two feet away I spied a beautiful little specimen of *Calendula albans* and pounced on it, holo camera at the ready. Nicholas observed me closely.

"You see this for what it is, then," he remarked with gloomy satisfaction. "A rarer thing than ever the old knight's Portingale orange, but because it is no more than a little pale flower, he regards it but scant."

"For the light shineth in the darkness, and darkness comprehendeth it not," I quoted smugly. "John, chapter one, verse five. Tell me," and I slipped into Latin for clarity, "where does Sir Walter find these unusual plants?"

"He collected some of them himself, when he was a young man." Nicholas matched me verb for verb easily. "And now he has a standing offer out in this part of the country for anything rare or strange. The result is that men come continually to his gate with two-headed calves, or with common plants that have been altered to make them look rare. One man brought a cherry tree with tin bells fastened to its branches with wire and tried to make us believe they were the natural fruit of the tree. Sometimes Sir Walter has been deceived and paid money to a charlatan. Still, sometimes one will come bearing a true wonder for sale: and then the silly old man buys it out of habit, without true understanding of what he has bought. So he bought this flower."

"Do you make a study of botany too?" My heart beat faster.

"No. But I know enough to discern that a white marigold is a marvel, whereas a unicorn is a lie."

"What is this unicorn? I have heard it spoken of three times now. I would pay money myself to see it."

He smiled contemptuously, but on him it looked good, and at least the contempt wasn't directed at me now. "Why, you may see it for yourself." He extended his right hand and took mine. "Come, Lady, and do not fear. He is a tame beast."

Only slowly I let go of his hand. We walked on through that garden, past banks of flowers lifting their unbelieving heads to the sun, past beds laid out in patterns intricate as Morisco tiles. Down a lane between clipped privet hedges we caught a glimpse of little white flanks. Nicholas flung out his arms and announced: "The unicorn of Hind!"

The tail end backed out of the marjoram knot the animal was destroying, and a little head appeared, to look at us inquiringly.

"Ay!" I exclaimed, and bent down to stare. It thought I had a treat for it and came trotting up to see.

"Don't tremble, Lady. It will do you no harm," said Nicholas with a straight face.

"He's a goat." I examined him. He was as white as milk, his tiny hooves had been gilded, and some cruel surgery had been done to his horn buds before they had sprouted, and some crueler binding had fused them into one stubby twisting spike. But he was a sweet and trusting little goat all the same.

"A goat!" Nicholas held up his hands. "Can this be true?"

"Señor." I looked up at him. "I was born in Spain. I know a goat when I see one."

He just folded his hands.

"Go, goat." I swatted the unicorn's flank, and he ran off to do further damage to the herbs. "And yet, strange to tell, there is such a thing as a unicorn."

"Surely not!"

"Truly, but it looks nothing like this. A big creature, rude and ugly. It is called in the Greek, *rhinoceros*."

He nodded, sounding it out. "Unfortunate. Sir Walter would not be pleased to discover that he paid twenty pounds eightpence for a goat."

"Why tell him? The worthy Erasmus says, in his *Praise of Folly*, that no man is so happy as he who lives under an illusion."

"Very true." Nicholas's eyes lit up. "You have read Erasmus? What do you think of his *Ichtuophagia?*"

Thank God, thank God I'd accessed that Strongly Suggested column. "I think it is outrageous. All the same, I agree with what he says," I replied with perfect composure.

"So you admit that it is unnecessary to salvation to eat fish on fast days?"

"Oh, señor, really, what nonsense."

"Even if the Pope commands it?" he pressed.

"Particularly so. Do you imagine God cares what we have for dinner? How can one worship when religion is so ridiculous?"

He opened his mouth to speak, then paused. "You have no faith, then," he said after a moment. There was a silence while we considered each other. "I have an excellent book I would like you to read," he said at last.

"Ah! He is going to convert me to the Church of England!" I exclaimed.

But that darkened his mood. He took a step closer and loomed over me.

"The Church of England?" he growled. "The one whose leaders even now recant like the hypocrites they are?"

He must have been close to seven feet tall with his biretta on.

"The crawling Council have sold this land to Spain, for the right to keep their miserable lives. Our Northumberland—you know who he was?"

"The Protestant faction leader," I stammered. "He made Lady Jane Grey queen."

"Poor maid. Yes, he did. And when he fell, he turned ranting Catholic at once, in the hope it would save his head. *She* died with more bravery. What man was that to lead us? But the ones who remain at Court have been more subtle in changing their coats. They remain on the Council, they conform. By the collusion of the men who should most defend them, the laws of our late king are set aside. How should I counsel you to join the Church of England, Lady, when it is made up of such rogues?"

"What has become of all those Bible-reading heretics we hear so much of in Spain?" I asked, startled by his vehemence. "All those learned merchants disputing doctrines?"

"Fled to live among the Germans," he said bitterly, "for safety. Yet had they had the courage to stay here and fight for the Faith, we would all be safe enough." *Except for the ones who died fighting for your faith*, I thought.

"All the same, I would be interested in reading this book of yours," I said at last. "Even if there is no true faith in England."

He took hold of my arm. He was very physical for such a godly man.

"Lady, the Faith is here," he stated. "But we must build churches in our hearts, for surely those built in the world have all betrayed us."

Now this was such a remarkable observation—for a sixteenth-century man mired in the perceptions and prejudices of mortals, I mean—that I was really impressed.

"Worldly institutions fail because they require power and gold to operate," I explained, graciously, I felt. "Power and gold attract wicked and greedy people. Wicked and greedy people are corrupters and betrayers. Therefore, worldly institutions become corrupt and betrayed. Churches, being in the world, are worldly institutions. Thus it is demonstrated."

He raised an eyebrow at me. "Very good. And very true, for all that you rattled it off like a parrot."

Parrot! I tried to flounce away, but he still had hold of my arm. "And where have you ever seen a parrot, I'd like to know?" I said scornfully.

"We have several in the aviary. Yes, he collects birds, too. Come, tell me, where did you learn such a nice little piece of sophistry? Never in Spain."

Sophistry! "We have not always lived in Spain," I extemporized. "We fled to France for a while. After my father got out of the dungeons of the Inquisition."

"How old were you at that time?"

"Four. It was not either a sophistry! If philosophers had ever thought about this for two minutes, humanity would stop building stupid worldly institutions like churches."

"Not necessarily. Anyone can see the disease, but what is the remedy? Tell me, doctor's child. Demonstrate for me the solution to the problem you have propounded." His eyes were blazing, intense, *interested in me.*

"You are asking me for a solution for human evil? Don't give your heart to any church, any leader, any idea. Collect rare plants like Sir Walter, or study them like me, but leave the damned world and its struggles alone."

"No! A hermit may do as much, or an animal, and never lessen human misery one particle. One *must* work for a better world." He had me by both arms now. "Listen to me. Shall we not struggle over ages to burn away what is evil in ourselves, until at some far day the angel with the flaming sword will relent and grant that we reenter Paradise?"

I hung there, gazing into his face, which shone with a radiance of belief so glorious, I didn't think to point out to him that his own Bible specifically says people are going to get worse, not better, until his God finally ends the whole mess in a shower of blood and flames.

No, all I could feel was admiration. Somehow he had figured out the truth. For what he spoke of really would happen, of course: except for the part about the angel. The human race, sick of its own mortality, was going to develop the technology to produce Us. And We, obviously, were the next step, We were the perfected ones, the immortal and infinitely wise and intelligent beings he believed men would become.

I did not heed his racing pulse, nor mine. I loved the sound of his beating heart.

"Now, truly I think you could move mountains with your speech," I gasped. "You almost do persuade me to such a faith as yours."

His eyes held mine.

"I *will* persuade you," he said. I ought to have heard warning sirens then, my heart ought to have run for a shelter.

But he was warm and solid as palpable sunlight, and I thought hazily: He wants to save my soul. How quixotic, how extravagant, how romantic.

He smoothed my coif. "Forgive me," he said. "I am too forward with my hands, when once I begin to speak."

"No, no." I blinked and shook my head.

"I have been beaten for it ere now, and belike shall hang for it yet. Come, art thou well?" He lifted my chin in his hand and looked down into my eyes.

"Yes! Yes! Very well!"

"Come, Lady Rose. Let us go about our tasks as we were bid. Now I will show you a cabbage said to be like none other in the world."

It turned out to be nothing more than a bok choy plant, though how it had got there was anybody's guess. But there were real strawberries, growing from jars set cunningly in a wall; Nicholas could only find four ripe ones, but he picked them for me. And he dutifully pulled down a branch of *Eucalyptus cordata* that I could not reach, and he waited with patience while I took careful samples of what must have looked to him like the dullest of weeds. He led me to the aviary and, yes, by golly, there were parrots there: several African grays, half a dozen assorted Amazons, and even a big blue-and-gold macaw ceaselessly chewing its way up and down a bar. It cocked an eye at me.

"Buenos días," it said.

"Buenos días," I replied.

"Why, here at last is one who will welcome a Spanish lady to England," jeered Nicholas pleasantly, just before the macaw said something so pungent, explicit, and imaginative that I blinked. Nicholas's face went red. Evidently his Spanish too was pretty good.

"You must have had him from a sailor, yes?" I guessed.

Nicholas, recovering himself, looked at me a long moment; then we began to laugh. He had a nice laugh. I hadn't thought godly people laughed.

So we were good friends, you see, by the time we came wandering back to the house that afternoon. But when we entered the great hall to find Joseph sitting placidly at the head of the long table, Nicholas stiffened. The mood dropped away, like a curtain falling, or a fine frost.

"Buenos días, daughter, young man." Joseph looked up from his book. He had a glass of perry and a dish of wafers at his elbow. The fire, all cheerful, set lights dancing in the wine.

"Good day, sir. Where is my master? This is his accustomed place at this hour of the day," said Nicholas.

"I administered him a purge." Joseph smiled at him. "He is in his private chamber. You may seek him there." I wished he wasn't looking so damned comfortable, after I'd gone to such trouble to depict him as a tormented scholar.

Nicholas turned to me, bowed slightly, and withdrew. I heard his footsteps receding into the depths of the house.

"Wafer?" offered Joseph. "Well. Did my weary eyes deceive me, or were you two young things smiling at each other as you came in?"

"I could punch you sometimes." I slammed my basket down on the table.

"You could try," he informed me mildly. "I'd duck. So, did you have a nice day?"

"Actually, yes." I sat down across from him. "I got some beautiful examples of the ilex and an obscure periwinkle and a white calendula, can you imagine?"

"Remarkable." Joseph turned a page. "Striking fellow, your Master Harpole. Big. Seems to share some of your interests, too."

"Don't beat it to death. He *is* nice. Okay? How did your day go with Sir Walter? He's really a mess, isn't he?"

Joseph nodded. "Comparatively. He's made of stern stuff, or he wouldn't have survived this long. I did a little tinkering. Can't take things too far too soon, but the old man will certainly get his new lease on life. Ha ha. It's the young man I'm worried about."

"Haven't you got a one-track mind!" I rose to make an affronted exit.

"Now, now. Just my little way of looking after our best interests. By the way, I've left a list of the drugs I need synthesized on your credenza console. It's two pages long, so you might want to get an early start on it."

I made my affronted exit anyway.

Sir Walter reappeared at supper looking pale and shaky, and took only some toast and a cup of watered Rhenish; but Joseph told a series of anecdotes concerning the king of France and a Spanish mule driver. Joseph was so adept at telling a funny story that Sir Walter was red with laughter soon, making high shrill barks of mirth like a terrier, with his mustache points spiking the air. Even the servants were giggling.

Nicholas came to supper with us for the first time, very reserved and correctly courteous. He smiled at the anecdotes, though everyone else at table was crying from laughing so hard. But when I struggled to shell a handful of filberts, he leaned over and took them in his fist and cracked them, so, and cast them on the table between us where they rolled like dice. I looked up into his eyes. Was it quite right for a godly man to show off his strength like that? But then, there'd been no reason for me to act helpless with the nuts, since I could crush them to powder if I had to.

"... so the mule driver saith, 'But, Your Majesty, that was why I married her!' " finished Joseph. Sir Walter beat his hand on the table and whooped his appreciation. Joseph leaned back in his chair, beaming, watching us.

"Nefer?" I turned the Rami lens slowly, fixing on a cell wall.

"Uhuh." She did not look up from my magazine.

"What do you think of Master Harpole?"

"Who? Oh, the tall guy. Gee, wasn't Joseph being a stinker about that this morning? Sending you off into the garden alone with him like that. Especially with you so nervous around mortals."

"Well, it went okay. Really. In fact, he's not so bad at all, for what he is. Have you scanned him?"

"Not closely." Her attention was drifting back to the magazine.

"He's so . . . healthy. And perfect. He's a lot like one of us."

"Head's the wrong shape." Some article was deeply interesting her. I cranked back the slide and processed it for transmission.

"Do you remember what you told me about having recreational sex with mortals?"

"Hm?" she said, and then played it back and lifted her head to stare at me. "Oops. No, I never said any such thing. Whatever it was you think I said. Listen, don't let Joseph pressure you into doing anything you really don't want to do. It's perfectly understandable if the idea of, uh, you know, makes you sick. I may have said something kind of dumb about acquired tastes, but if I did, it was only to show you how comfortable some of us can feel around mortals. Okay?"

"Well, okay, do you think you'd feel comfortable around a mortal like Nicholas Harpole?"

Her brow furrowed. "I guess so. He looks clean."

"He's *intelligent*. I never met a mortal with a real working brain before."

"Big surprise, isn't it?" She focused in on the magazine. "Well, congratulations. At the rate you're going, you'll have that AAE off your file in no time."

"How did you know I had an AAE?" I was stung. "Those things are supposed to be confidential!"

She just looked at me bleakly. "Sorry," she said. "They're not. Another big surprise."

"Boy!" I flung another slide into the credenza, so hard it beeped in protest. Nefer sighed.

"You work for the Company, Mendoza. This is what it's like."

"I saw a unicorn today," I told her maliciously.

"Sir Walter has a rhinoceros out there, huh?" She lost herself in the magazine again. "Wow. They're releasing the complete series of Jason Barrymore films on ring holo next month."

So who cared.

12

I KNOW NOTHING of your life, Master Harpole, do you know that?"
I said coquettishly. It was difficult to be a coquette while trying to
keep artichoke leaves out of one's mouth. We were busy wrestling a
very determined taproot up out of the mud.

"Hm?" he said, and then "Ha!" as the nasty thing sagged over,
defeated in the grass. I bent to cut the parts I needed for processing.

"Your artichoke is not your phoenix among herbs," panted Nicholas, wiping his hands.

"Pardon?"

"This is not a rare plant, you know," he pointed out, switching
to Latin.

"No, not rare, but very good for gross humors of the blood." I
sliced off spines. "Or so my father says. Sir Walter is troubled with
them, I am told."

"And is your father troubled with them also?"

"Sometimes." I squinted up at him. "There, behold. I have told
you more, and you have told me nothing. You have drawn volumes
of information out of me. You'd make a good spy." Coquettishness
in Latin. I felt pretty proud of myself. He gave me a look.

"Why, Lady, for all I know some friar is hiding close by, writing
down every word we say."

"He'd be more likely to be spying on me than on you, I fear.
But, since I am a woman and therefore given to curiosity, I must
know all about you. Where were you born?"

"Hampstead."

"Where were you educated?"

"Balliol."

"What are you doing here?"

"Using my wits to earn my bread."

"This rush of personal confidences is making me dizzy," I told the artichoke. "So you were at Balliol? At Oxford? And you didn't enter the Church?"

"No. I lack personal discipline. But a good friend recommended me to Sir Walter, and so I keep his accounts and dine at his table, and no man has cause to complain of me." He folded his hands in a manner that suggested the story was at an end.

"Did you get all that, Fray Diego?" I called over the hedge. "Well, you must excuse me. You know how we women are. Once we think something's hidden to us, we die to discover what it is."

"Now you're quoting from our Chaucer," he said. "Aren't you?"

"*Wife of Bath*," I admitted. "But Aristotle too."

"Yes." He watched me, smiling. I folded the parts of the artichoke I needed in a clean napkin and considered the remaining mess. I wondered if I should leave it for the gardener to clean up. Nicholas said, "You surely aren't saying you accept Aristotle's views on the female sex."

"What, that we're evil? Really, señor, would you believe something like that about yourself simply because some old pagan said it? And a Greek too."

"Our Lord had several female friends," observed Nicholas. "And women lived among His disciples. Without sin, we must assume." My turn to give him a look.

"I suppose so," I said. "The issue is whether carnal intercourse is sinful. Do you imagine Jesus Himself was a virgin at the age of thirty-three?"

He gaped.

"Did you often say things like that in Spain?" he asked finally.

"No, of course not. It wasn't safe."

"Nor is it any safer here, especially with your prince in our land. Please, think before you speak."

"I do. Am I not safe from betrayal with you?"

He leaned closer and switched from Latin to Greek. "And if you are, it is because we are alone in this place, and I see no danger in striving with you in the little intellectual contests you propose. But I would not speak so recklessly in front of anyone else, and neither must you."

"Why? Would Master Ffrawney run off to tell the nearest bishop?"

He snorted. "Without doubt. And then your father would have much to explain! The last thing anyone expected to see in England was a Spanish heretic."

"Oh, well." I got up from the grass and brushed off my skirt. "And I was so hoping we might have a discussion of the nature of *agape*. When the term is defined as a 'love-feast,' do you suppose they mean—"

"Hush! Hush! Hush!" He scrambled to his feet and put his hand over my mouth. I looked at him over the edge of his hand. He looked away. "I think I would like to have your father beaten," he said finally. I pulled away.

"You'd have to catch him first," I said.

"Yes, and I have a feeling that that would be difficult. He seems to be an able little twister in the nets of the law. By your leave. But he had no business bringing up a daughter so."

"What do you mean? Should he have denied me an education?" I was actually insulted.

"By no means. But he ought to have taught you discretion as well as Greek and Aramaic, Lady, lest you come to harm."

"Am I not discreet? Only with you would I say such rash things, because I know *you* would never do me harm," I said, flirt, flirt, wishing I had a fan to flutter.

"And you are correct! I hope I know better than to meddle with the daughter of a man who administers purges." He folded his arms and smiled.

"He's an able swordsman, I'll have you know," I told him when I had stopped laughing.

"No doubt."

"Renowned throughout Madrid, Valladolid, and the Alhambra."

"In truth."

"Deadly with a blade of Toledo steel."

"Deadlier with a good dose of laxative. No, if ever I wronged you, I'd keep close to my chamberpot, lest calamity befall. You need not fear me. But in God's name, Lady, have a care what you say."

I was in high spirits at my credenza that night, let me tell you; my fingers just flew over the keys. I synthesized four vials of anti-hypertensive in the time it took Nefer to repair her mantilla, which had met with an unfortunate accident in the trailing canopy of the bed. She was going crazy with boredom in England but not me, boy. I liked it here.

* * *

It happened that a remedy for Nefer's ennui arrived only the next morning, much to her surprise.

The day dawned dark, pouring black rain, so we were all gathered in the great hall watching Sir Walter eat his healthful, low-cholesterol breakfast. Joseph was watching him, anyway, and maybe Nefer; I was too busy making eye contact with Master Harpole to pay attention. But here came Francis Ffrawney, bowing and scraping, to announce:

"Sir Walter, there is a common sort of man at the gate saying he hath property of Doctor Ruy's and would speak to him thereof." All eyes turned to Joseph.

"What sort of man?" Joseph inquired.

"A poor sort, sir, a very rascal in a leather hood, that swears great oaths and will not move from the gate without he be granted your ear. I must warn your worship, he may well be some heretic malcontent."

"Why, that honest fellow!" Joseph leaped to his feet in feigned surprise. "This should be that same innkeeper that brought my baggage ashore. He must have found the chest I so unwittingly left behind."

This was news to me, but I piped up: "Truly, Father, the men of England are as honest as they are tall." More flirting and wished-for fan in Master Harpole's direction.

So Xenophon was admitted, all muddy and horsey, with a lot of stamping and swearing. He clumped up to Joseph and went down on one knee, holding out a plain wooden chest. It was not one we had brought from Spain.

"My good signior!" he said. "You had scarce been gone an hour when our lad Wat, him that carries away the chamber-lye in the jordans, he comes a-running down the stairs. Quoth he, 'That there Spanish grandee hath left a thing like a box in his room!' 'That's a wonder to be sure,' quoth I, and I went and looked, and to be sure you had left this. And since meseemeth this must be a very important casket, doubtless filled with what ye shall sore need in England"—wide take to be sure we got the point—"I thought it were best to bring it straight here myself."

"May God and the good Saint James bless thee for thy care," effused Joseph. "Let me give thee something for thy troubles." He groped in his purse and handed out what looked like a doubloon but was actually a mint Theobromos patty in silver paper.

"Such munificence!" exclaimed Xenophon. "I'm a-going to go out and buy me a cow with this, see if I don't." He prostrated himself at Joseph's feet. "I could kiss thy shoe of Cordovan leather, sir, that I could."

"Away, worthy peasant." Joseph waved at him. I was wondering how long they were going to carry on like this when Master Ffrawney sniffed:

"Will you not open the box, sir, and satisfy yourself that all your goods are safe within?"

There was an awkward pause. Joseph and Xenophon exchanged glances. Xenophon shrugged imperceptibly. "An excellent thought," conceded Joseph. Coding the unseen lock, he lifted the lid.

The chest contained things that appeared to be books but weren't, a couple of things that appeared to be surgeon's tools but weren't, and what appeared to be three jars of medicinal herbs. All these must have been the electronic tools and chemicals Joseph would need for his work on Sir Walter. Packed carefully apart from the rest was a little ornamented box with a couple of gold birds, or something, on the lid. Joseph held it up to the firelight, and his smiling face did not betray that he had no idea what the hell it was for.

But Nicholas leaned forward, frowning in astonishment. "That is a model of the Ark of the Covenant of the Israelites!" he stated.

"Yes, of course," Joseph agreed. "It's a, uh, reliquary. Enshrined within is a fragment of the pelvis of Saint Mary Magdalene. I never travel without it."

Nicholas sat back, his face a mask of disgust. Xenophon stepped forward and said: "Pardon me, sir, but an angel appeareth to be loose." He reached out and gave one of the lid ornaments a little twist.

Click.

—*KZUS, continuing your round-the-clock coverage of the royal wedding. And it looks like the rain's letting up here, so we may be able to go down into the street in a minute or two and see if we can interview somebody. I've certainly got an impressive view of Winchester Cathedral from where I'm stationed. I can see the floral decorations that the town council put up and believe me, folks, they certainly had a lot of work last night in the rain. And, say, those flowers are just beautiful. What kind are they, Justinian?*

Well, Decius, it says here those are pansies and heliotropes and of course the famous red-and-white Tudor roses. Folks, it's nine-hundred hours and counting on this day of the royal wedding. We'll be back to you on KZUS with the latest developments after this musical interlude. The strains of a basse-dance filled the room.

And Sir Walter went right on spooning down his oat porridge, and Nicholas still sat with his arms folded, staring sullenly into the fire. Master Ffrawney was still gazing on the reliquary with a suitable expression of reverent awe. They couldn't hear a thing, of course. It was being broadcast in a frequency out of mortal range.

"I desire to offer fervent prayers of thanksgiving." Nefer got up and took the radio out of Joseph's hands. "Give me leave, señor, to commune with the blessed saints for a while."

It would have been dangerous to get in her way. He bowed her out of the room, and she swept up the stairs, music trailing after her. Joseph pulled at his beard thoughtfully. He extended a hand to Xenophon.

"I shall see thee to thy horse, good fellow. By your leave, Sir Walter?"

Sir Walter waved his spoon at them in a dismissive way. They exited together. I got up and went to sit beside Nicholas. We looked at each other: he was still fuming. Yet he moved his thigh just a little closer to mine on the settle.

"What a joyous occasion this is!" exclaimed Master Ffrawney, when he realized that nobody else was going to make conversation. "Now good fortune and the blessing of the saint will surely attend the faithful in this house!"

"Even so." Sir Walter did not look up from his porringer.

"Amen!" Master Ffrawney looked pointedly at Nicholas. Nicholas did not move, but his eyes swiveled to look at Master Ffrawney.

"Now I wonder," Nicholas drawled, "what miraculous cures we shall owe to the holy pelvis of the Magdalene?"

Oh, what a smell of testosterone. Bright red and flashing, the readout appeared in midair, showing me the changing blood chemistry of all three men, with figures on the statistical probability of violence erupting. My body was already moving of its own accord, but as I got up to leave, I touched Nicholas's shoulder.

"Master Harpole," I quavered. "There is a thing I saw from the window, that I would know more of. Will it please you to come see it with me?"

With a last contemptuous stare at Master Ffrawney, Nicholas got to his feet and followed me out of the room. I led the way to a gallery on the second floor, well away from the monkey smell, and looked out a window at the rainy landscape. I found a gilded cupola to point at.

"There! What is that, please?" I asked. He looked briefly.

"That is the roof of the aviary," he said.

"Oh. We went there, didn't we? How different it all looks from up here."

He didn't say anything. I looked down at the floor. "I would not have had you come to blows with Master Ffrawney," I explained.

"Small matter if we had." He smiled bitterly. "Belike I'd have cracked his hypocrite's crown for him."

"Wrath is a sin, is it not? Wherefore be glad you have not sinned."

He nodded, calming down a little, watching the storm.

"I am sorry about the box," I said at last.

"What, the Ark of the Covenant?" He lounged against the wall, turning to face me. "Sweet Jesu, Lady, what a piece of arrant popery! And your father a learned man too. Truly the more I know of him, the less I know what manner of thing he is."

"Master Harpole, there are no religious relics in that box."

"No!" He flung up his hands in mock amazement.

"But my father did not feel himself amongst folk he could trust, and he had to say something. The box is—" I thought fast. "The box is connected with his studies. His more arcane studies."

Nicholas gave a slow incredulous grin. "What? A wizard?" Damn it, didn't *anybody* believe in witchcraft anymore?

"Rather, I should say—" I looked up and down the corridor. I switched to Greek. "My father has made some study of what you might call alchemy. Also mathematics and the properties of physical bodies."

"Ah." Suddenly Nicholas was interested. "You mean he is an hermetic philosopher? He has studied Vitruvius?" What was I getting myself into? I did a fast access and discovered that he was talking about early, early science and technology, which only secret societies and clandestine brotherhoods were concerned with right now.

"Yes," I said cautiously.

"Then I understand you." His face brightened with speculation. "Why, all the several parts of your story now become a whole. His Greek physick, his sufferings at the hands of the Inquisition—and it's evident he hath been at the Emperor's court—and this careful model of the Ark of the—" His mouth dropped open. He closed it.

"Your father is a Jew," he said quietly.

I remember thinking calmly, How silly, just before the shock wave hit. I saw the men and the glowing coals in the little room. I saw the bullying face of the priest. I saw, I saw, *I saw*—

Babbling frantic denials, I began tearing at my sleeve, I guess to show the blue veins that would prove I wasn't a *chueta*. Wouldn't you think a sophisticated creature like me would be able to handle a few bad memories? Except that this was the central trauma that Dr. Zeus had used to fix my indoctrination, to remind me always why I worked for them. They'd never meant to cure me of it. They'd tucked it deep down inside, the battery that powered my machine heart.

"Look, look—" With a great ripping of brocade my bare arm emerged. Nicholas seized it and held me still. His face was horrified. "Look!" I sobbed.

"Rose!"

"Look..." A yellow light stopped flashing, and a noise died away. Far off, Joseph was running back toward the house in a panic. He saw us at the window. He stopped. He watched us.

Nicholas had put both arms around me and embraced me, lifting me clear off the floor. He was so warm, and the gallery was freezing cold. I stopped shaking. Systems normalizing. "Your father was not alone in prison," he guessed in a whisper, setting me down carefully. "They had you, also, and—" Something in my face must have told him to stop there. But I had control of myself now. Yes. I could speak.

"Have you any idea," I enunciated, "what such a base and unfounded accusation means in Spain?"

He nodded slowly, not taking his eyes from my face.

"You could be as pure of blood as the Emperor himself, but if you were ever even so much as accused," I began to gasp again, "just *accused*—"

There were footsteps approaching the bottom of the stairs. Nicholas glanced down and drew me away with him, swiftly up the corridor to a smaller stair. It ascended steep as a ladder. We climbed it in haste, I hitching up my skirts so I wouldn't trip.

Through a little cut-corner door at the top was his room. It was Spartan and small, its slanting ceiling high and sharply angled.

The bed had been extended for his great length by having a chest put at the foot of it. There were books piled and tumbled on every flat surface. There was a chair by the window. There was a candle, upright amid drips of cold tallow from hours of reading.

He led me to the bed and sat me down on it, then wrapped my torn sleeve back about my arm. He put his blanket over my shoulders for good measure, then looked around his room in a helpless way. "Wait," he said at last. "I'll come anon."

He hastened down the stairs again. Clunk, clunk, clunk, I heard his footsteps descending.

I sat there on his bed. I could pick him up descending through the house in great agitation, with bursts of interference when someone else spoke to him. Nefer's radio was broadcasting a pavane now; nothing much must be happening with the royal wedding. Joseph had moved about thirty meters from his previous position and was reading me.

Mendoza?

Go to hell.

No, seriously. Are you—

I'm just embarrassed. Horribly embarrassed. Now get out.

He politely withdrew. How could I face Nicholas again?

It was calming to try to read his books' titles, all scattered as they were. Let's see, this one was the *Enchiridion Militis Christiani.* Predictable. *De Servo Arbitrario,* also predictable. *The Wicked Mammon,* this one was supposed to be out of print, wonder how he'd got a copy? *The Prologue to the Romans,* in English. *A Preservative against the Poison of Pelagius,* wow. I had begun to cry, little snively tears. I wiped them away angrily.

Clunk clunk clunk, there was Nicholas shouldering through the doorway. He was carrying a pint of something that steamed, and a ball of thread with a needle stuck in it.

"I must go," I said, mustering all the Hispanic dignity I had available. "This is not seemly, señor."

"Your sleeve must be mended first, lest it be remarked upon," he said. "And I think you will not want your duenna to do it, involved as she is in her devotions."

"She is a good woman and greatly stupid," I covered. "She truly believes that thing is a holy relic, and my father hath not seen fit to enlighten her. Nor doth she know of his private studies. I trust, sir, you will not tell her."

"Not I." He sat down beside me and put the pint pot in my hand. "Now, drink that off straight. It will calm thee." Awkwardly he threaded the needle.

"What is this?" I peered into the drink.

"Burnt sack and eggs."

Oh, no. But scanning revealed no pathogens, and it smelled all right, so I tasted it cautiously. Not so bad; something like eggnog. I sipped at it and watched him mend my sleeve with big clumsy stitches.

"Now, God He knows I am no tailor, Rose, but this will hold thee until thou canst better mend it thyself. Thou hast learned to use a needle?" he asked dryly.

"Yes."

"It is well. I am glad that thou, knowing so much Greek, hast a plain skill or two."

"You are too kind," I said, cold.

"Kindness is the duty of any Christian, Lady, is it not so?" He switched to Greek. "Hear me. What I have been told today, I will tell to no one. But, having said this, I must caution you again to hide your past. Better you had let me think your father a papist knave than to tell me such secrets. I believe you are innocent and pity your sufferings, yet there are those who would gladly see you burn even here in England. Though, God willing, this shall not become so fearful a place as Spain."

"Spain." I laughed and took a gulp of my drink. "I'll tell you what the trouble with Spain is, señor. We *read* our Scripture. We discovered therein, long before the rest of you, that this God we all serve is cruel and irrational. We are made in His image, are we not? In Spain, we derive grim pleasure from dragging ourselves across the coals of His will."

"No!" He took my hand. "Never believe such a thing! You must understand that God is Love."

"Must I?" I had another drink. "That same God who sent bears to kill the little children that mocked His prophet's baldness? That same God that slaughtered His own worshipers for trying to prevent the defilement of His carrying box? Love, you said?"

Wind buffeted the eaves, and a fresh torrent of rain streamed down the window. We sat looking at it.

Nicholas's voice was quiet. "This is truly the Devil's work: not women rolling on the floor and spitting toads, but this, the despair that you wake and sleep with."

I shrugged.

"How shall I save you?" But there, look, he actually had tears in his eyes. I felt a sudden rush of affection and wished I could console him. I wished I could tell him the truth. He didn't have to worry: I was saved, I was one of the lucky few who really would inherit the World to Come, in that wonderful faraway future where every toilet shall flush and there are cinema palaces on the moon. I was immortal, enlightened, and perfect, wasn't I? But not Jewish. No, no, absolutely not, never, not me.

"Don't fear for me," I told him. "If your God is truly what you say He is, He must forgive me. I came alive out of the Inquisition's hand; have I not spent my time in Hell?"

"I cannot judge you, certainly," he replied, folding his arms. "I have never suffered as you have. I hope my soul should fare no worse, if God so chose to test me. And who can see what is to come?''

How cold it was, the storm beating at the window.

Nicholas went down the stairs first to make sure that no one would see me leaving his room, beckoning me down when he saw the coast was clear. He bowed to me, I curtseyed to him, and we parted.

When I entered our room, Nefer was staring intently at the radio, which was broadcasting liturgical music. ''You missed it,'' she told me. ''They just got married.''

''Who?''

''Philip and Mary.''

''Some duenna you are.'' I reached around to unlace my bodice.

''Huh?''

''Here I've been alone with a man in his room, and you didn't even notice,'' I giggled, just a bit shrilly. ''Help me out of this, will you? My sleeve got torn and I—''

''Torn?'' She sat upright. ''Did you—I thought I heard—''

''Boy, who writes your dialogue?'' My Shrill went up a notch toward Hysterical. ''Yes! See? Mad with passion, he rent my sleeve. Turns out he's an elbow man.''

''Oh, shut up.'' She came and helped me with the laces. ''Here I am, bored out of my mind for three days, and the minute I have something interesting to listen to . . .''

''Knock, knock,'' said a voice outside our door. ''Whisk those frilly underthings out of sight, girls, I'm coming in.''

Enter Joseph, smiling and shaking rain out of the crown of his hat.

''Quite a little tempest we had there.'' He looked me in the eye. The sound of the choir stopped, and a voice announced, *That was the Agnus Dei as performed by the choir of Winchester Cathedral. Things look pretty quiet down there by the altar right now; Their Majesties have received the Sacrament and appear to be praying. You'll recall there was quite a stir earlier when the Prince's new titles were announced. Supposedly they're a wedding gift from the Emperor, though it's popularly speculated that they are in fact a bribe to get the Prince to go through with the wedding.*

''Yes, sir, quite a little electrical disturbance,'' continued Joseph. Nefer yanked off my bodice and handed it to me. I clutched it to myself in dismay.

''I'm *trying* to listen to the broadcast!'' she hissed at him. He raised his eyebrows at her and opened the door to his room.

"Mendoza?" He gestured. I followed him in, hastily shrugging back into the bodice.

"Have a seat. Have a glass of muscadel. On second thought, don't have a glass of muscadel; you've been drinking burnt sack. *I'll* have the glass of muscadel, and you can tell me why you're metabolizing burnt sack in a torn bodice." He went to a sideboard and poured from a decanter.

"Where'd you get the muscadel?" I asked very calmly, sitting down and folding my hands. Yes, I was completely in control.

"Master Ffrawney found it. He's been bringing me all kinds of useful stuff to prove he's a good Catholic. Wine. Sweetmeats. Gossip. On the subject of gossip, you want to tell Papa all about it?" He settled across from me, tasted his wine, and set it down.

"You're really good in this role, aren't you?" I said, not without admiration. "You've really become the Spanish Intriguer. But what possible use could you have for local gossip in a place like this?"

"Oh, you'd be surprised." He stroked his beard. "Lots of strange stuff goes on, and it's all interconnected, and you never know when you'll discover something that may be useful later. Works for Miss Marple every time. Mostly, though, I get into the habit of being nosy about everything because the character I'm playing is supposed to be nosy. If I'm true to all Doctor Ruy's mannerisms, I *believe* in him, and all the mortals I encounter believe in him too. Characterization is very important in the field. I don't think you've exactly got a handle on that, yet."

"I have too," I said hotly. "I think I'm portraying a late medieval Spanish adolescent very well."

"No. You *are* a late medieval Spanish adolescent. It's not a role for you, not yet. You need to develop that little bit of emotional distance between yourself and the person you want mortals to see. That person is your mask; that person is the one who reacts to the things you encounter. You, yourself, don't get emotionally involved; you let your character do all the reacting so that you, personally, never lose control. As so lamentably happened just now."

I fumed. He had another sip of wine.

"So. Just what happened up there in the gallery with Master Harpole?"

"It was your stupid explanation of the radio. Why'd you have to say it had a holy relic in it? You know how Protestants feel about stuff like that! So I was explaining how it was really something connected with your scientific research and, you know what, Mr. Smart Guy? He leaped to the conclusion that you're a secret J-J-Jew."

Silence, but for some distant bishop droning out a blessing on Philip and Mary.

"Tsk, tsk, tsk," said Joseph at last. "This was obviously where little Mendoza got excited. Dear me. And what a clever guy this Harpole is, isn't he? Awfully good at noticing all kinds of little unusual things about people and keeping them on file in his head. So he's built a theory around us, has he? He added two and two and came up with five, but nobody else in the house was aware there was anything to count. This is just the sort of mortal that puts a mission in jeopardy. What can we do about Master Harpole, Mendoza?"

"I don't know!" I snarled. "Is the Spanish Intriguer going to put poison in his ale?"

"Nothing so crude. Speaking of drinks, who gave you the burnt sack?"

"*He* got it for me," I muttered. "And he mended my sleeve."

"All right, this is a good sign. And did he recoil in horror at your supposed ethnic origin? No, he obviously didn't. What does this tell us, Mendoza? Think."

"He's brilliant and tolerant and humane and ahead of his time. He's like one of us."

"Well, now we know how you feel about him. And he feels—?"

"He's interested in me," I guessed. "Sympathetic."

"Bingo. Vulnerability can be very appealing. So, what do we do about Master Harpole, Mendoza? I've been saying all along, in my jolly avuncular way with just a hint of the pander, that you two would make the cutest couple."

"You have got to be crazy! I just embarrassed myself to death in front of that man."

"Oh. I see. All right. Forget I ever mentioned it. Say, I've always meant to ask you: Did you ever remember what your mortal name was?"

"What?" I started.

"Your name, when you were a mortal. At Santiago? We couldn't figure out if you were so little you didn't really know, or if you knew your name but were afraid to tell us."

"I really didn't know." Sweat broke out on my forehead.

Joseph sipped his wine.

"Remembering something?" he inquired.

"No!"

"Well. I guess we needn't worry too much about Master Harpole. Now that I know I'm supposed to be a Rosicrucian alchemistkabbalist, I'll drop a few corroborating remarks here and there. Doubtless that will satisfy his curiosity. Okay? And I'm sure things will work themselves out.''

I stayed in my room the next four days all the same. It rained steadily, so I had an excuse, but meals were awkward. Nefer brought me bread and cheese a couple of times; I could hear her downstairs, graciously informing them that Doña Rosa was indisposed, with that monolithic dignity she could summon at will. She had a good grasp of cover identity. Joseph was right: I had to work at my character more.

But I sat on my bed and watched the rain falling forever, and I entered requisition codes at my credenza, and I ignored Joan when she came in to clean, and I listened to the radio. There was steady music all day, some of it live. There was an evening news broadcast, and a great talk show in the afternoon: one of the station staff had a mortal cover identity as a lawyer, and he'd invite his clients to talk about their lives and problems in a room rigged with microphones. Occasionally the results were hilarious. Sometimes, lying awake at night, I heard strange little electronic noises coming from Sir Walter's room—Joseph in there with his pocketful of cryptotools, performing some secret rearrangement of Sir Walter's insides.

I listened for Nicholas, too. His long stride came sometimes down the hall and paused outside our door before moving slowly on. He sat up each evening late, before his bed creaked with the weight of his length settling on it. He read a lot. I wondered what he was reading now.

The fifth morning dawned bright and clear. No help for it: this would be a great day for collecting rare specimens of variegated shepherd's purse or green fumitory. I crept down the stairs behind Nefer, trying to look as inconspicuous as possible, and so naturally everyone was assembled in the great hall and all heads turned to stare at me as I entered.

"Why, well met, Lady Rose!" Sir Walter rose and bowed. "Are you with us again? I trust our English air hath not given you the tisick?"

"No, I thank you, sir. I am recovered now," I murmured.

"Excellent well! You shall dine on oranges in the Spanish fashion."

Oh, God, there was a bowl of ten oranges set at my place at the table. I smiled feebly.

"Master Harpole himself hath brought them in this morning. I thought we should never get more than three together ripe at one time, but it seems the weather likes them well,'' Sir Walter babbled on. I glanced up at Nicholas. I glanced away.

Hey, Nefer transmitted sternly. *These people are trying to be kind to you. Behave yourself.*

Taking your role as duenna a little seriously, aren't you? I shot back. But she was right. ''Truly I am unworthy of such care from so gracious a host, Sir Walter, but I pray you accept my wholly inadequate thanks for this abundance of orangery.'' I curtseyed.

So with my bodice dagger I peeled one and set to, and as the others sat there with eggs and oatmeal, I ate oranges until the corners of my mouth stung. Nicholas kept looking at me, but I avoided his gaze.

Just as the meal was concluding, Master Ffrawney hurried into the room.

''Sir Walter, there is a great party come on horseback, express to see the garden. John hath collected their pence, and they wait but for a guide—*thy* duty, man,'' he nodded peremptorily at Nicholas, who stood up and glowered at him. ''And they have been at Penshurst Place and seem to be persons of gentle birth and consequence, and— *wilt* thou not go, Nicholas?—and one gentleman, being a Master Darrell of Colehill, particularly wisheth to speak to you, sir, wherefore I judged it best to advise you directly.''

''Thou didst well.'' Sir Walter rose in excitement, his mustache points quivering. He practically ran for the door, then halted, conscious of the fact that he had Spaniards sitting in his dining room. ''Er, Doctor Ruy, for appearances' sake—''

''Say not a word, my dearest friend.'' Joseph rose majestically. ''You shall see that Spanish discretion is as great as Spanish love of fruit. Doña Marguerita? Daughter? Let us retire. I feel an urgent need to pray.''

''A thousand thanks,'' breathed Sir Walter, and hastened away with Nicholas stalking after him. As they departed, something strange drew my eye.

Sir Walter was taller.

High heels on his shoes? No. No, he actually was taller, coming farther up to Nicholas's shoulder than he had, and his movements were nimbler. I watched their retreating backs with some wonder. Joseph's clandestine retooling was beginning to show. How about that?

''Yes, a day of retreat and meditation will serve me well.'' Joseph selected an orange from the few still in the bowl. ''Master Ffrawney.''

He inclined in his direction and swept from the room. Nefer rose and hurried ahead of him, doubtless hoping to catch the morning news program. I got up to follow them, but Master Ffrawney stepped before me hesitantly and bowed low.

"Good Lady Rose," he said. "A word in your ear, with my most profound apologies for taking such familiarity, but I must speak."

I felt the bridge of my nose arch just a little higher. "What meanest thou, good man?" I said with condescending grace.

"By your leave, Lady, it is Sir Walter's man Nicholas. In him Sir Walter is much abused, I tell you, Lady, though he harbors him out of kindness. The knave is a pernicious heretic and an obdurate Gospel reader."

"Something of this I had heard before," I informed him solemnly, "and I pray hourly for his poor soul. But thou needst not concern thyself, señor. We are well aware that many in England are subject to such vice."

"Yea, but it is no common viciousness that is in this man, Lady." Master Ffrawney looked over his shoulder uneasily. I stepped closer to him, suddenly interested in his story. Having satisfied himself that Nicholas was not lurking nearby, Master Ffrawney stuck out his neck and spoke just above a whisper.

"You must know, Lady, that of late there hath been much apostasy and such like wickedness practiced here in Kent. Not only the new heresies of the German distemperature, but certain ancient ones too." He dropped his voice still lower. "More I may not tell a virtuous maid, but there was a community of such lewd persons in these parts, young persons given to idleness and heresy, and such a one, Lady," he looked around again, "was *Nicholas Harpole!*"

Wow! "I am shocked and horrified," I said.

"Yea, Lady, you shall find it is so, and though he came near to being hanged for his brawling and lasciviousness, he had friends at the University who excused and huddled it up, and set him here like a viper to be nourished at Sir Walter's bosom." He leaned back with pursed lips, nodding.

I was ready to die with laughter there on the spot, but I clutched my rosary and said, in most grave tones: "Now by Saint Mary and Saint James, can this be true? Was he verily given to the lusts of the flesh? Thou must understand that I am only an innocent and hath been among the blessed sisters all my days, and know nothing of the twisted sexual practices of Anabaptists."

Master Ffrawney drew back at the very word, and we both made the sign of the Cross.

"The more reason, gentle Lady, that I must warn you, for you go into the garden alone with this man and there is rumor (saving your grace) you were seen abovestairs with him, though no honest man believes it. But pray, beware this Harpole!"

How very, very amusing. "Fear not, good man, I will heed thy timely warning. Who would have thought he was one of those vile freewillers?"

"Aye, forsooth! I could tell you such things; but you see the sort of creature this Harpole is, do you not? You will not be deceived by his smooth speech or his politic looks. He is a very Satan in persuasion, I say."

"I go forth fortified by thy counsel," I promised him. "And now, I join my dear father in prayer. Buenos días, señor."

I skipped up the stairs and fell through our doorway giggling. Nef was sitting hunched up on our bed with a strained expression. The radio was on, as usual.

"You will never, never guess what I just found out!" I whooped.

"Mendoza, this is an interview with a mortal who raises Red Alderney cows, and if you talk through it, I'll make your life miserable for weeks."

"Well, pardon me." I started to flounce out of the room, but paused. Somehow I didn't feel like telling Joseph. I wandered over to the window instead and looked out at the bright day.

All in the garden green, there were the mortals moving. The top of Nicholas's biretta appeared above a hedge and traveled slowly along it until he emerged, so tall in his black robe that the visitors scurrying after him looked like dolls. Two little ladies in claret-colored velvet, four little gentlemen in their flat caps with swirling feathers. One of the little gentlemen was in heated conversation with Sir Walter. Nicholas pointed at a particularly fine old elm tree and said something about it, and everyone stared at it intently, except Sir Walter and the fourth little gentleman. I looked down on them like a goddess leaning out from Olympus.

What a snotty child she was, the little botanist Mendoza. Also gleeful, gratified, newly self-confident, and intrigued. She'd known there was more to Nicholas than met the eye. A wimpy Bible apologist is one thing, but a dark secret anarchist with a tortured soul, participating in religious orgies—well!

As I observed the mortals with a cool and distant smile, Nicholas suddenly lifted his head and stared straight at me. I caught my breath and backed away from the window, into the middle of the room.

Nay, good sir, they's good milkers, my cows be. My Silver, now

she do give place to none in filling of the can. Why, I could tell—
The transmission dissolved in a burst of static as my hardware disturbed the frequency. Nefer jumped like she'd been shot and glared at me.

"Sit down, dammit!"

Meekly I sat at the credenza and took out my sample analysis reports to work on. At least *they* did not give me unaccountable sensations in the pelvic region.

13

It was the middle of August and the first warm day since we arrived. Little rare plants were consenting to bloom, which meant I had much to do.

So I found myself in the garden again, threading my way through the green maze with Master Harpole and wondering what to say besides: "Pray, where do the best specimens of *Cochlearia officinalis* grow?"

I think he must have felt a certain shyness also, for he finally ventured to remark:

"The season grows hot at last, methinks."

It must have been all of twenty-one degrees Celsius outside.

"I think you have but one season in your England," I said. "Nothing but rainy spring all year round. Your King Arthur poet saith of the Isle of Avalon that it is a summer country, but I find it not so."

Nicholas smiled absently. "You misunderstand, Lady. This same Isle of Avalon is not England but some country to the west, beyond the sea."

"Ireland?"

"Not so, neither; for I understand the wild men there themselves believe in a western island where the flowers never fade."

"Think you they mean the New World?"

He shook his head. "Ships have been to the New World," he said in Latin. "That is an earthly place too, like Ireland, except that it is bigger and its savages wear feathers, not wool." Latin had become our favored language for straightforward conversation, because one didn't have to keep coming up with flowers of speech.

"What a disappointment. Surely, this Blessed Isle, it must be somewhere," I maintained. "Perhaps it lies to the west of the New World?"

Nicholas looked at me sideways. "It's a poetic device," he informed me. "A fantasy, a metaphor for the heart's desire that can never be found here on Earth."

"You think there is no place on Earth where flowers always bloom and it is always warm?" I found a nice little example of rupturewort and bent to examine it.

"Certainly you may find such a place, if you go to the Equator. The Blessed Isle of the poet is a land without human grief or sin."

"Ah, well, that is a fantasy, certainly." I took a quick holo shot.

"Let us hope not." His voice was quiet.

I snipped a few sprigs and put them away in my basket. "But I remember now. You believe men will defeat human nature and become perfect here on Earth. Tell me, how do you hope to accomplish that? What will you do about old age? Or death?"

I was smug, because I thought I had the answers myself. But he sat down on the grass beside me, put his fingertips together, and said, quite seriously:

"It's obvious. If men no longer sin, there will be no old age or death."

"What?" I stared, laying down my trowel.

"Have you read a book by Miles Coverdale on the old faith? Just a moment." He fished a dog-eared quarto from an inner pocket and thumbed through it. "He says—this is in reference to the Fall of Adam and Eve—he says, to paraphrase the English, that the Lord God made man with both an immortal soul *and* an immortal body, and that when Adam sinned, his flesh became mortal and only his soul remained everlasting. Here, he says it. Now, since we know that enough sin can kill even the everlasting soul, would it not therefore follow that *freedom* from sin might preserve even the earthly body so it endures forever? Read this page, here."

But I stared unseeing at the black-letter text. He had it right again! Men could defeat death, just as he believed, though technology, not grace, would be the weapon.

Though, come to think of it, we had done away with sin too, hadn't we? And not only by abandoning the concept: we eternal ones worked tirelessly for the good of man. His hideous wars, his politics, his greed and ignorance and wastefulness were abhorrent to us. We were perfect. Well, no, not *perfect*, exactly, but . . . Then again, define perfect.

"Nor is this idea without precedence in Scripture." Nicholas tucked the book away. "For example, the prophet Elijah was taken into Heaven in his mortal flesh, alive."

But I too had been taken to Heaven in a chariot of fire. What a depressing thought, somehow. Nothing to do with a soul or a spirit: a mechanical conjuring trick, a deus ex machina. And so what was I? The machine's child?

It's frightening, that moment when the ground first washes out from under your feet.

I wasn't even a human being. And this warm mortal man, with his broken nose and unshaven chin, speaking so confidently of such crazy ideas, seemed to stand in a lamplit room. I stood without in freezing darkness, by a sealed window. But I touched his hand and he took mine without even noticing. He folded it between his hands and kept on talking.

"The end of sin, therefore, is the end of death."

"Is there no way out of all this sin?" I cried in agony. Must I be trapped in this conversation my whole life?

"None for me. I have sinned, and I will surely die; but I have been closer to the true faith than my father was, and the child born tomorrow shall come closer yet than I. So long as each generation works tirelessly for the perfection of the soul, His Kingdom cannot fail to come on Earth."

Shut up, shut up, I thought. It was my own creed he was outlining, and it terrified me. There *was* no hope for him, he *would* surely die, but he didn't matter beside the greater good. I didn't want to think of my eternal labor through generations of men yet unborn, when Nicholas would be so much forgotten dust. I wanted to breathe in the scent of his mortal body and listen to the rhythms of his voice, without understanding.

"What madness this is, this idea," I said. "Living forever on Earth. Where will we all go, tell me, if no one ever dies? Next you'll be telling me that men will travel to the moon and stars." If he started to prophesy about space travel, I really was going to scream. But he only shrugged and smiled.

"As easily as traveling to the Isle of Avalon," he said. "For men must be without sin before they can do either."

Well, he was wrong about *that*, at least. "Enough of this talk of sin, in God's name," I begged him. "We are here, now, in this beautiful place. Isn't this enough? This garden, and the sun, and you and I here, and the poor little unicorn?"

"But the sun will set tonight, Rosa," he said. "And our lives will be over in a moment. And we know the truth, you and I, about that unicorn. What will sustain us but working for the eternal realm?''

Eternal work. My God, couldn't the man talk about anything else? What business did he have being so holy, with that big body of his so well made? With a sob of exasperation I caught hold of him, rock-steady as he was, and kissed him to make him quiet.

His first reaction was to kiss back. He did it very well, he took the initiative at once, and his hands set to work busily doing all the right things. He kissed like an angel of God. It figured.

He lifted his mouth, though, before even one lace had come unfastened, and set me at arm's length. "We must not," he said.

I looked at him, speechless. He could not snatch it away, whatever this was. I had stopped shaking and begun to grow warm inside, warm right through, even to that secret cupboard full of shattered glass and broken dishes. Yet it wouldn't do, would it, for Master Ffrawney or poor Sir Walter or even unexpected penny-paying tourists to come upon us sprawling in the long grass? Nicholas must have learned to dread scandal, if what was said of him was true. I looked down sullenly and said, "So love is a sin too."

"No!" He caught up my hand. "Before God, I tell you, flesh is innocent enough. But you are yet young and I . . ." I looked longingly at his big fine hands. He drew them back. "Would to God I had never sinned," he said.

We went on through the garden then, as we were supposed to do, and through all that long day I filled my basket with rarities, each priceless sacrifice saving its kind from extinction. The finest work in the world, as per my contract.

He didn't look happy either.

I bade Nicholas adieu at the top of the stairs that evening, and went into my room and worked at my credenza, like the good little operative I was supposed to be. I worked until late hours without a break, though Nefer brought me a plate of some kind of supper. I made immortal seven different varieties of cinquefoil, root, leaf, and blossom, for the benefit of the unborn generations who would thank me someday.

Wouldn't they? Wouldn't they appreciate the miraculous survival of seven rare subspecies of a common wildflower? Surely in the glorious future we were all headed for, such things would matter to everyone.

I was only a little distracted by Nefer pacing the floor, though I thought it very unusual for her to be disturbed about anything. Joseph came in to retire, cheery and relaxed, chuckling at some private joke. It must be nice, to find life so funny.

At eleven o'clock Nef came and tapped me on the shoulder.

"Lights out," she said flatly. I shut off the ultravey, and we were left in the wobbling candlelight to undo each other's back lacing.

"What's wrong with you?" I inquired.

"I'm doing nothing here," she sighed.

"Oh. Yes, I'd noticed that." I pulled her lacing free at the bottom, handed it to her, and turned my own back. Her fingers dug at the knots she'd tied that morning.

"It's not fair. There's so much work I could be doing. I hate these dead shifts, where you get stationed in the middle of nowhere for six months at a time with no assignment. At least in Spain there were cattle. I haven't seen anything but two oxen and three horses since I got here. Just wait, they'll pull this on you sometime."

"I don't see how. Domestic animals may be scarce in some places, but plants grow everywhere," I pointed out.

"Ha!" She jerked out a lace. "Ever been in the Sahara? Ever seen pictures of New York Terminus 2100? Or Luna? Not even a cactus. Wait'll you do a ten-month layover in metropolitan Bikkung."

Nonsense. She was exaggerating, surely. Though I recalled holos of urban canyons of the time to come, monoliths of millions of tiny windows, and now that I thought about it, I couldn't recall seeing a blade of grass anywhere there. But if that's what the future held—

"Nef," I said, "did you ever have second thoughts?"

"About what?" She stepped out of her skirts, and her hoops fell to the floor with a gentle whoosh. The candle flame danced.

"Just . . . everything."

"You mean Doctor Zeus?" She stared at me as if I were crazy.

"Well, no," I lied.

"I mean, yes, I'm fed up at the moment, and some of my assignments have been in some awful places, but the job is, well, the job, isn't it? How could anybody have second thoughts? I mean, who'd rather be *dead*?"

"Yeah, right," I said.

The candle was out, and the house was quiet. And all the talk, all the hours of good work were done. I was alone in the dark, sweating sick with the terror of eternal years.

Nicholas Harpole was sitting in his room, reading. He shone like his own candle through the walls. I could hear his breathing. He was aroused. That was what it was, the change in his scent. He closed the book. *Snap*. He put out his candle. *Ssst*. He rustled out of his clothes and into his creaking bed.

As he was poking his feet down into the bed to get them warm, my feet were touching the icy floor. No one made a move to stop me. I drifted from the room and up the long dark corridor, up through the house, with shades pressing close around me on all sides. I didn't run. I found my way to the top of the house, and I opened up the door of that high narrow room where he lay.

He sat up in his shirt, staring at me. I stood there in my nightgown. Oh, the floor was cold. What could I possibly say to him?

"I'm lost," I said. Ha ha; but it was true.

"Think, Lady," Nicholas whispered. "Consider your honor. Consider what you do." But he was already moving over and making room for me beside him, folding back the sheet with those superb hands.

"It is very frightening, being lost." I came closer. "Also I am cold, señor."

"You would be warm in bed," he conceded.

"Can you remedy my being lost, too?" I sat down on the edge. He put out his arm in the darkness and folded me to him.

"Why, Lady, I have found you. How then are you lost?"

He swept me in close, jumping a little at the touch of my icy toes on his shins, and leaned down for a kiss. Oh God he was warm, and his mouth tasted good, and his bed smelled of books and maleness and late nights. He was bare under his shirt, as I was bare under my shift.

"Well met!" He came up from the kiss laughing. "Hadst thou not come here, I swear I'd have lived thy constant friend in chastity, but my poor Friar John would scarce have left me alone."

"Friar John?" I was incredulous.

"Why, to be sure. The upright monk with his hood, who ever entreats me to seek out holy places." We were both giggling now. "Who would ever live in contemplation in some close dark cell, who, um, weeps great tears of remorse at my sins . . . Who . . . who . . . oh, the devil with the metaphor." We kissed greedily; but my fear had not gone yet.

"Everything I was ever told was a lie." I clung to him. "And I have gone too far on a road with no turning, but there must be a way back. There must. I can't take that road, though it lead to Paradise." Not many men would have taken thought for my spiritual state just then, but Nicholas lifted his head and said seriously:

"Sweet love, we shall go to Paradise. Here, now, in this idle pleasant way with our flesh; but also through grace. I will make you love God again."

"You're after my *soul*," I murmured, looking up at him. This was more wickedly exciting even than our nakedness. I could tell it was working that way with him, too: his nostrils flared, and he lowered himself to kiss me, but slow this time, and we settled down for serious work. I wonder if the careful reader has figured out what was bound to happen next. If you have, are you laughing? Are you really?

Our bodies are designed as indestructible sanctuaries. We are trained to flee every assault on their integrity; and if we cannot flee, then to fight. It's hardwired, we can't help it.

But even now I grit my teeth. He leaned back on his elbow to look at me, gingerly touching his cheek where I'd hit him. I had to turn away and cry.

"Thou art of two minds, it seems," he remarked, in such outrageous understatement that I nearly had hysterics then and there. He put his arms around me (brave man) and tucked me up into his shoulder.

"Hush, then, thou. Is this all? Why, love, it is no shame to be afeared so early in the dance. We'll have no leaping yet, shall we, no bouncing galliards? No. No. A slow pavane is more to the taste of a lady, I think. An easy dance, that may be learned by any little maid. We'll not spoil with haste."

"My body is frightened," I tried to explain. "Not me."

Patiently Nicholas held me until my sobs had gone quiet. Then he leaned up to look me in the eye and said:

"Now, why didst thou play the wanton with me? I would not have hurt thee for the world, Rose."

"I came to you because I love you," I said, as a defense; but I realized, with a certain gleeful horror, that it was true. "I have never loved anyone before in all my life, and I am so frightened."

"Flesh is a comfort to flesh," he said. "Though not, I think, the remedy for thy fear."

"My fear is not of you," I protested.

"What then?" he said. I took too long to come up with an answer, because thoughts began to turn behind his eyes and they grew small and suspicious.

"Did thy father bid thee come here?" That was so close to the mark that I had to catch my breath, which he interpreted correctly. His scowl deepened. I knew I must make the best of it, so I said:

"He hath counseled me to make much of you, señor, I will admit."

"What manner of man sends his virgin child—" Nicholas began in thunder.

I rushed on: "But in an honorable manner, señor, as any maid might do. He wisheth me to be married well and, having some care to my happiness, bade me look to wed with an Englishman."

"For safety," Nicholas muttered.

"It may be so."

"What storm is it he runs before? He hath some black business, thy father, hath he not? And this it is that maketh thee pale and sick."

I clung to him. Let him think what he wanted, I was in over my head. "It's true," I whispered in his ear. "I want no part of his life. Let me stay here with thee. Keep me, love."

He gave a long sigh, a brooding angry sound, but his hands began to move again on my skin. "Tell me the truth, Rose," he said. "What does thou fear?"

"So many things, I have forgot them all," I said wearily. "But I struck you because I thought you would tear me and make me to bleed."

He gave a rueful laugh. "I hope I may couch a lance with more skill than that. Will you prove me, love?" I kissed him where I had hit him. With great care and gentleness he began the game again.

"Some order ought to be taken for the better education of virgins, that they read no old romances," he grumbled pleasantly. "For there they will read of this maiden come near to dying when her lover beds her first, or that maiden staining seventeen ells of linen by her defloration, swooning for love, and I assure you it is not so. Look you, Friar John shall preach you a sermon on it." He began to speak in a little squeaky voice for his penis:

"Now you must know, child, that what passeth between a man and a maid is no ordeal but a delightful measure, as many happy country girls witnesseth, who are never the worse for making familiar with a plain and well-intentioned prick. Nay, further, our Lord that loveth us surpassing well hath ordained this matter to be pleasing to the partakers thereof, as we may read in Holy Scripture, where it saith: O that thy mouth would give us a kiss, for thy breasts are more pleasant than wine, and—"

So as I rocked in his arms, helpless with laughter, he pressed his advantage; with such courtesy that my castle, as they say, fell without further defense.

And as the apple tree among the trees of the wood, so was my beloved among the sons. Et cetera. What would I give, to have that night back, out of all my nights? No treasure fleet could hold it, what I'd give; no caravan of mules could carry it away.

14

IN THE BLACK morning he guided me down the stairs, though on the bottom step we clenched and melted, and had to run right back up to bed again.

When I finally crept back into my room, the eastern sky was starting to get light. Our windows faced east, so everything stood in black outline against them: very distinct, the posts and the drapes of the bed, and Nef's Egyptian profile where she sat upright watching the dawn. She turned to look at me.

"You all right?" she inquired.

I just smiled, the way you do when you're newly nineteen on a summer morning in England and you've just discovered Paradise on Earth. Were there stars in my eyes? I suppose there were. I came and settled gingerly on the foot of the bed.

"You know something?" I said. "All my life I've been fed this line of utter garbage about mortals. They're just the same as we are, and some of them"—meaningful pause here—"are *better.*"

The pity in her face was a thousand years old. I didn't understand it, so I ignored it.

"I just spent the night with a mortal man who's got God's own intellect," I swept on. "And the body to match. He's enlightened, he's fearless, he's seven hundred years ahead of his time. The only thing that makes him different from me or you is the hardware."

She just nodded and said, "Well . . ."

"The thing is, I've been operating all this time with an incredible sense of superiority over this race that produced Caligula and Hitler and the other monsters, and all the while ignoring the fact that this same race is capable of turning out Da Vincis and Shakespeares. How can we all be so arrogant?''

She shrugged a little and said, "Sometimes . . ."

"I mean, there's a whole world here I've never even thought about. There must be millions of these sane, intelligent individuals whose lives are every bit as meaningful as our own, and if it weren't for a few aberrant types screwing it up for everyone else, they'd probably be well on the way to the perfect civilization. This is tragic. We have to help these people. I mean, they made us, didn't they? We came from them. In a sense, we *are* them. Aren't we?''

How infinitely wry was Nef's smile, on that two millionth morning of her life.

"Yes and no," she said.

"What do you mean?" I bounced impatiently on the bed.

"You'll find out."

"Oh, baloney." I jumped up and crawled in on my side of the bed. "Don't go all metaphysical on me. And anyway—anyway! Why didn't anyone ever tell me what happens when you—you know—for the first time? I went into automatic defense mode and nearly hurt him!''

At least she winced. "Sorry about that," she said. "I thought you knew."

"Well, I didn't, and it nearly ruined everything," I said crossly, yanking most of the blankets over on my side.

"The man has to be careful, and you have to relax a lot," she explained.

"Thank you, we figured that out." I burrowed down into the pillows. "And now I'm going to sleep for hours and hours. I won't be down for breakfast. You can tell them whatever you want." To her everlasting credit, Nef did not pick up the candlestick and club me over the head. She only sighed and climbed out of bed to begin her two millionth day.

When I woke, I was as happy as if it were my birthday, and someone had crept into my room and left a rose by my pillow.

Well, who cared about work after that? Not I, and not Nicholas Harpole, except that it gave us an excuse to get out alone together in the garden. His God even favored us with a miracle, for it stopped raining; and this is always a marvel in that damned green land, but more so in that particular summer when the Cloud Prince was in residence.

Now that I come to write of what we did together, I have a

peculiar reluctance to put pen to paper. Yes, this is definitely pain I feel. There is a locked door, you see, hinges red as blood with rust: it screams upon being opened and tries to close again, but through its narrow space I see the color green.

Long grass where we lay, in the heart of the maze, and the little white flowers of the hedge had a sweet smell, like semen. I had filled my overskirt with damson plums, and we took turns eating them and reading to one another from *De Immensa Misericordia Dei*. I can still see the explosion of green at his window, the summer leaves crowding thick as though they would burst in on us where we sat naked on his bed. We had a dish of strawberries and a flagon of Rhenish wine, and he cradled a mandolin on his lap, for decency's sake, he said; his big hands closed on the frets and plucked the strings. Sweat formed on his fair skin. He taught me songs.

This truly hurts. But I need to record that green filtered sunlight streaming in through the great hall, where we made eye contact over breakfast. His foot sought mine under the table. He peeled oranges for me in long curls of gold. I ate them for him in suggestive ways, eloquent with lips and tongue. God knows what the servants thought.

So you may laugh at my heart's nakedness, but I'll tell you this much: all my nasty expectations fell away like stone birds that summer. With each sexual act and variation, layers of fear came away to reveal a commonplace, comfortable pastime.

It wasn't that the obsession died—Christ, we couldn't keep our hands off each other. What clutchings in the maze, what passionate and explicit notes in Greek we left for each other! But it became *innocent*. Maybe wholesome is a better word. Pleasant and unremarkable as eating. No sense of sin. What a revelation for me, eh?

We played mental games with each other, too, he still asking oblique questions about alchemists and I poking with casual remarks about weird Anabaptist sects. Stimulating discourses, as it were, to counterpoint our play.

Enough of the idyllic sex scenes. What we did, we did, and now you know.

Nef was very accommodating about it, because now she had the bed to herself and could play the radio as late as she wanted. Mind you, all there was usually to hear was a weather broadcast and a nightly program of madrigals by a popular group of castrati; but those things would comfort you too if you were trapped in a back country manor house and the only other woman around was younger than you and having a torrid love affair besides. Joseph made a few cheerful remarks about how great one's first little mortal fling was. Beyond that he didn't comment much, being very busy himself at that time.

In August, Mary the Queen and Philip her consort went on up to London, where it promptly rained buckets on all the Londoners who nonetheless staged elaborate pageants for His Gloomy Grace. I remember where I was when I heard the broadcast floating out of Nef's open window: in the center of a privet hedge with Nicholas. We were having a fierce postcoital discussion about Savonarola. Nicholas defended, I attacked.

In September there were news reports every day on how badly our quondam countrymen were getting on in England. Somewhere there was a plaintive hidalgo with gonorrhea who wondered what had become of the private physician whose passage he had paid for. Joseph could disappear in transit like a check, if he found it convenient.

There were rumors of revolts, of barricades and imperial treachery, but nothing came of them, and the sun kept shining down. No, it was in our own bright garden that the trouble began.

People noticed when the color began to come back into Sir Walter's hair and beard, but even the servants assumed it was only a dye job, if a subtle one. When Sir Walter got to handling and pinching the kitchen girls, his household chalked it up to male menopause. Dotage, they used to call it. But the day he fell down at the breakfast table in a fit, no one knew quite what to say.

I, Nicholas, and Master Ffrawney, Nef, Joseph, the steward, and two scullery boys all looked down at him in horror. He kicked. He foamed. He grunted. *Oops*, transmitted Joseph. Out loud, he said:

"Why, he hath the falling sickness. How unusual that he never told me of it."

What do you mean, oops? I questioned, and Nef echoed me. Joseph ignored us as he and Nicholas hastened down to their knees beside Sir Walter. With some struggle they edged him away from the table so he wouldn't brain himself, and did all the helpful things one is supposed to do for an epileptic. While Nicholas was busy unhooking fastenings, Joseph discreetly broke a little capsule over the throbbing vein in Sir Walter's temple.

"He hath never been so taken," gasped Nicholas, dodging a flailing shoe.

"Well, perhaps he had a surfeit of something that drew the sanguine humors up into the brain." Joseph pretended to take his pulse. "Eels, or oysters, or venison pie, perchance. Hmm?" But he struck a false note then, because his tone was too light and careless. I guess he was badly rattled, or he wouldn't have slipped up like that. And he only slipped a little; but Nicholas caught it, though the rest of the company were oblivious. He threw Joseph a quick, wondering look.

Watch out, I transmitted.

Slight miscalculation of dosage, Joseph returned. *The little guy must have been at the beefsteak again. I warned him about that.* Sir Walter gave a final thrash and went limp, apparently unconscious. Joseph called for a cushion and placed it under his head with great solicitude. "There is no cause to be alarmed, good people," he said loudly. "Doubtless this unfortunate incident was only the result of intemperate diet."

Sir Walter shot out his arms and legs and crowed like a rooster.

"Jesu bless us!" shrieked Master Ffrawney. "He hath a devil in him!" He and the scullery boys all made the sign of the Cross. So did Nefer and I, belatedly. Joseph was too busy trying to catch Sir Walter's flapping arms.

"I have it now!" he shouted. "It is, uh, an effusion of melancholic bile in the liver. The Count of Alcobiella was afflicted with the very same. Please, my young friend, let us get your master to his bed." Between them, he and Nicholas hoisted Sir Walter, who was grinning idiotically, and struggled with him up the stairs. Near the top, the old man began to howl:

"Dookies! Dookies! Dookies!"

I was too frightened to laugh. Nefer looked around at our terrified faces and pulled out her rosary. "Let us pray," she said firmly. "Entreat the Blessed Virgin in our efforts on Don Walter's behalf. *Ave Maria, Gratia plena . . .*"

We mumbled with her, occasionally glancing up as thumps and crashes came from the room above. At last there was silence. Three quarters of the way around the rosary, Nicholas came slowly down the stairs. His face was set and closed. I ran to him. "How does the good man?" I cried. He turned to stare at me; then he looked at the others and said:

"By the grace of God, Sir Walter is sleeping now and his fit hath passed. The doctor says he will be well." And as Nef and the others resumed prayer, he took me by the arm and led me outside.

"What is it, in God's name?" I said, peering up at him. He led me a little way from the house and looked at me.

"I have just seen a thing I cannot understand," he said.

"Before God, I don't doubt it!"

He glanced around before he replied in Greek. "I mean, above the extraordinary sight of a gentleman of reverend years crying cuckoo before his whole house. Men have lost their wits before. No, my love, when we carried my master up to his room, we stripped away his doublet and shirt so that your father could bleed him.

"Now, when Sir Walter was a young man, he saw some service with our late king in France, and took a wound from it. (Or it may be that as he sat in a tavern one night, he was set upon by thieves; I've heard him tell both stories.) However he came by it, he certainly had a great scar across his ribs."

"Had," I said uneasily.

"Yes. Past tense. Now he has but a little red line there, like a track of scarlet ink. How should this be, Rose?"

I took a deep breath. "Well, did you think it was sorcery? It's the physick, no question. Every hedgerow charlatan has a potion to take away wrinkles and scars. My father's remedy works, that's all."

Nicholas relaxed a little. "Certainly it's a great remover of scars. So long as it doesn't take Sir Walter's life away with the scar, all may be well. Pray that your father knows what he's doing, Rose, or people will swear there's been murder done. And witchcraft, very likely, or whatever else comes into their heads."

Mendoza!

I'm busy! I transmitted.

So am I, and I need somebody to hand me things. Now. On the double!

"Your advice is well taken." I squeezed Nicholas's arm. "I will go warn my father at once." He stared after me as I hitched up my skirts and ran back into the house.

Up the stairs and up the stairs and *up* the damned stairs, clattering, past staring servants. *All right, where are you?*

In here. I heard a bolt slide back at a near door, and the door opened just wide enough to admit me. It was a narrow room, like a cell. Once inside, I gasped and fell back at what I saw in it, as though physically pushed against the wall.

Sir Walter was laid out on a baize-covered table, smiling and stone dead. Had to be dead: his skin was gray, his stare was glassy as a doll's, and his chest had been opened out and folded back to expose its contents. Joseph was leaning down into the bloody cavity, working frantically with little tools. Organs were draped everywhere.

"Oh, my God, you've killed him," I said.

"Shut up and hand me that box," Joseph hissed. Too stunned to argue, I handed it to him: a red Bakelite component about the size of a matchbox, with a couple of tiny wires trailing from it. He snatched it from me, and it disappeared into the mortal mess.

"Pliers," he demanded. "Goddamn faulty regulator!"

"You really think you can revive him?" I edged closer to peer into the gaping hole as Joseph rummaged around in it frantically. Oh, gross.

"Yes. Grab that hemostim and stick it up his nose!"

I began to giggle in spite of my horror. Somehow I found the slender pointed tool and inserted it just above Sir Walter's mustache. Joseph growled, "Farther!"

Suddenly festoons of tiny colored lights were blinking inside Sir Walter, all over his lungs and heart and liver, as though his organs were throwing a block party. It was pretty, in a ghastly sort of way. One of Sir Walter's thumbs began to waggle back and forth.

"Good. Great." Joseph twisted the pliers and leaned with all his strength. Something gave a little click, and the blinking stopped, the lights shone with a steady soft glow. "Now take the hemostim out of his nose."

I obeyed gingerly and dropped the tool into a sterilizing pail. The lights continued to shine. Joseph exhaled loudly and began to close up Sir Walter.

"If you don't need me for anything more . . ." I moved toward the door.

"No, stick around. Your boyfriend noticed some stuff he couldn't account for, didn't he?"

"You mean, like scars vanishing? He's not an idiot. Don't worry, though, I explained it all away." I leaned against the wall and folded my arms, grinning. "I did *my* job. Your little mistake won't leave any lasting suspicions in his mind."

"It wasn't *my* little mistake after all, wiseass. See this?" Joseph slam-dunked something into the sterilizer. I peered at it. A little Bakelite box, twin to the first but obscured by a film of blood and tissue. "Defective. If I ever get my hands on Flavius again—"

"Wow. What was it supposed to do?"

"Regulate the release of pineal tribrantine 3, not dump a week's worth into his system." Joseph reached for the skin plasterer.

"No!" I whooped with laughter. "No wonder he went tilt! You're lucky you didn't have to get him down out of a tree!" Joseph just glared at me and troweled new flesh into Sir Walter's wounds while my snickering subsided. After a moment a thought sobered me.

"How come you're giving him tribrantine anyway? I thought only we got that."

"Special case." Joseph put away the plasterer and grabbed up the retoucher. "It can be given to mortals, and it'll do for them what it does for us; it's just that their systems can't learn to produce it like ours can. Costs a fortune to keep pumping it into 'em, too.''

"But it wouldn't make them immortal, would it?"

"Nah. But they'd be good-looking corpses when they finally died, believe me." Joseph looked up at me. "Thinking of the boyfriend, huh?"

Sir Walter twitched and groaned. His eyes had closed. I stared at him, watching the color return to his face. "No, actually," I lied.

Joseph appeared at supper grave and solemn as a church elder, close at Sir Walter's elbow. "Nay, I thank ye, I am very well now." Sir Walter waved easily at everyone. "It was but the falling sickness, brought on by immoderate diet. Doctor Ruy hath explained it all."

There were some dark looks in Joseph's direction from the household staff, but the truth was that Sir Walter did look perky as a cricket again. He reached out now and dragged a bowl of watercress across the table to his place.

"What's this? Cresses? You, Dick, this wants oil and salt! Alexander the Great was much given to the falling sickness, did you know that, madam?" He turned to Nef abruptly.

She blinked. He had scarcely ever spoken to her before. "Why— no, señor, I knew it not."

"Verily, Lady. Julius Caesar, too. And Pompey, so I believe." He stroked his beard complacently as one of the scullions fussed with the salad. "The ancients, being deluded heathen, held it to be a sign that Jupiter, who as you know was their principal idol, had marked a man for greatness. God's marrow bones, fool, I said *salt!*" he shouted, glaring at the boy. It was a loud and deep shout, a resonant sound, very striking on the ear, as it came from old, dry lungs. The boy cowered. Everyone at table stared.

"Perhaps it would be wise to take but little salt," reminded Joseph.

"Well, well." Sir Walter dredged up some cress between his thumb and forefinger and stuffed it in his mouth. He wiped his hand on a piece of bread and turned back to Nef, chewing busily. "Where was I? Aye, aye, that great ones were ofttimes marked. Or so the Romans held. I myself was born with a mark like a cobbler's awl upon mine elbow."

"Doubtless a prophecy of your piercing wit." Joseph smiled.

"Ha, ha, ha! Though I may tell you, Doctor Ruy, that I have made good fellows to laugh in my day, forsooth! I was once sought after for my good conversation." He coughed modestly.

Well, he was boring enough now. Not my Nicholas, though. I gave him a sultry smile, but he was watching Sir Walter, frowning a little. A moment later he noticed and smiled at me, and gave me a compensatory nudge under the table. Then his gaze wandered away again.

"Lewd fellows, those Romans," Sir Walter went on, digging out another handful of cress and wolfing it down. "They cut an image of Hercules in one of our chalk hills and—well—hum." He glanced over at me and then back at Nef. "I shall tell you of it another time, Lady. Take some of the cress, I pray you, it is very good. Now, Master Ffrawney, did I not call for a capon to table?" Hurriedly the serving boy presented a whole roast chicken from the sideboard. "Aah," cried Sir Walter; and as he leaned forward to pull off a drumstick, we all heard a distinct tearing sound. He froze.

"Your doublet is broke open behind, sir," observed Nicholas.

"Is it so?" Sir Walter scrabbled at the front buttons with greasy fingers. "Well, out upon it, it was an old thing and shabby besides. I shall have a new one! Nicholas, bid Master Fish the tailor to call upon me. I must have six doublets cut in the new fashion. See that it is done."

He got his six new doublets, and new shirts and hose as well; and the tailor went away shaking his head, because everything had to be made bigger in the neck and the shoulders. There was talk in the servants' hall, let me tell you.

There was more talk when Sir Walter began to sleep with the laundress. She was a well-mannered person remarkable chiefly for her cleanness—she must have taken her line of work seriously—and for her breasts, which were like river rocks. Pretty soon she was making regular calls at Sir Walter's creaking ancestral bed with the Iden arms on its hangings. I think the servants felt an obscure pride that somebody their master's age should have a backstairs squeeze at all. But they really did not approve of his flirting with Nef too.

15

ONE FAIR BRIGHT morning, I was running along an aisle of the privet maze, ever so picturesque: my hair down, cheeks flushed, eyes sparkling, et cetera. Just like the beginning of a historical romance. Never mind what I'd been doing. I found a green alleyway and ducked inside. My breathless giggling and the whining of the gnats sounded loud in my ears. There was a rustling from the hedge, and I poised to shriek: but it was Nef's long profile that came around the corner.

Pop went the ambiance. "What the hell are you doing here?" I snarled.

"Hiding," she said gloomily.

"Well, go hide somewhere else!"

"Ssh." She put out her hand. We listened for a few seconds but heard nothing.

"Who are you hiding from, anyway?" I resumed in a stage whisper.

"Sir Walter."

"You're kidding!" I began to giggle again. She favored me with a look that would have frozen anybody older and less stupid.

"He keeps trying to get me to ride down to Dorset with him to look at this Hercules thing. From the way he leers, I get the impression it's something improper."

"It sure is! It's a Neolithic nude with a twelve-foot penis."

She rolled her eyes. "Why me?"

"Because he figures you're a gentlewoman, what do you want to bet? And with all the improvements Joseph's making, the old man's fancy must be heavily turning to thoughts of love. I bet he feels like a million bucks. I bet he's beginning to regret that he never married and furthered the heroic Iden line. And you're the only available female of his social status, right? *Quod erat demonstrandum!*''

She took a swing at me with her rosary, which was solid silver and would have done me injury had it connected, though of course it only whirred harmlessly through the space where I'd been a nanosecond earlier. ''Mendoza, you're a rotten kid.''

''Don't you feel honored? How many years do you think it's been since the old boy thought of anything but his garden?''

She slumped down to a sitting position on the grass. ''This is too embarrassing.''

''Seriously, though, would you mind being embarrassed somewhere else? Nicholas and I were—''

That was when the unicorn appeared. Tiny and demure, he came around the corner nibbling daisies from the grass. He halted when he saw us. Nef sat bolt upright, staring.

''What—'' she said, and I started to explain; but she put out her hand, and the little creature ran to her at once. It nuzzled her, and she swept it up into her arms. ''Little baby, what's the matter?'' Her hands found the twisted stumpy horn, and she gave a cry.

''It's the unicorn,'' I said uncomfortably. ''The one I keep telling you about. Sir Walter's pride and joy. You know.''

''Oh, the poor little thing!'' There were actually tears in her eyes.

''See, somebody took a baby goat, and they did some sort of primitive surgery on its head—''

''I can see what they did, damn it!'' She was examining its little feet. ''And somebody gilded its hooves once, too, look at this, that's why they've grown out this way. What kind of bastard would do a thing like this?''

''Somebody who wanted to make some money.'' I shrugged. ''Look, if it makes you feel any better, remember that at least he's running around in a nice green garden this way. If he were still a goat, he'd probably have ended up as somebody's barbecue by now. And it's not as though he's in any pain.''

''How the hell would you know?'' She gave me a truly savage look. ''How would you like to have a pair of your wisdom teeth bound so they grew into each other?''

How graphic. I backed off a pace. ''Okay, okay, so it's cruel. What can we do about it, though?''

''You'll see.'' Grimly, she rose, the unicorn docile under her arm, and swept away with him.

''But you can't—''

Crash. Nicholas burst through the hedge, breeches already at half-mast. His whoop of triumph was strangled as Nef turned to glare at us. "God save you, madam," he choked, sweeping off his biretta.

"Buenos días, señor," she replied icily. The unicorn bleated. She turned away and marched on. We stared after her.

"What ails the lady?" he inquired at last.

"She hath discovered Sir Walter's unicorn, and the truth of it hath moved her to a great passion of rage," I explained.

"Charity to dumb beasts?" His eyes began to spark again. "Why, perhaps she should have been a shepherdess. God knows she's no duenna." And with that we changed the subject and had great joy of each other, there and then. Still, in the back of my mind a small beacon flashed red, red. I'd never seen Nef angry before.

It was a week before anybody found out what she meant to do, exactly a week to the day, and in that seven-day span summer left us: overnight. Nicholas and I went to sleep sprawled on top of his blankets and in the morning woke huddled under them.

I sat up in astonishment, in the dry cold air. The green leaves at the window stared in at me with a shocked look. What was wrong with them? I slipped out of bed to stare back. Yellow edges like fire beginning all around, chlorophyll breaking down, sugars blooming. I turned away. Nicholas lay watching me, an odd expression on his face.

"It's so cold," I said. "And the air has a smell."

He nodded. "Autumn," he said. "Time to put the pavilion about the Portingale orange, lest it die of cold. Come back into the bed, love, lest thou do likewise." I scrambled back in beside him gladly enough. He pulled me close to his body.

"It is very deciduous in this country, is it not?" I remarked. I could feel him bemusedly sorting out the meaning of the word, and then his heartbeat quickened. He burrowed down to face me and said in Greek:

"Leaves fall in England, yes. But do they not also fall in Spain?"

I answered warily. "Yes, we have autumn in Spain. But not so much. There were not many trees where we lived. Pines there were. So, you see, I have never seen such a season."

"I thought you said you also lived in France. And there are many trees in that country."

"We were in the south of France," I countered. "In the spring and summer."

"Aah." He narrowed his eyes.

"And perhaps I went to Egypt once," I added.

"Egypt." One corner of his mouth lifted. Sneer or smile?

"Yes. Or somewhere in the Holy Land. I remember seeing great seas of sand when I was small. There is no autumn in the desert, you know."

"Truly?"

"Yea, truly." I kissed him, and wriggled upward to the pillow and the safety of English. It was a great language to be evasive in. "But we have no time to debate these things, señor. The season changeth! Winter is at hand! The acorn shall drop for the rooting swine, and each little herb of the field shall bear seed according to its kind, señor! The holly berry waxeth red, doth it not? And I must gather fruiting body and example of them all. Quickly, señor, quickly!"

"I'll show thee seed enough." He reared up like a dolphin cresting a wave.

When we waltzed down to breakfast, very pleased with ourselves, the whole house was bustling. A brisk fire roared and snapped on the hearth. Sir Walter finished his oat porridge and poached egg in a gulp and lounged back in his chair, eyeing Nef.

"I think me this would be good weather for hunting," he remarked. "Have you never seen one of our English hunts, Lady Margaret?" I rolled my eyes at Nicholas.

"Never, señor." Nef did not look up from her dish of eggs and bacon.

"I think they have no such hunts in Spain. Our English hound is the only beast for the chase, I may say, and our English red deer the prince of quarries."

"I know little of these things, señor," she said calmly, buttering a slice of bread.

"Of course, I never kept a deer park." Sir Walter looked out of his window with a sigh. "The Idens of old, though valiant, were but modest gentlemen and had no such means."

"Come, sir, think of your ancestor! Old Sir Alexander hunted traitors, did he not? What need to take a deer when he had taken the monster Cade, eh?" cheered Nicholas, biting into an apple. It spat wine.

Sir Walter did not brighten much, though. " 'Tis true. A valorous man. Still, I could wish . . ."

I don't know what he wished, because even as I sat there savoring their mortal grace and silliness, there came a terrible outcry from the garden.

Before it was sound, there was a great blast of smell: two adult males in extremes of fear and dismay. I caught my breath. Nef lifted her eyes to mine. Sir Walter maundered on, Nicholas's fine teeth champed away at his apple, the serving boy with quiet pride lifted the cover from a dish of pudding. Then the shouting became audible to them.

"Sir! Sir! You are robbed, you are robbed outright, you are plundered!" yelled Master Ffrawney, bursting into the great hall. He had one of the servants by the collar, a little old wreck of a man. Nicholas had pointed him out to me as the animal keeper. The keeper staggered forward weeping and collapsed on his face.

Sir Walter leaped up, reeking with alarm. "Speak, man! What say you?" he demanded. But the keeper was incoherent, and Master Ffrawney spurned him impatiently.

"It appeareth, Sir Walter, that through the negligence of this lying knave one of your chiefest treasures hath been mutilated. Someone hath stolen the horn of your unicorn!"

A chorus of gasps from the assembled company. Eyes met horrified eyes, except for Nef's eyes, which were staring straight ahead. Another horrified gasp, this one of realization, from me, and quite drowned out by Sir Walter's roar:

"Let me see it! Is he butchered?" He did not wait for a reply but ran for the door, closely followed by the keeper, who was wailing out that it weren't his fault; and so followed the rest of the household, nearly, streaming down the manor steps through the sweet crisp air.

The unicorn was tied near the aviary, kicking and bleating. Sir Walter dropped to his knees beside it and raised profound ululation when he saw what the vandal had done to his heart's zoological darling. I pushed close to see. Dear, dear. The horn had been removed neatly, all the way down to the skull. Cleanly, with surgical clipping of the fur. And a tidy smooth bandage of, as I live and breathe, Graft-O-Plast.

"My unicorn of Hind!" screamed Sir Walter. "My thirty pounds!"

"Twenty pounds eightpence," said Nicholas faintly.

"Chide me not, master, for sweet Saint Mary's sake!" The keeper groveled. "Devils roast me forever if I ever slacked at my post. I put him in his pen last night, and shut the door fast, and when I comes in this morning, he were like that! God smite me with blindness if it weren't just so!"

"Thou liest, whoreson knave!" Master Ffrawney kicked at him again, but the keeper dodged. "Well we know thou hast taken the horn for thyself!"

"By Jesu and the heavenly host, master, I never did!" The keeper grabbed Sir Walter's ankles. "What should I do with the thing if I stole it?"

"Why, rogue, sell it for gold! All the world knoweth the horn of the unicorn hath great virtue for healing. Any learned doctor—" Master Ffrawney almost bit his tongue off, he stopped so fast.

Too late. The implication went off like a psychic bomb. The air before my eyes danced with red numbers, red readouts for eight mortals' mounting blood pressure all trying to claim my attention at once. I could scarcely breathe for the smell. And of course here came Joseph at the run, aware something had happened but only just beginning to get an idea of what. He paused. Every head turned to fix on him. Sir Walter's eyes were like a furious dog's.

The reading went off the scale. Killer apes. *"Spaniard,"* someone muttered.

I edged a little backward; in another few seconds I'd be unable to resist the urge to wink out of there and reappear in a safer place, and the mortals would startle away from where I'd stood. Too bad, but I couldn't help it. Oh, the smell. A hand closed on mine, and I jerked and looked up into Nicholas's eyes, cold and sane.

"Doctor Ruy," said Sir Walter. "Hast thou meddled here?" What a thick, barbarous tongue English could be.

Joseph took a step backward. He could read them all, he took in the bandaged skull of the goat in a glance, he met my eyes and knew. He turned his head to Nef, who stood still and quite composed beside me. There was an impact. I staggered. Nicholas's arm went around me.

Joseph strode forward and went down on one knee beside the goat. "Never, sir. Why, this is German wax," he said.

What?

Sir Walter blinked a few times. "How now?"

"This." Joseph tapped the bandage. "I have seen it in the Low Countries. Ferriers use it, and cattle thieves. It cannot be found in England. Some villain of a Fleming hath been here, as God is my salvation."

"A Fleming?" The keeper was bewildered.

"My friend, it is well known what price the horn of a unicorn brings in Flanders, and for what terrible purpose. Sir Walter, my heart is sick with grief at your loss. We must be grateful that the miscreant did not slaughter your little beast outright, though you may be sure he refrained only so that another horn might grow back, when peradventure the cunning thief may return, hoping to work yet another outrage! Precautions must be taken, my friend!''

They all shook their heads, trying to make out what he was saying. The violence index was dropping. Joseph turned to John, the gatekeeper. ''Hath there been any come to see the garden in recent days who spake like one from Flanders?'' Joseph inquired sternly. ''Or ragged men, who might be soldiers back from foreign wars?''

''Uh—'' John's mouth opened. An idea was put into his head. ''Aye! Aye, they was two such.''

''Two.'' Joseph nodded. ''You see, he had an accomplice.''

''Damned Flemings!'' Sir Walter clenched his fists.

''German wax?'' said the keeper.

I closed my eyes with relief. The little screen of numbers trickled down, out of imminent hazard. The mortals were only confused and angry now. Someone muttered that he had seen a soldier drinking in the village, and someone else was telling a third what his old father used to say about Flemings. Sir Walter was shouting orders to search the grounds.

Joseph walked through them to Nef. They looked at each other. Impact again. The whole garden skewed and slid over sideways, with its tiny creatures gesticulating and running about all flat and far away. Standing through that ephemeral reality were two towering clouds with edges sharp as razors, in terrible conversation: Joseph and Nef. Their words were sound below sound, unspeakable violent silence, a quarrel to break the inner ear. Off in a corner, a little squiggle of smoke, wailing and scrabbling: me. Surely Heaven was going to crack right open with that percussive wrath. Then the garden was back in real time, and I was standing, clutching my ears. Joseph and Nefer had not moved. He still looked at her, and at last she looked aside, diffidently, and arranged a fold of her skirt.

They were not any kind of human creature at all.

''Rose.'' Nicholas touched my shoulder. I swung around to him and wrapped my arms tight about his neck. Without even a word or a question he carried me away, good man, away to the long walk under the rose arbor. I lay there with my head in his lap, crying like a fool. How I wished, how I wished I were a mortal girl.

''Ah. There she is.'' Joseph, at the end of the walkway. Hurriedly I sat up. He strolled in and knelt on the grass beside us. Nicholas sat straight and squared his shoulders.

''My poor child. This nasty business hath unsettled thee quite, I

see. Please do not be frightened, daughter. All, I promise thee, shall
be well.''

"So we trust, sir,'' Nicholas said. Joseph just smiled at him.

"It is an act of loving charity to comfort my child that is so
distraught. I must offer my profound thanks, young man.''

"Why, sir, I accept them with a good will,'' said Nicholas coolly.
"And must express my admiration, in good sooth: there were hounds
on your track just now, and you faced them down as boldly as any
fox God ever made.''

Joseph's smile quirked up into his beard. His gaze, though, was
flat and assessing.

"Come, come, young man, your metaphor! Any fox that faced
down his enemies would be torn to pieces where he stood. The fox
hath more discretion: he hath speed, he dodges and feints, he hath a
thousand places to hide himself.''

"And leaves a stink wherewith he may be tracked, alas; and so
is slain,'' added Nicholas.

"It seems thy young man is hostile, daughter.'' Joseph cocked an
eyebrow at me.

"By no means, sir.'' Nicholas took my hand in his. "But I do
grieve for the kits of the fox, who are slain with him though they
have stolen no hens. Nor unicorn's horns.''

"My young friend, what should a fox want with such a thing?''

"What indeed, since surely such a fox hath the wit to see that
the creature was only a goat!''

Joseph blinked. "Aye.''

"What a comedy! And I would have laughed, but that you were
nearly murdered before your daughter's eyes.''

There was a long silence. "You are a clever boy.'' I didn't like
Joseph's smile at all. He settled into a more comfortable position, and
his voice took on an edge like cutting glass. "Loquere mihi, puere.''

"Facio libens.'' Nicholas matched his Latin without a second's
hesitation. "Senex.''

"You have a bright and questing mind. Why have you turned its
light on my personal affairs?''

"I did so at first because I perceived you to be a threat to my
master, my faith, and my nation. Having satisfied myself that you
were not such, or at least not directly, I continued in the second place
because I fell in love with your daughter, whose unlikely talents,
remarkable opinions, and charming lies present an enigma I feel compelled to understand. Not merely to know the truth about her, but also

better to comprehend the strange events taking place under Sir Walter's roof.'' Nicholas leaned forward to emphasize the last point.

Joseph looked very calm. He stroked his beard a moment before inquiring:

"What conclusions have you drawn, may I ask?''

"None that I think you would care very much to have spoken aloud. I will not judge your life; but I will say that it has not agreed much with your daughter. Accordingly, I had determined to ask you for her hand.''

Oh dear. Oh dear. How sweet, but oh dear. Joseph looked vastly amused.

"In light of your present sleeping arrangements, this is a generous offer indeed, but I am afraid you have overlooked the fact that I am not the only man in this rose arbor whose past does not bear close examination.''

Nicholas went pale.

"Oh, yes, my young friend, you have enemies. Talkative ones. And you and I have something else in common, you see: I too am fascinated by mysteries. I suspect my sources have told me a great deal more about you than my daughter has told you about me.''

"Rose . . .'' Nicholas glanced at me. He ran his tongue over his lips.

"Now, my child, as you pointed out, is of remarkable opinions and doubtless would not be very shocked if I told her of your intimate connection with a group that interpreted Holy Scripture in a highly . . . original way. In fact, I think she would find the allegations of your personal stamina and appetites quite amusing. And, having experienced it herself, she would well understand that your considerable personal charm drew not a few converts to a fairly disreputable sect.''

Nicholas winced deeply. He turned and took me by the shoulders. "Rose. What he is saying is the truth. But I . . .''

"I know.'' I glared at Joseph. "I don't care.'' I turned and put my arms around Nicholas's neck and kissed him. He returned my kiss in confusion. Joseph leaned back, watching us.

"There, my friend, you see? She has a forgiving nature.''

Shut up, I transmitted.

"But I am somewhat more cautious. Call it the point of view of an old fox, perhaps, watching from the safety of his den as a young fox makes a stand before an oncoming pack of hounds. This is a valiant young fox, surely, but he is soon to be a dead fox as well.

"I will not grant my daughter's hand to such a fool. However, I trust that we may still remain good friends. Good day, young man.

Daughter, when you are sufficiently composed, you may wish to speak to me privately, but there is no immediate need to do so.'' He made his exit.

Nicholas was distraught, and I was furious, but please note what Joseph had just accomplished: my panic horror, brought on by the vision of the inhuman force he really was, had vanished. I now wanted to kill the smug little son of a bitch, but I wasn't afraid of him. Further, he had just spared me the ordeal of explaining to Nicholas why I couldn't marry him. I could no more marry him than I could believe in his God, could I? I was no more human than Joseph was.

As soon as Joseph's back was out of sight, Nicholas cleared his throat. ''Rose.''

''What?'' I turned to him, almost irritable. He was watching me closely.

''Shall I plead my case?''

''It matters not.'' I jumped up and shook rose petals out of my skirt. It had become cold in the garden. ''All his talk was lies and ill will.''

''Ill will, yes, but not lies.'' He got up to follow me. ''I must confess I did such things.''

''I knew it before. Master Ffrawney came to me with just such a story,'' I announced.

There was a silence. Nicholas smacked his fist into his palm a few times, meditatively, quite hard. ''And didst thou believe it, love?'' he inquired.

''I hardly know.'' I stopped to look him in the eye, which of course I had to tilt back my head to do. ''What should I believe?''

''That I was only a boy. That I came among folk who were hypocrites, though they spake the Word of God, and I believed them.'' His mouth set at the memory.

''These people did no more than preach the Word of God?'' I adjusted my comb, ever so casual.

He looked away. He shrugged. ''No,'' he said.

The silence fell between us again. I could have stamped my heels and shrieked. ''Such dreadful things are told of, for example, Anabaptists, I am certain my imaginings are far worse than the truth,'' I nudged hopefully.

''I doubt it.'' He looked glum. ''Now, I wonder how long I shall pay for having been seventeen.''

I wondered what he looked like at seventeen. ''Speak, dearest love.''

He took my hands and led me to a bench. He drew a deep breath, not meeting my eyes. "Know, sweetheart, that my birth was . . . obscure. And my father would do little for me but this: he provided me with a tutor and sent me to school, that by having some education I might earn mine own bread, and he should hear no more of me.

"I revered my tutor as a father, for his learning was great, but also for this: he spoke like an apostle with Christ's words still ringing in his ears. He taught me to read the Holy Scriptures for myself in the original, and showed me by many examples how far the Church had gone from what was written there.

"So far as this went, he was a light unto my soul.

"I called him Father, he called me Son; and he had besides some several other sons in this kind, and not a few daughters, for he was tutor to many well-born children."

Yes, I could see it coming. I leaned forward sympathetically.

"We came together in secret places to hear him preach the Word of God truly, and to discuss its meaning with him. We lived like disciples."

Secret meetings, drinking parties, and hanging on their master's every word.

"Or as Adam lived before the Fall, in perfect charity and communion." He took a deep breath again. "The serpent in our Eden became manifest, even so; and it is a lasting confusion to me, and a bitterness, that God could so gift a man with the Holy Spirit and leave him so open for the Devil to meddle with."

"Go on."

"The better to show us what divine love was, he concerned himself with lifting from our eyes that veil which makes us perceive gluttony, drunkenness, and lechery as vices." His lip curled back in a sneer. My God, he was handsome. "Mark me, love, in Eden they are no sins, but we are not in that place. Such a subtle distinction cannot be easily understood by a boy, look you, but even I began to see his folly. Others saw it before me. They left our community, and there was scandal."

I could imagine.

"And I despaired in my heart, seeing that our master had deceived us. Even I, by my example, had led folk to idle, filthy pastime. But I saw further, that as my master had done, all the leaders of the Church had done, by a thousand twistings of the plain truth."

"Then the truth is not so plain, is it?" I pointed out gently. But his face was grim; he was living his memory.

"It is as plain as the blazing sun!" he cried.

"And as hard to look at," I said. "My love, this sun in the sky, we live by its grace; but it does well enough where it is, and we do well enough minding our own business down here. Seek to stare at it, and thou wilt burn out thine eyes."

"Better to go blind bringing the light to those who have never seen it," he answered. "And so I determined. I went forth into the lanes, and I began to preach the Word of God. I called upon the righteous to live as we had lived, without sin in a Paradise of love, where flesh is no enemy to the soul."

"Oh, my love."

"And I was taken and beaten," said Nicholas composedly, "a drunken boy spewing and blaspheming before the horrified multitudes. I was put in irons, but privately, for I was a gentleman's son. And I was conveyed to prison in another town by night, lest the neighbors come and burn me where I lay. Some months I sat in prison, while good men came and reasoned with me, making so evident the peril I stood in that I recanted all my former words, so great was my terror.

"Well, my father had done some service to the king. Clothes were found for me, and I was sent from England awhile, until folk had forgot my disgrace. And so back into Kent, where I have lived these several years a blameless man."

"Thanking God that thou still breathest," I finished in awe. He had come just as close to death as I had.

"Aye," he said, and then, "No!"

I looked at him. His eyes had gone small and angry. "No," he repeated. "I have suffocated, breathing this air. I lied so that I might go on living in this world, I who had lived in Eden! To creep into this little hole and never bear witness to the truth again, that was the price of my life. My soul."

This kind of talk made me very uneasy. "But if thou hadst been hanged, I'd never have known thee." I gave a little laugh.

His gaze came back to me. He put out his big hands and drew me close. "That much good has come from it, at least. And God knows, this is the first honest work I've done this seven year."

On which note, we melted into a kiss, but I thought: Work?

Before I could voice my question, there was a trampling of feet, and we jumped apart guiltily. Sir Walter came into sight around a hedge, accompanied by two servants bearing pitchforks. "Nicholas!"

"Sir." Nicholas stood and bowed. I curtseyed, and Sir Walter acknowledged me with a brisk nod.

"Nicholas, I have sought thee. We must carry the search into the surrounding fields."

"Aye, sir. Shall I muster the household?"

"No. I have done that. Go thou with Tom and Peter out into the way toward Sevenoaks, and hunt there. And think how we may remedy this, when thou shalt speak with Master Sampson. A new horn, of wax or bone, for appearance' sake?"

"Very good, sir." Nicholas bowed again.

I walked slowly back to the manor. There were servants scurrying everywhere, poking into hedges and peering up trees. A few gave me surly looks, but said not a word to me.

The house was virtually empty. I could hear the radio blaring from Nef's room, so I went up there. Nef, however, was not in sight. Joseph was stretched out on the bed, reading one of her magazines. I froze in the doorway; but he looked up with a charming smile.

"Mendoza. Baby. Do come in." I stepped inside and shut the door. "Sorry I had to beat up on your boyfriend, your very tall boyfriend, but I figured it wouldn't hurt to deflect his line of questioning. Bright guy, isn't he? Beautiful command of Latin." He turned a page.

"Where's Nef?" I stared around sullenly.

"In there." He pointed with the magazine. "Dictating her report to the disciplinary board. Be a good kid and don't bother her, okay? She's going to be at it awhile."

I looked at the silent door. I couldn't hear anything but the radio, which was playing dance music. I went over and turned the volume down.

"Look, I, uh, wanted to apologize." Joseph laid the magazine aside. "Nef and I really blew up at each other, and I'm afraid the shock waves kind of got to you. Didn't they? And I know that can be unsettling to a young op, especially in the field. We let ourselves go, and we shouldn't have. I'm sorry. She's sorry too."

"I bet she's really sorry." I looked at the door again.

"Not as sorry as she could be." His mouth became hard for a moment. "But she's a good operative, she's done good work for a long time; they'll let her off with a slap on the wrist. I was the one who had to deal with the consequences. I thought I saved us from getting lynched rather neatly, don't you? Are they still down there searching for dastardly Flemings?"

"As a matter of fact, yes."

"I guess we'll have to provide them with one." He got up and went to the window. "Is that your guy down there in the search party?" I went to the window to look but couldn't make out anyone amidst the leaves. Joseph put a hand on my shoulder.

"You're sore about this, I can tell."

I didn't know what to say. "You were awful to Nicholas."

"That's true. Yes, you're right. I'm truly sorry. I got the impression, though, that he was going out of his way to be awful to me."

"He doesn't like you."

"Gee. And I cut such a dashing figure as a freethinking victim of the Inquisition. Well, you can't please everybody. You appeared pretty agitated when he asked me for your hand, by the way. Did he just spring that on you?"

"Yes." I grew hot with embarrassment. Why didn't he leave me alone?

"Yeah. Poor kid. It's a good thing I was there to field that one for you. Marriage with a mortal! It's been done from time to time, actually. On a limited basis. Of course, you always have to desert them later, or pretend to die, or something like that. But, yeah. Naturally, it was out of the question this time, so I'm glad I was there for you, but with your next one—"

I felt dazed. "You mean I could have said yes?"

"Well, in principle, sure. Not to this guy, though. I've been married myself, you know, quite a few times. It's occasionally useful, and once in a while you just can't avoid it. But, believe me, it's the easiest thing in the world to get out of."

"But—but how can you do it? What if you really love one of them?"

"Is that a problem? I've loved my mortals, too. But, honey, the bottom line is—they're mortal. They're going to die. Nicholas is going to die. Now, do you want to stick around and watch it happen, or do you want to skip out and keep a beautiful memory? Of course you want the beautiful memory. Mendoza, it's painful to watch mortals get old. You have no idea yet."

"I've been thinking, actually." Although I hadn't been; I was desperately inventing this on the spur of the moment. "I had this thought. Nicholas is very unusual, you said so yourself, he's almost like one of us. He's absolutely physically perfect, and you wouldn't believe the things he says sometimes. His whole interpretation of the Christian cosmology is so close to the truth, it's scary. I'll bet he could adjust really well if he were told about us."

"No. I see where you're headed, but no."

"But just listen a minute! I know he can't be fixed like one of us, I know you're not supposed to do the Process on an adult, but look at the stuff you're doing for Sir Walter. And we have paid mortals who know about us, who work for us. So why couldn't you do the same for Nicholas, and we could take him away with us when we leave here, as a sort of—sort of . . .''

"A pet?" Joseph snorted. "Mendoza, we may be very attached to Fido, but sooner or later he's going to dog heaven, all right?"

"You bastard."

"No." He took my arms. "Sweetheart. Please understand. It wouldn't change anything and would only hurt you worse in the end. Trust me, I've been there. I feel very responsible for you, you know. I spotted you in that dungeon in Santiago. And I've watched you grow up into a damn good operative. Seriously, I think you've got what it takes to be the best in your field. I know I kind of encouraged this, it seemed like a good way to deal with the guy, and I thought the experience would be good for you. But I'd hate to see you get burned out this early by a bad relationship."

I pulled away and sat down, not looking at him.

"Besides," Joseph added, "his skull's the wrong shape." He came and sat down beside me. "And another thing," he went on. "I'd think you'd find the fact that he's a religious bigot kind of wearing at times."

"He's not a religious bigot!"

"Oh no? Remember his remarks about me being a secret you-know-what? And all that Jesus, Jesus, Jesus stuff. It must drive you crazy."

No, of course that wasn't true. Much.

"Yeah, they're funny that way." Joseph leaned back with a rueful chuckle. "I remember one of mine once. Golly. She was a sweet thing, you know, and I was just nuts about her, but she had this devotion to Ishtar and you simply could not argue with her. I had to become an initiate, go the whole route. When she finally died, I was heartbroken, really, I just moped around for weeks, but on the other hand—it was so great not to have to paint my ass blue and go whack the heads off doves at the temple every night. Always date atheists, that's my advice.

"By the way," he went on, "how's the work coming?"

"Oh." Slight uncomfortable pause from me, and a close examination of the brocade pattern on my sleeve. "It's—I had kind of taken this week off, because I've pretty much got the range of specimens in their summer growth phase. Now that autumn's here, I'll have to get busy again."

"Hmm. Any chance you can give me a preliminary completion date?"

"Well." I cleared my throat. "Well, I'll want to do a full scan on the plants that live through the winter, of course, and then we missed the spring because we didn't get here until July, so—er—I think we're looking at April or May."

That was the Eastcheape Waits performing Vous Avez Tout Ce Qui Est Mein. *A crisp voice from the radio spoke over a burst of static. We break now for an update on the Newsmaker of the Hour, Edward Bonner, that hard-line Catholic Bishop of London. Minor riots followed in the wake of his announcement yesterday that he is initiating an inquiry into the conduct and opinions of Protestant clergy. Results are in from our citizen correspondent's survey of Londoners: eight percent declined to state, fifty-two percent were opposed, forty percent said they favored the inquiry. Of the opposed percentage interviewed, most felt that this was the first move in a conspiracy to bring the Spanish Inquisition to England and deprive Englishmen of their civil liberties. The Council is expected to call a special meeting this evening to discuss the civil unrest. We've received no word yet from our correspondent on the Council, but as soon as we have the minutes of the meeting, they'll be broadcast live. Meanwhile, all operatives with Spanish identities are advised to avoid the following municipal areas—*

"Now, that's interesting." Joseph leaned over and switched it off. "I didn't think there were that many Spanish-cover ops out here. I wonder who else came over with us?"

"My God, aren't you the least bit alarmed?" I cried.

"No. Look, this will all blow over. The Council will reprimand this bishop, and he'll lay off for now. I'll bet they won't even hear about it in Kent for another week. Trust me." Joseph got up and stretched. "We have more pressing concerns right now."

"Such as?"

"Such as getting hold of a three-inch piece of deformed goat horn," he said.

16

AMAZINGLY ENOUGH, JUST such an object was found two days later, in the purse of a man floating facedown in a nearby river. He had been bludgeoned about the head and shoulders, making identification difficult, and his clothes were in rags, except for a fairly new buff soldier's jerkin.

Francis Ffrawney was quick to point out that this must be the thief, for Doctor Ruy had described just such a man as the probable culprit; doubtless the scoundrel had fallen out with his villainous Flemish accomplices. This theory was accepted by everyone except Nicholas, who gave me some very troubled and searching looks.

However, I was able to look right back at him with wide-eyed innocence, because I knew perfectly well that Joseph hadn't killed anybody; the Company would never permit such a thing. He'd just found a convenient corpse that was *already* dead and used it as a decoy, that was all.

At least, I thought that was what must have happened . . . but when I questioned Nef about it, she glowered and refused to tell me anything. She made herself pleasant enough to Sir Walter, however; became quite attentive. She coaxed him to let her tend to the poor little mutilated unicorn during its recovery, and the result was, it ended up sleeping in a wicker basket beside her bed. Joseph had a fit. Joan the chambermaid took to muttering darkly about how she was a *house* servant, not a stable girl, and I was doubly glad I wasn't rooming there anymore.

The wet weather began again. For about a week the hills were golden, the forests were rustling clouds of gold. Then the rain took it all away. There was suddenly a great deal of blue sky in England; a chilly wide sky, pale blue, like Nicholas's eyes.

The first morning there was a break in the rain, we went out for a bit of a frisk in the garden, but we had to take some care in our merry chase, with the mud and piles of wet slick leaves. As we neared the end of the path, we saw a traveler out by the gate, peering vainly in. He could see us perfectly well, too, so we slowed to a dignified walk and pretended we had been coming to meet him.

"The porter is not at his post, sir," called Nicholas.

"I can see that!" shouted the man in exasperation.

"I mean, sir, that there be no penny-paying guests after the rains begin," explained Nicholas as we drew nearer. "I fear most of our marvels are lacking their proper foliage. You may see the Great Aviary, or the Walk Historical. But the roses are a dead loss."

"I have come expressly to see Sir Walter Iden," grated the man.

"Oh," said Nicholas, and since we were at the gate by this time, he produced his ring of keys and let the traveler in. This gentleman shoved through and stood shaking the rain out of his hat, for the branches had been dripping on him where he stood. He glared at us. I had seen him before. Yes, he had come one day back in summer, with a party of other folk.

"Master Darrell." Nicholas bowed slightly, having placed him too.

"I am he." Master Darrell jammed his hat back on his head. "Pray announce me to your master."

"At once, sir. There is hot wine and a good fire in the hall," Nicholas placated. Master Darrell brightened considerably at the prospect as we walked back to the house.

"You have come on some business, sir? Or for the pleasure of Sir Walter's company?"

"A little of both, I think," the traveler replied, puffing out his breath in a frost cloud. "And I hope to sweeten your master's inclination to business by pleasant discourse with him. Heard you the news about Her Grace the queen?"

"I think not," said Nicholas cautiously. I put my arm through his as we walked. I knew what was coming.

"Why, she is with child."

Nicholas came to a full stop, gaping at him. Master Darrell eyed him wryly.

"Ah, that was how London did receive the news; then the folk all tore their caps off and cried huzzah, and blessed her name. As I think you will too, sir, being a prudent man."

"But . . ." said Nicholas.

At this moment Sir Walter emerged from the house and came springing nimbly down the steps, ready for his midmorning trot around the garden (per Joseph's orders). Master Darrell peered at him, and it was his turn to gape.

"Sweet Jesu, man, thy beard is red! How hast thou grown young?"

"It is a restorative physick, recommended by my personal physician," said Sir Walter airily. "Run along with me, for I may not stop, and I shall tell thee more." Master Darrell clutched his hat and panted off after him. I tugged at Nicholas's hand.

"My love, be of good cheer. The queen is old. A child is impossible."

Horror was slowly dawning in his eyes. "But if she brings forth an heir to the Spanish prince, then farewell England's liberty."

"She won't," I said, treading on thin ice. "She can't. I know it, love. She'll die."

"And what if she doth not die? Or what if she should die, and the child live?" Nicholas clenched my hand. "An infant crowned and the Inquisition to stand as regent over us all? This must not be." His grip was painful. I wanted to tell him about Mary's ovarian tumor and the hysterical symptoms, but all I could say was:

"Your God would not desert England so. Consider well, love, the late Queen Katherine bore but the one live child and that was Mary. All the rest died babies. Have faith. Pray."

"I cannot pray for the death of a child," said Nicholas wildly.

I racked my brains. "Hear me, love. My father has tended gentlemen of the Emperor's court and heard them tell tales current there, from the very spies come from England. And the saying is, that the Queen is so troubled in her monthly courses, and so subject to swollen distemperatures of her womb, that they doubt she could have borne a babe even when she was young."

"If the Emperor believed that, why did he send his son to marry the old cow?"

Well, that was a good question. "It's only dropsy," I said. "I'll stake my life on it."

"So thou mayest, and so may we all," growled Nicholas.

Later we heard rumors he liked better: that beaten Spaniards were leaving the country in droves, having failed to make their fortunes in this unpleasant country, and that their prince wished bitterly he could go with them. All true, according to our radio commentator.

We poor Spaniards, though, were stuck in an English *winter*. The bare fields like a gray sea frozen. The sky all lowering slate. Lead, steel, silver weather. The smell was oppressive. I don't mean that it stank, though there was a lot of death in the smell, and it wasn't the normal mortal reek of men and beasts. It was a cold, black kind of smell. It urgently needed jolly wood smoke to cover it, and piercing sweet winds off the sea to carry it away.

Visually winter was beautiful, especially if seen from behind thick windows and with a good fire at your back. The bleaker it got, the more the mortals in the household seemed to want to go out and rush around in it, especially after the snow started. No wonder the damned things died.

Yes, snow utterly failed to charm me. On the day I first saw snow, the *Ilex tormentosum* was fruiting at last, and I had crunched through frozen puddles to get at it, had wrapped myself in every garment I possessed plus a cloak of Nef's, smelling of goat though it did. For those sharp branches with their distinctive oblong berries I braved frostbite and an increasing atmospheric disturbance niggling at the edges of my sensory array. Nicholas, holding the basket beside me, looked perfectly comfortable in his ordinary clothes.

"This same holly we cut in the summer, I well recall," he observed. "Why do you take it again? Is there a particular virtue in the berry?"

"Oh, yes." I thought of diseases yet unnamed, in lands yet unknown. How to explain to him about Taxol, or *Vinca rosea*? "Blessed virtue. Their quality distilled will do more than garland thy house at Christmas, I'll tell thee. It's said the common kind keeps witches out; these will keep out Death himself."

"A likely story." He shifted the basket to his other arm.

"Well, it's true," I grumped at him. "Would I be out here in this filthy cold to get them, if it were otherwise?"

"It maketh thee look a spirit." He peered at me dreamily. "The leaves so green and the berries so red, and thy little blue hands and blue wrists and little angry blue face. I think if I tumbled thee under this green bush now, thou'd vanish like an ice cloud."

"Then should Friar John find himself out in the cold." I backed away a pace, just in case he intended to try it. Though he did look so handsome, with the frost bringing up the color of the good hot blood under his skin. He leaned down and lifted my chin in his own warm hand.

"Well, one must be prudent," he said, and kissed me. He radiated such heat it was delicious, and I leaned in to him and we could have kissed and kissed like that forever. I could have, anyway. I suppose his back would have gotten tired. As we came apart to breathe, something drifted between us. It was followed by several other somethings, white and falling swiftly. It looked exactly like the excelsior we used to kick around in heaps near the transport pad at Terra Australis, from the supply crates that were unloaded there. Of course, this was impossible. I frowned at the things, which were dropping everywhere now, and said:

"Where are all the feathers coming from?"

Of course I knew my mistake as soon as one of them touched my bare skin, and a second later I blurted, "It's snowing!" in dismay. I made a grab for my basket. But Nicholas had it, and he was staring at me in a mixture of alarm and delight.

"Thou knewest not what it was," he said. "Thou hadst never seen it before."

"Of course I have," I lied, getting the basket away from him. I had seen it in movies and paperweights and holos, and I had even done a five-thousand-piece jigsaw puzzle of a winter landscape once, but it hadn't prepared me for the reality. "I spake in jest. Come away now, quick. We must to the house."

"Thou'rt frightened." He paced along beside me, leaning down to look at me. "Sweetheart, it is but snow."

"So it is; and even in England folk must have enough sense to come in out of it, must they not?" I came to the end of the hedge and could see no garden anymore; only outlines rapidly obscured by the flying white. I panicked. "Where is the house?" I wailed; then my infrared cut in, and of course the house was the flare of light seventy meters northwest. Nicholas at my side blazed like an angel. He reached out for me.

"Peace, love, peace!" he called. "Follow my hand." But it was his light I followed, all the way back to Iden Hall. Contrary to the expectations fostered by literature and art, 1) snow does not fall in beautiful crystal kaleidoscopic flakes, and 2) it does not fall silently. It sounds like rain, only stealthy.

"Still blue," Nicholas marveled, helping me out of layers of cloak by the fire in the great hall. "They tell no lies that call thy Spanish gentry bluebloods."

Actually in my case it was antifreeze, but I looked haughtily at him. "Well, I shall not so chill my blood again until the spring returneth. This snow is a horrible marvel."

"Oh, but snow is a merry thing in England." Nicholas spread out his hands to the fire. "Many jolly country pastimes may be had, at the year's dark end. You may sled upon snow, or walk through snow to your neck deep, or make some defense and fight battles with snow. You may go skating on frozen millponds and with good fortune not drown.''

"*You* go skating on frozen millponds," I told him firmly, and we kissed, right there in front of a servant that was bringing big logs into the hall, and parted then. I had risked my fingers for *Ilex tormentosum*, and it had to be preserved for the ages.

Nef's room smelled like Nef's cloak, only more so.

"And how is our patient today?" I inquired, holding my nose as I went in.

"He's the sweetest, cleanest little baby in the world," Nef said. "And he's much better, thank you."

He looked better, sitting there nibbling on a corner of the brocade coverlet. The Graft-O-Plast had come away from the wound, and fur was growing back; the horn buds were obdurately two, as nature intended, and not one, as the fantasy of man demanded. "How nice," I said without enthusiasm. "Say, do you mind if I open a window while I work?"

"Yes." She didn't look up from the magazine she was reading. "It's snowing, in case you hadn't noticed."

At least it was warm in there. She hated the cold even more than I did and had built up a roaring fire on the hearth. I opened my credenza and resolutely set out my specimen prep slides. "So, what are we listening to?" I nodded at the radio.

"Pierre Attaignant memorial concert," Nef answered. "It's been going on for hours."

"Then I haven't missed the news."

"Nope."

"I've never seen it snow before." I switched on the ultravey.

"Lousy, isn't it?"

That was yet another set of bransles, a voice announced, sounding slightly desperate. *And with that we conclude this afternoon's segment of our tribute to the most prolific publisher of dance music of his time. Our thanks to studio musicians Dorin, Mark, Lucan, and Aristaeus of Thebes. Now for the news.*

News story of the hour: the first snowfall of the season has begun over southern England. Those of you stationed up north, of course, have already been experiencing nippy weather, and more of the same is expected over the next two weeks, as the cold pattern settles in over northern Europe. If you're having difficulties picking up our signal,

we recommend you tune in at 9 PM for our special program on how
to construct amplifying antennas out of common household items.

BZZZT! A burst of interference drowned Newsradio Renaissance.

"Sounds like you need to tune in to that one," I remarked. The
signal screeched and then came back:

Newsmaker of the Hour: Number one topic with the man in the
street appears to be the unexpected return to England of Reginald,
Cardinal Pole, after more than a quarter century in exile. A former
humanist, this rabid Catholic has been petitioning the Queen since
the start of her reign for absolute restoration to the Catholic Church
of all monastic properties confiscated during the reign of Henry the
Eighth. Since most of these are now in the hands of the private sector,
Pole's return is expected to galvanize resistance among members of
the Council.

News from the Continent: the Emperor Charles's health continues
to worsen, and the Prince Consort has expressed concern, but any
return to Spain has been ruled out at this time due to the Queen's
pregnancy, supposedly now in its third month. This isn't stopping his
countrymen, of course, and the official count of Spaniards leaving
England this week was . . .

"Those lucky, lucky guys." Nef shook her head.

"You're not serious. You want to go back to Spain?" I looked
over at her, incredulous.

"Anywhere but here."

"I thought you were all hot to get up to Northumberland."

"If I could actually get out of here and *go* there, I'd be happy.
It's the waiting that I hate. I hope at least I'll have some Blue Albions
to work with, after all this."

"Blue Albions? Is that a kind of beer?"

"No, dummy, it's a cow," she said in disgust.

"Aren't you a little worried by the news?" I flipped a slide. "I
mean, with this religious fanatic descending on England."

"No. Who cares what the monkeys do? We know how it all
comes out in the end, anyway."

"But not how it's going to happen. Don't you find it interesting
to follow the politics? Here's Mary with this Council dead set against
her. How's she going to push through her pro-Catholic legislation?
We know it's going to happen, but at the moment I can't see any
way. Aren't you curious?"

"Hell, no. If I want to find out something that badly, I'll access
a tape."

"Well, I think it's fascinating."

"You sound like a cultural anthropologist." She tossed her magazine aside.

"Gosh, excuse me."

"How's my little pal?" Nef leaned over and picked up the unicorn. "How are we feeling? It's almost time for our favorite show!"

"You were the one who said I had to learn to cope with mortals."

"I didn't mean you had to take them up as a hobby." She dandled the unicorn. "I remember when you couldn't stand the idea of coming to England. The New World, that was all you talked about, morning, noon, and night. Changed your mind, haven't you?"

"Maybe," I admitted. "England does have its charms."

"Get a load of her! We know the charm she's talking about, don't we?" she told the unicorn. "It's big, and it has a busted nose, and it looks like a horse."

"Oh, he does not." I jammed a slide in the wrong way and had to pop it out. "So where would you go if you had the chance? If you could make the Doctor station you anywhere you wanted?"

"India," she said right away, looking wistful. "No question. Anywhere in India. Or, maybe, Greece; Greece is swell." She kissed the unicorn's nose. "You'd like it there, wouldn't you, sugar face."

"Pleeeease!"

"Ssh. Ssh." She jumped up and turned up the volume. "It's time for the livestock report!"

But another crackling roar of interference rose, only slightly louder than her wail of protest.

Snow fell. And fell. Cardinal Pole came back to England and was welcomed with great ceremony by the Queen and our prince. Things started happening quickly, and it was worth braving the smell in Nef's room to catch the news broadcast every day.

Poor Mary. Our prince was not such a great actor, and she must have been increasingly aware that the honeymoon was over. But Cardinal Pole was sympathetic and attentive, and had big plans for a Counter-Reformation in her kingdom.

"This is crazy." I went into Joseph's room, having left Nef pounding on the sputtering radio and screaming at it. "They can't turn the clock back thirty years. They'll never bring it off."

"You wait." Joseph shook his head. He had taken to listening to the radio broadcasts with me, snow static and all, as the big soap opera got moving. "You'll see. They'll get help."

"From whom? The Emperor's going to die soon and so's the Pope."

"You'll see," he repeated. "Do a fast scan if you don't believe me."

I didn't want to do that. It was riveting, spell-binding to watch history as it unfolded. Why spoil it by fast-forwarding to the end? Besides, there were other stories to follow. A snowbound manor house is its own many-layered play, full of intrigues, confrontations, and twists.

It had gradually dawned on just about every inhabitant of the hall, thanks to Joan's intelligence reports, that Nicholas and I were sleeping together. Master Ffrawney averted his eyes from me any time we were in the same room, but all the others seemed rather relieved. Angry young men are uncomfortable to have around, and apparently getting laid regularly did wonders for Nicholas's temper. And what better way to quench a young firebrand than to have him fall in love with a nice Catholic girl? There were a few raised eyebrows over Joseph's apparent complaisance, but he was a foreigner, after all, and anyway people were too busy watching the other scandals to question it much.

The laundress continued steadfast in Sir Walter's bed, but somewhat less securely as his regeneration advanced. Indeed, she began casting slit-eyed glances of hate at Nef when their paths crossed, though that was seldom, and Nef barely noticed anyway. Now that I come to think of it, maybe the laundress's animosity didn't stem from a jealous heart after all. I certainly wouldn't have wanted to have washed Nef's linen, full of essence of unicorn as it was.

Nef, meanwhile, continued to respond to Sir Walter's efforts just warmly enough to get to keep the unicorn in her room. They flirted ponderously at table, and I believe things got physical once or twice. She was interested in his livestock, he in her noble lineage. Joseph and I had to invent a long string of Castilian ancestors for her and write it down so she could memorize it, because she was no good at making things up on the spur of the moment herself. Though she was good enough at home electronics . . .

Bloodcurdling screams in the night!!

I sat bolt upright in bed, scanning in a two-kilometer-wide radius. Nicholas was up and on his feet, staring. When another volley of shrieking sounded in the dead winter night, he strode to the door and opened it, and leaned out looking downstairs into blackness.

"What, help, ho! Is it fire?" someone on the second floor was shouting.

"What's the matter? Be there thieves again?" yelled somebody else, from belowstairs. There was no reply, but the screams died to hysterical sobbing, and a second voice from the same location was now heard making soothing noises.

"My master!" One of the servants came pounding up to the second-story landing. "Are you murdered? Is it the Spanish doctor?"

"Stay thou, Rose," Nicholas told me. He made a hasty descent, and in a second I could hear him beating on Sir Walter's door. "Sir Walter! Open, sir, if you can!"

I shivered and pulled the covers up around me. The weepy voice was moaning incoherently:

"It were on the chimney! O Jesu and St. Mary save us, I saw it!" To which the other voice—why, it was Sir Walter—replied in a hissed undertone:

"Peace, now, Alison, peace! Thou hast had no more than a dream! Hush! Thou hast roused the house, silly wench!"

"But I tell you it was the Devil! I saw his black wing!" the laundress (for it was she) shrilled.

"Sir Walter!" Nicholas couldn't hear the old man's frantic attempts to shut her up. "In God's name, sir, do you live?"

"Aye! Aye!" Sir Walter shouted in annoyance.

Mendoza! There was a dark shape pressed to our tiny window. I nearly screamed myself.

"But what's amiss, sir?"

Let me in, for God's sake, it's freezing out here!

"There is naught amiss! I merely . . . er, merely . . ."

I jumped up and opened the window. Nef's face, inexplicably upside down, stared in at me.

"Sir, are you held to hostage?" demanded one of the servants who had gathered in a small throng with Nicholas.

"Oh, God, I'll never get in through this," whimpered Nef through clenched teeth. "Can you break out the frame?"

"Nothing of the sort!" Sir Walter snarled. "Now go back to bed! Nicholas, bid them go!"

"I can't break out the frame, how'll I explain it?" I stammered. "What are you doing out there, anyway?"

"Sir, I must be assured that all is well with you," Nicholas explained patiently.

"Well—"

"No! There's a curse upon this house!" wailed the laundress. "I saw the Devil with mine own eyes, a-hanging from the chimney-pots—" Her voice broke off in a muffled bleat, as though someone were forcing her to eat her pillow.

"Nef!" I gaped at her in dawning and horrified comprehension.

"I assure you, all is well!" Sir Walter could be heard scurrying across the floor. There was a creak as he pulled the door open an inch and (presumably) stuck his nose out.

"It was the best placement for the signal," Nef explained through chattering teeth. "I made one of those radio antennas out of a broomstick and copper wire off the grip of that old sword of Joseph's—oh, shit, my fingers are completely numb—"

"There! Ye see I am unmurthered. Now, get ye back to bed!" grated Sir Walter.

"And, you know, it was dark up there, and I slipped a little, but of course I didn't fall, except—"

An indecisive muttering as people began to obey Sir Walter. Nicholas, the alarm in his voice replaced by a certain masked amusement: "It was no more than this? The woman had bad dreams?"

A thump as a window flew open one floor down and around the corner. *GET IN HERE!* thundered Joseph.

"Foolish fantasies," Sir Walter whispered. "The silly slut gets her up to piss and frights herself with supposed shadows. This is all!"

Don't you shout at me, Nef transmitted sullenly, but she went. She moved slowly past my window and disappeared. I stuck my head out into the night and glimpsed her crawling downward on a diagonal, until she reached the corner of the house and maneuvered around it and out of sight.

"Then I bid you good night, sir." The door slammed, and I could hear Nicholas returning. I shut the window and was back in bed in one bound. When he climbed in beside me, he was beautifully warm, even after standing around in a drafty hallway.

There was plenty of talk in the servants' hall the next morning, let me tell you, and plenty of venturings outside to peer and point at the chimney where His Satanic Majesty may or may not have been doing midnight gymnastics. Somehow nobody noticed the radio antenna wired unobtrusively into the leads.

There was plenty of dark speculation about the probable connection between Satan and Spaniards (perhaps he had just been looking in on us to see if there was anything we needed?), and there were plenty of molten glares between Joseph and Nef. Still, the English are rather fond of haunts and horrors in the season of ice and snow, so the denizens of Iden Hall let us go unlynched a while longer.

And our radio reception *was* much improved.

So the world turned, and so turned the small wheel of Iden Hall within the great wheel that was England, and the year rolled on toward the solstice.

17

"WE MUST KEEP Christmas well this year, what think you, Nicholas?" said Sir Walter at the dinner table.

All eyes turned to him at this announcement. We beheld, one and all, a robust fellow no more than forty years of age. He resembled a fox now more than a terrier; his hair and beard were red with just a little graying, or more correctly a yellowing, such as red-haired men get. He was bigger, he was bulkier, and his new clothes had been cut in better taste and of subtler colors. Altogether a different man.

"As you will, sir," said Nicholas. "Your revenues shall support it."

"Excellent well. I would have feasting, methinks, and dance. Take some care to find a consort for music. A fine consort, wanting nothing; there must be cornets and sackbuts, crumhorns and regals, and a great bass rackett—aye, and dulcians, too. I want this dull quiet hall to resound upon itself like a beating heart! Look to it, Nicholas."

Nicholas pulled out a little octavo book and a pencil and began making notes. I looked up from my dish of sops in milk. Dancing?

"I want . . ." Sir Walter leaned an elbow on the table and stroked his beard. "*Young* folk about me. Send word to the Elliseys and the Brockles and Master Syssing and his daughters, bid them all come. Tell them there shall be a great dance this Christmastide at Iden Hall."

I hadn't danced since I left Terra Australis. I looked hopefully across the table at Nicholas as he jotted down instructions.

"And I would have Christmas masquings and guisings, too, all fantastical, such as the King used to have," Sir Walter remembered fondly. He meant Old Henry, of course. As far as most men's memories were concerned now, poor little Edward had disappeared right back up his dead mother's womb.

"Master Sampson hath gilding and forms for masks." Nicholas wrote steadily.

"Why, lad, there must be more to it than that! God's death, these country folk have never seen the like. The whole matter of masques is that they must be some play or pageant, some spectacle. Doctor Ruy!" He looked over at Joseph. "You have been at Court. You know whereof I speak, surely."

"Yea, I assure you," Joseph agreed. "There are many spectacles at the Emperor's Court, some of them greatly astonishing."

"Just so!" Sir Walter smote the table. "I would astonish these folk! Now, you are a doctor and a learned man. Could you not then, as a friend, devise some dramatical interlude for the masquers?"

"Ah." Joseph blinked and then smiled. "My very dear friend, you do me too much honor. I would be delighted to do as you ask, but my skills are paltry—"

"Oh, but we must have a play, a diversion such as the Emperor hath, and what man better to know that than yourself? No, it shall be a splendid thing, I have no doubt. Now, may we not also have some subtlety at table, or some gorgeous marchpane semblance of a thing, as . . . a ship at full sail, or a wood with deer and little men . . . ?"

"Now where shall I find a pastry cockatrice a yard long, bearing the Iden arms upon its bosom?" said Nicholas in exasperation. He put out the candle and scrambled hastily in beside me.

"Can the cook make such a thing?" I burrowed up close to his chest. He put his arms about me, and we settled down. He replied:

"No. She cuts pastry leaves to deck baked apples: that is the whole of her craft. He wisheth a fantasy from the Queen's own table, and belike I'll have to go begging to the same."

We lay looking at the square of moonlight cast on the wall. "Why should he stop with a cockatrice?" I said. "If he would make folk stare, what about the Great Whore of Babylon riding on the Beast?"

There was silence for a moment, and then he began to giggle. "Painted in scarlet and purple, with seven wires stuck up the necks of the Beast to hold them still," he said. "That'd set tongues wagging!"

"Yet I would see this English Christmas." I wriggled around to look at him. "England is famous among all nations for celebration of this season." Though of course Dickens hadn't been born yet.

"Is it so?" He looked amused. "Have they no mummery, no masques and spiced ale in Europe?"

"Last year in Spain I prayed at High Mass until midnight, and then came home in falling sleet," I remembered.

"Bid thy heart be of good cheer, then, for we have no Romish Mass in this land," he said.

This made me acutely uncomfortable, because Parliament had already met to restore the Mass, and it would go through by a landslide. It had been on the radio this morning. Well, what he didn't know wouldn't hurt him.

"Though, to be sure, prayer is more fitting for celebrating the birth of Christ than drunkenness and revels," he continued thoughtfully.

"But thou must not put an end to Christmas revels!" I protested, and added, "When first I heard we should come into this land, I thought, At last I shall dance! Which I have not done yet, save only the shaking of the sheets with thee."

He grinned. "There shall be dances and sweet cakes to spare, my heart. As in sooth there must have been in France when thou wast a child. Is it not so? Or was it in Egypt thou toldest me last time?"

"Very likely," I said. "Or far Cathay."

"And do they hold Christmas revels in far Cathay?" He put his nose to mine. I thought about my childhood at the base. We celebrated a holiday loosely fashioned after the old Roman solstice festivals, and at Terra Australis it was in the summer anyway. I remembered hot dry horizons, sports matches, swimming parties.

"Be assured they do," I said. "And small apes climb palm trees at midnight to ring Christmastide bells."

"Sweet liar." He rolled over, and then we did something else.

"Whatever you do, don't touch the peacock," said Joseph, entering the room. "They've got it killed and hanging up already, and the party's over a week away." He looked at me, busy at my credenza, and at Nef, who was combing the unicorn's fur. "Not that the smell will bother you much," he went on. "But it'll be bacillus under glass by the time it's served."

"The Lollard statutes were voted in today," I told him angrily.

"The what?" he said, and did a fast scan. "Oh. The anti-Protestant laws, huh? Say, have either of you had any ideas about a Christmas masque I can write?"

"They aren't just anti-Protestant laws," I fumed. "They're special statutes that put the bishops above the law. They can arrest people, judge them, condemn them, *and* execute them—and the civil courts can't interfere! The Parliament just voted them in!''

"Did you think it couldn't happen here?" Joseph grinned briefly.

"For God's sake, it's crazy! These people are giving up their civil rights! It's a step back into the Middle Ages!''

"Funny thing about those Middle Ages," said Joseph. "They just keep coming back. Mortals keep thinking they're in Modern Times, you know, they get all this neat technology and pass all these humanitarian laws, and then something happens: there's an economic crisis, or science makes some discovery people can't deal with. And boom, people go right back to burning Jews and selling pieces of the true Cross. Don't you ever make the mistake of thinking that mortals want to live in a golden age. They hate thinking.''

"But this doesn't have anything to do with intellect!" I protested. "It's a question of survival! Don't they realize they've just voted absolute power to their enemies? My God, where's their common sense?''

Joseph and Nef just laughed, such a hollow sound that I wanted to run from the room. Joseph flung his hat up to the near bedpost, where it caught neatly and swung. "You think this is bad? You should have seen the stuff the English stood for under Henry the Eighth. Screw the monkeys anyway. Can't either of you come up with some jolly Yuletide high jinks for the old man?''

"Why don't you adapt something from Dickens?" Nef suggested. "Who's to know, anyway?''

I reached for my cloak. "I think I'll go out for a while.''

The snow packed us in and insulated us from any news by word of mouth; so the mortals got busy with their Christmas in the merriest of moods, and tacked up big swags of holly in the great hall, all blissful ignorance.

I had expected that we, as Spaniards, would be asked to stay in the background through most of the festivities. I got a big surprise: far from being an embarrassment, we were suddenly considered social assets. Sir Walter planned Spanish dances and Spanish refreshments and was confidently expecting some theatrical extravaganza from Joseph. Every time he asked about it, Joseph smiled wider and with increasing desperation. Nef and I gave him all sorts of helpful ideas, the best of which, as I recall, had the Man of La Mancha meeting the Ghosts of Christmas Past, Present, and Future, but Joseph finally came up with something on his own that required large amounts of pasteboard and secrecy.

He had lots of time, at least. In the sixteenth century, Christmas was celebrated from Christmas Day to January 6. In future times, of course, it would shift forward until it began in November and ended abruptly on Christmas Eve, which was how it was calendared at Company bases. I observed the Solstice by climbing from bed to watch the red sun rise out of black cloud, and marked his flaming early death that evening through black leafless branches. So the mystery passed, and the mortals hadn't even begun their celebration yet.

The first thing I saw on Christmas Day was, appropriately enough, the New Testament. Nicholas had it open on his chest and was reading in silence from the first chapter of the Gospel of Saint Luke. I yawned and stretched, and leaned up on my elbow to peer at the staggering black letters. It was a beautiful little story he was reading, and a perfectly simple one. How all those bishops and grand inquisitors drew what they did from it is beyond me.

I lay back and watched Nicholas's profile as he read. He was always pale when he first awoke, as though it took a little time for the blood to rise into his face. So at this hour he looked severe and autocratic, carved from ivory, and his light eyes flickered restlessly over the Word of God, or their pupils dilated in the crystal when a particular verse moved him.

He closed the book and blinked back tears. What was it like to believe in something that much?

The rooms smelled of spice, smoke, cut green branches, and mortals. They began arriving before noon, in wagons drawn by great stamping horses that had Nef running to the windows with cries of delight. Little mortal males in furred robes, the older ones clean-shaven, the younger ones with styled and pointed beards. Little mortal females in the latest fashions. I realized with a pang that my green gown, which I had planned to wear that day, was now hopelessly out of style. I spent a frantic hour sewing glass aglets on my peach outfit to cover the moth holes.

But my fussing was minimal compared to the scenes that were going on in the kitchen, and as for the great hall—*caramba*. A cart-load of consort drove up, unloading musicians and their instruments, and for a desperate half hour no one could figure out how to let them into the minstrels' gallery, which hadn't been opened in thirty years. A makeshift bandstand was being hammered together in a corner when somebody finally located the key, in a tin box at the back of a shelf. Most of this business Nicholas had to supervise, as well as a host of minor things forgotten until the last minute. Sir Walter was too far gone in hand-kissing and backslapping among his guests to be reminded he had not made a final decision on whether he wanted the consort playing before, during, or after the feast. So they started about ten o'clock and just tootled away, growing ever louder as the level in their ale barrel dropped.

The entrance of the Evil Spaniards was delayed, thanks to me.

"I can't wear this!" I wailed. "I stuck on every shiny doodad I own, and there's three big moth holes I didn't even see on the sleeve!"

"So take the sleeves off." Joseph examined his beard in the reflective surface of the credenza.

"Are you nuts? Every single one of those ladies downstairs has an outfit with matching sleeves," I said. "I can't look like a frump in front of Englishwomen!"

"So start a new fashion."

"If you'd put in the requisition for field dress like I'd asked you to—"

"Oh, here." Nef dove into her wardrobe and found a big pink ribbon, which she tied hastily around my arm. "Look, they'll never know."

"The color doesn't match," I fretted.

"Think of it as an accent."

"And it's cutting off my circulation."

"You want to see some circulation cut off?" Joseph started across the room menacingly. "It's going to be hard enough making an entrance in front of all those monkeys without being late, too."

"Will you both please shut up?" Nef demanded. Easy for her to say: she had a gorgeous plum-colored gown that was practically new. She grabbed my hand, hooked one arm through Joseph's, and dragged us out into the corridor. "Anybody would think you'd never been to a mortal party before," she scolded Joseph.

"Artist's nerves. I never wrote an entertainment before," Joseph muttered. We started unobtrusively down the stairs. People were milling all about.

"Well, you didn't really write this one, did you?" said Nef. "You copied it from—"

"Good gentles all, give greeting to the most renowned Doctor Ruy of Ansolebar, most learned physician to the Court of the Most Gracious, Serene, and Catholic Emperor Charles!" yelled Master Ffrawney, popping out unexpectedly from the foot of the stairs. We froze in midstep. All those mortal folk turned to look at us.

Only Nef's grip on my arm kept me from backing rapidly up the stairs. A great suffocating wave of smell came up to me. It was mortal fear, and a good quantity of mortal hatred, too. Riper than the holiday food. More pungent than the evergreen boughs. So bright in their Christmas finery, the little mortals regarded us out of animal eyes. Then, unnervingly, they all smiled. The males bowed; the females curtseyed.

"Oh, Master Ffrawney, you flatter me," said Joseph, with no trace of a Spanish accent at all. "To be sure, good people, I am only Sir Walter's old friend. Why, were we not boys together?"

"Certes, so we were." Sir Walter picked up his cue (for all I know, he believed it by this time) and emerged from the throng. "Come, Doctor Ruy, there is excellent muscadel here, none better may be had at the Emperor's table. And we shall have a Spanish viand later," he announced to his guests.

This did not help the smell. Yet we edged our way down with tiny frightened steps, and the mortal guests drew away from us as though Joseph had a cloven hoof.

"How festive it all looks," he remarked gamely.

And here came Nicholas in his severe Protestant black, towering head and shoulders above the guests. He met my eyes. People stared at him now, and the fear smell sharpened to anticipation. They were expecting a clash, but he took both my hands and kissed them.

"Well met here, Lady Rose. Doctor Ruy, I will be so bold as to carry your daughter away for a cup of hippocras." And he pulled me after him. The crowd registered astonishment. The tension broke.

"Ha ha ha," rattled Joseph. "Yes, go on. These young folk *will* be kissing in corners," he explained to the crowd.

It was all right now. Mortals love lovers, especially young ones. Everyone made way for Nicholas and me as we went in search of a punch bowl. "Thy hands are ice-cold," said Nicholas under his breath.

"And so should thine be, facing so many English," I replied. "If gazes were cannonballs, they'd have blasted us off the stairs."

"Oh, fear not." He located a steaming flagon of wine and filled a goblet for me. "These folk are the best small gentry of Kent! They'd no more harm thy father than wear a doublet that was out of fashion, which is to say they durst do neither."

"Good." I gulped at the wine. He watched me drink.

"Aye, sup that down. Thy face is pale as milk."

"If you think of anything else to build up my confidence, please tell me," I snapped in Greek.

He considered. "I like the aglets," he offered.

The operative words for this phase of the merriment seemed to be drink and mingle, as the scullery boys set up the long trestle tables in the hall. All we lacked was a cocktail waitress with a tray of little sandwiches. I took Nicholas's arm, and we moved cautiously around the edges, looking for a quiet place to talk. This soon proved impossible, however, because no less than four mortals came up to wave their crucifixes at me and tell me how their parents had been gardeners, or ladies-in-waiting, or household-account keepers to poor old Queen Katherine.

"God's my life, is it Nicholas Harpole?"

Nicholas turned abruptly, carrying me with him. We beheld a stout young male with a full beard, very steel-and-leather military in his bearing. Nicholas regarded him with narrowed eyes. "And he knoweth me not," added the speaker. "But I'd have known thee, Nick. Jesu, man, it's Tom!"

And he put out his hand, but Nicholas drew back as though he were a snake, and radiated such anger I was nearly knocked down. The other only laughed.

"What, art afeared still? I can tell thee, I've well washed away the stink of our tutor's blasphemies. I see thou hast done the same."

"Why are you here?" asked Nicholas, very quietly.

"I am a wooer." Tom jerked his thumb at a crowd of girls around Sir Walter. "Sweet Anne yonder. Not any goddess Venus, as you see, but I'll warm myself with her dower lands. Time to turn one's thoughts to such things, eh? I wot well we are not boys anymore." His eyes glinted wickedly. "How does it go? 'When I was a child, I spoke as a child'—"

Oh, Nicholas was going to hit him. There went the arm muscles contracting! I braced myself, but his back molars clashed together like boulders, and he said:

"In Christ's name, be silent."

"Tush, man, no one will mark me. And who'll mark thee? Thou hast found thyself the warmest bed in the house, and a Spanish bed to boot." He swept my knuckles to his lips. "Lady, buenos días. Nicholas, thou wast ever a lad of excellent common sense. With any luck, wilt wear a cardinal's hat before thou'rt forty."

That really did it. Nicholas grabbed the front of Tom's doublet and yanked him up to eye level. I said, "Nicholas!" and Tom said, "Peace, man, remember!" and one or two people turned to stare. Nicholas put him down.

"If I insulted thy lady, Nick, I'm sorry on't." Tom shrugged his

doublet back together. "And Christ be my witness, I meant no harm.
But what I said in jest, my heart meant." With a sincerity that was
worse than his bantering he put a hand on Nicholas's arm. "Thou
wert ever the best scholar among us. There's new men at Court, Nick,
the old papists die and make room for young ones. There's benefices,
Nick, there's gold, there's Dame Fortune with her knees wide apart!
Get thee to Court and try her, Nick, and shalt rise higher than poor
Tom with his plain wife and two farms in Kent." He looked across
the room at his girlfriend and sighed. "God grants each man his gifts.
I have only a prick; thou hast both a prick and a brain. Get thee to
Court, I say." And with a final melancholy smack on Nicholas's arm
he wandered away, and so just missed having his head ripped off. My
turn then to drag Nicholas to a sideboard and pour him a drink. Some
Christmas so far, eh?

By this time the tables were all set up and ready, so we were
seated in order of our status, and the first of the dishes were brought
in with great ceremony.

"A dish of small birds!" announced Master Ffrawney from his
post by the hall door. In came the small birds, pigeons probably, all
roasted and set on end with little pasteboard heads and wings. "A
dish of pike in gallantine!" cried Master Ffrawney next, and in it
came: phew, week-old fish in a sauce that smelled of cinnamon candy.
"A dish of pie Caneline!" ushered in one of the aforementioned
industrial-strength pies, borne by a gasping server who just barely
made it to the table.

And after that we were brought a dish of olives of veal, and a
dish of boar Porpentine, and the very boar's head itself: splendid as
on a Gordon's gin bottle, with big bulging eyes of half lemons stuck
in its blind sockets. I'd have given a lot for a gin and tonic as the
sweet cavalcade of indigestion rolled on.

They brought in the peacock: the whole skin had been flayed off,
then tucked back, feathers and all, on the roasted bird to make it look
lifelike. Only, they hadn't been able to unclench the little sphincter
or whatever kept the tail folded up, and the plumes moreover had
become sadly draggled on the ride from the poulterer's, so they had
taken the tail apart and stuck the remaining feathers on a big pasteboard fan, and painted in the missing ones.

Ducks by the dozen, chickens by the tens, packed like sardines
into dreadnought pies or propped up in little mounds of golden dead
bodies. Peculiar combinations of fish and flowers. Clods of roast beef
colored blue with heliotrope juice to make them look like venison.

Wonderful eggy pancakes, dusted with cinnamon and sugar. Cinnamon and sugar were in nearly everything, actually.

They brought in a trumpet to fanfare the arrival of the Spanish viand, a nice digestible recipe they'd coaxed out of Joseph, and when it hit the table, everyone really stared: it looked great, a sort of sweet rice pilaf, a big mound of rice and nuts and raisins, but all around the edge of the dish were perched big insects sculpted out of almond paste. "Rice after the fashion of Saint John the Baptist!" screamed Master Ffrawney triumphantly. "A pudding of Biscay!" There was polite silence as everyone tried to figure out what the bugs were there for.

"I do not recall that I specified such a curious subtlety as this," said Joseph at last.

"Please you, signior, but you said that we must have syrup of locusts to pour about the top, signior, and we had it not, wherefore Mistress Alison made locusts out of marchpane," explained the serving boy. "It were the best we could do, signior."

"The locust I meant is an evergreen tree bearing sweet beans," Joseph informed him.

"Oh," said the boy.

It was a great success anyway. The guests had drunk so much hippocras by this time that they thought the bugs were funny, and walked them up and down the table until their little toothpick legs fell off, or set them on ladies' headdresses or bosoms.

Nicholas was not amused by anything. He sat beside me looking dangerous, with the corners of his mouth pulled down from bad temper and a bright flush on his cheekbones from wine. I smiled at him timidly, but he sat staring unblinking into the fire.

When the first lull fell in the eating and drinking, Sir Walter lurched to his feet, rubbing his hands together. "Now, my neighbors, my friends, we shall have some diversion, shall we not?"

There were shouts of "Aye!" and general jolly laughter, and Sir Walter peered down the table at Nicholas. "Nicholas, my boy, what have we?"

"A cockfight, sir." Nicholas stood and signaled to men who waited at the door. Then he sat down beside me and folded his arms. In came two men, each bearing a gallant little bird with a bright cockade tail. They were held up for the guests to view, and what howls, what wagers, what quantities of coins were flung down on the banquet table!

I looked at Joseph. He was gazing into space with a vague smile, but his eyes were utterly blank. Nef was staring fixedly into her goblet and would not lift her head. The men put the cockerels down and backed away fast. The shouting in the hall grew deafening, and what happened next was as bad as you can imagine. Blood spattered everywhere, feathers flew. The little birds cut each other to ribbons, and one was blinded before the fight was done.

I leaned back shaking and found Nicholas's arm about me. "Take heart, Rose, and play the Spaniard. Whatever shalt thou do at a bull baiting?" he muttered. I burst into tears, but at least it got him out of his rage; he was contrite and kissed me, while the hall rang with bloodthirsty laughter.

A lamprey pie and maumany were served up next, as the blood was hastily mopped away. Then we were treated to an exhibition of fencing by two Frenchmen, very exciting, especially since they had no buttons on their foils. At least they didn't blind each other.

Then we had hasletts and troycream and date justles, just in case we hadn't had enough sweets to suit us, and the Four Tumbling Brothers of Billingsgate came in and vaulted all over one another for a while. People applauded greatly and threw them pennies. I saw a few spoons disappearing into the brothers' sleeves and hats as well.

By this time the tables were long highways of gnawed bones and fragments of piecrust, so Master Ffrawney entreated us all to decamp to the other corner of the great hall. There, arrangements had been made for card games in various nooks and crannies for those inclined to sit sensibly quiet after such a meal. For those not so inclined, the consort began to play dance tunes. At last!

But nobody began. People stood milling about as a good old-fashioned morisque opened; heads were lifted uncertainly, but not a foot moved, not a hip swayed.

I couldn't bear it. I seized Nicholas's arm. "Is this the way you dance in England?" I cried.

He looked around. "It is the custom for the master of the house to dance first," he explained, as his eye lit upon Sir Walter just sitting down to a nice game of primero with Nef and some other lady. "Sir Walter! Would you dance, sir?"

"What?" The little knight glanced around and became conscious of the gaffe. "Oh." He looked longingly at the cards in his hand but then brightened. "Nicholas, thou shalt lead for me. Hark ye, gentles, this tall fellow shall be lord for a little while in my place! Do you all take your steps from him!"

The master of the consort, who had been watching for a cue all this while, stopped the music abruptly. Nicholas stood aghast as all eyes turned to him. I took his hand. "Come, love."

The music began again, and I drew him into the dance. In those days dancers saluted each other first, as fencers do, very stately. A little stylized kissing of hands, the fellow bowing and the lady making a curtsey, then into the patterned intricate steps.

It was slow for a morisque, which was good because Nicholas hadn't danced in—how long? But the music caught us up, and the grace of his body came back to him. What bliss.

It disturbs me to remember how happy I was, how my blood moved in that hour. Music at that time was still brazen with colors picked up in the East during the Crusades, harsh with rhythms in a way it would not be again until the classical rock of the twentieth century. Dancing was erotic, formal, and feverish together. Nothing much more than hands touched, but what tension can crackle in fingertips. I forgot all about the terrible Christmas and the stinking food: there was only the music and my lover, who might as well have been naked there beside me, so fine he looked. Other couples had moved out beside us and were following in the steps. The music shook the very house; the bass rackett vibrated in the walls. Unreal at the corners, all kinds of little dramas were being acted out. Over there by the window at primero, Nef was beating the trunk hose off Sir Walter. Her face perfectly impassive, she accepted a card from him.

Over there by the carved panels, Joseph was surrounded by four or five anxious old males who had got enough of a look at Sir Walter to know that whatever physick he had, they had to have it too. Joseph's face was bland and slightly apologetic. I heard cracked elderly voices offering him many things, strange things, some of them.

And over there by the fire, nasty Tom was talking to someone, grinning and pointing at Nicholas. A bad man. Dangerous. His face went pale suddenly, and he clutched at his throat, and the concerned friend had to thump him on the back. We kept on dancing.

A basse-dance, a tourdion, a saltarello; bransles in sets of threes, and allemandes. Night fell early and black beyond the windows. Cressets were brought in, to flare and smoke. They made the dance more sensual, with complications of moving lights and shadow.

Pavanes we danced. A pavane is an ideal dance for lovers, because it's so slow, you can flirt or talk without losing your step. My very favorite pavane was "Belle Qui Tient Ma Vie" (the one from *The Private Life of Henry VIII*, *Romeo and Juliet*, the Leslie Howard version, and *Orlando*, both the 1993 version with Tilda Swinton and the 2150 remake with Zoë Barrymore), and it had just begun when Nicholas said: "Thy father will not give consent for me to wed thee."

"I know." What on earth did it matter? I took his hand, turned, swayed. He shifted the conversation into Greek.

"What do you think," he turned and bowed, "of an elopement?"

I stared but did not miss a step. Yes, a good dance for this kind of talk.

"Run away?" I said at last. "But where would we run, love?"

He took my hand and we turned. "To a safe place."

"Do you know of any?"

He was silent down the whole passage of the room, but when we turned again, he said:

"Some place where we are not known. Neither you nor I. We would have to leave Kent."

He had to switch into Latin for that, calling it the Place of the Cantii. It sounded very strange. I had a momentary vision of him blue and howling in a chariot, making life miserable for Flavius. "But how would we live?" I began a slow curtsey.

"I could teach boys. I could keep another man's accounts." He looked a little desperate. "There must be some way for a husband to feed his wife. And children." He glanced at me to see how I reacted to that.

"If God grants that I have children," I said primly, avoiding his gaze. "It is not the fate of all women." Certainly it was not my fate, since the installation of my contraceptive symbiote. Up until this time I'd been saying I took one of Doctor Ruy's secret potions to prevent a baby, but if we got married, Nicholas would see no reason . . .

If we got married . . .

Threading through the dance, I thought about it seriously. It wasn't unheard of. Joseph had admitted that. What if we really did run off together, elope, and wed?

I would have years and years, happy years with Nicholas. Someday he'd die, and my heart would break; but later was better than soon, and the good times would come first.

In the end, I could return contrite to Dr. Zeus. I was sure I knew enough about Company methods to avoid being caught until then. I'd accept the disciplinary actions there'd undoubtedly be, but it would have been worthwhile. Then I'd go on with my life. I could do that, couldn't I? I mean, if you're an immortal, they have to let you get away with peccadilloes like that, because what are they going to do? Kill you?

Instantly I had a plan. "I know what we can do," I told him. "We can get away to the Continent. England is not safe anymore. Europe, love, that's the place to go! We could go to Geneva! Many

English are living there in exile now, and you'd find work easily. Translating. Teaching. Something!''

But he had been thinking about it too, as he measured his steps to mine. When I mentioned Geneva, something went dark in his face. "Running," he said. "Hiding. Just like your father, living by his wits. We would be paupers, and year by year your eyes would grow more frightened. No, sweetheart, it would not be a good life. I must think of something better.''

Slowly we turned. He bowed. I bent to him. *Mendoza*, said an urgent voice. *Don't do it. Don't even think about it.*

I looked around, startled, to meet Joseph's dark gaze. *How dare you listen in on my signal?* I raged at him.

What signal? he retorted. *You're talking as loud as the music.*

I turned my back on him, but lowered my voice as I said:

"Nicholas, we'd be safe in Switzerland." Which was true; Dr. Zeus practically ran the place. Well, perhaps we wouldn't be so safe there. "Or Italy. Or France. Nicholas, a black storm is breaking over England. Any dumb animal knows enough to get in out of the rain. We must go to Europe, love.''

"Your metaphor is badly chosen." He rose to his full height. "It is no storm that comes, but a war. No man seeks shelter in a war. He fights." He looked over at Tom in contempt. "Or he surrenders.''

"If we were safe in Geneva," I ventured to Nicholas, "among so many righteous people, surely I might learn to trust your God.''

He looked at me bleakly. "Or you might learn to hate me for a coward. I must save your soul and mine own too, and flight is not the way. Give me time, love, to think what we can do.''

"All my time I give you," I promised. And the dance came to an end, in slow final steps. Now I can never listen to that music without feeling sad, though it was my very favorite pavane. I have never danced to it since.

I realize now that I must have talked him out of elopement, without meaning to. His idea must not have seemed stupid until he heard someone else agree with it.

It wouldn't have worked, of course.

After so many dances, people began to flag, and by this time the tables had been spread with clean cloths; so everyone trooped back in and found places for round two. The mortal guests were stupefied with all the eating and dancing, too sleepy to be quarrelsome. The musicians were tired too: they were doing mostly lute pieces now, very quiet, very soothing.

Only Joseph and Sir Walter were agitated. I looked over at them curiously. They were whispering together just as if they really were old friends. Nicholas got up and went over to them and leaned down. Sir Walter spoke rapidly in his ear. Nicholas listened, his face impassive; he nodded once, and then rose to exit the room. I leaned, trying to catch his eye; he gave me a peculiar smile and disappeared into the servants' hall.

How disappointing. I was hoping we might dance again, if the musicians woke up a little. I rested my chin on my palm and watched the mortals gossip, or doze, or stuff themselves.

Then they began to go out, the mortals. Not to leave the room, you understand, but to go *out*—like lamps. They were flickering out all around me and becoming transparent; one and then another vanished into the silence of the torchlight. Pop, here went a little lady in a great starched ruff, in the very act of talking behind her hand to her neighbor. Pop, there went a rakish fellow with mustaches, even as he poured wine in a long red stream from a high-held pitcher into his cup. Pop, there went both Master and Mistress Preeves, between one snore and the next. Before long there were no people at all, only tables, and then they too were gone. The fire burned down dim and cold, and the room itself changed, grew small and dark, the timbers blackening and warping. All the gilding and bright decoration went away.

Whoosh, the fire went out. I was alone in a cold blue light that streamed in through the windows. I looked at the windows, and they were distorted, for the leading had sagged and thrown the bright diamond panes out of true. But they faded and were gone, lingering for a moment as thin gray lines crossing the face of the moon. I looked back into the room, but it had gone too; I was alone in an expanse of snow mounded over ruins, and there was no house, no garden, only moonlight and dark trees in the distance . . .

I jerked upright in the midst of chattering mortal folk having their Christmas. I grabbed for a cup of wine. My teeth chattered against the rim. Sir Walter was standing, raising his hands for silence; he beamed around at all the guests.

"My neighbors all! Ye have supped this night on many a rare dish, and sported even as folk do at Court. Yea, I am assured that they keep Christmas no better even at the Emperor's very Court—" The door at the far side of the hall slammed open, and one of the serving boys ran in.

"My master!" he shouted. "Such portents, such signs and wonders! A great stag has been sighted, afar off, and he hath fire all along his horns!"

There was startled silence. Then the buzz of comments started up, and Sir Walter cried above it:

"Now what could this mean?"

We heard pounding footsteps, and another servant burst into the hall. "Oh, sir!" he cried. "Such strange things are abroad this night! There has been a great cloud hanging over the wood, and it shouted with the voice of a man!"

Before anyone could react to this, a third servant appeared. "Now Christ save us all! I have just seen, with mine own eyes, a tree that burned and yet was green! Surely this prefigures some fearful thing!"

It did, too, because there came a tremendous crash, and both the great hall doors flew open. At the same time the blazing fire dimmed and went out, just as in my vision, and though I had seen Joseph throw something into it, I still scanned nervously, involuntarily. Something was approaching, each step a thunder that shook the house. There was a flare of light from somewhere beyond; it threw a vast shadow that rippled across the wall, moved closer with each heartbeat.

Then it was in the doorway, silhouetted against the spectral glow: the figure of a knight, immensely tall, bearing in his hands a great double-headed ax. Several people screamed. Another flare of light, from a ball of green fire that hissed upon the floor. By its flickering light we could see the knight as he moved stiffly into the room.

His armor was wound about with ivy and stuck with holly branches here and there. His helmet was monstrously high, higher for the branching antlers at the crest; the visor was down, and no face could be seen. More green lights popped and rolled before him as he proceeded down the length of the hall. The faces of the guests shone out like masks as the light passed them: frozen in astonishment, terror, or laughter. He came to a stop just before Sir Walter's place at table. The candles burned high there, outlining Sir Walter in a golden halo.

"WHO IS LORD IN THIS PLACE?" cried a great hollow voice from within the helmet.

"I am he," said Sir Walter, trying to sound dignified but coming across smug. "What art thou, apparition, that troubles our festivities? Whither hast thou come, and wherefore?"

"I AM A SPIRIT THAT DOES NOT REST," boomed the voice. "AGE AFTER AGE I COME AGAIN, TO TEST MEN'S HEARTS: FROM OUT OF THE DEEP HILL I COME, UNDER THE STARING MOON."

"Come, spirit, tell us thy purpose!" demanded Sir Walter. The knight took a step backward and swung his ax up high. The lights came up slightly; the blade winked as it rose.

"I CRY A CHALLENGE TO THIS MORTAL COMPANY!
WHO SHALL TRY ODDS WITH ME? WHO HATH A FEARLESS
HEART?''

Sir Walter slapped his hand on his sword hilt. "Why, who shall
match thee but this hall's very master? I take thy challenge, phantom!''

"NAY, LORD, THIS CANNOT BE," replied the knight. "BY
LAW MORE ANCIENT THAN THE STANDING OAKS, I AM BID
CHOOSE MINE OWN CHAMPION FROM YOUR GUESTS. WHO
IN THIS PLACE SHALL STAND A CAST WITH ME?''

He began to stalk along the tables, turning his helmet this way
and that.

"WHO HATH A VALIANT HEART?" he called. "WHO
DURST HAZARD A CHANCE?'' Nobody spoke up, though somebody was crying hysterically. Goodness, hadn't these people read their
own literature?

Finally he stopped and again lifted the ax high. Slowly he brought
it down, down, down, and pointed at a very small boy, who sat
wedged between his parents. Relieved laughter from all the adults as
the tension broke.

"THIS SHALL BE MINE OPPONENT," declared the knight.
The little boy shrank back, his eyes huge in his white face.

"Why, Edward, it seems thou must play the hero now," his father
joked.

Edward shook his head mutely and made himself even smaller;
but rowdy grown-ups all over the room were shouting for him now.

"I can't, Dad," he said in a tiny voice.

"What, sirrah, wilt thou not?" His mother reached down and
pinched him, hard, which brought him yelping to his feet; and his
father hauled him up onto the table, telling him:

"If thou'rt a coward, thou'rt no boy of mine!"

I am always so sorry for mortal children.

Well, the knight put down his ax and lifted Edward to the floor,
where he stood shaking in his little holiday clothes.

"NOW, EDWARD," admonished the knight. "THOU SHALT
TAKE MINE AX"—he lifted the weapon and put it in the child's
hands—"AND I SHALL BEND MY NECK TO THE BLOW. THOU
SHALT PLAY THE HEADSMAN, AND TRY WHETHER MY
HEAD COME OFF OR NO."

"I dursn't!" gasped Edward, and there were jeers and catcalls
from all around the room.

"NAY, EDWARD, TAKE THOU HEART." The knight turned

to sweep the room with his gaze. "WHAT THOU MUST DO, ALL THESE FEAR TO DO THEMSELVES." The noise subsided a little. The knight turned back.

"STRIKE ONLY ONCE," he said. "CLEANLY, AND QUICK." Then, ever so slowly, he bent down, and the broad antlers raked the air in their descent. Edward made a little terrified sound; but he dragged the great ax aloft, tottering with effort, and let it come crashing down.

A crack, a smash, and a shower of sparks. All the lights burned high at once, and the knight's head came off and shattered on the floor, spilling out sweets and trinkets and little sugared cakes. Nicholas rose up smiling and tousled.

"A Merry Christmas, neighbors, to you all!" he shouted.

I laughed so hard, there were tears in my eyes. All around me mortals whooped and applauded. Joseph closed his eyes in relief that all his special effects had worked. Little Edward blinked at Nicholas. After a careful survey of the grown folk, none of whom were watching him, he knelt and began methodically scooping loot into his doublet.

Now I remember the detail of the boy, but then I saw only Nicholas in his pasteboard armor. Nicholas looked charming and silly and very sexy too, in a kinky sort of way. Somehow it all recedes from me as I write it down, like a fade-out in an old film. I remember that Nicholas came clumping back to his place at table, and that amid all the clamor we slipped off upstairs. There I played the squire, or maybe page is the better word, and helped my knight get naked in the darkness. Jolly Christmas pastimes then, I can assure you, as peach wool and green carapace scattered together on the floor.

Yet the first memory that comes when I think of that night is the wary face of the child. I wonder who he was, and what became of him.

18

THE BIG SURPRISE the next morning was that most of the guests were still there.

Waking slowly in Nicholas's arms, my first drowsy scan of the house told me it was pullulating like a beehive. When we crept down cautiously in the first winter light, we saw rows of makeshift beds all along the gallery, most of which were still occupied by sleeping mortals.

"What are they doing here?" I whispered. Nicholas shook his head in amazement. As we came to the stair landing, we met Master Ffrawney coming up with a tray, followed by Joan, whose expression was even more martyred than usual. Ffrawney smiled at us maliciously. Nicholas ignored his ill will and pointed in the direction of the gallery.

"What means this?" he said. "Have these folk no homes?"

"Oh, to be sure they do." Master Ffrawney leaned the tray on a corner post. "But snow is deep and bitter cold, or so Sir Walter wisely said last night, when he was far gone in wine. Further, he assured his many friends that the hour was late, and all those present solemnly agreed with him. Lastly, he said he was not such a starveling beggar as to bid his guests depart when his splendid house could accommodate them all. Whereupon beds were made, and those folk who could still walk went off to sleep in them. I am bound for His Grace's chamber now, to tell him that the folk who remained at table clamor for breakfast."

"Doth he think this is Whitehall Palace?" Nicholas was aghast. "His revenues will not feed all these folk the whole Christmastide, he cannot afford it."

"Well, no doubt *thou* hadst told him so, hadst thou been there. But *thou* wast abed early, if I recall me." And he gave me an arch glance.

"I must speak with him privily." Nicholas started back up the stairs.

"Then thou must ask the youngest Ashford girl to get out of his bed."

"Oh, sweet Christ!" Nicholas halted. He turned back and took the tray. "I'll bear him this."

"As thou wilt." Master Ffrawney shrugged and turned to descend. "I'll go and see what manner of fare we have remaining."

This was grim. With an apologetic look Nicholas left me. I picked my way through the bodies to Nef's door and slipped inside.

They were sitting there listening to the radio, Joseph, Nef, and the unicorn.

... the consequences of the Act of Supremacy were tremendous, and its proposed repeal is viewed as a token measure only by the Council. Of course, they have no idea yet of the extent to which Pole will implement the repeal. Roderick, can you give us the story from Court?

Well, Decius, the cardinal appears to be having a temporary eclipse of his power over the Queen right now, because of course with the Christmas festivities the Queen and the Prince Consort are publicly together quite a bit, so the growing rift between them isn't as apparent as it was. The cardinal's doing most of his damage in the Parliament, though, and a few of the Council members are beginning to get an inkling of just how far to the religious right things are going to swing. Sir William Cecil, in fact ...

"Smart man. Cake?" Joseph held out a small plate. I inspected it gingerly and took a slice.

"None of those awful people went home!" I announced. "Couldn't you have done something? They're going to eat us out of house and headquarters!"

"What will be, will be. The little guy was in what you'd call an expansive mood last night. I guess he'll just have to send out for a few more sides of beef."

"I won thirty-seven pounds last night," remarked Nef.

"So, what did you think of my diversion?" Joseph leaned back and sipped wine. "What about those pyrotechnics, huh? What about that sleight of hand?"

"Not bad. The piñata I liked particularly. Nicholas was a surprise too."

184 ON COMPANY TIME

"He's tall and real loud. Perfect for the part," said Joseph. I bristled, but Nef said thoughtfully:

"Sir Walter will need more entertainment if all these people stay until Twelfth Night. I'll bet I could make a fortune at cards."

How could millennia-old superbeings be so boring? I wandered over to the window and watched the snow fall. Spreading my fingertips against the glass, I tuned in and scanned.

Many voices, inquiring about breakfast and sanitary arrangements. Dark voices belowstairs, complaining of the extra work. Master Ffrawney saying something high-pitched about the snow. And there, there it was, Nicholas's voice in earnest entreaty.

"Sir, I tell you plainly that you waste your substance. What will you do? Where will you get more money?"

"Why, with any luck I shall better my fortune." There was a faint defiance in Sir Walter's voice.

"In God's name, sir, how?"

"I have my plans." Now there was desperation. "I am revolving in my mind some several stratagems, any of which may bring me fortune enough."

Nicholas radiated bewilderment.

"By feeding peacocks to the Syssings and the Preeves the whole Christmastide?"

"Um, no. But, Nicholas, I must think of myself! Gold I have had for many years, and the good name of my fathers; but mine own name is unknown, Nicholas. Thirty years have I spent in careful restoration of Sir Alexander's glory, ensuring that his name be not forgot. Were it not well now to add mine own glories to the name of Iden?"

There was a long pause.

"If I take your meaning aright," said Nicholas carefully, "you seek a life in the world again. Why, this is well; commerce suited you. I shall, if you wish, make inquiries as to companies seeking capital and mercantile argosies. You may buy and trade and so increase your revenues until within them you shall live as liberally as you please. Shall I ride forth, when the roads are clear?"

"Yea. Nay. I would, and yet . . ." Sir Walter's voice grew small.

"Sir, this is excellent good sense."

"But it fretted my soul to be a merchant," Sir Walter complained. "It is no fit work for a gentleman. Sir Alexander won his glory with a sword, in the service of his king."

"So he did, sir, but men live otherwise now. Any knave with a pistol may drop a knight-at-arms, and the tourneys are all for show. Take heart! Lords win honors by their wits these days, and doubt not that you shall do the same. Be thrifty! Send your neighbors home now, and you shall feast them in greater splendor on another day."

"But I promised them supper, Nicholas," said Sir Walter miserably.

A long, long exhaled breath from Nicholas.

"Sir, what shall they eat? There is no more beef slaughtered and dressed. Who hath fowls to sell us, even should we buy? The snows have filled the ways to your farms."

Another long pause, and then a snuffling sound. Sir Walter was crying.

Creak creak creak. Nicholas pacing furiously.

"We shall make broth," he said, "out of the leavings. And put in some unlikely herb, or some color to make it strange. And you shall tell them it is a dish from the Court of the Emperor, that it is the Spanish fashion to sup but lightly after a feast day. Doctor Ruy will not naysay you."

"I could do that, couldn't I?" said Sir Walter through his tears.

"Aye, and—and—offer that they may, nay, *ought* to be purged and bled by the doctor, which (you shall say) is also the fashion of the Court after a great feast. I warrant they'll get them home in haste then."

"Thou hast brains, boy, thou hast." A honk, as Sir Walter blew his nose on the sheet.

"And you shall make them promise of great cheer in some time to come."

"Oh, good."

"And so honor is served, with no ruin to your purse thereby."

"Nicholas, thou hast ever done me good service. 'Tis only a pity—"

Pause. "Sir?"

"A pity thou art so inclined to Gospelling. It suits not with the time, I fear."

Dead silence. Then:

"I may cut my coat to follow fashion, sir, but not my conscience." Nicholas's voice was rigid.

"Well, but thou dost neither. I shall have new livery made for thee, what say you? Not so much black. It puts folk in mind of Lutherans."

"When you can afford new livery, sir, you may do what you list."

"I shall, then. Go thou now, and send Jack that I might dress me."

"Sir." Nicholas was withdrawing, coming down the hall in a glow of anger. I left the window.

"Sir Walter can't send out for more beef," I told Joseph abruptly. "He doesn't have enough money. He and Nicholas were just fighting about it. Can't you do something to help? Prescribe fasting for health reasons, maybe?"

Joseph sighed. "I can try. He needs to be fine-tuned after all that whoopee last night anyway. All right, I'll pay him a visit."

"Great!" I ran from the room so I could catch Nicholas halfway down the hall.

"My love! My father fears that immoderate merriment may do Sir Walter harm, and hinder careful physic. He will counsel him to send his neighbors home."

"My master is already so persuaded, but if thy father's word will strengthen the argument, be it so." Nicholas leaned against the wall and folded his arms. "I never heard that wits came with wrinkles, but as he loses the one, it seems he loses the other too."

"Oh, love." I put my arms around him, so sorry to see him unhappy, and moodily he held me. As we stood there, a smell came floating up the stairs, a greasy rank smell.

"What reeks so?" I said in distaste.

"Suet pudding from last night. They fry it for breakfast," he replied. "We must get these folk out of the house ere we have nothing to feed them."

"You could make a mess of thin pottage," I said mischievously. "Color it with saffron and tell folk it is a rare dish out of Spain."

It was a stupid slip. No older, experienced operative would have made it. Nicholas glanced down at me with suspicion in his eyes. Only for a moment, but the suspicion was there.

"Why, so I had resolved to do," he said. "Dost thou listen at doors, Rose?"

"Nay, love, I have been with my father!" I buried my face against him to conceal my dismay. "Sweetheart, have courage! All will be well."

All was well, too, thanks to Joseph. When Sir Walter's guests heard that forthcoming meals were going to consist of leftovers and purges, they found courteous excuses to brave hip-deep snow back to their own homes. Only a few folk lingered, minor gentry so impoverished that even a purge sounded like fun to them so long as it was free. They made a less unreasonable demand on the larder while still allowing Sir Walter to play the host, so everyone was happy. Besides, the more inedible portions of the festal food could be recycled endlessly, if the cook kept grating cinnamon on it to disguise the smell.

So the days of Christmas rolled on cheerily enough. There was no work to do in the garden; there were no guests to shepherd about and explain things to; there were no more frenzied party preparations. Most hours Nicholas and I spent in his little bare room at the top of the house, where the relative chill refreshed us after the stuffiness downstairs.

My love, my love. At night we cuddled together under the blanket and read by the light of his single candle, or talked far into the dark hours. He would never give over his attempts to persuade me that I needed his Christ; and I could not resist the temptation to argue the need to save men's lives rather than their souls. Yet he had some remarkably advanced ideas for a man of his time, he really had.

Mine only love. The household slept below in silence; our little room seemed cut adrift, the cabin of a ship sailing through the vaster silence of the winter stars. How could anyone think that my lover was a paltry mortal thing? He was an immortal creature like me, and we dwelt in perfect harmony in a tiny world of bare boards and dust, leather and vellum.

You can love like that but once.

I was vaguely aware that terrible and portentous things were happening in the world outside. I heard fragments of news broadcasts coming up from Nef's room, and warning messages were surfacing out of my chronomemory program. It seemed sensible to ignore them, since there was nothing at all I could do about them. One should always avoid unnecessary unhappiness. Especially if one is an immortal. They taught us that in school.

19

ON THE ELEVENTH day of Christmas, January 5, 1555, there was a thaw. There was pouring rain, rushing in gutters, and then it froze again; but the snow had been so reduced that the lanes were open and people could visit one another for Twelfth Night.

Our Christmas parasites used the opportunity to go home at last. Without them the house seemed luxuriously empty, and Nicholas and I got the chance to explore the minstrels' gallery.

It was entered from a third-floor passageway, through a tiny dark door that looked like a cupboard. Nicholas had to bend nearly double to squeeze through, and my hoops gave me no end of trouble, but once we were up there, it was neat. We stood and surveyed the view of the great hall, and Nicholas drew my attention to the fine carved roundels that were practically invisible from down on the dance floor.

"Red roses," I observed. "Red roses were the badge of your Lancasters, in your Roses wars, were they not? I did not know the house was so old."

"It isn't." Nicholas grinned. "But Sir Alexander was a Lancastrian partisan, and so we have roses encarnadined in his honor. Not that any Christian soul hath noticed them these thirty years. I must write them in mine abstract of Worthy Sights to Be Pointed Out to Paying Guests."

I peered over the rail.

"So far up and such a little space. I wonder they got all those hautboys and base viols up here. They must have been sitting in one another's laps, trying to play."

We looked at each other. I sidled over to him.

"I recall," I remarked, "that when we looked up at the musicians, we could see but their heads and the topmost parts of their instruments."

Nicholas leaned his elbows on the rail and gave me a sidelong gaze.

"What better place than this," I decided, "for a lesson on the recorder?"

"Madam, what can you mean?" inquired Nicholas in his suavest voice. I pounced, and we tussled out of sight, up there on the tiny platform.

A door opened below us, and two sets of footsteps sounded in the great hall. We froze, except for Friar John, who fainted dead away. I sat up in a panic, and Nicholas grabbed me and pulled me down. Our hearts thundered, surely louder than those footsteps over hollow cellars.

"I had come sooner, but the snow did not permit," said a voice. Familiar, somehow. "And, to tell the plain truth, there have been fearful things that captured my thoughts. I have ridden from Rochester, you may know."

"Aye. Well, the time spent has been favorable to thy case. I too have had much to consider." That was Sir Walter. "I'll tell thee, Master Darrell, I have looked at thine offer with new eyes."

Master Darrell? Offer?

"Have you so?" the other voice sharpened. "And what say you to it now?"

"It likes me well," said Sir Walter. "I were a liar if I said otherwise."

"This is a change, certes."

"Well, well; the case is altered."

"Ah."

Creak as they sat down together.

"Shall I—? I shall call for sack," said Sir Walter, and he did, and they sat there saying nothing while a servant brought sack, and they said nothing while he left, and only after the door shut behind him did they speak.

"Tell me, how much—" began Sir Walter, at the same moment that Master Darrell said, "I am prepared—" They both halted.

"Forgive me, sir," said Master Darrell.

"Nay, a thousand pardons. Speak, friend."

"What I offered, I offer still: half the sum in sealed bags now, and the rest when the cherries ripen and apricots go to market, God send us favorable sun and rain. Even failing that, I have wool in the north, and that's sure. And you spake once of certain provisos . . ."

"In sooth. Thou must keep the name."

"Oh, sir, the name is all. Therein is the value. Who would pay a farthing to see Darrell's Garden?"

Nicholas turned his head, frowning.

"Well! I am satisfied," said Sir Walter, and there was a silence as they both drank. Sir Walter set down his tankard and said:

"I am no man for this country life. Look at me, Master Darrell, am I old? Am I palsied? Do I falter?"

"Uh . . . nay."

"Hadst thou met me but today, thou shouldst say I were no more than thirty. The Greek physick hath given me a new life! Shall I dream it away in this quiet place? Or shall I not rather set out anew?"

Bad feelings in the minstrels' gallery.

"What is it you mean to do?"

"Meseems I have not known mine own heart . . . I thought this garden should be my fame, my child, my all. I see now it is not the end I desire. I, I meant to hold a Christmas revel that befitted mine ancient lineage. It was nothing so grand as I envisioned, for I saw that my neighbors are but lowborn country folk, and I find myself but a little country squire pinched shrewdly by his expenses. I was made for greater things, Master Darrell!"

"But what remedy, sir?"

"Thou shalt hear it. I'll get me to London and try for a courtier. There is power, there are the New Men! Through sale of this estate I'll have ready cash in hand, and haply a Spanish wife of noble birth, which cannot but stand me in good stead at Court."

"You mean to marry, then?"

"If the lady grant my suit, aye. She hath looked well on me thus far, and I may hope, I tell thee. God knows she is not fair, but she's young, and I doubt not of an heir once I bed her—"

He was talking about Nefer. My astonishment at this was such that I inadvertently broadcast it, and a second later I felt both Joseph and Nef tuning in to the conversation.

"—and thereby my puling nephew shall have no claim."

"This lady is one of your guests, then," said Master Darrell.

"Yes. As to that—" Sir Walter sounded uneasy.

What's going on? from Nef.

Shut up! from Joseph.

"There is a thing thou shouldst know," said Sir Walter. "This Lady Margaret is a sort of nurse, after the Spanish fashion, of virtues sober, to that girl thou hast seen in my garden. The girl and her father, Doctor Ruy, are my guests here."

"For that he is your ancient friend. Aye, I remember me."

"Yea, even so, and yet thou shouldst know . . ."

Hold it hold it HOLD IT! Joseph was exploding out of a chair, and distantly I heard him pelting down a corridor.

"There is a certain arrangement that I have with Doctor Ruy. He must remain here, he and his daughter, as long as they will; and all that they want of the garden, they must have. Seeds or grafts or bushes entire, and thou must on no account hinder them. Nor mayest thou question them concerning anything thou seest, though never so strange."

"I like this not so well," ventured Master Darrell.

"I could say more, if I durst." Sir Walter gulped his wine. "So thou meddle not in his affairs but let him do as he pleases, it will be well for thee. He hath powerful friends, hath Doctor Ruy—"

"What, is the man a Spanish spy?" blurted Master Darrell. "God's death, sir, how could you?"

The shock in Nicholas's face is something I wince at even now.

"No, his masters have—"

"God save you, Sir Walter. I have come of express purpose to seek you out. God save you also, sir." Joseph appearing out of nowhere, not even out of breath.

A silence that sizzled like bacon.

"This is Master Darrell of Colehill," said Sir Walter with a little cough.

"Ah. Sir, your servant. You are the gentleman who desires to purchase the garden, is it not so?"

A baffled silence. "I had not told anyone—" began Sir Walter.

"But me. You recall? When we drank so much sack together. We were grievous deep in our cups, I fear. Have you decided to sell?"

"I had thought to." Sir Walter let his words out one at a time, like frightened mice.

"You have, of course, told him of our arrangement? I trust, sir, you understand?"

"No, sir." Very grim, very brief the reply.

"Then I must explain. I belong to a fraternity of scholars. We quest after knowledge of divers sorts, to work great good for men. Our brotherhood is wealthy, and not so respectful of priests as it might be, wherefore the Church hath put us under interdict, and so we work secretly—"

"No more, brother! I know whereof you speak." Master Darrell's voice had lightened up amazingly.

"You do?" said Joseph, after a pause in which I could hear his

wheels whirring. He gambled and said, "Then in the name of the
Widow's Son, I need say no more."

"You have a friend in me, sir." Master Darrell's voice was jovial,
and there was a brief smack of palms as they exchanged lodge signs
or something. Everyone, and I mean everyone, relaxed.

"My studies have brought me to Sir Walter's garden for the rare
simples that grow therein." Joseph picked up the ball and ran like a
thief. "As you may see, casting your eyes on Sir Walter, I have been
able to reverse the natural decay of the flesh. I ask but that I be
allowed to continue my studies here. I shall pay you well for the
privilege."

"Why, is it so? Then all is well. Tell me, can you . . . uh . . .
restore that natural growth of hair, the want of which upon the head
of a man who is yet young, shall make him appear older than his
years?"

"Are you troubled with baldness? I can cure it without fail, my
friend. You may consult with me when you will. But I had near forgot
the purpose I came here for! I would remind you, Sir Walter, that you
are to fast this night. No sack with eggs."

"If I must," grumbled Sir Walter.

"Lovers grow lean for love, and so must thou," said Master Darrell. "Tell thy lady thou diest for her."

"Lady?" Polite professional interest from Joseph.

Sir Walter drew a deep breath. "As you know—Doctor Ruy—I
have made suit to the Lady Margaret. Marriage is my intent."

Oh really? reacted Nef, without as much laughter as I would have
thought.

"Truly? Then sir, God speed you in your suit. Her dowry is not
base gold but spotless virtue, which you well know is a far greater
treasure."

"No, er, lands or inheritances, then?" said Sir Walter.

"Not nowadays, though I assure you her forefathers (pure Christians all of them) fought valiantly for the Cross, placing faith above
base gain."

"Oh."

I'd better lay away my thirty-seven pounds, thought Nef.

"Be ruled by me and take the lady for herself, man." Master
Darrell spoke with a certain bitterness. "I had not told you all my
news yet. A Spanish lady will serve you better than six hundred
pounds a year, if you would try Court now."

"What do you mean?"

"There is great news in Rochester, and we must rejoice. For, look you, this Christmastide the Parliament hath done wonders. England hath repented her sins and returned to the bosom of Rome, I say. The late King Henry's Acts are voted down every one, the Mass is restored, whereat we must rejoice.''

In the great hall there was a shocked silence, until at last Sir Walter said: "Thou knewst all this, and came into my house so lightly to bargain with me?''

"How otherwise, sir? Is this not great news? Were we to go about sadly, we should be suspected for heretics, should we not?''

"So we should." It was difficult to read Sir Walter's voice. He was silent another long moment, and then he said: "So we shall have the abbeys and the monasteries back again.''

"Aye, forsooth.''

"And good sisters shall tell their beads so quaintly again, as they did when I was a child, and there shall be great paintings in the church to show the glories of Paradise and the torments of the damned.''

"Aye, forsooth.''

Joseph's voice, sounding embarrassed: "Now, as I am a Spaniard, and a loyal son of the Church, I trust you gentlemen will not recall that I spoke of any brotherhood of scholars.''

"Oh, nay.''

"Nay, nay, sir. It is well, nowadays, to have a Spaniard for a friend," said Master Darrell.

"I certainly count myself as such.'' Joseph matched his irony note for note.

Mendoza, are you okay? sent Nef.

"How long, think you, before the bishop's men are sent out amongst us?'' asked Sir Walter.

"It is expected that the order to conform goes out before the end of the month.''

"Ah. I have some time, then, to put my house in order.''

I will never understand the English. Sir Walter had cried like a child because he could not serve his guests peacock two nights in a row; but at the news that his civil liberties had been taken away, the man was sensible and calm.

"So.'' Master Darrell drained his tankard and set it down. "I would, if I may, sir, see the accounts for your garden, the better to know what income I may expect.''

"My secretary keeps excellent accounts.'' Sir Walter got to his feet. "Let us go find the books, and thou shalt see for thyself.''

"And I shall take my leave of you, señors.'' Joseph was bowing.

"I must to my studies, er, prayers. Remember, Sir Walter, you must fast."

"Aye. Aye." And they went out of the great hall, all together.

Nicholas and I sat silent in the gallery for a few minutes. He was nodding, slightly, and his lips were moving, but no sound came out. Finally he gave a little choked laugh.

"Why, so is the silly world turned upon its head," he said.

"How could they do it?" I whispered. "How could a people be so foolish?"

Nicholas lowered his head to his knees and wept. His sobs echoed in the great hall, where only a short time before he had played the winter king in his pasteboard armor.

Arrows you may dodge and fever you may antibody for, but mortal grief is a misfortune you cannot escape. That's a translation of something solemn from my school days. It was, as I remember, the first sentence of an essay about the hazards of taking mortal lovers. The author compares this act to having a gangrenous limb grafted onto one's perfect immortal body. He then proceeds to a little parable about the immortal heart as beautiful machine, flawless and balanced, designed by a master with all protection against weakness and damage—until the heart's foolish owner attaches leads from it to the inferior heart of a badly made mortal engine, thus compromising the integrity of the better design and exposing the owner to all the shocks, faults, and stresses of the lesser model.

See, cyborgs have their Thomas Aquinases too. Though I'd been told, practically from the first day I went into the field, that all that was nonsense and it was actually really okay to sleep with mortals. Nothing to it at all.

It's very important to give young operatives the straight dope, you know?

You can imagine that after a miserable interlude Nicholas and I crawled out of the gallery and walked away down the corridor. He turned suddenly to stare at me. His eyes were red-rimmed and swollen with crying. I had expected them to be bewildered too; they weren't. There was a clear, cold place in them, a country of ice I'd seen at a distance before. No distance now. "In this life," he said, "we must be on our guard."

"Yes," I replied uncertainly.

Terrible music was beginning to play, an anthem for that frozen land; but a door down the hall opened, and Sir Walter emerged.

"Nicholas!" he said. "We must speak, now."

"Right gladly." Nicholas turned on his heel and advanced on Sir Walter so rapidly, and drawing himself up so tall and ominous, that Sir Walter shrank back a little. He retreated through the doorway, and Nicholas followed him in.

I had no urge to go and listen to them. For the first time in a long while, I badly needed the company of my own kind.

This sentiment lasted until I got to Nef's room. Opening the door, I beheld Joseph bounding up and down in place like a rubber imp on a string.

"The son of a bitch! The ungrateful, dressed-up chimpanzee! The rotten little two-timing descendant of Saxon drag queens!"

"Ignore him." Stonily Nefer turned a page of her magazine.

"Ignore me?" Joseph screamed. "IGNORE ME? YOU GO RIGHT AHEAD AND IGNORE ME, MISS TUTANKHAMEN! I'M ONLY GETTING A LITTLE AGGRAVATION OUT OF MY SYSTEM!"

I put my hands over my ears. The unicorn buried its head in Nef's skirts.

"Ah! Ah! Ah!" Joseph went right on bounding with the precision of a jackhammer. "I'll kill him! I'll give him cavities and postnasal drip! I'll rig his autonomic nervous system so he does something painfully embarrassing every time he sneezes!" He stopped, staggering slightly as an idea hit him. "Where's the black hellebore? Where's the nux vomica? Is *he* ever going to get a bedtime cocktail tonight!"

"You're upset about the mission with everything else that's just happened?" I wept. "The Parliament selling out to Cardinal Pole? The Church getting all those awful powers again?"

"Yes, I'm upset about the mission, and so should you be!" Joseph rounded on me. "It's in jeopardy thanks to Little Sir Walt, and after months of cleaning out his lousy arteries, this is the thanks I get? Now I have to completely renegotiate the contract with the new owner, which is going to cost the Company money, which is going to reflect badly on me, although you still get to collect your Furbish's lousewort or whatever so what do you care? I guess it's just too much to hope that you might be providing your poor facilitator and group leader with sympathy, understanding, and commiseration. Hell, not you! You're in shock because the monkeys are throwing coconuts at each other! We told you mortals did stuff like this, didn't we? What did you learn at school, anyway? How can you have come out of the dungeons of the Inquisition and still be surprised by anything they do?"

"You were surprised by Sir Walter," remarked Nef.

"Jesus H. Christ, was I ever." Joseph collapsed on a settle. "The nerve. The consummate nerve of the guy. We had a deal! So now he's going to sell the property and go into politics at Court, is he? Well, he'll be sorry he crossed me. I wouldn't accept that marriage proposal if I were you, baby."

"Oh, I don't know." Nef laid down her magazine and looked at him. "I don't particularly want to go to Court. Maybe I can talk him out of it. Maybe I can make him buy a cattle ranch."

"They don't have ranches in England," I said. She shrugged.

"Well, you'd have to watch him around the clock," said Joseph bitterly. "The guy has no loyalty to anything. Can you beat it? After he gave me his knightly word of honor, too. How could he do this to me? I mean, his garden was his whole life!"

"My God, can't you see why?" I cried. "You pumped hormones and who knows what else into him, you gave him his youth back, and now it's not just his old clothes that don't fit, it's his old life! That's why he wants a change. Blame yourself!"

"Hey! I only met his price for what we wanted." Joseph glared at me. "And his price was youth, which shows he was restless already."

"I thought the Indian maize was his price."

"That was the official price." Joseph examined his fingernails.

"What?"

"Bureaucratic levels of reality," said Nef. "Don't worry about it."

I looked from one to the other.

"Are we . . . are we really good for humankind?" I wondered for the first time.

"Sure we are, honey."

"But everything that little man valued in life we turned to dust for him. Before we came, he didn't mind about getting old. Did we really have any right to step in and change him?"

"Wait, wait, wait. Hold it right there. We didn't just step in and change him without his permission. The dissatisfaction with life was already there in his tiny mind. We only give people what they want, and usually what's good for them. I did what any doctor would do."

"If a sixteenth-century doctor had the technology," put in Nef.

"But you can't make a values call on whether or not I should have let him stay a sick old man," continued Joseph. "Even if the guy could see it objectively the way we can, do you think for a second he wouldn't have made the same choice? There isn't a mortal born that won't try to cheat Father Time."

"But he made the wrong choice."

"Did he? Are you going to make his choices for him? That's a violation of his natural rights, kiddo. Don't forget that mortals have free will. They traded their Paradise for it, and they can jump into manure up to their necks if they choose to. We don't care. We're not here to make them happy, we're not here to make them prosperous, we're not here to help them on the road to self-realization. We're here to do business for the Company.

"Sir Walters and Nicholases are out there everywhere. But your *Ilex tormentosum* is so rare, it's only growing in one place in the whole world. If it wasn't for the work you've been doing, it would become extinct, when we know it has properties that can save a billion mortal lives. Isn't that, morally, worth the happiness of one old man?"

"But . . ." Unpleasant light had begun to dawn on me. "Because of what we did for Sir Walter, he's sold the garden to Master Darrell. What if Master Darrell decides to cut down the ilex and replace it with something he thinks is more exotic, after we've gone? Then the ilex will be extinct, except for what the Company has. But Sir Walter would never have sold the garden if we hadn't come and messed with him. What are we doing to cause and effect, here? Does the Company really know what it's doing?"

"Of course it does," said Joseph instantly. "And if you worry about this, you'll drive yourself nuts. Really."

"Just take it on faith, I always say," Nef told me. "I mean, everything works out in the end anyway, doesn't it? We know the ilex becomes extinct, because there isn't any in the future except what the Company has. So you must have saved it. So why ask questions?"

"Believe me, Mendoza, there are better minds than yours grappling with this."

"All the time, honey. Do yourself a favor, don't get metaphysical."

"Really."

So I backed away from the void, which was a very deep and very dark void indeed, doubtless chock-full of unhappiness for anyone unwisely peering into it for too long. And what is worse, for an immortal being, than unhappiness?

Joseph got to his feet. "Once again, poor little Joseph finds himself having to hand out sage advice and counsel to younger operatives when he'd rather be crying into his pillow. Does anyone care? Fat chance. I'm going to have myself a glass of sherry and access all the information I have on A) freemasons and B) hair restoration, and then I'm going to review the microsurgery I was planning to do on the little shit tonight. I hope, I just fervently hope and pray, that I can keep an open and forgiving mind. It sure would be terrible if I connected some of his nasty organic pipes wrong. Or, better yet, planted some exotic disease cultures in timed-release capsules in his gluteal muscle sheath. Boy, now *there's* an idea . . .'' He went into his room and slammed the door.

"He's so dramatic." Nef picked up her magazine again.

"Are you really planning to marry Sir Walter?" I wanted to know.

"Oh, gee, no," she said. "He's kind of cute—now—but I don't think the Company would okay it."

"You'd have to ask the Company first?"

"Of course, Mendoza. So they could see if his proposal was advantageous to them, so they could analyze whether my tour of duty would be compatible with a life with him, so they could evaluate granting him higher security clearance. Frankly, though, after what he just did, I don't think there's a chance in Hell he'd be approved. Doctor Zeus doesn't like double-dealers."

"You don't mean Joseph is really going to poison him!" I was aghast.

"No, no, of course not. That almost never happens." She became fascinated by her magazine. "Hey, can you beat this? The whole Bogart canon is coming out as a set on Ring compatible! We're getting it for thirteen point seven. Isn't that fabulous?"

"Real neat," I said wearily.

But I was young then and had yet to appreciate the wisdom of Bogart, particularly as regards the problems of three little people not amounting to a hill of beans in this or any other crazy world.

20

NOTHING WAS THE same anymore.

Sir Walter called his entire household together and gave them the news about the sale first. That their religion had just been changed was nothing to them compared with the shock of losing their jobs; they had never been a particularly devout household anyway. There was a private chapel at Iden Hall, dusty and disused, but it had furnished Sir Walter and his people with an excuse for not going to church every Sabbath.

No longer. Almost at once the order went out: Mass was to be celebrated in every church in every village in England, with one hundred percent attendance expected. In each parish a ledger was to be kept with the names of the persons who did not attend, and that ledger was to be turned over to the agents of the bishops, agents sent to each church to ensure the conformity of its flock. Whoever did not attend Mass would be flogged or given other suitable chastisement and returned to the care of the village priest. Those persons found to be resolute heretics would be burned, after a trial proved guilt.

Simple? Straightforward? See how easy it is to restore the true faith to a country? You just have to be firm. There weren't even any Jews to hunt for.

Well, it certainly would have worked in Spain. Doubtless in many parts of France too. But this was England, practically the home of civil disobedience. It has always seemed bizarre to me that the race that invented the tea cozy should also so resolutely refuse ever ever to be slaves.

So the English refused, at first, though of course they surrendered in the end. In one village a man realized that he could settle an old

score with a neighbor by reporting him to the bishops' men for
heretical opinions. Somewhere else, a man terrified of being betrayed
sought to save himself by confessing, and in doing so implicated most
of his family and friends.

The old story, at least to a Spaniard. All the same, it took the
English a little longer than most to light their fires.

It was decided that the household would be kept together for some
months, while all the legal details of the transaction were arranged.
During that time everyone was to go to Mass on Sundays, on pain of
being discharged immediately.

Nicholas flatly refused. There was a terrible scene in Sir Walter's
private chamber, and I don't know what they said, because I turned
up the volume on the radio to drown them out; but they emerged with
the agreement that Nicholas would remain at Iden Hall for as long as
it took to prepare the inventory and financial records for the sale.

"I am not to speak with more folk than is needful, nor am I to
arrange anymore with the butcher or greengrocer. Master Ffrawney
shall see to that. Neither shall I conduct the penny-paying guests on
the Walks Historical, Botanical, or Zoological." Nicholas paused and
squinted at the sky. "Not that I expect any penny-paying guests for
months, if this weather hold."

We were walking in the garden. It was raw and ugly as only
January in England can be; but it smelled better outdoors than in the
house.

He had changed, my Nicholas; he had grown pale. The early-
morning bloodlessness was with him all the time now.

"What shall we do?" I sighed.

"Why, what you shall do I know not. Truth to tell, I know not
mine own course neither." He wrapped his hands in his frayed sleeves
for warmth. "I must trust in God."

"You could do that in Frankfurt," I suggested. He fixed me with
a cold look, askance down his high cheekbones, that made my heart
beat fast. For days I had been trying to talk him into fleeing to safety.

"Setting aside the risk I should run of arrest," he said, "there
remains the question of expense."

"That could be arranged," I hinted. His look of scorn deepened.

This is the time to rehearse the wise and careful speeches about
parting, those slick ways to begin the end. This is when you need to
tell yourself, and then tell him, how natural it is to grow in different
directions, and that it doesn't mean failure, it doesn't mean love is

any less. All that beautifully phrased bullshit, over nerves screaming for release. But God help you if no such speech comes into your head, and you cling to the sullen rock of his shoulder in the night ocean.

"Your father must be dismayed by the sale of the house." Nicholas looked away again.

"He is." I did not take my eyes from his face. "And the new laws make him afeared. We shall not stay in this place much longer."

"Shall you not? Where shall you go?"

"If we went to Frankfurt, would you come?"

"Your father has no need of a secretary, I think."

We walked on in that winter pattern of hedges and lanes without another word.

And now the news. And it's grim, we regret to say: today England's first official victim of the Counter-Reformation was burnt at Smithfield. John Rogers, Canon of Saint Paul's, long-time Reformation agitator and translator of the Matthew Bible, died in the presence of his wife and children in a ceremony lasting twenty-five minutes. Your news team had an operative on the scene and, Diotima, can you tell us about it?

Well, Reg, you know I've been in the field a long time, and I've been there for most of the big events of the Tudor regime, but let me say right now this hits a new low. This is on a par with the day the old Countess of Salisbury was executed—

You were there that day, weren't you?

Yes, Reg, and frankly I thought that was pretty bad, I mean, the old woman was running around on the scaffold trying to escape and they had to physically drag her to the block—

And it's, uh, interesting that the countess was Cardinal Pole's mother. Wouldn't you say that incident is the motivation for many of his policies now? Could you say he's settling scores with the Reformation in a deeply personal way?

Undoubtedly, Reg. Anyway, I was there today, and let me tell you operatives listening in: these people are animals. There is not a doubt in my mind. Sick animals.

And now we had to go to Mass again, after happy months of neglect. Once again miserable journeys through Sunday rain, to file into a dear quaint village church of local stone and arctic atmosphere. Lots of bare whitewashed walls, and a priest very nervous and imperfect in his Latin. Nonetheless, it was standing room only, and the wretched faithful, packed in like sardines, were only too glad to be seen there. On prominent display by the pulpit was a great big book, and you can bet it had nothing to do with Common Prayer. Nearby sat an alert gentleman in nondescript clothes, who conferred often with the priest. After these conferences, the priest mixed up his tenses and endings even more, and the gentleman made many notes in a smaller book he kept in his doublet.

For once, I was not bored at Mass. The mortal population for miles around was crammed into that quaint little church, and you could have floated an armada on the high waves of emotion there. Our arrival occasioned a particularly heady gust, of course, as the Evil Spaniards, particularly when Sir Walter accompanied us with every single member of his household but one.

"Why, Sir Walter, you are well met," said one of our Christmas visitors as we sidled in.

"Aye, forsooth, friends, I hope I am as pious and conformable a man as any in England," answered Sir Walter, loud and firm.

"I do not see your tall fellow," remarked someone else.

"No, alack." Sir Walter looked straight ahead and made a passable sign of the Cross. "The poor man is grievous sick."

"Alack, indeed. And is he expected to live?"

"Sir, I scarcely know."

Everyone turned and looked knowingly at everyone else; then everyone turned cold gazes back to the Spanish visitors, as though it were *our* fault.

The unfortunate Canon Rogers was followed to the stake by Bishop John Hooper. There was a live broadcast from Gloucester, and I had to run out of the room before it was over. His executioners botched the job: they used wet wood, and green wood, and at the last the poor old bastard left off his prayers and screamed for more fire, because only his legs were burning.

As the days went by, a butcher was burned alive, then a barber, then a weaver, and more common folk followed them to the fire. The prisons began to fill with the condemned from all ranks, all classes. It was true that some died political deaths, old scores from the previous reign settled at last. But most people were dying for things like being seen reading their Bibles, or even for only listening to the Bible being read.

The Spanish were bewildered. In Spain the Holy Inquisition was a gloomy duty, propelled along by the riches it brought the Holy Office from the confiscated property of the condemned. That was easy to understand: who wasn't motivated by profit? But how to explain the brutal zest with which these country constables dragged penniless apprentices to martyrdom? What to make of reverend old bishops fighting like Punch and Judy, squalling curses at each other from their respective sides of the flames? It was all so *personal*.

Even our prince decided that he'd had enough of this crazy country, and gave the order that all his remaining countrymen were to get themselves home to Spain.

No escape for us synthetic Spaniards, though. Too much to do. There was another thaw and more rain; all manner of splash and trickle ran everywhere, and blind green shoots found their way up to the sun. My work began again. I was mostly alone in the garden now, Nicholas being kept indoors. Sometimes the old gardener appeared, tramping about with sacking and a shovel, but he would neither speak nor look at me. That suited me fine. My loathing for mortals was growing like the garden.

I took blossom and cutting of an apple men would not taste again for centuries, until it was—will be—rediscovered in Humboldt Province. I took wildflowers, tiny ephemera of the hedgerows: soon men would know them only through images in tapestries, their names would be forgotten, and there would come a day when even hedgerows themselves would be plowed under by an England that no longer remembered what it was. But when the industries have come and gone, the little flowers will seed and bloom again. Men will not even notice they've returned; but the land will know. This is the purpose of my life.

Men burned; flowers were rescued.

It was all drawing to a close. Nicholas spent his days with the documents for the sale, long hours drawing up inventories of goods. All the furnishings were to be sold; all the plate was to be sold. The cabinets of curiosities and the tapestries were to be sold. All the careful gathering of a lifetime was to go for ready cash. If Sir Walter had been dead, it would have been very sad, but since he was selling his own dreams, nobody felt anything. Nicholas woke me muttering in his sleep: "*Item*, one salver of Italian plate. *Item*, one pair of bronze candlesticks, representing satyrs . . ."

One day, when he was at work, someone went into his room and took all his books away. I saw white smoke billowing from the kitchen chimney, smelled burning paper, never guessing that his translations of Saint Paul were cooking dinner. He never guessed either, until we opened his door that evening.

What a surprise. What petty devastation: flakes of wax, chips and flattened beads of candle wax, scattered all over the bare table. Moth wings. Great square vacancies in the dust of the tabletop, and a broken candle lying on the floor, wrenched from its drippy socket between two volumes. But no volumes. All that crazy-tumbled pyramid of thought and argument was gone.

We just stood and stared by the light of the new candle we had brought. When it sank in that practically everything he owned was so much ruffled ash in the kitchen grate, I was the one who broke down and cried, and wanted to go accuse somebody. Nicholas was too stunned to hear my tempest. He wandered over to the table and stood looking down at the place where his books had been. There was a long stream of wax lying there, a solid river broken off at its source. He picked it up and turned it in the light, examining it intently.

Finally he said, "Wherefore art thou angered?"

I stared through my tears. "Thy books are burnt!" Get red in the face, Nicholas, please, storm downstairs and grab Master Ffrawney by the throat.

He shook his head.

"It is a sign. One more test. The Word of God is not so much paper and calfskin. These gross forms have been destroyed. Perhaps this is to signify that I loved them too much. Perhaps I sinned in pride, having so many books."

This kind of talk terrified me. I went across the room to him, to physically close the gulf I could feel opening between us. There was something glinting on the bit of wax he held; I looked at it closely and saw it was a moth. Its charred body was trapped in the frozen flow of tallow, legs clumped all askew, and the powdery wings that stuck out were shredded and broken.

How cold that room was.

You must understand that I would not sit there and watch. Mortals can make a poetry of death; they have to. What is too horrible to look in the face must have a mask. Still, mortals have the urge to pull away that mask, as the stupid girl does in the film, and the angry specter jumps out roaring.

We are not like that. No romantic Death for us. Like cockroaches or mold, he must be driven out: spray for him, scour him away, put him out in the sunlight. Unclean.

I made a plan.

"Joseph." I opened his door. He looked up at me unfocused: he had a ring holo made like a pair of spectacles on his nose and was relaxing with a film. "We have to talk."

"We do, huh?" He sighed and switched off the holo. Folding it up, he put it in his doublet and pulled out a stick of Theobromos. "Mood elevant?" He offered it to me.

"No, thanks."

He shrugged and commenced peeling the silver paper off one end.

"How soon before we leave here, Joseph?"

"That's up to you, isn't it? Sit down. How long before you've taken as much as is worth taking out of the garden?"

"Only a few weeks. I'll have a complete growing cycle on the ilex by then, and enough samples on everything else for full in-lab reconstruction."

"Say a month, then." He leaned back and put the end of the stick in his mouth. "Sooner, if you can manage it, because in case you haven't been listening to the news, the rest of the Spaniards are ditching the joint. It would be nice if you and I could do likewise. Save us the cost of paying off Master Darrell, too."

"What about Nef?"

"She's going to HQ, and they're finally sending her north with a new cover."

"Oh." I got up and paced. "Well, look; I need you to do something for me."

"Oh really?" He raised his eyebrows. "What?"

"Save Nicholas."

"He'll die, Mendoza," Joseph said. "Eventually. They all do. You know that."

"But he doesn't have to die now. Not while he's a young man. He has no idea how dangerous it is here now, he won't listen to reason, and I've talked to him until I'm going crazy trying to get him to flee to Zurich or somewhere safe. He won't listen to me. This is why you have to help me."

"I have persuasive charms, baby, but I'm not that good."

"Like hell you're not. I know what you are. You can sell anything."

"Mendoza, people have to want to be saved. Did you want to die in Santiago? No. Did Sir Walter want to get old and sick? No. Do you understand what I'm trying to tell you? What can I offer this guy? Big healthy buck in the prime of life like him. He doesn't like me, he doesn't trust me, and if a nubile little thing like you can't make him catch a fast boat to the Continent for his own good, I've got a feeling that I too shall argue in vain."

"I'm not asking you to argue with him. Look, I have it all worked out. Give me a drug that will make him look dead."

"You mean like in *Romeo and Juliet*?" Joseph was incredulous.

"Just like that. Slip him the drug just before we're ready to leave, do the coffin trick, and smuggle him out with us when we go. Keep him on life support until we get to Europe, leave him in an inn in Zurich, where he can wake up with a headache and no memory of how he got there. But he'll have a purse of Swiss gold. And I'll never see him again, Joseph, I promise."

"Mendoza, did you ever see the movie? The poison bit didn't work out so well. All kinds of stuff could go wrong with your plan. I might miscalculate the dosage."

"You wouldn't."

"This is a plan dreamed up by a desperate person."

"Is there any reason it positively wouldn't work? Huh?"

"Where do you think I'm going to get a drug like that? I don't exactly keep a box of them under my bed. Oh, a Juliet special? Yes, I just whipped up a batch."

"You *can* make a batch. You must know a formula. Give me a list of what you need, and I'll get everything."

"Mendoza . . . I'll try. Okay? I can't guarantee anything, and I wish you wouldn't get your hopes up about this—"

"You can do it." I thumped him on the shoulder. His stick of Theobromos broke, and he looked at me reproachfully, but I was already exiting on a wave of confidence.

So that was my plan.

Actually, that was only one of my plans, but they all began: *As soon as I get Nicholas out of here . . .*

21

THE DAYS WENT by as I clipped and dug and collected.

Sir Walter proposed to Nef and was refused with a great deal of tact and charm. She told him she was too old for him (certainly true), too poor, and anyway had been betrothed since childhood to an hidalgo of Castile who had sailed away to the New World. Though the hidalgo had never returned, doubtless slain by savages somewhere, honor compelled her to wait for him. This news was received with great dismay by Sir Walter, but his tears were in vain. He became resigned; he let her keep the unicorn as a symbol of their lost love. It was pretty obviously a goat now anyway, both little horns poking out bravely; and thus Sir Walter could be gallant and rid himself of an embarrassment at the same time. Within a day he had convinced himself that there were plenty of wealthy noblewomen in England who'd fall for him.

One day it rained. And the next day it rained, and the next. Then it rained again. Venturing into the garden meant sinking ankle-deep in wet leaf mold (a substance found only in the British Isles, thank God), so I opted to stay indoors and watch Nicholas take inventory.

Rain pattered down, and light came gray and watery through the windows of the great hall. I sat on the staircase hoping to avoid the drafts, my skirts all tucked up around my ankles, and helped Nicholas with the inventory list. Chin on fist, I watched as he crawled up and down the stepladder before an enormous curio case. How bleak and unforgiving the light, picking out every threadbare place in his black robe. No new livery for him now: Sir Walter wasn't going to waste the money.

"*Item*, one head of a Scots king," he announced.

"Thou liest!" I lowered my quill to stare.

"There." He pointed to the topmost shelf, and I looked up to meet the blind stare of very former majesty. The man had died young: had very good teeth and a lot of red hair and beard, still bushy.

"What is he doing here?" I looked away and jotted the entry.

"Little enough nowadays, I warrant you. *Item*, one head of a queen." He reached to the back of the shelf and pulled it out for me to see. "Supposed to be Queen Guenevere."

"Who supposes so?" I jeered. "That's a man's skull with a yellow wig glued on't!" A Roman man, to be exact, about fifty years of age and dead of—plumbism? No. I scanned deeper and found the flint projectile point. Poor old centurion. I hoped my tour of duty in Britain turned out better than his had.

"This was a man? So these are not the locks caressed by Arthur? Well, farewell Sir Walter's two pound tenpence. He ought to have known it were no true queen's head at that price. Though mind you"—he put it back and moved down another shelf—"there was a time when queens' heads went for less in this land.

"Now, Rose, make a new heading of Popish Impostures—" He halted. "Nay, I see I am too slow. Someone hath been and changed the sign in this case. Rather write, Holy Relics Miraculously Preserved from the Late Heretics. *Item*, fifteen pieces of the true Cross. *Item*, six crystal vials of the blood of Christ, with lead stoppers. *Item*, seven glass vials of the same. *Item*, a finger of Saint Winifred. *Item*, a finger of Saint Ethelbert. *Item*, a toe of Saint Cuthbert, with an otter's tooth affixed therein. *Item*, a tooth of Saint Ascanius."

He climbed down and came to sit beside me, shaking from an urge to laugh or cry. "A trove the Pope himself must envy. Yet I tell you, Sir Walter bought them cheaply when the monasteries were broken up. For a long while there was a card whereon was writ large how these were counterfeits made by greedy monks to rob honest Englishmen."

"One of those fingers is a chicken bone." I put my arm around him. A couple of the little bones actually did show a faint spectrum of Crome's radiation, though, so maybe they were the true toes of saints after all.

But there were footsteps. A door opened, and people came into the great hall. Sir Walter, Joseph, and Master Darrell. Joseph was saying:

"Now, having compounded this, you must rub it well into your scalp—" They noticed us sitting there. Joseph gave me a tiny apologetic shrug, and Master Darrell doffed his hat to me, courteous fellow. But Sir Walter strode forward and said:

"How now, Nicholas, not finished yet? I would have this abstract done afore next Christmas, boy."

He had been such a charming little old man. What a bastard he was, young.

"You bid me be exact, sir, and there is much to account for." Nicholas bowed slightly.

"Well, thou must be precise. Look you, Master Darrell, here are wonders indeed. Where is the sword of Charlemagne, Nicholas?"

"Sword of Charlemagne?" Nicholas frowned.

"What, art turned parrot? Tell me where it is, boy. Ha! I see it there. Look up, Master Darrell, it is the French Caesar's very blade." He pointed to a sword mounted on the wall high above the case. Nicholas consulted his list. Sir Walter went on: "This same blade, sir, was presented to our late King Henry Fifth, when he did conquer France. It came into this country, I am told, when—"

"That's the sword of Roland, sir." Nicholas looked up.

"When—what?"

"It is Roland's sword. Not Charlemagne's."

Sir Walter's eyes quite popped with annoyance. "I think I know mine own goods, boy. That is the sword of Charlemagne. Roland had a horn, Charlemagne had a sword."

"With respect, sir, the horn of Roland is in the second cabinet in the east gallery, and this is Roland's sword. You bought them both from a peddler in Wapping. Charlemagne's—"

"God's blood, must I prove it to thee? I see I must." With a great show of impatience, Sir Walter seized the stepladder and bounded up to the top. The sword was still well out of his reach, though, so he got up on top of the cabinet and stood cautiously.

"Sweet Jesu, sir, have a care!" cried Master Darrell.

"Aye, aye." Sir Walter turned unsteadily and looked out at us all: couldn't resist the urge to see what the view was like from up there, I guess. I wondered briefly if he could see into the minstrels' gallery.

He remembered why he was there and grabbed for the sword. "Here! Now thou shalt see—" But it was only hanging between two sixpenny nails and came loose sooner than he expected and plummeted downward. He jumped back, nearly fell, as with a hiss the sword dropped behind the cabinet and thunked into the baseboard. Nicholas looked disdainful. I had to hide my face in my hands to keep from snickering, and it was well I did, for little Sir Walter grew as furious as a cat up there on his hands and knees.

"Why was that not hung more securer?" he cried. "I might have been killed, thou fool! And now we must move the cabinet to have the sword back again!''

"Peace, sir, another time,'' soothed Master Darrell. "I am certain it was Charlemagne's sword, none other.''

"It must be got out!''

"We shall have some of the household move the cabinet later, my friend.'' Joseph came and steadied the ladder. "But descend now, I pray you, lest you fall.''

"We shall have it moved *now*, and I shall prove to thee . . .'' Reckless in his anger, Sir Walter scrambled to his feet again. Bad move. He overbalanced and tottered. To avoid falling, he threw himself backward against the wall. His feet pushed at the top of the cabinet, and it toppled slowly outward. I screamed, and the men shouted, for Joseph was standing underneath.

Now, a scene in slow motion:

Joseph's eyes met mine. It wasn't that he couldn't get out of the way in time: we had both been alerted when the center of gravity began to shift. He could have been safe on the stair beside me in that first fraction of a second after the cabinet started falling. But there were two mortals staring fixedly at him, who would have seen him blink out.

My God, what are you going to do?

Make it look good. Cross your fingers.

As artifacts and pieces of saints began to rain down on him, Joseph found the exact place of least momentum, lightest impact; positioned himself there, threw up his arms, and waited. Crraassh, it came. A mortal man would have been broken like a matchstick. Joseph, though, took the weight and folded with it, telescoped and bent like a spring but did not crush. Nothing can shatter our cyborg skulls. BOOM. Dust settling.

Normal time again. Sir Walter sprawled amid cobwebs, fractured in a few places, but nobody was paying him any heed because I was screeching fit to wake the dead, frantically clawing at the cabinet. Nicholas and Master Darrell were beside me at once, and some of the servants ran in, and by combined effort we hoisted the cabinet up about two feet. I let go at once and flung myself underneath, ruining my hoops.

"Rose!''

Joseph looked like a cubist painting. He unfolded as I slithered to him.

Damage?

Pull me out.

I got him by the shoulders and pulled, and he swore, but I backed out rapidly with him. When we emerged, he feigned unconsciousness. Kneeling beside him, I wrung my hands and lamented in Spanish, while the following subvocal conversation was going on:

Damage?

Soft tissue injuries, multiple, minor. Right ankle sprained. Right wrist sprained. Left shoulder sprained, separated, massive hematoma—

Here comes Nef.

Have you got—

Yes. What dosage?

Six point three.

Beside me Nef joined in the hysterics, seizing Joseph's face in her hands and neatly pressing the drug patch into place behind his ear.

Better. Thanks.

"Oh, Jesu, is he slain?" Sir Walter staggered up, looking ghastly pale. I could hear Nicholas shouting for someone to fetch a surgeon. Joseph turned his head and moaned feebly. Nef shrieked her joy that he was alive and began to pray. I cried out that it was a miracle, blessed be the Holy Virgin and Saint James, et cetera. Nicholas crouched down beside me.

"Sir, can you hear me? We have sent for a surgeon. All will be well."

"A surgeon?" Joseph's eyes flew open.

"He speaks!" Master Darrell bent close. "Master Doctor, it is God's mercy you yet live. We thought you smashed like an apple."

"No, God be thanked," Joseph murmured. "But let me have no surgeons—I pray you!"

"But sir, your hurts must be seen to," protested Nicholas.

"My daughter shall tend to me. Have I not taught her physick?" Joseph tried to sit up and gave a cry of real pain.

"Peace, Father, all shall be as you wish," I reassured him. Nicholas stared at me, and I gave him my most beseeching look. So he helped make a litter out of a tapestry and a pair of boar spears and carried Joseph up to our rooms. Once Joseph was set down, Nef chased everyone else out of the room so we could get most of his clothes off him.

What a mess. He looked like a peach that hadn't been packed in excelsior before it was shipped, and was subsequently dropped and stepped on. Pulpy devastation. A veritable field of blossoming purple. Even as we watched, though, he was healing. Bruises roiled beneath his skin, spread, changed color, faded like clouds across the sky at sunset.

"Kind of pretty, isn't it?" Nef surveyed him.

"Shut up," he groaned.

"Oh, you're doing fine. The sprains are binding back up, aren't they? I think the swelling's even going down. That shoulder's going to give you trouble, though. I had one once like that and it took most of a week to heal."

"Is that all." Joseph writhed.

"We'll put a fake splint on the arm." Nef turned to me. "He can wear a sling to immobilize that side. If we were at HQ, they could go in and staple him up right now, but out here—gee. These things can be awfully tedious when they happen in the field." Her unicorn wandered in and tried to jump up on the bed.

"Keep that thing out of here!" railed Joseph. "And that goes double for their damned surgeon. Leeches biting me, that's all I need."

"Fuss, fuss, fuss."

"I'm in pain, dammit!"

"Not like you'd be if you were a mortal," Nef pointed out.

"If I were a mortal, I wouldn't be feeling anything because I'd be dead now," Joseph snapped.

"There art thou happy," Nef told him cheerily.

By the time we got the splint on him, the bruises had all but disappeared. I left him in bed watching a holo and went out to see if I could help clean up the wreckage downstairs. I found Nicholas waiting just outside the door.

"Shall he live?"

"Aye, Saint James be praised for a miracle."

He came close to me. "Yet thou hast no belief in Saint James, nor in miracles neither. If there had been no miracle and thy father had been killed, what then? Hast thou any family but him? Any friends?"

"None," I replied. "If my father were slain, I should be alone in this foreign land. I have no husband, nor am I like to."

He leaned down and kissed me. What a long, lovely, lose-your-balance kiss. We hadn't kissed like that in weeks.

Say you'll come away with me! But though he held tighter, he didn't say it.

"What of the case of relics?" I gasped, when we came up for breath. "There was fearful disarray there. Ought we not to sweep it up?"

"Let Sir Walter go picking in the dust for his trash," he growled. "I have done with him."

I threw my arms around his neck and hugged tight. He made a harsh sound and we fled away, up to his room.

I was certain I'd won. People who struggle with their consciences and triumph over them get a certain look on their faces, disappointment mingled with relief. They don't say much. I thought Nicholas's silence was a sure sign that he'd decided to do something wrong by his standards.

But he never did say he'd come away with me.

We spent the rest of the day in his room, being what used to be called wanton. I was thrilled, I was intoxicated. Everything would be all right. If only he would say something, though . . .

The rain stopped some time before twilight. A north wind came up, sharp and cold as crystal, and shredded away the clouds. It drove their rags far out to sea, so that a red sunset flared in through the windows, and later piercingly bright stars.

"Sweetheart, we should rise," I whispered at last. " 'Tis past the hour of six, surely. Folk will wonder where we are."

"We may burn in Hell for all they care," he said out loud. I jumped a little, it had been so quiet in that room.

"Maybe," I said. "But I must see how my father fares."

He nodded at that but made no move to get up with me as I rose and dressed. I left him there in drafty starlight and went down into the depths of the house.

Smoky and too warm: they had built up the fires. Supper cooking. I was so ravenous, I could have eaten the Christmas pie. There might well have been some left, bubbling away and evolving into a strange life-form on a forgotten shelf in the pantry.

It was quiet outside Nef's room: no radio on. I looked in on Joseph and found him wide awake in darkness. "Where's Nef?" I lit a candle.

"Down having supper," he replied. "Say, you wouldn't mind pouring me some sherry, would you? About three bottles?"

I looked around for a decanter and filled a glass. He took it in his good hand and tossed the drink back in one gulp.

"Are you still hurting that bad?" I looked at the empty glass in awe. He held it out for a refill, and I obliged.

"Wait'll you do this to yourself some day, little cyborg. Healing hurts. Pain and I are becoming old friends. It invites me over to watch football matches in holo, and we've loaned each other money. Old friends. Heck, yes, I sure do hurt." He chugged his drink again.

"Should you drink so much with the patch on?"

"Won't affect it. It's the shoulder that's giving me hell. Everything else healed right up. But the Pectoralises Major and Minor and a host of their neighbors have parted company with Mr. Clavicle. They need a mediator in a big way."

"I'm really sorry." I poked up the fire. "Can I get you anything?"

"Just another shot of amontillado. Listen, this is kind of going to put a crimp in my abilities to, uh, make secret knockout potions and so on . . ."

I grinned, pouring out his refill. "Don't worry about that. It may not be necessary. I think that issue's going to resolve itself real soon."

"No kidding?" He looked at me searchingly. "Somebody's listening to reason? Well, glad to hear it. Just the same, with my arm like this, I wouldn't want us to have to pack our bags and run for anywhere for at least a week. Keep that in mind, won't you? In case any of your plans involve dramatic departures."

"Hey, baby, trust me." I smiled and exited on that line.

Down the dark staircase into firelight. It occurred to me that in a month's time I might be in a different city, away from the rain and smoke and dark corridors of England. This cheered my heart so much, I danced a saltarello all the way to the bottom of the stairs and ran breathless into the great hall.

Same old tableau there, a few people more or less. Francis Ffrawney standing all self-important in new livery. Being a groveling toady had paid off in a big way. Sir Walter looking very stiff and uncomfortable and somehow suddenly older; nevertheless his beard wagged on implacably about something to Nef, who was nodding in boredom as she poked her spoon around in a dish of baked beans. She was a great listener, that woman.

As I came skipping in, they all turned to stare at me with varying degrees of the same expression of disapproval.

"God give you good evening, gentles." I curtseyed. "I am come lately from my father, who hath slept and waked with a rare appetite. Which portends (as Avicenna saith) a speedy recovery, God be thanked. Wherefore I would take him some new loaves of bread, some hot broth, perhaps a joint of beef or a chicken, and some strong ale . . . ?" Nef raised eyebrows at me, but Sir Walter waved his hand at Master Ffrawney.

"See to it, Francis. How now, Lady Rose, doth thy father so well? I am glad. I would not for the world have him miscarry in my house."

I felt a storm of giggling coming on. "Trust me, sir, his miraculous preservation was due to none other thing but the great abundance of holy relics of the saints that fell in profusion about him. Yea, surely, the very finger of Saint Ethelbert stood upright to ward off the terrible blow.''

Mendoza, you brat, watch your mouth.

"Say you so? It may be.'' Sir Walter nodded solemnly. ''I myself was shrewdly bruised, I fear, and want your father's physick much. But sit, child, and thou shalt hear how I have won a sharp bargain with Master Darrell . . .''

Yawn yawn yawn. The little weasel had got a clause put in the sale contract for a room to be set aside for his use, if he should ever come back to visit Iden Hall: the idea being that as a kind of celebrity exhibit himself, he deserved free bed and board. I could see how he had cleaned up in the wool trade all those years ago. He seemed ready to go on about the clause for hours, so when Master Ffrawney returned with a huge tray, I jumped up and took it from him.

"Señor, you are too kind. I shall away to my poor, dear father with this bounty at once. Yet though it be excellent wholesome, I believe it shall do him less good than your prayers.''

"Why, so we shall pray for him,'' Sir Walter called after me as I sped off. I paused long enough to curtsey again, didn't spill a drop of ale, and hurried on. I took the stairs two at a time. Fresh-baked bread, oh boy. Capon broth and a roasted capon too. Joseph blinked at me foggily as I set the can of broth beside him.

"Have some chicken soup,'' I said, snatching up his candle. ''Trade you.''

"Room service?'' he called, but I was already gone.

So at last back to Nicholas, who had put on his shirt and breeches and was sitting on the bed looking out at the little square of night sky. I set down the tray on the table where his books used to be; the candle danced and flared in the draft.

"Supper,'' I announced. He turned in the candlelight, and my heart lurched painfully. It was very strange, because this surge of love swept away all my merriment and left me feeling the need to hold him and cry. I rushed to him, blinking back tears.

"What, Rose, is thy father worse?'' He put his arms around me.

"No.'' I hid my face against him. ''But I am sick with love.''

He was silent a moment at that, stroking my hair.

"So am I,'' he said at last. ''Who shall heal us?''

"We haven't got the fever by the book.'' I wiped at my eyes. ''All this heat, all this sorrow should have come at the beginning. By now we should have been cool to each other and free of pain.''

"Would to God we were," he said. "And yet that's blasphemy, to rail at love. No more of this talk."

We had our little supper, crowded together at the table, while the draft ruffled the candle. We could hear the wild air prowling round and round outside, buffeting for a way in through the window. We didn't talk much. I watched him eat. Half dressed and unshaven as he was, he looked dissolute. Hard. I wondered what he'd have been like that way. There are plenty of gentlemen adventurers around, bastards by birth and inclination both. I'd have loved him anyway: better for him to have been a rogue like Tom than a righteous martyr. At least we wouldn't be sitting in this chilly room now, amid the ghosts of his books, in a fearful country.

Well, who knew? Maybe in a month's time we'd be in some other drafty little garret somewhere, sharing our bread by some other candle or by no candle at all. But we'd be free. Running together.

To the end of his tether.

That popped into my head so sudden and discordant, I scanned for Joseph, but he wasn't there. What a nasty thought. I'd have to learn to keep all such nasty thoughts well to the back of my mind in the future. We'd have forty years at least, and everything would be wonderful, wonderful. Love on the run through Renaissance Europe. Grand romance, as in the films. High adventure, and it was only just beginning.

At last Nicholas leaned back from the table and sat with his arms crossed, looking at me.

"Thy father," he said. "How long shall he lie abed until he heal?"

"Why, some days, surely," I said uncomfortably. Why did he want to talk about Joseph, now of all times? "He is hurt sore."

"Yet he would have no surgeon to tend him, but only thee," Nicholas mused. I knit my brows.

"Doctors have but poor opinion of each other. He trusts no physick but his own."

"But must he have thee by him the whole time he mends?"

Aha. "Nay, love, or I should have been by his side this whole while."

He nodded thoughtfully. "Couldst thou leave him?"

My soul leapt right up like the candle flame. I looked him straight in the eyes without smiling and said, "Aye."

We were going to elope after all. And what an opportunity: Joseph disabled and Nef absorbed in her radio and magazines. When might such a chance come again? Though I hadn't finished my work . . .

Nicholas got up and went to the window to peer out. The wind was higher; black branches whipped against the stars. "Well," he said, "it is no night for faring abroad. It is bitter cold, and all the lanes will be foul with mud."

"I fear no cold," I said at once. He looked over at me and smiled wryly.

"Nor I," he said. "But we should leave tracks in mud, and be followed."

Oh, right. Of course.

"Too wet to fare abroad." He came and leaned forward, taking both my hands. "But if this wind continues, it will dry out the roads soon. In some two days or three, one horse might bear two riders to the sea, leaving no mark of their passing."

Yes, a horse. How foolish I'd been to think of running out now just as we were. How clever he was at planning. Clearly this was going to work out well.

"Art thou fearful?" He leaned closer.

"I? Nay!" Was my face doing something I wasn't aware of? His eyes were a little sad.

"My Rose is scarlet sometimes, and other times white pale. Come to bed, sweetheart. Thou to rest, and I to think. It is a long way yet until morning."

A long way until morning.

I must finish this. I began it as a kind of therapy, and, like pulling one's own tooth, it becomes unbearable as the inevitable conclusion nears. But I find myself back in that room again, seeing that sad candle, that girl expecting a miracle. So let's finish it.

Joseph lay awake in pain, in darkness. The amontillado had long since been metabolized down to sugar and water, leaving him mercilessly sober. The capon broth was busy providing him with protein and hydrating vital tissues; but even its most enthusiastic proponents cannot claim that chicken soup is a narcotic.

"Screw this," he told himself at last. Groping one-handed, he pushed back the sheet and crawled out of bed. From beneath the bed he drew a slim wooden box, awkwardly thumbed the combination, and removed a small leather case. This he unrolled, and spread its contents out upon the counterpane.

Steel rods, the size of pencils. They had peculiar grips and buttons and tiny winking lights. He studied them for a long moment and hummed a little song to himself. It was a very old song. He had learned it as a child, and it evidently held some soothing association with a pleasant memory, for he had found that humming it helped him self-induce a light trance state.

After about five minutes of contemplation he got up and wandered around the room, slightly glassy-eyed. His little song was doing its trick. He found five wax tapers in a drawer and carried them to the hearth, where he crouched down and held the tips into the coals until they ignited. Light bloomed. He stood up and arranged the surface of his writing desk, sticking the tapers upright in a tankard, fanning them out. He found a mirror in his travel bag and propped it up in the candlelight. When he was satisfied with the arrangement, he took off his sling.

The humming had become a chanting now. With his good hand he collected the instruments and moved forward to regard himself in the mirror.

Pulse, slow. Heartbeat, slow. Respiration, very slow and deep. His right arm was warm and had good color, but the rest of his skin now was pale, especially over the left side of his chest. He depressed a button on an instrument, and there was a hiss, followed by a strong smell of cloves. He put down the instrument, took up another, and applied it to his shoulder. No blade was visible, but his skin parted in a long red line. He extended the line down in a semicircle, back and forth. His skin peeled back in a sheet, gradually exposing the musculature underneath.

There was no bleeding. As he worked, there were pinpoint flashes of green light. The chanting resolved into words, in a language long forgotten, about some boys with new spears who go down by the river to hunt bison but catch ducks instead, and take them back to their girlfriends who live under the cliffs, who are not impressed and won't dig garlic for them anymore . . .

It was dark where I was, except for the hole the fire shone through and the red red coals, and they gleamed in the priest's eyes but not in Joseph's where he watched in a corner. My eyes hurt. And I couldn't breathe. I tried to get out of the chair, but my hands were pinned straight through by the spines of holly leaves. Merry Christmas. Jesus Christ, said Joseph, they'll bury you alive.

"Rose!" The terrifying darkness faded into Nicholas's staring face. He had me by the wrists. "Rose, in God's name!" Only his room. Only England outside, with her buffeting wind and her stars wheeling late through the night. Only the candle, burned low through the hours so its big flame staggered like a drunkard.

"Los Inquisidores," I stated. I lay back down, and it began again at once, the fire, the darkness, the suffocation, and with a scream (silent, I had no breath) I fought my way back upright. Without another word Nicholas swung me out of bed and stood me on the cold floor.

"Walk with me." Three times around the room, and I was wide awake, shivering in my shift. It was clammy with sweat.

"I couldn't wake up," I explained. He helped me back to bed and sat beside me. My heart was hammering still, so loud he must have been able to hear it. Carefully he arranged the blanket and smoothed my hair back. He was shaking too, his face twisted by pity and revulsion.

"Thou hast dreamt of Spain."

"I did. I was there again. I was where they—they—"

He was not looking at me but at the shadows on the wall. "They killed thy mother."

"She wasn't!" I cried in panic.

"Ssh! 'Tis well, 'tis well. See, love, that was long ago. Thou art safe—" and he halted, because he couldn't really tell me that truly, could he? Not in this England. He got up to put on his breeches and shoes. I only watched him, too exhausted and confused to move. He went to the door, and I protested and stretched out a hand.

"Wait, love. I will fetch thee a posset," he promised.

Joseph, deep in his trance, became aware that someone was outside his door. His exterior consciousness began to return. Circled by the blaze of light from five waxen tapers, he turned around as the door opened.

I sat bolt upright. I hadn't screamed, I wasn't having a nightmare. But somebody was.

There was a horrendous crashing. The door flew open, and a figure hurled itself at me. That was too much for my nerves. I winked out.

I was across the room watching Nicholas fall on the bed. He got up slowly, staring at me, shocked forever. There was no color in his face at all. His eyes were like glass. He came at me. Again, I winked out.

I was on the other side of the room. He spun around and caught at me again.

I was standing on the bed. He came after me.

I was perched on the windowsill. He leaped.

I was on the ceiling, wedged into the angle of the beam where no human woman could ever have held on.

The chase ended there. He regarded me, panting. I regarded him, neither breathing nor moving. He took a step backward and collapsed. "Nicholas," I said in a tiny voice.

He sat up at once, fixing his gaze on me. Dragging himself backward until he reached the chest at the foot of his bed, he threw it open and fumbled inside. He pulled out a sword. So his books hadn't been his only possessions.

Gasping, he set his back against the wall and took the sword out of its sheath. He held it in both hands, the pommel resting on his drawn-up knees, the point directed at me. Neither of us moved for some few minutes, while the sound of his breathing grew quieter. How the wind roared and threatened to get into the room with us.

"What art thou?" he said at last.

To answer such a question, in such a position.

"Come, tell me, for I must know." His voice grew stronger.

I drew a deep breath. "I am not mortal."

"So much I'd guessed." He actually laughed, a low cold laugh. While I was fleeing him, his face had been like an animal's, almost unrecognizable. I thought he had gone mad. But he hadn't: his eyes were clear now and very, very hard. I moved an arm, and the sword point jerked up at me. "Nay, do not come down," he said sternly. "Whilst thou art up there, I cannot be persuaded this is a dream. Nor would I kill thee. Can I kill thee?"

"No," I informed him.

"No, not with a sword, if thou art a spirit." Looking at me steadily, he reversed the sword so that the cross-shaped hilt was toward me. When I did not flinch, he spun it back. "Ha! That's a fable. Thou hast worn crucifixes and read Scripture with me. So much for the devil in the old play. But I charge thee, Spirit, to tell what thou art."

"A spirit whose heart breaks," I said faintly. "A spirit who can bleed."

He glanced at the door, nervous. "True enough. Thy flesh is palpable, I know that well. Oh, God help me, that I suspected what thou wert and still loved thee. Thou wouldst scarce eat of our mortal bread. Thou hadst never seen snow nor frost. A hundred things betrayed what thou wert, and still I loved thee."

"I am still what I was," I pleaded.

"But the *world* has changed. What I have learned in this one hour—" His eyes widened. "To think I sought to save thy soul! And thou wert ever seeking after mine. Lord God, why hast thou shown me this fearful thing?''

"Nicholas, let me come down."

But he did not answer me, staring slack-jawed as revelation came to him. "Once," he said, "I betrayed the faith for the sake of my sinful flesh. The way to atonement has lain before me all this while, but I did not take it, for love of thee. I would have run away with thee and saved myself again. My flesh hath ever been mine enemy. And how sweet, how reasonable were thine arguments that led me to damnation! Nor could I have ever seen the trap, unless God made it plain. Which He hath done!''

He struggled to his feet, looking up at me. His face was shining, shining with fire.

"My love—for truly I may call thee so, since thy failure hath been my salvation—my love, thou hast lost. Return whence thou camest, and tempt me no more."

I think he expected me to vanish then, but I was in danger of falling on him, so racked with gripping were my arms and legs. "I can't go like that," I wept. "I have to climb down."

"Then I shall leave thee." He backed toward the door. "If I can. If I can get out of this house alive, I shall. And then the way lies clear and straight. Farewell, Spirit!''

He turned and bolted. I heard him thundering down the stairs, and then the screaming began: deep, full-throated screams of alarm in purest Castilian Spanish. I fell at last and scrambled to the doorway.

There was Nef down on the landing, immovable as rock in front of Joseph's door. She was in her shift, and her hair was down around her shoulders. She brandished a lighted candelabra at Nicholas, who was edging warily past her, holding out his sword.

"Murderer!" she howled. "Seducer! Lucifer incarnate!''

And I realized that doors were opening and people were running from all parts of the house to stare. Nicholas realized it too. He made a break and got past her, and, running to the edge of the great staircase, vaulted into space from the top step. Like a star he dropped out of the light, and I was sure the fall would kill him.

"Nicholas!" I ran shrieking.

He hit the floor below with a crash that shook the house. I sped after him, but Nef reached out and took my wrist in a grip of iron.

"Stop," she said quietly. And even as I sagged to the floor crying, I heard him get to his feet and run on, and there was a boom as the doors of the great hall were flung open. The wind was let into the house at last. Rejoicing, it swept up through that dusty place, bringing in the smell of a cold spring morning.

22

T HE STORY TOLD itself. Everyone had seen it happen. The duenna, steadfast and formidable; the wretched daughter in tears; the father pale as his sheet, a terrible wound in his shoulder, begging—for the honor of his family name—that no more should be said about this lamentable occurrence.

Several of the household offered to ride out and find Nicholas, that he might be hanged; though there were others who shrugged and spat, and whispered to one another that something terrible had been bound to happen sooner or later, with Spaniards in the house. Sir Walter told me I was an evil daughter and ought to be beaten soundly. He would gladly beat me himself if Doctor Ruy so wished. Doctor Ruy thanked him graciously but declined.

My own plan was to lie in the corridor where I had fallen and cry until the world ended. I was prevented from doing this by Nef, who dragged me into her room and shut the door after us. She then directed a shrill volley of Castilian abuse at me, which greatly edified the listeners outside. Joseph explained, and explained, and explained. When it began to grow light outside, everyone gave it up and went back to bed.

"It was just the worst luck in the world," Nef told me. "And I've seen some bad luck in my day. But, honey, the relationship couldn't have gone on anyway. We were leaving soon. He was about to be fired. This way there was a hell of a scandal, but at least our cover wasn't blown."

I listened without comment. Failing my plan to lie on the floor, I was perfectly content to lie in bed and cry until the world ended.

"Now, I know nothing I say helps," Nef went on. "You may not believe this now, but you're not the only person this has ever happened to, you know."

Great.

"And it could have been worse. What if I hadn't come out? What if he'd gone back in there and attacked Joseph? We'd have had to kill him then, and what a mess that would have been to cover up. Even if he talks about what he saw, wherever he is now, who's going to believe him? Half the servants are convinced they saw the whole thing just the way Joseph says it happened. So we're safe. Your reputation's a little soiled, but what the heck. You'll be out of here in another month."

I couldn't live that long.

"Hey, baby, what can I say?" Joseph shrugged, not easy with his arm in a sling. "I should have locked the door. My one mistake. Well, okay, I shouldn't have been doing self-repair in the field. But have you ever had a shoulder separation? You try living with a thing like that for a whole week. Really painful. Nothing like the pain I'd feel if I ever, ever thought you had some crazy idea about ditching the Company and running off with a mortal. Not that you *could*, of course; they built all sorts of subprograms into you to make you betray yourself if you ever tried dereliction of duty after all the money they spent on you. But you're a good little operative, I know you'd never do a thing like that. Say, did the guy happen to mention why he felt it was necessary to run back down with his sword to try and kill me?"

I didn't respond.

"I guess he thought I was kind of, like, the Devil or something, huh?"

I closed my eyes.

Joan entered the room as silently as a mortal can, and I lay with closed eyes pretending to be asleep. Do Not Disturb. But I didn't hear her pulling out dirty linen or pouring wash water, so after a moment I squinted through my lashes to see what she was doing.

She had an amulet of some kind and was waving it over our things: the baggage, the credenza, even the dirty linen. Her lips were moving in some kind of chant. She turned to look at me, and I saw her extend her hand in the old, old sign against evil, fingers pointed like a devil's horns. Then she crept out.

*　　*　　*

Well, I knew now conclusively: I could never have walked away and left Nicholas anywhere. It would have killed me. It was killing me now.

I slept and dreamed he had come back. It had all been a misunderstanding: everything was all right now. Somehow he had accepted the truth about me and didn't mind. We kept packing our belongings to go to Europe, but when I'd get to the door, he wouldn't be with me, and I'd have to go back and look for him.

I couldn't get warm. Nothing would warm the bed. I couldn't figure out what to do with my arms and legs while I slept, either.

"Hi there," said Joseph pleasantly, backing into the room. His arms were full of cut green twigs. "Beat it, goat." The unicorn skittered away from him and then came bleating back, looking for a handout.

"Whew. Now that the weather's warming up, maybe we can persuade Nef to keep Fluffy here outside." He dropped the twigs on my credenza. "So. You're probably wondering what I'm doing with all this shrubby stuff. Well, I knew you weren't feeling like doing any work or anything, but the garden's just greening away and I thought: Say, I'll bet I could take some of those specimens myself. All it involves is cutting off leaves and branches, right? Something like that. And what a good idea to speed things up when it's getting more dangerous to stay in this country every day. Not that I want to put any pressure on Mendoza, I told myself. So I just found a pair of clippers and hacked off a bunch of stuff I thought looked interesting."

I looked at what he had brought. Hacked was too mild a word. I shuddered to think what the plant must look like now.

"Yeah, I grabbed up a little of everything. Of course, I'm not a botanist, so I can't really tell what's important and what isn't, but I figured if I just kept slashing away, I'd get something we need. Now, let's see. How do you turn this thing on?"

He twisted a few knobs, and the console lit up with a warning beep.

"Gee, this must not be right. It's asking me if I want to override. Well, let's let it warm up a few minutes. I can just take the time to look through what I bagged and see if I got anything useful. Here's some of that ilex stuff, for instance."

What a ruin he'd made of the stem. Had he used his teeth, for God's sake?

"Yes, sir, this is pretty interesting. Really funky leaves and, uh, I guess this is a flower or something—"

"Let me see that." I put out my hand. He brought the twig. Florets like pale green wax, arranged alternately at the bases of the leaves. "Were they all like this?" I demanded.

"Could have been. I didn't notice; I'm not a botanist, you know that."

I swore softly.

"Is it important? Is it, like, the final all-important step in the growth cycle you've been holding us up here so you could get? Boy, wouldn't that be swell? But don't worry. Don't bother to get up. I'll process it for you, if I can get the credenza working."

I got out of bed.

The official word to the residents of Iden Hall was that I was doing penance for my wicked behavior. I must travel all through the garden on my knees, saying rosaries every hour on the hour, with my grim-visaged duenna by my side. The weather was not sufficiently damp and cold to satisfy those who felt I should be flayed alive, but they had to live with their disappointment.

As for me, I was out in the garden before it was light, working until my breath smoked in the evening gloom. Nef, who would much rather have been in her warm room listening to the radio, was grim-visaged indeed. She had to play her part, though, as I had to play mine.

Work shut my heart in another room and locked the door, so I was free of the wailing thing all day. Only at night was it able to get at me. Nights were hell.

I cleaned out Joseph's entire stash of Theobromos. He sighed and endured, because I was doing a month's work in a matter of days. *Ilex tormentosum* was caught in its full cycle, absolutely optimum for the Company banks, forever and forever a benefit to humankind. Little herbs of the field, sweet grasses fell to my knife to rise eternal in electronic alchemy. Some nights, the best nights, I never went to bed at all; the blue light of the ultravey kept me safely out of that horrible terrain while Nef lay grumbling, holding up a pillow to block the light.

I had always thought we were made perfect: but if they could make us sleepless, and heartless, what a lot of good work we could get done.

Bright weather and steadily warmer. The smell of the land changed: that dead black coldness was blowing away. The north wind blows, and you look upward, at chimney pots and leafless branches, but the south wind blows, and you look down, where all wakeful things stretch green in the light of the young sun.

I was doing the very last work on the roses. They weren't as important as the ilex; *Rosa pellucida* would produce no miracle cures, but in a hundred years its distinctive flowers would open in no mortal garden. It would be rediscovered in the twenty-first century, in the abandoned garden of an old house in Oregon. What long chain of engineered circumstance would stretch back to me, here in the sunlight of a spring day in 1555?

"My favorite broadcast is on in six minutes," Nef informed me in a martyred tone. I looked up, startled.

"Oh?"

"It's on Red Shropshires," she explained. God only knew what Red Shropshires were, but I decided to be accommodating.

"Nobody's likely to bother me here. I've got my rosary handy. Why don't you go tune in?"

"Thanks." She was away like a shot. For such a big woman, she could move pretty quickly when she needed to. But, then, we all could, couldn't we? I went on clipping and scanning, because I had work to do.

I sensed a mortal coming into the garden. Who? . . . Straining, I perceived Master Ffrawney. In a panic I pulled out my rosary.

There I knelt, the image of pious repentance, but he came nowhere near me. I tracked his approach to a spot about three meters away, blocked from me by a dense hedge. There he stopped and settled, and I heard him sigh. What on earth was he doing? But perhaps even crawling sycophants liked to take in a little sunshine now and then. I tucked my rosary away.

No sooner had I resumed work than another of the little monsters arrived. This time I scanned to follow his or her progress. His, definitely. Male, about thirty-five, five feet six inches tall, weight one-forty, chemical profile . . . Master Darrell.

He was advancing steadily along the main avenue to the house, and would miss me completely. I relaxed. As he approached the intersection of his path and the one Master Ffrawney was seated in, I heard Master Ffrawney rise.

"Good day to you, Master Darrell."

"Ah." The other altered his course and proceeded at right angles. "Good day to you, sir. Most rare weather for March, is it not?"

"Even as the true faith bloometh, so doth England," responded Master Ffrawney. "Er . . . have you come a-purpose to see Sir Walter?"

"Aye, forsooth."

"Alack, sir, he is indisposed." A wave of embarrassment from Master Ffrawney, and some covert sexual excitement too. Sir Walter must be with the laundress again.

"Oh." A creak as Master Darrell sat down. "Well, well . . . perhaps *you* would know. I have been studying the household account books and would have some speech thereupon with some responsible person. Having heard of Master Harpole's disgrace—and I trust no evil came to Sir Walter thereby?—I say, having heard of it, I wondered who hath been appointed to keep accounts now?"

"I have that task, sir, until a new secretary be found. And may I say, sir, that Sir Walter haply had resolved to rid himself of that vile heretic already—"

"Good. Good. So you keep accounts now? Tell me, have you been long in this household?"

"Twelve years, sir."

"And you know well, then, how much money hath been spent to maintain the garden?"

"Why . . . yea, yea, I do. Better, I may say, than that foul heretic who, when he was not lusting after wenches, was polluting his heart with Lutheran books."

"Aye, forsooth, but let him alone for now. You shall remain in the household, shall you, when it is given over?"

"No, sir, I am Sir Walter's man." Pride swelled in him like a pimple. "He desires me to go to Court with him. You see I wear new livery, special for the purpose."

"A great honor." Masked annoyance in Master Darrell's congratulation. "Yet I could wish—I will be frank with you, Master Ffrawney, and do you the office of a friend. I could wish you less honored and more fortunate."

"I do not understand your meaning, sir."

"Master Ffrawney, I am often in London. Sir Walter hath not been there this many a year. He doth not know how the ground lies outside of Kent. It is not so easy to make one's fortune at Court as at a wool mercer's. I have seen many a noble knight unable to pay his tailor. Need I say that where the master goes hungry, his man starveth? You face no safe or comfortable prospect, Master Ffrawney."

"Oh, sir." Master Ffrawney sounded thoroughly alarmed. "Surely Sir Walter is so liberal and excellent in his person, and so faithful a son of the Church, that he must win wealthy friends in London. Yet an he doth not, what remedy for me?"

"Fear not, Master Ffrawney, for here I stand like a loving cousin to counsel you. Whatever wage Sir Walter promised you, I'll double it. You shall be my secretary here, supplying the place of that Harpole who is gone, and shall remain safe in this noble hall. And (to tell you in your ear) you shall fare better thereby than Sir Walter, ere long.''

It was at that precise moment that Master Ffrawney switched allegiances, if the chemical composition of his sweat was any indication. He wanted to be wooed, all the same.

"Sir, shall I desert him I have served so faithfully and so long? I'll tell you plain, he payeth me handsomely indeed." This outright lie was a mistake, for Master Darrell had been reading the household accounts, after all.

"Handsomely, say you?'' smirked Master Darrell. "If you think you are well paid now, you shall think me as liberal as Croesus. I mark how Sir Walter hath paid out divers sums this long while for certain curiosities, the verity of which I do doubt. Sure I have seen his unicorn: if the man had no better judgment than to buy a plain goat for twenty pounds eightpence, it is a miracle he hath kept himself out of debt as long as he hath. Thrift shall be the new order of the day, I tell you, and there shall be no more cockatrices nor sea dragons bought from peddlers. And why should not some of these grounds be planted out in bright stuff, less rare but easier to maintain, that maketh a better show? And why should folk pay but a penny at the gate, when they might just as well pay twopence?''

I nodded. As I'd thought: the end of the garden as I'd known it.

"This is excellent sense, sir," Master Ffrawney agreed. "I oft did think, in days past, that Sir Walter spent his substance unwisely. But in this he was much misled by his man Nicholas, you must know. Well, of him we shall speak no more. He shall be brought to justice some day, and God will deal with him then.''

A wave of puzzlement from Master Darrell. "Shall be? But he *hath* been.''

Now wonder and excitement from Master Ffrawney. "Hath he been taken? I thought all had been kept quiet, lest shame come to the Spanish doctor. And is he hanged indeed?''

"Hanged!" Master Darrell was frowning. "Nay, he is condemned to burn.''

My heart wasn't beating. I couldn't hear it beat.

"Burn? Go to!''

"Aye, in Rochester. Jesu, what hath happened here? Didst thou not hear how he was taken preaching in the marketplace at Sevenoaks? They say he ranted heresies like a bedlam man, and not in the way of a plain Lutheran neither, but the old heresies—thou knowest whereof I speak. Hath he done some offense here too?''

Master Ffrawney's joy was incandescent. It fairly shone through the hedge. I could almost see the little green leaves shrivel and curl with its intensity. He proceeded to tell the whole juicy story, but I didn't stay to listen. I had been carefully packing up my tools. I set them in my basket, got to my feet, and walked away.

I walked right out of that garden. Out through the fantastical gate with its gilded whirligigs and pennants, out into the lane beyond, where long meadows sloped down to a river and pollarded willows grew. No, that was south. I mustn't go that way. Rochester was due north. I had to find a road that would take me north.

I kept walking.

When I had gone some eight kilometers, it occurred to me that they might be burning him even now. Sobbing, I began to run.

23

IT WAS A long way, fifty kilometers or more. I had to wade rivers. I saw the osiers and weirs and other uniquely English features of the landscape. I walked through orchards just leafing out in green mist, no blossoms yet. I crossed chalky downs, with stands of beech trees. Sometimes I ran, and sometimes I walked. Sometimes I followed a road, and sometimes I cut across broad expanses where sheep grazed. I saw examples of *Dianthus carolphyllus albans* and *Cerastium holosteoides* and *Polygala caeruleis*.

I saw thieves, possibly murderers. Near dark I passed through the outskirts of a little town and saw some men standing around a well. I remember their hard stares in their bearded faces. Probably they didn't often see a young lady in Spanish dress out alone at sunset. Not in Cosenton, or wherever it was.

One of them followed me. About a mile onward, I picked up his signal, coming swiftly after: his pulse was racing, he was excited. Rape, probably, or robbery. I tucked my crucifix inside my bodice and looked around for a place to hide. There were trees nearby, very dense and dark, darker now with night falling. I left the road and went in among them. Nothing there but birds, settling in for the night. I climbed into a good old oak, tearing my dress but who cared now, and sat primly on a branch with my hands folded, waiting.

Presently he came along, and I could see him by infrared, his blood glaring out hot through his clothes. He slunk at a quick trot, as a dog on bad business does, with his excitement hanging around him like a bad smell. I sent a blast of loathing at him. He must have been a psychic dog: he faltered and turned about in the road and actually came a few paces near my tree. I sent images into his mind of violent assault, murder, bloodshed. It must have excited him, because he nosed even closer. In desperation I conjured up the supernatural: white clammy specters coming at him out of the trees, arms wide to embrace him. That did the trick. He took to his heels and ran back the way he'd come. I sat trembling in the oak branches for a while, hating the mortal race.

Except Nicholas, of course.

There was a waxing moon for a few hours, and by its light I found my way on through cold England, across green hills. Somewhere off north was the sea, and away to my left was a river that snaked down to it, growing wider with each curve. The Medway, it must have been. Yes, Rochester was on the Medway. The smell of the river and the turning stars guided me after the moon went down.

Sometimes, a long way off, I could see candlelit windows. There were mortals in the warmth behind those windows, up late: sitting up with sick ones or reading solitary or having late-night suppers of toast and mulled wine. I would have liked some toast and mulled wine. Any other time, I would have thought sentimentally about the people in the candlelit rooms, living out all the poignant details of their little mortal lives. Not tonight. I passed on through the dark with the knowledge that if I knocked on one of those doors, was welcomed into one of those warm bright rooms, they would be bright for only a moment: then, as at Christmas, all the lights would go out, and I would be alone in the dark with time and its dead. Better to walk the night.

Morning took a long time coming. The first thing I noticed by its gray light was that I had wrecked my clothes: there were rips and trails of lace everywhere, and mud, and wet dead leaves. Too bad. The second thing I noticed was a castle sticking up on a mound by a big gray curve of river. There were pointy parts of building below it— a cathedral.

I accessed all my store of maps and literature. Yes, that must be Rochester. Smoke curled upward from it. Oh, let it be chimney smoke, harmless chimney smoke. Or a hundred men with pipes? No, not pipes. A few years yet before tobacco became a habit among civilized men. What would it be like to live, as some future generations would, in perpetual clouds of herbal smoke? It must be a sweet kind of smell. Perhaps it would be like incense. A shame about the carcinogens, of course, but with all the medical advances of that era, the mortality rate would probably balance out even with now.

So I babbled to myself, on the road to the city, and the sun climbed higher in the sky. It did not dry me out much. I was encountering mortals on the road now. They did stare at me as we passed each other. Either my clothes were in a worse state than I thought, or they didn't often see señoritas here.

An old woman was puffing along slowly toward me with a basket under her arm. She was as much a wreck as sixty mortal years could make her, but my goodness what pink skin she had. That's the English for you.

"Good morrow, good mother."

"Eh?" She looked up (she was only about four feet tall) and noticed me for the first time. Her blue eyes widened in a stare.

"Art thou come from yonder town, good mother?"

"Eh? Aye." She couldn't make up her mind to curtsey to me, not being entirely sure what I was, so she wobbled a bit and flapped her apron to be on the safe side. I reached up to smooth my hair and found a long oak twig sticking straight up like an antenna. Wonderful.

"Thou wilt pardon me for my wild appearance, good woman, as I was set upon by thieves."

"Truly?" Instant rush of interest, and not sympathy, exactly, but a certain enthusiasm. She came closer.

"I must know, goodwife, whether there hath lately been a man burned at Rochester?" I held my breath and waited.

"Nay, lady, but there is to be."

Whoosh. "I pray you, tell me when?"

"Why, on the morrow, lady." Her eyes assessed me. "Spanish, are you?"

Must be the cut of my gown. "Why, so I am," I answered cautiously.

"Then you've lost none of your sport. The man burneth tomorrow betimes." She shrugged her basket closer to her and walked on. I walked on my way too, light-headed as all hell. Nearly a whole day before? Surely I could come up with some kind of plan.

Rochester was a very old place. It smelled old. Moldy, too. The air of decay probably came from the ruin that about a third of the town was fast becoming. It had been a monastic town, so the Reformation had smashed it pretty well. There seemed to be one main street that dove straight through without taking the traveler anywhere much. To either side of it the town was self-enclosed and secretive, blind as a maze. Only, looming over all, was this big cathedral that looked like it might fall on you at any time. I didn't like the cathedral. But I wasn't there to like it, was I?

So many mortals now, along the main street, and all staring at me. I saw a man coming out of a house. He seemed to be important; his surcoat had fur trimming on it.

"Reverend sir." I curtseyed deep before him as he regarded me in astonishment. "Can you tell me where the man is, that was brought here from Sevenoaks?"

He took forever to answer. Really, had he never seen a Spanish ghost before?

"If you mean the foul heretic, lady, he is held fast at the bishop's house."

Ah. I was getting somewhere. I pulled my crucifix out of my bosom. He goggled at one or the other. "I pray you, sir, is he a great tall fellow, without a beard?"

"Aye, fair maid, he is. Wherefore would you know?"

"Oh, sir!" All right, he was looking at my bosom. I made it heave and brought it closer to him. "I have sought the recreant this many a mile, through wild country as you may plainly see, all that I might dispute with him concerning the true faith, to lead him out of error into salvation." I found my rosary and waved that at him too. He blinked and replied:

"That were a great pity, lady, for the man hath remained constant in his heresy and is to die for it."

I swooned. Not really; but it put the ball in his court, and my feet were killing me anyway. There was an outcry all around me, and I was lifted up and carried into the house, with much covert squeezing of my behind and even more covert tugging at my gold crucifix. Both remained attached, however. I was revived with a shot of aqua vitae and came to with suitably faint requests for data concerning my location. Many staring English faces assured me I was in the Lord Mayor's house and need not fear, for they were all honest folk here.

I checked my cross and rosary, then sought the face of the man I'd first spoken to. He must be El Alcalde de Rochester. I played my scene to him and played it well, too: wept for the man Harpole, explained that I had striven to save his soul but he had fled me, adamant in his heresy, though because there had been some tender feeling between us that had nothing to do with theology I thought I might still manage to reconcile him to the Church. Might I not be given this chance?

But the Lord Mayor was shaking his head.

"Child, he is condemned. You may save his immortal part, aye; but the knave hath argued so coldly, and so shrewdly, and hath such a wicked reputation beside, that you will never see him pardoned. Be content; there is no remedy."

"But I must see him!"

"Well, that may be done," said a lady, clearly the mayor's wife. "But who are you, child? Are you not Spanish?" *Hola.*

"I am the daughter of Doctor Ruy Anzolabejar," I said, as proud as though it were true. "And what honorable love there hath been between myself and this poor man I will not say; but I charge you to think whether you would deny a soul one last persuasion that might be its salvation, and break a maiden's heart into the bargain."

The Lord Mayor and his wife exchanged glances. She got up and encouraged her neighbors to leave. When she came back, the Lord Mayor said delicately:

"Lady, your intent is praiseworthy, but I must tell you that though this is a godly place wherein most folk do love our queen, our prince, and his holiness the Pope, as well they ought, yet there are certain vile persons here who have acclaimed the man Harpole as a martyr. This has hardened him to his villainous intent. These ill-wishers may do you some harm if you attempt to dissuade him."

"Let them," I said. "I care not, so his precious soul is saved." So there. The Lord Mayor cleared his throat.

"Why, then—then you may take some buttered eggs with us, and rest you from your wearisome journey, and perhaps after dark I may take you to where he is kept."

"I must go to him now," I insisted. "What, shall I lose one instant of the brief time I have left to convert him?"

"Fie for shame, husband!" cried the wife. "Put a cloak about her and take her round about by the old way. There's none will see her in the vineyard."

"So shall I do." He looked at her indignantly. "And was about to so propose, ere thou prated at me."

In the end we both went covered up in cloaks, through a mass of ruined walls and green garden, all around under that big cathedral. We went into the back garden of a big house, and the Lord Mayor courteously explained my purpose to several persons of importance, including Bishop Griffin himself. As in take after take of a comic film, I played my scene out some three or four times. Finally everyone agreed I should have my shot at the condemned man. So after an agony of wasted time, I found myself in front of a little low door, with a mail-clad soldier turning a key in the lock.

The key was ornate. The lock clanked. These physical details claimed my attention, I found them absolutely fascinating, and of course the reason was that I had no idea why I had come to see Nicholas or what I was going to say to him. But I went in, and there he was.

He was sitting quiet and composed on a narrow cot, the single piece of furniture in the room. His eyes widened as I came in with the Lord Mayor, but he did not react otherwise.

The Lord Mayor lectured Nicholas sternly about his fate, and told him how he didn't deserve this virtuous lady coming to reason with him, but since she was here, the Lord Mayor would see if youth and virtue might succeed where reverend wisdom had failed to shake Nicholas's sinful heart. I was assured that if any violence was attempted on my person, I had but to cry out and I should be rescued instantly, and this bad fellow would be the worse for it. Having said his say, the Lord Mayor took his leave of us. The door closed after him. We were alone.

We looked at each other in silence. Nicholas was muddy and torn too, and bruised besides; pale, thin, and unshaven. His face had changed.

"Welcome, Spirit," he said at last. His voice had changed, too.

"May I sit down?" I requested. Then I realized there was only the bed to sit on. He got up and gestured for me to sit. My legs were trembling, so I sat and pulled off my shoes, which hurt my feet very much. He leaned against the wall with his arms folded, watching me.

"How should a spirit have such muddy toes?" he wondered.

"Didst thou think I flew here?" I looked at him. "Think again. I have walked the whole way from Iden Hall."

"Ah." He looked at me steadily.

"See?" I stretched out my feet. "No hooves."

A smile came and went, chilly, strange.

"To tell truth, I am glad thou hast come," he said. "This mortal air was getting a sweetness to it that made my heart cold to my duty. It made me wonder whether I had only dreamed—what thou knowest of. I was growing weak in my resolve. Now thou art here to test me, like a good friend, and I see it was no dream and am strong again."

I couldn't think what to say at all. My eyes filled with tears.

"Aye." He nodded. "Weep, Spirit. I will not falter."

"Oh, this is stupid!"

"I may tell thee, thou hast done me great good. Before mine eyes were opened, I believed as any weak and sensible man doth: that God exists, because we have been taught so, but there are no miracles and our only duty is earthly charity. More, I believed there were no devils nor spirits but only wickedness in men. For who has ever seen a serpent that spake with a voice, to tempt men from God?" What a strange look for me as he said that last. Almost kindly. "But, having known thee, I learned the truth of what thou art, and mine eyes are opened.''

I had certainly shown him there were more things in heaven and earth than were dreamt of in his philosophy, hadn't I? He eased himself down into a sitting position on the floor.

''Regard what thou hast done. In every respect where I doubted, thou hast made me believe.'' He leaned forward. ''Were it not for thine ever witching me away from my duty, I could think thou wert a spirit of a different kind entirely.''

''I am,'' I said, without much hope.

''It may be so,'' he admitted. ''But what thou art I cannot guess.'' There was another long silence. ''Where is thine argument?'' he said at last. ''Where is thy subtle persuasion? Wilt thou not beg me to lie, and recant, and get mercy from the bishop?''

''Thou wilt not,'' I said. I was so tired. ''They will kill thee, and I have no power to help—'' My voice broke. By reflex he got up and came to me with a gesture of comfort, then froze.

''Ah,'' he said. ''This is temptation too.''

I let my head fall backward, for exasperation and weariness. He sat down again. After a moment he ventured:

''Wert thou mortal once?''

I nodded.

''And art thou damned eternally?''

''No.'' I laughed. ''Yes! Oh, I must be.''

He frowned. ''What wert thou, being mortal?''

''I told thee what I was.'' I looked down at him. ''A child of Spain. And by chance, and by lies, I came into the dungeons of the Inquisition there.'' He looked uncomfortable then. ''Oh, yes, señor. Didst thou think I was only a mask of Satan, with no real heart to be broken? What thou lovedst was real enough. Suffering and all. Muddy feet and all.''

He jumped up and went to the window, and stood there staring out.

''Hast thou never heard,'' I tried to put it a way he might understand, ''of spirits who partake neither of Heaven nor of Hell?''

''The heathen and the dead children,'' he whispered, ''who are neither damned nor saved.''

''Just so.''

He turned around and looked at me with such dread in his eyes, I grew angry. Was he superstitious? This man? I clenched my fists. ''Now hearing you'd been arrested for yelling in the street, I came weeping all the way here and never slept, and was followed by a

murderer, and had neither rest nor food, and God knows why I troubled myself, for I knew you'd only say I was Satan come to tempt
you. I wanted to save your life! But I'm too late! You have your
martyr's crown, your horrible death! Oh, I could have gone away with
you—I would have run away from my duty and lived with you in
any street in Europe, I'd have read your awful Scripture and listened
to your awful sermons and worshiped your awful God—''

"Stop!" He seized me by the shoulders. "Stop! Stop!"

"Don't you tell me to stop!" I screamed at him. "*You* talked and
talked—''

"But if I could have *saved* thee—''

The door flew open. We both turned, expecting the guard. It
wasn't the guard, though. It was Joseph.

"Excuse me." He marched right up to us, looking determined,
and threw a punch at Nicholas. He had to jump a little to connect
with Nicholas's jaw, but he connected, and Nicholas crashed backward into the wall.

"Mendoza, out. Now." Joseph turned to me.

This was too much. This was grossly unfair. I collapsed sobbing
on the bed. Joseph exhaled angrily and went to the door, where the
Lord Mayor was peering in with a rather frightened face.

"I must have some private speech with my child, it seems. Pray
pardon me." And he swung the door shut, bang. Turning back, he
said:

"Okay, Mendoza, get up. I've just ridden thirty miles on an extremely unpleasant horse and I don't feel like having an argument.
You are in a lot of trouble."

"No!" I cried. "You can't make me leave now!"

"Now? Not leave now? What do you want to do, stay here until
they torch the guy?"

Nicholas was struggling to his feet, staring from one to the other
of us in bewilderment. Cinema Standard was enough like Tudor English for him to be able to understand about one word in three of
what we were saying.

"I don't know! God, God, help me, I can't save him!"

"What language are you speaking?" inquired Nicholas in Latin.

"Shut up, creep. Oh, and by the way," Joseph continued in Latin,
turning to him, "would you tell me why you were trying to get into
my room with a sword? It takes something more to kill me, as you
no doubt have guessed."

"I never went to your room to kill you," said Nicholas. "I was
trying to get out of the house without being killed. I went to your

room only for medicine, to calm your daughter. You know what I
saw when I opened your door."

"I know. You ought to have knocked. But do you understand you
are a dead man?"

"Truly I know it," said Nicholas, with a little of his former sneer.
"But I die in a just cause. And I will testify to the truth until I have
no voice."

"You mean to denounce us to the world, then?" Soberly, Joseph
put his hand on his pouch, where he kept his little glass vials. I opened
my mouth, but no scream came out.

"By no means. Who would believe me? The ranting of a madman
is not regarded. I mean to put my last breath to better use."

"Very wise of you, I'm sure." But Joseph's fingers were still
working at the fastening. Nicholas saw the fear in my eyes.

"Thou art not her father!" he blurted out in English. "Though
I'll lay odds thou art the same demon who stole the child and made
her what she is."

Dead silence. Joseph surveyed him.

"Boy, you're good at figuring things out. Isn't he? Except that if
anybody's the devil in this room it's *you*, buster." An extraordinary
bitterness came into his face. "I've seen you before. I know you, all
right, preacher man. Age after age, you come back. You always lead
the crusades. You're so damned golden-tongued, other people just
flock to die for your causes. You die with them, it's true, because
you're stupid enough to believe your own great lies; but you always
come back again somehow. Oh, I know *you*."

No hair-tearing, no jumping up and down. Only his voice dropping to an unexpected bass with Nicholas staring at him, unable to
comprehend.

"You think I'm not her father?" Joseph thundered. "I took her
out of the grave and gave her eternal life, which is more than your
lousy God would have done! You're the one who seduced her into
believing that your miserable little cult matters a damn, when she
knows nothing matters less. You're the one who's made her hate what
she is. How's she supposed to live, now, after what you've done to
her heart?"

Not understanding him, Nicholas had stopped listening and was
watching me where I cowered on the bed.

"So thou canst disobey him," he said softly. "So thou hast a
free will and may choose."

"Mendoza, get up. I'm taking you out of here."

Nicholas held my gaze, and I could not look away. "Stay with me until I have suffered tomorrow. Be with me at the end. I cannot rest otherwise, nor wilt thou rest. This thou knowest, love.''

Joseph seized me and pulled me to my feet. "Mendoza, we're getting on two fine horses I paid ready cash for and we're riding south. We are not going to watch an auto-da-fé. Come on.''

My heart felt like a balloon.

"You can't make me leave if I don't want to. Can you?'' I said to Joseph. "I'm already in trouble. I'm staying until it's over tomorrow. When it's over, I'll go back with you, and the Company can do whatever it wants to.''

Joseph let go of me. "It might teach you a lesson, at that,'' he said. "All right.'' He looked at Nicholas. "Young man. Do you know how many burnings at the stake I've had to sit through? Seven hundred and nine. Yours may be the first one I've ever enjoyed. In anticipation of that, I thank you.''

He swung the door open and pulled me out with him.

I went obediently enough. I let Joseph lead me back to the Lord Mayor's house with the Lord Mayor practically bowing and scraping beside us the whole way and telling us about his cousin who had married one of Katherine of Aragon's grooms. Apparently he offered to put us up for the night, too, but I missed what he and Joseph said to each other in that regard, because I was in a fog.

Something had happened in that cell that made it all right between us again. My own Nicholas had been looking at me at the last, and not that cold godly stranger.

At the Lord Mayor's house we were shown to an upstairs room, quite nicely furnished. Food and hot wine were brought for us; soap and water in a basin for me. I watched as Joseph talked to people. He explained, he apologized, he made arrangements, and at last he closed the door on the last mayoral wish for our pleasant stay in Rochester.

Turning around, he leaned against the door and stared at me.

"You shouldn't have said all those awful things about Nicholas,'' I said thickly. "Not true at all. Petty of you. Coming back age after age?''

He put his palms to his temples and pressed, as though he were trying to keep his brains from exploding.

"I mean, what, you believe in reincarnation or something?'' I went on.

"You're how old now, Mendoza?'' he inquired, with tremendous self-control.

"Nineteen. Maybe.''

"Nineteen, huh?" He took his hands down and began to pace. "Jesus. This must be what it's like to have a real daughter. What are they teaching you kids back there? As for reincarnation, it's realer than you think, smart-ass. There are only so many personality types among mortals. They just use the same ones over and over. Zealots like your Nicholas keep turning up, and every time they do, they make trouble for everybody. He's screwed *you* up, the son of a bitch. When this guy burns tomorrow—"

"Oh, he won't burn," I said dreamily. "He's going to recant. That's why he wants me to be there. He'll save himself, and then what will you do? He knows all about us. And he understands—isn't that incredible? A mortal capable of understanding the truth about us? See, you won't have any choice. You'll have to recruit him for us now. Give him tribrantine. And you know he'll be the best mortal worker we've ever had, once we explain the whole truth to him. Imagine all that intellect and all that zeal working for us!"

But he moved away from me and took hold of the bed rail with both hands.

"Mendoza," he said, "you can sleep in the saddle. We'll go slow. I'll lead your horse. Just come away with me right now, and I swear I'll fix everything with the Company about your going AWOL. Maybe I can even get you out to the New World. There are people who owe me favors out there. Please, Mendoza. For your old pal who got you out of Santiago? Don't stay here."

"Didn't you hear a word I just said?" I demanded. His shoulders sagged.

"You'd better get some sleep," he said.

It was still dark when I opened my eyes, but I was wide awake at once. Joseph sat motionless in a chair by the window.

Rochester. Today. Nicholas.

"It's April first," I said. "Fool's Day." Joseph nodded.

"Five A.M., as a matter of fact. Want to go back to sleep for a few hours?"

"Don't be stupid. I have to see him." I jumped out of bed and got dressed. I felt very light, very unreal, and my heart was pounding.

I had thought we could just leave the house quietly, but when we went downstairs, the Lord Mayor's household was awake and bustling. So we were offered breakfast (I was too nervous to eat) and given cushions by the fire while the Lord Mayor got into his mayoral robes, because of course he had to attend the public event, and we, being his guests, had to wait for him. It took him forever to get dressed. His wife fussed around him and adjusted his chain of office and his big flat cap with its curling plume. The plume was an ostrich feather. It must have come from Africa by way of Spain. Wasn't the world a small place nowadays?

It was gray when we left the house. A light wind had risen in the night and blown away the fog. The Medway sparkled dully, waiting for the sunlight. The stars were going to bed, faint in a sky pale as blue chalk. Everything green was turned to the east, where it was bright and growing brighter.

The people, though, were drawn to the precinct of the cathedral. There, right by the bishop's palace, they had set up the stake. I saw it from a distance before I knew what it was. What drew my attention to it was the stream of mortals: from every door and lane they emerged to hurry toward it, like rats after the Pied Piper. Some mortals only glanced at us as they came out. Some bowed and slowed, and made to trail behind us as though they were members of our party. Some mortals spat at us and ran. They all looked alike, though.

But the stake. How could anyone pay attention to anything else? It was black with pitch and stood straight up out of a platform of logs. There were tidy bundles of brushwood stacked close by and a perimeter of bleachers, yes, actual spectator seating. Why, they'd thought of everything. We might have been in Spain.

Joseph had taken my hand in his and was squeezing tight. Was he worried? We were shown to seats. Seats of honor in the front row, no less, though some people in the crowd muttered against us. Then came out the bishop and the other ranking clergymen of the area, in solemn procession. Everybody stood. Respectfully, after the religious had been seated, the rest of us sat down again. Just like at Mass.

We waited. The sky grew lighter. What a sweet wind had sprung up, all fresh the way it is in the early morning.

In the midst of a prayer led by the bishop, they brought out Nicholas. You could see him from a long way off too, like the stake. He towered above his guards.

Oh. He was stripped to his shirt and hose. Indecent, somehow. Didn't they give the condemned in this country sanbenitos to wear? Wondering that was a mistake, because it called to my mind a long-buried memory of shuffling figures all chained together, the tall points of their hats bobbing like antennae. I had screamed when I saw them. Where had I seen them? When? Was I sweating cold then, as I was now?

Then as now, people stooped to pick up stones and flung them. Like men braving heavy rain, Nicholas and his guards put their

heads down and slogged on. Stones clattered on the metal pot hats of
the guards. They swore at the crowd and swung their pikes before
them. Nicholas could have run away then, but he didn't. He didn't
even look up until a flint struck and gashed his scalp. Blood ran down
the side of his face. As he stood staring, his eyes met mine. The guards
grabbed him, and he walked on. He came to the stake.

Suddenly he moved, he struck into the crowd and caught me up
close to him. Only for a second, a split second, and then his guards
were pulling him back and he was shouting hoarsely:

"Ego te baptismo! In nomine Patris, et Filii, et Spiritus Sancti!
Amen!"

I was shocked numb. I put up my hand to my face. His blood
was smeared on my face, in my hair. He had a look of desperate
triumph in his eyes, though the guards were beating him with their
pike staves. Stumbling, he let them back him in among the logs. He
fell against the stake.

What was happening?

He let them clamber up beside him and chain him there. A big
loop around his chest, another about his legs. Three little kegs of
gunpowder were brought and fastened up with him. Then the guards
jumped down and began to lift the brushwood bundles into place with
their pikes.

Weren't they going to give him a chance to recant?

The bishop stood up and began solemnly to tell him off, but
Nicholas didn't listen; his gaze was fixed on me with a kind of black
delight, and I felt so stupid, sitting there, because I was only just
beginning to understand.

". . . to the everlasting shame of them that bore thee, and clothed
thee, and taught thee, and sheltered thee! Wilt thou not so far amend
thy life, man, as to renounce thine error? Speak, for thine hour is at
hand," commanded the bishop.

It was what Nicholas had been waiting for. He swung his head
from side to side, taking in his audience. "Yea, the hour is at hand!"
he shouted. "Not mine hour alone but all England's hour, when it
shall be tried in the sight of God! Gentlemen, my sin was very great.
Ye know it well, all of ye, for it is your sin too and its name is Silence!
O England, we knew the truth! We had the stone wherewith to build
the New Jerusalem! And we neither spoke that truth nor built that
city, being prudent, fearful men, and see what woe hath overtaken us
now! The Lord hath sent a plague of Romish cardinals to drink our
blood—"

"Fie! Wilt thou slander, thou?" cried the bishop.

"Do I slander? I humbly cry you mercy. I do but confess my sin. We have all sinned, we righteous men who kept silent when you crept back into England. Now you have returned in your power to forbid us the very Word of God! And who shall we blame but ourselves, who have let you return? O England, men will wear no chains but what they bind on with their own hands!"

His voice was beautiful. God, how beautiful. People were listening with their mouths open and greedy satisfaction in their eyes. Even the bishop, though his face was growing steadily more purple; he didn't want to miss a word, not a single damning word.

"Well, *I* will wear no more chains, gentlemen! *I* never will be silent again! Yea, you smile and say I am chained now, and soon will be silent enough. Yet I wear no such coils as all of ye. How will it go with ye when ye stand in shame before Almighty God, wearing such a weight of silence? England, is your flesh so dear to you as that? Is the flame so terrible?"

"Thou shalt know!" the bishop told him and, turning, gave the order. A soldier brought a torch and thrust it in among the piled brushwood. I lunged forward, and yet I could not leave the spot where I stood: there was an audible crack as muscle strove against bone. Joseph muttered an exclamation beside me and put his hand on my shoulder.

"Go, set the fire to blaze, for I will not peril my soul to keep out of it any longer!" Nicholas's voice came back like a great bell, drawing the crowd's attention from the first little curls of smoke. "I will escape the prison of earthly flesh that confineth ye all!"

And he turned and found me with his eyes, and his look went through me like a sword.

"I call on thee to break down the prison wall! What, wilt thou live on for endless years in this dark place and never come to Paradise? Thou art a spirit, and wilt thou not come back to the love of God? *Thou mayest choose!* Look, I stand in this door of flame and I tell thee it is but a little way through. Wilt thou not rise and walk with me?"

And he held out his hand, through the fire. But he was wrong: I couldn't choose. I was rooted where I stood. I could no more have walked into those flames than lifted that stone cathedral on my back. I had no free will.

Fire shot up and danced through his outstretched fingers, caught at his wide sleeve. He closed his eyes for a moment in pain. The contact was broken, and I looked away wildly. I was closed in by a circle of eager faces, rapt faces, Catholic and Protestant alike. He could be a heretic or a holy martyr to them, so long as they got to watch him die. This quaint people, pink-faced lord mayors and good-wives and honest tradesmen, were leaning close to see the intellect of an angel reduced to so much greasy ash. This people, whose wicker holocausts had shocked even the Romans; they had become Christians, but they hadn't changed. I met Joseph's sad black stare.

Nicholas made an agonized sound, and I looked back at him. The flames were high now. "Spirit, I charge thee, follow me into Paradise!" he choked, and then his voice rose clearer and louder than before. "I am thine only husband and thou art my bride! *I am the same that waked thee among the apple trees where thy mother bore thee, where thy mother brought thee into the world!* Come, and I will stay for thee! Oh, Jesu have mercy—oh—OH, JESU HAVE MERCY—"

Never say God doesn't answer prayers. The powder blew then and killed him. He became a column of fire and light as the sun rose over England.

While the crowd made appreciative noises, Joseph was finally able to pull me away from there; and we left that place.

24

$\mathbf{A}$T SOME LATER point, not connected by memory to anything preceding or following it, I was riding along a lane with Joseph. All the trees were in bloom: white blossoms and sweet scent everywhere. Apple trees. Every kind of flowering tree.

Joseph was talking to me as we rode along.

"You aren't feeling anything much right now," he was saying, "because you're in shock. It's a protective reflex. It'll last for a while. Eventually you'll feel again, and when you do, you'll be hurting pretty badly. But your work will help, Mendoza. Only your work will take the pain away. You'll need it like food and water and air.

"I'll see to it they don't take your work away. This wasn't your fault, this was a hell of a thing to happen to you your first time out in the field."

He was correct, it was. I looked at all the details of his clothing as we rode, fascinated by the patterns in the cloth. He watched the road for a while, and then he said:

"Yes, I can cover everything up, I know what I can do. Don't worry. And think of the relief, Mendoza, this whole nasty business is over. It ended badly, but it's over. Nothing to be afraid of now, nothing to break your heart hoping for. The mission was a success, too, and we're out of here. New location, nothing to remind you of unhappiness."

Oh, yes, I had to get out of England. He peered at me.

"Maybe I can get you posted to the New World. Hey, there's a great base where you could do research work, lots of peace and quiet there, maybe I can fix it so you won't get another assignment right away. What do you say, Mendoza?"

Yes, that sounded like what I needed.

He leaned toward me from his horse. "Okay, Mendoza?"

I blinked in surprise. Wasn't I agreeing with him? He took the reins from my hand and shook his head.

We got back to Iden Hall, I remember that very clearly. I thought it would hurt, but it didn't hurt, because it wasn't the same place. Nothing at all looked familiar.

Only my work area met me like an old friend. I went straight to it and got busy wrapping up my projects for travel. I worked steadily there until we left, however many days that may have been. One day, when I was in the middle of an entry, Joseph and Nef told me that I had to dismantle the unit for packing. So I logged out, and they told me to pack my other things too.

Joan came in while we were closing up our trunks, no doubt to discreetly inventory the linen to be sure we didn't make off with anything at check-out time. Nef attempted to press a shilling on her by way of tip, but Joan drew her hand back as from a snake.

"Thank you, mistress, but I will none," she snapped.

"How now?" Nef stared at her. "Wherefore art thou displeased with us? Have we not ever treated thee well?"

"Ay, mistress, it *seems*; but God knows this is not the house it was when ye came into it, and a many strangenesses have happened, and whose doing were they?" She turned a killing look on me. "And there was a holy martyr lately burned for his faith at Rochester, they say, but *I* say he had been living still, had not some here meddled with him."

Nef stepped swiftly to my side and put an arm around me, but I had taken the blow without blinking. Why blanch at the truth?

"We need no reproaches from the likes of thee." Nef glared at her. "Leave us!"

"With a right good will," retorted Joan, and flounced out of the room.

When the servant came to help us carry our bags down, it wasn't a servant I knew. I saw no one as we descended the staircase for the last time, went through the great hall for the last time, went out and climbed into our saddles and rode out through the garden the way we'd come. Not a sign of Sir Walter or Francis Ffrawney. Had they gone away to London? But that had been a lifetime ago. I didn't look back as we rode, knowing that the house had already faded to transparency and would vanish altogether if I turned.

So through the whirligig gate, Joseph, Nef, and I. Just beyond it a farmer was pulling up in his cart, and he gave us a bright expectant look as we came abreast of him.

"Be ye folk come from the great house yonder?"

"Aye, good man," replied Joseph.

"Then I have a marvel for ye, gentles. Grant a look, sir, only a look—" And he jumped down and pulled a cover of sacking from the back of the cart. There, lying in the straw, was the complete skull of an ichthyosaur half embedded in a rock.

"Sir, you see? The very dragon's head of the dragon Saint George slew. It came out of a rock nigh to my house. What say you, sir, is it not worth an angel at least?"

"Without doubt." Joseph stroked his beard. "But I fear thou hast come a long way for naught, man. Iden Hall hath been sold. There is no market here anymore for such things as dragon's heads."

The man's mouth fell open. He gave such a howl of dismay that the unicorn struggled and bleated in Nef's arms. "Say not so! I have carried it clean from Lyme, sir!"

"Sad but sooth, my good man. Though I'll tell thee, there's an inn on the road to Southampton, the Jove-His-Levin-Bolt, where they might pay thee for a look at this skull," Joseph offered.

"Nay, out upon Southampton! If I've come on a fool's errand, I'll no further with the damned thing!" the farmer yelled, and he hauled off and kicked the wheel of his cart. His horse reared, the traces flew up, and the cart dipped backward, tipping the skull out into the road. It rolled ponderously, wobbling end over end, to the edge where the embankment dropped away; poised there a thudding second, and then went over, picking up speed as it went, bumping away down the long sloping meadows of Kent. The last we saw, it struck a log and bounded into space, completely clearing a hedge and crashing out of sight below. For all I know it is rolling still.

"You'll be sorry you did that, in the morning," Joseph called to the farmer, who had gone storming off.

"When will they ever regret what they do?" Nef brooded.

"Oh, some morning or other," said Joseph lightly. And we rode on.

Not that morning, though, nor for many others.

Poor Queen Mary never had her baby, because of course it was only a tumor. She went right on burning her subjects, though, in the hope that God would somehow produce a baby from somewhere if she did His will resolutely enough.

She never birthed her Counter-Reformation, either. In November

1558 she died, quietly in her pointless bed, and Elizabeth got the throne. That was it for the Catholic Church in England. The burnings stopped abruptly. The Protestants were reinstated. England did an about-face into a Golden Age.

But you missed it, Nicholas. You should have listened to me.

I missed it, too, because six months after leaving England I was stepping out of an air transport at New World One, and I was fine, just fine. I'd had therapy, I'd had drugs, I had lots of new clothes, and the AAE recommendation had mysteriously vanished from my personnel file. Happy me. Best of all, I was in New Spain.

I was discovering that a transport terminal was a pretty good indicator of the status of the outpost. New World One glittered: fabulous Mayan murals, gold leaf everywhere, inlaid floors. I wandered around the lounge, staring. A transport hostess with a spectacular feathered headdress. Jade cups in the coffee bar. Art objects, for God's sake, mounted on brackets above the announcement speakers. A little cross-legged god vibrated slightly as I was asked to report to the arrivals office.

The arrivals office looked like a hothouse. Thick bluegreen glass, terra-cotta, flowers crowding the walls. A smiling woman in tropical whites came to the window. I had on tropical whites, too. With our hoop skirts we looked like a pair of wedding cakes.

Wedding cakes. Grooms and brides. A thought like a loose plank in a bridge, to be stepped around.

"Hi there." A musical voice. "Botanist Mendoza? Did you have a good flight?"

"Reporting. Yes. Where do I sign in?"

She dimpled about something. "Well, your personnel coordinator is waiting right through those doors. You'll want your arrival packet first, of course." She drew out a handsomely embossed portfolio and pushed it across the desk to me. "You might want to remove the complimentary Theobromos right away. It melts out in the sun."

"Hot here, huh?"

"This is a tropical paradise," she informed me.

"Nice. Thank you," I said, took the portfolio, and headed for the exit.

Neat doors. A bas-relief sculpture of two jaguars rampant, battling with each other. When I got close enough, the jaguars disengaged as the doors slid apart, vanishing into silhouettes. A blaze of white light struck through the doorway. I stepped out. I faced heat. Light. Complex smells and sounds. A horizon of towering green as far as the eye could see, a mild and tolerable green, out to the edges of a blue sky transparent with the intensity of sunlight. Off to the west, a city of red and white pyramids: New World One. And here, right before me, four mortals and a man of my own kind. The mortals, all four, dropped on their faces.

"Hail, child of gods!" they cried.

I stared at them, dumbfounded, and then up at the Old One. He looked amused. He was a vision in white: white doublet and white trunk hose, white skin, white canvas conquistador's helmet. His hair and pointed beard were flaming red. He was lounging in an open sedan chair. "Welcome to New Spain," he said.

"Who the hell are you supposed to be?" I inquired.

"Quetzalcoatl," he replied. "As it were." The mortals got to their feet, and they too were a sight to behold, each one clothed like a Mayan prince in gold and feathers. Their faces were sad and noble; they had big high cheekbones, curved noses, and sullen mouths. I swallowed hard. I looked past them at the guy in the sedan chair.

"Botanist Mendoza reporting in," I said. My voice didn't shake at all.

"Personnel Coordinator Victor, at your service." He made room for me on the seat beside him. "Hop in, and we'll take you to your suite. Boys, collect the lady's luggage."

As we were jogged along, he said:

"A protégée of Joseph's, eh?"

"Yes."

"And you've just spent two years in the field? In the Old World? How grueling."

"Yes, it was."

"My word." He leaned back. We went sailing by mahogany trees like standing gods. "Well, life is just a little more gracious in these parts. You'll like it. Joseph pushed quite a few buttons to get you in here, you know. Any questions I can answer for you?"

"Do you have flush toilets and hot showers?"

He smirked. "And four restaurants. And an eighteen-hole golf course. And cocktails served in the main courtyard every afternoon at four." He glanced at his chronophase. "We'll be in plenty of time. We're mostly scholars here, and we enjoy our little rituals."

Wow.

"What about the—" I gestured at our mortal bearers, their plumed hats waving as they ran. "Isn't this kind of exploitive?"

"No, no, it's prestigious for them. They're all intercepted sacrifices. This way they get to be Servants of the Gods without dying.

We acquire most of our mortal staff that way. They're the most de-
voted fellows you could imagine.''

"No kidding?'' A red stucco wall rose before us, and we were
carried in through the gate. Victor gave me a tour around: acres of
plush lawn, fountains, courtyards, flowers, water-lily pools, parrots.
The chaos of the jungle outside, but within the perimeter of that high
wall, absolute manicured control.

"Boys, Botany Residential Pyramid.'' Victor waved an arm. He
leaned back beside me as they took us down a boulevard toward a
white palace. "The red building over there is the botany lab, and the
gardens are on the other side. The residential suites are really first-
rate. There's a PX on the first floor and laundry facilities, though I'm
afraid we've had some complaints because Botany Residential has to
share its pool and gymnasium with Support Tech Residential. Yes, a
few ruffled feathers over that. I hope you won't feel slighted.''

I looked at him sidelong. "I'll manage,'' I told him.

We pulled up in front of Botany Residential, and Victor took me
into the concierge's office, where we registered my retinal pattern,
and so up to my suite. Four rooms, all for me. The walls were smooth
bare plaster, and there any resemblance to a cell stopped.

"Complete entertainment center here.'' Proudly Victor swung
open the doors of a vast console. "It's tied in to our library. Over
forty million entries to choose from, and here's the receiver for Radio
Maya. Liquor cabinet over there, sauna over there. You're scheduled
to meet with your departmental director at 1830 hours for your briefing.''

"Great.'' Business at last. "Where's the director's office?''

"Oh, he's reserved a booth at El Galleon.'' At my blank stare
Victor added, "Our premier restaurant. Formal dress, of course. If
you call the porter service from the lobby desk, a pair of the boys can
take you there in ten minutes, though I should tell you—'' he lowered
his voice a little—"it's considered correct to attend cocktail service
at half past four precisely and remain until six, and then arrive early
for dinner.''

"Oh.''

"Etiquette,'' he explained. "It's very important here.''

"I see.''

"I'm sure you'll fit in quite well. I'll just toddle on now and leave
you to your own devices; daresay you'd like privacy while you un-
pack. If you have any other questions, the answers are most probably
in your arrival packet. I'd suggest you read it through before your
briefing.''

"I will, thank you."

He bowed, and I curtseyed, and I was alone again.

By the time I had showered, dressed, tested the bed and the holo reception, it was almost 1600 hours. I decided to walk to the main courtyard on my own legs. I wasn't really up to being a goddess in a chariot yet. Besides, I found the Mayan profile disconcerting.

So of course the cocktail waiters were all Mayans.

"What would the Daughter of Heaven prefer?" mine inquired politely, putting down a napkin at my elbow. I was unnerved but stared hard at him: no resemblance at all, really. Not straight on.

"What have you got there?" I nodded at his tray.

"Dry vodka martini. Tequila on the rocks, rum and soda, rum and tonic, margarita. Might this slave suggest the margarita?"

"Sure. Thanks."

He set it down and glided off. I settled back and picked up my arrival packet. There was a round spreading oil stain on the cover: whoops. My Theobromos had melted. I opened the front and peeled my complimentary stick off the first page of the brochure in order to read all about New World One and its calendar of social events for the coming year.

After a while, though, my attention wandered. The breeze through the white arches of the court was very pleasant, and the splashing of the central fountain was pleasant too, as was the chattering of the little green parrots in among the flowering vines. How soothing it all was. I could sit here, just like this, for years and years. I probably would, wouldn't I?

I only became aware that my eyes had filled with tears when I noticed some commotion in the treetops, far off outside the perimeter wall. I blinked and looked again. There were monkeys out there fighting, screaming and pelting one another with rotten fruit.

Shuddering, I reached for my drink.

Sky
Coyote

To George H. Baker,

who once spent a very long afternoon trying to read

Hiawatha to an impatient four-year-old so she'd have

some sense of his ethnic heritage,

this book is respectfully dedicated.

1

YOU'LL UNDERSTAND THIS story better if I tell you a lie.

Well, a myth, anyway. There was this god once, the Greek god of Time. He was a cruel old bastard and he ate all his children as soon as they were born. Zeus, the youngest son, managed to escape; when he grew up, he came back and ended the rule of Time by killing his father. Then he cut him open and set the older children free. King Time is dead; long live King Zeus.

In the twenty-fourth century, a research and development firm proudly appropriated Zeus as its corporate logo when it developed a method of time travel.

The method didn't quite pan out, though. Traveling through time is prohibitively expensive, and there are certain crucial limitations. For example, you can't go into the future, only backward into the past, and forward again to your point of departure in the present. Another problem is that history cannot be changed. Period. It's the law.

However, this law can only be observed to apply to *recorded* history . . .

So the discovery wasn't a total loss. The company altered its logo slightly and became *Dr.* Zeus. They were able to make a nice profit looting the past by collecting "lost" works of art and arranging long-term investments. They loaded a database with every event in recorded history and found they still had plenty of uncharted past to move around in. They realized that if the past couldn't be changed, it could at least be manipulated to Company advantage.

But who were they going to get to do the actual manipulating? Traveling back in time is rough, if you do it the cost-effective way without extra buffers. Twenty-fourth-century agents bitch about it constantly, and demand extra pay. Fabulously rich corporations never seem to have enough cash, paradoxically enough; though you may really *need* to send that man back to deposit a certain sum in a certain bank on a certain day in 1806, you're reluctant to do it unless you've got a guarantee it will pay off in six figures. And how many times do you want to lay out money to send people through? Isn't there a way to cut costs on this?

Dr. Zeus got its answer reviewing another failed project: immortality.

Technically it's possible to make an immortal person. It is not commercially practical. It only works on infants or little children, not middle-aged millionaires; and since middle-aged millionaires are the only ones who could afford to pay for the process, it's sort of a loss as a market item. In addition, the chosen babies must meet certain stringent physical requirements, and endure years of surgical alteration and training. Not even the most determined millionaire parents, once they knew what it entailed, would put their little Gloria or Donald Jr. through such an ordeal.

So, you can't sell immortality. On the other hand, if you're looking for Company agents who will work loyally without health insurance and never, ever retire . . .

They sent a team back to Lower Paleolithic times. A permanent base was established; equipment was shipped back, too. The original team went about collecting little Neanderthals and Cro-Magnons. These kids were then implanted, augmented, amplified, fortified, hopped up, switched on, tuned in, and thoroughly indoctrinated. They were given the whole harvest of human knowledge and culture from the other end of time; the books, the music, the cinema. They grew up, these *superüberkinder,* and when the last nasty mortal tissues had been well and truly excised, the base technicians handed them the keys to the lab and said: You take over. We're going home.

So, see what was accomplished with just one round trip? You don't send your agents back and forth through time; you recruit them at the beginning and let them walk forward through time in the ordinary way. Outlay for the project was kept to a minimum, and now Dr. Zeus had immortal operatives working for it, strategically placed at every important event in history. Of course, they were promised a golden future when they finally *got* to the future. Though that hasn't happened yet . . .

And the immortals made more immortals, though not in the usual way, because they had all been very carefully sterilized; suitable infants were selected from the mortal population and processed at remote bases inaccessible to marauding primitives. More bases were built, more secret Company projects were inaugurated, and the fix, as they say, was in.

Dr. Zeus ruled the world. Covertly, of course.

By now you've probably got a mental image of these immortals. You're only mortal yourself, and the idea of a deathless, perfect race makes you uncomfortable—and maybe just a little hostile—so you imagine them intellectual and emotionless. Stuck up, too. You're probably thinking they all look like vampires or superheroes, tall and steely-eyed, the men with bulging biceps and the women gorgeous in a chilly sort of way.

Well, you're wrong. The truth is, they look just like you, and why shouldn't they? They used to be human beings.

2

T HE YEAR IS 1699 A.D., the place is South America: deepest jungle, green shadows, slanting bars of sunlight, a dark rich overripe smell. Jaguars on the prowl. Orchids in bloom. Little birds and monkeys making continuous little bird and monkey noises in the background.

And here's the Lost City in the middle of the jungle: sudden acres of sunlight and silence in the middle of all that malarial gloom. Red and white stucco pyramids. Steps and courtyards and avenues, straight as a die. Straighter. Really impressive architecture out in the middle of nowhere. Gods and kings carved all over the place.

And here's the intrepid Spanish Jesuit, our hero. You couldn't mistake him for anything else. He's got those little black raisin eyes Spanish priests are supposed to have, but with a sort of twinkly expression the masters of the Inquisition usually lack. He's got the black robe, the boots, the crucifix; he's short—well, let's say "compact of build"—and is of olive complexion. Needs a shave.

He approaches cautiously through the jungle, and his cute little eyes widen as he beholds the Lost City. From somewhere within his robe he produces a square of folded sheepskin, and opens it to study a complicated design penned in red and blue inks. He seems to orient himself, and proceeds quickly to a wall embellished with scowling plaster monsters whose terrifying rage seems to keep even the lianas and orchids from encroaching on them. He makes his way along the perimeter, then: ten meters, twenty meters, thirty, and comes at last to the Jaguar Gate.

This is a magnificent towering megalith kind of a thing of red plaster, surmounted by a green stone lintel on which two jaguars are carved in bas-relief, upright and rampant in fighting poses, with eyes and claws inlaid in gold. Nay, but there's more: no actual gate occupies this gateway, no rusting bars of iron, oh no. Instead a solid wave of faint blue light shimmers there, obscuring slightly the view of the fabulous city beyond. If you have *really* good hearing (and the Spanish Jesuit has), you can just perceive that the blue light is humming slightly, crackling, buzzing.

And what's this in nasty little heaps around the base of the gateway? Lots of fried bugs and a fried bird or two, and—gosh, the Spanish Jesuit doesn't even want to think about what that blackened and twisted thing is over there, the one reaching out with a skeletal claw to the blue light. Probably just a dead monkey, though.

Peering at the detail of the pictographic inscription that runs up one side of the gateway, the Jesuit finds what he has been searching for: a tiny black slot in the face of a parrot-deity who's either beheading a prisoner or fertilizing a banana plant, depending on how good your knowledge of pictographs is. After observing it closely, the Jesuit reaches into a small leather pouch at his belt. He brings out an artifact, a golden key of strange and unkeylike design. How did this Spanish Jesuit come by such a key? Did he read about its fabled existence in some long-forgotten volume moldering in the libraries of the Escorial? Did he track its whereabouts across the New World, following a long-obscured trail through unspeakable dangers? Your guess is as good as mine. Holding his breath, he inserts it into the slot in the parrot-god's beak.

At once there is a high-pitched shrilling noise, and the Spanish Jesuit knows, without being told, that someone has been alerted to his presence there. Maybe several someones. The blue light falters and blinks out for a second. Seizing his opportunity, the Spanish Jesuit leaps through the gateway, moving remarkably quickly for a man in a long cassock. No sooner has he landed on the pavement beyond than the blue light snaps back on, and a mosquito who was attempting to follow the Spanish Jesuit meets a terrible, though not untimely, death in a burst of sparks. The Spanish Jesuit breathes a sigh of relief. He has gained entrance to the Lost City.

Making his way through this awesome pile of arcane geometry, he finds a shaded courtyard where a fountain splashes. Here are tables and seats carved from stone. He sits down. There's a stiff sheet of calligraphied parchment lying on the table. He leans forward to peer at it with interest. A shadow appears across an archway, and he looks up to see the Ancient Mayan.

Again, this is a guy you identify immediately. Feathered headdress, jaguarskin kilt, silky black pageboy bob. Hooked nose and high cheekbones. A sad and sneering countenance, appropriate on a member of a long-vanished empire. Is this the end for the Spanish Jesuit?

No, because the Ancient Mayan bows so his green plumes curl and bounce forward, and he inquires:

"How may I serve the Son of Heaven?"

The Jesuit looks down at the parchment.

"Well, the Margarita Grande looks pretty good. On the rocks, *with* salt, okay? And make that two. I'm expecting a friend."

"Okay," replies the Ancient Mayan, and glides away silently.

Boy, I love moments like this. I really enjoy watching the illusion coming into sharp contrast with the reality. I imagine the shock of the imaginary viewer, who must think he's walked into a British comedy sketch. You know why I've survived in this job, year after year, lousy assignment after lousy assignment, with no counseling whatsoever? Because I have a keen appreciation of the ludicrous. Also because I have no choice.

3

So I'M SITTING here waiting for the Mayan guy to come back with our cocktails, and I'm understandably a little jumpy, because I'm meeting someone I haven't seen in, oh, a while, and we didn't part on the best of terms. When mortals are nervous, their senses are heightened, they notice all kinds of little details they're ordinarily unaware of. Imagine how it is with us.

Like I notice: the sound of tennis balls, far off, rebounding. Leisure. The sound of toilets flushing, wow, think of all that expensive plumbing. The smell of the jungle isn't any worse than, say, a terrarium in bad need of a cleaning, and it's pretty much blocked out anyway by the dominating aromas of this place: colognes. Antiperspirants. Cultivated flowers. Refrigerated food all nice and fresh. I can even smell fabric: starched napkins and tablecloths and bed linens, and not one spot of mildew on anything, and this is in the tropics, yet.

As I sit marveling at the luxury of New World One, she comes into range. I pick her up about twenty-five meters to the right and two meters down, steadily ascending, must be stairs beyond that arch. She's moving at four point six kilometers an hour. I hear the footsteps on the staircase now, and through the arch I see her rising: head, then shoulders, then the white brocade of her gown.

She paused on the top step and looked at me.

She'd been one of those Galicians with white skin and red hair; could have passed for an Irishwoman, or English, even, until you saw her eyes. They were black. They had a hard stare, an expression of ... *disdain* is too mild a word. Disgust, that's it, whether at me or the world or God, I could never tell.

But it had been a long time, and maybe she'd even forgotten about what's-his-name. I took a deep breath and smiled.

"Well, well. Little Mendoza." And I stood and summoned every ounce of belief in the scene we presented. Father confessor extends welcome to young noblewoman.

"Jesus Christ," she said.

"No, sorry," I replied. "The robe's got you fooled."

"What a little pudding face you have with your beard and mustache shaved off."

"I missed you too," I said gallantly, gesturing to a seat. After a moment's hesitation she approached and sat down, and I sat too, and the Mayan very providentially brought our cocktails.

"You got my transmission, then." It's safe to begin with the obvious.

"I did." She arranged the train of her gown, not looking at me.

"So." I leaned back after the first sip. "Been a long time, hasn't it?"

"One hundred and forty-four years." No, she hadn't forgotten about what's-his-name. "Since Portsmouth. I'm taller than you are, too. I wonder why I never noticed that before."

"You're wearing high heels."

"Could be." She raised her glass and considered it. She was being too much of a lady to bite the lime, but she did lick the salt.

"I like your ensemble. Bonnet *à la Fontagnes,* isn't it? Boy, they really keep up with fashion here, don't they? That's the exact style they were wearing in Madrid when I left."

"I should hope so." She sneered. "You think courtiers fuss about their clothes? Hang around here a few years."

"If I remember right, you used to like new fashions."

"Less important now. I don't know why. I'm very comfortable here, actually. Sanitation, good food, peace and quiet. Nothing to disturb my work but the social occasions, and I manage to get out of most of those."

"So you don't party much?"

"I hate parties."

I reached out and took her hand. She looked at me in swift surprise. Then she relaxed and said, "You're back with the Church again, obviously."

"Have been. I'm about to change roles."

"Really?"

"Yes. Yes, I died heroically in an attempt to carry the Word of God to a bunch of Indians who weren't having any, thank you very much. Even now faithful Waldomar, my novice, is telling Father Sulpicio why he was unable to recover my arrow-studded body from the jungle. Anyway, I've just hiked in and I haven't even reported for debriefing yet. Can't wait for a shower and a shave.''

"I would have thought you'd go for them first.''

"Wanted to see you.'' I shrugged and had another sip. Her eyes narrowed slightly.

"What exactly are you doing here, Joseph?'' she inquired. This time she bit the lime. "If you don't mind?''

"Recuperating!'' My eyes widened. "I've just come from ten years as part of a Counter-Reformation dirty tricks squad in Madrid, doing stuff that would make a hyena queasy. Then I had a sea voyage here, which was *not* any kind of a luxury cruise, and two weeks on a stinky jungle trail. I'm a little overdue for a vacation, wouldn't you say?''

"Overdue for a shower, anyway.''

"Sad but true.'' I looked into the bottom of my glass. "What does one do to order a second round here?''

She waved a negligent hand, two fingers extended. The Mayan appeared from nowhere with two new drinks. He went through the whole business with the new napkins and the old glasses and swept away. I stared after him. "What does he do, stand there just out of sight listening to us?''

"Probably.'' She raised her glass. "So after your vacation you're going back out into the field?''

"Well, yes, as a matter of fact.''

"Going to play with politics at Lima?''

"No. They're sending me up north.''

"Mexico? What on earth are you going to find to do up there?''

"Farther north than that. California.''

"Ahh.'' She nodded and drank. "Well, you'll enjoy that. Great climate, I'm told. On the other hand—'' She looked up suspiciously. "Nobody's *there* yet. No cities, no court, no political intrigues. So what could you possibly . . .''

"There are Indians there,'' I reminded her. "Indians have politics too, you know.''

"Oh, Indians.'' She gestured as dismissively as only a Spaniard can. "But what a waste of your talents! They're all savages up there, Joseph. Who did you offend, to draw an assignment like that? What will you do?''

"I don't know. I haven't been briefed on it yet. The rumor is, though, that Dr. Zeus is drafting a big expedition. Lots of personnel

from all the disciplines. Big base camp and everything. No expense
spared.''

"And you're probably going to go in there and collect little Indians for study before they're all killed off by smallpox.''

"I wouldn't be surprised.''

"You slimy little guy.'' She shook her head sadly. "Well, best
of luck.''

4

I GOT A guest suite, and I showered, I shaved, I was brought a fresh clean set of tropical whites and decked myself out in style. I left the long heavy wig on its wooden head; I like fashion as well as the next guy, but you have to be realistic sometimes. And the rest of the getup felt swell after my Jesuit mufti: silk knee breeches, gauzy shirt, frogged coat with cuffs you could conceal a dictionary in, let alone a scented hankie or an assignation letter. The heels on the shoes gave me some height, too. Oh, to be able to parade around Barcelona in this suit. You know what priests really miss? Not sex. Style. I admired myself in the mirror a few minutes before going off to report in like a good little operative.

Guest Services turned out to be located right off the lobby of my pyramid, so I didn't even have to step outside. This was good, because even with the air-conditioning on I was sweating by the time I stepped into the director's outer office.

It was lush with pre-Columbian art treasures and potted orchids. A big revolving ceiling fan moved the damp air around. High vaulted windows looked out on a walled garden where long shadows stretched across a brilliantly green lawn, and a turquoise pool of chlorinated water shimmered. No piranha would have lasted five minutes in there.

There was a receptionist's desk of carved mahogany, but no receptionist. Okay. I looked around and picked up a copy of *Immortal Lifestyles Monthly*. Its glossy cover stuck to my fingers. Pulling them loose made a creepy tearing noise, and from behind a doorway a polite voice inquired, "Yoohoo?"

"Hello? Is the director anywhere around?" I called in reply. A few seconds later the door was pulled open and an immortal guy peered out. He looked at the vacant desk with a slight frown of annoyance.

"I'm so sorry," he said. "I can't think where she's got to. You'd be—?"

"Facilitator Grade One Joseph, reporting in."

"Ah." He reached out and shook my hand. "Good to see you. Guest Services Director Lewis, at your service. Please come in."

His inner office was a little cooler than the outer one, but I noticed he wasn't bothering with his wig either; it drooped from its wooden head on a corner of his desk, with his tricorne perched rakishly atop it. Next to that was a commissary take-out box containing the remnants of a salad and next to that a jade cup half full of cold coffee, with a film of cream streaking the surface. The rest of the desk was in snappy order, though, neat little stacks of brochures arranged by size and a keen matching inkwell-and-quill-stand set of Ming dynasty porcelain. A desk calendar told me today was November 15, 1699.

"Please have a seat. Would you like something cold?" he suggested, bowing slightly in the direction of his liquor cabinet with its built-in icebox. I nodded, mopping my face with one of my crisp fresh handkerchiefs. It promptly wilted. He brought us a couple of Campari frosties and sat down behind his desk. He was wilted, too. Lewis was one of those fragile-looking little guys who could have understudied for Fredric March or Leslie Howard. Limp fair hair over a high-domed forehead with hollow temples, deep-set tragic eyes the color of a bruised violet. Determined chin, though. We swilled down our Camparis in grateful unison.

"Ah." He set down the glass. "Equatorial or not, we don't usually have such heat at this time of the year. You hiked in on foot, too, didn't you? I daresay you're ready for a bit of rest and rec after *that* ordeal."

"I sure am, if I have the time," I said indistinctly, crunching ice. "Do I have the time, before this next job?"

"Let's just see, shall we?" He turned, and a terminal screen rose up smoothly out of a groove in the polished surface of his desk. He unfolded a keyboard and tapped in a request. Little green letters ran across the sea-blue screen. "Well! Here's your file. Oh, my goodness, you're one of our more experienced operatives, aren't you? *Look* at the missions you've been on. So you're the man who preserved the cave paintings at Irun del Mar?"

I thought back twenty thousand years. "Yeah," I admitted. "Long story, actually. They were my father's paintings."

"That's wonderful." Lewis looked impressed. "That's in the south of France, isn't it? Or is it northern Spain?"

"Neither one, back then. We were the people who became what you'd call Basques."

"*Those* people." Lewis leaned his chin in his palm. "Gosh, that's fascinating. I was stationed in the south of France myself for a couple of centuries and I always meant to go down there on holiday, but the work just never let up. You know how it is."

I nodded. The irony of being immortal and having all the time in the world is that you never really have any time, because there's so much work to do. Except for the occasional layover at places like this, of course. Lewis turned to the screen again.

"Let's see. Quite a distinguished field record throughout prehistory! Then it says you sailed with the Phoenicians, worked in Babylon, you were a priest in Egypt, a politician in Athens, secretary to a Roman senator, brief period as a legionary, three hundred years in Gaul and Britain . . . Why, we came rather close to meeting one another there. That's where I was recruited. I was supposed to have been a Roman."

"Supposed to have been?" I tilted my glass to get the last ice.

"Well, half Roman. By that time, everybody was half Roman and half Gaul or Visigoth or one of those people. There weren't any more Roman Romans." He gave a brief sharp smile. "In any case, my mother abandoned me in the spa at Aquae Sulis. Or so I've been told. Thank heavens a Company agent came along before somebody drowned me like a kitten."

I nodded in sympathy. Lots of us started out that way. He leaned forward and resumed his perusal of my personal history. "And then you served in Byzantium—my, I wish I'd been able to see it then. I was stuck in Ireland, of all places. Did you ever meet the Empress Theodosia?"

"Yes. Evita Peron but with class. Nice lady."

"*Really.* And then it says you put in some time working with the Idrissid rulers in Morocco, then back to Byzantium for the Crusades, and then to Spain. You've been with the Church, in one capacity or other, ever since. Worked under the Inquisition, did you?" Lewis raised an eyebrow.

"Yes, and you know what? The pay was crappy. Somebody was making money out of all those persecuted heretics, but it wasn't me," I told him.

He shook his head, his turn to look sympathetic. "And here's your recreational data . . . say! You're a soccer man? It says here you played on the base team when you were stationed in Andalusia. The Black Legend All-Stars."

"I'm short, but I'm fast." I grinned, setting my glass on his desk.

"Oh, how I *wish* you were going to be here a little longer," Lewis mourned. "We've been trying to introduce soccer and get our own base team together. We had jai alai matches with our Mayans, but they insisted on killing one another afterward. Nasty business. Well, we do have tennis and croquet, if you enjoy either game."

"I'm a tennis man, too."

"Splendid. We have marvelous outdoor courts. Oh! Oh! Here we are, here's your next posting. Six weeks away. Well, you're in for a grand time. You'll be able to enjoy the annual 'Saturnalia, Christmas, Yule, Whatever' party. There's also the Grand Fin de Siècle Cotillion on New Year's Eve as we swing into yet another new century. You'll just make that one," he told me. "Your transport's scheduled to leave the next day."

"It is, huh?" I looked regretful. "Maybe I'd better miss the dance, then. I hate catching a flight when I've been partying the night before."

"Oh, I wouldn't recommend doing *that*." Lewis looked at me mildly, but there was a barely perceptible warning in his tone. "It's the Big Event of the year. There'll be no end of hurt feelings if you don't attend. Our present administrator (also known as the Incarnation of Kukulkan Himself) is most particular about complete participation by base staff and guests in his little entertainments."

"Uh-oh. It's like that, is it?" I shifted in my seat.

"Awful. Cheer up: the food's good, and most of us manage to bail out by one A.M. Just stay away from the mescal punch. His own recipe, unfortunately." Lewis shook his head. He leaned forward to look at the screen again. "You're scheduled to meet with the big, excuse me, with Base Administrator Houbert at half past ten tomorrow morning. Formal brunch in his receiving salon. He'll brief you on your mission to Alta California and provide you with all the access codes you'll need. After that your time is largely your own until your transport arrives. Social rituals apart, of course."

"Okay. What kind of social rituals?" I inquired, casting a longing gaze at the icebox. Lewis took the hint promptly and got up to fetch another round.

"Cocktails every four P.M. precisely. The administrative staff are obliged by tradition to observe cocktail hour at the Palenque Poodle, but as a guest you're free to swill where you will." He handed me another cold one. "I can recommend the hotel bar just across the lobby. Great stock of gins, and their wine cellar is really quite decent. Let's see, what else? Sunday brunch is a must, at any one of the four excellent restaurants available for your dining pleasure, and I must say eggs Benedict combines remarkably well with the breathtaking view from the topmost terrace of a pyramid, but one *is* expected to sort of circulate from table to table chatting with other diners, and that can become tedious after a while. Personally, I never manage to get all the way across the restaurant without at least one sausage rolling off my plate.''

''Maybe I'll set a new fashion and eat in my room.'' I considered.

''Out of the minibar? Lots of luck. You'll be interrupted at least three times by well-meaning Mayans wanting to know if you forgot to make a sedan chair reservation.'' Lewis sighed and let the screen slide back into its hidden place. He opened a desk drawer and drew out a sheaf of papers.

''Here's your guest information packet with access codes for the base map.'' He slid it across the desk to me. ''Green entries are the different departments, red entries are eating establishments, blue entries are recreation and entertainment areas. We have a first-class cinema that's presently hosting a late-twentieth-century film noir festival, which ought to interest you. You're a Raymond Chandler fan, according to your file.''

''Dashiell Hammett, too,'' I told him.

''You're in luck, then: tomorrow's program features all six versions of *The Maltese Falcon*. Here's your key card for the gymnasium machines and shower lockers. This is your flyer describing social events for the upcoming month. Your physical measurements have been forwarded to our Wardrobe Department, and a complete set of morning dress, evening wear, sportswear, lounging wear, and personal linen has already been delivered to your dressing room. Your tastes in literature and music as noted in your file have been installed in your suite's entertainment center. A bottle of Sandeman Analog Oloroso has been added to your liquor cabinet. Have I forgotten anything? I don't think I have, but God knows I'll be here if you've any further questions.'' Lewis drooped back into his chair.

''Long tour of duty?'' I asked.

''Seven hundred years,'' he replied wearily.

5

NEW WORLD ONE wasn't such a bad place, really. That was what I was thinking to myself as I strolled through the Grand Plaza next morning on my way to the Palace of Kukulkan.

I mean, spacious—? Acres of wide-open gardens and lawns, huge old rubber trees, broad avenues with hardly a soul in sight. Every so often I'd pick up the pounding of steady purposeful feet and duck into an arched portico or behind a big flowering bush to watch as a sedan chair went by with a lot of nodding green plumes and magnificent coppery muscles moving smoothly under it. In it there were always immortals like me, usually riding alone, staring out with set features as they were jogged inexorably to some other sector of this paradise.

I got to Kukulkan's palace just fine on my own, accessing the data on my base map. It was something to see, all right. A snow-white stucco ziggurat covered with more dragons than Grauman's Chinese Theater, rising huge out of the middle of a small artificial lake. From the front portico a waterfall cascaded down over green copper steps; visitors presumably had to wade up to the front door with shoes and socks in hand. That was assuming they could get across the moat in the first place. I didn't see a bridge. But wait, there was a kind of gondola thing moored amid the lily pads at one edge. Somewhere just out of sight, I knew, a tragically dignified Mayan prince awaited my least command to leap into action and ferry me across.

We aren't really supposed to exploit our paid mortals this way. In fact, the Dr. Zeus offices in the future have a real horror of just this kind of thing going on. We're the servants, never the masters, and God forbid we should behave in such a way as to even suggest we don't know our place.

Only problem is, the mortals in the past just adore surrendering themselves to a higher power. It's embarrassing, sometimes, the way they go on. We pay really well, of course, which may have something to do with it. Anyway, it always makes me uncomfortable to have some poor mortal slob throw himself at my feet and do the O Great White God bit, especially as I'm more sort of a little brown god.

But, hell, how was I supposed to get inside? I took off my tricorne and scratched under my wig, wondering what to do.

"You must be the important guest he's expecting at his midmorning levee," said a voice from the general direction of my right knee.

I looked down and saw a tiny black child, five at most, wearing white satin breeches and a scarlet coat. Not a mortal; he was one of our neophytes, so young he was still undergoing brain and skull surgery, to judge from his heavily bandaged head. The mass of white wrappings looked just like a turban. The rest of his costume must have been designed with that effect in mind, to judge from his pointed slippers and the pink cake box he was carrying.

"Tasteful, isn't it?" he observed sourly, acknowledging my stare. "You're early."

"I won't be if I can't get up to the front door." I nodded in the direction of the moat.

"Scared of slipping on the steps?"

"It's not my idea of a dignified entrance, anyway."

He gave a snort of impatience. "Come on," he said, and I followed him around the side and through a dark tunnel of purple flowers trained over an arbor. We emerged at another face of the ziggurat, one with an ordinary-looking door set back in a recess. A small pirogue drifted on a rope at our feet.

"Give me a hand," he instructed, and as I lifted him up, I realized he really was just a baby, light as chicken feathers, with a baby's domed brow and wide eyes. He perched on the prow, balancing his cake box, while I found a pole to move us across the moat.

"How come you're not in school?" I inquired as we drifted along.

"This *is* school," he replied disgustedly. "I'm an executive administrative trainee. Houbert's supposed to be giving me valuable insights into running a base. This morning's lesson seems to be What to Do If One Runs Out of Marzipan Petits Fours When One Is Expecting an Important Guest for Brunch. I hope you like the damned things.''

"Hey, I'll eat anything. Sorry he made you run around like this."

"That's okay." He shrugged his little shoulders. "This semester's almost over. Next semester I'll be̅ sent to study with Labienus at Mackenzie Base. I've heard he's a *real* administrator. Then, next year, I'm scheduled to go to the Low Countries and learn field command from Van Drouten. *Then* I'm going on to Morocco. That's where I want to work once I graduate. With Suleyman. Do you know him?"

"The North African section head? Yeah. Worked with him under Moulay Idriss. Nice guy."

"He's working for Moulay Ismail now, with the Sallee corsairs. He recruited me." The baby's eyes were wide for a moment, and for just that moment he looked his age. "We were on a slave ship, and m–my, my mortal mother, died. Suleyman was there in chains too, pretending to be one of us, and he looked after me then. But he had his pirates lying in wait! He had them board the ship and free everybody! He took me away with him and sent me to the Company. I was aptitude-tested and scored extremely high in leadership capabilities. That's why my augmentation is proceeding at an accelerated rate, you see."

"I'd wondered. Neophytes aren't usually sent into the field this early." We bumped gently into the coping on the other side, and I fished around for the mooring rope. "How old are you, anyway? Four?"

"Three," he told me proudly, and held up his arms to be lifted out of the boat. "I guess they need good administrators these days. If Houbert is typical of the best they've got, they *really* need me. I won't work here, though. I'll be in Africa. With Suleyman."

"You've got it all planned, huh?"

"He's the best there is in his field," the kid said proudly. "I've been reading his file. Talk about a celebrated record! I want to model my career on his. He gave me my name, you know. Latif, that's what he called me when he was taking care of me. I don't remember what I was called before. Anyway, the Company's really going to need good African operatives soon, with all the history that's going to happen over there."

"Well, Latif, I hope you get your chance." I stepped onto the coping beside him, and we made our way to the door, which turned out to be the entrance to a fairly ordinary elevator. Latif put down his cake box long enough to press the button. I looked at him thoughtfully. Smart, confident kid, despite his size-10 case of hero worship.

Probably with a brilliant future ahead of him, too; Suleyman had an eye for good recruits. Why hadn't any of my recruits ever thought I was a hero? I'd certainly believed the operative who recruited me was God Himself, I'd been so grateful to be saved from those screaming people with stone axes. But Mendoza hadn't liked me much even before that business with the Englishman, and it wasn't my fault the guy got himself burned at the stake. You'd think she'd show a little gratitude now and then, considering what I'd saved her from.

On the other hand, how much gratitude had I shown to old Budu, the guy who recruited me? I hadn't exactly been there like a loyal son when he needed me, had I? So maybe the problem is simply that I'm a slimy little guy, and that's life.

6

WHEN THE ELEVATOR doors parted, we were greeted by a blast of recorded music—sounded like Mozart—and a wave of heavy incense smoke. And I mean heavy. Blue clouds of it.

"Oh, shit, he's set fire to the copal again," muttered Latif. "He's through there. That's his morning levee room. I'm just taking this off to the kitchen. See you later."

I took a moment to adjust my wig, set my hat at the proper angle, and shoot my lace cuffs. As I did, a querulous voice called:

"The *stairs*. You didn't come up my stairs. That's part of the whole experience."

"Sorry," I responded, following the voice through the outer room to the door of the audience chamber. I looked in.

It was a very nice room, everything green and white and gold, with snaky Mayan stuff all over the walls. At the far end an enormous philodendron looked ready to eat the two jaguars that lolled half-asleep beside its pot. Slightly nearer, a golden throne encrusted with jade commanded my attention. Or maybe it was a jade throne encrusted with gold. Anyway it was a hell of an impressive piece of furniture. Too bad the guy perched upon it looked like J. Wellington Wimpy.

"Joseph." He rose slowly to his feet and took a couple of majestic steps down to meet me. "Joseph, at last. This is the one we've heard so much about." He seized my hand in both his own and shook it up and down. "And I am merely Kukulkan the Divine Feathered Serpent, or I may be Director Houbert. I would prefer to be less the god-bureaucrat and more the artist; but one can't have everything, even here." Standing up, he had a little more dignity, because he was pretty tall for one of us, and beefy with it too. The white robe and golden sandals put you in mind of classical statuary. I wondered what possessed him to wear that feeble-looking little red mustache and skimpy beard. Oh, of course: he was supposed to be Kukulkan on Earth, the feathered serpent who was believed to appear as a white man with a red beard. Maybe the Mayans found him convincing.

"You really ought to have braved my stairs, you know. There are a whole series of theatrical effects triggered if you tread in the right places. Bursts of flame. Armored automata. Cascades of flowers. I spent decades working out the mechanisms," he told me.

"Gee, I wish I'd seen. I was helping the kid bring your bakery order up, though."

"Ah, little Latif." He smiled fondly. "Isn't he a charming child? One seldom sees them out in the field so young, but he does have extraordinary potential. Such a shame he can't stay longer! Off to the harsh new worlds beyond our ancient walls. Everyone's leaving, it seems." He sighed and shook his head.

"Are they?"

"Oh, yes. Inevitably. Our revels here are nearly ended, you know; cloud-capped palaces and gorgeous illusions will melt away quite, before the end of the next century. All this splendor abandoned to the spider and the worm." His eyes grew moist with sorrow.

"Ah, don't take it too hard. You know the Company isn't going to leave all this stuff. They'll have tech crews ripping out the gold and packing up the furniture years before we ditch the place," I said cheerfully. "You can set up your trick staircase in the next outpost. I hear Canada's got some great scenery."

"A frozen wasteland." He shuddered. "Don't even speak to me about it. How I envy you your time in California." His eyes brightened. "*Speaking* of which, I've arranged a little entertainment to make your briefing more interesting. And I'm being remiss! Naughty me. I haven't even offered you coffee. Shall I make it up to you?"

"Sure," I said, guardedly, because he had a little secret smile on his face. He looped his big arm through mine and waltzed me across the room, straight toward a bare wall. Just as it seemed we were about to smack into it, the wall swung away as silently and swiftly as if it were a curtain instead of plastered mortar. A neat effect, I had to admit. Too bad I was an immortal with an immortal's senses, because of course I'd heard the mechanisms and counterweights going off when we crossed a certain section of tiled floor; but it was almost as good without the surprise.

Beyond was his dining room. There was a long banquet table

loaded with great-looking food on gold-and-jade service; coffee was
steaming, orange juice was freshly squeezed, and peaked napkins were
set at three places, one of which was occupied by Latif, who looked
bored and impatient. The only problem was, table and chairs appeared
to be suspended in midair over a pool, and there were piranhas flitting
back and forth in the water.

Director Houbert stepped back to watch my reaction, his little
smile spreading below his little mustache. I felt like punching the guy;
I really wanted breakfast.

Now, Sam Spade or Philip Marlowe, whose adventures have kept
me company on many a lonely outpost over the centuries, would have
said something really snappy here to deflate the big balloon. I've never
yielded to the temptation to emulate my literary pals, though; immortals can't afford to make enemies. Especially of other immortals. So
I tilted my tricorne back and grinned, the picture of foolish admiration.

"Boy, what a conundrum! You designed all this yourself, didn't
you?"

"Surely *you* can solve my puzzle," he crowed, his little eyes
twinkling. "You who've served in such fascinating places and epochs.
This should be child's play for you. I've read your file, you know.
You're quite a celebrity. Come now, show some of the mental dexterity that saved you from the Pictish headhunters!"

Jeez, he *had* read my file. If there's anything more uncomfortable
than meeting a fan, I don't know what it is. Maybe being eaten alive
by piranhas. Latif met my eyes and started to open his mouth. "Don't
you dare tell him!" cried Houbert. Latif shrugged and poured himself
a cup of coffee. I could just jump across, but I'd land smack in the
middle of the cups and saucers and epergnes et cetera, smasho.

"Well, let's see." I scanned the room. The fish were real, all
right, and so was the water. I groped in my coat to find something to
toss in, and brought out a little ball of wadded-up silver paper. It
barely touched the surface before it vanished in a boiling mass of
nasty little fish. Okay. No glass panel covering the pool. I scanned
again and on impulse switched to infrared this time. Bingo!

No solid sheet of glass, but a kind of transparent ferro-ceramic
path to the table, no more than a half meter wide and set just a fraction
of a centimeter below the surface of the water. Step off a centimeter
to either side and breakfast would be on me, if I were a mortal. Thanks
to the highly visible temperature differential between the transparency
and the water on infrared, though, I ran no risk of feeding the fish.
Boldly I stepped out on the unseen path and marched across it to the

table, kicking out of my way a couple of overeager piranhas who jumped at my shoes.

"Oh, well done!" Houbert applauded. "Splendid!" He came bouncing after me, and I could see Latif watching him, wondering whether he'd slip, but Houbert got safely to his chair and rang a tiny golden bell. I tensed for more theatrics: he was only summoning a trio of Mayans, who prostrated themselves on the threshold of the room. "You may serve now," he told them.

The poor bastards couldn't see the path like I could, but they must have known it was there, because they came in coolly enough and proceeded to wait on us. Great food, if deliberately weird: the eggs were pink and green and the orange juice was from blood oranges, which Houbert drank with a smirk from a golden sacrificial vessel. The Mayans whisked his napkin open for him and dished out his Franco-Mayan cuisine with reverence and patience, as befitted the Father of Heaven.

"Do you like our regional variant of *oeufs crocodiles?* These fellows can prepare anything if they're shown how once. Try the *pommes de terre Quetzalcoatl!*" Houbert leaned across to push a golden platter in my direction. I lifted my hand, but a Mayan had anticipated me and scooped a big starchy mass onto my plate.

"Swell," I affirmed. "You know, you've got quite an unusual setup here. I can't remember when I've been at a base with such, uh, flair."

"Well, of course we've had a long time to develop everything." Houbert looked pleased. "I daresay we've been the premiere research facility for a good three millennia. That's what makes it such a pity . . . But we won't speak of it, no, we absolutely mustn't. I warn you, I sob like a child when I contemplate the future."

I looked at Latif, who nodded gravely and rolled his eyes.

"Sorry to hear that."

"I was hoping—if it isn't presumptuous—you've been to such fabulous places, lived in them, worked in them, passed effortlessly as one of their denizens. How did you bear it? You saw Rome in all her splendor. Byzantium, too. How does one cope with the inevitable death of all that beauty and elegance?" Houbert looked at me beseechingly.

"Well . . ." I bit the end off a croissant and chewed slowly, giving myself time to come up with an answer. "It wasn't all like that, you know. There was a lot of garbage and disease and starvation, too. Maybe that's it, you know, sir? You see the bad with the good long enough, and by the time a change comes, you're ready to welcome

it. No more gilded carriages in the streets, but no more crippled beggars either. Sometimes it's a good idea for weeds to cover a place.''

"I see your point." Houbert looked disappointed. "But in that
case, there's really no analogy possible, is there? For of course we
have no crippled beggars here. No ugliness, no injustice, no hunger.
Only perfection. No reason for the hypothetical gods to take their
revenge on us."

I nodded and stuffed the rest of the croissant in my mouth, but I
thought privately that I'd seen some perfect pleasure gardens go up
in flames too, and sometimes it seemed like a good idea at the time.
Not that I've ever been the one with the torch, of course. That's not
my job; I'm what Dr. Zeus used to call a Preserver, not an Enforcer.
But, then, nowadays nobody even remembers that there ever were
Enforcers, except for really old operatives like me.

"I suppose one learns not to care," mused Houbert, spreading
mango jam on a helping of teosinte polenta. "After all, however many
palace revolutions one flees, there's always another palace somewhere. For us, at least. The charm of the new continually soothing
away regret for the old. Do you not find it so?"

"Sometimes, yes."

"And of course we immortals must above all things cultivate our
sense of enchantment." Houbert spooned a massive glob into his
mouth, and jam dripped into his beard. One of the Mayans deftly and
immediately napkined him. "That's one of the things, the *truly* important things I've been endeavoring to impart to our little colleague
here. Life is ours, eternally; whether a gift or a curse is largely up to
our own efforts. Boredom is a dreadful thing to carry through the
centuries. One must preserve one's sense of wonder at life. One must
make it a grand continual game, full of rapture, revelry, and sur-
prises."

He had a point there. You do have to play certain mind games to
keep from going nuts. A good sex life helps, too.

"Your problem, sir, if I may speak plainly," said Latif, "is that
you don't have enough real work to do."

"Child, child, how can you understand?" My god, tears were
actually standing in Houbert's eyes. "There is *endless* work to do.
But if you don't find a way to make it delightful, what do you face
but ages upon ages of drudgery? We must retain the freshness and
capacity for enjoyment of childhood—qualities that, I regret to say,
you do not seem to possess in any great quantity."

Maybe watching his mother die in chains had something to do

with it. Latif snorted and tossed a bit of javelina sausage to the piranhas, who made it vanish.

"And you really must learn to appreciate these things, child, or life will be the dullest eternity of bread and water you can imagine. If you *can* imagine," Houbert pleaded. "Nobody can face eternity without dreams."

Actually dreams can be a problem, but I didn't feel I should butt in at this point, because, except for the raving excess, I agreed with Houbert. It's just that not everybody has to prance around in a perpetual Disneyland to have a good time, and when you enforce whimsy with an iron hand, nobody enjoys it.

"Well, sir, I'm doing my best to understand you," Latif told him. "I'm wearing the costume. I play the games. What you don't seem to get is that I've got a *purpose* here. Purpose can be fun, too. I've had plenty of style, but I'd like some substance now, thank you. I want to learn about managing people. I want to learn about command decisions. Okay? I now know how to arrange a diplomatic banquet and brunch for a real live field agent who's actually been out in reality and done things with it. I know all about providing my subordinates with magic and mystery and fun. It's the problems I want to learn about."

"My child, my child, won't you find out about the problems soon enough?" Houbert raised his hands to heaven. The Mayans misunderstood his gesture and stepped in with hot towels, one for either hand. "But I know what it is. You're young. And who is so impatient to be perfect as a youthful operative, still in the process of sloughing off his imperfect mortal flesh? Look at you, your augmentations have barely begun, and yet you can't wait to leave your flawed humanity behind. So eager to be the perfect machine! If you'd only listen, *this* old machine could warn you that the day will come when you'll learn to savor that humanity. Playfulness, irrationality, sheer nonsense for nonsense's sake lend a dimension to life we immortals need, need desperately. How else can we endure the centuries rolling over our heads and the horrors they bring?"

"Baloney," muttered Latif.

"Well, he can't really appreciate your point, sir, because there aren't any horrors here, are there? There aren't even any problems." I took on the voice of reason. "This is a five-star vacation resort compared with some other places I've been, kid. You'll get your chance to wade in trouble up to your neck, believe me. Enjoy the hot showers and the flush toilets while you've got 'em, because for the next two hundred years or so they'll be few and far between. Take your time. God knows you've got time."

"When we stop playing, we die emotionally," sniffled Houbert, waving away Mayans.

"Oh, I don't know if I'd agree with that." I looked at Latif. "But take your fun while you can get it, that's what I always say. Your friend Suleyman, for example. Boy, the laughs we had in the souk at Fes! He had complete control of the political situation the whole time, dispatching reports and coordinating intelligence, but did he neglect to hang out by the pool in the evening with a couple of cold ones and a good book? Nope. You learn what you like, and you make sure you always have enough of it, so you can work as hard as the Company needs you to."

"He reads?" Latif asked in an offhand way. "I wonder what he likes to read."

"Poetry," I informed him. He looked shocked. "No, seriously. I mean, what would he want with adventure stories? With *his* life? And philosophy is mostly crap when you live forever. No, he likes great poetry."

"You see?" Houbert cried. "What is life without poetry?" Latif ignored him, but I could tell he was thinking about it. I looked at the Mayan waiters.

"What do you think, guys?" I inquired. It was their turn to look shocked. After a moment's hesitation, the one with the most green plumes in his headdress spoke.

"Well—we think the Son of Heaven must, in every respect, agree with the Father of Heaven."

"Oh, I do. But what do *you* think? You think all this pleasure chasing and show business and incense is a good idea?"

"Of course. You're gods. These things are fitting for You."

Boy, if the front-office mortals in the twenty-fourth century could hear this.

"You think maybe we ought to tone down our style a little? Live more like you do?"

"Why would You want to, Son of Heaven?" The Mayan looked appalled. "Look how pleasant it is here. Can You imagine any of us wanting to go back and live in the world of men? We were made to live in blood and flames and shit. We have escaped these things because we were Your chosen ones, and we would very much prefer to stay here with You. But if You were to go down to that other world and suffer as men do . . . what kind of god would do a thing like that? It's not appropriate behavior, You see."

"But a god might have work to do there," pointed out Latif. "Important work, like running things. Anyway, you don't really believe we're your old gods, do you?"

"Certainly." The Mayan looked faintly offended. "You may not resemble the gods we were led to expect, but You neither age nor die, You reside in the ancient places of our fathers, and You work miracles on a daily basis. That is quite close enough for us. Miserable wretches that we are, we take pride in knowing that we serve such splendid masters. The Father of Heaven always takes great care to behave in a suitably godly way, and I could only wish some of His children would follow His example a little more."

"Thank you, best of slaves." Houbert sighed happily and clasped his hands together on his stomach. "You see, child? *They* understand. We require pomp and circumstance. We require pageantry and ritual. There is a certain touching beauty in the way mortals instinctively grasp this about us when we ourselves deny it."

Latif's response was brief, explicit, and to the point. I looked brightly from one to the other; I hadn't enjoyed brunch like this in a long time. Houbert winced profoundly. He turned to me, pointedly ignoring his apprentice.

"Well, here's a perquisite of divinity you won't turn down, I daresay." He gestured hypnotically, and a drop-dead gorgeous Mayanette came gliding into the room, bearing a golden tray of jade vessels. I thought he was talking about the girl, but as soon as she was close enough, I caught a scent that grabbed hold of my nose and yanked me to my feet.

"Jesus, what IS that?" I yelped. It was all I could do to keep from grabbing the tray from her. She dimpled and leaned low to place it before us, giving me a spectacular view of cleavage I had absolutely no interest in at that moment. A blue mystery of aroma was coiling from the spout of an urn, a smell of every sweet deal in life, every sure thing, and every winning ticket. Latif clenched his little fists and looked away. Houbert's smile was like the sun in splendor.

"Theobromos, my friend. A little more complex than the formula to which you are accustomed, however. This, you see, is the original recipe. This is the sacred beverage our dear Mayans reserved for the incarnation of God on Earth Himself alone. *And* for grownups." He turned and blew Latif a Bronx cheer.

"I hope your teeth rot," said Latif gamely, and poured himself another shot of java. He couldn't stop himself from adding four lumps of sugar, though, I noticed. But my attention was yanked back to the sacred vessels as Miss Mayan Universe poured me a cup of something

smooth and rich and dark as any sin I'd heard confessed in three
hundred years of faithful service to the Church. She held it out to me
balanced on both her palms, and her smile of invitation was as tender
and reverent as though I were her god, just her special god, the one
she dreamed about.

Our mortal masters designed us to be pretty much resistant to
intoxicants, you see; at least, the ones they knew about. Alcohol is
pleasant but provides no more than a mild buzz, and the big nasties
like cocaine and opium do nothing for us at all. How surprised (and
horrified) they'd been to discover that *Theobroma cacao* interacts with
an immortal's nervous system in a totally unique manner.

I accepted the cup from the girl and breathed in deeply. "Holy
smoke" was all I could say. But the first sip unlocked my tongue and
all my senses, and I won't even attempt to describe what it was like,
because you'd just moan and toss on your pillow all night from unbearable envy. No kidding. You really would.

Our masters were envious enough; the stuff will be illegal anyway
in the twenty-fourth century, on the grounds that it's fattening and
contains refined sugar, but it never has that effect on *them*. There was
talk about forbidding us its use, at the very beginning; wiser heads
prevailed, though.

"Houbert, you are one swell host," I gasped. He quaffed from
his exquisite jade cup and beamed upon me. How could I have thought
he looked like Wimpy? Charles Laughton in *Rembrandt*, that's it, he
was a dead ringer for the guy.

"You won't find this little specialty at the commissary, I think."
He raised his cup to the Mayans. "My kitchen does have its own
secrets. Notice the bouquet! How many complex alkaloids, how many
extracts of certain rare orchids can one perceive? You'll find the range
of perception varies, but in this morning's brew I believe there are—"
He took another sip and inhaled judiciously. "Let me see, I detect
five distinct perfumes. Would you say? But perhaps it takes a rather
longer acquaintance with the God in the Jar to become proficient in
judging such matters."

How was he managing to express himself so elegantly when he'd
had a snootful of this stuff? I was lost in admiration for him. Latif
sipped his coffee and watched us critically. I turned to look at him
and felt like crying out of sympathy. Imagine not being able to drink
this yet! I wanted to tell him something to console him. Any minute
now I would, too. As soon as I remembered what the other thing was
I'd been going to say.

Only, how could I talk and interrupt such beautiful music? How

the hell was Houbert doing that with his voice, perfectly counterpointing the Gounod in the background? What was he saying, anyway?
Whatever it was, it was sheer poetry. It brought tears to my eyes. Had
I thought he looked like Charles Laughton? Was I blind? Ronald
Colman in *Lost Horizon,* with the voice to match. The enchantment
just kept coming, too, because Latif's voice rose like a little temple
flute:

"Well, I'm certainly learning important things this morning. Not
one, but two millennial creatures of infinite experience and knowledge
reduced to drooling idiots before my eyes. I simply can't wait until I
grow up."

"You're just jealous," retorted Houbert, but I thought it was so
funny, I started giggling and couldn't stop. I had become a flooded
house, and about a hundred little Josephs were running around in my
bloodstream frantically trying to bail me out. Damn. The buzz was
wearing off. There it went. My internal chemistry revolted and
dumped a few toxins to teach me a lesson. Suddenly I needed sugar.

"Where are those petits fours?" I wanted to know, and a Mayan
with a cake plate was at my elbow like a devil after a soul. I took a
handful of tiny, poisonously bright cakes and wolfed them down.
Houbert had receded in dignity again; he was about at Peter Ustinov
in *Spartacus* now. Hadn't there been a point to this feast of fools,
anyway? Oh, yeah. "I was supposed to have a briefing of some kind,
wasn't I?"

"Oh, that," said Houbert dismissively. "I assume the ever-so-
efficient Lewis provided you with most of the mundane facts. As for
the classified material . . ." He began to smile again. "I've set you
another little test. Your access code strip is here, within reach. To
find it, you have only to use the imagination and ingenuity that stood
you in such good stead when the High Priest of Dagon tried to have
you stoned!"

7

IT TOOK ME about two days to recover from Theobromine poisoning, but after that I had a swell vacation. I watched a lot of cinema. Played a lot of tennis. Watched serene Mayans putting up holiday decorations to which they had absolutely no cultural connection. Ate many tasty meals at the several excellent restaurants provided for my dining pleasure. Went to three holiday parties and won a door prize at one of them (bottle of aftershave). Looked up a number of old pals I hadn't seen in centuries. They hadn't changed at all (big surprise!).

Also, I accessed the code strips relating to my upcoming assignment. They gave me a lot of research material to integrate and store in my tertiary consciousness. They also gave me a duty I was not looking forward to.

I was returning my racquet to the Mayan attendant one afternoon when I was dumb enough to ask, "How do I get to the Botany Department from here?"

He looked over my shoulder and whistled. I turned to see four big Indians swerve in my direction and set down the sedan chair they had been carrying. "The Son of Heaven wishes to go to the Botany Department," he told them.

"Okay," they replied in unison, and before I could say a word in protest, they had done a neatly synchronized dip and the attendant had picked me up bodily and shot-putted me into the passenger compartment, so smoothly the other passenger wasn't even jostled. "Well, hi there." Mendoza smiled at my discomposure. "Happy Solstice Season."

"Hi." I braced myself as the chair was lifted, but it rose smooth as anything and just flew off. You couldn't have known there were straining mortal muscles or a drop of mortal sweat connected with the motion in any way.

"Don't you find this just a little embarrassing?" I asked her, struggling to get comfortable.

"I used to." Mendoza yawned elaborately. "Nowadays I just say what the hell and ride. It's easier than arguing with them, and they find it so fulfilling."

"Fulfilling?" I looked down on the nodding plumes.

"I think they enjoy debasing themselves. What else is there for them to do around here, after all? They're decadent. We're decadent. Everybody's decadent at New World One. Here, have some Theobromos." She proffered a bar with an ironical gesture.

Irony or not, I accepted. Enough time had passed since that fatal brunch for me to be able to look at the stuff again, and besides, even with the ordinary formula, New World One has the best you can get anywhere and you never, never turn it down when it's offered. Nectar and ambrosia, baby. I leaned back in the chair and felt my spirits rise.

"Yes, this is an amazing place. Kind of confining, though, isn't it?"

"Is it?" Mendoza raised an inquiring eyebrow.

"All this manicured luxury, I mean. I'll be glad to get out in the field again, personally."

"That's right, your California trip." She looked out idly at the passing scenery. "Fun with Stone Age people. Have you found out more about it?"

"I've had some briefing, yes."

"How nice for you. Why were you going over to Botany?" Such a cold black stare she had.

"Oh, just to look over one or two things connected with the job," I lied.

"Hey!" Her eyes suddenly came to life. "You can see my work."

My heart sank. "Gee, that would be interesting," I lied further. "So you've got a garden or something? I didn't think you worked with any actual green plants anymore."

"I do compilation and analysis of other operatives' field specimens, but everybody's allowed some private projects. And look, here we are at Botany! Come on." She fairly leaped from the sedan chair before the bearers had set it all the way down.

"Happy Holidays. We must remind the Daughter of Heaven to remain within the conveyance until it has stopped moving," one of the bearers informed her in aggrieved tones.

"Yeah, yeah." She waved a hand, not looking back. I followed her, thanking God she wasn't something like an entomologist.

Botany was less a pyramid and more a toppled megalith, long and low. We went through it past the labs and offices and out into the back, where a vast field was surrounded on three sides by pink stucco walls. I had figured on a greenhouse or something, which was kind of a silly expectation in the tropics. Under the open sky grew fruits and vegetables of obscene size, enough to fill the salad bars at the many excellent restaurants available for my dining pleasure and then some.

"Now, get a load of this." Mendoza hitched up her skirts and led me across the rows to a double line of green stalks. "Look at these big guys."

"You're still fooling around with maize?" She'd been doing that back in 1554.

"I could never quite give up on it. It's so beautiful, see, but the stuff is worthless as a food staple. Well, nearly. Compared to soybeans or oats or wheat. Far less nourishing. And the bigger and more golden you make it, the less food value it generally has, even when you develop high-lysine varieties. But look at this *Zea mays* and look at these primitive varieties over here, these are cultivars that were abandoned because their yield was low or they were difficult to hull, and look at the oldest one here, teosinte," she said it like a saint's name. "If you analyze its genetic structure, you know what you find?"

I was afraid she was going to tell me. She did, too, for the next forty-five minutes.

"... so one day, one fine day when I've perfected it, this specimen's descendant will leap from the stalk, rip open his husk, and yell, 'Here I am! Supergrain! More nourishing than a speeding ear of triticale!' And it'll all be my work." She fondled the golden tassels with such intimacy, I had to look away.

"But you haven't limited yourself to maize, have you? If I remember right, you used to be a real whiz on all the New World grains and other related stuff."

"Oh, sure."

"Like for example, you'd know about the kind of grain the Native Americans in California eat."

"Well, they don't eat grain up there exactly, their main analogous staples are acorns and chia—" She broke off and swung around to look at me, terrible suspicion in her eyes. "Why, Joseph?"

"No, no, I've got good news. Trust me. You remember back

when you were just out of school, when you filled out a certain form PF215?''

"Personal Goals and Preferences," she responded, and then her mouth fell open and stayed that way. ''Ohhhh . . .''

"And you *said*, I mean, you know, it was you who filled this thing out, you did your best to convince the graduation board that you ought to be sent to the New World to work on its flora in remote areas, because you were this super expert on New World grains, and—''

"No! No, no, no! That was in 1554!''

"And you've been drafted for the California project, and that's how it is, babe.''

If any of those giant zucchini had connected, I'd have been seriously bruised.

8

As you may have gathered, Mendoza is not the kind of woman to waste time on petty things like forgiveness. But somehow she rose above her inclinations enough to let me download the briefing material she'd need for her assignment. Maybe it was the fact that it was that festive time of year when old grudges are put aside, mistletoe is hung, the smell of gingerbread and Yule logs perfumes the air, and slaves get to whack their masters on the head with inflated pig bladders. Maybe it was the fact that she really did love her work more than anything else (or anything at all). Anyhow we saw more of each other as the century rolled through its final days, assembling our field kits and swapping bits of information that might prove useful on the job.

It was Mendoza who pointed out to me that observing our Mayans would teach me absolutely nothing about the Indians we were going to work with, just as studying Swedish farmers would teach me nothing about Turkish soldiers. Different continent, different nation, different culture, different experiences. It's a point non-Americans tend to miss, and what did I know? I'd been based in the Old World all my life. Well, most of my life. I had all those access codes to clue me in, though, and I was an expert in no time.

So, though you couldn't call our relationship cordial, we wound up going to the Grand Fin de Siècle Cotillion on New Year's Eve together.

"Wait here, guys, okay?" I hopped nimbly from the sedan chair as soon as the Mayans set it down. The lead bearer inclined graciously. I tossed him a couple of drink tokens by way of a tip and went into Botany Residential, adjusting my wig.

"Hokay, Natasha, honeybunch, your ride is here," I called cheerfully, ringing the buzzer.

"You're early," Mendoza told me, opening the door long enough for me to step inside. She turned and went back to packing a garment bag with what looked like fifty pounds of white silk petticoat. She herself was all dolled up in ballroom best, absolutely the latest Paris fashion rendered in tropical-weight cream shantung, though she hadn't yet put on the elaborately heeled shoes (higher than mine) of Italian calfskin. They were lined up neatly by the side of the bed, next to her field kit and duffel.

"I'm always early. Catches people off guard," I replied, looking around. The place was emptier than a hotel room, though she'd been living in it for over a century. She'd packed up, but the staff hadn't yet been in to vacuum, so there were dust rectangles on the console where her field notebooks had been and two dust outlines on the wall where pictures had hung. From a hook dangled a single strand of spangly holiday decoration. It had broken when she pulled it down and was too high up the wall to bother with. "Boy, I hate moving during the holidays," I said sympathetically. She shrugged and zipped the bag shut, subduing all those waves of silk.

"I passed the Grand Ballroom on the way over here," I continued. "Brother! What an engineering stunt *that* is."

"Isn't it?" She sat on the edge of the bed and fished around for her shoes. "Whole thing goes up like a hallucination in twenty-four hours. You haven't even seen the inside yet. That's his big specialty; Houbert earned his first credits designing portable field shelters like palaces. He's a genius, under all the aesthete crap."

"I guess so!"

"Not that I'll miss him." She pushed her feet into her shoes and stood up, looming over me. "Let's get out of here. Revelry and merriment await us."

9

WHETHER THEY DID or not, I was sure impressed by the Grand Ballroom. It looked real, and permanent, until you got close enough through the traffic jam of sedan chairs and saw that the whole massive thing was just a white tent—though on a scale that made Barnum and Bailey's biggest effort look like a field bivvy. Carved cantilevers ten stories high circled around the outside, gleaming with gold leaf, and scarlet pennants fluttered from the dome, and the whole business glowed with interior lighting like a fairy castle.

"Wow" was all I could say. Mendoza clambered out of the chair ahead of me, unimpressed.

"Come on. I want a drink."

We joined the milling throng and flowed inside with everybody else, where I had the shock of discovering that this was a two-level tent. On the ground floor were a bar, hatcheck booth, retiring area, and kitchens, all gorgeously appointed in a central chamber. Around the perimeter ran a couple of long sloping ramps leading up to the second floor, curtained in swags of sea-green satin. Gaping, I followed Mendoza as she beelined for the bar, and soon we were on our way up the ramp with a margarita each and so many other immortals, you couldn't hear yourself think for all the subvocal chatter.

I thought that what I'd seen so far had been pretty neat, until I got upstairs. The ballroom itself was floored with a vast and gleaming expanse of polished teak—over cork, to judge from the pleasant bounciness of our steps. The ceiling was held up with gilded palm trees and winked here and there with tiny electric stars. From the center a mirrored ball hung, revolving above rose-pink lights, throwing spots of light that swam slowly like fish around the walls. There was a bandstand full of white-jacketed musicians tuning up; a placard of gold script on a blood-red background announced that they were KING PAKAL & HIS PARTY BOYS D' POPUL VUH.

A few immortals drifted on the dance floor; others were sitting at a bank of tables on a kind of mezzanine, near the buffet table. I made for the food first, like the old field operative I am. Mendoza teetered along after me, sipping from her margarita.

And was that a spread! Great hors d'oeuvres and other little crunchy things. Nothing as substantial as cold cuts or dinner rolls, but what it lacked in solid food, it made up for in imaginative presentation. I remember a big pyramid of chicken salad paprikaed all over to look like our red stucco central residential complex. I remember Mayan hieroglyphs sculpted in liverwurst. I remember a scowling Mayan warrior profile bas-relieved in tomato aspic, with a bulging hard-boiled egg for its glaring eye. Green vegetable pâté had been piped in for the head's trailing quetzal plumes.

But the desserts! Let's skip the obvious stuff like the pineapple gondolas and the *gateaux pyramides*. Let's skip the little dishes of salted nuts and chalky mints. There was Theobromos in abundance like I've never seen in my long life: layered into cakes, whipped into creamy mousses, waxily coating fresh strawberries and candied fruits. There was Theobromos cream pie three inches deep, Theobromos cheesecake decorated with Theobromos bonbons, Theobromos roses on sugar stems, bombe Theobromos filled with frozen Theobromos ganache, Theobromos tartufos rolled in chopped Brazil nuts, and a whole lot of lively and obscene little figures made of plain, solid, highest-grade Theobromos. *And* champagne. Boy oh boy, what would our mortal masters say if they could see all this?

Over the buffet was strung a bannered message in gold script: WE ARE THE BRIGHT ASCENDING BUBBLES IN THE BLACK WINE OF MORTALITY. What the hell that was supposed to mean I couldn't guess, but it looked poetic. Mendoza and I loaded our plates with a little of everything and elbowed along the terrace to a vacant table.

"This looks like a good place." Mendoza dumped her plate down and collapsed into a folding chair. "Nice view, breeze from the windows, close to a door for quick exit after the New Year strikes. I've gone as far as I'm going in these heels tonight, thank you."

"You said it, kiddo." I dove into my Theobromos zabaglione fantasia, and conversation sort of languished for a few minutes. With each passing moment, though, the ballroom grew more beautiful and the wan crowd of immortals livelier. King Pakal and his buddies struck up a medley of Cab Calloway hits, and a few Old Ones actually got out on the floor and boogie-woogied in their silk pants and hoop skirts.

"Say, Joseph, is that you?" Lewis wandered up with a massively loaded dessert plate and a dry martini. "And Mendoza! Good to see you again. Would you two mind terribly if I took this chair? My lady friend threw tact to the winds and locked herself in her room with a good book, so I'm going to spend my evening carping from the mezzanine and overdosing on neurostimulants."

"Sure." Mendoza speared a bonbon on her dessert fork and waved assent. "How the hell are you, anyway?"

"Just peachy-keen, thanks." He set his plate down and took a seat. Wriggling forward to the edge of it, he placed his fingertips on his knees. "And I've had the most splendid news. You'll never guess."

"What?"

"I'm being transferred!"

"No kidding? Where to?"

"England. The jolly old UK." He lifted a forkful of Theobromos torte and bit into it decisively. "Well, with a brief layover in Jamaica to build a cover identity. Oh, my, this has orange liqueur drizzled through it! Try some. In any case, I'm off next month. Hurrah!"

"England, huh?" Mendoza laid her fork down and frowned. "Well, you watch out, dear. It's a crazy place. Cold and wet, and dirty, too. I was miserable there."

She hadn't been miserable all of the time, as I remembered, but even under the cheery influence of the Theobromos I knew better than to say this. I just scraped my parfait glass clean and dug into the Theobromos pudding.

"Well, you were there in, what, the fifteens? This is a whole new era. London may be nasty, but there'll be coffeehouses and exciting literary parties. And, you know, I'm actually rather looking forward to getting my hands dirty in the field again." He raised his martini in a gesture of salute. I thought he looked as though he'd break in half if the dirt fought back with any determination, but then he was stronger than he appeared. We all are. Mendoza just shook her head.

"You take care, all the same. They're not a civilized people, no matter what they think of themselves."

"Oh, I know. I've some wild and woolly times to get through before Victoria toddles onstage. I'll be working out of the London safe house, though, so I shouldn't think there'll be too much cause for concern. Do you know London at all?"

"No." Mendoza sipped from her drink. "I was stuck down in

Kent the whole time." I wondered why she was able to discuss England with everybody except me.

"Pity. Well, that's what access codes are for, though I always find personal recommendations helpful too. And! Even though my primary assignment will be coordinating arrivals and departures, somebody up there's finally remembered my literary training. I'm to collect rare volumes as they come off the presses and ship them off to 'specified locales.' What fun! Perhaps I'll run some cozy little antiquarian bookshop in the West End. Assuming there is a West End yet. I suppose there must be." He carefully removed the nuts from a slice of Theobromos log before attacking it with his fork.

"You'll have a swell time," I assured him. King Pakal led a particularly raucous sign-off to the "St. James Infirmary Blues" and started in on some twenty-third-century neobaroque fusion stuff. I turned to stare at the ballroom, which glittered with movement as more and more people braved the dance floor. "Boy, look at the turnout. Is it like this every year?"

"Not so elaborate," Mendoza admitted.

"No indeed." Lewis waved his fork. "Look at all the slogans." I followed his gesture and realized that there were banners everywhere like the one above the buffet, with drooping gold script announcing such heartening sentiments as TEMPUS FUGIT, CARPE DIEM, WE ARE THE TICKING CLOCK MEASURING THE SOUL'S DARK MIDNIGHT, WE ARE DIANA'S FORESTERS, ALL GOOD THINGS MUST END, and TOMORROW AND TOMORROW AND TOMORROW.

"Nothing like wallowing in it." Mendoza shuddered.

"Well, it *is* the beginning of the end for this place," Lewis pointed out. "The Age of Exploration marches on, nipping at Houbert's heels. How he must dread the thought of all those earnest fellows in pith helmets searching for Lost Atlantis here. I must say I've been bored silly at old New World One, but I'll be sorry to think of the monkeys finally getting in."

"The human ones or the ones with tails?" Mendoza showed too many teeth in her smile. We all shared a brittle laugh and clinked our glasses, toasting nothing much.

The orchestra abruptly left off the fusion and struck up Mozart's "Chorus of the Janissaries" from *The Abduction from the Seraglio*.

"Whoops." Lewis and Mendoza got to their feet, as did everybody else who had been sitting down, so I stood too. All the Mayan waiters prostrated themselves. Base Administrator Houbert was borne in through the main entrance in a gilded sedan chair. He had on a getup of gold tissue and purple plumes, and wore a crown of violets.

Big golden tears had been painted down his cheeks. I guess this was to signify that he was in mourning for the end of an era.

Lewis pressed his lips together, but Mendoza didn't even bother to conceal her giggles, until it became obvious that the chair bearers were taking Houbert on a grand circuit of the dance floor, past all the diners on the terrace. As he processed along, he dipped into a bag from time to time and tossed little round black pellets to the crowd. Black olives? Goat droppings? No, they were hitting with a sharp crack that made diners flinch and avoid them. The sound suggested a hard coating.

"Oh, God, they're *black* jelly beans this year," Mendoza muttered.

"Of course. The siècle is fin, after all," replied Lewis out of the side of his mouth. As the palanquin neared us, we gentlemen doffed our hats and bowed, which Houbert acknowledged with a graceful wave and a shotgun scatter of candy. I jumped up to catch one before it broke my margarita glass and popped it in my mouth. I was expecting licorice, but that would have been too pedestrian for Houbert; these jelly beans were flavored with Black Elysium liqueur. It figured.

I had drawn attention to myself with my leap, though, and Houbert's little eyes settled on me. There was a split second of recognition, then an icy stare, before he turned his face deliberately away. The sedan chair bounced on past our table.

"Well, that was as pointed a snub as I've seen in the last three hundred years," observed Lewis. Suddenly his face lit up. "Great Caesar's ghost, that story is true! You did electrocute his pet piranhas!"

"What!" Mendoza stared at me.

"They say he stepped into the damned breakfast-room pool and fried those fish with some direct current when they attacked him. Oh, well done!" Lewis applauded me.

"It was an accident," I muttered in embarrassment. "It was part of this dumb game he had me playing to find my access codes. I was coming down off a Theobromine high at the time, and I slipped."

"Ah. Plied you with Hell's Own Swiss Miss compound, did he? Serves the beggar right." Lewis resumed his seat and dug into a Theobromos napoleon with gusto. Mendoza collapsed into her chair, weeping with laughter.

"You of all people losing your stirrups. And I missed it? I'm desolated! I'd cut my own throat, if that would kill me! How, oh how did this happen?"

"Did you ever have the special stuff he serves his guests?" I said defensively.

"Oh, no." Lewis dabbed at his mouth with a napkin. "We've never been considered artistic or creative enough to appreciate it. We're mere bureaucratic cogs in the big chronometer of life, unlike you, apparently. No, old chap, you sampled a pleasure reserved for the elite few." He began to chuckle afresh. "That'll teach him!"

By this time Houbert had made a full circuit of the ballroom, and his bearers took him across to where a golden throne was just descending from the ceiling, its arrival on a raised dias timed to coincide with the end of the music. He dismounted from the palanquin and turned to face us all (except for me). A single pink spotlight hit him.

MY DEAREST CHILDREN! he boomed. Wc all winced, and he hastily adjusted his decibels. *Weep with me! Weep, oh weep! All weep!*

Nobody was weeping, and the Mayan waiters gave us some dirty looks. Finally there were some howls and boohoos of lament from the tables closest the dias. Houbert raised his big hands in seeming ecstasy, as though he were conducting an orchestra playing something slow and sublime. *That's it! Allow it to well up in your hearts! FEEL the sorrow of eternal life, the endless tragedy of the endless mortality in which we can never share! Let the tide of tears for all that you have known, and all that you can never know, wash into your hearts!*

"Have you heard about the latest nanotechnology they're allowing us in the field?" Lewis inquired of Mendoza. "There was a nice article in *Immortal Lifestyles Monthly.*"

"No, I haven't seen this month's issue," replied Mendoza, draining her margarita.

For another day of reckoning dawns on the all-too-near horizon, my children! Once again the evil genius Time draws near with his hourglass and scythe, bringing destruction once again to a garden of paradise! Once again we poor deathless ones will wander homeless upon the face of the earth, as ruin devours what we once held dear! Houbert held out one palm and shimmied it slowly downward. He may have meant the gesture to be expressive, but it made him look as though he were shaking a tambourine.

"Well, it seems that someone's come up with a surveillance device of perfectly astonishing tininess, and here's the best part: it's packaged in miniature robots that look *exactly* like head lice." Lewis widened his eyes for emphasis.

"No kidding?"

Will no merciful God look down to stop the pitiless and eternally unfolding pageant of the years? Who among you but has fled weeping

*as barbarians despoiled Troy, or as fire and brimstone rained down
upon Nineveh and Tyre? Who among you but has learned the bitter
lesson that All Good Things Must Come to an End?*

"As God is my witness. Even under a microscope, you can't tell,
unless you know where to look for the manufacturer's mark. Plant
one on a mortal subject, and you can hear every word that's uttered
in a thirty-foot radius around him."

"The anthropologists ought to love that."

LAMENTATION is my theme this evening. Houbert threw up his
beefy arms. *For this sweet utopia that will lie in ruins one century
hence, and for us, poor creatures that we are, denied the blessed
solace of eternal sleep, of kindly dust and gentle oblivion, of sharing
the fate of those who have gone forever into that good night!*

"But! There's more. The article says that these are only the pro-
totypes, and we can expect a whole new line of multipurpose lice.
Tiny traveling cameras, for example. Lice that function as miniature
hypodermics—" Lewis jabbed eloquently with his dessert fork. "One
'bite,' and your mortal subject is knocked out for hours, or inoculated
with a vaccine."

"And the timing's so right, too. Just as the powdered wig is
becoming *the* fashion statement," said Mendoza in admiration.

*CHERISH the divine emotions that make you what you are, my
children: the unnatural survivors of fragile humanity, from them but
never again of them, watching eternally as human creativity is destroyed and yet eternally renewed, so that even as we unnaturals
MOURN, we must unnaturally CELEBRATE!*

"That's just what I thought, myself. Dare we take it further? Why
not receivers as well as transmitters? Lice that pick up Company
broadcasts of popular entertainment. Lice that store and deliver coded
information. Think of the possibilities!"

"You know, I think I did see this article. Wasn't this in the issue
with Alec Guinness on the cover?"

*DO NOT shrug, as some will, and declare that weeds and death
SHOULD conquer because the gilded and graceful SHARE the streets
with poverty and disease.* A glare in my direction left no doubt about
Houbert's opinion of me.

"Yes, as a matter of fact, with an article on his postwar come-
dies."

"That's the one. I haven't read it yet. It's packed in my carry-on
so I'll have something to read on the transport."

*Consider us here on this last night of a century, the deathless,
the eternally beautiful, in all our comfort and felicity. Yet even WE*

shall scatter like leaves before the wind, and who can know when we shall meet again? This gorgeous pavilion will vanish with the dews of morning; yet our more PERMANENT halls shall prove no less insubstantial! Houbert buried his face in his hands, smearing his golden paint.

"Well, don't miss the 'Coming Attractions' section. Personally, I'm thrilled by the potential uses. I can just see myself sitting in some London salon with my lice-ridden peruke, eavesdropping on Doctor Johnson!" Lewis rubbed his hands together.

"How colorful." Mendoza moved her elbow as a Mayan waiter put down a silver ice bucket containing a champagne bottle. "What's this? We didn't order champagne."

"The Father of Heaven (who is, by the way, giving a beautiful speech to which everyone ought to be paying attention) gave orders that this beverage be served to all His immortal children," replied the Mayan primly. "Whether They deserve it or not."

"Oh yeah?" Mendoza glared back at him. "Well, you can go jump in the nearest fountain, pal."

Houbert continued: *Now, you will ask, my children: What are we to do? How are we to live, knowing that ALL beauty is ephemeral? And I shall tell you to dance! DANCE, and express the sorrow in your perfect and unfailing hearts! RENEW in your beautiful dance the pattern of the cosmos itself! Dance, my children, even as you hear the bell tolling and know it shall NEVER toll for thee!!* And the spotlight went out, causing him to vanish.

"Certainly," said the waiter, drawing himself up in injured dignity just as the tolling of a very large, very loud bell reverberated through the place. "I'll obey the Daughter of Heaven immediately. I'll go right out to the nearest fountain, even in these clothes which require pressing and starching, and I'll just leap in." He turned to push his way through the crowd on the mezzanine, which had become pretty dense by this time, so I was able to grab his arm.

"What are you, nuts?" I demanded, and Lewis joined in: "Now, now, let's not lose our tempers."

"Look, you stupid bloody Indian—" Mendoza yelled in exasperation as a frenzied waltz began to play.

"Mendoza—"

"Why, of course this slave is stupid. But not so stupid that he has forgotten he's under oath to obey any order whatsoever given him by a Child of Heaven, no matter how unpleasant or irrational. But stupid most assuredly. The Daughter of Heaven has said so." The waiter jutted his ferocious nose in the air.

"Aw, come on, you don't have to go jump in any fountains," I told him.

"No, with all respect, Son of Heaven, I must obey."

"Not if both he and I countermand her order," Lewis proposed. "That would satisfy your oath, wouldn't it? Two Children of Heaven surely overrule one. We both order you *not* to go jump in the nearest fountain. Don't we, Joseph?"

"Yeah, we do, and not only that"—I looked sternly at Mendoza—"the Daughter of Heaven is going to reverse her order too. Aren't you, Mendoza?"

She got an evil gleam in her eyes.

"And she's not going to order you to do something painful and difficult with the champagne bottle, either!" I yelled.

"The Daughter of Heaven reverses her previous order," Mendoza enunciated clearly. I released the waiter's arm. He shook out his bar towel with a crisp snap, refolded it, and draped it over his wrist.

"Thank You. If You have no further orders, this slave is going to continue serving wine to other Children of Heaven, who have *also* disregarded the Father of Heaven's request to dance." And he moved away, back as stiff as a ramrod.

"Goodness, that was awkward," observed Lewis. "But cheer up; soon enough we won't have passive-aggressive members of a vanished empire to order about anymore."

"Three cheers." Mendoza leaned back wearily. "And I'm not getting up to dance, even if a whole priesthood of Mayans disapproves of me."

"Good evening, all," said a voice, seemingly from under the table. A moment later our fourth chair was pushed back, and a little figure clambered up into it.

Lewis nodded. "Good evening, Latif. I assume you have permission to stay up this late?"

"Naturally." Latif settled back into his chair. The candy-box costume was gone; he wore now the school uniform for the neophyte class, with pleats pressed razor-sharp. "Any of you opening that champagne, by the way?"

"Oh, why not?" Lewis peered into his empty martini glass. He pulled out the drippy bottle and prized up the foil and wire with fastidious care. When the cork finally blew, he poured fresh drinks all around, and we sat for a while watching our fellow immortals dance.

Something I've noticed over the years: we don't dance well, on the whole. None of us are clumsy on the floor, or anything like that;

just the opposite. We're too . . . smooth. Too perfect. Well, you can't avoid saying it, we look mechanical. Like big sharks gliding around and around. Never a missed step or beat. Mortals move with a difference, with an awkward something that makes their motion beautiful. Maybe it's passion. I don't know. I only knew one immortal who danced well, and she won't anymore. But maybe it's just the heels she wears nowadays.

As the level in the champagne bottle grew lower, Lewis began to look green.

"Oh, dear," he said faintly. "I don't think I ought to have eaten that last helping of Theobromos mousse."

"You were drinking martinis before the champagne, weren't you?" Latif pointed out in his bright little voice. "Theobromine and gin don't combine well, you know. Try metabolizing sucrose."

"I haven't taken in enough starches. Oh dear."

"Here." Mendoza pushed back her chair, and Lewis sort of toppled over into her lap, where she fed him sugar cubes from the little dish on the table. He lay there pale and wan. I ordered more champagne, which I shared with Latif. Mendoza just watched the whirling dancers as she stroked Lewis's limp hair, her face sad and cold.

Hmmm. I looked at them out of the corner of my eye. Had they had a relationship or something, at one time? Lewis was hardly her type. On the other hand, he seemed funny and kind. I found myself hoping she'd made at least one friend during all these years and realized I was in for a lot of trouble on this next job if I let myself worry about the state of Mendoza's heart. I looked away.

"You're a lot more presentable in the uniform," I told Latif. "How'd you get Houbert to let you out of the Hindu prince suit?"

"Nothing he can do." How could a baby grin wolfishly? "A communication came through this morning. It seems my timetable's been moved up. I'm to be posted to Labienus ahead of schedule. I leave day after tomorrow. Tell me, sir, have you ever been to Canada? Should one pack a heavyweight wardrobe?"

"Thermal underwear and flannel everything," I advised. "And plenty of blankets and waterproof shoes. They won't want you freezing if they're in such a hurry to get you up there," I told him. I wouldn't have put it past him to have intercepted and altered a couple of transmissions to facilitate things, and I wouldn't have blamed him either. What a cool little customer Latif was. Just like I'd been, once. What would he be like in twenty years?

"Well, we'll just see, won't we?" he remarked cheerily, and stood in his chair to pour us both more champagne.

Lewis felt better after a while and lurched upright, just in time to hear *La Valse* by Ravel pulse into its opening chords.

"I wondered when they'd play that," he groaned. "That's Houbert's favorite piece of music, you know. After *The Phantom of the Opera*." The lights in the ballroom deepened to an ominous and weird purple.

"Well, it's appropriate for tonight, anyhow," said Mendoza. "The way it evokes glittering empires about to crumble. Music full of death. God, that's spooky. Look at everybody!"

I peered out on the dance floor, and I swear I felt the hairs on the back of my neck stand. Houbert had worked some trick of lighting, some perversely brilliant special effect, that gave the illusion of death masks on each perfect clockwork dancer who skimmed the ballroom floor in time to that terrible, beautiful music. Swooping and circling, they moved, so many skeletons in satin clothes.

No, wait. They weren't *human* skeletons. Something was picking up the alloy frame in each of them, the machine that had replaced their mortal, breakable bones, the indestructible casing that held their brains and eyes. Was it some quality in the purple light that caused them to glow through the flesh?

No, not the light—or at least not the light alone. The champagne we'd all been given! He'd had it adulterated with something, some chemical harmless in itself, or we'd have detected it in the first taste. That was what was making our hardware glow.

Slowly I looked down at my own hands. Fine jointed mechanisms riveted to a pivoting frame that disappeared into my lace cuffs. I tried to look at Lewis and Mendoza without turning my head much. They were staring out at the dancers with haunted eyes; they hadn't noticed that they too were part of the show, a dapper gentleman skeleton machine and a lissome skull-faced lady machine. And Latif? Well, he wasn't glowing much, because less of him had been replaced, you see. Just a little machine, yet.

And as the music soared to its crashing close, a deafening chime was heard—two, three, four. The chimes kept coming, and the clock was striking midnight. Happy Hellish New Year, 1700! Things like snakes began to fall from the ceiling, and of course they were only black streamers. Our Mayan waiters began to blow paper horns and crank noisemakers. The waltz ended, and the lights came up. "Auld Lang Syne" was playing, the classic soupy Guy Lombardo arrangement.

Lewis looked gray and tired. Mendoza was pale, shaking. I thought she must have noticed the ugly illusion at our own table—

well, not illusion, after all—but she drew a deep breath and said very quietly:

"Oh, how I hate parties. Here we sit tonight, and do you realize how unlikely it is any of us four will ever be together in the same room again?"

Was it loneliness she was afraid of? I reached out my hand to clasp hers.

"Hey, kiddo, you'll see *me* again. We're going on the same assignment together, remember?"

She bared her teeth at me.

10

BUT WE FOUND ourselves on the same transport the next morning, strapped into our seats and watching New World One drop away beneath us.

"It was time for you to move on anyway," I told Mendoza consolingly. "It was stuffy. Decadent. Dull. Nothing should be decadent *and* dull."

"Your father was a Moorish groom and your mother performed circumcisions on sailors," she informed me.

"Hey, that's okay. I know you're not really sore. You're going to love it in California."

"I won't be able to get a cocktail there for at least a hundred years," she brooded. "And longer, for a Ghirardelli's hot fudge sundae."

"Well, you hated parties anyway."

She just snarled and opened her magazine, shutting me out. I didn't mind; do I ever mind? I'm only the guy who gave her eternal life, after all. I settled back in my seat and closed my eyes. Forty winks after last night's party seemed like a good idea.

I thought about Latif, the self-assured little administrator-in-training, all his buttons polished, intent on asking the right questions and making the right moves. Funny that he so worshiped my buddy Suleyman, who was anything but a bureaucrat. Still, when you're tiny and mortal and frightened, and this big god comes looming out of the darkness to offer you a hand—well, it makes an impression. I thought about what it must have been like, in the stinking hold of a slave ship, with all the comfort and safety you'd ever known lying beside you bewilderingly dead . . . and just as the loss got through to you, and

the scream began to rise in your throat because you knew you were
alone, just then the big man appeared and called your name.

I don't know how he knew my name. I don't even remember
what my name was. But he was there, looming against the darkness,
a god in a bearskin, and his axe and his hands were red. Lying around
his feet were the bad guys, all smashed, the tattooed devils who'd
caught my family away from the rock shelter. He didn't smell or look
anything like anybody else I'd ever seen. He looked like a mountain
and his brow was a cliff, with his pale eyes staring out from its
shadow. He saw me where I was hiding. He put out his red hand and
called my name, in his flat high voice. I went to him. He took me out
of the painted cave and past the fires where his army was burning the
bodies of the tattooed men. He explained that the tattooed men had
to die because they were bad and made war. I was glad they were
dead and burning, because it meant that I wasn't going to die.

He told me I would never die. He took me to the other place,
where there were clean quiet people who didn't smell. They fed me,
washed me, and put me to bed where it was safe. Later they made
me immortal.

But I could never seem to get completely out of that darkness
that was scary and smelled so bad. Then I was in the prison and
staring through the doorway at the little girl who sat huddled in the
straw, such a thin, sick little girl, her arms and legs like white sticks.
All the life she had left was burning in her eyes, furious black eyes.
I loomed against the light and put out my hand to her. She told me
to go to hell. I knew then she had to be immortal; you need a tough
will to work for Dr. Zeus.

"Hey." Mendoza shoved me. Light all around us, clouds drifting
past the window. "Wake up. We're over Alta California."

11

CALIFORNIA.

Named after a queen, supposedly, and you could see why. She's the schizoid goddess Fortune herself: sometimes a smiling benefactress who gives mortals all they could hope for in life, sometimes a snarling bitch driving her children from her with a whip and a flail. The trick is, see, you have to know what you really want from her when you go there.

First we saw a pretty coastline: mountains that rolled back from the coastal bluffs, scored with deep valleys. Everything was green, but it was winter, you have to remember.

We saw a place where the land stuck out like a snail's head just emerging from its shell. That was Point Conception, our destination. No trees here: bare scrubby headland, and even from the transport you could see the bushes tilting sideways in the sea breeze. We felt the wind buffeting us as we sank toward the landing platform.

When we stepped out, wow. An ice-cold gale that made my eyes water. I noticed that all the field personnel lined up to greet us wore sunglasses, the wraparound kind like goggles. I hoped I'd be issued a pair. The winter sunlight was sharp as diamonds.

"Where are the palm trees?" said Mendoza through gritted teeth. "Where are the swimming pools?" There was the sea and a lot of bare rolling hills, and that was about it. We slogged across the platform, the wind whipping at the train of Mendoza's gown, and presented ourselves to the foremost of the goggled welcomers.

"Hi." I thrust out a hand. "Facilitator Grade One Joseph reporting to AltaCal Base."

"Good." The welcomer smiled, took and dropped my hand. "And Botanist Grade Six Mendoza?"

"Reporting."

"Good. This way." We followed him to our shuttle, which was a rickety car set to run on a wooden track held above the earth on cement piers. It looked like a roller coaster. It drove like one, too.

The wind would have torn our voices away if we'd tried to speak out loud, but the man made no subvocal communication attempts either. Nothing like *So this is your first time in California?* or *Wait'll you folks taste the abalone chowder we fix around here.* He might as well have been a mortal. Mendoza just stared off inland; God knows what she was thinking. I watched the blue Pacific glitter in the sun. It certainly was blue, I gave it that.

We rattled away north to a beach at the mouth of a canyon. The main base was here, a plain modular station backed up on its piers into the cliff at the south side of the cove; the kind of place that could be removed later, and a judiciously engineered rock slide or two would hide any evidence it had ever been there. It was painted for camouflage, but otherwise featureless. Like the personnel. Everyone I saw was wearing Company base issue, which is blank utility clothing with a lot of pockets and no style. Houbert would have been appalled. Men and women alike wore the same one-piece garment. No lace, no padding, no embroidery. I'd worn it myself once or twice, back in prehistory, but I could see Mendoza staring at it aghast.

Or maybe she was looking aghast at the mortals, of which there were a surprising number among the base personnel. Not natives that had been fixed for maintenance labor like the Mayans, either, but actual officers. Kids from the future. It must have cost the Company a fortune to ship them all here.

Aren't those— she subbed at me, and I replied, *That's right.*

Our little thrill ride took us right up under the base, where at last the roar of the wind was shut out. Our driver popped the door open for us, and I ventured, "Lotta youngsters here, aren't there?"

"Yep."

"Real windy place, too."

"Sure is."

"I was expecting something a little more temperate."

"Yeah?"

"Say, you don't talk much, do you?"

"I'm busy." The guy half-turned. "Mr. Bugleg asked that you report to his office immediately upon arrival. Go up those stairs, and the admitting desk will direct you."

I figured it out at last. He was an immortal like we were, all right, but a recent recruit: probably born in the twenty-third century. So that's what they looked like in the future? Was *he* ever caught between two worlds.

We clambered up the steps with our luggage, and Mendoza growled, "Always the same damn story. I've never in my life seen an escalator in one of these places." She grabbed up her train with one hand and hoisted her suitcase in the other. I pushed my tricorne to the back of my head and followed.

At the top of the stairs we were met by a smiling mortal woman with a clipboard. She might have been good-looking in a silk mantle, with maybe a little lace apron. She wore the sexless coveralls, though, like everybody else we'd met so far.

"Um, welcome to AltaCal Base Eight. You must be Facilitator Joseph, and you must be Botanist Mendoza, am I right? Hello and welcome—"

"Yeah. Hi," replied Mendoza. "Look, that driver told us we've got to report directly to a meeting. Was he kidding? Don't we get to see our quarters first, wash up a little? That's pretty inconsiderate, don't you think?"

"Oh, Mr. Bugleg wants to see you right away. It's very important." Rapidly the girl clipped little ID tags to us and our luggage. Her own tag read STACEY. I guessed she'd seen a few of us in her brief lifetime, but not enough to be cool about it. She was radiating discomfort. A little fear, a little more repugnance. I could smell it, and so, unfortunately, could Mendoza. "You can leave your bags here, and we'll deliver them to your rooms. Mr. Bugleg wants to discuss your mission over dinner."

"Great. Thank you very much. Where is the man?" I inquired, hurriedly because I could feel a confrontation building.

"Go through that door at the end of the hall," said the mortal girl, just before Mendoza said, "Did you know you've got an impacted wisdom tooth, Stacey? I'd have it checked out if I were you."

Stacey's hand flew to the corner of her jaw, and my hand flew to Mendoza's arm and I pulled her away with me down the hall.

"Mendoza, that was not nice. Scanning them without permission is impolite."

"I don't give a rat's ass! Did you smell the way she felt about us? If she's got a problem dealing with immortals, why's she with the Company? Nobody told me there'd be mortals crawling all over this place."

"Are you going to do this to me again? Don't do this to me again, Mendoza."

"What'd she think we were, for crying out loud? *Androids?*"

"You've never worked with any Company mortals, have you?" I paused, scanning the long featureless hall in confusion. What was that pinging noise?

"Sure I have." Mendoza turned her head irritably, picking up the sound too.

"I don't mean native busboys. I mean officers and shareholders of Dr. Zeus, from the future. We make them uncomfortable." I paused outside a door and scanned the room beyond. There was a mortal inside, interfacing with an entertainment console. That was it. Somebody was playing a holo game.

"But why? They made us, didn't they? We do exactly what they built us to do, don't we?"

"I know. I'm not sure what the reason is. Maybe some of them feel we're not much more than superpowered slaves and they feel guilty about that?"

She took that in for a minute, as we walked on down the hall.

"Well, that's just ducky," she hissed, and I knocked on Mr. Bugleg's door before she could tell me just how ducky it was.

We were let in by a mortal kid, I guess he was a junior clerk or something, and there was Mr. Bugleg standing at the other end of a table set for four. He'd put the table between us and himself, but otherwise you couldn't have told he was a bigot at all. Nice plastic smile like the girl Stacey. He was mortal too, of course. The food looked lousy. *Oh, boy, this is going to be some tour of duty,* broadcast Mendoza. *Shut up,* I broadcast back. She looked around the room, which was otherwise bare of ornament or furniture save for a plain day bed and a wall console with an enormous private entertainment center. Quite a change from New World One. Bugleg cleared his throat.

"Mendoza. Joseph. How are you? I'm Bugleg. Have a seat." His smile faltered off. He looked like a scared toddler at a birthday party. He was a thirtyish mortal, not quite beginning to sag yet, fairly pastyfaced, and his head was a funny shape. (But, then, all their heads look funny to me.) He wore the same drab clothing as his staff: no medals, epaulets, or gold braid.

"I'll ring for my aide now," he told us, and he did, and after an uncomfortable moment of silence a door opened and another man walked in. This one was an immortal and decently dressed, too, with a good wig and a spiffy brocaded coat. He had a black silk steinkirk knotted casually about his throat. To judge from the heels on his shoes, he wasn't any taller than me, but he strode up to us with authority. The man had style.

His eyes were gray and cold, and his grip was a little too firm as he shook our hands.

"This is Mr. Lopez, my aide," ventured Bugleg.

"Joseph. Mendoza. It's a pleasure meeting you. I'll be briefing you on the mission as we"—he paused significantly—"dine."

He pulled out Mendoza's chair for her. Bugleg sat down and watched in horrified fascination as Mendoza seated herself, settling her acreage of rustling silks less inconveniently.

"Why did you wear all those clothes here?" he asked. "You should put on clothes like we wear. You'd be more comfortable."

Mendoza was too surprised to say anything, for which I was grateful.

"You must remember, sir, that we field operatives spend our whole lives in the past," Lopez explained smoothly. "I've told you about this before. For us, the past *is* real time. We wear these clothes because they're what's being made this year, which happens to be 1700 A.D., by the way. Mortals would notice us if we dressed differently. Besides, if we wanted to wear clothes like yours, they'd have to be specially imported from the future, which would be expensive. It's much cheaper simply to wear what everybody else is wearing in this time period. In fact, we're quite used to these fashions. It may be hard for you to believe, but she's just as comfortable in her clothing as you are in yours."

"Oh," said Bugleg.

The food was just as lousy on closer inspection as it had seemed at first glance. At each place was a shaped tray with compartments containing various pureed or textured substances, brightly colored. We all made courteously exclamatory noises over it, though I noticed Lopez's elbow twitch as he stopped himself from reaching for a claret decanter that wasn't there. I lifted my plastic sipper bottle to see what our beverage was. Distilled water. Bugleg lifted his and slurped as happily as though it were champagne. He put it down and said:

"It's so great you're here at last. Now we can really get some work done. We couldn't start without you, uh, Joseph. What do you need to know about your mission?"

Mendoza raised her eyebrows, but I said, "Well, as I understand it, we're kind of lifting an entire biosystem off the face of the Earth in situ, right?"

Bugleg's jaw hung slack. *He doesn't know what the big words mean,* transmitted Lopez, and out loud he said, "Right. To be specific, we're collecting the Chumash village of Humashup. The people, the animals they hunt, the plants they gather, the fish they catch, their culture in its entirety, even samples of the local geology and seawater."

"Yes," affirmed Bugleg.

"No wonder you've brought so many specialists in on this," remarked Mendoza.

"Impressive, isn't it?" Lopez almost reached for claret again. "You'll find access codes for all relevant anthropological information in your assigned quarters, and I believe you'll find the texts by John P. Harrington and Alfred L. Kroeber the most useful. To give you an overview, however: the Chumash are the aboriginal inhabitants of this region of the California coast. Our preliminary studies show a Neolithic level of technological development but an extremely complex social and mercantile structure. They're hunter-gatherers but also industrialists, if you can imagine that. They produce a wide variety of objects manufactured specifically for trade with other local tribes. They've developed a monetary system that other tribes have had to adopt in order to do business with them, but they've retained sole rights to the manufacture of the shell money they use. The word *Chumash* is a corruption of the name given to them by their neighbors, which can be roughly translated as 'the people who make money.' Which they certainly do, literally and figuratively. By local standards they're millionaires."

"Savages with an economic empire." Mendoza looked amused.

"Hardly savages. Their standard of living is quite high. Life is easy for the Chumash. They haven't had to develop agriculture or domesticate animals, because the wild food sources are abundant. The climate in the interior is temperate, so clothing is largely unnecessary, though they enjoy elaborate jewelry and hair adornment. And they bathe more frequently than contemporary mortals in Europe."

"Well, who doesn't?"

Lopez put his elbows on the table and leaned forward. "These people have saunas. They have municipal centers for organized sporting events. They have ballet. They have stand-up comedians. I think most people would define that as the Good Life."

"Sound like stereotypical Californians to me." I bit down on a hard lump of something. Analysis proved it to be an unrehydrated nugget of protein paste. I made it vanish discreetly into my paper napkin. "Do they have any less attractive qualities?"

Sighing, Lopez settled back in his chair and pushed his food away.

"They have their problems. They seem to get most of their aggressions out on their neighbors by controlling commerce, but there is some territorial warfare. Their infant mortality rate is suspiciously high. Seems to be a high level of domestic violence, too."

"Nobody's perfect." I drank the rest of my water and looked around for more. Lopez's elbow twitched again. No crystal decanter to refill my bottle, and Bugleg seemed oblivious to the possibility that his guests might want more. Lopez and I both sighed. "So, what's their religion like? I understand I'm playing a god?" I continued.

"More or less. They're loosely pantheistic, animistic, and their astrologers are quite accomplished astronomers as well. They do debate philosophy to some degree. Their principal semidivine totemic hero is Sky Coyote. You'll get all the available data on him when you access your orientation material, but he's your standard Trickster figure who's also the friend and helper of the human race. Hence our choice of him as our liaison."

"I don't know what that word means," complained Bugleg. The conversation came to a screeching halt, and we all stared at him.

"Which word, sir?" inquired Lopez.

"*Hence*. You went, *hence*. That's one of those old-time words."

"Why, yes, sir, but we're old-time people, aren't we, sir?" Lopez smiled at him with great effort. "So you mustn't mind it."

"*Hence* means 'So that's why,' " I explained. "Like, 'So that's why we chose Coyote as our liaison.' See?"

"Oh." Bugleg looked sulky. "Then you should have gone 'So that's why,' not that old-time word. You shouldn't use those old-time words. They're weird."

Lopez drew a deep breath. I began to have respect for the man. He rushed on: "You're going to make contact with the Chumash and persuade them to relocate. Then you'll keep them cooperative as we go through the subsequent stages of the operation. We're staging it now, because communication among villages is limited at this time of the year and we're aiming at closure within two months. In fact, we chose Humashup because it's comparatively isolated and word of our presence is less likely to spread. It's also the nearest community to Point Conception (known to the Chumash as *Humqaq*, or Raven Point), which was chosen as our base site because it figures in their mythology as the gateway to the next world. The locals avoid the area for that reason, making it an ideal place for our installation."

"And if anybody sees anything high-tech and strange, it can be explained away as spirits," I guessed.

"Exactly. Once we've collected them, all the villagers will be airlifted to Mackenzie Base for further study and assimilation."

"Sounds like I'll need to do some pretty fancy talking to get these people to go with us, if they have such a good life here," I said.

"The Company has every confidence in you," Lopez told me firmly. "You yourself are the product of a similarly primitive culture, after all, which ought to provide you with some insights. We're also fitting you with complex appliance makeup and biomechanical prostheses to turn you into their patron god. In fact"—Lopez took out an octavo memorandum and consulted it—"you'll report to suite A_3 at eight hundred hours tomorrow for preliminary fittings and tissue matching. Shower and shave first, please."

"Is this an uncomfortable process?"

"I'm afraid so."

"Oh, well. I guess I'll need every possible arrow in my quiver." I shrugged.

"You're not supposed to use arrows!" said Bugleg, in some alarm.

There was another pause. *I give up,* transmitted Mendoza. *Is the guy brain-damaged or what?*

He only speaks Twenty-Fourth Century Cinema Standard, explained Lopez.

But so do we!

Not exactly.

But we've read their books! We've seen their films! Charles Dickens! Somerset Maugham! Warner Brothers!

Those are mostly drawn from the few centuries preceding his time, Lopez told her. *In his era, most mortals find them too difficult to understand. Particularly technocrats such as our friend here. The liberal arts are consequently—how shall I say it?—rather suspect.*

Mendoza was stunned into silence. All of their conversation took about a nanosecond, so without even missing a beat I turned to Bugleg and grinned like his best pal. "Just a figure of speech, sir. A metaphor. You know."

He blinked.

"I won't really shoot anybody with any real arrows," I assured him. "Say, isn't this Proteus-Brand Synthesized Protein we're eating?"

"Yes."

"In béarnaise sauce. Well, well. You know, it'll be great once we're really settled in here at this base and your catering crew get their act together. Plenty of great stuff to eat in California, you know.

There's abalone and swordfish out there in the sea. Venison's abundant in this coastal range, too, I hear. Swell fresh cuisine.''

I swear the guy turned pale.

"We feel more comfortable with our own food," he said.

Okay. I got down the last of my foodlike substance and looked around longingly. No wine, no brandy, no liqueurs or coffee. No dessert either.

"What a great meal," I said. "Got any Theobromos?"

!!!!!!! broadcast Lopez. Bugleg looked shocked.

"Is that a joke?"

Whoops.

"Of course it is." I grinned most charmingly. "Take it easy. I guess you've heard us field operatives are a pretty wild bunch, but really nobody does Theobromos. Honest. Just pulling your leg."

"Just—"

"I was only joking with you," I clarified.

"Oh."

I hope they don't search our luggage, broadcast Mendoza.

By that evening, as I reclined on my uncomfortable twenty-fourth-century mattress accessing anthropological data, I had Bugleg all figured out. You know those Victorian big-game hunters who'll insist on bringing all the apparatus of their civilization into the jungles with them? Formal dress for dinner, *London Illustrated News,* teatime? Every little British social custom rigorously observed, so they don't go native? That was what was going on here. Bugleg couldn't have volunteered for this mission, he must have been horrified to have been chosen; and so he'd compensated by wrapping his whole sanitized twenty-fourth-century world and all its values around himself, and we were expected to conform, like native bearers obliged to wear white jackets to serve dinner.

What kind of rank did he hold in the Company, though, to have pull like that? It must have cost a fortune to ship a whole chunk of the twenty-fourth century here, just so he could cope. He seemed like such a moron.

The Chumash were a lot easier to understand. Even before I'd finished the material by Harrington and Kroeber, I felt I knew them. Everything Lopez had told me was true, and if you don't believe me, access the files yourself. They really did have an economic empire and a sophisticated lifestyle, for people living in a Neolithic world. To tell the truth, they were a lot more advanced than the tribe I'd been born into, back in France or Spain or wherever it had been.

I didn't think I'd have any problems, though. The truth is, *Homo sapiens sapiens* is pretty much the same the world over, regardless of skin color or technological development. Racists and provincial types have problems with this fact, but it is a fact. All mortals have the same potential, and only chance determines who's playing a spinet or who's clubbing dinner to death with a big rock. And, you know what? Mortals adapt to the environment in which they're placed. Switch babies between savages and technologicals, and nobody notices! I know, because I've seen it done. I've seen the son of a club-carrying cave dweller fuming because his accounting software wasn't quite adequate for his needs. All humans have the same brain package.

Nowadays, anyway.

12

NINE HUNDRED HOURS, day two of my time in Alta California, and I was gingerly withdrawing my hand from a Fineplast casting. Matthias, the tech, nodded approvingly at the hole I'd made and handed it off to a mortal assistant. Matthias was one of our Old Ones, like me; except he had the big face and unflappable calm of the Neanderthals. I'd always gotten on well with these guys. Nowadays, of course, they couldn't work in the field much, due to the fact that the human gene drift had moved away from their kind of looks and made them really noticeable if they went out among mortals; but they seemed happy enough working as technicians and pilots around Company bases.

"Now, here's a model of the hardware we'll use for the paw prosthesis. It fits over here"—he took my wrist and demonstrated—"and we'll graft the implants here, here, and here. The nerves will run right down through the flesh frame to your own, so there'll be no loss of sensation and no lag time in response. The digits may look short, but we've practiced with a model and you can manipulate them perfectly well. You can eat, drink, take care of sanitary functions . . ."

"I'm so glad."

"Yeah, we thought you'd be." Matthias put down the skeleton model and took up a graphics plaquette. "Now, we have quite a few possible heads, here. We can go the full-head approach or we can go with appliances, which might be more comfortable for you but would have fewer effects. Your choice." He held up a series of sketches for my perusal.

I surveyed my choices. The full-head model was spectacular; on the drawing board it could do enough tricks to have me convincing

Rin Tin Tin I was his brother. Still, I passed on it. I've worn prostheses with fancy effects before, and they never work right, no matter what the techs tell you. Besides, I'm a minimalist. A good actor doesn't need all that stuff to make mortals believe in him.

We settled on a combination of appliances I felt would work, and while Matthias was making notes, I inquired casually, "So, where do discriminating palates dine around here?"

Matthias looked into my eyes, glanced at his mortal assistant, and said:

"Petrie, I want a Fineplast five-eight, medium olive range." And when Petrie had gone off to make it, whatever it was, Matthias leaned close and said: "So far we've been able to have a couple of seafood bakes. There's a place farther down the beach, still inside the perimeter but out of sight of the base, and there's some shelter from the wind. If you can get away Saturday night . . . You like venison?"

"Are you kidding?"

"Okay, well, Sixtus brought down a buck last week and he's hiding it in the refrigeration module. It ought to be great by the barbecue. For God's sake don't tell the mortals, though. We'd never hear the end of it."

"I gather the administrative staff are strict vegetarians?"

"You can say that again," he said, shaking his head sadly.

"So, what's the deal, here?" I prodded. "I've never seen so many twenty-fourth-century bureaucrats on a mission in my life. How much did Dr. Zeus spend on this show, anyway?"

"Buckets of cash, from what I've heard," Matthias told me. "Apparently it's something political. I don't ask, friend, I just do my job." He toyed with his stylus absentmindedly as he spoke, making it rotate over and under each finger in turn. You never see that kind of manual dexterity anymore; Cro-Magnons didn't have it, and it wasn't passed on to the hybrid *Homo sapiens sapiens*.

"There seems to be a lot of, uh, bad feeling between them and us," I observed.

"*You* try living with these people for six weeks," Matthias said with a sigh. "I've been here since setup, man, and I'm so sick of them, I could cry. I'm just hoping they'll transfer me back to Greenland when this job's over. Get you into your coyote suit and I'm out of here, with any luck. I can't believe the stares I get from these kids. I'm about ready to make myself up as a Cro-Magnon, just so they stop flinching when they pass me in the hallway."

He dropped his voice as Petrie came back and informed him that my five-eight was ready. It turned out to be the medium for my lower-body cast. Quite an experience.

13

So here I am, Mr. Sky Coyote.

I like this role. Trot trot trot on my new feet, leaving strange prints along the creek bed. A seagull floating inland gives a high far-off cry, and I cock my ear most comically. Up the winding canyon, and any real beast meeting me here in the gloom under the oak trees will have the fright of its life. If I wanted to give chase, I wonder how I'd do? The muzzle points, the sharp teeth bare, and they snap and slash. We had to compromise on the tongue so I could still speak, but I've practiced panting in the mirror. I'm confident I'll make a good impression.

Once upon a time, see, the line between men and animals was a lot less clearly drawn. If you were out with your spear thrower on a summer morning in Spain a couple of hundred centuries ago, you might have met with a creature like me and been scared, yes; but not really surprised. Things were more fluid then. Perception wasn't the same. Mortals have since learned not to see what doesn't fit into the world pattern they're most comfortable with, so of course there are no human-headed bulls, no transparent women walking along the surface of rivers, no balls of fire that hang in the air and scream with human voices. Any time mortals live out in the open, though, it becomes harder for them to shut out the inexplicable stuff, so they have to develop some context for it. That's why they tell stories about creatures like me, with my teeth and my tail. That's why they'll accept me as Sky Coyote come for a visit.

Yeah, I'm pretty game for a guy walking into Chumash territory buck naked except for some prostheses and strategic fur implants. But, hey, I'm a Facilitator! We're more flexible than the Conservers or the

Techs, psychologically, physically, morally. Disguises and intrigues are what we live for. And these really are the very best effects the Company can provide.

Let's try Angry Coyote. I crouch, and look at those ears go back, back, look at those hackles rise! I snarl, I sidle. Tail down like a broken plume.

Happy Coyote. Mr. Perky! Everything upright and bouncy! Whoops. Maybe too upright and bouncy, but what the hell, maybe the Chumash will think it's funny. Got to remember my cultural context here. I frisk. I frolic. I try a few yards on all fours and actually do pretty well. Could even run like this if I had to.

Anyway there I was, following the creek back into the hills, miles and miles of getting into character, and suddenly I picked them up about a mile ahead of me and fifty feet up the hillside to my left: mortals. Two males.

When you're going to impress somebody with your otherworldly godliness, it's better to try it from high ground. Silhouetted dramatically against the sky, like. Sprinting up the steep slope through the sagebrush or whatever it was, I thought of Warner Brothers 'toons and giggled. There was a nice outcropping of red rock just out of bowshot from where they'd pass. I got up there and struck an attitude. They were coming steadily nearer; they'd heard me crashing around.

In a moment I saw them, and they were buck naked too, literally, insofar as they both had on these kind of stuffed deer-head hats that Chumash hunters wore for camouflage. Pretty clever, if you're after deer. I was after *them*.

"Hello, nephews," I barked.

The little deer heads stopped bobbing forward. They rose slowly, and we beheld each other, I and my two earthbound kin.

"You haven't caught anything today, I see," I observed, scratching myself with my hind leg. Sort of.

"It's Sky Coyote," one of them observed faintly. I cocked my ear at that.

"Well, of course I am. Why are you so surprised to see me?" They were more than surprised, actually, if the sudden reek of urine from downwind was any indication. I'd overdone it on the otherworldly-god bit, but I sure had made an impression. To keep them from running away, I continued with the conversation: "I've got some very important matters to discuss with you boys."

"Really?" replied the other of them, still trembling.

"Really. Very important. But excuse me a minute, won't you?" I cocked my leg majestically, hoping to damp down, as it were, their awe. They stared, and then one of them straightened up and pulled off his headgear.

"Oh, for God's sake, it's just a man in a coyote hat," he said in disgust. "Who do you think you are, mister?"

Time for action. I leaped down and landed in front of him. "Who do *you* think I am?" I retorted.

Up close, the whole carefully crafted illusion was undeniable. I watched his face as his reality shifted out from under him, never to settle back in the old way again. I seized his shaking hand and dragged it up to my ear. "Look. Feel. Pull it. Now do you know who I am?"

"My God!" he burst out. "You really are Sky Coyote! I mean— excuse me—"

"Why are you so surprised?" I repeated. "Haven't you been hearing about me all your life?"

"Well, yes—it's just that nobody's ever actually *seen* You. In our village, anyway."

"I don't get down to this world much lately. It's sort of out of the way. Nevertheless, I'm here, because I have big news for your village. I'm here to save you all!"

So they took me to meet the folks.

Their names were Kenemekme and Wixay, and they were upright, fit, and clean-limbed young guys, with nice clear skins. Gleaming white teeth, hair like black silk. Pretty much representative of their race. Kenemekme was tall and nervous. Wixay was sturdier; he kept exclaiming and smacking the earth with his bow as we walked along.

"I just can't get over this," he said excitedly. "You're really here! Sky Coyote, in the flesh! There are so many things I've always wanted to ask You."

"Such as?"

"Well, is it true that You wanted to fix it so we'd never get old and sick by letting us swim in the Lake of Youth, but the Earth Cricket voted You down in the Sky People's council?"

"It's true. He said things would be too crowded if men never died." I nodded emphatically. "And he was right, actually, but you can't blame me for trying!"

"And is that story true, how you were the referee when Hawk and Turtle had their race, back in the first days of the world?"

"That's right. And were they grateful for my honest judgment? I don't think so!"

"But this means it's *all* true, then, doesn't it? About the World above This One and the Sky People and everything?"

"Yes, nephew, it's all true," I told him solemnly.

"Wow." He shivered with pleasure.

"You're serious about this, aren't You?" Kenemekme studied me as we trudged along. I nodded. He bit his lip.

I didn't blame him for being uneasy. Mortals occupy a pretty low place in Chumash cosmogony. There's a principal supreme deity who's the Sun, usually, and there are a few subordinate deities who keep the universe running smoothly and punish their fellow supernaturals who get out of line. The only celestial big shot who concerns himself with the human race is Sky Coyote. He created men, he meddles in their affairs, he negotiates with the other spirits for good harvests and low mortality rates. Not all-powerful and not especially virtuous, either, but he's the only friend men have. Just the role for me.

14

So here's the semigod or tutelary spirit or whatever he is, arriving in the valley of Humashup with two of his mortal nephews.

Humashup was not a big town, but it was a prosperous one. There was a residential district back in the oak forest, three or four broad streets lined with woven houses. Over on the west side was the big municipal sports field and beyond that the sacred enclosure and cemetery, tidily fenced. To the south a long thatched enclosure marked the village meeting house. Down by the creek I saw the communal acorn-processing rocks and, a respectable distance away, the private steam baths. The little open-air shrine I could see was in fine repair, and the altar pole was loaded with offerings. Times were good in Humashup, obviously.

We advanced from the west, through what you might call the industrial complex: a stone yard with stonecutters busily at work, a boatyard with canoemakers busily at work. Until they saw me, of course.

And then, hey, the people came out to look. The workers dropped their tools and stared; the women pounding acorns stopped in mid-pound and stared; the boys driving a hoop around the playing field stopped and stared, and the hoop went wobbling away unnoticed.

I waved. "Hello, everybody. It's Uncle Sky Coyote. Remember me?"

Now, these people were not idiots, and the first conclusion most of them came to was that I was a mortal man in some kind of coyote suit. Thank Dr. Zeus for high-quality grafts, implants, and appliance makeup. I think I'll just skip over all the times I had to have my tail pulled to prove I was real, likewise the times people said things like

I've Heard a Lot about You but I Never Actually Thought I'd Meet You. Let's cut to the big meeting in the council house that night.

I had the seat of honor, on a boulder near the fire. Everyone else sat on mats on the floor, and the place was packed, more than packed; through every crevice and slot in the tule wall I could see a pair of eyes gleaming, from all those who weren't important enough to sit inside.

As soon as everyone had gotten comfortable, Sepawit, the chief, stood and cleared his throat. He was a thin man approaching middle age, with an intelligent face. Like most of the other men, he wore nothing but a belt and some shell-bead money, but his hair was long and arranged in an elaborate chignon with beautifully carved wooden pins.

"Well. Well, folks, I guess our distinguished visitor doesn't need much of an introduction to you all—" Scattered nervous giggles at that. I laughed, too, tongue lolling and fangs bright, to show I appreciated the situation and to show off some of my head's effects. "And though it's certainly been a long time since He's visited us, I'd say we're unanimous in extending a heartfelt welcome to Sky Coyote from the people and fraternal organizations of Humashup!"

There were polite nods and mutters of assent. The chief went on. "Uncle Sky Coyote, I'd like to introduce Nutku, spokesman for the Canoemakers' Union. Nutku is also First Functionary of the Humashup Lodge of the Brotherhood of the Kantap."

Nutku rose to his knees so I could see him. Powerful arms on this fellow, and he wore more strings of shell money than Sepawit did, and had a bearskin cloak over his shoulders too. His hair was done up with mother-of-pearl pins. I scanned him and detected mild arteriosclerosis, a touch of hypertension: he dined on lots of fatty red meat and made executive decisions. Introduced first, too. Important guy.

"And this is Sawlawlan, spokesman for the United Workers in Steatite." Another one wearing lots of money, with big hair and a sea-otter cape. "And Kupiuc, spokesman for the Intertribal Trade Council and Second Functionary of the Humashup Lodge. And this is Kaxiwalic, one of our most successful independent entrepreneurs."

"Pleased to meet all of you," I said, all benevolence. I had my audience pegged, now: here were the upper classes, wearing a certain hard and confident look, a can-do look, you might say, and across their chests the rolls of shell money rippled and clicked like backgammon counters. The nobodies were at the back of the room, with open, vulnerable faces like nobodies everywhere. I could play to this audience. I'd played to their like for more centuries than I remembered.

I got to my feet. My shadow loomed up behind me on the dome of the hall, unsteady in the firelight.

"It's good to be back in Humashup, children," I said, "though it's true I haven't been to see you in a few generations. But it's a long journey from here to the World Above, let me tell you, and I'm a busy god. I only found the time to come down now because I have very important news.

"Now, you all know"—I held out my strange hands to them—"how we play a game up there, the Sun and I, at midwinter every year. We gamble. We outguess each other, He and I. And you all know what the stakes are.

"Yes, I can see you do. It's your *lives* He wants, the Sun, because He's always hungry. All that burning, burning up in the sky, and how does He do it? He feeds on men. Your lives light the sky, heat the earth, and the only one who can keep Him from taking you all is me. If I didn't gamble with him to save some of you every year, you wouldn't be here now to listen to me, any of you. This fine hall would be dark and cold, and you'd all be in the cemetery out there.

"But don't worry: I'm a good gambler and I win often. When I do, the Sun can't take any of you but the old sick people. Better than that: He has to pay me in good things, acorns and fish, deer and geese in plenty, which I send down to you. I win you rainy seasons to make the hills green. I win you calm weather at sea and big runs of salmon. All these things come from me, because I'm your uncle and I look out for you.

"You know all this. And this is how things have always been, every year. But not anymore!"

Eyes widened at this, and there was some muttering. The mortals smelled afraid. I went on: "Last month was midwinter, and I went to the corner of the sky where I gamble with the Sun. And He was there, all right, and there were the dice ready for the cast, but I saw something else too: the Sun had a talisman around His neck on a piece of cord, and it looked like a canoe, only a *big* canoe with the wings of a white bird."

A few people exchanged meaningful glances.

"Anyway I settled down to play with Him, and I noticed that He took off His talisman and lay it down by His right foot. We cast the dice, the little shells spun around, and at first I won. Then my luck changed! If I called five, three came up. If I called ten, I'd throw two. I couldn't call a winning throw no matter how I shook the shells.

"This went on and on. I lost ten of your lives, ten of you here in this very hall. Whose lives do you suppose they were? Then I lost fifty lives. Then a hundred. Sun threw every number He called, but never me. So I watched closely, and I saw what was happening.

"There were little men hiding in Sun's canoe talisman, tiny men white as chalk. When it was my turn, they'd run out and bowl the shells along like hoops until they landed me a losing number. When Sun threw, they'd bowl and flip the shells so that He won every time. And more and more of you were dying, and not only you but all the tribes, the Yokuts and the Ohlone and tribes you haven't even heard of. Finally I threw my hands up and cried, 'Sun, You're cheating!'

"He just laughed and said, 'If you think so, call in Moon to judge between us.'

"This seemed all right to me, because, say what you like about Moon being changeable, She is a fair judge at least. She came in and watched us play for a while. You know how sharp She can be, especially at certain times of the month when She's in a bad mood! She spotted the tiny white men right away. She shook Her head in disapproval and said, 'You're right, Coyote, Sun is cheating!'

"Sun just laughed at us. He said, 'I became tired of losing to you all the time, so I got myself a little magic to change the score. I'll pay the penalty for cheating, but I'll tell you this: my magic can't be stopped. The white men in this canoe will collect human lives for me, all I can eat forever. You can't stop them. You can win all the good harvests you like, but who will you give them to? So hot, so bright I'll burn on all those lives!' "

Absolute silence in the meeting hall. I lifted my head and howled. I made it the sound of all desolation, and the naked little mortals sat rigid with terror.

"But!" I went on after a suitable pause. "Moon looked at Sun with blood in Her eye and said: 'You cheated at the midwinter game! Do You think You can get away with it? I'm going to fine You! Sky Coyote can have seventy years for his people before Your white men come for them. Also, if You eat all the people, the earth will go out of balance, and we can't have that. So here's a further penalty: Sky Coyote can take *four* magic canoes of his own and fill them with as many of his people as he can carry to safety. Those people You can never eat. Then, after seventy years, You are free to do Your worst to the people Sky Coyote leaves behind.'

"That was what Moon had to say. So this is what I've come to tell you, my children of Humashup: I will not leave you behind. Because I love you the most, I'm taking all of you away with me in my canoes.''

Silence. Then a babble of panicked voices, louder outside where people had been listening through the walls. Sepawit looked around at all the confusion and rose to address me.

"So . . . we're to interpret all this literally, then."

"Of course!"

"And not as a series of metaphors."

"What did you think, I came here to read you riddles?"

The chief turned and stared at his shamans, who looked uncomfortable. From the back of the room, someone cried out: "I've seen those big canoes with wings! They're sails! And they *do* have white men in them!"

"Like I said." I crossed my arms, or forelimbs, or whatever. Must have been some Spanish ships straggling north from Mexico that weren't making it into the history books. Oh, well. I'd known these people weren't stupid. It might be a good idea to ease up on the mythic style, though.

"You have to save us, Uncle Coyote!" cried the general mass.

"Now, everybody, calm down!" The chief waved his hands. "There's no immediate danger. Sky Coyote has already promised to save us. And we have seventy years—didn't You say seventy years?—yes, all right, He said seventy years before the white men even get here, by which time I'm sure we'll be long gone. So you see, there's no cause for alarm."

"I'd like to ask a few questions." The spokesman for the Canoemakers' Union got to his feet. He looked determined, though he'd gone pale like the rest of them when I howled the doom of everything he knew.

"Ask, nephew."

"First, the Canoemakers' Union would like to thank You for Your concern and Your timely warning. But we'd like to ask—could You be a little more specific about this white-men thing? What exactly is involved here?"

"Yes, the United Steatite Workers would like to ask that, too," chimed in Sawlawlan.

Coolheaded pragmatists, huh? All right. I addressed my words to them, but I spoke to be heard by the fearful unthinking masses at the back. "You want to know more? I'll tell you. The Sun hasn't got just one of those canoes with sails, He's got thousands of them. They'll bring more white men than there are stars in the sky, and white men, let me tell you, are the masters of invasion. Everything they touch dies, even their embraces kill, and you should see their weapons! Don't think they're just coming for a raid on you, either, don't think they'll take the sea-otter pelts and a woman or two and go to sea again in their big canoes. They're going to *live* here.

"This won't be your land anymore, it'll be theirs. You'll be their slaves, as long as you live. And you won't live long. But while you live, you'll do what they tell you to do, you'll eat what they tell you to eat, you'll think what they tell you to think. And after they've destroyed you, they'll start on the very earth. They'll remake it to what they think a land should be. No more oak trees, no more wild places.

"Don't you understand? As soon as the white men get here, that's the end of this world. It won't even be a memory, because there'll be none of you left to remember what this place was like.

"Only Sky Coyote can save you."

Just about had them. Their eyes were wide and staring now.

"All right." Sepawit swallowed hard. "But surely, Sky Coyote, this is a little sudden—"

"You don't believe me, do you?" I looked down my muzzle at him, severe now.

"We do, but—"

"You never expected me to visit you, did you? You didn't even believe in me. Even now some of you are thinking, Who is this Sky Coyote really? Does He have to disrupt our comfortable lives like this? Couldn't we just stay here and take our chances with these white men? Well, believe me, if this is too much trouble for you, I can go to some other village."

Some of them began to panic. Sepawit was sweating. "No! No, please, Sky Coyote, don't take offense. You must understand, this is all something of a shock to us. We need some time to take it in. To, er, discuss it among ourselves. Won't you tell us more about what you plan to do?"

So I unbent, and graciously told them. Not the whole story, naturally, but the usual rigmarole about giant sky canoes carting everybody off to a wonderful promised land where they wouldn't ever die, even after their present bodies grew old and passed away. And I told them about my spirit servants who were going to be visiting to collect samples of the local flora and fauna, so the rest of their world could be rescued, too.

And they bought it, pretty much. The chief was mortified at my anger and ready to do anything to show himself cooperative, but I could tell I'd still have some work to do with the businessmen. Probably with the shamans, too. Get them alone, personal interviews, wheedling and threats and a little sleight of hand, one on one.

The questions and answers went on until pretty late, and I was invited to stay overnight in the special guest quarters for visiting dignitaries. With me went a couple of young ladies, groupies, as it were, in otter-fur capes, who wanted a closer look at some of my effects. You don't need to know about this part, but the Prosthetics and Appliances Division of Dr. Zeus passed yet another field test with flying colors.

"Wow." Puluy leaned back dreamily into otter fur, carefully arranging her hairdo. She was the prettier and more poised of the two. "That was neat, Coyote. I've never picked poppies with a Sky Guy before. You're so, like, you know, *furry*."

"Dummy," Awhay told her scornfully, stretching out her legs. She was the plumper and more serious one. "Of course He's furry! He's Sky Coyote, okay? So anyway, Uncle Coyote. Did You, like, really mean that, about the white men coming and all? I mean, the end of the world is, no shit, really coming?"

"That's right." I tried crossing my forelimbs behind my head and found I could do it. "You can kiss this place goodbye."

"That is so weird." Awhay stared at the ceiling, thinking about it. "And I can't believe the first person You talked to was Kenemekme. That guy is such a *loser!*"

"Omigod!" Puluy started up on her elbow. "I've got my birthday party coming up next month! My dad's sent me some money and my grandmother's jewelry. Oh, shit!"

"Don't worry," I said with a yawn. "You'll get your birthday party. We won't be leaving right away."

"My dad lives in Nipumu." Puluy frowned slightly. "Are You gonna be rescuing his village too?"

"Can't." I shrugged. "I'm only allowed to take so many. Sorry, sweetheart." She considered that a moment before her face cleared.

"Oh well. At least he's already sent the presents. And it's not like he's even seen me since I was ten. Like he cares." She lay down again, perfectly content. Awhay turned on her side and regarded me.

"What was it like in the beginning, Uncle Sky Coyote?" she asked. "I mean, *really*. Forget the shit we're told by the priests. You were there! Was there actually a big flood and all that?"

"Sure." I wriggled around and pulled up a folded fur behind my head to get comfortable. "We used to live down here in the Middle World, but after the flood we decided to be Sky People instead. But somebody had to live down here, so we got together to make you guys. All the Sky People contributed different ideas. Humans were designed by committee, and that's why your bodies work so badly. We mold-cast the first couple in parts, see? And I was going to give you all nice useful hands like mine, that you can dig with and run around on without hurting; but at the last minute Lizard substituted a cast of his hands instead!''

"I've heard that story." Awhay held up her hand and peered at it. "But it's weird, you know, because we *don't* have lizard hands."

"Well. They look more like a lizard's hands than mine," I improvised. "And anyway, this is Sky Lizard we're talking about, and he has hands just like yours."

"Oh. Okay." Awhay settled down, but her eyes were still on me. "Tell us more about what it was like in the old days?"

"Well, let's see." I accessed more files. "Did you ever hear about the time I rescued Eagle's daughter from the Sea People?"

"Uh-uh. Tell us."

"Okay. Way back when we Sky People used to live here, Eagle had a beautiful daughter. She was so lovely, golden light shone from her, and golden poppies bloomed out of her footprints. And everybody wanted her, because her beauty was famous all over the world; but Eagle decided to marry her to his sister's son, Falcon, who was chief over on Limuw Island back then. So he sent a wedding party, a bunch of people in canoes, with Pelican and Cormorant leading because they knew the way, and a big fancy canoe decorated with golden poppies with Eagle's daughter in it.

"But halfway across the channel, a bunch of swordfish came swimming up out of the sea and attacked the bride's canoe! They made it capsize, and Eagle's daughter fell into the water and sank like a stone and vanished from sight. So did the swordfish. The wedding party put about and searched, and Cormorant and Pelican dove down to see if they could find her, but it was no use.

"Boy, was there a to-do about that! The groom, Falcon, was crazy with grief. Eagle racked his brains to think of what he could do. But what could he do? The sea was a big place, and he had no power there.

"And so at last Eagle swallowed his pride and sent for me. There'd been some bad blood between us for a long time—in fact I hadn't even been invited to the wedding. But I didn't hold it against him when he sent for me and admitted that only I, Coyote, was smart enough to steal his daughter back. I especially liked it that he got down on his knees and begged me. So I said, 'Sure! No problem.'

"I got some magic stuff together in a couple of cane tubes, and I had Pelican and Cormorant take me out in a canoe to the place where Eagle's daughter had gone overboard. Falcon insisted on coming along, even though I figured he'd get in the way. So as we sat there in the canoe, I handed him one of the tubes of magic stuff.

" 'Okay, kid, stick that in your ear and keep it there!' I told him. 'It's dangerous where we're going, but the tube should protect you.' And I put the other tube in my ear and told him, 'Now, when we get where we're going, you let me do all the talking, understand?' He told me that he understood, real meek, so I grabbed him and we jumped overboard. I stuck my head up out of the water and told Cormorant and Pelican not to come after us, no matter what happened.

" 'No chance!' replied Cormorant. 'We'll stick around a day and a night, but then we're out of here.'

"So down we went through the water, Falcon and I. First the water was clear as glass, then a gloomy kind of blue-green, then dark as night. We could feel the water squeezing us and freezing us, and we'd have been killed if not for my magic tube stuff. At last, a long way down, we saw a golden light shining in the black water.

"When we got closer, we saw that the light was spilling from the door and the smoke hole of a house that had been built on the sea bottom. It looked just like the house we're in now, except that it had a whalebone frame instead of wood and was thatched with kelp instead of tules. We went to the door and looked in. Eagle's daughter was in there, and the golden light was coming from her. Poor thing, she was crouched on the floor grinding up snails in a mortar, just the way you'd grind acorns, only these were nasty slimy snails, and the whole house was slimy and untidy inside. She kept working, crying the whole time and wiping away golden tears.

" 'That's my bride!' shouted Falcon. I clapped my paw over his mouth to shut him up, but it was too late, the Sea People heard us.

"There was hissing laughter behind us. We turned around and saw them. They were evil, dirty old men, with long white beards and eyebrows, and every one had a sword in his hand. Quick as a flash I said:

" 'Hi there, Undersea Fellows. This boy here and I are travelers, and we'd like shelter for the night. Will you grant it?' And this really screwed them, see, because once I'd asked for hospitality, they couldn't attack us. They looked at one another with their cold eyes, trying to think of a way around the rules. At last one of them said, 'Of course!' grinning with his sharp teeth. 'Please enter into our house, and share our food and the heat of our fire!'

"So we went inside, and they crowded in after us, careful to sit between us and the door so there was no quick way to exit. We sat down by the fire, but it was an undersea fire: it burned cold and blue and made the place darker. The only real light came from Eagle's daughter, who looked at us hopefully but didn't dare stop pounding snails in her mortar.

" 'That's a pretty girl,' I said to the Sea People.

" 'She's all right,' said the oldest old man. 'It's been a long time since we had a slave who made decent sea-snail mush! Come, we were just about to eat our evening meal of whale meat. There's plenty for everyone. You'll insult us if you don't eat heartily!' They were trying to trap us, see, by making us insult them at their own hearth, so they'd have an excuse to kill us. But I said, 'Sounds great! Bring on the blubber!'

"So one of them went out, and after a minute he starts to pitch dead whales in through the doorway. Obviously this was a magic house, because it expanded as the whales came in, so that everybody was able to sit comfortably with a dead whale in front of him. 'I hope you don't expect such decadent luxury as *cooking*,' sneered the oldest Sea Person. 'We eat our meat raw under this roof, it's healthier that way.'

" 'Of course!' I answered cheerfully. 'That's how it tastes best!' I could see Falcon looking green, so I leaned over and whispered to him: 'Just pretend to eat. Cut off chunks and pass them to me.'

"Well, the meal commenced. You should have seen the disgusting table manners those guys had! Grease and blood and blubber all over their faces. Each one chewed down a whole whale all by himself. I ate up all mine too—but then, I can eat anything. Falcon couldn't manage more than a couple of mouthfuls, but he tore off big pieces and passed them to me under his thigh, and I gobbled them down so the Sea People couldn't say we were turning up our noses at their food.

"When the meal was over, I licked my chops and grinned. 'What a great meal!' I told them. 'Truly you Sea People are masters of hospitality.' But the oldest one just grinned like a saw blade and said, 'If you liked our meat so much, you'll have to try our tobacco. Our feelings will be very hurt if you don't like it!' And they handed around a tube of the awful stuff they use down there. It was like sticking a salted fish up your nose! I took a big helping, though, when my turn came, and signaled to Falcon that he do the same. Then, just like with the meat, he passed me his share under his thigh, and I was able to partake of it without harm, because nothing makes me sick. But I was getting tired of this, and besides the Sea People were still between us and the door, giving us no chance of grabbing Eagle's daughter and making a break for it. So I said:

" 'You've been so kind in sharing your comforts here in your home, allow me to repay you by singing to you all!'

" 'All right,' said the oldest of the Sea People, not knowing what to expect. Now, personally, I think I have a beautiful voice, but all the other Sky People have told me they'd rather be dragged over hot coals than listen to me sing. They say I sound like wild animals being skinned alive. Anyhow, I began to serenade the Sea People in my own special way.

"Poor Falcon went pale, and Eagle's daughter covered her ears and cowered down. The Sea People made faces as though they'd just bitten into something rotten; but what could they do? I was hoping they'd leave, but they were so tough and ugly, even my singing wasn't too much for them. I sang and sang, love songs and lullabies, fishing songs and songs of war. A couple began to rock back and forth in pain, one of them clutched at the side of his head like he had a toothache, and the oldest one's nose started to bleed. But there they sat, blocking the way for us to escape with Eagle's daughter.

"I sang at them for hours, thinking they would at least have to go out to relieve themselves. But nobody was moving, even after that meal! Finally I realized they were going right where they sat, like fish! Their poop didn't have any smell, like the poop of fish or shrimp, but it gave me an idea.

" 'Excuse me a moment while I refresh my voice, won't you?' I asked, and I slipped the tube of magic stuff from my ear and poured a little into my mouth.

" 'Oh, please, don't strain your throat,' begged the oldest of the Sea People, wiping blood and tears from his face.

" 'Don't you like my singing?' I asked in an offended voice. 'After I've racked my brains for every tune I know, just to entertain you?' Because I could feel the magic stuff working inside me, you see. And the Sea People brightened a little at that, because they thought I was going to insult them and there'd be a fight, so they could kill me at last.

" 'Well, I guess I can tell the truth in my own house,' said the old one with a grin. 'The plain truth is, your singing is terrible and hurts our ears!'

" 'Oh yeah?' I retorted. Yes, the magic was working! 'And do you want to know what I think of your taste in music?'

At that every one of the Sea People grabbed hold of his sword.

'What?' they said in a chorus. 'What do you think of our taste in music?'

'' 'THIS!' I replied, and let loose a thunderous fart. Now you know I'm an ancient and powerful creature, and I'd had a huge meal of rotten whale and magic powder on top of that, so you can imagine what happened. The whole house rose on its foundations and settled again in the crater my fart made. Eagle's daughter and Falcon fainted dead away. Over on the islands, people thought they were having an earthquake. When the bubble broke on the surface of the sea, birds fell out of the air like stones, and fish were killed instantly, and washed up on the beach for weeks. There were colorful sunsets for a year and a half from the poison in the air. But the Sea People got out of that house as fast as they could. They didn't even bother with the door—they jumped out through the smoke hole!

"I grabbed up Eagle's daughter and Falcon, one in either arm, and beat it through the door and swam up and up until I saw clear water above me and the face of the Moon, white with horror. She used to be red like the Sun, before that night when I farted. I broke the surface and found the canoe still floating there, though it was half swamped, and Cormorant and Pelican were lying in it unconscious. I tossed in Eagle's daughter and Falcon, jumped in myself, bailed out the water, and paddled us all back to the mainland single-handed.

"Eagle's daughter and Falcon recovered and were married, and lived happily ever after. I'm not sure if they had children, though. At least I wasn't invited to any naming ceremonies! And you can hang that story on the hook, because I'm finished telling it.''

"God, Sky Coyote, that was *so* gross!'' giggled Awhay, rolling close to me. "Did it really happen like that? Was that really the truth?''

"As much of the truth as I ever tell, child of earth.'' I grinned lazily at her.

"My mother used to say You're a truth made of lies. Maybe she was right, for once in her life.'' She snuggled closer. "You know what? I think Puluy's gone to sleep . . .''

When it got quiet at last, I lay there between the girls and watched the stars. From time to time a little wind moved in the oak trees, but mostly there was only the old sound, the oldest sound, mortals breathing slowly by their hearth fires, with now and then the whimper of a child or dog.

Sleep tight, children. Sky Coyote is with you.

15

I SLEPT, AND saw all the terrible things I'd warned the Chumash about. From the sea came the white sails, and they anchored and the white men came striding up over the land. Their armor gleamed silver and their priests carried banners with crosses. My people fought and died, or turned to flee into the mountains. But from beyond the mountains came more white men, under a striped banner, bearing long rifles. What were my people going to do? Were we all going to die?

No! Because here they came, the Enforcers, heroes to save the day. Budu pointed at the Spanish and the Americans with his ax. He pronounced his sentence on them, as he always did: If you make war on other tribes to take their land, you must die. He gave an order, and the big men in bearskins moved, as they always had, like a wave rolling in to crush the guilty and protect the innocent. The Spanish cut them with steel, but they kept coming. The Americans shot them with bullets, but they kept coming.

Oh, it was wonderful! All the terrible things I'd prophesied weren't going to come true after all, no near extinction for the Chumash, no mission slaves, no conquerors! The Enforcers were seeing to it that life would go on in the ancient ways forever and ever, so that good people could sleep safely by their fires under the kindly stars. The problems with history being changed had all been smoothed over, somehow.

Now all the invaders seemed to be dead, and Budu was helping his men take heads. The bodies were stacked in heaps and burned. He was laughing his high-pitched laugh; his pale-blue eyes were dancing. The Chumash were bowing down to thank him. But then from the dead I saw a figure leap up, a priest who somehow hadn't been executed, a small man in a black robe. He slipped in under Budu's arm. He had a long knife in his hand. I tried to yell a warning but I couldn't, and anyway I recognized the man in the black robe. I saw myself running my knife in between Budu's ribs. No. No.

It didn't happen that way. I would never have done that.

Would I? If I'd been ordered to do it, would I have betrayed him?

I was shivering when I woke up, but the girls were hogging the furs. Growling softly, I nipped at Awhay until she woke up enough to relinquish some bed space to her principal divinity.

16

IF THE CHUMASH had been impressed with me, I really made a sensational entrance at the weekly production meeting.

I had to open the rear seam of my breeches to let my tail out, and it stuck through the rear pleat of my coat. I had to abandon my wig, but my tricorne fit very tidily between my coyote ears. Yes, all eyes were on me during my report on Initial Contact and Preliminary Negotiations. I disconcerted Mr. Bugleg no end. I could tell, because he kept dropping his stylus. Then again, maybe he usually had trouble holding small objects. Anyhow I concluded my report and stepped down, and there was vast creaking in that prefab hall as fifty people shifted uncomfortably in their folding chairs.

"Questions?" inquired Mr. Lopez.

One of the administrative team put up his hand, an elderly mortal. He wasn't a scientist or anything; he was just some investor the Company had sent along on the trip so he could think he was helping to make decisions. He stood and frowned at me.

"I'm sure everyone at Dr. Zeus would like to thank Joseph for his report, and it sounds like he's doing a great job, but I don't see why he had to include in his report his adventures with the underaged native girls. I would like to go on record as protesting that."

"So noted," intoned Lopez, and I made my ears droop. There was a wave of subvocal giggling from the immortals in the hall. The old man glared around—you'd have thought he could hear us—and raised his voice as he continued:

"I would also like to go on record as protesting the choice of the Chumash tribe as preservation subjects."

"So noted," replied Lopez hurriedly, but the old guy went right on:

"I've been watching the preliminary field reports. These Indians aren't like the Hopi or the Navajo. Those were clean, peaceful Indians with an advanced society and beautiful mythology. They farmed and they built houses the way we do. These Chumash are different. They're dirty-minded, lazy, pleasure-loving Indians. They don't have anything important to contribute to human culture. I think it's a waste of Company funds to bother with them."

"So noted. Thank you," said Lopez.

"And they're not spiritual people at all! Their sexual habits are depraved. They're decadent. They remind me of those emperor people who used to lie around in togas—you know. What were they called?"

"Romans, sir," said Lopez faintly.

"Romans, right. The Company would be spending its time and money much better if it went after a nicer tribe. There are Indians down in Los Angeles now with much more meaningful lives. I saw a thing on the holo where they've even discovered monotheism and they have a prophet and everything. If *they* were the ones we were saving, I'll bet they'd develop into a great civilization."

Lopez cleared his throat.

"With respect, sir, we operatives aren't permitted to judge the quality of one mortal culture against another. You all have equal value in our eyes, regardless of your beliefs and practices. We simply follow the directives of Dr. Zeus, and in this particular case Dr. Zeus has decided that the Chumash are worth rescuing."

"Yes, I know all about you immortals and how smart you are. Well, I'm just an old man from the twenty-fourth century, but I'll tell you this: we should have programmed you with a sense of right and wrong. Because it sure seems to me that you androids don't have any." *Oooo!* What a faux pas. There was a real vibration of subsonic rage in the room from my fellow Old Ones. Lopez drew a deep breath.

"Sir, we are cyborgs. Not androids. There is a difference."

"Whatever." The old guy waved dismissively. "The point is that you people just don't have any values. So I want to go on record as protesting this Chumash thing. *And* the way Dr. Zeus is being run nowadays. I know I can't do anything about it, but I've been a stockholder since this company started, and I don't like one bit the way it's turned out."

"So noted," said Lopez. And over the red wave of immortal wrath that filled the ether, he broadcast: *Please, everybody, the old horse's ass is retiring next month.*

The meeting moved on to other topics, and afterward there were refreshments, if you found distilled water and little sea-algae crackers refreshing. I didn't stay.

I went back to Humashup by a path different from the one I took the first time. People are funny about their gods: might be one or two lurkers hoping to get off an arrow or two at me. So I went over the hills and just strolled in through the oak trees behind the houses, where there were some children running around. They didn't notice me. I crouched down to watch them.

Little brown kids, mostly naked, playing with some rocks by water. I'd been like that once: no bright electronic toys, and no possible way to understand one if I'd encountered it. That was before all the operations that turned me into a brainy little cyborg like Latif. Old Eurobase One in the high Cévennes in France, that had been where Budu sent me. They'd unloaded me, crying and airsick and disoriented, straight into the base hospital. When I awoke, my intelligence had been zapped upward a few million points, and I had the potential to become immortal.

The very first thing I remember seeing, in my new improved state, was a flat white wall on which images danced, a lot more colorful than my poor dad's bison and horses. There were other children lying in beds nearby, and they were giggling weakly at the bright figures. There was a little pink man with a weapon, and a rabbit and a duck; the duck was trying to get the man to kill the rabbit, but the rabbit was so clever, he managed to turn the duck's scheming back against him every time. The duck's bill was blown completely off his face. I laughed at that until I hurt.

Eurobase One was a lot more primitive than the deluxe private-school bases the Company built later. It was more like a military base with a school attached as a kind of afterthought, and we kids were used to seeing Enforcers go charging out to fight off the latest stupid attack by the Great Goat Cult. Bad guys were stupid. I remember a nurse sitting down on the edge of my bed and explaining this to me. The Rabbit was the hero, because he wasn't trying to hurt anybody, and he used his intelligence to confuse his enemies so they hurt themselves instead of hurting him. It made sense to me, and as a role model the screwy Rabbit was hard to improve on. Which was a good thing, since Eurobase One had a limited budget for teaching tools in those days.

I wondered how these kids would adjust to a new world, and to new heroes like rabbits and stuttering pigs? To say nothing of all the shiny educational toys the Company provided for its mortal wards. The kids wouldn't be turned into little geniuses like I'd been, but life was going to offer a lot more than the game of scrambling up on a high rock and stopping everyone else from getting up there too.

These kids seemed to be having a great time, though, getting muddy in a stream. Nobody was watching as one little guy, maybe fifteen months old, toddled away downstream and found a big pool of still water to stare into.

Something on its surface fascinated him, and, after watching awhile, he made a grab for it. He lost his balance and fell in. It wasn't all that deep, but he wasn't all that big, and once he'd choked and got water up his nose, he became panicky and uncoordinated. Face-down in the water, and somehow unable to climb out.

Now, I can watch human tragedy on the large scale and yawn. Nations fall? Big deal. Revolutions fail? So? Societies collapse? I'll join the looters. Most people have it coming to them. Their babies don't, though. So I sprinted over and fished the kid out before he could drown. At the sight of me he coughed up water and began to scream bloody murder.

The other kids paid no attention until one of them glanced over and noticed I was Coyote, and then they all came running. "Sky Coyote!" they all yelled, mostly in unison.

"Are You really Sky Coyote?"

"Are You going to take us away in a canoe?"

"Will You make some magic work for us?"

"Can I go up in the sky with You?"

"Look, whose baby is this?" I demanded, holding him out at arm's length because he was wetting all over the place in his terror.

"That's my little brother, Sky Coyote," admitted a boy about eight years old.

"Well, why weren't you watching him? He almost drowned," I said sternly.

He just stared at me.

"Where's your mother?" I barked at him.

"She's working in her house," volunteered another child.

"Well, where's her house?" Now they all just stared until I bared my fangs at them, and then they all took a step backward. One of them pointed to a house down the street.

"Over there."

"Thanks," I growled, and hauled the still-shrieking kid in that direction. As I departed, I heard one of the group say:

"He's *mean*."

The only reason the baby's mother didn't hear me coming was that she was having an argument with a man at her door. She was a nicely plump lady in the two-piece outfit most of the working women wore, a woven tule skirt under a tabard of the same material, fastened at the shoulder with a feathered pin. The skirt was weighted at the hem with little plumb bobs of drilled stone to keep it hanging in dignified folds. This regal effect was spoiled a little by the fact that she was yelling so loud, the veins were standing out in her neck.

"You have to be crazy!" she was shouting. "I can't turn out three-color baskets that fast! Nobody can!"

"My other manufacturers do," the man said.

"Oh no, buster, no no no, you just said the *wrong* thing. Didn't you ever think me and the other ladies would get together and compare notes?" Her eyes widened in fierce triumph. "You've been using that line on all of us! And we found out you've been lying about a *lot* of things. Like the price controls on deergrass!"

He was withering under her assault when I barked, "Excuse me." She barely glanced at me, and then she and the man did a set of double-takes so classic, it put me in mind again of the rabbit and the duck. "This your baby, lady?" I held him out. She didn't take him, but he scrambled loose from me at last and ran to cling to her. "What's going on, here?" I inquired.

"Just a business discussion, Sky Coyote." The man held up his hands. I recognized him as Kaxiwalic, the one introduced to me at the town meeting as a successful entrepreneur. Not all that successful, to judge from his skinny appearance and the fact that he wore only a couple of strands of shell money. Right now he looked as though he'd like nothing better than to vanish silently into the sagebrush. "I'll see you later, Skilmoy."

"Hey, now here's somebody who'd be interested in your dirty tricks!" Grinning hugely, the woman grabbed him by the arm. "What do You think of smooth operators, Coyote? This lousy slave driver charges us extra for our materials and then gets a kickback from the Deergrass Gatherers' Union—" The baby's squalling threatened to drown her out. She leaned down and slapped him a good one. "Shut up! Kyupi, will you get out here and do something with him?"

An adolescent girl came out of the house. Her eyes got big when she saw me, but she grabbed up the baby and scuttled back inside with him. I could hear her rocking and shushing, rocking and shushing.

"These women are all lazy," said Kaxiwalic in a chummy way,

evidently assuming I was a male chauvinist god. Skilmoy rounded on him furiously.

"Lazy! Sky Coyote, do You know how hard I have to work to feed all these miserable children? Do You know how much fish costs these days? I'm an *artist*—"

"Your baby almost drowned."

"He what?" Her face crumpled up. Tears came into her eyes. "How can I watch him when I have to weave baskets every hour of the day and night? The kids won't help me with him at all."

"Maybe you shouldn't have had so many," said Kaxiwalic, looking smug.

"I'd like to see you pregnant every year, you bastard, and count how many big basket deals you'd make—"

"Now, hold it." I stepped between them. "What's the point of all this? Weren't you listening to what I told you in the meeting hall? The end of the world is coming soon. What do you need all these baskets for?"

"I can sell them, Sky Coyote," explained Kaxiwalic. "I mean, wherever we go, people are going to need baskets, right? And wait'll they see my merchandise. I see the end of this world as an opportunity. Think of the new markets opening up in the next one!"

"I wouldn't count on it. Maybe I didn't make myself clear: you're going to a wonderful paradise. Do you think there are underpaid, overworked women in paradise to make baskets for you?"

"But that's exactly why I need a big inventory before we leave! I have to—" I took him by the arm. He flinched at the touch of my paw. I looked into his eyes and shook my head.

"Uh-uh," I told him. He stared at me.

"But if I don't have baskets to sell, I—"

"Uh-uh. You can't use World Below methods in the World Above."

He opened and shut his mouth a few times. He glanced quickly at the woman and then said to me, lowering his voice, "Can I discuss this with You later?"

"Anytime."

"Thank You. I have to be going now." He hurried off, doubtless to call an emergency meeting of the local businessmen.

Skilmoy had calmed down a little, but now she looked worried.

"Sky Coyote, are you saying Kaxiwalic won't need us to make baskets for him anymore?"

"Yes, my child."

"But he can't lay us off! How are we going to live, with no money coming in?"

"What will you need money for, in paradise? As far as that goes, why do you need it now? Don't I send you plenty of good food? Look at all the acorns there are, look at all the roots and seeds and bulbs. I haven't seen one starving person in this town."

"Well, so nobody's starving, but I have to pay the fishermen and the hunters, don't I? And I have to pay the fees to get my son into the Kantap Society, so he can go somewhere in life. For all the child support I get, my ex-husband might just as well be in hell, which is where I wish he was anyway."

"Now, now, my child." Boy, these people needed a social benefits program or at least a day care center, but that wasn't my job. I was only there to play God. "Don't you understand that all these concerns won't exist anymore, very soon?"

She looked at me with slightly narrowed eyes. "When You say we'll all be in paradise . . . You don't mean we'll all be dead or anything like that, do you?"

"No. You'll live long, long, and happy lives, and you'll never be sick or in need." And that was the absolute truth; the Company had great retirement plans for its mortal employees. "Then you'll move on to another plane of existence."

"That's just . . . that's too good to be true." She stared hard at me, wanting to believe it all the same. "No trouble? No bad luck? No work?"

"I didn't say there wouldn't be any work."

"Ha! I knew it."

"But it'll be easy work, helping the Spirits. You'll have everything you could possibly want. If you didn't have *something* to do, paradise would be a pretty boring place. But you won't have any worries."

"Well, no offense, Sky Coyote, but I'll believe it when we get there." She got an odd look on her face. "Coyote? Are You going to rescue the people at Syuxtun Township too?"

"No," I told her. "Only Humashup has been chosen."

She clapped her hands and let out a whoop of laughter. "My ex-husband and his girlfriend live in Syuxtun!" she cried in delight. I put my head on one side and regarded her. "You're a pal, Sky Coyote! Come in and have some food. Do You like roasted agave heart?"

"With cherry sauce?" I said hopefully. She looked coy, and I followed her inside.

The girl was still rocking the baby by the fire. As we came in, he pointed at me and began to scream again.

"Oh, shut up, stupid, can't you see this is Sky Coyote?" Skilmoy went and rummaged among her kitchen things.

"Hello, Uncle Sky Coyote. He's too little to understand, Mama," said the girl.

"Hi there." I sat down on a tule-reed mat.

"Well, he'd damn well better learn to understand, if he wants to get anywhere in life," retorted Skilmoy. "Kyupi, where's the agave heart we had last night?"

"I had it for breakfast, Mama."

The woman turned and slapped her. "Didn't it occur to you that I might bring a guest home? I'm so sorry, Sky Coyote. Would You like some acorn porridge instead? Or—oh." She looked appalled as something dawned on her. "You don't want . . . ? I mean, I've heard stories that Spirits do lots of stuff backward in the World Above. I've heard that the Sky People eat . . . well, shit."

I'd encountered this quaint belief in a few other cultures. What a dilemma for a thoughtful hostess!

"Actually, acorn porridge will be fine," I assured her. I had no idea there was any difference between Spanish acorns and the New World variety, which are, well, an acquired taste. But after the first shock I choked the stuff down with a happy doglike expression. Laying the abalone-shell bowl aside, I looked around the room. Domestic chaos was everywhere, except for the corner that was clearly where Skilmoy worked. There were tidy bunches of deergrass and split rush there, sorted for length and tied in bundles. Some of them had already been dyed assorted colors, reds and yellows and blacks. In a small woven tray were a few simple tools, a bone knife and an awl, a couple of spools of thread, and some bone needles.

"So this is your work?" I picked up a stack of baskets and examined them. They were so tightly woven, they could have held water, and so beautifully finished, you could turn and turn one in your hands without finding a loose end anywhere. The spiraling patterns were sophisticated and dizzying in their complexity.

"You like them? Yes, they're mine. I'm the best, even Kaxiwalic admits it." She came and sat down beside me so her knee touched mine. "The ones with the colored patterns are the most expensive," she explained.

"I guess the colored dyes cost a lot, huh?" I turned one over and stopped cold. Worked into this basket was a pretty fair representation of the flag of Spain. There was no mistaking it; I've marched, ridden, and persecuted heretics under it enough times to know those little castles and lions when I see them.

"What's this one?" I said, when I'd collected my wits.

"That? That's a new design. Some strangers came ashore in a canoe at Syuxtun and bought a lot of baskets at Kaxiwalic's shop down there. They were such good customers, he copied some designs off their gear. The idea is, next time they stop there, he'll have a whole new line of merchandise to appeal to them. Kaxiwalic's a lying bum, but he gets good ideas." So much for the purity of Chumash culture.

"Well, you know—" I frowned, holding the basket up to the light. "It might not be a good idea to trade with those people. I'm pretty sure this is the tribal tattoo of the white men, the ones the Sun is sending? That must have been one of their scouting parties that came ashore. They may not be causing much trouble now, but soon . . ."

"Oh, Sky Coyote, how terrible." She looked into my eyes, and hers were wide with—concern?

"It was hard to hear You through the wall when You spoke to us the other night, but You looked so impressive, standing there towering above everyone else. Won't You tell me more about this? These white men you speak of frighten me." And she leaned forward. All those kids notwithstanding, she still had a figure.

"I think I'll go out for a walk," said the little girl, and she got up with the baby in her arms and took him outside.

It must have been the ears or something. I hadn't seen this much romantic action in a couple of centuries.

17

"Y OU KNOW WHAT you look like?" Mendoza peered at me from her beach chair. "Like the guy in that Beauty and the Beast movie. The one by Cocteau."

"Nah." Ashur paused as he moved from refilling her glass to refilling mine. He stood back and studied me. The campfire danced behind him. The surf boomed distantly; it was late, and the tide was way out. We were celebrating Matthias's upcoming transfer back to Greenland One, and the party had gone on too long.

"Wrong clothes," Ashur pronounced at last. "The one in that movie had a high lace collar. Remember? With this shirt he's more like the Beast in the Duvall version."

"I think he looks like Puss in Boots," somebody on the other side of the fire giggled. I glared across at her.

"You're all wrong," I stated. "I look like the guy in the Kracowiac ring holo of *The Isle of Dogs*."

There was silence and then a scattered chorus of agreement from my fellow Old Ones. "Except the costume's still wrong," amended Matthias. "That production was done in late-twenty-first-century dress."

Never play trivia games with immortals. Do you know how many movies we've seen?

"Henry Hull in *Werewolf of London*," somebody ventured, but he was drowned out by somebody else insisting, "No! No! Oliver Reed in *The Curse of the Werewolf*!"

"Ssh." Ashur waved his arms above his head drunkenly. "Keep it down. Wind's shifted and noise carries. Don't want the"—he jabbed a thumb in the direction of the base—"the New Kids to hear."

"Let 'em hear. What a bunch of snotty-nosed, puritanical brats they are, to be sure." Mendoza tossed back another shot of home-brewed aguardiente.

"They don't mean to be. We just sort of—" Sixtus groped for words.

"Gross them out?" I suggested.

"They're too delicate for this end of time, that's all. We see venison, they see Bambi. We see swordfish steaks, they see Friendly Flippy lying murdered."

"We see ourselves, and they see—" Matthias scowled into his drink. "Savages, I suppose."

"Don't take it to heart," Ashur said, patting his shoulder. "They're just a bunch of rude, racist, species-ist adolescents."

"Then they ought to get back to their own damned end of time and let us manage affairs at this end, like we've always done," growled a zoologist named MacCool.

"Even the abalone they get sentimental about," mused Sixtus. "Can you imagine? I don't remember any animated mollusk classics, do you?"

"Wrong. There was a whole French school of cinema d'abalone in the late twentieth century," I lied. Matthias gave a high-pitched giggle.

"No, with the abalone it's bacteria they're afraid of," Mendoza informed Sixtus, ignoring us. "They're positive everything here is contaminated. I tried to get clearance to put in a little vegetable garden on the leeward side of the base. You know, for fresh tomatoes and maybe a lettuce or two? You'd have thought from Bugleg's face I was suggesting we grow amanita mushrooms. What about the microbes, the man said. I don't know where he learned a big word like that. As though I couldn't spot a goddam pathogen a mile ahead of him any day!"

"It's because they can't see them that they're so frightened," pointed out our principal anthropologist. Imarte was her name.

"Yeah, well."

"They think germs are scary?" demanded Sixtus. "They ought to see some of the things we've had to fight in their service, over the ages. A damn sight nastier than microbes, most of them! Eh?" He elbowed Matthias. Matthias and I exchanged uneasy glances. Most of the younger operatives don't know about that particular episode in prehistory, and official Company policy doesn't encourage letting them in on the secret. Besides, Sixtus was wrong to assume Matthias was part of the operation. Full-blooded Neanderthals weren't drafted to be Enforcers. They were too short, and they just couldn't ever seem to get worked up enough.

"How on earth can they know what we've seen?" mused Ashur, belching gently. "We've made life in that precious future of theirs so safe for them, they can't even imagine what real danger is."

"They're ungrateful brats," MacCool said.

"I think you're missing the point," Imarte tried to tell him, but he rounded on her:

"Aren't you appalled by them? Weren't you brought up to see them as the wise and benevolent Masters of the bloody Universe? Remote figures in their twenty-three-hundred offices who Know It All? God help us if these people are representative of Dr. Zeus."

"Of course not. They're field lackeys, that's all."

"So why do we have all these geeks from the future on this job?" Mendoza wanted to know.

"Because this one is a big moneymaker for the Company," I said, glancing sideways at Matthias. "Or so the rumor goes. There's a lot hanging on this one."

"There's a lot hanging on every one," grumbled Sixtus.

MacCool flung a deer rib into the fire and watched it sizzle. "We've been running things for them for how many millennia now? Thirty? Forty? We were always good enough for the job before. This boy in charge can't seem to make up his mind whether I'm some sort of temperamental office equipment or belong in a cage next to the specimens I collect. Were they always like this? I can't ever recall being called an android before, can any of you?"

"We're starting to get close to their end of time," Ashur told him. "Only a few more centuries to go. Makes 'em nervous. Have little drink."

"It's all that processed food they eat making them constipated, that's why they're nervous," chortled Sixtus.

"And these are the cretins we're saving the world for." Mac-Cool's eyes smoldered.

"You're-talk-ing-TREA-son," sang somebody from the other side of the fire.

"And if I bloody am?" He half-started up.

Matthias stared at him. "Boy, what's eating you? No need to fight about it, is there?"

"Sorry." MacCool raised his drink in a gesture of apology. "I've had this little spit-and-polish mortal jerk overseeing my project. He seems to feel that if he isn't right there to watch my every move, I'm going to club and eat all my specimens before they can be shipped. I thought of telling him about the times I've watched his ancestors clubbing and eating one another! Where does he get off thinking *I'm* barbaric, the chinless little twerp!''

"Okay, okay, mortals stink," agreed Ashur.

"Not the New Kids," said Mendoza in a thoughtful voice. "Have you noticed? They have no proper scent. They don't even sweat."

"I mean it!" MacCool turned slowly to stare at us all and settled his gaze at last on Mendoza. I should mention that he was a big good-looking guy with a black mustache that would have done an Armenian poet proud. She looked up at him. "What are these people? They don't watch their own movies, they don't read their own books, they don't listen to their own music, their art embarrasses them, and as far as I can tell they're afraid of one another. They stay in their rooms playing games! How in the living hell did they ever create us?''

I knew some answers to that question, but it didn't seem like a good time to give them, not with the mood he was in.

"MacCool, their lives are so short," pleaded Imarte. "They don't have time for anything. Why shouldn't they be frightened? What if you knew you only had two centuries of consciousness, maybe less?''

"Then I wouldn't waste it in a holo cabinet shooting at imaginary soldiers," snarled MacCool. He looked down into Mendoza's eyes. "Would you?''

She returned his stare with a flat, opaque look, but smiled and drew her shawl around her shoulders. "Certainly not."

"Is *that* what they do all the time?" somebody asked.

MacCool turned and said: "As God's my witness. When they're off duty, they hook up to a console and play holo games. They shoot at targets or collect little blue dots of light. That's all they do, for hours on end! Take a look at their entertainment programs sometime. Not one book or film will you find, and no music more than two years old their time. Nothing but games, and not even that many of them.''

There was a moment of silence.

"Well, maybe they're exercising. Practicing reflex speed or something," Ashur suggested. "They have to operate a lot of machinery. Maybe in the field they don't want any other entertainment. They seem to be big on stripped-down efficiency. Function over form. Look at those god-awful clothes.''

"They're more androids than we are," muttered MacCool.

"Although . . ." Mendoza said slowly. "They *do* seem to have a point about wearing simpler clothes in the field. I'm ruining all the stuff I brought up from New World One. It's hard collecting specimens in all that lace. I've broken three sets of heels climbing around in these canyons. I don't know who I thought I was going to impress in my Madrid fashions, because the sagebrush sure doesn't care. This is stupid. I'm ordering more sensible clothes. Khaki. Low heels. That kind of thing.''

I stared at her in disbelief. MacCool put his hand over hers.

''But the lace suits you, you know. Jesu, don't let them persuade you to their notions of fashion. They *have* no fashion.''

Mendoza looked down at their touching hands. I couldn't read her expression.

Was he thinking of putting the moves on her? He was definitely her type, as I remembered her type: large, loud, and physically impulsive. A crusader. I prayed to every god I'd ever burned incense to that I wouldn't to be treated to a ringside seat as history repeated itself in Mendoza's love life. Even a wimp like Lewis seemed far and away a safer choice. But who was I to get involved? She wasn't a kid anymore.

''It has nothing to do with the New Kids,'' she told him. ''Why indulge in vanities like fashion if simpler clothing will make my work easier?''

MacCool reached out uncertainly and brushed her hair back from her face. ''I also like the way you look in white silk,'' he added.

''Well, the Don Juan of the canid world has to get his beauty sleep,'' I said loudly, briskly shaking the sand from my tail. ''See you guys in the morning. Don't forget to cover the still and bury the barbecue leftovers. We wouldn't want Bugleg to find out about these swell parties.''

''Huh?'' Matthias started up from where he'd begun to doze.

''They know perfectly well what we do out here,'' said Sixtus sullenly, staring into the fire.

''Probably, but isn't it fun to pretend? 'Night, all.'' Putting on my hat, I walked back down the beach toward the lights of the base. There was salt in the wind. I turned up my collar. One thing you can say for mortals: when they get together at a party, they don't have the same damned conversation every time.

18

"SKY COYOTE! DELIGHTED you could make it," Sepawit welcomed me from the doorway of the sacred enclosure. It was an impressive doorway, framed by whale ribs. Do you have any idea how big whale ribs are? I stepped up to go in, but he stopped me with an apologetic little smile.

"I have to precede You walking backward. It's customary. I know You probably don't demand anything like that, but the shamans are so set on protocol, and my Speaker is away on business for me, so if You don't mind . . ."

"No problem." I gave him a conspiratorial wink and let him back in ahead of me.

"Welcome to our house, Uncle Sky Coyote; welcome from the north, welcome from the east, welcome from the south, welcome from the west," he recited in a loud voice.

"Slower!" somebody hissed from inside. "Don't babble it like that."

"And the white wind welcomes You. And the red fire welcomes You. And the black earth welcomes You. And the blue rain welcomes You." Sepawit looked mortified. This might take all night. I put my paw on his shoulder and stepped past him into the enclosure.

"Thank you, all you directions and personified natural phenomena, your welcome is gratefully accepted. Well, well, and who do we have here?" I looked around at the religious dignitaries assembled before me. They looked back at me, formidably. Time for a few good guesses. I bowed to one elderly gent, portly and very distinguished in appearance, with a nice mild face like the bishop of Madrid.

"My greetings to the astrologer priest," I ventured.

"Uncle Sky Coyote." He inclined graciously. "You are truly with us."

"So I am." I turned and bowed to two more gentlemen of the same august sort, whose feathered topknots poked at the ceiling. "Reverend sirs! May your divinations produce answers. May your sacrifices find favor. May your rituals go smoothly."

"Welcome, Uncle Sky Coyote," they fluted. That left a couple of lean men with staring eyes. These were the ones with tattoos, knotted hair, animal parts strung about their persons, and a general look of having partaken way too frequently of certain vegetable alkaloids.

"Learned doctors," I tried. "Best of luck in your pursuit of knowledge." That seemed to please them. They began to rock back and forth where they sat.

So far, so good. I whisked my tail out of the way and sat down casually. Their eyes all widened. I must have sat on something sacred. I checked over my shoulder and yes, I was sitting on some kind of intricately painted skin. Okay, I'd forge ahead.

"Now, naturally enough, you don't have to tell me why you asked me here. I can tell you. You want the truth about my revelation of the other evening. You're all initiates, and you know there's more here than can be understood by those who have not traveled the secret paths." Right? Right, guys? After a breathless pause Sepawit nodded.

"We knew that story about the white men was a cover for something. It's the Chinigchinix thing, isn't it?"

Who? What? I opened my mouth for a bluff while I accessed hastily, but was saved the trouble of some fast thinking by one of the shamans, who leaped to his feet.

"I am one with Sky Coyote and I speak for Him! I can tell you what is in His heart. The white men represent the followers of Chinigchinix who dwell in the south. Do they not paint their heads with white clay? And their Sun is not our own true Sun but an angry god who drives out all gods but himself and visits terrible punishment on unbelievers! Sky Coyote is trying to tell us that Chinigchinix is readying his people to invade us. So says Sky Coyote!"

There was silence for a moment as we all took that in.

"Thank you, Pahkshono." Sepawit gave a slight cough. "Now, Coyote—"

"No!" One of the priests jumped up. "My knowledge is greater than his! You only have to look at Sky Coyote to see the truth. Has He not sat in the midst of the sky map of the summer solstice? This signifies the intrusion of celestial forces into our Middle World. And does His tail not point in the direction sacred to the autumn harvest?

By this, we may know the time of the divine invasion. Plainly, the Sun is attempting to kill us by sending a great drought which is to wipe out this year's harvest.''

All this made me nervous. I crossed my legs.

"Liar!" shouted yet another shaman. "See how Sky Coyote has negated your specious interpretation of His revelation, which is utterly clear to anyone with any *real* hermetic training. By sitting on the sky map, Sky Coyote is plainly demonstrating His contempt for you and your dependence on astrology. Are not the stars celestial bodies like the Sun? We can infer from this that by 'white men' he means the stars. Sky Coyote warns us that dependence on the so-called wisdom of the stars will lead us to damnation.''

"That is precisely what He is *not* saying," said the astrologer priest severely. "By sitting on the sky map, obviously Sky Coyote acknowledges that the same cosmic system supports those in the World Above as in our world. Even the Sun Himself must follow the preordained celestial patterns. If you think Sky Coyote came all the way down to Earth to overturn the existing order, you're vastly mistaken.''

"And yet, isn't that what He's saying?" countered one of the priests. "The existing order is about to be overthrown by these white men, whatever or whoever they are. What we ought to be asking ourselves is, What is the reason? I think it must be that our people have strayed into evil ways and wrong thinking. The young have no respect for their elders, divorce is on the rise, and there is no proper respect paid to the sayings of the priests anymore. We have grown decadent. Do we not deserve this terrible punishment?''

"No!" cried another shaman. "Sky Coyote *wants* us to be irreverent. He is the spirit of divine anarchy! His message is that He will save us just as we are, in fact He will carry us away to a world of everlasting pleasure where we can sin more enthusiastically and reach ever wilder levels of chaos!''

"Now, hold it! Hold it! Hold it!" I interjected.

"Hold what?" they replied in unison.

"He said it three times," observed one of the diviners.

"So much for a message advocating anarchy!" crowed the astrologer priest. "By 'Hold it' Sky Coyote signifies that we must contain ourselves and our wasteful urges.''

"You timid equivocator!" thundered a shaman. "He meant, 'Hold on to the concept of liberation through excess'!''

"Wait—" I said.

"For what?" demanded a shaman.

"How long?'' inquired a diviner.

"Where?'' asked the astrologer priest.

"Sky Coyote, I wonder if I might have a word with You outside for a minute?'' murmured Sepawit. I got up and went out with him. Behind us a furious discussion of my posture ensued.

"Look, er, Coyote . . . I'm no theologian or anything, so I'm afraid Your answer might go right over my head, but I need to know: how serious is this Chinigchinix threat? Am I going to have to organize a war party? Because if I have to, it's only fair to tell You, we wouldn't have a chance. The Chinigchinix cultists are fanatics, and there are thousands of them. They keep growing in numbers, too, because they forcibly convert their captives. My Speaker isn't away on business—I've had him out gathering intelligence for the last ten moons, and what I've been hearing makes my blood run cold. The priests don't know. The people don't know. I'm the only one who's put all the facts together, and I don't know what to do. You must have come here to save us from them. Tell me, Sky Coyote, that's why You're here.'' The poor guy was shaking.

"You've worked hard for my people, Sepawit. Do you think I'd let you down?'' I soothed him in the voice I'd used in confessionals in Madrid. "You don't have to worry about Chinigchinix. We'll be safely out of here before anything happens.''

"But You have no idea how fast they move,'' he rattled on. "At least—excuse me, of course *You* do. It started down south among the Tongva, at a village called Yang-Na. They had this prophet who's supposed to have been born on Huya Island, who went around telling everybody that there's only one god and anyone who doesn't believe that will suffer horrible punishment. He convinced his people to fight for this god, and they've been taking every village in their path. All the tribes to the east have gone over, and most of the island tribes, and it's been spreading north. They're fanatics! They still trade with us because we make things they want, but in my opinion it's only a matter of time before they declare holy war.''

"I know, my child,'' I told him. It was a story I'd learned a long time ago. Almost the first story I'd ever learned, now that I come to think of it; and later I'd seen it acted out in Egypt, and in Byzantium, and in North Africa. One man becomes convinced he's found a truth so important, the whole world must be forced to acknowledge it.

"And they always conquer.'' He looked at me with haunted eyes. "It's as though they really do have the most powerful god on their side. This prophet's followers aren't afraid of anything in battle—my spies tell me it's because they're all on drugs. And they say—'' He looked away from me. "They say You're the Evil One. They say You used to be a servant to their god, and that You did something terrible and were cast down among the nunasis."

"Boy, that figures." I shook my head. "What do you think, Sepawit?"

"I know You're our uncle. I know You've always helped us in the old stories. But even in the stories You lose sometimes. What will happen if You lose now?"

"We won't stick around here long enough to find out. Sepawit, I think you're a brave man, and a wise man, or you wouldn't be so scared. Will you help me save our people?"

The sound of argument from inside the sacred enclosure grew louder. Sepawit glanced over nervously. It sounded as though somebody was throttling the astrologer priest.

"Of course I will. Tell me what to do."

"Just follow my orders. I really am going to get you all out of this, Sepawit, but you have to see to it that everybody cooperates with me. I don't want any more argument or second-guessing out of that bunch in there." I nodded at the sacred enclosure. "You're the chief, after all. They have to obey you, right?"

"Supposedly," he replied. "It would be a help, Coyote, if You could tell me which of them was right."

"All of them, naturally," I replied. "And none of them, of course."

Well, how else is a god supposed to answer a question like that?

It was a lot to think about, walking home. Isn't it funny how patterns repeat themselves? Unless you're immortal, though, you don't usually get a chance to appreciate just how often they repeat themselves.

I mean, there my people were, not bothering anybody, hunting and gathering like everyone else in 18,000 B.C.E., moving from a winter cave to a summer camp and back again as the seasons changed, regular as clockwork. The only thing we did that was in the least bit remarkable was paint on rocks and on the walls of our winter cave, and actually only my father did any painting. Aunt Druva did a lot of scrimshaw with mammoth ivory, of course, but that didn't count.

The paintings did count, because they were almost the first things the tattooed strangers noticed when they came walking into our hunting grounds. This wasn't a good thing, as it turned out. We had no clue why they started screaming and killing us, but I learned later that they had this god whose principal commandment was that every living soul on earth must be tattooed, or the universe would collapse. Anybody not submitting to mandatory skin art was guilty of not doing his bit to keep the universe in place and must therefore die. Anybody who lavished art on something other than skin was guilty of blasphemy and must also die. They had developed a lot of sound theological reasons for this, I'm told, and we'd have probably listened patiently to them as we submitted to being tattooed; my people weren't dumb.

Unfortunately the evidence that we were blasphemers was daubed all over the walls of the cliff we sheltered under in summer: leaping deer and lolloping bison in every shade of ocher and umber my dad had been able to mix. He'd been the kind of guy who just couldn't resist a blank surface, my poor dad. The tattooed guys never even tried to convert us to the Way; they took one look at those paintings and waded in to restore cosmic order with their hatchets.

My people would have been wiped out, as a lot of other tribes had been wiped out, if it wasn't for the big men in bearskins who appeared out of nowhere to smash the tattooed guys all to bits.

I didn't know any of this at the time, of course. It was only explained to me later how the big men had their own commandment, their own method of keeping the universe from collapsing, and it was a lot simpler than seeing that everyone got tattoos. They just went around killing anybody who tried to kill anybody else. It was okay for *them* to kill, because they were Enforcers, but nobody else was allowed to. They'd been after the tattooed people for a long time. Eventually they got them all, too.

Which was a shame, in a way, because then the real trouble started . . .

19

LOPEZ WELCOMED ME into his quarters with a bow, and I bowed in my turn, sweeping off my tricorne.

"Nice place you've got here." I looked around as I straightened up.

"I like my comforts," he replied, going to a sideboard where a decanter was set up beside two fine glasses. I realized his rank must be pretty damn high too, to have his personal furniture shipped out to a base at the back of beyond like this one. I'd been a successful operative for longer than I cared to think about, and I didn't even *own* any furniture. So how had Lopez managed to hang on to those two comfy chairs, that carved walnut sideboard, that Turkish carpet? Not to mention the nice little Rembrandt study, looking sadly out of place on the gray prefab wall. Best of all, it was golden amontillado he was pouring into that Florentine glass. I nearly shed tears as he handed it to me.

"To the Company." We raised our glasses. He gestured me to one of the two comfy chairs and himself sank into the other one. We put up our feet in front of his heating panel. "That's more like it, I trust?" He sipped his wine.

"You can say that again," I sighed. Beyond the dark window a Pacific gale was howling in the winter night. I edged my feet a little closer to the panel. They were bare, of course, because I couldn't get shoes or stockings on my coyote hind paws. I guess they looked a little odd emerging from my red knee breeches, because Lopez casually remarked:

"The younger members of our organization just can't seem to get used to the sight of a coyote in a brocade coat."

"Yes, I'd noticed that." I cocked my ears and grinned at him. "The alternative is to go nude, though, and I think the New Kids would like that even less."

"I've heard they would prefer it if you wore Company-issue coveralls to clothe your nakedness," said Lopez mildly, and we both laughed, but it was clear he was dropping a hint. I narrowed my eyes. Not on his eternal life. I looked strange enough as it was.

"Poor future kids." I shook my head with an air of indulgence. "They're finding this mission a little hard on their sensibilities, aren't they? Things must be sort of rough compared with what they're used to up there in the Platinum Age."

"They find us outlandish," Lopez admitted. "Extravagant. Eclectic. Unfathomable."

"Frightening," I added. He smiled slightly and shrugged. "Distasteful," I went on. "They're barely polite to us. Not that I take it personally, I'm an open-minded kind of guy, but anybody else just might suffer some hurt feelings."

"Yes, I gather there've been some problems with morale," he mused. "Androids . . . ," he said, at the same moment I said it. He looked gently pained and shook his head. "That *was* unfortunate."

"I thought so." I looked into my glass. Drinking with this muzzle took a bit of concentration, but if I sort of made a long spoon of my tongue, I could get the sherry down my throat without spilling any.

"And so there have been a few late-night parties where some grumbling went on. A few ill-considered words. A few rash opinions."

Aha. Lopez was an attitude cop. He was sounding me out over discontent in the ranks.

So I relaxed and sank deeper into my chair, savoring my amontillado and letting it take me back to a certain garden in Madrid where the sun was warm, and just around the corner was a great little wineshop, and just next door to that was a really fine tailor's, and next to that a lovely old church whose bell sounded the Angelus sweet and mellow through the sleepy air, and if the wind was right, you could barely smell the heretics burning . . .

"Well, you know, Lopez, I think we all agree that what matters most is the Company. We all want this mission to succeed, we really do. But it's hard, meeting somebody like Bugleg, to feel confident that this mission is in the best hands. Now, you know and I know that, despite appearances, these mortals are perfectly competent guys." Boy, was I smooth. "So what if they're a little culturally limited? I'll bet they're swell at interfacing with information-exchange terminals. But some of our old field operatives have trouble appreciating that, you know? Especially with somebody like Bugleg. What's the story with that guy? Level with me. He's somebody's nephew, right?''

The corner of Lopez's mouth quirked, but his gaze remained opaque. "Now, now. He has his talents."

"I'm sure he has." Maybe the guy collected stamps.

"Joseph, I truly understand how you feel." He reached over for the decanter and refilled our glasses. *I'll bet you do,* I thought to myself. I accepted my drink, and as I took the glass, I looked him straight in the eye, sincere as hell.

"I'm an old, old agent, Lopez," I said. "I love my work. The Company is everything in the world to me. All I ask is to know for certain that Dr. Zeus is being run by people who'll treat it right." I practically had myself crying, but Lopez saw right through me. He leaned back, sipping his sherry, considering me with bland eyes.

"I feel I can speak frankly with you, Joseph. You're a Facilitator, after all, and you've been around long enough to know a few things the rest don't know. The conservationists, anthropologists, botanists, and others, they're not really designed to grasp the big picture. Are they? Too focused on their own particular areas of expertise. Only a Facilitator has the necessary detachment to view a political situation with any real perception. Only a Facilitator—well, an older one, you or I, for example—has the experience to act effectively in that political situation."

"Maybe," I said, shrugging, remembering that pleasant little garden where no one could provoke me into revealing anything. Lopez smiled grudgingly at my control.

"You'd be a fool if you weren't concerned about the future, and I happen to know you're no fool. I've read your personnel file, you know."

Hadn't everybody?

"It's an impressive record," he went on. "Only three disciplinary incidents in your whole career! And I was tempted to discount that last one. Tell the truth: weren't you taking the heat for that protégée of yours? She's on this mission, in fact, isn't she, the botanist Mendoza? Presumably she's older and wiser now. Let us hope."

"It was just one of those things," I said, trying to sound as though this was something I hadn't thought about in decades. "Kids! What can you do? They always seem to want to learn the hard way. She's straightened out, though. They always do, eventually."

"How true," he said, sipping his drink. "Setting aside the incident with the young lady, however—I was particularly struck by your ability to see clearly and function correctly in, let's say, personally complicated difficulties."

What did *this* mean? How far back in my file had he read? It can't have been easy to interpret my expression through all the appliance makeup, but he was managing. He smiled reassuringly.

"You've made some difficult choices, in your time, but you always chose correctly. That business with the old Enforcers, for example."

Yikes.

I let myself look sad and shook my head. "Poor old guys. But, you know what they lacked? That same quality you were just talking about. Detachment. They were damned good at their jobs, but it made them a bunch of loose cannons in the end. I was really relieved to hear they'd been retrained before they could do themselves more harm."

His stare was like an icepick, but he wasn't going to pry anything else out of me. Not on this subject. He seemed to accept this and went on convivially:

"Your feelings do you credit, especially since they're tempered by wisdom. You know what I admire in you? Your ability to trust." I almost grinned, but he held up his hand and went on: "You've been able to understand that this operation—by which I mean the whole thing, from its beginning, before either of us was created—couldn't have been conceived, planned, or carried out by people who didn't know exactly what they were doing. You have never, for one moment during your very long career, questioned the authority over you. Not because you're a drone or a toady, either. You have always understood that, whoever might be running things, their plan was sound."

"Like I said." I lapped up some sherry to break the mood.

Then he truly surprised me.

"You know what you have to keep in mind, Joseph? They're children, the mortals. No more than children. Life is so simple in that bright future of theirs, they've never had to trouble themselves to learn how to do more than play. For some of them it's very, very creative play, mind you, but . . . it has a certain uncomplicated quality, shall we say. Because, like children, they're bored by complicated things. More than bored: they feel threatened. Give a child mashed potatoes and butter, and he's happy. He doesn't want to try the rich sauce with capers, in fact he'll cry if he's forced to taste it. You see what I mean?

"But, listen, Joseph. A child is easy to control. Keep him happy, and he'll believe what he's told to believe. The mortals believe that they're running the Company, that they make the decisions, that they have the ideas. The child believes the world revolves around himself. Nursie knows better, but of course she doesn't tell him so.

"Though," he added thoughtfully, "he will learn the truth, someday."

What was I to make of this? I took a gulp of wine and looked askance at him. He might be letting me in on some genuine secret politics, but on the other hand he might be baiting a trap for a seditious renegade.

Well, he was sounding out the wrong man. I've worked for the Spanish Inquisition, and this is one game where I know the rules, thank you very much.

I shook my furry head. "I'm afraid this is all too deep for me. I'm just an old field agent, and maybe I'm a little out of touch with the way my betters are running things these days. But, you know, I've always felt we operatives shouldn't trouble ourselves with that end of the business. If you tell me that whoever's in charge knows what's best for Dr. Zeus, why, that's good enough for me, and I'll take your word for it."

"You're an honest fellow, Joseph," purred Lopez. "You touch my heart. Another glass of amontillado?"

"Have some greens, Sky Coyote." Nutku passed me the dish. It was full of wild onions and miner's lettuce. The greens had been steamed limp and were getting limper in the stifling air of the sauna.

"Thanks." I helped myself, and he leaned back with a grimace.

"My personal shaman says they're good for me, but what does he know? It's my spirit I pay him to take care of, and at pretty damned exorbitant rates at that. What I say is, after working my butt off to get where I am, it'd be a fine thing if I couldn't eat steak when I wanted to."

"You've got a point," I agreed.

"Let's have a little more mist, shall we?" Kaxiwalic poured some more water on the hot stones. They hissed and sent up dense clouds, making it harder to see in the already blurry air. Not that my eyes gave me any problems, but I was praying that the fancy circuitry in my prostheses wouldn't be affected by all the damp heat.

"Now *thaaat's* more like it," Kupiuc groaned, easing his big body backward. Even here he'd brought his charmstone with him, a small polished artifact he had the nervous habit of rolling between his fingers. "What a day I had. What a day. My ex-wife is after me for child support again."

"No kidding?"

"The she-whale. She wants me to get all three boys into the kantap down there at Syuxtun. She's obsessed with status. What I say is, let the kids be fishermen or something. At least they won't have to put up with job stress the way their old man does. Anyway, she's wasting her time on the youngest one. He's a lousy little hoodlum; I had to beat him when he was up here last summer. Caught him stealing! It's a shame when you have to say it about your own flesh and blood, always assuming he is, of course, but the kid's just no good."

This met with frowns from his fellow sweat-lodge members.

"Huh." Nutku cleared his throat. "Kantap's a good start in life for a boy, though, you know. It might turn him around. He'd be running with the right crowd, too, not a bunch of losers like hunters. The kantap made *you* what you are, that's for sure."

"Oh, well, of course," Kupiuc hastened to say. "Don't get me wrong. But I'm not made of money, am I?" His charmstone was describing ever faster and tighter circles in his palm.

"Just don't put the kantap down," growled Sawlawlan, and went into a coughing fit that lasted two whole minutes. I scanned him idly. Twenty years of carving steatite had left his lungs lined with talc. He had hemorrhoids, too. Rich as he was, he must have been miserable most of the time.

"You've got to have a word with the boys up at Skaxpilil, by the way." Nutku splashed a little water in Kupiuc's direction. "It looks as though they've been letting redwood consignments through again. I think they're stockpiling. Might be time for a little Miwok lightning."

"Stockpiling?" I inquired.

"We've got an agreement with the towns up north, Sky Coyote. Don't You do this kind of thing in the Upper World? They hold back on their redwood export, and we can keep the price of redwood canoes nice and high."

"That's pretty clever!" I said ingenuously. "Of course, wouldn't that mean most people can't afford them?"

"Right, so they buy pine. Which means they have to get a new one every sixteen moons. Either way, big profits." Nutku looked hard at Kupiuc. "So any bastard planning to flood the market with cheap redwood had better have his inventory torched before he gets the chance. Understand?"

"Nutku, I've got it under control. Trust me." Flip, flip, flip went the charmstone.

"We may not be the dealers You guys are in the Upper World,

but we know a few tricks, huh?'' Nutku grinned at me. He leaned forward conspiratorially. "So, what about a little straight talk on this white men thing, Sky Coyote?"

"Straight talk?" I looked as innocent as I could. It's not easy with pointed ears and fangs.

"Come on, Sky Coyote, You can level with us. The metaphors are okay for the little people, but we're community leaders. We know how the game's really played. These white men, is that some kind of code phrase for the Chinigchinix crazies down south? You can't mean there's an invasion planned? Why should they invade us? They need us. They can't produce any trade goods worth mentioning."

"Stranger things have happened," I told him. "But, no. The white men are somebody else entirely, and they really are going to invade you. In fact, their advance forces have already been scouting your coast. You know those funny-looking canoes that landed at Syuxtun? The strangers you sold all those baskets to?" I leaned back lazily and smiled at Kaxiwalic.

As my words sank in, he froze in the act of pouring more water on the rocks.

"What?"

"Remember those fancy new patterns you had designed for souvenirs? Those people, remember? Didn't they look just the teensiest bit, oh, *white* to you?"

"Actually some of them were black—but—" His mouth hung open.

"So they're real?" Nutku looked grim. "Well, so what? They're only men like we are, then. They want to invade us? We'll see about that. Our war parties can kick ass like nobody's business."

"What's it going to take to get through to you guys?" I barked. "This is not just an invasion. This is a cosmic matter. There are Big Players in this game. The white men and the Chumash are just pawns."

Kupiuc stared. "So there really is a World Above."

"Do I look like I've come from the next village over? Of *course* there's a World Above. Look, I'll level with you. You all understand, I'm sure, that there are times when you have to let out information in a strictly controlled way. You're not lying, exactly. Just telling the truth strategically. You all follow me?"

They nodded tensely.

"All right, so we've been a little vague with you about Life Up There. It isn't all that different from life down here, if you want the truth. It's a power struggle. You have to play the game to win. You guys would understand that.

"Now, your lives are a commodity to us, like any other commodity. Some of us have vested interests in you. Others are more interested in controlling the rate of flow." I made my eyes mean and small. I canted the tips of my ears forward. "With you guys it's shell money. With us it's human lives. My stock goes up when there are a lot of you running around. But the other party—and you can go on calling Him the Sun—does good business when lots of you die off.

"So I've had inside information on a move He's planning, this white-men business. If I can pull my capital—all of you, I mean—in time, I can protect most of it and transfer to a long-term investment. He'll flood the market with His invading force, and I'll take a loss, but I won't be wiped out. See? Then He'll have wasted a lot of His resources. I can pull back, draw on my reserves, and hit Him in the next game, and He'll be at a disadvantage because He won't know about my secret strategy this time around. And *that's* how the game is played by the Big Boys, nephews." Whew.

They sat there in shock a minute or two. At last Sawlawlan moved uneasily on his rock and said, "Well, I never thought the universe worked quite like that . . . But, you know, now that I think about it, it's sort of comforting. I mean, this is a system I understand, anyway."

"Yeah," said Nutku.

"And it's not like we were unimportant or anything," ventured Kaxiwalic. "We're vital parts of the big plan, aren't we?"

"Sure you are."

"Hell, yes, we must be, or Sky Coyote wouldn't be here! Right, Coyote?" Kupiuc looked narrow-eyed and astute. "The good-and-evil stuff is just a front. It's business up there just like it's business down here." He squeezed his charmstone tight.

"And you smart boys figured it out instinctively." I smiled with all my sharp and pointed teeth. "The priests are all chasing moonbeams, but leave it to the real leaders to understand the truth." They all basked in that for a moment, then Nutku cleared his throat again.

"So, um, Sky Coyote . . . what about *our* investments?"

"I knew you were coming to that."

"Kaxiwalic mentioned something about losing our markets . . . ?"

"I won't lie to you. Sure, you'll take a loss—but not the way everybody else will. So, where does that put you? Ahead of the game, right? Which will make you insiders when we get to where we're going. And, Kaxiwalic, chum: don't get too worried about our little

conversation the other day. I mean, one of your producers was standing right there! Do you think I'd let one of *them* in on this?''

That lightened up a couple of faces, and I rushed on. ''Plus—and
listen up, this is a big plus—think of the aggravation you're leaving
behind! Ex-wives. Fanatic cultist trading partners. Redwood over-
stock. Okay? And as for all your existing inventory, hey, all I can say
is, sell out now. How, you ask, it's winter! Sea's too rough to go on
the trade routes. Land's a mess with mud, and there's hungry bears
and mountain lions on the trails. Well, I can bring in buyers who'll
take it all off your hands! And at retail prices, too! Canoes, bowls,
baskets, the whole works, AT RETAIL! You can liquidate all your
assets, and when we get to the new place, you'll be the ones with the
capital to get the ball rolling in the new game. And believe me, boys,
it'll be a new game. There are easier ways to make a living than
chipping stone bowls. Can you trust your Uncle Sky Coyote?''

Nutku clenched his fists. ''You guarantee you can unload my
inventory before we go?''

''I said retail, didn't I?'' I replied cheerfully, leaning forward to
slosh some hot water on the stones and cloud the issue. I didn't know
where Beckman, our art curator, was going to get all that shell money,
but that wasn't my department.

20

As it turned out, all this had been foreseen, and Beckman had enough cash with him to buy a couple of museums, let alone a luxury canoe. If he'd worn all his money, he couldn't have stood upright, of course. Instead, he stood unburdened in one discreet but high-denomination strand of shells, a deerskin jockstrap, and green body paint, with the rest of the loot carried in satchels by a couple of burly techs.

They waited patiently with the rest of the salvage team in the icy breeze coming off the Pacific. I could see them waiting as I hopped out of my knee breeches. Actually, some of them weren't waiting so patiently.

"And here he comes! The star player! Yaay!" I went sprinting out to them. Fourteen freezing specialists and thirty security techs glared at me, and nobody cheered. With the goose pimples, green paint, and skimpy Chumash costumes, they looked like a bunch of avocados in a diorama.

"Does it get any warmer away from this goddam beach?" Mendoza wanted to know.

"Sure it does. This is California," I told her. "Now, everybody, probably we won't encounter any locals until we reach the village. I never give them any clear idea of when I'm going to visit them, so I don't think they'll shoot at you or anything, but let me go first and do all the talking. Everyone accessed their language files last night, riiiight?"

"Riiiight," they echoed in sour unison.

"Heads up, everybody, here comes Bugleg," hissed MacCool.

Yes, here came our fearless leader, out to review the troops, shepherded by his faithful dog or puppet master, whichever view of Lopez one preferred. They emerged from the base, and Bugleg stood there blinking rapidly in the wind. I don't think he got outdoors much.

I saluted briskly. "Hello, Mr. Bugleg. Any words of inspiration for us before we hit the beach?"

"What did you say?" He looked bewildered. "This is the beach. I thought you were going to the native huts."

"Figure of speech, sir. Beach, front lines, salt mines, trenches. Engaging the enemy. Going off into the wild blue yonder. Beginning the beguine. Setting off on our mission." *Damn it, Joseph!* broadcast Lopez, and I gave him a coyote grin and responded, *Sorry, I've really gotten into my role.* Bugleg's face meanwhile was desperate as he dodged my metaphors and caught the only phrase he understood.

"Oh," he said. "Oh. I hope it goes all right. Okay? Be careful, everybody."

It was a wonder the massed wave of scorn projected at him through the ether didn't knock him off his feet, to say nothing of the silently transmitted raspberries. Careful? Mortal man, we're immortals! We tread water through the Great Flood! Ashur over there got out of Pompeii a month before things got hot, sold his house at a profit too: he could hear the mountain grumbling in its heart. Imarte can smell a Turk coming a mile away, was well clear of Byzantium before the fall. I saw the writing on the wall myself, at Tyre: never mind what it said, but I left on a fast horse the same day. Beckman's never booked passage for a shipwreck, or stood on a wobbly scaffold. Careful? Mortal, you don't know what careful is.

Though of course nobody looked scornful, because that would have been rude. Instead everyone said out loud, "Thank you, Mr. Bugleg," in a quiet and nonthreatening way. He turned to me and complained, "They're all green. Why?"

"Local folklore, sir, remember? They're supposed to be supernatural beings."

"Oh." He nodded. I think he comprehended, even though *supernatural* is five whole syllables long. "And everybody is going in just like we planned?"

"Right. We have a zoologist, an art curator, a botanist, a marine biologist, a geologist, a primary cultural anthropologist, a primary physical anthropologist, and six class-two anthropologists to work in teams with the other specialists."

"But what if the natives shoot at them?"

"Well, sir, that's what the security techs are for, isn't it? And they'll also help us transport artifacts." Bugleg blanked on that one.

"You know, the things the Indians make. Beads and stuff? Souvenirs?"

"All right." He shivered. "You better get started. I don't like it out here. Too cold."

"Yes, sir, it's very cold."

"I'm going inside." He turned and left.

We set off, up the long canyon. Behind us there was a mortal face at every window.

"Symbolic, isn't it?" Beside me, Mendoza settled her pack.

"What?"

"Mortals behind us, mortals ahead of us. We're always in the middle, trudging up some blind canyon with our collecting gear, bare-ass naked."

"You're not bare-ass naked; you're in colorful local costume," I reproved. "I bet you're wishing you had your Madrid fashions on now, huh?"

"And how," muttered a dozen immortals.

But their spirits rose as we got inland, away from the wind. The sky was blue, the sun was warm, and nobody was shooting at us: basic elemental pleasures like that. More, though: we were finally away from all the bureaucratic crap and going out where we could do some work at last. We were on the job again. It produces a sense of euphoria in us. We were designed that way.

And we certainly had time to do what we'd come to do. Seventy years at least before Father Serra, bless or damn his well-meaning soul as you like, limps up the coast to found his mission system. Twice that long before the Yankee boys see Spanish estates the size of minor kingdoms, all empty and pastoral, and decide these lazy *Gentes de Razón* must be pretty damn dumb not to see the money they could be making if they'd cut down the oak trees and build towns. Two hundred years and then some before the engineer Mulholland throws open the sluice on his new aqueduct and yells, "There it is—take it!" as somebody else's water cascades down to a host of real estate developers and orange growers. Putting in five words the creed of everyone who'll ever lay eyes on this poor California.

Well. Come genocide, come developers, come pollution and urban war. Let 'em do their worst: we can clone even Eden, if we get there before the Serpent and take samples.

21

I LED EVERYBODY up the back of the big hill that overlooked the village. We paused on the summit to look down at the little houses and work yards and the tiny figures going to and fro. "Humashup," I announced.

"Okay, we're fanning out," announced the head security tech, and he and the other members of his team vanished into the sagebrush, leaving their packs for the rest of us to carry. Within seconds even we couldn't tell where they were, but we knew they'd be down there doing invisible surveillance.

"It's *perfect!*" said Imarte, eyes shining. "Look, there are children playing the hoop game—and that must be the cemetery—oh my god, they're making canoes over there!"

"See the shell mound?" Beckman said, shading his eyes. "That's not a midden. Those are money shells. And that man's cutting abalone shell for inlay work . . ." The others crowded close to see, muttering excitedly. Only Mendoza stood apart. I looked over at her.

She'd barely noticed the village. She was staring beyond it into the land, green and rolling with huge oak trees like gods, rolling away to green and blue mountains. She was breathing in the scent of the aromatic brush on the hills, the sage and the agave with its white spires of clustered flowers. She was taking in the cloud shadows and the pattern the wind made coming across the savanna before it funneled into the canyon and carried away the smoke from the cooking fires of Humashup.

I know it's pretty wild and empty, but it won't be so bad, I transmitted to her. No reply, but a sound I couldn't describe exactly, kind of a throbbing sound, kind of a storm sound. What was she tuning in to that I couldn't hear? She turned her head slowly to stare at me, and her eyes were a thousand years away. I shivered. Last time I'd seen that look, it was on a nun whose palms had suddenly and inexplicably begun to bleed. *You okay, Mendoza?*

Her brows drew together in a faint frown, as if she'd just noticed me.

"This is the most beautiful place I've ever seen," she replied. "How could anybody cut down those trees?"

I went and took her by the arm. "Nobody's going to start for a while, but you've still got plenty of work to do. Come on."

There's always a letdown after first contact with an endangered species. You get real moved at the thought of saving all those mortal lives, and then you actually meet the mortals and it's sort of a disappointment. Except for the anthropologists. They love mortals. Good thing, too.

In spite of my careful preparation for this moment, the people of Humashup did not take it well when they beheld a crowd of green beings descending the green hillside. Men stared and rummaged for their spears, women ducked inside their houses, children ran screaming after the women who had ducked inside the houses.

"Children! Children! There's nothing to be afraid of!" I barked. "Don't you know friendly spirits when you see them?" Sepawit had come out of the council house and was standing there with his mouth open, watching us approach. I caught his eye. He turned and waved his hands frantically.

"It's all right, everyone! It's only Sky Coyote and his spirits! It's *green* men, not white men! Come on back, all of you!"

Actually it took about an hour to calm down the populace of Humashup and entice them to an orderly assembly, during which time my fellow immortals stood awkward and embarrassed in their viridian near nudity. Except the anthropologists: they ran around with little cries of delight, taking notes and holo shots of everything.

"Thank you all for coming," I said at last, pacing before the silent and staring village. "You mustn't be afraid of my servants! Why, except for the fact that they're green, they look just like you, don't they? And you all know I'd never do you harm. I've brought them here to collect things. You see, I'm not just saving all of you, I'm saving this world. I'll want to build it again someday, so I'm having my servants collect a little of everything: the plants, the animals, the stones and shells. They're also here to collect wisdom, to collect your knowledge of these things. You must help them by an-

swering any questions they ask you. Be truthful. Don't lie about anything. After all, if you lie, I might make some mistakes the next time
I create this world."

The crowd took that in, and there were a lot of thoughtful nods
as they accepted it. The concept of an infallible deity was going to
be something new to the Chumash.

"I mean, you wouldn't want me to make a world where the creeks
flowed blood, or the oaks grew bones instead of acorns, would you?"
Scattered laughter and shudders.

"We do things a little differently in the World Above. When we
spirits relax, we like to sit down to a big heaping bowlful of rabbit
pellets with a few rattlesnake heads scattered on top for that extra
burst of flavor"—screams of delighted laughter—"but somehow I
don't think that would suit you folks very well. So it's very important
for you to give good, truthful answers to the spirits. Otherwise, who
knows what people could find themselves eating?

"Now, tell me: Who are the best hunters here? Who's the best at
bringing down the deer, the ducks and geese?" Quite a few skinny
guys stepped forth uncertainly. I nodded to MacCool and the anthropologist Giovanna. They advanced out of the group.

"Good! Now, this man is the Spirit Who Catches Animals. He
needs to catch two of all the animals you hunt. That woman is the
Spirit Who Collects Hunting Wisdom. All of you hunters go over
there with them and talk for a while, all right?"

They went obediently, and I beckoned to Mendoza and her team
anthropologist, Dalton.

"Now, who among you ladies is the very best at gathering roots
out of the earth, or greens in the rainy season? You members of the
Deer Grass Gatherers' Union, where are you? You herbal healers, you
women of wisdom, where are you? Only the wisest, mind you."

A number of hefty dames pushed their way forward, elbowing
one another out of the way. There was a brief nasty squabble about
which of them was the wisest woman of wisdom, and in the end I
had to promise them they'd all get a turn at talking. I sent them away
with the Spirit Who Collects Plants and the Spirit Who Gathers Herb
Lore.

The rest of it went pretty peacefully. There was the Spirit Who
Fishes, and the Spirit Who Collects Dirt, and the Spirit Who Wants
to Know about Your Sex Life, and so on. Various elements of the
population went off to sit under oak trees and talk with them, until at
last there were only Beckman with his satchels and me. My executive

pals from the steam bath had been waiting in a group, eyeing the satchel.

Nutku put up his hand. "That's the Spirit Who Buys at Retail, right?"

"Yes! This is the spirit whose coming I foretold to you." I grinned, tongue lolling. They converged on Beckman like sharks on a swimmer.

"Hey, spirit. I've got canoes! Beautiful canoes, all redwood models, with every luxury feature. Retrievable paddles, spear racks, mother-of-pearl inlay, I've got two-seaters, three-seaters, hell, I've even got a couple of war canoes at prices you won't find anywhere else!"

"You want baskets? I've got the best. Two-color, three-color, even four-color, large and small. Unbelievable patterns, also custom work!"

"*No* finer pots and bowls anywhere, guaranteed not to crack, and they're fireproof! Polished, carved, and inlaid by the finest craftsmen. We also carry utility vessels, hand mills, storage basins, durable kitchenware in designs that'll grace the poorest camp or the richest house. Ask me about our line of novelties, too!"

So they bore him off, and I heard his voice lifted and the rattle of his coin.

Neat stuff was acquired and sent back to the base for storage every night, already tagged and context-catalogued. Chumash kitchenware. Chumash clothing. Chumash tools. Chumash medical supplies. Chumash sporting goods. Chumash diapers. Chumash birthday presents.

The anthropologists became great favorites, because they were so friendly. They recorded endless hours of Chumash voices speaking at great length on every conceivable subject. Their eyes recorded weeks of footage of Chumash life. Women pounding acorns. Men carving stoneware. A birth. Sports. A death. Courtship. Commercial fishing. They collected the people, too: DNA samples were taken, and each individual was catalogued and described under his or her entry by gender, age, profession, and genetic code. All two hundred and thirty-six or -seven inhabitants of Humashup, tidily listed for the big cargo manifest.

This is not to say that things went smoothly, however . . . though the Chumash weren't the problem.

*   *   *

"A *feast?*" Bugleg looked blanker than usual. "At night?"

"Yes, sir. The Chumash would like to throw us a party." I pulled out a chair and sat down, since I hadn't been invited to. "They'd like to show off some of their dances and stuff, and the anthropologists are thrilled. It'll be a great opportunity to record cultural material actually on location, you see. Their ceremonies and rituals aren't just performed every day. They're making a special occasion for us."

"Rituals," Bugleg repeated. "Ceremonies. Is that the same thing as a *cult?* That sounds scary. They're not going to kill people, are they?"

"No, no, no," Lopez hastened to assure him. "This will be a peaceful celebration, sir. And though it does require that we relax our regulations concerning base curfew for one night, it should prove well worth it."

"Why do we have to do that?"

"Why, so the operatives can all attend, sir," I explained. "They've been working pretty closely with the Chumash, and if they didn't show up after being invited, it would cause hurt feelings. Plus, the operatives *really* want to go. So it'll be all those who have gone on the collecting trips and the security teams who'll guard the perimeter, and everybody'll be out all night. Now, to do this, we need you to sign your name on this plaquette that says it's okay, because the rules say officially we can't have that many base personnel out after dark at one time." And I pushed the plaquette before him and put a stylus into his nerveless hand.

He wasn't happy. "I don't know. It doesn't sound safe."

"Oh, no, sir, it's safe. I mean, what can hurt us? We're immortal, remember?"

"I know that." He pursed his lips. "I didn't mean for you. I meant for us. We'd be alone here with all the security techs away from us. What if the natives attacked? If they play their drums and dance, they might attack. What would happen then?"

"Oh, but sir, they won't do that," Lopez assured him. "The operatives will be right there with them. If the Chumash tried anything of the kind, they'd all be stunned into submission, you see?"

"Though they won't do anything like that, sir, honest," I stated. "They're nice people, when you get to know them. Really."

"But they have rituals and dances," said Bugleg in distaste. "And they catch animals and kill them." His eyes widened as a horrid thought occurred to him. "A feast is where they catch an animal and cook it on a big fire, isn't it? Are they going to do that?"

Lopez and I looked at each other.

"Well, only an animal that's already dead, sir," Lopez told him at last. "It's not as though it's being hurt in any way."

"But there'll be—bones, and muscles, and . . ." Bugleg's face was going pale, either with the slaughterhouse mental pictures he must have been forming or with the effort of forming them, it was hard to say which.

"It's true, sir, meat in its natural state does have bones in it," I agreed. "But the natives are okay with that, and so are we. We're used to it, remember."

"But I'm not!" He clenched the edge of the table. "This is gross. And I just thought of something! You're all, 'Only dead animals will be cooked,' but that still means somebody will kill the animals, doesn't it? And you can't do that! You can't have *rituals* and . . . and all that other stuff! I won't sign permission. It's too nasty and scary."

"Oh, we won't kill anything," I told him earnestly. "The Chumash will be doing the hunting. Honest."

"But they'll be killing animals and you'll eat them. No. Nobody in the Company can do this while I'm in charge. You Old People get away with a whole lot, but you can't do this." He folded his arms. "No weird rituals."

I gave Lopez a long, meaningful glance.

"Wait a minute, wait a minute, I know what the trouble is!" I slapped my brow. "You thought—but how silly—I somehow gave you the impression that there were animal sacrifices going on. Wasn't that dumb! No, no, sir, no actual real live animals will be killed for this feast. No, we explained to the Chumash our feelings about that. It so happens they've got an ingenious way of fabricating protein out of, uh, acorn meal and soya flour, which they then sculpt into the shapes of animals, and *that's* what's actually consumed at the feasts. See?"

Bugleg wasn't quite that dumb. "But you were all, 'Meat in its natural state does have bones in it,' " he quoted. "You said about eating blood and bones and muscles. I heard you."

"Well, sure, but not at a party," I explained. "Hey, I can't fool you. You know that savages eat meat sometimes, and you know we Old Ones do too now and then. But, my God, you don't think we'd do it where anybody else could see! At a *party?* In front of other people? Gosh, even the Chumash would think that was crude. No, seriously, sir, the only animals we'll be eating will be pretend ones."

"Oh. Okay." There was actual comprehension in his eyes. He knew about hiding appetites where nobody could see them. I wondered what the games in his private entertainment console were like. "I guess that would be all right."

"Thank you for understanding, sir." Lopez guided his hand to the signature line. "This will help ensure that the mission is a tremendous success. Your superiors in the Company will be very, very pleased with you."

"That would be nice," he replied, obediently signing. "But it's more important to be sure no animals die."

It dawned on me then that he was actually standing up for a principle here, not just being ignorant and squeamish. I felt bad about lying to him, for a second or two. Lopez caught up the plaquette as soon as it had registered Bugleg's signature. "Authorization cleared! Let the festivities commence."

22

IT BROUGHT BACK memories, let me tell you, hurrying through the dark canyon to the distant lights, with smoke and excitement on the wind. Party time! Behind me on the trail, they might have been tribal members and not anthropologists, all giggly with anticipation. How often are you invited to go back to the first days of the world, when evening dress consisted of feathers and beads?

The Humashup Municipal Sports Field had been co-opted for the party, neatly swept and fenced around with woven tule screens to keep out the wind. Only the side facing the sacred enclosure was open, framed by a doorway of whale ribs painted red, and a big fire burned there to light the dancing ground. Outside the field were cooking fires where people were lined up for helpings of barbecued venison and abalone-shell bowlfuls of acorn mush. One or two from each family were sent on the line to get as much as they could carry back to the others, who had staked out places with picnic blankets and woven drinking jugs. Everybody stopped what they were doing, though, to stare as we made our entrance: Sky Coyote and his spirits!

I wore my usual fur ensemble, but the rest of the team members hadn't been able to bring themselves to tough it out in green makeup alone, so they were wrapped in an interesting assortment of capes and cloaks of European design. *Eclectic* wasn't a strong enough word for the combination of cottonwood fiber G-strings and Florentine velvet brocade.

"Children! Good to see you again." I held out my forepaws as we swept in. "I hope we're not late?"

"Not at all, Sky Coyote, not at all." Sepawit rose from his party blanket, handing off a greasy toddler with a half-chewed rib bone to

Mrs. Sepawit. "Please! We've saved a place of honor for You, here by the banners." He stepped through the crowd, escorting us to our seats. People scrunched over to make way for us, and there were several admiring and envious comments on the fashion parade. "We've even set out a buffet for You, here in the corner. Plenty of venison and side dishes, courtesy of the ladies of the Eelgrass Gatherers' Union, and lots of jugs of manzanita punch and chia tea. If there's anything else we can provide, we've got servers ready to fetch it for you immediately."

What a fabulous view! Imarte rhapsodized. *Look at this, look, we're right in line with the sacred enclosure!*

"This place pleases us," I announced. "Be seated, spirits. Sepawit, have I got time for a whizz before the ceremonies commence?"

"Certainly, Sky Coyote. This way." Sepawit and I stepped away discreetly through a break in the screen wall to where a latrine trench had been dug, special for the evening's festivities. We faced out into the dark and addressed the trench.

"Looks like everybody's in a celebratory mood," I remarked.

"They're thrilled," replied Sepawit. "Nervous, You know, because this isn't like performing for some other village's visiting dignitaries. I'm sure You've seen better dancing in the World above This One."

"You'd be surprised." I scanned the dark in infrared, spotting our security techs silent and motionless out there in the night. "Some gods don't care much for fun. My group are all set to enjoy themselves, though!"

"I think they'll be pleased with what the kantap's prepared," Sepawit told me. "They're really quite talented, our guys, remarkable artists, considering they're businessmen too. Um . . . by the way, Coyote. I suppose You're aware of everything that's going on in this world . . . You'd tell me if we were in any danger from, ah, other tribes, wouldn't You? Like for instance those people we talked about?"

"The Chinigchinix cult? Of course. They can't hurt you, Sepawit, not with me here. What's got you worrying?"

"Oh, just that I'm overdue for a report from my Speaker. I sent him south to gather facts . . . He should have returned by now, that's all." Sepawit finished and stepped back from the edge. I felt bad for him. He was looking out into a darkness a lot blacker than the night, from the edge of a pit much deeper and filled with nastier stuff.

"I can't answer for your Speaker, Sepawit. You know that bad things happen. You've got my word for it, though: I'll keep *you* safe, you and everybody here tonight," I told him.

"I believe You," he sighed, rubbing where his ulcer was hurting him.

We went back in, and Sepawit picked his way through the crowd to the fire, where he raised both hands for attention.

"Everybody? We're just about ready to start"—assorted cheers from the multitude, spirits and villagers alike—"so settle down and get comfortable. Before we begin, I'd like to remind all of you to thank the Civic Works Committee for the great job they did on fixing up the hoop field at such short notice. And let's not make their job tomorrow any more difficult by leaving trash around, all right? Wherever you're sitting, be sure to look around you when you leave and pick up any bones or leaf wrappings or whatever you may have discarded in the course of the evening and make sure you throw them in the latrine where they belong. Agreed?" There were grumbles of assent from various quarters. Somebody far to the back yelled:

"We want a SHOW!"

"Yeah!!" shrieked one of our anthropologists gleefully. I turned around with a stern look. Got to preserve cosmic order, after all. Everybody took the hint and focused attention on the sacred enclosure, except for MacCool, who was solicitously offering Mendoza a bowl of acorn mush. She was declining politely, looking through him.

"All right, all right!" Sepawit looked toward the sacred enclosure for a cue. "Just sit tight, folks, because I think—are we? We are? Here we go!"

He stepped back into the shadows as a drumming cadence began and was picked up by a shrill chorus of whistles. From an unseen place the music grew louder, until it was an alert, a warning, like flashing lights. Someone invisible threw something on the fire, and colored flames leaped up. Out of the darkness came a long low growl, a sound to raise the hackles on an old operative who remembered cave bears. Hold on: where was it coming from? Was it drooling out of the shadows behind us? From over here? Over there? *Had something come down from the hills?* Every member of the audience shivered and crouched down, but nobody could look away from the leaping flames.

There! It was a bear, shambling forward out of the enclosure. It was a grizzly, turning his head this way and that to smell the air. He shrugged his humping shoulders and muscled up on hind legs, weaving from side to side. You could see the costume feathers and Nutku's face, you knew it was only him, but there was another dimension here. In cities, in theaters in Europe at this very moment, with carriages drawn up outside and grease-painted players on dusty boards, it would be called suspension of disbelief. Here it was something a lot more profound, and it tugged at my heart painfully.

It was a grizzly, and it was the power in Nutku's shoulders, and it was the thing you *think* might be a bear when you're all alone on the trail and you've caught a glimpse, maybe, of a profile in the trees. It was that thing in the wild that makes your blood run cold. Though it fascinates, too, because you can't look away from what might be— what is—Death Himself standing on hind legs.

And here came crouched things, moving slow, shaking rattles of turtle shell in perfect time with the weaving dance of the bear. First one, then another, then a third set up a droning hum, three harmonic tones blending in an eerie wail. It rose in pitch. It became a melody with chanted words.

> *Listen up now, listen for your life,*
> *Show's about to start, the star is here, I am here,*
> *Tooth and claw, Murder on two legs, Murder on four legs!*
> *Am I man? Am I beast? I'm POWER in the flesh!*
> *Do you feel me stamping, feel the weight of my step?*
> *Do you see the torn earth, see tree bark hanging in shreds?*
> *Do you hear that groan, that cough that means*
> *It's time to hit the trail? Can you outrun me?*
>
> *No, don't move! Watch now and pray.*
> *He grunts, up there in the trees where you can't see him.*
> *Is that an earthquake, or just him coming?*
> *Last night he came to a house,*
> *They thought it was a thunderclap, that noise,*
> *Rocking wind and rattling hail,*
> *Even when the walls cracked and split,*
> *Even when the Night came in for them.*
>
> *Oh, get out of my way!*
> *I am the One with the Raking Hand,*
> *I am the Mountain Come Walking,*
> *I am Power and No Reason!*
> *Is there anywhere safe from me,*
> *Any corner of the world I don't own?*
> *Pray I don't walk on my two legs to your house.*
> *I am Power and No Reason!*

The words trailed away, but the tune grew louder now and the music stepped up its rattling pace. The audience was frozen in place, even we immortals, because Bear was pacing among us. We could see the glint of his little malignant eyes, and those weren't costume feathers brushing us but rank fur. The clumsy shuffle wasn't funny, didn't make you think of country fairs and fiddlers, oh no; it was scary as hell, because we all knew it wasn't old Nutku in there, it was a dark god.

The menacing flutes and rattles led him through us, in and out of the rows of people, slowly questing after a scent, turning and turning his head to sniff the wind. Just about at the point where the tension was becoming intolerable, the music changed. Or was it the wind that changed? A whole string of little high notes made Bear lift his head: he'd caught the scent at last. He began to edge his way back out of the crowd, following that shrill refrain, and you could smell the relief in the audience as he shambled with deliberate steps for the arch of whalebone. *Chac chac chac,* the rattles led him on; *chac chac chac,* he nosed the doorway; he was almost through, the whistles very faint now; then abruptly, the fire blazed up as he whirled to stand, silhouetted black, claws up and threatening, and the flutes screamed out, and there was a thundering roll of the drums.

And blackout!

I gasped, able to breathe at last.

What had happened was that the kantap's special-effects genius had thrown a cover over the fire, a big woven lid lined with wet moss, and held it there a second in the darkness and confusion while Nutku made his exit. Then it was yanked away, and there was a dim light from the rekindling flames and a lot of smoke and coughing. People were laughing or sobbing with the release of tension. Stiff limbs were stretched. Old grandmothers with apple cheeks and droopy breasts shifted sleepy babies, a bunch of adolescent boys near the front whooped with sudden laughter like honking geese.

When the smoke had cleared and the buzz of talk had died away, a figure was revealed sitting alert and upright in the whalebone doorway. There were a lot of shy giggles and sidelong looks at me, then, because it was Coyote sitting there. It was Kaxiwalic, actually, in an eared hood with a long dog snout tied on over his nose, and in a little fur breechclout with a long tail attached behind and a long stuffed-fur penis attached in front.

I just grinned and laughed. Kaxiwalic waited until the snickers had died down before speaking.

"*Eeevening,* neighbors," he whined. "Got any food?" Which

was apparently an old routine, because with delighted yells the audience began to hurl garbage at him. Gnawed bones and mussel shells clattered through the air, and he made a show of scampering about on all fours to retrieve them. He had the dog moves down perfectly: I could have learned a thing or two from him, especially when he leaped straight up to catch a flying deer rib in his teeth. He got a standing ovation and applause from my fellow immortals for that one.

"Thank you, thank you." He waved the bombardment to a stop. "You're all so kind! And what a turnout we have tonight, huh? What a lot of distinguished visitors from the World Above. Or is that a forest of trees?" An unseen drummer struck a double note you'd have sworn was a rim shot. Kaxiwalic peered through the darkness at us, shading his eyes. "No, no—some of them have tits. Definitely not trees. And look! There's my very own old Grandfather Sky Coyote! Grandpa, how's it going? Long time no see! Mama says you can come home now, by the way—the girl's brothers have all died and the baby was born without a tail!"

Whoops of appreciative laughter. A young mother wiped tears from her eyes, giggling, and her nursing baby pulled loose to chortle in empathy and clap his little fat hands. Kaxiwalic watched us all with bright eyes, judging the timing before he resumed:

"All right! On that spiritually uplifting note, I'd like to introduce a powerful ally. He's one tough customer, but we owe him a lot for driving those herds of seals up on the beach every year. Ladies, gentlemen, sky spirits, let's give a big welcome to—Killer Whale!"

Blackout again, and when the light rekindled, we looked on a scene of roiling waves, or maybe they were woven tule screens painted green and white and being moved from side to side by unobtrusive, hunkered figures. But you could hear the sea, thanks to the *boom-boom* of the big drums and the rattle and hiss of the small drums and percussion. It set up a counterpoint roll of surging surf that would have put Debussy to shame; we were all swaying in our seats in time to it. A flute came in with a string of ascending notes that were Killer Whale rising up through the depths, and sure enough he appeared, with a leap that took him clear of the green mats and with a spray of water.

It was Kupiuc, smooth naked, his big humped body painted gleaming black and white. Only around his neck he wore the bony jaws of a real killer whale, and he made the sharp teeth clash with the music. His eyes rolled white as he tossed his head, as he leaped and thrashed to the pounding drumbeats. He was telling us he was a king in his country, a fearsome hunter, that he had wives and power, that he knew how to go where none of us could go: down into green canyons and forests of waving weed, without any fear of storm. He told us, in his dance, about the silver flights of sardine he'd taken, about the runs of red-fleshed salmon, about his wars with Swordfish.

He sported before us in the sheer ebullience of being himself, a fine sea lord, but then his dance took on a menacing quality: he began to wheel and cruise, seeking something. He was on the hunt. Gradually we saw his prey, revealed a little at a time by the waving screens: one sleek brown head, then a second, then a third. Big frightened dog eyes and blunt muzzles. The seal dancers began to sing:

> *Listen! Listen! He's on the wild water!*
> *He is everywhere, behind us, all around us!*
> *Oh, Grandfather, get us out of here!*
> *Why, oh, why did we ever leave the land?*
> *Maybe he'll kill a shark, and not me.*
> *Maybe he'll take a salmon, and not me.*
> *How much farther till we reach the shore?*

One seal moved to the foreground, the dancer under the headdress floundering like a clumsy thing in panic. Kupiuc danced in place, his body semaphoring triumph. The seal dancer cried:

> *Look at him, painted up to kill!*
> *Look at him, so beautiful!*
> *How can my death be so beautiful?*
> *Here under blue air, with white foam flying,*
> *Green water crashing, how can I die?*

Here came the second seal, bobbing forward, singing:

> *I lived, I had a mate, I had children,*
> *And now I'm cold, I'm old, too slow,*
> *Too slow! Twenty long seasons since my head was big*
> *At Tuqan Island, and how slow I am now!*
> *And look at my scars! And my teeth are broken!*
> *But my lord is fine in his black and white!*

Now the third seal, a big seal, joined them:

> *How well I've fed! Sardines fed me, salmon fed me,*
> *All the little perch and mackerel fed me,*

Made me too fat to escape! What will I feed?
Oh, how unfair it is, when life is so good!
Sleeping in the sun, and mating.
Why will this lord take it all away from me?

They cowered down all three, as Kupiuc leaped high. An unseen
voice chanted:

Who said life was fair?
You run before me like leaves on the wind
To your certain deaths: but listen, listen,
You who love me, you old one, you fat one,
I'm not driving you to hear you cry,
I'm not driving you for cruel reasons.
Look up on the beach
Where Coyote's children wait for you
With swift spears, with quick clubs.
I'm driving you for them,
Because I'm sometimes kind:
Poor naked creatures,
Aren't they cold without your fur skins?
Aren't they lean without your rich fat?
Here in the white water it all ends,
Here in the breaking wave it all ends!

And the seals moved in one synchronized leap of agony, straight
at a painted mat that was flung up before them, where the stylized
figures of men with spears leaned out. Men and seals vanished under
the mat as Killer Whale curvetted and jumped his triumph, and the
music rose to accompany his gradual return to the sea, through the
green mats whose motion was slowing. At last he vanished, with a
last jet of spray, and the lights went down.

Beside me, Imarte shivered in ecstasy. "I can't believe this," she
whispered. "I've never encountered a society where the businessmen
were also the entertainers."

"Hey, you're in California, remember?" I grinned at her and
reached for a nice fat venison rib.

The lights were coming up again. Coyote came dancing out between the red whale bones, deliberately making his penis bob in time
with his steps. When he threw out his hands and stopped, it kept
dancing up and down as though it had a life of its own. He pretended
to notice and did an elaborate double take. The audience tittered.

"Hey! What do you think you're doing? *I* stopped dancing," he admonished it.

"So?" it replied. "You think you're the only one who feels like dancing now and then?" This guy was some ventriloquist! "Why should the party stop, just because *you* get tired?"

"Because I'm the one in charge around here, that's why!" shouted Coyote.

"Oh really?" The penis craned up as though it were staring balefully at him. It was a clever puppet, it had to be a puppet, but I was damned if I could see how it worked. "So you're the big chief, huh?"

"That's right!" Coyote told it, backing up a little as though he were intimidated, but of course the penis stayed right with him.

"I don't think so," it replied.

"You what? You've got your nerve!" shouted Coyote. "I'm the one who decides where we go. I'm the one who decides when we wake, when we sleep, when we play. I'm the one . . ." But his penis was shaking its head.

"Suppose you're relaxing on a nice warm sandy beach, but I see a pretty girl and decide to go talk to her. Do you think you get to sleep in the sun? Uh-uh."

"Well, maybe, but—"

"And suppose you're hungry and digging for roots, but I see a pretty girl. You're going to go hungry a while longer!"

"Well, that's happened, but—"

"But nothing! *I'm* the one who calls the shots around here. And from now on, I'm not just hanging around."

"Oh, yeah?"

"Yeah! I'm going to have my own social life. To begin with, I'm not riding around down here anymore, I'm going to perch on top of your head."

Coyote was aghast. "You can't do *that!* I'll look ridiculous!"

"You think I'm not tired of looking ridiculous? Now it's your turn. Besides, the brains belong on top! When I see a woman I want to talk to, no more arguments! We're going right to bed with her. Bear's wife, for example. Eagle's wife! We'll jump in the furs with her right away."

"We can't do that!" cried Coyote. "Eagle will kill me! Bear will too!"

"What do I care? Did you ever care what happened to me when you went diving in the cold surf?" The penis shivered dramatically. "If Bear or Eagle beat you up, too bad for you. We're doing things my way now!"

"We're not!" Coyote shouted.

"And another thing! I'm tired of being bald! I want a nice toupee of otter fur. The most expensive kind!"

Oh, the people were rolling on the ground, crying with laughter.

"You must be crazy!" Coyote yelled, after a pause to let them quiet down. "Where do you think I'm going to get that kind of money?"

"You just get it, that's all, or else!" The penis reared threateningly.

"Oh, yeah?" said Coyote furiously, glaring down at it. "Or else what?"

By way of answer the penis squirted a stream of water into his face. The audience roared. "Aaargh!" Coyote shook his head wildly, wiping his eyes. He took a swing at the penis, which dodged out of the way.

"Ha ha ha! See how *you* like a faceful of that stuff!" the penis told him. Coyote swung at it again, and it dodged the other way. Back and forth, back and forth it dodged as he tried to hit it. "Missed me, missed me!" it jeered.

At last Coyote mimed *I'll fix HIM* to the audience. He brought both fists up together in the air over his head, clasped them together as though he were gripping a sledgehammer handle, and brought them down on his penis with all his might. BOOM, went the drums, and the flutes screamed once. Coyote froze, his face a mask of astonishment.

For a minute there was absolute silence, except for the audience, who were leaning and clutching at one another in their howling merriment. Coyote remained standing perfectly still, and then he began to blink very fast. Flutter flutter, went his eyelids, though nothing else moved. Then his toes curled.

The drums began a roll, building steadily to a crescendo, and at their height Coyote leaped backward, falling down and spinning wildly on his back. "YIPE YIPE YIPE! I've killed him, I've killed him, oh, help, somebody!"

"What's the matter? What's all the noise about?" A figure came running out between the whale bones. It was Sawlawlan, but judging from his little fur hat and the black paint on his hands and around his eyes, he was supposed to be Raccoon.

"I've, uh, injured myself," groaned Coyote.

"Oh, my goodness, how terrible!" Raccoon threw up his little black hands in dismay. "What did you do?"

"Well . . . I was asleep behind a rock on the beach, and my penis is so long, it was lying out along the sand, and some men came along and thought it was a redwood tree washed up. They tried to split it into planks, and now it's dead!'' Coyote told him.

"Poor Coyote! It certainly looks dead.'' Gingerly Raccoon reached down and lifted it by the tip. He let go, and it flopped lifelessly. Coyote howled.

"Don't worry, Coyote! I'll get help. Everyone, call with me!'' Raccoon implored us. "Call out like this: Help! Help! Coyote's penis won't stand up!''

"COYOTE'S PENIS WON'T STAND UP!'' we all yelled. Coyote looked indignant.

"That's right! All together now! Coyote needs help to get his penis up!''

"COYOTE NEEDS HELP TO GET HIS PENIS UP!'' shouted the reverend elders, and the fathers and mothers, and the bright-eyed children.

"Hey!'' Coyote protested. "Don't tell people that. Call for help some other way. Tell them—I broke my fishing spear.''

"If you say so. Help! Help! Coyote broke his fishing spear!''

"What's that?'' Through the whalebone door came Kupiuc, still all black and white but with feather ornaments now, and a beaked mask instead of teeth.

"Oh, Cormorant, I'm so glad you're here!'' cried Raccoon. "Coyote hurt his—''

"My fishing spear,'' said Coyote.

"His fishing spear?'' Cormorant cocked his head and looked at Coyote out of one eye. "I didn't know you were a fisherman, Coyote.''

"Of course I am! I'm a famous and clever fisherman, only I've broken my spear and I can't fish just now!'' snapped Coyote.

"You look like you've hurt your penis, too,'' said Cormorant, moving his neck snakily, considering Coyote from another angle.

"Nonsense! Nothing wrong with it at all!''

"But—but—'' Raccoon pulled at his ears in bewilderment.

"If you have got a spare fishing spear you could lend me, I'd be much obliged,'' Coyote continued, gritting his teeth.

"Certainly. Here you go.'' Cormorant held out a spear, and Coyote took it. "Going to go fishing now, are you?''

"Of course, of course, as soon as I've rested a little. Don't let me detain you! Please go on and do whatever you were going to do. Bye-bye.''

Cormorant shrugged and left.

Raccoon wrung his hands. "Coyote, are you crazy? What are you going to do with a fishing spear?"

"Here! Tie it to my penis!" Coyote snarled. "Maybe this will help make it stiff again. Ow! Be careful! Not so tight!"

"I'm doing my best!" fretted Raccoon.

"There! See if it will stand up now," Coyote demanded. Raccoon held it up again, but it fell over with a dismal flop, accented by a falling run of notes on the flute. Fresh gales of mirth from the audience.

"It's not working, Coyote," cried Raccoon. "Whatever shall we do?"

"What's all the noise?" came a wobbly falsetto, and out minced big Nutku in drag. He had a long gray wig of fiber cord and a deerhide cloak painted with a pattern of datura plants, big leaves and white trumpet flowers as fine as on a Georgia O'Keefe calendar. There were white flowers wound into his braids, too, and tucked behind his ears.

"Oh, Moonflower, we're so glad you're here," said Raccoon. "Coyote's hurt his—"

"Good heavens, Coyote!" exclaimed Moonflower. "Why on earth do you have a fishing spear tied to your penis? You'll never get a woman to sit on it like that!"

"That's not my penis," grated Coyote. "That's uh, my baby!"

"Your baby!" Moonflower whooped with shrill laughter. "Old woman as I am, I thought I'd seen everything! Your baby, eh? Why does the poor little one-eyed thing have a fishing spear tied to him?"

"He has curvature of the spine," replied Coyote with an attempt at dignity. "I don't have a cradle board for him, so I tied him to a fishing spear."

"No cradle board?" said Moonflower. "It so happens I have a spare cradle board here, one my grandson outgrew." She produced one from under her robe. "This will fix his little back!"

"Er, thank you, Moonflower, but, you know—I think what he really needs is a dose of your special medicine." Coyote looked beguiling. "That wonderful elixir you serve, the one that kills pain and brings visions? Just leave some with me, and I'll administer it."

"To a baby? Don't be silly, Coyote. He'd get so stoned, he'd never be right in the head again," Moonflower chuckled. "Here, you just let an old woman who knows about these things see to him, eh? Come, poor little ugly baby, Old Woman Moonflower will bind you so you'll grow up right!" She proceeded to bind Coyote's penis to the cradle board, while he grimaced wildly in discomfort. "You have to tie them tight, that's the secret!"

"I think you're squishing his head too much—" gasped Coyote.

"Why, haven't I raised more children and grandchildren than I can count? You may have sired a thousand little yipping brats, but you know nothing about them. Now you just keep that poor little creature tied up nice and tight, and he'll be fine." Moonflower drew her robe about her and left.

Coyote gestured frantically at Raccoon. "Take it off, take it off!" he begged.

Raccoon clasped his hands, looking befuddled. "But, Coyote, don't you want your baby to grow up with a straight back?"

"It's not a baby, you idiot!" Coyote growled. "It's my penis, remember?"

Raccoon crossly crouched down and started untying the bindings. "First it's a fishing spear, next it's a baby. Really, Coyote, why you want to tell so many lies is beyond me! If you ask my opinion, I think we ought to call in Horned Owl."

"All right! All right!" Coyote was twisting on the ground, pounding it with his fists, kicking his feet. "Anything!"

"All right, everybody?" Raccoon faced the audience. "Let's see if we can find Horned Owl. Is he flying around up there in the night? Everybody crane your heads back and see."

And while we were all staring up into the black night sky, past the fluttering banners at the million stars, there was a blinding flash of light from the whalebone doorway. All our heads snapped forward, and we saw a new figure standing there, wreathed in plumes of colored smoke.

It was Kupiuc again, wearing the astrologer priest's feathered topknot with two big feathered horns. He had a big medicine bag at his belt, and whatever trick of makeup Lon Chaney would use to give his Phantom of the Opera horrible lidless eyes, Kupiuc had figured it out first. What a wide, glassy stare!

"Yes!" he announced. "It is I, Horned Owl, the powerful shaman! Is someone in need of my services?" And he spread his arms wide, so the folds of his feathered cloak spread out.

Raccoon bowed and scraped, rubbing his hands. "Oh, yes, please, Wise One! You see, Coyote here has broken his—"

"Nothing serious, Your Grace, I've just suffered a slight fracture of my seed beater," interrupted Coyote, but Horned Owl drowned him out with a thunderous cry:

"Silence, dissimulator! By the position of the stars"—he turned his staring face to the sky—"and the augury of the sacred shells"—he threw a handful of clam shells on the ground, leaped into a crouch over them, and peered down intently—"I can see it is a penis and not a seed beater that has been broken!"

"All right." Coyote lay down flat and dejected. "It's useless to try to hide anything from a clever and powerful creature like you. I woke up this morning and found it had died in the night. I must have rolled over on it and suffocated it by accident."

Horned Owl sprang to his feet. "The sacred shells tell me that you yourself assaulted your defenseless member!"

"Oh no!" Raccoon threw up his hands in horror.

Coyote began to weep loudly. "It's true," he sniveled. "I struck it in anger, and now it's *deeaad!* Oh, please, great and ingenious healer, bring it back to life! Don't let my poor flute go tuneless the rest of my days—"

Horned Owl flung out his hands, fingers crooked like claws. "I can alleviate your distress, but an injury this serious requires tremendous effort! The very patch of universe we occupy at this moment in time must be realigned with the heavenly bodies!"

"Oh, my!" said Raccoon breathlessly.

"And so I must have SILENCE while I perform the sacred dance to manipulate time, space, and the material plane!" Horned Owl raised his hands, and he had silence, all right. Then the flutes and rattles began, and the action of the play stopped while he performed the sacred dance.

It was a bravura display of the kantap's secret special-effects craft. Horned Owl paced slowly. He stamped, and weird lights shone. Globes of fire came down and spun in the air like planets, scattering sparks as they rotated. Over beyond the sacred enclosure, spectral figures of gauze or smoke rose pale into the night, and the spooky music led them in a counterpointing dance. All very mysterious and scary. By coincidence, it was during this part that I picked up a sudden signal from somewhere out in the night, a strong flash of nearly hysterical rage and terror. Who was it? None of my Chumash, I could tell that much. I saw other immortals turning their heads in puzzlement.

Security? I sent to our big silent guys, invisible in the trees.
Acknowledged.
Did you hear that?
Affirmative. Investigating. Beginning perimeter sweep now.
Okay. Thanks.

And that was all. Meanwhile Horned Owl had made green flames rise in the central fire, and little things popped and chattered like ghosts speaking. The dance drew to a close with Horned Owl striking a dramatic pose.

"Unworthy creature," he said, "the spirits have spoken to me. In your vile act of self-abuse, you have unbalanced your own cosmic order! Your interior self is blocked. Its channels cannot flow, because of all the gross matter backed up there! Or, to put the matter plainly—"

"He's full of shit?" guessed Raccoon.

"It is so!" Horned Owl gave a dramatic leap. "And the spirits have therefore decreed that Coyote must have"—out through the whalebone doorway came bent figures carrying an enormous agave trunk with a wooden nozzle at one end—"an enema!" He seized it from them and brandished it aloft.

Coyote sat straight up as the audience rocked with laughter. "I'm feeling much better, suddenly!" he said.

"Silence!" shouted Horned Owl. "Your masculine apparatus yet lies lifeless before you!"

"No, really, he's fine now!" Coyote held up the limp head and waggled it to and fro. "See? He's standing up and waving hello! Complete recovery! Miraculous revival! Your lovely dancing must have done it, Your Reverence! What a genius you are!"

"Come now, it's for your own good, after all," scolded Raccoon.

"You think it's so great, *you* have the enema!" cried Coyote. He got up on all fours to flee; but Raccoon caught hold of his tail, and in a single flowing gesture Horned Owl pretended to ram the nozzle where it would do the most good.

"Whoops," quavered Coyote, frozen in midflight.

Horned Owl pulled the probe back, and Raccoon let go of Coyote's tail. Yelping, Coyote began to race around in circles, dragging himself along on his buttocks at unbelievable speed.

"Is it supposed to have that sort of effect on him?" inquired Raccoon worriedly.

"In extreme conditions, the reaction is extreme," stated Horned Owl. "But even now I can sense that his channels have begun to flow."

The rudest noises now came from the musicians. Coyote pulled up sharp and began to flip and spin on his back like a break-dancer. "Gotta go, gotta go," he yipped. "Look out, everybody!"

He backed up to the whalebone arch. "Drop and cover your eyes!" cried Horned Owl. "Here it comes!"

With an agonized howl, Coyote fell forward on his face. From behind him a jet of flame shot up, and then some unseen device

belched forth a fireball that rose and exploded. When we opened our
eyes, we beheld Coyote with his tail on fire, rolling and whimpering.
A front-row toddler hid his face in his mother's lap, wailing in terror.
She rocked him but could not stop laughing.

"I bet he feels better now," said Raccoon.

"Ow ow ow! Oh, my poor tail!" screeched Coyote.

Horned Owl accepted a woven pail of water from one of the
crouching figures and doused Coyote's tail. "Now then, Coyote, how
do you feel?" he asked.

"I wish I was dead," whined Coyote, where he lay panting on
his side in a puddle of water.

"And serve you right, too!" yelled his penis, jumping up between
his legs. Raccoon clapped his hands.

"Hooray! Hooray! Coyote's penis is alive again! Let's all dance
and rejoice!"

He began to do a little hopping dance of triumph, in which Horned
Owl joined; the musicians struck up a lively syncopated air; and out
came Moonflower, and the seals, and the various bent-over creatures
that had facilitated the stage business. At last even Coyote struggled
wearily to his feet, and they all did the Chumash equivalent of the
Bergomask dance, with Coyote's penis bobbing along merrily.

> *Listen! Listen!*
> *We are the Kantap*
> *Of Humashup Village!*
> *Who say they're better*
> *Than we are, at magic?*
> *Other kantaps eat our dust*
> *When it comes to dancing, singing, or jokes!*
> *Have you ever had a night like this one?*
> *Have you ever been so scared, or laughed so much?*
> *Show us the pastime that can compare*
> *(Except for gambling, of course)*
> *With the entertainment we provide!*
> *Let anyone who didn't enjoy himself tonight*
> *Be eaten by nunasis on his way home.*
> *But all of you who had a great time,*
> *Let us know by cheering!*

We cheered and cheered. And had they known, those hard-
working kantap guys, that cameras filmed them that night, and the
whole bawdy, silly, terrifying show would be watched by scholars

and analyzed long after they were dust, would they have been proud? In a way it was immortality, and yet I wondered if it would be the same watching the show in cold daylight, on a gray screen in a clean room. You wouldn't have the stars overhead, or the sound of the wind in the banners and the oak leaves, or the smell of wood smoke. And you wouldn't *know* the players, you wouldn't be thinking, Hey, there's old Nutku, there's Kaxiwalic, there's the rest of them, and the firelight bright on the delighted faces of the old people and the young people. It'd be like somebody else's family pictures, meaningless to your heart, and the jokes wouldn't be half as funny. We save so much for those future mortals, we preserve so much heritage they would otherwise lose; but in the end, maybe we can't really give it back to them. Not the part that matters, anyway.

Not that I was thinking anything so gloomy as I congratulated the performers afterward, standing around laughing outside the entrance to the sacred enclosure as the audience staggered away through the night to their beds—some to lie down on furs in tule houses and some on shaped foam in modular cells. A couple of mood-elevating substances were passed around, of which I partook like a regular guy, though they had no effect on me—other than maybe to paint a more brightly colored mental snapshot of Kaxiwalic half out of costume, laughing, his face shining in the firelight, or Nutku flouncing around and waving his wig, talking to it in his gravelly baritone.

I felt at home. When you're an old, old immortal, you've long since learned to make your home inside your unbreakable skull. You've learned to accept that the simpler time, the better time, the long-gone faces won't ever come back. So you make a village in your head. And that's where it's always that good time, with your people telling jokes beside the fire, with everybody happy and everything all right.

But warming yourself by an image of a fire doesn't satisfy when you see a real fire burning, when you have a chance to creep close to it and feel some real warmth for the first time in longer than you want to remember. It wasn't really my fire; but for a little while that evening it had almost been. My village and my dead were almost there with me again.

Anyway, eventually we looked around and realized that nearly everybody else had gone, except for one or two chat-happy anthropologists who'd found insomniac Chumash to talk to. So I made my farewells for the night and set off down the canyon trail that wound away to the sea.

It was late. Old stars had swung around to stare down disapprovingly at us unfamiliar wanderers in the night. I scanned and picked up the perimeter guard making an orderly retreat through the trees, and a long uneven string of Old Ones winding their way back to the base along the trail.

In fact . . . there were a couple of operatives up ahead, formless moving shadows by starlight unless you looked at them in infrared, when they became Mendoza and MacCool. They were going slowly because she was picking her way with finicky care. I could hear them, too. MacCool was saying:

"You know, what you want to do is ask one of the Indians to make you a pair of tule sandals. Then you can just stride along without worrying about rocks and thorns."

"Thank you, but I'm all right." I knew the expression on Mendoza's face without seeing it.

"No, really, they're happy to do it. Jacqueline got a pair, and they're quite well made, ought to last for years! Better than you'd get in shops."

"Mm."

"I'll ask for you, if you'd rather not talk to them."

"We'll see. Wasn't that a wonderful show tonight?"

"Best I've seen in centuries," he agreed. "But, can you imagine what our lords and masters would have made of it?" He laughed, and Mendoza chuckled along with him.

"I daresay they'd be horrified," she said. "At least the ignorant prudes they assigned to run this mission would be."

"Too right!" His amusement faded. "If the Company officers are the benevolent and all-knowing people we've always been told they are, why do they send a bunch of idiots to run a mission as important as this one is supposed to be? Tell me that. Rude idiots, too. If any of them had gone in to make contact with the Chumash, they'd have been massacred."

I heard Mendoza sigh. "That's why they had us do it, MacCool."

"Why, of course. We're their slaves, the builders of their empire, the ones who go in and do the hard things. Now that I'm actually seeing the inhabitants of the future, it's obvious to me why we were created!"

"To preserve life from death," Mendoza said with another sigh. "To save man from the consequences of his own destructive stupidity. To save the rest of the life on this planet from man."

"That's the official reason, but—isn't it convenient that we also give our masters infinite wealth and infinite power? All their platitudes about world conservation aside, do you think they'd keep us if we threatened their supremacy even once? Why do you suppose we're never given any information from the future after the year 2355? No books, no cinema, no history?''

''Well, that's the year all our work bears fruit, they say, the year the earth becomes a paradise again and we immortals can all rest and enjoy things firsthand. And of course nobody has ever believed that for a minute. Everybody knows there's some dark secret Dr. Zeus is keeping from us about 2355.''

''I suspect that's when we all get retired,'' said MacCool grimly.

''Yeah, or there's a cosmic disaster and they ditch the earth (and us) and take off in a space ark with all the stuff we've saved for them. I heard all the theories back in school! Something big happens in 2355. Some say that's when we immortals rebel and take over at last. Some say there are factions among even us, twenty different cabals, each with its own plan to take over the world. Some say the Company has a self-destruct mechanism built into each of us that we can't detect, and that 2355 is the year they push its button. MacCool, who the hell knows?''

''Twenty cabals?'' He sounded nonplussed.

''But, you know what? None of it changes the fact that we *do* preserve life. We *do* prevent extinctions and rescue great art. Whatever the truth is, we're doing the only work that really matters. Why should I care if that also means that some bureaucrat somewhere is getting fat off my labors? As if anybody could get fat on that atrocious food, anyway!''

''But doesn't it ever make you angry?''

''Angry?'' She stopped on the trail and turned to him. ''You can't imagine my anger. It's infinite rage; it's surrounded me so long, I no longer have any idea where it begins, where it ends. So what? I'm just a machine. You are too. What use is anger to either of us?''

''We're more than that,'' protested MacCool. ''They're the machines. They have less human feeling than you or I do.''

''Not me.'' Mendoza leaned toward him. ''My human feeling is falling away, a grain at a time. Every year I find myself having less in common with mortals, even with my own kind, for that matter.''

''You feel rage, but you work on. That's exactly the kind of attitude a good general prays for in a soldier.'' MacCool sounded weary. ''That's what Dr. Zeus is counting on, don't you see? And don't you see that you should place that unshakable faith of yours in worthier masters?'' He took her by the shoulders and looked down into her eyes.

She sneered. ''Faith? You dope, that's resignation! I don't *care* how the Company's run! Are you actually promoting some kind of rebellion against those poor idiots? Do you think it'd change anything? Has there ever been a revolution that produced something better than what it overthrew? The only thing people learn from being oppressed is how to oppress others!''

She stalked ahead. He followed cautiously, and I followed more cautiously still.

''That's true of mortals, I grant you,'' he ventured. ''But how can you think we'd do the same?''

''I'll tell you how.'' By infrared she was a figure made of flames, dancing on the path in her anger. ''You think there aren't some of us who hate the goddam human race by now, after what we've seen? How long do you think it would be before we started rounding them up in camps for their own good? And we'd have to weed out the genetic defects, of course. And supervised breeding programs, we'd have to have those. We'd run things, because they're evil and incapable of learning, while we're these godlike superior beings!''

''And if it came to a time when we had no choice?'' he demanded. ''What if that's the only way to save them, in 2355?''

She threw back her head and screamed in silence. He moved toward her.

''You're shivering. That cape's no use here. Mine's wool—'' He slung it off his shoulders, and the colors of his body changed instantly as the cold bit into him. He draped it around her shoulders, and I'm afraid she didn't even thank him. He drew a deep breath and said, ''It could come to that, you know. Aren't they becoming less than human? And all the same, I'd rule with human compassion.''

''And what makes you think you'll be running the show, you sap?'' Mendoza paced back and forth in her agitation. ''There are those among us smarter than you, my friend. I mean—here we are, eternally young, infinitely informed, and *designed to preserve ourselves at all costs*. Now, if we all suspect we're going to be terminated in the year 2355, doesn't it seem likely that some of us have already taken steps to make sure that that never happens? What if we're already running things? But if that's the case, we aren't exactly ruling mortals with human compassion, are we?''

''If that's the case, it's not our fault,'' replied MacCool. ''The rule about being unable to change history applies to us as well. But we don't know what happens after 2355! If we move then, we might be able to make a new beginning for the world. Doesn't it make sense to start preparing now?''

''Stop this, MacCool!'' She put her head down and started on up the path, but stopped and turned to him again. "Here's a thought for you. They (whoever they are) can hear everything we say to each other. All the electronic shit in our heads, you know? All those audio and video transcripts we record. You think we can't be accessed as easily as we ourselves access? Why bother with plots? They'll know." She turned to go again. He caught her arm.

"But don't you see? If they know what we're saying and not punishing us—then either we're already in control or they're hopeless simpletons. There's no risk involved, Mendoza!"

She ignored his hand on her bare arm. "How do you know you can trust *me,* fool?"

At this juncture Old Coyote—old Joseph too, for that matter— was wishing He could turn around on the path and go back to His children of Humashup, snuggle down beside their mortal hearths, listen to their sleepy mortal talk and snoring, and give advice on their little mortal concerns, such as how to get their daughter to stop dating that boy or whether to save up for a canoe they couldn't really afford.

"Because I know you, Mendoza. I know your history, what you've endured." MacCool's voice was full of compassion, but I cringed inwardly. He was treading on really dangerous ground with her; did he know it? He pulled Mendoza close to him. "Why would you serve mortal despots, after what you've suffered at their hands? You wouldn't betray me to them, not you. Not after what happened in England. You've been alone too long, Mendoza, but you needn't be!"

He didn't wait for her reaction, but bent her back in a dramatic kiss. That was enough for me. I decided to take an alternate path home and veered off uphill through the sagebrush, heading for the ridge route. As I did, though, I heard her come up for air with an infuriated yell of "Aw, for crying out loud! Was *that* what this was all about?"

I left them below me, climbing through the darkness until I made the top of the ridge, where I could look out across the folded canyons at the black night ocean. I needed to sit alone for a while.

It wasn't the embarrassment of being an inadvertent spectator to the seduction attempt. Mendoza appeared to have that particular problem well under control, and if MacCool was smart, he'd lay in some frostbite salve. Of course, he wasn't smart.

He was a lot more than not smart, and it had nothing to do with Mendoza. How can you work for the Company for however many hundred years MacCool had been around and not know how it handles little troubles that aren't supposed to happen?

We're going to have a flashback sequence now.

23

I HAD COME a long way to find him, following rimrock trails through what would one day be the Italian Alps. He'd set up a base in a cave there, with his heroes around him. It was well below the snow line, but as far as the local mortals went, he was as safe as though he were on the moon; they knew his reputation.

You don't want to go up there! the village headman had signed to me. *Angry god up there. Really angry. Takes heads. You stay down here like us, don't make trouble, hunt for ducks or cut wood—no problem. You go trespassing his place, he kill you.*

I'll be all right, I signed back. *He won't kill me, because I have no weapon. He only kills men who go after him with weapons.*

The headman stared at me a minute, then slapped his brow to indicate that I was right. He'd never noticed it before, but the angry god did seem mostly to pick on people with weapons!

Isn't he a good god most of the time? I signed my inquiry. *Kills bears for you, keeps invading tribes out of your valley?*

I guess so, signed the headman, *but when we go out raid cattle from other tribes, he go after us too.*

Well, that's your problem! I explained.

The headman thought about that. *You mean we not supposed to invade anybody either?*

That's it.

The headman looked appalled as this sank in. Then another thought occurred to him. He looked at me worriedly. *Are you his priest or something?*

No, no, I assured him. *Just a friend.*

He stared after me as I went on my way, and when I had climbed so high that the little village looked toylike in its alpine meadow, I could still see him standing there, lost in thought amid the edelweiss. Or whatever those flowers were. I hoped I hadn't started a religion.

I kept climbing, and before long I saw a pair of the heroes, standing with their spears on either side of the path like towering menhirs. All they wore were bearskins. You have never seen guys that big and strong in your life, unless you're as old as I am, because they're all gone now.

Imagine immortals made from Neanderthals, with just a little genetic interference to give them some Cro-Magnon characteristics, like extreme height and the tendency to go crazy when they're excited. All the rest of their personal qualities were pure Neanderthal, though, the weight lifter's build, the helmet head, the big clever hands; also the courage that nothing could shake, and I mean nothing.

You want an example? When a guy in a Cro-Magnon hunting party fell into a bear den, his friends would step away from the edge and wring their hands. They'd compose sorrowful elegies about him afterward, or maybe horror stories about bears; but no way would they endanger themselves to get him out. When a guy from a Neanderthal tribe fell into a den, though, his friends wouldn't even stop to think: they'd jump right in after him and lay about them with their fists, if they had nothing else, until the bears stopped biting or their friend managed to scramble out.

Of course, it doesn't take a genius to figure out that eventually there were a lot fewer Neanderthals than Cro-Magnons, which meant that Neanderthals contributed a lot less genetic material to *Homo sapiens sapiens*. They contributed some, though.

"Hey, Big Nose, how's it going?" I greeted the one I recognized. That was only a nickname, his real name was Dewayne, but his nose really was this massive lumpy thing between his wide eyes.

"How's it going yourself, you little sack of shit?" he responded in the flat high voice they all had. He grinned, dropping to one knee. I went up to him, and we hugged hello, trying to make each other's ribs creak. Guess who succeeded. "Been a long time," he told me. "Look at you! Tailored skins and everything. How long you been a Facilitator now?"

"Since graduation," I told him. I was looking him over, too; almost no scars remained to give away the fact that when I'd first seen him, he'd been bleeding from a dozen wounds, including the stump of his neck. His head had been in a bucket between his feet on the stretcher. The medics cursed at us kids and told us to beat it, not to watch or we'd have nightmares the rest of our lives. I took somebody up on a dare later, though, and sneaked into the base intensive care unit to see the fallen hero in his regeneration vat. There he was, floating dreamily in blue solution; his head had been reattached, and his wounds were healing already. Little Preservers like me were programmed to avoid physical injury at all costs, but the big Enforcers were so brave, they didn't care what happened to themselves, so long as they did their job. That was why they were heroes. We were taught to admire them but never to imitate them.

"All grown up." Dewayne got to his feet. He giggled. "Though I'd be surprised if you hadn't, after seven thousand years. You here to see the old man, by any chance?"

"I'd like to," I replied. "I hope he'll see me."

"You? Why wouldn't he?" he said, and then his smile faded. "You're here on Company business, huh?"

"Kind of unofficially," I replied. "Where is he, Dewayne?"

"Well—"

It's all right. Send him up. The transmission came through loud and clear. Dewayne pointed up the trail and stood to attention again, resuming his unblinking watch over the valley below us. I passed through three other patrols before I came to the cave under the glacier.

He was sitting in the sunlight at the cave mouth, frowning slightly at the clouds that were massing in the northern quadrant of the sky. He lowered his head as I approached and smiled at me with his pale eyes. He didn't look surprised to see me. Budu never looked surprised. He surprised other people.

He was bigger and older and smarter than any of the other Enforcers, and even the people who loved him were frightened of him. I don't want to give you the impression I didn't love him. I've paid lip service to thin sad gods on crucifixes and bearded gods who flung thunderbolts and green gods all wrapped up in bandages, but the god my heart really believes in wears a bearskin, has bloody hands and a calm, merciless stare.

"What nice clothes, son," he observed, and I ran to him and we embraced. He still smelled the same: not like a *Homo sapiens sapiens* at all. I came up to his collarbone now, but I still felt four years old.

"Thanks. Look! Custom stitching!" I preened, trying to make him laugh. He did smile a little.

"Look at you, how grand you are nowadays. You must have risen high in the ranks," he remarked in his toneless voice.

"Oh, not all that much," I said. "Otherwise I'd have a nice soft desk job. I'm just a field operative, and they keep me busy, let me tell you."

He nodded. "Sending you on errands like this one."

I coughed a little at that. "They didn't exactly send me. I wanted to come, to talk to you myself. There've been a lot of strange stories going around. I wanted to get your opinion on things."

"My opinion or my statement, child?" he said, and chuckled at my discomposure.

"You know what's been happening," I told him, deciding to throw circumlocution to the winds. "The war's over. It's been over for centuries, really. If there are any of the Goat Cult left anywhere, they're keeping to themselves, not bothering anybody. A lot of the Enforcers are balking at new assignments, though. They won't believe the Goats are really gone."

"They *are* gone," Budu told me.

"I knew you weren't one of the problem cases," I said, reassured. "So maybe you could tell me what's going on with the other guys, that they won't come back to the bases with their regiments? One or two have even refused direct orders. You'd think they'd be glad to come in out of the cold, after all this time!"

"And some have done worse things," he prompted.

"Yes," I sighed and looked down at my feet. "It's a pretty ugly story. Marco commandeered a mortal village and quartered his regiment there. Said his intelligence was that there were Goat spies hiding out with the civilians. He began interrogations."

"And it came to killing," Budu said.

"Yeah. But apparently nobody there had ever even heard of the Goats. A lot of innocent mortals died."

Budu nodded slowly. "Marco is a fool," he said. I was so glad to hear him say that! But my relief was damped down when he went on to say:

"He doesn't need the Goat Cult."

"*Nobody* needs the Goat Cult!" I agreed desperately. "And he knew that as well as you or I. He did his job so well, all of you did, that nobody will ever have to worry about the Goats again. All he had to do was bring his men home. And now he's facing a disciplinary hearing, when he ought to be retiring with honors."

"And is he sitting in a detention cell, awaiting trial?" Budu inquired.

"Well—not exactly," I admitted. "He's still out there. He says he's on the trail of a new Goat incursion. He's refusing to come in."

"How unfortunate," said Budu, "for everyone concerned."

"It really is. The rumors are that there were even women and children killed at this village," I went on.

"But we always killed them." Budu looked at me. "He-Goats, she-Goats, little Goats beside their Goat mothers. We spared only the infants. The indoctrination was too complete in the others. If you'd been crouching beside a Goat body instead of by your mother, I'd have knocked in your little head too, lest you grow up into a big Goat."

He watched my reaction with a cold twinkle in his eye. "Now you look shocked!" he joked. "Don't worry. I knew you were a good child when I saw you. But really, there was no way but to exterminate them wherever we found them, and they were everywhere in those days. Not now."

After an uncertain pause, I said, "So, have you any suggestion about what to do with Marco? I don't suppose you could talk to him?"

"I might," Budu told me. "If I see him. I could tell him he's wasting his time hunting for Goats."

"It would really, really be a good idea if you could," I told him. "It would ease a lot of people's minds at Company headquarters. Some of those committee members don't understand—well, no, they do understand what you guys have done for them. But they're getting a little scared, to tell you the absolute truth."

"They know they can't do much to stop us, if we refuse orders," said Budu.

"Exactly," I agreed.

A silence fell. I hurried to fill it in.

"Under the circumstances, you can see how the Company might be a little uncomfortable that you've chosen to postpone coming in, yourself."

"I've been busy," he replied.

"It sounds like you've been doing a great job with the locals," I said lamely.

"I've been busy thinking," he said.

"Oh. Okay," I said, and then he got up and paced out to the edge of the bluff, and I had to run after. He stopped and looked around him. You could see for huge distances in all directions, well into what would one day be different nations.

"You ought to look at this and think about it, too," he told me. "Look, out here. That will be Italy, one day. The little man Napoleon will come from there, and go over there"—he swung his big arm around in the direction of France—"to raise his armies, trying to be a god. Many, many people will die before he learns he's a man." He swung his big arm around. "And that will be Germany, where there will be a man so stupid, he doesn't know what happens when one group of animal breeds only with itself, or one family marries only its own cousins. You know what he'll do in the name of what he calls his race. How many will die? Ten million? And how many others will learn the idea of big murder from him, and do as he did in their own nations? And look out there," he went on, turning. "Spain. They will feed people to their god, and then go conquer a world, beyond that sea, where the rulers feed people to *their* god.

"Keep looking, Joseph. That will be Africa. Think of all those slaves dying for the wealth of nations, and the curse they fulfill. And there, in Jerusalem, three people of one book, children of one god, will tear one another to pieces. Farther, where you can't see, from the steppes, another little man will come, with his horses and his men, conquering with no other plan than to make heaps of skulls wherever he goes. British, Americans, Japanese, Russians. Look up at the sky, think of all those people burning to death on Mars. Big murder, son. You can't look in any direction without seeing a nation that deserves to be gelded."

"Well—yeah," I agreed. "That's why Dr. Zeus was founded. Why we were made. To preserve the good part of humanity from all the awful things these people will do."

"That was why *you* were made, son." He turned to look down at me. "And since you were made to hide things away to keep them safe, it must have occurred to you how much simpler your job would be if we Enforcers were permitted to keep monsters from running loose in the world."

"Of course," I said uneasily. I could see where this was going. "But what can we do? Those people will have their time. Hitler, the Vikings, the Church of God-A. All we can do is work in their event shadows to make the best of things. We can't prevent their existence, however much we'd like to. We can't change history."

"How do you know, son?"

"Because it's impossible! Every one knows that. It's one of the first things we learn. The laws of temporal physics prove it," I stated.

"And you've made a study of temporal physics?" He put his enormous hands behind his back and regarded me.

"No, but I know what everybody else knows," I answered, feeling panicked.

"Because Dr. Zeus told you." His gaze traveled out to the world again. "Think about this, son. If the Company were lying to you, how would you know? And if the Company were lying, and history *can* be changed—would it be to the Company's advantage to change it?"

"Well, of course," I responded. "Except—well, wait. No, because the whole operation has functioned by using the event shadows cast by history as it exists. If history were changed, all those chains of connected circumstance would be broken. We don't know what would happen.''

He nodded slowly. ''The Company owns many fine things, saved from war and wickedness. But if there were no wars, no thieves and murderers, who would own those fine things? In the future there are wise and powerful men who send us our orders, you and me. If history were changed, would those men lose their power?''

The line of black clouds was advancing from the north, bringing a storm that couldn't be blown away or outrun. He sighed, watching it come.

''Maybe our masters are great and good and have told us the truth. But if they've lied to us—and how can we know they haven't?—then a thousand generations of innocents will die to make our masters rich.''

''But we have no way of knowing that they've lied, either!'' I protested.

He looked down at me and smiled. ''No way at all,'' he said. ''So I'll speak to Marco, when I see him. Tell me, do you know what they're going to do with us, my Enforcers and me, now that we have served our purpose?''

''You'll be retrained.'' That was what I had been told.

''Will we?'' He held up his big hands and looked at them. ''Will they make us Preservers, like you?''

''I—I guess so.''

''Then we must obey,'' he said. ''I wonder about something. When the year 2355 has come and gone, will the Company still need its Preservers?''

''Not as Preservers, no,'' I said after a moment. ''The Company will have made a new civilization, one that's so advanced, there won't be wars.''

''Or natural disasters, or accidents?'' he asked. A breeze came out of the north, cold as ice, the outrider of the coming storm.

''Maybe they'll need us to preserve things from those, then.'' I said. ''We have to trust the Company, father! What else can we do?''

''I don't know,'' he told me. ''But you should think about this, son.''

I didn't want to. It was pointless. What could I do, even if he happened to be right? But I owed him a son's duty, so I told him I'd think about it.

I left him and made my way back down the mountain. Near the

pass into future Switzerland, I encountered a mortal traveler swinging a nifty copper ax as he strode along.

Is pass open? he signed to me.

Yes, I signed back, *but you'd better hide your ax.* His eyes widened at that; he must have heard about the angry god. Hastily he slipped it over his shoulder into his backpack.

Thanks, he signed.

You should probably turn back, though, I added. *There's a storm coming.*

His gaze traveled off to where I was pointing at the wall of clouds. It had come a full third of the way across the sky. He evaluated for a moment and then shrugged.

I bet I make it.

I shrugged back at him and went on my way. If that guy got caught in the storm, he might be stuck up here until skiers found him in the late twentieth century; but it wouldn't be my fault. I'd warned him, hadn't I? Whatever doubts Budu might have on the subject, it was my experience, so far, that history couldn't be changed.

24

On the other hand, Budu had been right in his suspicion that the Company didn't always take the high moral ground where troublesome immortals were concerned. The Enforcers were gone now; I hadn't seen one in centuries. Were they really leading happy and productive lives somewhere? What happened to immortals who asked the wrong questions, like Budu? Or like MacCool, for that matter?

And what *was* going to happen in the year 2355?

I stood up slowly and looked out into the night. There were the lights of the base. No nice warm fireside for me; I had a berth among the other ageless, in a gray future room without decoration, where walls met floors and ceilings without molding or baseboard, stripped bare of decoration and other nonfunctional nonessentials.

Oh well. It would at least be warm and dry. I turned to head down the ridge.

What was *that?* There was that emotion again, that broadcast from somebody far out in the night. Anger, but with it a certain glee. Whoever it was had evaded our patrols. Great. Well, he wasn't close enough to do me any harm on my way home. I'd make my report in the morning, which it was already, actually. One of the really important things an immortal needs to know is when to go to bed.

I made my report, and the security patrols were stepped up. They found evidence somebody had been lurking around, all right; some Native American covert surveillance guy was peeping at us. Would he be back? It was anybody's guess, but the proper precautions were taken. Meanwhile, those of us working in the field tried to speed up the job a little.

I was watching Mendoza and Dalton at work. They were on their knees in a meadow, examining some plant with one of the wise women, who was pronouncing:

"Now, this we call *tok*, and it has many uses. The flower buds are good to eat—"

"*Asclepias eriocarpa*," said Mendoza under her breath. "Ask her if this isn't the same thing they use to make fishing tackle." She could speak Chumash perfectly well but preferred to let Dalton do the talking. With one memorable exception, Mendoza avoids contact with mortals.

"Don't you use this for fishing tackle, too?" prodded Dalton obediently.

"Of course! You see, you just cut the stems and peel them open . . ." Their voices faded into the background. Far but sharp, I heard a man weeping. I smelled mortal misery.

I scanned. He was a mile distant, but his emotional state streamed in the air like a banner, blue and purple. I focused in and could just make out somebody huddled in oak shade on a hill due west of us. Mendoza was too focused on what she was doing to hear, but Dalton sensed him too and glanced across at me, questioning. I got up and strolled away in a casual manner until I was out of sight, when I broke into a run.

No, no, this would never do. Everyone was supposed to be happy about leaving. Upbeat. Glad to be clearing out before the murderous white men or Chinigchinixians or whoever arrived. If one mortal sat down and actually thought about it and got sad, others might too. Mortals are like that, for all their lack of sympathy for one another. And unhappy individuals ask questions, which is never a good idea when you're trying to lead a people to a promised land. I had to find this poor wretch, whoever he was, and cheer him up. Or something.

Half a mile down the canyon, I could identify the guy: Kenemekme, the first man to speak to me. I'd got to know him, slightly, since. He seemed to be the loser my groupies had said he was: a decent hunter, but nobody much otherwise. Not wealthy. Once a husband and father, but something had happened to the baby and the wife had run off with somebody else. Nobody listened to him in the councils. I guess you might hide in the bushes and cry, if your life was like that.

By the time I got to where he was, he'd stopped crying and was resting his chin in his hands, staring at the far-off sea horizon. He jumped a little as I hunkered beside him.

"Nice view, isn't it, nephew?"

He looked down at his feet. "All right, I guess."

"Yes, lovely view. The sky is blue, the sun is warm, the salvation of your people is proceeding apace. So, why such a long face? You can tell your Uncle Sky Coyote." I put my head to one side, watching him.

He swallowed hard and at last replied, "I thought it would be different."

"What would be different, nephew?"

"Well, I thought—it's just that before You came, I had my own ideas about the way things worked. All that about Father Sun drinking blood and devouring corpses, like the priests told us—I mean, that *couldn't* be true. He's no more than a monster if He does things like that. I had Him pictured more like a kind of grandfather, loving but stern. Terrible to the wicked, yes, that I could believe. And . . . I thought some kind of higher order prevailed in the Upper World. But from what You say, things are just as bad up there as they are down here. Even God cheats." He gave a shaken little laugh that caught on a sob.

I sighed and shrugged. "Nephew. What did you think, when the priests and shamans told you about us Sky People? When you hear a story, do you believe only the nice parts? Truth isn't like a baked fish, where you can eat the flesh and leave the bones and skin. You have to eat it all."

"But if some of those stories are true, then worship is pointless, isn't it? Why worship beings like that? And all those rituals, all those kantap mysteries, why bother anymore? I mean, now we *know*."

"Well, the kantap's another affair. But—"

"And as for prayer, forget it. Why pray to a cannibal who cheats at dice, no matter how powerful He is? And why behave at all? You Sky People have Your nerve dictating rules to us, the way You carry on! When I think of some of the stories I've heard about You, Coyote—!"

I hated to do it, but it was time to drag out my Spanish Jesuit training.

"All right. Think what you're saying, nephew. You don't like us Sky People, so no more moral restraints for you. You can lie, steal, and cheat, yes, rape and murder too, if you feel like it."

"Well, no, I won't, because—well, it's wrong, and if everybody did it, nobody could live anywhere, and—we have to have some way to protect people. And I won't be like You Gods!"

"I see. But doesn't that mean you're deciding to be good without anybody telling you to? Nobody punishing you if you sin, nobody rewarding you for virtue? Think of that, nephew.''

He struggled with the idea. It scared the daylights out of him, of course. I've never met a mortal it didn't scare. So he said:

"Wait a minute! Why am I even listening to You? Of course! You're a liar! In every story I've ever heard, You tell the most outrageous lies!''

"So it follows that—?''

"Well, it follows that none of what You've been telling us is true.'' He grasped at a ray of light. ''And maybe things *are* like I'd imagined, and maybe Father Sun *is* loving and benign and cares for us . . .''

I shook my head. ''You're forgetting something, nephew. I didn't tell you that Father Sun eats people. That's been said by your own priests, by all the reverend truth-tellers of your own village.''

He stared at me and bit his lip. ''Then maybe they don't know anything either . . .''

"Then figure it out for yourself! Here I come all the way from the Upper World to save my people from annihilation, and what happens? I get called a liar. Thank you *so* much.'' I rose as if to go.

"No! Wait, just this once, couldn't You tell the truth?'' He caught hold of my leg in desperation. ''The shamans don't know anything more than I do. They've never been to the Upper World, but You have! You're the only one I can ask! If You really love Your creations, why can't You at least tell us the truth about it all? Why do children die? Why doesn't love last? Why are our lives so short and miserable? Why do You allow evil? Isn't there *anywhere* things are the way they ought to be? What's the truth?''

"Is that what you're really in search of, nephew? Truth?''

"Yes! Truth!''

Hell, I hate to see people unhappy. ''Then look into my eyes, nephew.''

Truth is not all that hard to do, as special effects go. You just put mortals in a trance, scramble their brains a little, and invest some random object with Mystic Significance. It can be anything: a rock, a bush, a flower, a word. The tricky part is making sure your subject has a nice neutral Life-Affirming Experience and not a Call to Action. Otherwise he or she is likely to go out and preach that it's necessary to the world's salvation that (for example) everyone must be tattooed or the universe will collapse. Look at whoever this guy was down in Yang-Na.

Me, I'm a professional. I don't make that kind of mistake. When

I blow somebody's mind, I empty the ammo chamber first. Kene-mekme staggered back and shook his head. His eyes filled with tears.

"The beauty," he sobbed. "Oh—oh, the beauty!"

"Happy now?" I ventured. He threw his arms around me.

"Yes! At last, I understand! It all makes sense now and—what *beauty!*"

"Yes. But you can't put it into words, can you? That would be blasphemy."

"Oh, yes, You're right. How could I ever describe . . . How can I ever thank You?"

"And you won't try to go out and tell other people about it, will you? No preaching or anything like that? This is our little secret."

"Yes! Yes! Thank You, thank You, thank You!"

"Don't mention it. You run along now and be happy, okay?"

"Yes!!" he cried, and went away down the hill singing.

Piece of cake. His brain, I mean.

Mendoza paused, her spoonful of Proteus lifted halfway to her mouth. She frowned slightly.

"Are we having an earthquake?" she wondered. All over the commissary, immortal heads were raised, immortal brows creased in the same frown. There weren't any mortals in there with us except for the food servers, who weren't noticing. I shivered and grabbed my ears: all those long inner dog hairs had begun to vibrate unbearably. She threw her spoon down in disgust. "That's all we need. A goddam temblor."

But nothing was shaking or rattling, not anywhere in the room. We looked around at the other immortals. I shrugged.

"Something seismic somewhere, I guess, but not near enough to involve us," I told her. She shrugged too, picked up her spoon and went on eating. You could almost hear the whirring in the room as twenty people accessed their files on earthquakes in recorded history. It occurred to me that we weren't operating in recorded history, ex-actly, but I didn't say anything about that. Panicked immortals are awesome to behold.

"Yeah, I remember now," I went on. "There's a lot of regular volcanic activity a little way up the coastline. No big deal. Lava pil-lows in the cliffs, hot springs in the interior. I bet that's what we're noticing."

"Hot springs, huh?" Mendoza looked mildly interested. "No spas yet, of course. Funny your Chumash don't seem to know anything about them. You'd think a hot spring would be an ideal place to build a sweat lodge."

"Actually, they have." An anthropologist named Catton leaned over the back of his chair. "Not our people here, the tribe living up there. They even have a health resort, so to speak, but they don't get many customers from other tribes, because their rates are so high."

This brought a general chuckle from the listeners around us. There were a few jokes about mints on pillows and complimentary sherry in the rooms. God, I'd have liked a glass of sherry right then.

Mendoza got up and went across the room to the cooler for more water, all straight lines in her new field garb. She hadn't been able to bring herself to adopt the space age coveralls; her compromise made her look like a sensible Victorian tourist in khaki. I leaned forward to speak to her when she returned.

"Uh . . . say, I don't see that guy with the mustache and the attitude. What's his name? MacIntyre?" I said, very casually.

She gave me the look she usually gives at such moments.

"Him." What a lot of contempt could be crammed into one syllable. "The name you're straining after, not very convincingly, I might add, is MacCool."

"The two of you have been seeing a lot of each other, huh?" I said.

She stared at me, surprised, but only for a moment.

"What the hell is it to you?" she demanded in a savage undertone. "Are you all set to leap in and sabotage my little romance again?"

"Look, your private life is none of my business—"

"Gosh, thanks so much!"

"But—" I struggled to find a way to tell her the guy was bad news. "I thought . . . Weren't you and Lewis . . . ?"

For a moment she looked blank.

"Lewis. My God, what an imagination you've got! For your information, Lewis and I were very good friends and that was all, I can assure you. Do you think I'd ever in my life fall in love with anybody again, after what happened in England?"

"You might think it was safer, with somebody who wasn't mortal," I blundered on. "One of us, maybe."

"I might, but you know something?" Jesus, her eyes were hard. "I'm discovering I don't like the company of my own kind much better than that of the mortal monkeys. I don't want the complications, the interference, the distraction. I have work to do! What's the point of sitting around with a bunch of millennial bores and listening to

them complain about things they can't change? Some of us are just
as stupid as mortals, if not more so.''

"Glad to hear you say that,'' I ventured, meaning to go on with
something complimentary about her work ethic. Before I could,
though, she looked me in the eye and said quietly:

"Level with me, Joseph, for once in your life. You're older than
most of the people in this room. I can't remember ever seeing you
have a real emotion. You are one perfect Company machine. You
don't feel a damned thing anymore, do you? No, please, I'm not trying
to insult you. I just want you to tell me something.

"Our hearts, they do go dead after a few centuries, don't they?
The human emotions stop bothering us.''

I had to tell her some of the truth. So I said: "The game is
learning to avoid pain, babe. No more, no less. They told you that in
school, didn't they? Look around you. The rest of these people aren't
necessarily more successful at it than you are. I don't even manage
it, all the time. It isn't getting free of your heart that saves you. It's
your work that saves you, because it's the only thing that will never
let you down. Okay?''

Her eyes bored into me a few seconds before she decided to
accept that. She looked down at her plate, and I had the sensation of
having a sword point lowered from my throat.

"I don't want a human heart anymore,'' she said quietly. "It's
not a question of pain, either. It's . . . it's the scope of the work here.
This country. These mountains. Those trees, Joseph, those magnificent
trees. All the years wasted at New World One, when I should have
been here! Parties and babbling and new clothes, all keeping me from
this place. I don't want . . . people tugging my attention away from it
now.''

She was in love again, after all; but not with MacCool or anything
human, mortal or immortal. I chose my next words very carefully.

"Exactly! You're focusing on your work, which is what you
should be doing. I think this is great, Mendoza. You're instinctively
choosing to turn your attention to the important stuff, and it's going
to make you a lot happier than some people I could mention who
spend all their time bitching about management.''

"Like MacCool?'' She looked up again, sneering. "Was that
what was bothering you, the prospect of my falling for somebody like
him? Well, don't trouble yourself, dog boy. That guy is a disaster
waiting to happen, and I've had enough disasters, thank you very
much. He smells like burning houses and screaming civilians trapped
in wreckage. Wrong, wrong, *wrong* for little me.''

"MacCool? He was transferred," said a geologist at a near table, leaning toward us.

"He what?" I started. Mendoza became perfectly still, staring at me.

"This morning. He was pulled for a special project elsewhere, or so I heard. His orders came through last night. I don't know where they sent him."

"Ah," I said.

Mendoza, still looking at me, was even whiter than she usually is. *Joseph*, she transmitted, *you're scared.*

You can tell that through the dog face? You're imagining it. I'm surprised, that's all.

You're scared. MacCool was shooting his big mouth off, and now he's been taken away, and you're scared.

I am not! But if he had to go to a disciplinary hearing somewhere, I'm damn glad you're not with him. He was stupid. We're not stupid. We keep our heads down and do our jobs, right? Because we know that whatever happens, in the long run the Company is on the side of the angels, or whatever there is up there. Years of habit kicked in, and I made the sign of the cross with my coyote paw. She did, too, shakily. Once a Spaniard, always a Spaniard.

And maybe that was why it was easier for her to accept the idea of people just disappearing, no trial, no trace. It should have been easy for me. It's not like I haven't seen it happen before.

Part of the trick of avoiding pain is to make sure that all the people whose personal misery can hurt you too are off safe somewhere, doing something that can't possibly screw up their lives again. If you can get them settled securely in some comfortable rut, you can go your own way without thinking all those creepy little thoughts that come to you in the sleepless night.

I had thought Budu was safe. Everybody knew that most of the Enforcer rank and file had been retrained as Preservers, but the Company had found what seemed like an ingenious solution for the best ones, the officers. Who has the most opportunity to plunge into the wreckage of war and take what would otherwise be burned or smashed? A soldier, right? And when you're an ex-Enforcer, you can do the job even better than an original Preserver could, because you're a really big, ugly soldier who can get away with taking loot or prisoners for himself. Your fellow warriors aren't going to argue the point. You can be a barbarian, mercenary, pirate, or legionary and be in at the kill as empires totter, as libraries and monasteries are sacked, and help yourself to what the Company wants.

And Budu and his officers did pretty well, for what seemed like a long time. They weren't kept together, of course. After *Homo sapiens sapiens* became the only game in town, a bunch of guys that big and that strange-looking would have drawn attention. Separated, they were less noticeable, especially in armies whose men came from diverse ethnic and racial groups, like Rome's. So they passed themselves off as Hyperboreans, later as Norsemen, and if the men they soldiered with hadn't ever actually been to Scandinavia, it helped.

Or so I heard. As the ages went by, I kept in touch less and less, because I was pretty busy. I knew that Budu had become a Roman legionary and loved his work: he found the ethics of the republic admirable and enjoyed fighting alongside all those hard-working enlisted men. That was the image of him I kept in my mind for the next few centuries, Budu happy and occupied, smashing barbarian skulls so that neat little garrison towns could be carved out of the European wilderness. Though I served as a centurion myself for a while, our legions were never quartered near each other, so I never had the chance to drop in on him.

Of course, if I'd let myself think about it, I'd have come to the uneasy conclusion that once the Caesar family got into power, Budu wouldn't find Rome quite so admirable. I didn't let myself think about it, though, because of my habit of avoiding pain. And after Rome fell, I just assumed he'd switched sides and was helping to tear down what he'd helped build.

But I never asked, never looked him up, because . . . why because? Probably because deep down I knew what was happening.

25

I'D BEEN A spy for Alexis Comnene, one of his army of invisible men doing their quiet bit to keep the status quo in old Byzantium. Right now the best way to prevent the Basileus's boat from rocking seemed to be encouraging those reliable and dependable enemies, the Turks, to slaughter those worst of loose-cannon friends, the Norman knights. It was a political scene a million miles removed from armies on the Tiber and memories of Budu.

I saw him last in Antioch. That was where everybody saw him last. I was surprised as all hell to meet him there, too. He was sitting in a transport lounge placidly reading a magazine. The transport lounge was seven stories below ground level, the year happened to be 1099, and Budu was wearing the mail habit of a Crusader. The strange thing was that he sat between two nervous-looking security techs. I knew what had happened, but I wouldn't admit it to myself. I just smiled and advanced on him with my most innocent look of delighted astonishment.

"Wow, father, what are you, under arrest or something?" I exclaimed.

He lowered the magazine and looked at me. "Yes," he replied.

He might just as well have thrown a punch into my solar plexus. I stopped dead and gave a weak little giggle. "You're kidding, right?"

But one of the techs stood up and placed his hand on my shoulder. "Sir, can we ask you to move on? This operative has nothing to say to you."

"I'm a Facilitator," I told him, remaining reasonable and calm. "It's okay. I have clearance for stuff like this."

The tech looked into my eyes. He was checking my retinal pattern, not my sincere expression, and after a second he nodded. "We're just his escort, sir. He's on his way to a hearing."

"Of course," I said with a nod, feeling queasy. "Look, can I have a few minutes alone with the old guy? Maybe I can learn something useful."

The tech didn't like that much, but my record was clean and my rank was high—higher than his, at least, which was what counted. "Go on, take your friend with you and have a couple of Turkish coffees. I'll bet I can get something out of him in the time it takes you to get down to the mud. Okay?"

"Okay," the tech replied, and nodded at his friend, who rose readily enough to go with him. I had a feeling they weren't enjoying this duty. Budu watched them go, shaking his head.

"Look at them, just walking away after a few smooth words from a stranger. If they were under my command, I'd order them both to step off a cliff."

"If they were under your command, they'd do it, too," I said, sitting down beside him. "What the hell's happened, father? What are you doing here?"

"I refused a direct order," he replied.

I don't get caught flat-footed often, but that time I sat there gaping like an idiot. After a moment of my stunned silence, he decided to take charge of the conversation.

"I have something to ask you. Listen to me, son. How long has it been since you've seen one of my kind? Almost a thousand years, hasn't it? And yet there were hundreds of us. Where have they all gone? Do you know? Tell me if you know."

"They're—they're working on Company bases, or in military operations," I said. "Aren't they?"

"No, they're not," he told me. "I've been searching. I've seen classified information. Most of them were never retrained at all. Marco was never retrained. Where is he? And the rest of the commanders, the ones like me who were sent out to save with one hand and slay with the other, do you know where they are? I'll tell you as much as I know. One by one, as the centuries have gone by, the others have fallen in battle. Just as in the old times, Company medical teams have collected them and taken them back to the nearest base for repair and regeneration. *But they have never been released.* No record of reassignment for any of them, anywhere. I am the last."

"They must be on some base somewhere," I said faintly, but I knew he was telling the truth, as hideous as it sounded.

"No personnel list on any base on Earth carries their names," Budu told me.

Then he did something without warning, without asking my permission, taking advantage of the state of shock I was in. He reached out and set his index finger between my eyes and forcibly downloaded information to me, an encrypted signal bearing something I *really* didn't want to know about. I gasped and shunted it to my tertiary consciousness.

"No!" I clenched my fists. "You can't stick me with this!"

He just laughed. "You'll have to decode it, one day. You won't be able to resist. I wonder what you'll do then? I hope you can hide the fact that you're carrying a secret message, son."

"Why?" I looked at him, almost tearfully. "Why did you do this?"

He half shrugged. "Insurance. The Company won't retire you, son, you look too much like all the rest of them, and you're too good a liar to be caught. You may succeed in doing something where I fail."

"Thanks a lot," I muttered. He swept the transport lounge in a leisurely glance. The two security techs were still at the coffee bar.

"I should tell you what I'm going to tell the disciplinary board," he said. "When I was assigned to Jerusalem, it was the last indignity I could endure. I have obeyed orders and have asked no questions all this long while, as the Company's purpose has been repeatedly betrayed and degraded. The excuse given was always that history cannot be changed. Why did I labor for them to make Rome mighty, if all that power and order was to be handed to a family of monsters? Why did I lend my strength to drive the Saxons out of Britain, if Camelot was to fall in one generation? Once it was not so, but since history began, the Company's way is always to bring something great into being and then to let it die. They set me to kill, because I like to kill, and they think that my pleasure will distract me from the dishonor of these days." He held me silent with that pale-blue stare of his, so pale a blue, cold and self-assured, it was almost no color at all.

"Look now! Islam has brought order here, knowledge, tolerance. And I must wear this cross and wade in innocent blood, that I may get for my masters a box hidden under Solomon's temple. Do you know what some of these Christians have been doing? Eating human flesh. Moslem children. You remember what we would have done to mortals for such an offense, in the days of our power?"

I nodded, shivering.

"That's what I'll tell the disciplinary board," Budu continued composedly. "It may make some of them sorry for me. It won't change what they mean to do with me, but it may put them off their guard. Here come my little dogs."

The security techs were returning now. We watched them approach. Budu said to me:

"I could strike you, if you like. I could pretend anger with you. It might help you disassociate yourself from me, if you're afraid of coming under suspicion."

"I don't want to disassociate myself from you," I whispered.

"Then you're a fool," Budu replied, and picked up his magazine again. "Goodbye, son. Access the code, if you dare. I wonder if you will."

I stood up and walked away from him shakily, nodding at the techs.

"That one's been in the field too long," I told them in an undertone. "I'll transmit my report this afternoon. Watch yourselves, guys."

But they didn't, apparently; or, to be more precise, they didn't watch Budu. He never got to that disciplinary hearing. I don't know why, I don't know what happened, I only know there was an extremely discreet all-points bulletin broadcast later, using a lot of euphemisms and addressed only to the attention of operatives with a certain level of security clearance. He got away somehow.

I've never seen him since. I haven't looked for him. He hasn't attempted to contact me, and I'm grateful for that. Maybe he was caught a long time ago; how do you hide, after all, from a Company with advance knowledge of every event in history? Though a lot of history is unrecorded, and who knows the event-shadow areas better than we immortals, who have to work in them so much of the time?

I've never accessed his message, all the same.

I've gone through seven centuries with this permanent Pandora's box in my head, and I have nightmares now and then, where I give in to temptation and decode the damn thing, and something awful always happens. Moaning and shuddering, I wake up with a start.

26

I WOKE UP on my Foamfill synthetic bed with a start. As my night-mare faded around me, I realized that my ears were doing that awful inner vibration thing again, and after a millisecond's analysis I knew why. You couldn't have seen me as I dove for the bag under my bed and fled through the doorway of my cubicle; I was moving too fast.

Out in the corridor, doors were popping open all along its length, and there was a white flurry of immortals in various kinds of eighteenth-century nightdress moving like wraiths—very, very fast wraiths—each clutching an emergency bag, rushing for the door at the end of the hall in an unstoppable torrent. But there was hardly a sound, and under the eerie calm of the blue hall lights it looked like a dream sequence from a film.

Down the stairs we went, with muffled thunder of bare feet and slippers, to crash open the ground-level doors and burst into the ice-cold night full of the noise of roaring black surf. Nobody stopped; nobody said a word; we kept going, plowing through the cold soft sand across the beach, gaining speed as we reached the solid ground and sped uphill for the nearest high place.

We'd found a good refuge around a rocky outcropping in seconds, and that was where we were assembled when the first shaking began. At first, vibrations only we could perceive; then the trembling that the base warning system picked up, causing it to emit the shrill bleeping signal that woke the mortals; then the steady *bang-bang-bang* of a fairly big one. It wasn't so bad where we were; a few pebbles went bouncing off the outcropping, and we swayed slightly and clutched one another. We heard the mortals screaming inside the base structure, which rocked and groaned on its pilings like an uneasy elephant. A couple of them came running down the stairs and then stopped in the lobby, staring out in horror at the floodlit sand, which was dancing as though it were alive, each grain leaping up.

"STAY WHERE YOU ARE!" cried one of us, his volume up to the maximum setting. I crouched down and grabbed my poor ears. Where was Mendoza? The shaking got harder; it was coming in waves now. The exterior floodlights flickered and went out, throwing the lobby into black shadow, so we couldn't tell if the mortals obeyed or not. Somebody—it was the geologist who'd spoken with me at dinner—pushed his way to the front of our group and stared down. He stretched out an arm, pointing and yelling, "Sand boil!"

And these things came spouting up from the beach under the moonlight, like jets of water but not glittering the way water would; no, these were liquefied sand fountains. We stared in fascination, swaying to keep balance, until somebody gasped, "Oh, shit, look!"

A sand boil had erupted right beside one of the base's support pilings. As we watched, the whole modular dome began to lean, tilt, as if the uneasy elephant had decided to kneel down, or as if a horseshoe crab had decided to bury itself in sand. There was one shocked outcry from us all, blended with profanity in dozens of long-forgotten languages and dialects, then silence. We watched motionless through the longest ten seconds I could remember in a while, as the base settled, and tilted, and settled. We heard things breaking. The mortals trapped inside were making the kind of noises that come to you in nightmares for years after. We didn't even notice that the shaking had stopped.

With a final groan, the base settled at last and didn't tilt anymore. The mortal crying—and it was mostly crying now, the hysterical screams had stopped—drifted up on the night air, faint as the sound of summer crickets. The wind and the surf were so loud.

"Six point two," announced the geologist.

"All right." Lopez pushed his way to the front of the crowd. He wore a long nightshirt with lace cuffs, and without his wig I saw he had a crewcut bullet head. "Security! Initiate damage assessment and rescue attempts." They saluted and filed away down the hill. "Idomenus?"

"Sir." The geologist stepped forward.

"What, in your opinion, is the least likely location to be affected by aftershocks?"

"This hill's pretty good, sir. Granite bedrock close under the surface."

"Good. We'll establish our emergency camp here. Operatives!

Kindly open your emergency kits and prepare shelters and triage facilities. I assume we can expect aftershocks?'' He turned to Idomenus.

"Oh, yes.''

All around us, immortals were fanning out along the wide saddle-backed hill, and here and there tents were already popping open like mushrooms in the moonlight. Lopez asked me, "Can you estimate what effect this is likely to have on the mission?''

"I don't guess it'll bother the Chumash much, not physically—their houses are pretty earthquake-safe. They'll view it as a mystical event; they have an earth goddess named Khutash, and maybe they'll assume she's angry—'' My ears began to go crazy again, and I grabbed them.

Lopez's eyes widened. "Operatives! Aftershock in five seconds!'' he shouted. Sure enough, the earth gave a rolling tremor, and we braced ourselves. Fresh screams broke out down at the base. I realized I was getting motion sick. Lopez watched me with interest.

"God, that's useful. Your ears are functioning as an early-warning system superior to ours,'' he said as the rumbling subsided.

"You wouldn't want it made standard issue, believe me,'' I said wretchedly.

"Perhaps not. Continue with your report, please.''

"Uh . . . so, the earth goddess is mad about something. I'll have to come up with a reason. I can do that, no problem. As far as the rest of the mission goes, we won't know how it's been impacted until we get a report from security. Was our equipment damaged? Was our collected material damaged? That has to be determined.''

"Yes, of course.'' He nodded thoughtfully.

"You want me to go help them set up tents now?'' I looked around for a bush behind which I could throw up.

"No. Remain with me. You're too useful in detecting aftershocks, for the time being. Let's see: it's now oh five hundred hours precisely. As soon as the sun rises, you're to go to the Chumash and reassure them about the seismic event. Perhaps the earth goddess is angry with the Sun about the coming invasion?''

"Yeah, or something.''

"Something to pacify them.'' He turned briskly and surveyed the eastern horizon, which was already a little paler than the rest of the sky. Low down, there was a spreading, rolling puff of what I would have thought was fog, only it was blood-red and blowing from inland out to sea. It was dust, from who knew how many landslides. I worried briefly about my Chumash, until I remembered that Humashup was laid out sensibly clear of possible slide areas.

"Looks like they're bringing out some stretchers," called Ashur, whose tent area had a good view of the base.

"Tsk. Operatives, prepare triage for incoming wounded! What is it, are we about to have another shock?" He whirled about in concern as I staggered for the nearest bush.

"Nope," I replied feebly, and whooped my guts up. "Well, actually . . . now we are."

"Aftershock!" he announced, and it came rolling through, and we rode it out. "All operatives with medical training report to the triage area, please!"

"That includes me." I held up my paw.

He looked severe. "I rather think your appliances rule out your performing brain surgery at the present time," he told me. "Now, let's go see what's become of our mortal contingent. In the event Mr. Bugleg has deceased, you are second in command."

"Okay." Gosh, I'd made officer again. He strode away to the line of security techs that was just winding its way up the hill, and I wandered after him. We passed Mendoza, who was briskly setting up her tent like all the others. I waved at her. She looked up and grinned.

"Some ride, huh?" she shouted. I nodded and kept going. Nice to know she was all right.

The preliminary reports were: no dead; fifteen slightly injured, with assorted scratches and contusions; three badly wounded, two of whom had been in the lobby, because the glass doors broke when the dome tilted over; and two mortals with, respectively, one broken arm and one broken ankle. Not bad. There were people unaccounted for, but we were still evacuating them from the base, which had remained structurally sound despite its support failure. In the growing light, the base looked like one of those crablike things out of a Hieronymus Bosch landscape, gigantic and marooned on the beach, with tiny people crawling in and out of it. Obviously not a Houbert design. But the lead security tech was confident it could be righted with a day of heavy equipment work.

And I wasn't an officer again after all. Bugleg was escorted stumbling and weeping up the hill by two techs. Lopez and I both scanned him as he approached.

"Minor contusions on your knees and elbows, slight abrasion of your chin," Lopez diagnosed. "Very good, sir! You clearly did the sensible thing and stayed in your room during the shaking. The base modules are designed to provide maximum protection—"

"*You* didn't!" sobbed Bugleg. "You left us! You left us and ran outside!"

"Well, but that's what we were designed to do, sir. We left early so as to have nice shelters all prepared for you when the quake was over. See?" Lopez pointed. "Everything's ready: tents set up, triage hospital in operation, evacuation proceeding on schedule. You'll even have breakfast on time."

"But the base fell over and *you left us!*" Bugleg's voice rose to an accusatory scream. "You knew it was going to happen, you old-time people, and you didn't tell us!"

Lopez hauled off and slapped him in the face. Even I jumped.

"Stop that blubbering at once," said Lopez in a low, cold voice. "You'll frighten the others. Now, then. None of us operatives had advance warning from the Company of this, any more than you did. It's known that California has earthquakes, so precautions were taken, and they've paid off, I might add. None of you has been killed. But there is no written history for this particular region in this particular year. This is one of those dark zones we operatives have to contend with all the time in the field: times and places where anything might happen. You've just experienced a little of the danger we have to face continually.

"As for staying behind and getting you out of your beds, we could no more have done that than we could have told the earthquake to go away. We were designed with the irresistible compulsion to avoid danger at all costs, even at the cost of your lives. You designed us that way, sir, you and your associates, so you've no cause to complain if we perform according to specifications."

I don't think poor Bugleg was taking in half of what he was being told. He stood there in his jammies, shivering and blinking back tears. Lopez looked him up and down.

"Now, I suggest you retire to a shelter and calm yourself. We'll attempt to send a communication to the Company as soon as it can be determined whether or not our system was damaged."

"Okay," Bugleg sniffled.

"Come on, guy, there's a nice one all set up over here," I said, leading him by the sleeve to a minidome a few paces from Lopez's impromptu command center. He was so upset, he didn't seem to notice the physical contact, which would have had him recoiling at any other time. "Looky here! Protection from the wind, nice comfy air mattress, cozy Thermofilm comforter! Why don't we sit down in here and wait until Mr. Lopez gets everything under control, okay?"

"My clothes are dirty," he said sadly.

"Well, sure. That was bound to happen. They can be washed as soon as everything's back up and running."

"Lopez is mean." Tears formed in his eyes. "All you old-time people are mean. I wish I'd never made that pineal tribrantine three."

"Huh?" I gaped at him. Was he telling me he was the genius who'd invented PT3, the stuff that keeps our immortal cellular clocks set at high noon? I was all set to blurt out the question, but at that very second my ears began to go nuts again. I clutched them and yelled, "Hey, Lopez! Heads up!"

"Operatives! Aftershock!" roared Lopez from where he was conferring with the security techs. The tent began to widgy back and forth, and Bugleg cowered, his eyes wide.

"It's okay! It's okay! Look! It's almost over. It is over, see? You're safe. Nothing can fall on you out here," I told him.

"I'm not safe!" he wailed. "It's cold. It's dark. We're out where animals and savages can get us! I left my sipper bottle in my room. And the rocks hurt my feet. And there's disease vectors and microbes, and the sun radiation will give us cancer. And we're killing the grass on this hill with these tents. And the shaking keeps coming. And . . . I have to be with old-time people." He wrung his hands.

"You don't like us, huh?" I studied him. He shook his head miserably. "How come?"

"You're weird and scary. You do bad things like kill animals," he gulped. The effort of answering a question seemed to focus him, calm him a little. "You chop down trees to make your houses and fires. And you smoke bad stuff and eat and drink bad stuff, even though you know it's wrong."

"Controlled substances." Like coffee, tea, chocolate . . . Boy, if our spartan little beach parties upset him, what would he make of a New World One? Did he even have a clue how Houbert was living down there?

"And you and the old-time mortals do all those rituals and superstitions. Lopez said you were a, a *priest!*" He mouthed the word in utter digust. "And you watch those things where people kill each other. That's sick!"

"You mean . . . gladiatorial games?" I was mystified.

He shook his head. "No. The Agatha Christies. The Sherlock Holmes. You people *like* those. I know."

"But you guys play shooting games at your holo consoles."

"That's different." His voice dropped to an uneasy whisper. "That's to get out the bad thoughts."

"Bad thoughts?" I made a guess. "You mean, violent impulses?"

He stared at me, trying to decipher what I'd said. "Violents," he agreed at last. "People are bad. We're all bad. But if we play the games every day, just killing pretend things, we don't hurt anybody."

"So people are bad, and we have to keep from hurting anything," I prompted. "And that was why Dr. Zeus was founded?"

He nodded, wiping his nose. "People did war," he said. "Pollution. Killing things until they were all gone. We could stay inside and not hurt anything, but the bad things had happened already. We had to make them not have happened. That was why they made you old-time people, so you could stop the bad things. But they made you wrong. I don't like you."

"Okay. But you helped make us too, right? You helped make pineal tribrantine three?"

"*I* made it," he corrected me. "I figured out how. We had to make you fast and strong and not get old." And he proceeded to tell me how he'd done it, in technical language that made my head spin, though the grammar and syntax were stripped down to six-year-old level. Though I had to access volumes to get even a grasp of the chemistry and technology involved, it was obvious it was the simplest thing in the world to him. Such was his concentration, as he spoke, that he didn't even notice the next three aftershocks, or the screams of Stacey as she was having a piece of lobby door removed from her leg.

"Only now I'm sorry I did it," he finished with a hiccup. "I'm thirsty. Get me something to drink."

"Sure." I groped around and handed him a sipper bottle of distilled water. He sucked on it contentedly as I stared at him, trying to dope the thing out. Was he an idiot savant? But the other mortals shared a lot of his attitudes, and many of them were nearly as ignorant. Was he just an extreme case of a future type, brilliant in his own field and proudly, defensively moronic about everything else? It was a historical fact that after the Victorian era, scientists would become more and more specialized in their disciplines and less informed about other fields, the opposite of Renaissance men. Would the trend continue long enough to produce *this?* And would ecological responsibility warp into this bizarre self-hatred? What a substitute for a faith! Puritanism Lite! All the guilt without the God!

And yet . . . what did I want from the guy? He believed it was morally wrong to hurt anybody or anything. He lived by his principles and tried to make sure everybody under his command followed them too, even if his command was pretty much a joke.

It was sad that he was so terrified of the wild nature he was trying to preserve, and so bigoted against the humanity he was trying to help. So unnerved, too, by the deathless creatures he'd helped create to do his work.

Jeez, he'd helped create *me*. Here I was, sitting in a tent, face to face with my creator. Or one of my creator's faces.

So I had a couple more pieces of that very big jigsaw puzzle I'd first sat down to twenty thousand years ago. Pieces of the edge, from the look of it. I was pretty sure that Bugleg and his peer group couldn't possibly be running things, poor little sanctimonious Victor Frankensteins that they were. They certainly would never have countenanced the creation of Budu and his fellow Enforcers. To say nothing of all the dirty-tricks squads that had operated for the good of the Company since then. Or Houbert's screamingly decadent parties.

Which meant that Lopez had probably been leveling with me when he implied that he and his cronies were the ones really in charge. It made more sense, and was in some ways a comforting thought. On the other hand, it meant that my kind were responsible for some pretty nasty work, including the betrayal of their own Enforcers.

On the *other* hand . . . you never have enough hands, you know? Look at it from the Company's point of view: here they are stuck with these enormously strong guys who don't even look human anymore, at least not by the modern definition, and as if that isn't awkward enough, they like to kill, kill, kill. Though only in the most righteous of causes! So to keep them happy, you have to keep finding evildoers for them to tear into little pieces. To make matters worse, the immortals are terribly cunning and now beginning to disapprove of *you*.

I would've started sweating, myself. And if there's this future of perfect peace and harmony coming in 2355, what place would soldiers have in it anyway?

I didn't see what choice the Company had. But the Enforcers couldn't have been done away with. They were immortal, after all. Probably they were hidden away somewhere having a nice long rest. Maybe being saved as some kind of special-unit ace in the hole just in case the future of perfect peace and harmony didn't quite work out. Yeah.

The awful bottom line, of course, is that if you're going to rule the world, you have to have absolute power, and everybody knows what absolute power does. Dr. Zeus set out to change things, to give the whole sorry history of the human race a happy ending. The Company discovered that it had to rule the world first; and then it turned out that nothing could be changed. As for that happy ending—we won't know until after 2355, will we?

So, really, what can one poor little coyote like me do about it?
You could decipher the message.

Bugleg began to snore. I scanned him and found that he had asthma, which the dust and spring pollen were probably aggravating. He couldn't even breathe the same air as us, poor bastard.

The east got brighter, and pretty soon my enemy the Sun rose, red and hungry. I got up and went over to Lopez to see how things were going.

He stood in the open air reading a transmission. Our communications system must be okay. He was still wigless, but somebody had fetched his tricorne out of the mess for him, and it threw a pointed shadow on the page in his hands.

"Want me to go check on the Chumash now?" I asked him, and he turned to me a face livid with rage.

"They knew," he said, "about the quake. In *their* time, their survey equipment is clever enough to read old strata like a book. Isn't that wonderful? Of course they had no idea it would be this severe, or that we'd be sitting right on top of it. They didn't tell us, because it would only have upset the mortals; besides, they knew we could handle any problems that might arise. Naturally. It's what we were designed to do, after all."

He crumpled up the paper and flung it into the sagebrush. I slunk away, my tail between my legs. Another round of motion sickness was coming on. Was it an aftershock, or all the shifting conspiracy theories?

You could hardly tell there'd been an earthquake, away from the base. Back along the trail everything looked just as normal and sunny as can be, with little birds singing and dew sparkling on the leaves. In a couple of places there'd been a minor landslide, a few bucketfuls of rocks and dirt fresh and dark on the path; that was all.

Humashup was busy as I walked in. Outside their doors, people were shaking ashes and charcoal out of their sleeping furs, or sweeping cold cinders into the streets. I let myself pretend for a moment I was walking into the old village I dream about, which was now probably buried under somebody's wine cellar in Spain or France. Sepawit, sluicing off ash with a basket of water, greeted me cheerfully.

"Hey, Sky Coyote, You should have been here this morning! We had quite a shaker!"

"Hell of a quake," agreed Nutku, beating his best bearskin robe until the dust flew. I was about to reply when a bizarre figure pranced by, decked in flowers and tootling away on a deer-bone flute. It was Kenemekme; he had taken to doing things like that lately. We watched

him in silence for a moment. Nutku sighed and went on shaking dust
out of his robe, and I tried to remember what I'd been about to say.

"I know. Khutash is very angry. She found out about Sun's white
men last night," I told them. They looked surprised.

"Khutash is angry? Is that what makes earthquakes?" Sepawit
blinked. "Well, I guess You'd know, but we always thought it was a
natural phenomenon."

"What?" Oh, boy, I wasn't at my quick-witted best today.

"We always thought it was the World Snakes down there under
the crust of the earth, the ones who hold everything up? We thought
they just get tired every now and then and bump into one another,"
Nutku explained. "The astrologer-priest says they push the mountains
up a little higher every year."

"Oh," I said.

27

Humashup was back to normal by midmorning. AltaCal Base took a lot longer to recover. Even after the techs had managed to right and reinforce the supports on the modular dome, we had trouble convincing the mortals to go back inside. They crouched in the pop-tents on the hill, shivering, and even when we explained that we could tell it was absolutely safe (hadn't they designed us to detect structural infirmity in any building we might enter?), they wouldn't budge. Finally I said I thought I'd seen bear tracks nearby, and that got them moving. Within an hour the corridors of the base were resounding with electronic beeps and blasts from all the reactivated holo cabinets, and another layer of mutual dislike and mistrust settled into place.

"So, can that thing see me all right?" Nutku inquired, peering into the holocamera lens. It was one of two reflective eyes in the face of a little crouching figure Jomo was carrying on his shoulder. The other two holocameras, similarly disguised, were parranged at the two other points of a triangle centered on Nutku.

"Just fine," Jomo assured him. Jomo was the Spirit Who Wants to Watch As You Build a Canoe. Chang, his team anthropologist, was excitedly talking to Nutku's apprentices where they were attempting to work. They were trying to be terribly cool and make it all look easier than it was. I sat in the shade nearby, glad I didn't have to stand in the sun in my coyote fur.

"All right. This is my boatyard we're standing in," said Nutku, gesturing around him. "Over there are my apprentices. Their parents are paying me plenty to take them on, believe me, because once you've joined the Canoemakers' Union and learned how to build fine-

quality canoes, you're set for life. For an extra fee they can get their
kid into the kantap, but only if I agree to sponsor him, and I only
sponsor the really talented ones. Some guys will let any moron into
the kantap if he pays enough, but not me.

"Where was I? So anyway, I've got them cutting up these logs."
He walked over to the work site. The boys were hacking away self-
consciously, trying not to look up at the camera. "Pine isn't your best
material for canoes, but this is a midrange model with just a few
luxury features—"

"Where do you get your wood?" Chang wanted to know.

"What?"

"Where do you get the wood you use?"

"Stuku the lumber dealer," Nutku replied, as though it were terribly obvious. "Except when we get some redwood from dealers I
know up north, or sometimes we get lucky and a redwood log washes
up on the beach. But we're talking pine right now, okay? So what
I've got my boys doing is, they're splitting these logs up into planks.
Show one for the spirit, Sulup."

One of the kids held up a plank that had been split off, rough and
splintery, about an inch thick. He grinned at the camera. "Remember
me, spirit! My name is Sulupiauset and my father's a rich man and I
make the best canoes anywhere!"

"And you get tar detail, too, smart mouth," growled Nutku. "Pay
no attention to these brats, spirit. Anyway, once the pine's all cut into
planks, we adze them down until they're only about so thick." He
measured a three-quarter-inch space between his index finger and
thumb.

"What are they using, there?" Jomo asked, moving in for a close-
up. The boys gladly stopped working to turn to the lead camera and
display their adzes, the various flint and obsidian blades in handles
made of deer antler.

"Damned expensive tools, but their parents can afford the best.
It's an investment, anyway," Nutku explained. "That black rock's
imported all the way from the desert on the other side of Kuyam.
Back to work, kids."

"Don't you find the flint lasts better?" I asked, surprised. My
tribe had always preferred it. The camera wobbled over to focus on
me for a moment—the heads of the two other little figures followed
suit, turning silently—then swung back to the workers. Nutku stepped
out of camera range and told me sotto voce, "Of course it does, but
the kids love the way the black stuff looks, right? And it *is* sharp."

Chang meanwhile had become fascinated with the sight of the

wood curling back from the planks—it looked so easy—and had taken up an adze himself to try a few tentative scrapes. The boys put their tools down and stood around to watch his efforts, very respectful. Jomo went for another close-up. After a couple of minutes Jomo set down his camera and reached for an adze himself.

"You're doing it wrong," he told Chang. The boys snickered and nudged one another.

"I don't think so," Chang replied huffily. Nutku turned and saw what was happening.

"What do you think you're doing, watching a race?" he shouted at the apprentices. "Get back to work! I want those planks cut and sanded by dinnertime!" He strode back and crouched down in front of the holocamera, which was still recording. "Can you still see me, little spirit? Okay, the next thing we do is cut the planks in the pattern for a canoe and drill the holes so the planks can be sewn and tarred together."

Jomo and Chang were still splintering away at their respective planks, so I went over and picked up the holocamera. "So, uh, what do you use for sanding? Sharkskin?" I inquired.

"What else is there to use? And don't think *that* doesn't cost plenty. Hey, do You use something else for sanding in the World Above?" Nutku stepped too close, and the frame filled with a picture of his chest. I set the holocamera on my shoulder and pointed it at the work team, trying to focus on the boys and not on Jomo and Chang.

"Well, we've got a few things . . ." I hedged, but Nutku pushed on:

"See, Sky Coyote, I've been wondering about something. I know you said we're all going to lose our markets in the World Above, but are You really, absolutely positive nobody's going to need canoes where we're going? What's Spirit Who Buys at Retail going to do with all those he bought, or this one?" Nutku gestured at the one that was being constructed for the documentary. "Maybe nobody uses canoes to get around up there, but couldn't there be some way to create a market? The spirits must go fishing once in a while. What if we came up with some sort of sales strategy, you and I, huh? What do you think?"

I was about to let him down tactfully, when an idea hit me.

"You know, it just might work!" I remembered MacCool's comment about how popular Chumash woven sandals were becoming with our operatives. "Have you ever thought about diversifying?"

"What, make other stuff besides canoes? But canoe building is what I know," protested Nutku. He was clearly thinking about the concept, all the same, because a moment later he added, "Which is not to say I can't turn out wooden bowls and boxes, especially with inlay decoration."

"Even canoes, maybe!" I said, thinking about luxury bases like New World One, to say nothing of the Company's Day Six resorts for twenty-fourth-century tourists who wanted to go primitive. "You're right, spirits do go fishing once in a while. What I'm seeing here, though, is that you have a monopoly on a marketable commodity. Nobody else can make the things you and your people make, and as soon as the other Sky People see how beautiful your merchandise is, I'll bet it'll be in demand. If you organize with Sawlawlan and the others—I wonder if you couldn't start production again, once you're in the World Above? Some canoes, but also baskets, bowls, inlaid carvings, sandals, the kind of stuff people like to buy ready-made."

"Small items they could easily take away with them if they were traveling," breathed Nutku, his eyes lighting up.

"Things that would have a special value because they'd been made by you, the craft masters of Humashup, and wouldn't be available anywhere else," I suggested.

There was an outburst of profanity from Chang; the adze he was using had just broken. "See, if you'd been using it correctly, that wouldn't have happened," Jomo told him smugly.

"We'd have to make damn sure they wouldn't be available anywhere else," mused Nutku, rubbing his chin. "Some kind of bigger and better brotherhood system to put pressure on imitators, if you know what I mean."

"Hey! You wouldn't have to break a single arm," I told him. "We've got this law in the World Above about unauthorized use of somebody else's guild mark."

"Master Nutku?" One of the boys came forward tearfully. "The spirit broke my new adze! My father's gonna kill me—"

"Oh, shut up and take a new one from the basket," Nutku told him. He turned to grin at me. "The spirits are paying for it, after all."

Bit by bit, the town of Humashup began to take on an empty and untidy look, the way a house will when people are packing up to move. One day the chisels stopped ringing in the stoneworkers' yard: the last mortars, the last bowls had been made for the holocameras, and nobody would need any more. That ringing was subtracted from the sound of village life, but the subtraction wasn't noticed.

Next, the adzes stopped chuffing in the cured pine, the last canoe was finished, and Nutku's boatyard was silent. The boys were glad to clean the pitch and the fragrant shavings off their fingers, glad to kick back and relax for a change. They were still thinking of the upcoming flight as a kind of vacation, nothing more. Only Nutku had grasped the idea that the rules of the game were about to change forever. You'd think that mortals would understand the end as a concept—it's what defines them as mortals, after all—but they never do.

It was my job, of course, to let them in on the truth and conceal it at the same time. I was sort of an anesthesiologist. I capered for the Chumash, I kept them laughing with funny stories, I diverted them with songs and sleight of hand (or paw). I came up with facile answers for the ones who asked awkward questions.

Mostly facile answers, anyway. Sometimes you have to come up with more.

We'd all gone down to the beach to watch the canoe launching—not the beach at Point Conception, where the base was, but the closer and convenient beach the Chumash frequented. It had turned out really well, that last canoe, that midrange model with spear racks (safety bladders optional), and, since people still had to eat until the day of our departure, the fishermen were taking it out to see what they could get.

Jomo had carefully positioned two holocameras on the beach and waded out with the third one for triangulation. Our other anthropologists had been thrilled by the news, and there were a whole bunch of them gathered on the shore, avidly watching-recording the ceremony. Nutku and three other guys were carrying the canoe on their shoulders, while the fifth waited, knee-deep in the surf, both oars over his shoulders.

"All right now!" hollered Nutku proudly, showing off for the spirits. "This baby's going to cut through the water like a Shoshone after a duck! Come on, boys, march! Give me some room!"

"Give me some room!" echoed his bearers.

"Don't give up!" Nutku sang out like a drill instructor.

"Don't give up!"

"We're almost there!" Nutku told them.

"We're almost there!"

"EEEE-ha!" Nutku charged into the water.

"Eeee-ha!"

They wrestled the canoe out through the surf, and the new owner waded uncertainly after them. I was cheering with everybody else, until the security tech appeared at my elbow.

"Jesus!" I leaped into the air. "Give a guy some warning, can't you? You're too good at your job, you know that?"

But he looked grim. Grimmer, I mean, than security techs usually look. "We've caught the intruder. Mr. Lopez said you were to deal with the situation immediately."

"Me? Is there a problem?"

"The Chumash know about it. Our rabbit just walked right into the village. We've got him isolated in one of their huts, but people are curious about him. He won't shut up, either."

I got a bad, bad feeling. Sepawit noticed me talking to the tech and approached hesitantly. "Has something happened, Sky Coyote?"

"Uh . . . the spirit tells me that a stranger has come to Humashup," I translated.

"Maybe it's my Speaker!" Sepawit's face lit up with hope. "Is he all right?"

I thought fast. "The spirits aren't clear about what's going on. I think I'd better get back there right away."

"Let's go." Sepawit sprinted ahead of me. How to tell the guy he wasn't going to like what he found, that he should leave this to old Uncle Sky Coyote? I couldn't think of a way, so I just dog-trotted after him. Halfway there, the tech and I caught up with him, and he limped after us into Humashup, winded and puffing, holding his side.

Scared and curious Chumash were clustered a short distance from Sepawit's house, in front of which two of our security guys stood guard, tall, green, and impassive. From inside a voice was droning on and on in some kind of chant. Mrs. Sepawit (actually her name was Ponoya, I remembered now) approached us tearfully, leading their little boy by the hand.

"Sepawit, what's going on? Uncle Coyote, the spirits threw me out of my own house! They have a stranger in there, and they're not letting anybody see him—"

"Stranger?" Sepawit's face fell. "It's not Sumewo?"

"No!" she replied, as the security team leader came up to me and saluted.

"You'd better go in there, sir. He sounds like a spy. Potential compromise."

Sepawit pushed ahead of me, and what was I going to do, tell him to keep out of his own house? I did manage to get through the doorway at roughly the same moment, at least, so we saw our visitor at about the same time. I felt Sepawit's silent cry of disappointment. Myself, I was surprised.

After all, this was the guy whose rage I'd felt miles away, who'd been evading our patrols for weeks; I guess I'd been expecting some wild-eyed commando savage with dreadlocks. Not this little man. He wasn't Chumash; Shoshone, maybe, but there wasn't much identifying stuff like tattoos or ornaments, only a pattern of lurid purple burn scars on his chest. He was stark naked, in fact, but that was because the belt and pouches he'd worn had been confiscated. He was sitting on the floor, hands bound behind him, and he was chanting as we entered. Praying. I know praying when I hear it.

But he broke off when we entered, and stared up wide-eyed. He had an open, kindly face, mild of expression. When his gaze fixed on me, he gave a little gasp and a shiver, almost of pleasure. But he forced himself to look at Sepawit.

"Sepawit, my friend," he said in perfect, unaccented Chumash, and what a sweet, deep, authoritative voice he had. "I've come to ask you a question."

Sepawit stared. "What? How do you know my name?"

"Tell me, Sepawit, if you saw your neighbor's little child fall into water, and your neighbor wasn't there to see, would you rescue the child yourself?"

"What? What does that have to do with anything?" Sepawit's brow furrowed. "Who are you, and what are you doing here?"

"I'm trying to explain that to you. What would you do? Would you let the child drown?"

"Of course I wouldn't! Now, who the hell—"

"Who I am doesn't matter. *What* I am is His Voice. Now, follow my argument a little further. If your neighbor's house were on fire, and his women and children asleep inside, and he was with them and also sleeping, what would you do? Would you try to wake them by shouting? Would you try to beat out the flames? Failing that, would you go inside and try to pull them out, even at the risk of getting burned yourself?"

Sepawit controlled his temper with an effort. "Yes, I would. Anyone would."

"Of course you would, because you're a good man, Sepawit. Now. You should be able to understand my duty here. I too am a good man. I've been sent to pull you from the fire."

"In what sense?" Sepawit asked, eyes hardening. He was beginning to have some idea who his visitor was. "There's no fire burning here, stranger."

"You think not, because you are asleep. You've been lulled to sleep by the one who's set your thatch ablaze. You don't know what's happening. He came as a guest to your house, but he hasn't told you his real name. I know his name, however. He is the Great Thief and Cannibal. He's come in all his evil to destroy your family, Sepawit, to take them off the face of the earth, and why? To prevent them from hearing the Joyous Message.''

"That's it!" Sepawit glared at him. "You're from Yang-Na, aren't you? You're one of the Chinigchinix priests.''

The stranger beamed at him. "And, oh, Sepawit, I have got such good news for you. None of his threats are true! He's been lying to you all along. You've been lied to all your life! The Sun isn't your enemy, and there are no white men coming to do terrible things. All this was a stratagem of the Thief, here.'' He nodded at me, a little shy deferential nod, as though I were a celebrity.

I sighed and sat down. Talk about déjà vu. Why do I keep running into these guys?

Sepawit's voice was cold. "Uh-huh. I've heard your opinion of Sky Coyote. I don't care to hear more. What you're going to tell me is what's happened to Sumewo. Where is he?''

"Ah, Sumewo," said the stranger with a nod. "The one you sent to spy on us. He's safe; safer than he's ever been, in fact. He knows the Truth now.''

Oh, Sepawit was afraid: sick afraid. I could smell it in the air. But he just nodded and folded his arms. "What's your business here, really? You're a spy too, I suppose.''

"Sepawit, I meant it when I said I'd come to save you.'' The little man spoke softly, earnestly. "I really mean you no harm, not you, not any of the others. But when He told me I had work to do here, I must confess I had no idea you stood in such danger.'' The stranger dared a glance across at me. "We all knew the Thief had a grip on you up here, but I never thought he'd dare to walk among you all in his own flesh! How can you stand it? You must be able to see what kind of creature he is. And such a story he's told you! You must understand that it's not true, any of it. There is no evil old Sun who hates you. How can He be the sort of creature the Thief says He is, when all life proceeds from Him? Doesn't He warm you, doesn't He make food grow out of the earth for you? Do you think He'd do that if you weren't His beloved children?''

"I know your line," said Sepawit with admirable patience. "But if we're the Sun's beloved children, why does He let us suffer and die? Why did He beget us so weak and small? Why does He allow evil to trouble us? It makes no sense, and I don't intend wasting time listening to you tell me it does.''

"But all the evil in the world proceeds from *him!*" The stranger gestured at me with a frantic nod of his head. "He's the one who gave the grizzly bear his cruelty, he's the one who stole the fire of eternal life from your homes! Oh, my friend, how he's lied to you all! You think the world is ruled by a host of petty little gods, more foolish and wicked than men are. I tell you it's not true! There's only One, and He's the Sun and the Moon both, the brightest Being in Creation! He may be terrible to the wicked, but not to those who believe in Him."

He had that professional magic in his voice that gets 'em up and storming the barricades. But Sepawit wasn't buying it—he was too afraid about the fate of his Speaker. He turned in disgust.

"What should we do with him, Sky Coyote? I've got boys who can get information out of him. Or do You think You can do something?"

"I'll talk to him," I replied wearily. I had the training, after all. "Go out and tell your people it's all right. Offer your wife my apologies. Oh, and send in one of the spirits, will you?" He nodded and stalked out.

The stranger watched Sepawit through the doorway until he was gone. Then he tried to focus on the ground in front of him, but he couldn't. I just sat and stared at him, and after a minute or two, he had to do it, he had to look up and meet my eyes.

"Hi there," I said.

He looked scared but joyful too, and I knew why. "I refuse you," he told me. "I reject you utterly."

"The feeling is mutual," I told him. This was the last place I'd expected to have this conversation again. I'd lived through so many miserable decades of standing over poor mortal bastards in dungeons, people who hadn't done anything to deserve what I and the rest of my pals in the Holy Office were putting them through. Every once in a while, though, there'd be somebody there on the torture table with the light of Revelation in his eyes, somebody who'd angled to die like a martyr. Mostly I deserved the names they called me, but it was hard not to lose patience with them. What kind of nuts were they, to thumb their noses at a power that could put them in a spot like this?

And you couldn't argue with them. Like this guy, they had all the answers. Like the Englishman had, the one who broke Mendoza's heart. What is it with martyrs, anyway? Are they so set on death because they can't cope with life? Or do they really believe that somehow at the last minute they'll escape by some mystical ladder to paradise? The big Englishman had. I remembered that flat certainty in his pale-blue eyes. God, I'd hated that man.

The security tech I'd requested put his head through the door.
"Sir?"

"Long-range broadcast to base. Give them a situation report. This
is a spy for the Tongva, one of the Chinigchinix cultists. He appears
to be operating alone. Could be advance scouting for an invasion.
Could be a missionary. Interrogation is proceeding. Send instructions,
if any."

"Yes, sir." The tech went out again. The stranger had watched
us in fascination as we spoke, taking in every detail of the tech's
green skin, of my muzzle and paws. When we were alone again, he
cleared his throat. He would never for the world have admitted to
himself that he was trying to get my attention, but I turned my head
to stare at him again, and this time he stared right back, feasting his
eyes on my strangeness.

"You're glad to see me, aren't you?" I remarked. "My very
existence proves something. Before today you believed what you believe on faith alone, but now you've seen proof with your own eyes.
Of me, anyway. And if I really exist, then your Lord must, too, huh?"

"Even the Liar must tell truth when speaking of Him," he said.
I had the feeling it was a quote from oral Scripture.

"You've done a pretty good job of evading my spirits. Why did
you give it up? Why did you just walk in here and surrender?" I
leaned forward.

"I had my duty to fulfill, and I'd waited long enough. At last, I
saw no other way," he replied. "If I can't give these people the
Message by my teaching, I can give them the example of my death."

"Nobody's letting you give them any examples."

"You think not?" He shifted, crossing his legs. "I've already
planted the first seeds in Sepawit's heart. And all of them out there,
Ponoya, Kaxiwalic, the rest of them, they want to know who I am
and why you keep me prisoner here. I shouted no threats, I didn't
fight your spirits; I let myself be led like a child to my prison. You
think that hasn't puzzled them? I won't resist, either, when you have
me killed; and you'll look brutal, killing a harmless little fellow like
me, who's done nothing but testify to the Truth. And you'll have to
kill me, or I'll keep talking to them, telling them what you don't want
them to hear. Either way, His purpose will be served."

"Okay." I yawned and scratched my ear. "So let me see if I
have this right. You've been sneaking around Humashup for months,
maybe even before I got here, watching these people without their
knowing it. You've learned their names; you know who's related to
whom and all kinds of other little details about their lives. Whoever

trained you did a great job. The plan was, when you knew enough, you'd just appear in the village one day, knowing things about people here you couldn't possibly know unless you'd been given divine knowledge.''

"And if I scouted the place where I was to fight you, Thief, who can blame me? Yes, I learned what I needed to know about these poor people. And I learned about you! I've seen your hive of demons over at Raven Point. I know all about what you're doing there!'' His eyes were stern. "You've done your best to conceal what unnatural creatures you are, but you can't hide the truth from His Eyes.''

"I'll grant you this, you're a pretty good sneak. So then, when you'd awed everybody with the confidence game, you'd start giving them the Message. Winning over converts and disciples to Chinigchinix. I'll bet you've been carefully trained in the right people to go after, too; the ones with power who are emotionally weak enough to listen to you, the ones you can scare. If that doesn't work, the alternative is to build up a convert base among the poor and dispossessed. There are lots of them, and they have nothing to lose by a change of government.''

He blinked at me, saying nothing.

"Am I right?'' I went on. "So, okay, the next step is invasion. If you've converted the rich, it'll be peaceful and gradual. If you've only managed to get the poor to listen, it'll be a civil rebellion, with lots of assistance from the Brothers in Chinigchinix down south. If you haven't won any converts at all, you'll still have enough information on these people to make an invasion force's job easy. And— worst-case scenario—if you're killed before you can accomplish any of the above, you've been trained to die well, and your martyrdom will confuse and intrigue everyone. Then another missionary will be sent to replace you. They'll keep sending little men like you until one of them does the trick.''

He was trembling where he sat. I hated this. I didn't need his terrified expression to tell me I was guessing right; there's only one way to do a job like the one he'd been given, after all, and I should know. I've been a missionary myself. I've persecuted them, too.

"The only problem was,'' I continued, "nobody counted on my actually coming down here, in the flesh, with all my spirits, who hide in the woods and create surveillance barriers even the best-trained spies can't slip through. Suddenly you couldn't get close to these people anymore, that was one problem, and your other problem was that it was going to be a lot harder to sell your story to them with me here. You solved your first problem by letting yourself be captured. I don't think you're going to be able to solve the other problem, though.''

"Wrong." The stranger swallowed hard. "I've told you. Sepawit is doubting you already."

"You wish. I don't think you realize that your people are building themselves a nasty reputation. Sepawit's heard of your tactics: why do you think he sent a spy to gather intelligence on you? And Sumewo wasn't the first one, you know. If you've killed the guy—and Sepawit is pretty sure you have—not all the sweet talk in the world will convince him to worship your god.''

The stranger was silent for a moment before he shrugged. "Well. The Lord may have hardened Sepawit's heart for His own purposes. It doesn't matter. We *will* win here, you know that! We have conquered in His name everywhere we've gone.''

"Everyone's a winner until he loses," I told him. "You've just had a long streak, that's all. Hey, why don't you tell me why this all-loving Father of yours would deliberately harden one of His children's hearts to *not* do His will? I've always wondered about that, myself. Think He's setting poor old Sepawit up for damnation, just to make an example of him? Sounds a lot like cheating to me. Almost like something a Trickster god would pull." I was getting angry; not a good sign for me. This was the place in the argument where I used to have to resist the temptation to give the wheel a little crank, just to wipe some of the smug self-destructive confidence off their faces.

"You're testing me." The stranger looked serene. "You're tempting me to doubt. Unfortunately for you, by manifesting here in earthly form, you have proved to me forever and beyond question that He is Lord. You yourself said it.''

"Well, yeah, but I'm the Great Liar, ain't I?" I said with a grin. "What if the only thing my being here proves is that I exist? You can see me with your own eyes, but have you ever seen Him?''

"Everywhere," he replied with certainty.

I nodded grudgingly. "Nice. But not enough. Look, my friend, let's make this short and sweet. You're not going to teach anybody anything, and you're not going to win a martyrdom for yourself, either. I've worked too hard here for you to louse things up at the last moment. My friends the spirits are going to put you to sleep, and when you wake up, you'll be wandering along the beach at Syuxtun with no thought in your head but getting back to Yang-Na. You won't remember what happened here for months, if ever. I'm sure your god has a lot of fine qualities, but you ain't peddling him on this side of the street, not while I'm working it. Understand?''

He was opening his mouth to protest, when the tech came back in.

"Sir? Instructions from base. Prisoner is to be detained at all costs until the cultural anthropology team can get here. Do not, repeat, do not allow prisoner to sustain injury. This is a priority request."

"Huh. Okay." I turned to the stranger, hoping he couldn't read expressions very well. "And then again—maybe I will let you speak your piece. Not to these mortals, though. How'd you like to preach to my spirits? Think of it as a test. Can you convert one of *them?* I'll bet that'd win you commendation from your Boss, big time. Care to give it a shot?"

His face was something to see. Disappointment and suspicion and crazy hope. He leaned back against the wall.

"My faith is strong," he told me. "Do your worst."

My worst was sending him Imarte, who arrived in a flurry of field notes, dragging her little team pal Jensen with her. Imarte, by the way, was a good-looker of a type that doesn't pop up much in the gene pool anymore, Mesopotamian dusky with bright green eyes and an hourglass figure.

"I came the second I heard," she told me breathlessly. "I can't believe it! Until this time we've only had the Boscana manuscript as any proof this religion arose *before* the introduction of Christianity and not in response to it! What a fabulous opportunity to document a spontaneous monotheistic movement!"

"For you, maybe," I told her. "I guess you're going to interview him for the details. Will it take long?"

"Of course." She stared at me as though I were nuts. "You think I'm going to pass up a chance to study this man? He's a priest of a living faith, not some pathetic old mission wreck with half-forgotten traditions. Think of all he can tell us!"

"That's what I'm afraid of," I replied. "Look, I don't want to step on somebody else's discipline, but this guy's presence here is endangering my work. It'll be all I can do to keep the Chumash from killing him, let alone allowing him to live here while you pick his brains. You can't take him back to the base for study, because what will you do with him afterward? He's not going to Mackenzie Base with my Chumash, I can tell you that. I can't even guarantee he'll cooperate with you. You don't know these guys the way I do."

She gripped her notebook with both hands. "We'll manage. Joseph, we really have to do this! And you can bet that once the stockholders hear about this man, they're going to agree with me."

I threw up my paws. "It's your project. Don't blame me if things go wrong."

I led her into Sepawit's house, and Jensen followed us. The stranger had slumped down, but jerked up straight as we entered. He had his serene and kindly look on again. It slipped a little when he saw that his tormentors were to be a lovely lady with big knockers and her mousy assistant.

"Hello." Imarte smiled at him earnestly. "I've come to speak with you. Are you all right? Is there anything I can get you?"

"The pleasures of love would be welcome, but will not distract me from my purpose here," he replied, politely enough. He looked at me. "What kind of test is this, Thief? Am I to preach to *these?*"

"Oh, please do." Imarte sat down across from him. "We've come to hear you speak, this spirit and I, and I promise we'll listen respectfully. It's not our intention to mock you in any way. You mustn't imagine we're servants of Coyote!"

"Thanks a lot." I scratched myself. She gave me an impatient glare. The stranger looked from one to the other of us, sizing the situation up. He leaned forward to Imarte.

"Listen to me, Beautiful One. If you will believe in the One True God, even a creature like you will be treated with mercy by Him. But I haven't come here to preach to your kind; I came here for the people of this village. Let me go out and speak to them! The Lord would look favorably upon such an action on your part." His eyes were big and appealing.

"Alas, Coyote has powerful sorcery and won't allow it," Imarte said with a sigh. "But tell me of this Lord you follow, for I know nothing of Him, and I want very much to know." Her assistant began to record, unobtrusively.

The stranger knitted his brow. "What do you mean, you know nothing of Him? You're a spirit. Of course you know of the One True Lord. All spirits know of Him; they've simply been wicked and disobedient since time began, and refused to acknowledge Him."

"Well, but we don't know *much* about Him," Imarte temporized. "You see, um—Coyote has kept us ignorant." She gestured dismissively at me. "But this I promise you, holy man: if you will preach to us, this spirit and I will remember your words always, and we will tell them to other spirits. Now, wouldn't the Lord want that?"

He narrowed his eyes, I guess trying to figure whether she was lying. "How many other spirits would you speak to?"

"Through us, your words would reach more spirits than there are stars in the sky," she told him, more or less truthfully. "And everyone would know that you were the bringer of truth to the spirits."

Bravo, temptress! She hooked him with that one. No missionary born could resist such an offer. She knew it, too, from his expression, and pressed her advantage:

"What we would like to hear first is the true story of how the universe came into existence, followed by a description of Him and any earthly manifestations He may or may not assume, and then any notable miracles worked by Him or His prophet, and of course the body of His laws—uh—but why don't you just tell us in your own words? And please stop us at any time if you need a drink of water or anything like that. All right?"

"Very well." The stranger drew a deep breath, trying to ignore the dazzling prospects opening before him—or maybe it was Imarte's bosom he was trying to ignore—and, raising his fine, loud voice, he began:

"In the beginning was Vacancy and Emptiness, but He was before the beginning.

"Then Vacancy and Emptiness became Pallor and Oblivion; but He was not pale, and He was conscious. Then Pallor and Oblivion became Explosion and Falling Outward, but He did not move, He was in the still center. Then Falling Outward became the Night, full of stars; and the Earth was in it, and He looked upon the Earth.

"And He saw her bear many children, but they followed no Law. He was angry with the children of Earth for this, and so He came to Earth and was born as one of her children too. He was more beautiful than the Sun, but He was so terrifying to the guilty children of Earth that she had to hide Him at first. Still He was like a fire shining out of a grave, and made His Law known to them.

"Earth taught all her other children to worship Him. Now, those who obeyed, He spared. But to those who would not worship Him, His avengers came, bringing terrible torment; the Bear to bite, the Scorpion to sting, the Rose to grieve, the Rattlesnake to poison . . ."

I sighed and left as discreetly as I could. The missionary ignored me and kept going, and Imarte listened, rapt, stars in her eyes, drinking in his every word. It wasn't that she hadn't heard the same old spiel, as I had, in a hundred ancient tongues, in a hundred different centuries; but this was her line of work, and it gave her as much delight as rare maize cultivars gave Mendoza or fake temples gave Houbert.

Not to knock the guy's religion or anything.

And speaking of religion, here was my own little prophet of Re-

vealed Truth waiting for me just outside the door! Kenemekme pushed
a chaplet of flowers up from where it had slipped over one eye and
looked at me terribly earnestly.

"Is it true what they're saying, Uncle? Is that one of Your enemies in there? Why don't I just go in and explain about how nice
You are?"

"Thanks, nephew, but I have my spirits in there working on
him." I took him by the arm and led him away.

"I could play some music for him," he offered. "I composed the
most beautiful song this morning, all about the light and how it shines
and shines."

"That's just wonderful. Say, I'll bet the sea would like to hear
your song, don't you think so? How about you run down to the beach
and play some tunes to the waves?"

"What a beautiful thing to do!" Kenemekme looked enchanted.
"I'll go right now." He ran away, breaking into his weird little dance
as he went.

"Sky Coyote?" Sepawit was pacing nearby, looking unhappy.
"How long am I going to be kept out of my house like this?"

"Not much longer, Sepawit, I promise." There had to be a more
convenient place for Imarte to conduct her researches. "I've got my
spirits on him now, softening him up. They'll get him to talk in no
time."

"Sounds like he's talking well enough," Sepawit said with a
scowl. He was right; the stranger's trained voice was carrying right
through the walls, so that all Sepawit's neighbors were getting an
earful of the Youthful Miracles of Chinigchinix. He had reached the
part where the Boy Divinity takes His elderly blind aunt digging clams
and tricks her into entering a sea cave, which He then walls up so
she drowns at high tide, which is okay (as He explains to His disconcerted family) because she's really a sorceress, only nobody but Him
knew.

"The spirit is letting him think he's converting her. Lulling him,"
I explained. "Once she has his confidence, she can trick him into
revealing the invasion plans."

"If You say so." Sepawit looked down and sighed. "I don't
suppose You could try to find out what became of my Speaker?"

"Sumewo. Right. She'll ask, but . . . the Tongvans had to have
captured him, Sepawit. How else would the guy know to come straight
here, to this village? And they had to have made him talk, and to do
that . . . well, the outlook isn't good. I'm pretty sure he's dead, Sepawit."

Sepawit turned his face away. "I thought he must be." After a moment that wasn't enough, and he covered his face with both hands, and drew a deep breath and held it. Finally he managed to say, "But I have to know, Sky Coyote. You understand."

"He was your son, wasn't he?" I guessed. Behind us the droning voice went on, describing the birth of a prophet to a young girl who had never slept with a man. Sepawit nodded miserably.

"Not Ponoya's. My firstborn. From a long time ago. He was a brave boy . . . would have made a great chief. He became my Speaker when he was only sixteen." He choked off. "He volunteered—oh, Coyote!"

I sighed. So many old masks to try and fit on over this coyote face. All afternoon I'd been wearing the Persecuting Inquisitor; now I had to put on the kindly Father Confessor.

"You know what happens to a soul like that, when it leaves the body? Flies straight over the rainbow bridge to paradise, straight as an arrow," I told him. "After all, this wasn't a boy who died in a stupid accident, or in a fight over a woman, or of illness. He was willing to risk his life for his people! And a strong soul, and a good soul, comes back sooner, because it has the most work to do in this world. You'll see him again, Sepawit."

"Will I see him where you're taking us?" he asked, without much hope.

"Well, no, because you won't be dead. But there are higher paradises, and you'll move on to them eventually, and he'll be there."

"If he's dead." Sepawit turned his head in the direction of the house, where the stranger had begun to sing a hymn. "There's always the chance, of course, that he isn't. It's not knowing that's killing me. Maybe the Tongvans aren't as bad as we think, maybe they've treated him well. What if he's alive, and we leave here, and we leave him behind us? What if . . . it makes me afraid to go, Sky Coyote, white men or no white men."

"No. You wouldn't want to fall into the white men's hands," I said emphatically. "I didn't tell you as much as I could have about them, you know. Your people would have been too scared. South of here, way south of here, they came for a tribe that was bigger and richer than you could ever imagine. Only a handful of white men against this powerful tribe, but you know what happened? They walked right into the biggest village and took their chief prisoner, without striking a blow. That tribe are all slaves now, the ones left alive. And you and I could walk south right now, Sepawit, for only a few moons, and you could see with your own eyes the graves of

their babies stretching to the horizon. You think that doesn't make me
sick with fear for all of you? And they're coming for you, Sepawit,
don't kid yourself. They're creeping up on the Tongvans just as surely
as the Tongvans are creeping up on you.''

"Maybe the white men won't last forever," he sighed. "Maybe
there'll come an age of the world when they've all gone away and
we can be born again back here. And then I won't . . . then my son
can be the chief he would have been."

"Of course he will," I said. "But meanwhile your other son will
grow up free and happy, and he'll never have to watch his mother
being raped by conquerors, and he'll never be sick a day in his long,
long life. And why? Because you'll all be safe with me, in the place
I'm taking you. Think about it, Sepawit. You don't really have a
choice here, do you?''

"No, of course not," he replied. His gaze wandered to the house
again. The stranger was singing:

> *And he told her, the priest said to the girl,*
> *To the girl white with anger,*
> *To the pure girl in her robe of honor,*
> *The priest fell to his knees and said to her,*
> *"O young girl, you are most fortunate!*
> *For you have been the one to bear the child of the clouds,*
> *The son of the dead, the hungry one,*
> *The prophet of justice,*
> *The Sun in his person, the Moon and Stars in the flesh!*
> *Here on this island of the blessed, you will bear him!''*

He had a beautiful voice. All of Sepawit's neighbors were coming
out to listen.

28

I TRUDGED WEARILY back to the base by my devious ways and had myself a sponge bath. It didn't do much toward taking away the psychological stench, but not even peeling off my skin would have done that.

I used to soap up in various wooden or tin tubs after a session in the dungeons of the Holy Inquisition. Anybody in his right mind would have bathed, the places were so foul. The worst part wasn't working in the questioning chambers; it was being sent to fetch prisoners from the filthy cells where they'd been sitting forgotten for weeks or even months. Worst of all was opening a door and seeing a buzzing mass of flies whirl up from something that wasn't going to have to worry, ever again, about whether or not it was Jewish. Or maybe it was worse to open a door into darkness and meet the stare of a child, alone there, forgotten by everybody except some rabid priest who'd authorized red-hot pincers for her mother.

Maybe that was my last straw, maybe that was the moment I finally came to the place Budu had been when he watched Christians eating Moslem corpses. Not that I hadn't seen children die before. Maybe it was the cumulative effect of seeing them die over centuries, being able to rescue only the perfect few for immortality. Maybe it was just my amazement that the kid never cried.

She didn't cry once while we were interrogating her. She was so angry. Her anger fascinated me; there wasn't a doubt in my mind that she'd refuse to break. Even when we began to wear her down, when she was terrified by having been shown the torture chamber, when she was confused and exhausted, she didn't cry. I think she was four years old, at most.

And she'd fit all the physical parameters. With an iron soul like hers, I thought she'd make a great Facilitator someday, so I spirited her off to the hidden lab where Marigny and I ran the rescue operation. I couldn't believe it when he came out later with that look on his face.

"What do you mean, she's not up to specs?" I hissed. "I scanned her myself. She's optimum for augmentation, for Christ's sake!"

"She scored high on everything, but that's the problem," he muttered, not looking me in the eye. "She's a Crome generator, Joseph. Not much, maybe only force two, but the readings are there. Look at the brain imaging, if you don't believe me. Any score above .009, and the Company doesn't want them. You know that."

I knew. Some mortals generate Crome's radiation spontaneously. Actually everybody generates some, under sufficient stress, but mortals who produce above a certain amount tend to do flukey things like levitate small objects and see the future. If it were controllable or predictable, the Company could make use of it; but it isn't, so we don't. And when you're transforming a mortal into an immortal, you *really* don't want anything uncontrollable or unpredictable in the equation, because any mistakes you make aren't going to go away. Ever.

But what was I going to do, send the little girl back to her cell to die? One more lousy deed in my life that was becoming an unending string of lousy deeds, just so I could occasionally get a good deal on something or someone Dr. Zeus wanted.

She's stressed, I told Marigny subvocally. *That's why she's scoring so high. So, you know what you're going to do? You're going to fudge the test results so they read under .009, and nobody's ever going to know you did it. I've already forgotten what I just said. You owe me, Marigny!*

Out loud I said, "Well, you'd better go back and double-check to be sure. Did you remember to factor in the medication I slipped her?"

"Oh, my gosh, that totally slipped my mind!" exclaimed Marigny. He wasn't as good a liar as I was, but he was good enough. "I guess I'd better go back in and take another reading."

So he did, and this time Mendoza scored nice and low on the Crome test, and we shipped her off to Terra Australis Base to be processed for immortality. I couldn't believe it when I found out she'd become a botanist. I'd been certain that the kid was Facilitator material.

Then again, would I want a daughter to have to do the kind of work I do?

"Are you out of your mind?" I took off my tricorne and flung it down on the conference table so hard that papers fluttered everywhere and styluses rolled off. "This guy is poison! He already has my people arguing. Everything we've done so far could be jeopardized. All that cooperation, all that trust could go."

"With respect, Joseph, you're overreacting." Imarte kept a tight hold on both ends of her stylus. She looked demurely down the table at Lopez. "You should see the man, sir. He's no warrior, not by any stretch of the imagination. He came on a peaceful mission to evangelize for his faith. While I agree that he mustn't be allowed to do that, for the sake of our own mission, we have an incredible opportunity to learn from him. And we certainly can't mistreat him in any way! Not only is it in violation of our code and everything we stand for, it wouldn't give the Chumash a very good impression of us."

Lopez sighed and drummed his fingers on the polished synthetic substance of the tabletop. "Joseph's not asking that we kill the man, madam. You simply want him removed from the village, am I right?" He turned his head to me. Beside him, Bugleg watched us uneasily.

"That's all. Put him in a holding cell here. Conduct your interviews with him as long as you want, but in a place where my people won't have to listen," I implored. "The guy can project like a stage actor! And my poor chief would like his house back."

"I'm sorry about that," said Imarte, looking away. "We can try to make arrangements for Sepawit. But we can't move the man here, not to this alien environment! Don't you understand the importance of obtaining such material in context? Right now, his beliefs are intact. Even meeting you and me, disguised as we are, has reinforced his world picture and his belief system. The minute he's exposed to *this*—" she indicated the base with a sweeping gesture that took in the four long walls of the gray conference room—"the material will be compromised. His belief system will change."

"So dress up your quarters to look like the inside of a tule house," I snarled. "Don't let him see any plastic while he's here. Whatever. But I want him out of Humashup!"

"And we'll get him out," Lopez agreed. "I'm certain there's a way to accommodate everyone, Imarte. Our first priority must be the Chumash rescue, however."

"But they're as good as rescued. We've learned nearly everything we can from them. What can happen now?" Imarte said. "And this man is such a valuable source of information, it would be criminal not to learn as much as we can while we have access to him. Besides, not only would he speak differently here in this strange place, I'd listen differently. There's a mind-set that goes with hearing such stories seated on the earth, under a wooden roof, where I can smell the cooking fire and see the artifacts of ancient life around us. All that would be lost here.''

"Look, you may be grooving on the primal ancientness of it all,'' I said, ''but in the meantime this man presents a real danger to everything we've accomplished. And the Company has a low, low tolerance for people who endanger our work.''

"And if the Company knew what's at stake here?'' She leaned forward. ''You know how some of our stockholders feel about monotheism. They'd want him saved at all costs, you know they would! What if they put it to a vote?''

"What, indeed?'' said Lopez calmly as he poured himself a glass of water. ''They might just do that, if they knew about this man. They don't, however. Someone here did try to tell them; I intercepted an unauthorized transmission only last night, in fact.''

Imarte gulped. My ears went up. ''Of all the underhanded—'' I began, but Imarte cut me off:

"We don't need to contact the future for a directive, anyway. There are enough representatives of the future here for a vote right now, if you call a meeting. Call that meeting, Lopez!''

"Unfortunately, madam, that authority does not lie with me,'' said Lopez, and took a sip of his distilled water. A silence fell. We looked at Bugleg, marooned as usual on his island of incomprehension.

"Sir.'' Imarte got up and went to him. ''Surely you understand. This mortal has information on a lost culture, on a faith that would have transformed the world if it had been given the time! The loss to human civilization is, consequently, incalculable; but we can change that. This is comparable to finding Saint Paul or Mohammed and being able to record his actual doctrines in their purest state, not just the edited and half-obliterated translations that have been preserved. More so, because the ideologies of those religions employed scriptural text and have thus survived as cultural influences. Not so with the Native American faiths. We came here to ameliorate that tremendous injustice, sir, and what we've done so far on restoration for the Chumash has made a good start. But we'd be betraying our purpose if we didn't utilize all our resources to record everything we can about this visitor from an equally significant civilization, given the remarkable opportunity we have to do so.''

She leaned way over to emphasize her point with her cleavage. Bugleg fiddled with his stylus. "Um—" he said.

"Sir, I implore you. This situation must be brought to the attention of the stockholders here," she told him. "Call the meeting. Let's have a consensus."

He looked horrified. I sat down and leaned back in my chair.

"You need to know some stuff, sir," I told him. "This man is a religious fanatic. He belongs to a cult. They do sacrifices and rituals."

"They do?" His eyes darted to my face.

"Yes, they do. And you know how we've been saving the Indians, and it's all been going really good? You know how we're going to take them off to a base where they can stop doing savage old-time stuff and live just like you? Well, this man wants that not to happen. He wants to make them belong to his cult. See, he's one of those guys who thinks it's okay to kill people who don't do rituals like he does. He's a priest. I used to be a priest, and I know what they do. I was part of that Inquisition thing. You know about that, don't you? That was where those bad old guys would torture people to make them join their religion. This guy is doing the same thing. We Old People learned from you that bigotry and intolerance are bad, but *he* doesn't think so. In fact, he wants to start a war over it that will kill lots of people. I bet lots of animals get killed, too. You don't want that, do you?"

"No!" cried Bugleg. He turned accusing eyes on Imarte. "You were all, 'He came on a peaceful mission'!"

"He *is* a man of peace, sir. You don't understand—it's not as simple as Joseph is making it sound." She looked at me furiously. "Yes, he comes from a religious group, but you were the ones who decided that all mortal cultures have equal value. You were the ones who thought everything was worth preserving. I'm simply following our Greater Mission Statement!"

"You know what he believes about his god, this guy?" I said with a yawn and stretch. "That He sends animals to attack anybody who laughs at Him. Hey, and you know how she was all, Saint Paul and Mohammed? You know who those guys were? They started religions that got billions and billions of people killed fighting one another in wars. They said they were men of peace, too, but look what happened. This is the same kind of guy. Now, she wants to listen to his talking, and she wants to do it in the Indian village, and she doesn't think it matters if my Indians hear his cult ideas. I say it's dangerous. What if they listen to him and turn into cultists? He's like a microbe, this guy, he's like germs. Okay? And if you let her have her meeting thing, and her consensus thing, the germs are going to spread. Do you want that?''

"How can you *do* this?'' Imarte had tears in her eyes. "Joseph, you of all people should know what's at stake here!''

I knew better than she did. Bugleg was shaking his head obstinately. "No, no, no. You can't have a meeting. This man sounds really sick. No sacrifices and no wars.''

"Let's compromise, shall we?'' said Lopez, who had been watching us, chin on fist. "We'll have a replica native dwelling built nearby. This man can be brought in—perhaps at night or while he's unconscious—and you can continue your interviews there, madam. Minimal loss of context, and he won't be exposed to anything alien enough to affect his personal mythology. Will that do? He won't disturb the Chumash any further, and I'm sure you can invent a plausible reason for his disappearance, can't you, Joseph?''

"Sure! Sounds great.'' I got up and collected my hat. Imarte stared down at the table with big soulful betrayed eyes. Bugleg looked at us, from one to the other, still outraged.

"No meetings!'' he said sternly.

"Nope. You did good, sir,'' I told him. "That was smart, giving that order. It'll save the mission from those nasty cult guys. You should be proud of yourself.'' But he shook his head again.

"Being proud is wrong,'' he told us.

The long walk back to Humashup wasn't all that comfortable, with Imarte sniffling and refusing to talk to me. I was sorry I'd had to play hardball, but this wasn't the first time somebody's enthusiasm for his own little line of work had made trouble on a mission. Sometimes you have to take people's toys away.

The sound of very loud prayer drifted to us from Sepawit's house as we approached. Was it my imagination, or were the people standing around eyeing me with a certain amount of fear and suspicion? The security tech guys stood stolid and silent outside the door. A lady named Anucwa, one of the bossy wise women, approached us cautiously.

"Uncle Sky Coyote, I think you'd better kill that prisoner. He's saying some terrible things about you. I don't believe any of it, of course, but people are starting to talk.''

"Yes, I thought this would happen.'' I looked sidelong at Imarte. "What is he saying, sweetheart?''

"Oh, all sorts of nonsense . . . that you're the king of the nunasis, for one thing. Which is ridiculous, of course; but he knows a lot of other things that are true. He was sitting in there all night yelling about you, and about all of us here. Calling for people he's never met, but he knows their names and all about their families. We're all wondering how he knows so much about us. I told everybody he must be a sorcerer.'' She looked at me expectantly.

"Good for you!'' I patted her on the behind. "You guessed right. Will you be a love and go tell the rest of them that? And not to worry about the things he says. He's just trying to scare everybody. I'm taking him away from here today.''

"I'd better go in and talk to him,'' murmured Imarte, which was as close to an apology as I was going to get from her.

"You do that, babe.'' I watched as she and Jensen slunk away into Sepawit's house. Sepawit, right. Must talk to him.

I found him sitting outside Kaxiwalic's, where he'd been staying with his wife and the baby. The kid was crawling around on his lap, eating most of his breakfast for him. He didn't seem to mind. But when he looked up to wish me good morning, even he had a different look in his eyes.

"Has he told You about Sumewo yet?'' he asked.

"I expect to find out today,'' I temporized. Damn, I'd forgotten to ask Imarte about that. Well, I'd go ask the guy myself. "You're getting your house back tonight, too.''

"Oh, good,'' he said listlessly. "The baby's already broken a couple of Kaxiwalic's belongings. He's a bachelor, You know, so he leaves things lying around . . .''

"I'm sorry.'' I sat down beside him. "I'll pay for any damage.'' The baby offered me a grubby fistful of acorn mush, then changed his mind and ate it himself.

"Oh, that's all right,'' Sepawit said. He was a million miles away. "You don't suppose . . . What if he is still alive, Sky Coyote?''

"Does that seem real likely to you?'' I asked him.

"No, but . . . that man has been going on and on about what a loving god Chinigchinix is, as long as you don't cross Him. He explained that Chinigchinix doesn't want everybody killed, just made to worship Him. He says his people haven't been making war on the other tribes. They've just been making them see the truth—His truth— and as soon as the other tribes accept that, then they all live like brothers. Not that I believe a story like that for a minute, but there might be some truth in it. It wouldn't make any sense to kill off all the other tribes you meet—I mean, who would you trade with?—and you can only take so many slaves. I just don't see what the point is of this insisting that everybody believe in the same god.''

"He's a jealous god, that's all, and He doesn't want any attention paid to anybody else," I explained. "Children are like that, sometimes. New baby gets born, big sister wants mother to pay attention just to her and not to the new one. You can't give in to gods when they demand crazy things of you, or there'll be no end to the things they expect you to do. You know that tribe down south I told you about, the really rich one? They hooked up with a god who told them they had to give Him human hearts to eat, every day, and blood between meals."

Sepawit shuddered. "What an awful god! What did they do?"

"Well, they sure as hell didn't want to tear out their own hearts to feed their god, so they had to make war on their neighbors all the time so they'd have captives' hearts to feed Him. Pretty soon all their neighbors hated them. Also, they had dead bodies piling up—which they took to eating, because, well, there the bodies were, and how are you going to go hunting deer when you have to make war all the time? And the laugh was, their god dumped them in the end. He just let the white men come marching in and didn't lift a finger to save his people. Talk about ungrateful!"

"Well, if you behave like that, you deserve what you get," remarked Sepawit. "No, what I don't understand is why this Chinigchinix should want to bother *us?* We're good people. We know it's wrong to steal, lie, and murder. What did we do to get this god on our case?"

"Well, you're my children. He doesn't like me, as you may have noticed," I said with a rueful grin.

"It *is* true that You lie sometimes. And steal," Sepawit ventured, looking uneasily at me from the corner of his eye. "At least, the stories say so."

I shrugged. "I did stupid things when I was young. Didn't you? As it is with you men, so it is with us Sky People. I think Chinigchinix must be a very young god, or crazy, to be so selfish."

"Maybe." He nodded. He was still watching me. "But, You know, that man seems so friendly. So calm. If they're all like him, maybe they're not so bad. Maybe they didn't harm Sumewo after all."

Okay: if you had your choice between believing that your son had suffered a horrible death by torture or believing that he was perfectly all right with good, humane people, which would you rather believe? And if the enemy is good and humane, maybe they're telling you the truth when they say that your kindly old Uncle is actually the Lord of the Flies Himself. And if that's the case, what's your next move?

I didn't know how far he'd gone along this path of reasoning, but he wasn't going to travel any farther.

"This isn't fair. You shouldn't have to suffer the suspense." I jumped to my feet. "I'll get an answer for you, Sepawit. You need to know, one way or the other."

"Thank You," he called after me.

29

OUTSIDE THE HOUSE I could hear the stranger's voice raised in earnest entreaty.

"No! He will preserve you against harm. It's only the unbelievers upon whom He looses his avengers. You have only to agree to this, and I will initiate you into the Hidden Mysteries."

Imarte's voice was strained but courteous: "Please believe that I have nothing but the greatest reverence for your sacred stories. Myths tell us many beautiful truths about ourselves—"

"They are NOT stories!" shouted the stranger. "They are Sacred Truth! Can't you understand that if you deny them, you will be damned for all time?"

"He wants you to convert, doesn't he?" I said, ducking in through the doorway. "Hell, honey, go along with it. He'll be a lot more cooperative."

"I won't insult him by lying to him," she replied stiffly. In Chumash, she told him: "Sir, I want to know more of what you have to tell me. But you must understand that I am only a vessel of the truth. My personal faith is not the issue here."

"Yes, it is." He was staring at her with the most betrayed expression—where had I seen a face like that recently? "If you yourself have no faith, you can't carry it to others. I can never reveal what is hidden to the likes of you! You are hollow!"

"Never worked with one of this kind, have you?" I said, crouching down across from her. "True believers aren't real receptive to the idea that what they're telling you is just mythology. Doesn't matter how appreciative of their culture you are, Imarte. You want my advice, you'll fall down on the floor this minute in a foaming-at-the-mouth screeching fit of revelation from Chinigchinix Himself. Otherwise you're not getting a step further with this guy.''

But it seemed my advice was badly timed. The stranger turned his head to stare at me, and he was wroth.

"Now I see the trick!'' he hissed. "You've wasted my time with this woman, when I might have been out doing His Will! Oh, Thief, you are pathetic. Do you think a few hours' delay will prevent me from accomplishing what I set out to do?''

I had a snappy comeback on the tip of my tongue, but the guy vanished before I could use it.

It seems that all the while he'd been praying so loud, in there by himself, he'd also managed to free his hands. Then (so far as we could tell later) he'd managed to make a hole in the wall directly behind him, and cover it again with tules so it wouldn't show. This was Super Commando Missionary, after all. Since he'd fixed himself an escape route he could have used at any time, it must have been only the prospect of converting a couple of spirits that made him stick around.

"Oh, no!'' Imarte sobbed, but I was out the door ahead of her.

Security! Your rabbit's loose and running! I broadcast. *Contain only! No force! Do not lay hands on the guy!*

Shocked affirmatives bounced through the ether. The missionary was going for his martyrdom, I'd bet. However things turned out now, nobody could see me or mine so much as touch him, or I'd be playing into his hands. He was running ahead of me, dodging and feinting, and he was quite a little sprinter; but he hadn't played for the Black Legend All-Stars like I had. We paralleled each other all the way to the sacred enclosure, with the astonished Chumash watching us. Some of them took up the chase. Oh, great: now he'd have his audience. In front of the whale bones he pulled up, daring me to come closer and prevent sacrilege. I kept my distance, but an outraged priest came out to see what was going on and caught him by the arm. He whirled and struck the reverend gentleman hard. The priest oophed and dropped to his knees, clutching his stomach.

"You see, people of Humashup?'' the stranger cried. "It is a sign! The Thief has not caught me, and your own priest kneels to my Lord! The One True God has sent me as a friend to you, to tell you the danger you're in! Coyote told you a story about invasions, and persuaded you to go with him to an unknown place, lest you all be destroyed—and all the while *he* has destroyed you! Look around at yourselves! What's become of your village? Where are the things that made you what you are? You've sold them all to spirits! You are as naked as corpses, without even gifts to take into your graves! And make no mistake about it, people of Humashup, you're going to your graves. Do you know where he's taking you? I have seen the place! He's taking you to Raven Point, where the spirits of the dead travel! Let him deny it, but I've seen his spirits preparing the place!''

Sir? Containment achieved.

Gosh, thanks a lot. Are you in range to try a disruption?

That's against the code, sir—

Heads were turning, people were staring at me. "Of course we're going out on Raven Point," I replied. "That's where the Rainbow Bridge is. You know any other way to get to paradise?''

"But he's not taking you over the bridge!'' riposted the stranger. "You'll all go down under the water, where the Lord's avengers will tear you to pieces, flesh and souls! Don't let him do this to you, people of Humashup! There are no white men coming! At Syuxtun, at Humaliwu, at Muwu, your neighbors are living in peace, preparing to receive the Glad Truth of the Lord! They aren't uprooting their lives and casting off their property, like people about to die!''

Nobody was looking at me now, they were staring at the ground or looking at one another with fear in their eyes. There were murmurs.

I'll take responsibility. I don't want you to kill the guy, anyway; just give him a seizure. Grand mal, preferably.

On your order and under protest, then.

What a bunch of Goody Two-Shoes. The old Enforcers wouldn't have blinked at an order like that; but then, they'd never have let the missionary escape in the first place.

Fine! Wait for my signal—

"People, don't worry about it," I told the growing crowd. "He's crazy, that's all. Listen, guy, who's going to believe a little runt like you? Can your god come down and talk to these people the way I have? You're only a man! Why should they believe you instead of me, anyway?''

If everything had gone as I planned, he'd have fallen down then in a fit, a clear sign to anyone watching that he most definitely did not have God on his side. But Sepawit pushed through the crowd, carrying a stone cooking bowl. I swung to point my muzzle at the stranger.

"And another thing!'' I barked. "You serve such an angry god: why don't you tell us what fate befell the boy these people sent out to spy on you? What did His avengers do to Sumewo? What awaits those who defy Chinigchinix?''

"Hideous death!'' The fool couldn't resist scaring them with hellfire and damnation. "See the consequence of being His enemy? The spy could not hide his presence from us, and with coals and scorpions his tongue was loosened, with the flaying knife his soul was liberated! But he was more fortunate than you shall be, for at the end he accepted the Lord, and so his spirit is at rest. You will envy him, when the avengers come for you! And they will come—''

But the crowd gasped.

"Sumewo is dead?'' Anucwa put her hands to her mouth in horror, and somebody else said incredulously, "Little Sumewo?'' and there were moans of dismay, and a couple of people burst into tears. The missionary must have thought he'd hit the mark big time.

But Sepawit stumbled forward, unable to take his eyes off the stranger's face. "You did kill the boy, then,'' he stated.

"Not I, but the wrath of the One Lord!'' shouted the stranger in his triumph. He made no attempt to dodge the stone bowl as Sepawit smashed it down on his head. *Sickening crunch* is a cliché for the sound it made, but an apt cliché. He dropped. There were brains in the dirt. Sepawit sank into a crouch and covered his face with his hands.

I went to him and knelt beside him. "Sepawit. I'm sorry. I told you about these people.''

"I just bought that bowl,'' he said in a stunned voice. "Kaxiwalic won't want it now.'' He began to shake, and finally burst into tears. He threw his arms around me and wept his heart out, as unashamedly as though I were a sympathetic dog.

"Let's get this trash out of here and burn it,'' said Nutku grimly. He and a couple of other men took the stranger's body by the heels and dragged it away. People drifted off like ghosts, unwilling to intrude on Sepawit's grief.

30

THERE WERE CONSEQUENCES, of course. There was a whole inquiry and report. Imarte made one hell of a scene, but the final ruling was that if she hadn't been such a fatuous ass, the situation wouldn't have deteriorated to the point it did. Interestingly enough, none of the Future Kids was particularly shocked at what Sepawit had done. After all, he was only a savage, wasn't he, and didn't they do things like that all the time? And maybe the mortals from the twenty-fourth century were still human enough to wonder what they'd do if they found out that one of *their* children had been tortured to death.

But my fellow immortals were mostly on Imarte's side. I had set in motion the chain of events that led to the death of a mortal; and while the older operatives understood that this had been necessary for the good of the mission, they were a little disgusted by the debating trick with which I'd beaten Imarte. None of them were Facilitators, naturally. The anthropologists, of course, were outraged and horrified at what a slimy little guy I was. The younger operatives agreed with them.

Except for Mendoza. She'd barely noticed any of it.

I was sitting in splendid isolation at my table in the commissary, pretending not to notice as people avoided sitting near me. Not that I blamed them; I wouldn't want to watch me eat, either, with this coyote muzzle. Mendoza came in and got a bowl of soup and some crackers. She carried them straight to my table and sat down across from me, to my surprise and shock. I looked up at her to see if she was maybe expressing a comradely solidarity. I should have known better; she was staring absently into space, crumbling crackers into her soup in a way that suggested she'd forgotten how to eat.

"It's tomato bisque today, you know," I told her.

"Uh-huh."

"With real synthetic cream."

"How gross," she said, but not as though she meant it.

"So, how's it going lately?" I inquired. "Haven't seen you in the village much, now that the operation's winding down."

"I've been in the field, doing a survey," she said, bringing her stare back from a great distance and focusing on me at last. "I went for a walk. I was gone seven days and seven nights, and never stopped walking. I went a long way up this country, Joseph, more than a hundred miles. You wouldn't believe the things I've seen."

"What did you see?" I leaned forward. She leaned forward too, and there was a warmth in her eyes for the first time in a long time, but it wasn't for me.

"I saw a high desert, a bitter, chill place with no water, a desolation of spines. But one night of rain, and there were flowers there stretching for miles, rolling away in every direction: violet, blue, crimson, and every shade of gold, pale gold like the morning or saffron yellow, and green-gold like brass. They just swept on forever, and the color pulsed and flickered like a bed of coals. There were clumps and stands of boulders rising from the desert floor, and they were *pink*, Joseph, like strawberries bleeding juice into cream, colors of the strangest innocence for that place of death.

"I turned my face north and went on, and looked down out of the mountains into a valley floor. It ran five hundred miles, with a river winding down it, and was so wide, a mortal wouldn't have been able to see across, and on the bottom was a lost sea. Only salt marshes left, marooned in the land, and cracked earth white with salt and bleaching bones. There was still a smell of the sea in the air, which was hot as a furnace. I walked across the valley and found mussel shells in the rocks. Condors drifted in the thermals over it, and dragonflies mottled green and orange, big as birds.

"I walked up that valley, following the edge of the hills, and crossed over west into the green coastal range. North of here, Joseph, are oak forests that run on unbroken for miles, every kind of oak tree, every species that exists! Some are so old, so huge, one tree might shelter a whole valley in its shade. But you should see the redwoods!

"Where the mountains fall steeply into the sea, that's where I found the best ones. You've never seen trees so tall, not even you, and these are so old, they might have taken root when you were young. They make a darkness like night down in the canyons, cold as night, heavy with shadows and incense. Around their roots, even the little growth is ancient: horsetail rush and fern, living fossils. It might have been a million years ago; I felt I had fallen into the past there, with not a human sight or sound for miles. It's all alive with its own life, Joseph, nothing to do with us!

"I went north until I saw a mountain of marble, like a white pyramid, and that was where I turned back and followed the coast down. It was like a garden! Madrone trees all along the ridges, standing like queens, the leaves every pastel shade, the blood-red bark peeling back from the branches that might have been smooth-cast in copper. Silver-barked alders following every little stream down to the sea, and buckeyes just beginning to put out big sprays of pink-and-white blossom, fragrant as almond oil. Tiny meadows a thousand feet above the sea, talk about your hanging gardens!

"And there's a place, Joseph, where a vein of green stone works its way through the side of a mountain and down into cliffs that stand above the sea, and the trail to the beach winds over boulders like raw emeralds. The beach is all dark-green sand, and the water's clear and green like rolling glass. Not one human voice to hear, not a breath, not a heartbeat, not a cry! Only the sound of the sea booming in the green caves.

"I could have stood there on that headland forever, perfectly happy, until the green lichen had grown over me, until the long mosses trailed from my hair. I never wanted to move from that spot again. You must have found places like that, in all your centuries. Haven't you ever wanted that, Joseph, just to let go of your humanity and let the sunlight flood in on the black place where it once was?"

She looked so happy, and I was losing her, losing her into that wilderness. But the ice was melting, the stuff that had locked around her heart on the day the Englishman died.

I smiled my most sincere smile, coyote teeth and all, and said, "It sounds swell, honey."

"Oh, there's so much work for me here," she went on, her eyes intense. "The Spanish will graze cattle and work unthinkable changes on the environment, but what the Yankees do in their turn will make the Spanish look like conservationists. There will be mass extinctions of the native plants as species are introduced from Europe and go wild. There are endemics growing here that are found nowhere else, Joseph, plants that evolved on their own in some fabulously distant time, maybe when this whole range was an island to itself. Did you know it was an island once?"

"I'd heard that."

"The geology bears no relation to the mainland of America. This whole place just drifted in on the continental plate, appeared on the Pacific horizon like a cloud, and came to rest here. It will move out to sea again one day, tearing loose from America with enough seismic force to level the cities. Paradise on the move once more, and the angel with the flaming sword back in residence.'' She looked wistful. ''Perhaps the people will all be gone by then. The trees will still be here, though, if I do my work right. Do you think I have a chance of staying here, Joseph, if I put in a request with the Company?''

''You might,'' I replied, knowing I would have to pull in a couple of favors again. ''I don't see why not, if there's as much botanical work as you say. They need somebody here, and it might as well be you.''

''Exactly. This was what I did my graduate work in, anyway, you remember? The particular botany of the New World. This was the place I wanted to go, when I started out. Isn't it funny how I was right about this, all along?'' Resentment flashed briefly in her eyes. ''Why on earth didn't the Company send me here first, instead of Europe? Think how different my life would have been!''

No denying that. ''But you'd never have scored that *Ilex tormentosum*,'' I reminded her. Then I wished I hadn't, because such a bleak look came into her face, I wanted to lift my muzzle and howl that I was sorry, I was sorry, I was sorry.

''Damn you for the memory,'' she said. ''Oh, hell, what's the point in denying it happened? It would have all been ended by now anyway.''

''I tried to tell you.''

''I know. And I never believed you, even after he was gone.'' Cold sorrow in her white face, all the happiness pale ashes again. She gave me that look like steel, straight into my eyes. ''Do you know when I believed you at last? In 1596, when Sir Francis Drake died. There was quite a lot of chatter about it, you know, because he was a sort of anticelebrity down there in New Spain. Houbert held a big mourning party—all in fun, naturally. There was an enormous dessert, a ship, the *Golden Hind*, sculpted in Theobromos. Everyone was supposed to come dressed up as pirates, I remember. People were swaggering around speaking in terrible English accents, and the sound of those voices again—well. That was when it struck me, you know, that I'd been away from England for forty-one years.''

She was looking past me now, out the commissary window at the dark Pacific. Her voice had grown cool and distant. ''He'd have been an old man, my Nicholas, if he'd lived. I didn't dare try to imagine what he'd have looked like. How could time wreck that well-made body of his? Stupid question, since fire did the job in half an hour. Anyway I sat there at that table with Houbert's damned orchestra playing *Fifteen Men on the Dead Man's Chest*, dropping miserable tears into my rum cocktail, and that was when I knew you'd been right.''

"As I sat there, a kind-hearted stranger saw me crying and brought me a handful of cocktail napkins so I could blow my nose. That was how I met Lewis.

"He was so kind to me, Joseph, that day I knew that you'd been right. It would have come to grief in the end no matter what Nicholas and I had done. You were right after all.''

"I was hoping you'd forgive me eventually,'' I said.

She brought her gaze back to me with a snap. "I didn't say I'd forgiven you,'' she said. "You could have saved him for me, and you let him die.''

"Baby, I couldn't have saved him! You know that. There was no way he was going to let us rescue him.''

"Maybe,'' she replied. "But I know that if there had been, you'd have killed him just the same. He'd seen too much; he knew about us. That made him a security risk for the Company. He had to be silenced, and you were all ready to do it. It was simply your good luck he was so set on his martyrdom; saved you the trouble of injecting him with one of those nasty little drugs you used to carry around with you.''

What could I say? We both knew it was the truth.

She put her head to one side, considering me. "No lies, no denials? Well, good for you. Listen, don't feel too badly about this. I can't forgive you, but I do understand that you had no choice. You're a Company man, and you had to do what the Company wanted. You always have; you always will. I don't hate you for it.'' She reached out and patted my paw absently. "There's not enough of *you* inside there to hate, is there?''

Maybe not.

I said nothing—what could I say?—as she got up and walked away. The soup she hadn't even touched sat there at her empty place, getting cold.

31

THE LAST DAYS of Humashup were now drawing to a close. Nutku and his cronies had liquidated their assets and closed out their books. The priests had stripped their holy places of sanctity and shut them down. Streets and houses took on an eerily clean look, because what hadn't been packed up for travel had been sold to the Company. People had nothing to do but eat and talk to one another. We had come to the dangerous days, the time when second thoughts occur; and while the missionary had failed in his effort to convince them that I was Evil Incarnate, maybe some of them were now a little shaky in their confidence. Not Kenemekme, of course; nothing could upset him; he just danced his little dances and played his little tunes and was happy with me as he could be. But other folks were getting restless. Other folks were thinking about friends or relatives in other villages who would be left behind. Other folks were beginning to realize this was not a game.

How would I handle it? How would I keep them from contemplating the end of their world?

Try this some time and see if it doesn't work for you, when you're having problems with your Chumash.

"Sorry I'm late, everybody," I puffed, sprinting into the clearing where everyone had gathered at my request. It was just getting dark, so the white sheet I was carrying shimmered ghostly in the twilight.

"We're all here, Uncle Sky Coyote, like you wanted," Sepawit told me, looking uncertainly at the techs who'd come with me. They ignored him as they proceeded to set up the primitive battery-powered equipment they'd brought. Some of the people turned and stared at them; others watched me as I got busy tacking up the sheet between two oak trees.

"I can see you are, and I'm very pleased," I said. "I worked hard to get this treat for you tonight, I'll have you know. Had to send off all the way to the World Above for it!" Which was close to the truth; New World One was a tropical paradise, wasn't it?

"A treat? That's nice," said Sepawit, turning to let everybody know, but most of the village had heard our conversation and were murmuring to one another. When I turned to face them all, they looked up at me with bright anticipatory faces, the young people and the old ones, the shamans and the hunters and my pals from the kantap. I could see that the techs were just about ready, so I threw up my arms in a gesture of welcome. The white spotlight hit me, and there were cries of astonishment.

"My children!" I cried. "I hate being bored! Don't you? Doesn't everybody? Even spirits get bored, you know. We were sitting around in the Sky talking about what a great show the kantap put on for everybody, and the spirits were saying they wished there was something they could do to repay you all for the wonderful time they had that night. So I said, well, why don't we work some magic for them?

"And they agreed that was a great idea, so here we are. Tonight, I'm going to tell you stories the way we tell them in the World Above. Before we do, though, I have to show you my special hunting medicine."

There was a flash and a click as the first of the slides was inserted, and on the sheet an image appeared: a red cylinder as long as a man's hand, with a piece of cord protruding from one end and a little flame licking at the tip of the cord. I pointed to it.

"There. That's my Fire Flashes like Lightning. If I want to kill something, all I have to do is throw one of these babies and wait for whatever I'm hunting to run across it. It's better than a harpoon, and not only does it kill what I'm hunting, it cooks it for me on the spot! Like it?

"But look at this one!" The slide changed, and there was a bigger red cylinder, and this one had a stick protruding from one end and a cone-shaped head on the other. "This is my Flies like a Goose! When I want to go somewhere in a hurry, I just climb on its back, tie myself on with some cord, and hold a little fire under its tail. You should see me go!"

There were gasps of wonder. I could see Nutku and the others from the kantap sitting forward, peering hard at the screen to figure out how the hell I was achieving this illusion. I let my tongue hang out and grinned.

"Here we are. This is Pulls through the Air," I continued, pointing at the next picture. It was a figure like a red U on its side, and the tips of its ends were dull silver. "Whenever I want something to come to me, I hold this up, and it attracts it! Well—most of the time, anyway.

"Now, this is only some of my hunting medicine. Whenever I need more, you know what I do? I put some shell money in a pouch, and on the pouch I inscribe this." On the white screen the word ACME appeared. "This sign is the most powerful medicine of all. I can get anything I need with this sign. Yes, folks, that's my secret! Now you know how I became the powerful and successful hunter I am, and now you'll be able to enjoy the hunting stories I'm about to show you." I stepped forward, picking my way through the seated crowd, and sat down between the kantap and the other notables. "Roll it, guys!"

The equipment began to whirr, and there was a burst of sound that made everybody jump. A blurred image appeared on the screen, which resolved into a pattern of red concentric circles as a jolly little tune announced itself.

"What's that, Sky Coyote?" Kaxiwalic leaned over to ask, shouting a little above the bouncing music.

"It's the tribal tattoo for the World Above," I told him. He nodded thoughtfully, and then his attention was seized and held by the bright figures that leaped into view. His cry of astonishment was echoed by most of the people of Humashup. The audience fell silent as they leaned forward and stared openmouthed at a brilliant world of red mesas, yellow desert, blue sky. Across this landscape a streak of dust was moving at high speed, emitting a high-pitched double cry.

"Hey!" said Sawlawlan abruptly. "I know where that is! Isn't that down at Sespe?"

"Who cares, you idiot?" growled Nutku. "Don't you want to know what's making the painting move?"

"Well, sure, but—"

Conversation died as the dust streak halted in its rush and everybody gaped at what had been emitting the strange cry.

"Is that some kind of bird?" Sepawit inquired politely, just as it began to move again. Close behind it, here came a second speeding blur. I elbowed Kaxiwalic.

"You'll appreciate this," I told him, just as the blur froze to reveal—

"COYOTE!" cried the whole village, nearly in unison.

If they'd been interested before, they were spellbound now. The people of Humashup watched intently as the hunt progressed, scarcely drawing a breath until the first time the coyote turned full-frontal to glare at the audience, inviting them to share his frustration at the unstoppable speed of his adversary. There were some horrified mutters from the priests and shamans, but they were drowned out by a wave of tittering. Kaxiwalic guffawed outright.

"All right, all right!" I said good-humoredly. "I'd had a little accident when these pictures were painted, okay? It grew back later."

The laughter never really stopped after that, even when their mirth at a coyote with no penis died away, because here was the first stupid blunder with the hunting medicine: Coyote trapping the damned bird under a tub and throwing one of his fire-sticks in after it, then waiting expectantly for the explosion that never came. Half the people in the audience groaned and howled warnings to Coyote as he couldn't resist peering under the tub to see what had gone wrong, then crawling inside the trap himself to investigate. Of course, the bird had magically escaped, and it looked on brightly as the explosion came, blowing poor Coyote sky-high.

No, they couldn't stop laughing at poor old Coyote, through his misadventures with the ACME hunting medicine that never worked right, through his collisions with inescapable red boulders and cliff walls, through his doomed stares at the audience as he free-fell down, down, down some red canyon, so far down that he disappeared before the tiny puff of dust below signaled his impact.

They had no problem at all understanding the humor. I needed to explain that the long gray stripe with the white line that wound to the horizon was a game trail, and that the wheeled things that charged along it blaring before they flattened Coyote were a kind of high-powered nunasis. Most of it they figured out for themselves, though, even the fiendishly clever contraptions of levers and springs that always failed to function until *after* the bird sped by, even the rocket-powered shoes or mail-order wings that invariably flew Coyote straight into rock walls. And how they laughed and laughed, including poor gloomy Sepawit, who hadn't smiled since the day he'd learned his son was dead.

Mortals are funny about their gods. My people were reassured: this was the Coyote they'd always known, this clever loser, always starving, never quite able to do anything without taking an ignominious pratfall. Who could imagine me as a demon of darkness now? When you laugh at something, you don't fear it anymore.

I sat there among them and wrapped myself in their happiness. Good old paintings: you can't beat them for a teaching device, whether they're bison that seem to dance on a rock wall by the flickering light of a tallow lamp or rabbits that caper on a white sheet suspended before a projector.

Once upon a time I'd been the rabbit, hadn't I? The rabbit who always won, who might drive the mean-spirited duck or the little pink man crazy with his tricks but who was never mean-spirited himself. That had been my favorite role for years and years, clever immortal guy outwitting brutish mortals but never doing them any harm.

Gradually the world got darker and smaller, and my job got a little dirtier. So I told myself I was the man who had to go down the mean streets, though he wasn't mean himelf. I was still the hero, even if now and then I had to hurt somebody. And if it was kind of lonely sometimes, well, that went with the job. Philip Marlowe never got the girl, did he? He always seemed to end up alone in his rented room, no company but a bottle or a chess problem, until the door should open and another desperate soul ask for his help.

You really have to lie to yourself sometimes, if you're stuck with eternal life.

But there would come a point where it was just no use anymore, not with the things I had to do in my line of work, and I couldn't seem to find the role. I was the secret good guy on the bad-guy team, right, playing the Company's hand, not really a member of the Inquisition. But for every Jew I smuggled out of the dungeons because his genetic code was unique and the Company wanted it passed on, I had to watch as twenty were burned. Hell, I helped burn them. Being able to play the sinister Spanish devil, a good meaty part, wasn't much compensation.

I'd been playing Coyote for years now, really, hadn't I? No hero at all, and lately not even much of a villain. God knows I did what the Company asked of me—what else could I do?—but nowadays most of my jobs seemed to consist of catching anvils with my head. How far down was I going to fall? How far before my own personal little puff of dust signaled to the chuckling gods that I'd hit bottom?

Well, no way of knowing, and no point in wondering. I was immortal; no accident was ever going to set me free. Like the silly bastard in the cartoon, I'd just drag myself out of the hole I'd made and limp on to the next job, whatever it was.

32

OH, THE CHUMASH loved those cartoons. They couldn't get enough of them. I had to order more from New World One. Imarte issued a snotty formal protest about it—supposedly I was wreaking havoc with their cultural myth sphere—but she'd said it herself, we'd garnered about all we could of their culture. Besides, as soon as we took them away, they were going to be exposed to a lot stranger things than coyotes on rocket roller skates.

So I showed them the stories about the rabbit and the hunter and the duck, and while I had to do a lot of translating, they found them as funny as I had, long ago. They were so enthusiastic, in fact, that I went ahead and gave them the stuff they *really* had no context for, like the duck and the pig and the Martian, or the rabbit and the hunter singing opera, or the furious little man with the six-guns. It took a few screenings for them to figure out what was supposed to be going on, but once they'd grasped it, they laughed twice as hard and clamored for more. The kantap began having intense discussions about devising new shows with a whole new cast of characters and new and improved special effects. Imarte was furious.

Not a day too soon, the personnel transports arrived.

I was screening a matinee in the meeting house at the time, so I didn't find out about them until they'd been there six hours. I was on my way back to the base for a nice hot sponge bath, when I saw Mendoza standing motionless on the hillside above me. She was staring intently out to sea. *Something going on?* I broadcast in inquiry. She glanced down, located me, and responded, *The ships.*

So I went trotting up to see and, by golly, there they were: four gleaming transports hanging far out above the water, waiting for nightfall so they could come in.

"Well, finally," I said. "I was running out of party tricks."

"Now you can give your mortals their ride in the chariots of the gods." Mendoza pulled her cloak closer about her. The wind battered at us, up here. My skimpy fur stood on end; Mendoza's hair streamed out like fire. I did a little dance, partly to express joy and partly to keep from freezing.

"This means that this time next week I'll be out of here!"

"Just when I'd got used to you with a tail," she remarked, actually smiling.

"Oh, I won't be out of the dog suit for another six months, believe me. I have to help the Chumash settle into their new lifestyle. Boy, will I have some explaining to do."

"You'll manage," she said. She was still smiling. I looked at her closely. As usual, the smile had nothing to do with me.

"You look happy," I observed.

"The Company approved my request, Joseph," she said. "I've been reassigned. I'm staying here in California."

"Congratulations," I said, mentally thanking the people who had owed me favors. "So you're going out to the base at Yosemite?"

"Out there? No. Though I'll certainly visit it when I get the chance; those sequoias are supposed to be amazing. No, I'm on my own recognizance. I'll be scouting with a complete field kit and sending stuff in as it's acquired. I thought I'd make myself a base camp in the coastal range hereabouts, just me and my credenza for company."

"You're kidding." I stared. "Mendoza, there's nothing here!"

"There's work, Joseph. There's enough work to keep me busy for years and years. No miserable departmental dinners. No social life. No *people*, very nearly. Only the land. Only those forests."

What reverence in her voice, talking about a bunch of trees and seismic zones. She had the answer, all right; she had found the True Faith, and she was as certain about it as the damned Englishman had been about his. She looked out at the ships and finally said, "I'll say this much for New World One. With all the luxury and all Houbert's silly rituals, all the conversation and busyness, there wasn't much time to think. That was a good thing, for a long while."

"Well, but what about your work? Your maize cultivars, that big project you've had on the burner since forever?"

"I have all the time I need for that," she said serenely. "I'm immortal, aren't I? Besides, I was about ready to settle down for a long spell of analysis of the hybrids I'd produced, and one can do that best inside a credenza anyway. Without all the distractions, I ought to make some real progress for a change.''

She was already gone, settling her pack on her back and disappearing into the green leaves without a trace. I had to make an effort, all the same.

''But, Mendoza—you have no idea what it'll be like. I've been on field assignments in real fields, baby; there are no shelters, no generators, no emergency backup. You live like an animal in the woods, and you can lose yourself.''

''God, I hope so,'' she said softly. I didn't know what to say in reply, so I didn't say anything. The big ships hovered out there, silent, waiting to take me away.

33

THE DAY OF the sky canoes.

Old Coyote went prowling back to the town in the dim hour before dawn, and as he stood on the hill above them all, he thought the place was already a dream. Not a soul to see, not a sound to hear: the houses looked transparent in the bleak air. Some cameraman somewhere was about to turn a rheostat, and they'd all fade out, shadows on a screen in a darkened room, no more.

I put my head in through the chief's doorway.

"Sepawit? It's our big day. Wake up your people."

A mound of furs on a sleeping platform stirred, and the chief emerged. He stared, half-asleep. Ponoya was a smooth curve behind him; between them sprawled the baby. "I saw the white men," he said thickly. "The trees died where they came."

"That's right, Sepawit. Wake up."

Back and forth between the houses I flitted, just like a real coyote hoping to find garbage. Or a loving father waking his children on Christmas morning. I guess I was somewhere in between. Young and old I woke them up, rich and poor, and one after another they emerged from their houses and stood blinking in the light.

"All right, everybody!" I jumped up in the air and waved my paws. "Come on out to the playing field, all of you! I have big news!" I loped away, and most of them followed me, except for one or two who weren't facing the day without breakfast even if it was the end of the world. They turned right around and went back inside, and soon you could see the smoke of their cooking fires.

The others milled around on the open ground, and I capered and frisked before them. "Now!" I barked. "You'll never guess what I saw this morning, out on Raven Point!"

"White men?" somebody ventured fearfully.

"No!" I replied, though it was true.

"The spirits of the dead?" tried somebody else.

"No! No, my own dear nephews and nieces, I saw not one, not two, not three, but four big sky canoes! The very same sky canoes that are going to carry us away from here!"

This made for general excited babble from most of them, though some thoughtful souls fell silent and stared. I raised my paws again.

"And they are *beautiful* sky canoes too!" I went on. "Wait till you see them! They shine like polished abalone shell. They're bigger than the council house. They're all enclosed, so the wind won't blow us overboard on our journey. The sea won't even splash us. There are fine seats inside these canoes and, best of all, they have what you have never, ever seen in any other canoe in your lives: latrines!"

This impressed everybody.

"You mean—"

"Yes! No need to worry about falling off while the canoe is moving. No need to cross your legs until you reach your destination. A beautiful private room instead, with a door that closes and plenty of hygienic accessories!"

"How do you get all that in a canoe?" demanded Nutku, clearly taken with the idea.

"Sky Magic, friend. So! My Sky spirits are waiting for us out on Raven Point. Each of you needs to go back to your house now, and pack a bundle for traveling. Yes, you can eat breakfast first. But don't bother to wash dishes, don't worry about banking the fire, don't even stop to fasten shut your doors when you've finished. Just grab those bundles and be back here in an hour!"

It took slightly more than an hour, but they did it. In the time between, the security team from the base arrived, sent by Lopez for crowd control in the event of panic. I can't say I wasn't a little annoyed by this: I mean, I'm a persuasive guy and I know how to do my job, right? But they did look impressive lined up behind me, I had to admit. A whole squadron of immortals as green as trees, as silent as a forest at my back.

When finally the whole population of Humashup had returned with their luggage, I cleared my throat and barked: "Let's all line up now! Families first. I want all the families in groups. Next, the single or divorced men. Single or divorced women next. Ladies, that's so you can watch their behinds as they walk!"

With a little help from the security teams, they were lined up in no time. I took my place at the head of the line and turned back to address them.

"Are we all ready? Good! I've composed a little song in honor of the occasion, and we'll sing it as we march along, all right? Here we go!"

> *Put all my sorrows in a basket,*
> *I sing quietly as I go out upon my journey.*
> *Farewell, Raven.*
>
> *A woman stays awake to greet me,*
> *She is sweet as honeydew.*
> *Farewell, Raven.*
>
> *In this place there are no shamans to assist me,*
> *Only people who want to talk*
> *About their own misfortunes.*
>
> *Pile furs on my sleeping platform, put wood on the fire,*
> *I will come home when the stars have faded.*
> *Raven, farewell.*

So that was the way they walked out of time, my people of Humashup: singing, and they never looked once behind them. But I kept my eyes on the village as we went along, walking backward most of the way, and I swear I saw the thatching on the houses blow away, their upright poles collapse, everything crumble. The ghosts took it over. My village died again, the old life died again. It was the year 1700, and time was running out for the old ways, the little tribal villages under the trees. A couple more centuries, and there wouldn't be any Stone Age left anywhere, would there? Except in my memory.

Then the town was out of sight, and we climbed up a canyon and wound across the green hills in a line, and the hard spring wind came up off the ocean and buffeted us all.

Sepawit strode at their head, holding his child tight in his arms, staring into the uncertain future. Ponoya trudged beside him, carrying the pack with their belongings. After him came a few married couples and several old folks carrying grandchildren, teenaged aunts and uncles pulling toddlers by the hand, big sisters or brothers carrying tiny babies, thin wary children on their own. Yes, there was little Kyupi lugging the baby I'd saved, with the two young boys tagging after. Farewell, Raven, they sang.

In the next group came the rich men, Nutku and Kaxiwalic and the rest of the guys, and their cloaks were made of otterskin and they hefted skin bags full of money. Bracelets of money rattled on their arms, money swung in pendant loops about their throats, and they shuffled with careful steps so they wouldn't lose any. I wondered if they'd packed their makeup and ceremonial costumes. Then came the shamans and priests, decked out in their feathers, bodies painted with signs to keep the world in balance, searching the sky for trouble. Last came the plain men, hunters, fishermen, and laborers, ragged or naked. Farewell, Raven, they sang.

The women came last. The well-born ones were skirted in deer-skin, the poor ones in woven plant fiber, and all carried their lives on their backs. Some few carried infants. Some others wore a little money of their own. There were my groupie cuties, Puluy and Awhay, carefully dressed for the occasion, thrilled to trade the past for a new scene. There was the artist Skilmoy, angry about something again, and there was Anucwa, sagely giving her advice on what to do about it. Behind them they were leaving a hundred tasks undone for all time. Raven, farewell, they sang.

Get a good look at them all, because they're going away forever.

They stopped singing when we came in sight of the ships, and some of them stopped in their tracks. There was the holoproduced vision of the Rainbow Bridge, arching above the transport pad, its other end vanishing into a golden cloud far out over the sea. Some of my Chumash looked scared, but the security teams closed right in to push them along.

"Look!" I barked, prancing, frisking in circles. "Look at the lovely ships! Not only does each and every one have its own latrine, but we'll all get delicious food and drink on board, served by beautiful Sky Ladies who will wait on you with smiles. I can hardly wait, can you? Come on!"

So I led them at last to the transport pad, where the ships sat like silver ducks. Here were the anthropologists, out to meet us with open arms. Green arms with goose pimples, but open anyway.

"Look, spirits, I have brought my nieces and nephews for a ride in the Sky Canoes!" I saluted them.

"Welcome, Children of Coyote!" they cried. But the people hung back, staring up at the gleaming ships.

"They don't look like canoes," ventured Sepawit. "They look

like that flying tube the War Helmet Nunasis had.'' He meant the Martian from our latest matinee. ''Are you sure they're safe?''

''Of course they're safe! I'm going with you myself, aren't I? Would I ride in them if they weren't safe? You've all heard stories about what a coward I am.'' Inspiration hit me. ''And, you know what else? There's *heating* inside those canoes.''

This brought a look of longing to many faces, including the anthropologists'. Nutku pushed through the line.

''Well, I'm through freezing. I want to see what it's like inside one of those things,'' he said. That got them moving, because of course his fellow kantap members had to come too or lose status, and naturally the priests and shamans couldn't appear afraid, so they pushed forward up the boarding ramps, and as the leaders went, so went the townsfolk.

I breathed a sigh of relief. Backing around the side of a ship to get out of the wind, I bumped into someone. A cup of something hot was pressed into my paw. I gulped gratefully. Black coffee laced with aguardiente, wow.

''Swell!'' I gasped, handing the cup back to Mendoza. ''Burns all the way down. Say, what are you doing up here?''

''Turning to ice, same as everybody else. Came up to watch the end of it all.'' She had the hood of her cloak pulled so tight about her face, she looked like a nun.

''No, no, it's a new beginning!'' I cried cheerily, overcompensating because it didn't feel like one. ''The good people of Humashup are out, they're filing up the ramps, my bags are already packed and on board, and I know for a fact that the commissary at Mackenzie Base serves great food. Little Joseph is a happy Sky Coyote!''

Right on cue, it came into our line of sight, a canoe negotiating the surf and boulders below us to strike out into the open sea.

''One of your Indians appears to have changed his mind,'' observed Mendoza delicately.

It was Kenemekme, the poor dope. He was leaning way forward, inexpertly paddling a dugout he must have made himself, it was so crudely chiseled out of drift log. He was naked. All he had with him besides the paddle were flowers. Some kind of yellow flowers, he'd picked hundreds of them, they filled his canoe and hung over the sides, and a few bobbed yellow in his wake, floating in the sea foam. My muzzle hung open in astonishment.

''*Coreopsis gigantea, Eschscholzia californica,* and—let's see, that's *Oenothera hookerii,*'' Mendoza said, peering at him, shading her eyes with her hand. "He must have been up all night gathering those. Shouldn't you be raising some kind of alarm or something?"

On one particularly enthusiastic backswing he noticed us, and stood up to wave. The canoe nearly capsized, but he steadied it somehow and gave us a crazy smile. He was shouting something. Mortals couldn't have heard him through the distance and the wind and surf, but we received him clear as anything.

"Uncle Sky Coyote! I'll meet You there! Don't worry, I know the way! But the beauty is shining out there, shining and shining beyond the world, can't You see it? I have to go find out what it is!" he cried. Then he plopped himself back into his canoe and went paddling on out to sea.

"If I remember Company policy correctly," Mendoza continued, watching me, "you're supposed to sound an alarm so the security teams can decide whether they'll go with option one, which is to rush out there and recover the escapee, or with the never-talked-about option two, which is to have a sharpshooter pick him off and thereby eliminate any loose talk or loose ends."

"I think I'm going to make an executive decision," I found myself saying. "I think I'm going to let that one get away."

"But heavens, whatever shall we do? He is already in the catalogue. Ah, but we've taken samples of what matters of him, so I suppose that doesn't pose a problem after all. Perhaps you think he won't survive to tell anyone about us, in that wretchedly unseaworthy boat? You may be right. I estimate his chances of not drowning in the next three hours at seven hundred and fifteen to one. Though if the prevailing winds let up, he may have a better chance, and *might* make it to one of those islands out there in the channel. On the other hand, some of those islands are inhabited by worshipers of Chinigchinix, who are, as I understand, religious fanatics. If he lands on the wrong island, babbling about visions he received from Coyote, he'll be killed as a heretic. Though if he lands on the *right* island, he might be hailed as a new prophet and tell all kinds of tales we don't want him to tell. What does a Company man do in a situation like this, I wonder?" She watched me, coldly amused.

I yawned a wide coyote yawn. I shrugged.

"Hey, he won't last an hour in that thing."

"And if you send out an emergency team to pick him up, it'll delay takeoff. Sound decision, I guess . . ."

"I think so. Anyhow, you know what I always say? In a hundred years, who's gonna care?"

She was still laughing at that as I took back the coffee and had another hit. "Mm, good. Whoops—there go the boarding lights. Time for me to beat it. Well, Mendoza, it's been truly great working with you again after all these years. Keep in touch, okay? Vaya con Dios."

34

I WAS KEPT busy in the next few minutes explaining to the sixty-five Chumash on our ship just how safe things were. When I was finally able to buckle myself into a seat and look out a window, I saw the base personnel assembled to watch the takeoff. There was Bugleg, eyes streaming with tears from the cold air and the pollen count, looking on unhappily as Lopez gave firm orders. Only the brass and the specialists were there, of course; all the techs were busy packing up equipment or dismantling the modular dome. Nobody was staying a second longer than was necessary, except for Mendoza. She was still standing there sipping her coffee, but she was staring away, fascinated, at the wild mountains of the interior. She looked up and raised her cup in a farewell gesture as the ship began to rise. I felt the climb speed up, and she seemed to sink into the earth as California dropped away below us. And there, quite a ways out to sea, I saw Kenemekme still bobbing along in his canoe full of flowers.

It really would have been more trouble than it was worth to go after him. Would he really have been happy at Mackenzie Base? He had his quest to find the beauty that was shining beyond the world, and he was sure to enjoy it more than orientation seminars and learning to drive loaders. The plain daylight around him was probably the closest he'd ever come to his mystical goal, but maybe he wouldn't live long enough to realize that.

Though I once knew a lady of a metaphysical turn of mind who'd have argued that the plain daylight *is* the mystical goal, that God or whatever, being everywhere, *is* the ordinary world all around us, and our quest is not to arrive where He is but to notice Him right in front of our faces. If she was correct, Kenemekme wouldn't be disappointed. She died a long time ago, though, so I couldn't debate the point.

But it made me feel good to see him paddling along happily into the unknown. One little bit of Humashup was being left behind, one tiny fragment of the lost world, and maybe something good would come of it. Sort of like Pandora's box, you know? Shut in there with all the evils and sorrows of the world was Hope. The rest of the people were being taken away to a bright future, and Kenemekme was being left in the dark, but maybe he'd brighten up the darkness a little while with his songs, with his crazy dances.

35

THE REST OF the story's pretty funny. Want to hear?

The people of Humashup did just fine at Mackenzie Base. Massive culture shock at first, of course, but they picked up on the delights of technology right away. More cartoon matinees! Food you didn't have to pound on a rock! Toilet paper! Not to mention lifetime jobs with the Company doing things like cleaning fuel tanks and working in processing plants. Menial work, but they were unskilled, after all, and it paid well. Great medical benefits, too. Most of them lived to see a third century.

They weren't allowed to breed anymore, of course, but that was okay with them, because most of them felt that parenting was a real pain in the ass. They happily donated sperm and ova to the Company freezebanks and let the anthropologists continue to pick their brains, though of course the longer they were exposed to a foreign culture, the less accurate their memories were about their old ways. They lived out long and comfortable lives eating Company food, buying Company merchandise, and vacationing at Company resorts.

Did I mention that Nutku and his fellow kantap members went into business? Their shell money was traded for Company scrip as soon as they figured out the exchange rate, and with it they bought the plant that manufactured the BeadBucks used at Company resorts for minor purchases like cocktails, appetizers, and beach-chair rentals. They parleyed that into a number of Authentic Chumash™ handicraft stands at Company bases all over the globe. Sepawit's kid grew up to become one of their CEOs, in fact, an executive with amazing vision. Numbers of ladies like Skilmoy supplemented their paychecks by producing Authentic Chumash™ baskets and other stuff in their spare time, which they had more of, now that they didn't have babies every year, and eventually banked enough to open their own, competing line. There was a real trade war that went on for years. Eventually they all died of old age, rich, and that was the end of them.

A long, long time later, the Chumash nation was reborn. Not the real Chumash, of course; the ones we left behind had long since died of smallpox or interbred with their invaders to the point that they ceased to exist as a culture, except for one determined tribe that ran a gambling casino somewhere.

No, the New Chumash were mostly Caucasian members of a religious group in the Federal Republic of Santa Barbara. Their spiritual leader had this vision that declared that he and all his followers were reincarnated Chumash. They believed the Chumash had spent all their time swimming with dolphins and getting energy out of quartz crystals. Nobody thought to ask the casino owners whether or not this was true, because running a casino didn't seem a very spiritual thing to be doing.

So the New Chumash bought up all this land north of the republic (pretty close to where Humashup had been, as a matter of fact) and declared it an ecological preserve and spiritual sanctuary. They were able to do this, despite the astronomical price of real estate in California, because they were stinking rich, being a very successful religious movement. The Reformed Church of Chinigchinix, by this time a toothless and benign old faith, gave its blessing to these fellow Native Americans by adoption.

And they had a lot of healing seminars and ate a lot of whole-grain carbohydrates on the sacred ground, but most of them felt that something was missing. Maybe it had something to do with the fact that the sacred ground, like most of California after half a millennium of overdevelopment, was so chemically poisoned it looked like the back of the moon. All the whole-grain carbohydrates and the woven baskets they were served in had to be imported from Nigeria. Anyway, the reincarnated Chumash weren't quite happy.

It chanced that one of them, being a stockbroker, was at a dinner party with a lot of other rich and powerful people. There she met a friend of a friend who had connections with Dr. Zeus. She did a lot of wistful talking over her nonalcoholic Chardonnay; so did her money. One thing led to another, and within two weeks the New Life Chumash Nation had placed its order with the Company. As the Company had known it would.

Bring the Chumash out of the past for us, they said. Give us back our traditions, our ancient ways. We want to dress up in Chumash robes. We want the total Chumash experience. Spare no expense.

And with those magic words, Dr. Zeus got to work. From their labs they got out all this Chumash genetic material that they, uh, just happened to have. They brought out all the carefully propagated flora and fauna of the Chumash ecosystem from their botanical and zoological gardens. They brought from their records every possible detail of Chumash folkways and culture, and boy, they sure had a lot of material.

The sacred ground was detoxified and bulldozed back into its original contours; it was replanted; it was restocked with animal life. Cleaning and restocking the adjacent ocean floor was harder, but, you know, they'd said to spare no expense, and who was the Company to argue? There was some outcry from historical preservationists when the picturesque old oil rigs off the coast were dismantled. Cash donations shut them up. When everything had naturalized, Humashup was rebuilt down to the last woven hut, and the New Life Chumash Nation moved in.

The next step was making more Chumash. This posed a slight problem for the New Lifers, because they were all sexually dysfunctional in one way or another. No problem, said Dr. Zeus. We've got genuine Chumash sperm and ova here, and they can get it on in a petri dish as well as anywhere else. The ladies of the group coped admirably with the in vitro transplants; they drank raspberry leaf tea for nine months and found childbirth a very spiritually fulfilling experience.

But they were kind of disappointed in the resulting children, who didn't seem to share their values. And, let's face it, life on the sacred ground under the ancient oak trees was, well, *hard* and smelly, and there turned out to be absolutely no psychic contacts with dolphins. The tribe running the casino could have told them that, if anyone had bothered to ask them.

Eventually most of the New Chumash got tired of it and went off to be the other people they'd been in their past lives. Dr. Zeus got custody of the Chumash children, and the children inherited the ecological preserve. They had to be taught how to live on it, though, so the Company sent in all these anthropologists made up as Sky People to instruct them in their ancient culture. Including a Sky Coyote, but not me. That was some other Sky Coyote. I was somewhere else by then.

When they grew up, the Chumash took a good look at the world around them and decided they wanted out of the Stone Age. But these

Chumash had been inoculated against diseases, and there were no Spaniards around to beat them up, see, so things turned out a little differently this time.

A couple of generations later, genetic descendants of Nutku were the stockbrokers drinking Chardonnay at dinner parties in Santa Barbara. They still had their language and culture intact, which helped them become the most aggressive import-export entrepreneurs on the Pacific Rim. Many of them moved down to Hollywood, where they revitalized the entertainment industry to such an extent that there were soon dark mutterings in certain quarters about the town's being run by Indians.

They did have a problem with juvenile delinquency, however. Chumash gangs became the latest scourge of the venerable Republic of Mission Revival. The same intact culture that made them good businessmen also made many of them lousy parents . . .

But it was *their* culture, and at least they got it back, which is more than some people get. And, all things considered, they're doing okay. You should see how the Etruscans Nouveaux turned out!

Happy endings aren't so easy to come by when you're an immortal, because nothing ever quite seems to end. Well, things do; we don't, which is part of the problem.

New World One Base was closed down, right on schedule before the century ended. Deliberately ruined and abandoned to the jungle, leaving not a rack behind for Colonel Churchward or any of those guys to find. Houbert had decamped by then, with an entourage that included his few surviving Mayans. His next paradise was a château on the Loire, where I understand the Mayans refined the science of haute cuisine to an art before they, too, eventually died. Houbert was moved on to Monaco—it's one of those places the Company practically invented—and created another little celestial world on the Riviera. As far as I know, he's still there at the safe house, dispensing his own special syrupy wisdom to adoring mortal servants and unlucky subordinates.

Latif grew up into a superbly competent executive administrator, all brass and flash and hardball, and got the shock of his young life when he finally pushed through his assignment to North Africa and was reunited with his hero Suleyman. It took him a while to realize that sly, courteous old Suleyman was also a superbly competent executive administrator, and actually knew a few tricks Latif didn't. Eventually the student settled down at the feet of the master, and the two of them became legends in that part of the world.

I was thrown back in the arms of Holy Mother Church once I got out of makeup, but somehow my descent into darkness eased up for a while. I'm not sure why. Maybe because I was sent in as a jolly Franciscan instead of a villainous Jesuit. Maybe it was because the murderous power of the Inquisition—and the Church, too—had begun to wane at last. Less and less of my job had to do with the scourge and the branding iron, more and more with protecting lovely old religious art treasures from an increasingly rapacious secular world. Nice work, if you can get it, and I got it for a while.

But I go where the power is, and there was a new religion coming, a new force to hold people spellbound and visit them with dreams and terrors, to unite them with a common point of view and common assumptions about what life is and ought to be. It packed them into its pews every single night of the week without even one commandment, and Hollywood was its holy city. That was where the Company sent me, practically on the day Cecil B. DeMille rolled into town. I've been in the entertainment industry ever since, in one capacity or another. It's better than the Inquisition. Usually.

Lewis wound up in Hollywood too, for a while, as film scripts took on historic value of their own. He really did get work stunt-doubling for Fredric March and Leslie Howard, as it turned out. We occasionally had lunch at Musso & Frank's Grill and talked about old times over gin gimlets made with Rose's Lime Juice. We never discussed Mendoza, though.

I don't know where Mendoza is.

This is not to say I don't know what happened to her, or at least that I haven't made a few good guesses; but I don't think about her much.

She was okay for a while. She did vanish into the coastal range of Central California, and really did all that good work she'd been so confident she could do; in fact, she won a few commendations. I saw her now and again, when she had occasion to stop by some mission where I happened to be portraying a kindly friar. But she was nervous and irritable in human places; she couldn't wait to finish whatever business had brought her there and disappear again into the wilderness. Just about the only times I ever saw her smile were when she'd turn for a goodbye salute before fading up some canyon, into some drift of coastal fog.

I played that game again: I told myself Mendoza was doing just fine and put her out of my mind, and if I thought about her at all, it was only in the context of how happy she was in some redwood forest somewhere, so I didn't have to worry about her.

Something happened, though.

I never saw her again after the middle of the nineteenth century. She just wasn't there anymore, and some other Company botanist had been assigned to that region. He had his work cut out for him, too, because suddenly there were Yankee homesteaders and miners all over the place, clear-cutting, burning, and grazing their cattle even in those precipitous ranges. Mendoza would have been so furious.

Maybe what happened to her had something to do with that. I'd know for certain, if I were to access the official notification the Company sent me. I never have.

I only read enough to glimpse her name and some mention of a disciplinary hearing before I filed it away, unwilling to integrate the rest of the information it contained. That was in 1863, and to this day there it sits on some buried level of my consciousness, right next to the access code that Budu forced on me. I've never found out what that says, either.

I did *think* I saw her, once, in the early years of this century. That was a hallucination, though; had to have been. She couldn't possibly have been sitting at that table in the Hotel St. Catherine in 1923, and even if she had, she couldn't possibly have been sitting with the other person I thought I saw there. Anyway, by the time I managed to push my way from the crowded bar to the place where I'd seen them, the table was vacant, two wineglasses empty, the terrace door open. Had they run away? No. They'd never been there at all. Mendoza was somewhere else, I knew that, stashed away in some secret Company place because of something that would probably turn out to be my fault.

But they can't have done anything too terrible to Mendoza, because she was a good operative, she did good work. It's not like they could kill her, anyway, right? She's an immortal, after all, as indestructible as I am. She must be out there someplace.

Budu must be out there someplace too.

The year 2355 approaches, though, and not one of us can hide from it or outrun it. I guess I'm going to have to access Budu's message eventually, decrypt whatever it was he wanted me to know. I'll probably read that memo on Mendoza then, too. I have a feeling that I'll find a new role to play after that, which is okay. Between you and me, being a minor studio executive with a leased sports coupe is beginning to pall a little.